More praise for *Girly*

"Elizabeth Merrick masters a universe here, including the vast planets of girlhood, adolescence, daughter-, mother-, and sisterhood. *Girly* is a novel of great life and great pain. Merrick's characters and their voices sing and weave and dodge and ultimately embroider themselves on the reader's consciousness. To read *Girly* is to give yourself over to Racinda, Amandine, and Ruth, and to revel and weep in their power. Don't miss this."

—Kathleen Hughes, author of *Dear Mrs. Lindbergh*

"*Girly* is a novel that takes risks and breaks conventions in compelling ways. Merrick is a writer unafraid to venture into new territory and to bring us with her."

—Martha Witt, author of *Broken as Things Are*

"Elizabeth Merrick unleashes the devil in herself as she immerses us in her characters' gothic Christian world. With ambition and sensitivity, she takes us intimately into their tangled and multilayered webs of condemnation, rivalry, insecurity, and grudges that will never die. Meanwhile, she offers hope and light telling the stories of young girls struggling for a voice in the midst of it all."

—Paula Kamen, author of *All in My Head*

"Merrick delivers devastatingly sharp and evocative lines . . .she spins a tale around the Harts that shows their faults, while swaddling them in her honest, judgeless prose."

—*Chicago Time Out*

"A sweeping epic chronicling several generations of women, centered around sisters Ruth and Racinda as they grapple with living in gossipy small towns, restrictive church teachings, family upheaval, and finding themselves, with detours into affairs, sex, drugs, cults, bands and boys along the way . . . walks the line between poetically atmospheric and compulsively readable."

—Gothamist.com

"Merrick has captured a part of the universal female experience that is rare in modern literature . . . She captures the darker, more painful side of femininity from which beauty and strength grow."

—*Small Spiral Notebook*

GIRLY

GIRLY

A NOVEL

ELIZABETH MERRICK

Demimonde Books
New York

www.demimondebooks.com

Cover design by Wendy Kenigsberg and Elizabeth Merrick
Back cover designed by Wendy Kenigsberg and Tania Kamensky
Author photo © 2006 Joan Beard
Designed by Robin Werner

ISBN 0-9768801-0-5
Printed in Canada
Publisher's Cataloging-in-Publication
(Provided by Quality Books, Inc.)

Merrick, Elizabeth.
    Girly : a novel / Elizabeth Merrick.
    p. cm.
    ISBN 0-9768801-0-5

    1. Women–Sexuality–Fiction. 2. Women–Religious
life–Fiction. 3. Spirituality–Fiction. 4. Hart family
–Fiction. 5. Fundamentalism–Fiction. I. Title.

PS3613.E7757G57 2005   813'.6
        QBI06-700003

Published by DEMIMONDE BOOKS
320 7th Avenue #199
Brooklyn, NY 11215

www.demimondebooks.com

for my parents and my grandparents

I am the silence that is incomprehensible
  and the idea whose remembrance is frequent.
I am the voice whose sound is manifold
  and the word whose appearance is multiple.
I am the utterance of my name.

"Thunder: Perfect Mind"

BOOK ONE

She lets the other tongue of a thousand tongues speak—the tongue, sound without barrier or death. She refuses life nothing.

HELENE CIXOUS

1

DISOBEY

APRIL 1981

He wouldn't kiss her, fearing sin—the prude—but Ruth knew he'd kissed a clean girl who sat quietly for him on a cold bench. Ruth knew: behind the middle school, the neat, pretty girl had stared nearly immobile into the woods, her expression hapless, her mouth naturally settling into the thin smile of a doll.

Ruth knew because she'd made her sister watch.

The Dieckmann boy said no to Ruth Hart's demands that Sunday in 1981, when they had both wandered away from church services held in a neighbor's living room. Far removed from the prayers of the devout, Ruth swiped, backhand, across Kurt Dieckmann's face with her grandmother's gardening trowel, leaving his teeth and blood for silent witnesses on the grayed-out macadam.

It was premeditated. Ruth had brought the silvery, chipped trowel with her in her schoolbag. Later she turned it on her own face—messy, scowling, surrounded by white-blond kinky hair that refused to stay completely in a barrette—and knocked out nearly the same teeth as from his mouth. Oddly enough, nobody thought in the tears and the rush to the emergency room to ask how the trowel got there, or why she brought her schoolbag to Sunday worship, for that matter.

When Kurt screamed, the Christians gathered in the Dell family's ranch house could only assume the weak, shattered noise came from a girl's mouth.

How could a thirteen year old boy summon such force, the adults thought but did not speak. They thought *monster,* thought *juvie,* thought *military school* and *stolen license plates.* Said: Jesus forgive this child. But Ruth's mother, Amandine, and younger sister, Racinda, knew exactly what had happened when they saw the decimated mouths. The question of whose strength broke the teeth didn't occur to either one. They imagined Ruth's arm sweeping at Kurt, they imagined the sound of metal hitting bone, tearing gum. Imagined the pain in Ruth's and Kurt's separate mouths uniting them in immediacy, in fire, as if both had been in the near periphery of a car bomb. And the Harts kept quiet, they protected their own, refused a fellow worshipper's offer of a ride to the hospital. Amandine herself drove while Racinda held her sister's hand. Racinda started ahead silently, rebuking the Devil as her mother had taught her, sure he had a hand in it all, somehow, even though usually at the Dells' he didn't haunt her so badly with all the clapping, the singing, the Word.

Two.

It had all started a few months earlier, back in February, with a nail gun—not the kind that's hooked up to an air-compressor, but the kind that actually looks like a gun, the kind you have to load one nail at a time. The sort of nail gun that makes almost the same noise as a .22 when it fires. You wouldn't have occasion to know this, though, unless you have a friend, a member of the family, say, in the construction business, or were a young boy obsessed with that sort of equipment, or perhaps unless you were one of this boy's cronies or admirers impressed with his stories of having stolen one.

Ruth and Racinda had been waiting outside the high school for Amandine to come drive them home, but she was late. Winter was turning cold again, after a brief thaw, and the February palette of iron was rising again and gaining strength, rushing into objects with each gust of wind. It was still winter. The lot was near-silent: no teachers' sad little cars in the lot, no sports teams, just a thin trickle of traffic and the light shifting low, bluer, at the horizon. The district's thirteen school buses were lined up, empty, in front of so many black-mouthed garage doors.

Racinda's little fingers parched and dried in the cold. She wedged them under the graying pink cuff of her padded nylon parka. Racinda was sitting on her book bag, leaning against some steps, and when her hands warmed a bit she started folding all four of her untied shoelaces on top of each other into a braid when she realized that Ruth—whose fidgeting and breathing and quick detours into frantic chatter paced most of Racinda's earthly hours—had been still and silent for too long. Racinda looked up quietly and slowly with expert feigned spaciness and nonchalance, to see what her sister was honing in on.

Racinda could see Kurt Dieckmann in profile, under shrubbery, his face to the ear of a boy named Will. Kurt's bright yellow ski jacket dulled his hair to flat white, and his lips and cheeks were pinkened. The two boys hugged the frozen soil under a border hedge and Will's wrists were wobbly, holding up the gun in such an awkward position; one eye tightened shut, the other aiming carefully.

"Will's shooting somebody!" Racinda, leaning forward to see if she could see any human target past the row of school buses, whisper-yelled to Ruth. "Ruth!"

Ruth's grin expanded wide between her cheeks.

Racinda grabbed her arm.

"Ruth do some—"

"Shooting people sometimes happens, Creature," Ruth said, pulling her arm away from her sister and turning around.

Racinda's eyes widened and she felt about to cry, but instead of pulling that torment out, Ruth ended it, amused elsewhere: she was leaning back on her hands against the wall and imagining Kurt's skin.

Racinda shook, tightened her mouth and her throat.

Ruth's hips were pressed against the low wall, and she was staring at the boys, who were oblivious of her. Her whitish hair lit, flew in perfect tendrils—this was the weather for that kinky hair. The cold kept any moisture from frizzing it. Ruth's silky shirt rippled back off her arms. Despite the cold, Ruth's skin would be warm to the touch.

"Do it," Ruth whispered, her face and Racinda's face wide toward Kurt like a pair of satellites, "He's saying, '*Will, do it, shoot it to the tire. . .*'"

Ruth had been talking about Kurt nonstop for two weeks, ever since he showed her a joint at church at the Dells. She'd ignored him before that—he'd always stayed quiet those Sundays: sullen, but quiet, his nasty-boy attitude somehow missing in those moments when he would lean in on his mother's waist or whisper to her. The joint was like an early-morning homeroom loudspeaker announcement to Ruth that Kurt wasn't as boring as he looked at church: even though he was a year older, and a terror on the school bus—ready to attack at any moment—with his mother he seemed like a pussy, and Ruth had always seen as fit to ignore him as he had her.

The shot seemed to break the air apart.

Racinda jumped and made a little squeak and grabbed her sisters forearm.

Ruth hissed, then laughed when she saw that one of the bus's tires had already started to deflate from the direct hit.

Yeah, Kurt said.

Mr. Alperi, the long-haired, Penn-educated head mechanic who was outside smoking, sitting on the bumper of a bus at the far corner of the garage, didn't jump from the noise—just calmly tugged his sharp chin back toward Kurt as if pulled slowly on a fishing line. Mr. Alperi maintained a calm, knowing look. His eyes became hard, he took two last drags before crushing the Winston into a sand-filled bucket.

Smoothing back his hair, Mr. Alperi paused, freeze frame, a brief moment before lurching, like a Labrador retriever after a tennis ball, toward the boys, his legs a fast blur despite too-baggy coveralls.

"Ruth—he's going to shoot Mr. Alperi!"

"Oh please, Creature," Ruth said, with enough generosity to glance at and scowl at her sister, "Didn't you ever hear about how Will's brothers steal them from construction sites in Landemberg? It's a *nail* gun."

Racinda's panic now sunk into a frown. That Ruth could manipulate her into terror at any moment was depressing, though at least there wouldn't be any physical pain to follow, since Ruth was already ignoring her, staring intensely at Kurt.

As Mr. Alperi swiftly approached, Kurt practically evaporated: Will became alone suddenly under the shrub, carefully readjusting himself on top of the nail gun to hide it, slowly lowering his head as if his sandy-brown bangs might camouflage his transgression.

"Move," Ruth said.

Ruth only needed to grip Racinda's wrist the first minute or so of following Kurt's flight—secretly, nothing would have pleased Racinda more than this race up Union Street, toward the elementary school where Amandine, often confused, sometimes mistakenly went instead to pick up the girls anyway.

Kurt looked back at the sisters when he finally heard their feet stomping up behind him, and, though he kept walking, his *face* paused a minute—unsure whether to ignore them or maybe even turn around and walk back down to the high school. He settled on affecting a quiet frown they couldn't see, then picked up his pace a bit to expand the distance. His vanilla-canvas book bag slapped his hip as he headed on.

As they walked up the slight incline that became a tiny bridge overpass above the train tracks, Ruth banged her hand in a constant rhythm against the railing on the inside of the sidewalk that was there to keep pedestrians from falling.

A silence seemed to hold when she stopped beating the pace with her hand, when she opened her palm to smell the skin on metal.

"You need a ride, Dieckmann?" she said.

Steps on pavement, dust by the side of the road, leaves that have molded and decayed now with the life dried, frozen out of them—burgundy, caramel, russet skeletons. White pebbles on the side of the road. Cigarette packs, gum wrappers, plastic bottle lids on the side of the road. Three children.

Kurt turned to them but kept walking, fast, backwards, facing Ruth, but refusing to let her near him. The sun slipped a notch grayer before Ruth finally called to him.

"Where's your stash?" Ruth said.

A clear scowl took over Kurt's face, but before he could think of anything to say, Ruth started calling his name.

"Kurt Dieckmann!" Ruth said. "Kurt Dieckmann!"

Her tone was sarcastic, mocking, as if he were the outcast, not her.

Kurt puffed along, still backwards, still facing her, his chin jutting out a little bit. The cold was irritating his eyes. He blinked.

Kurt Dieckmann Kurt Dieckmann Kurt Dieckmann Kurt Dieckmann.

"Fucking freak," Kurt said, but Ruth couldn't hear him for shouting his name.

The car swooped down the road too fast, too quickly to the right before it slowed next to them and stopped, a little ahead.

Kurt Dieckmann Kurt Dieckmann Kurt Dieckmann Kurt Dieckmann.

Mrs. Dieckmann's hair was perfect, and her skin shone like Ruth's. She sat straight. Mrs. Dieckmann rolled down the passenger window by pressing a button on her own door. She tilted her head, confused as to why

Ruth was repeating her son's name so gleefully, and at once so vindictively.

You would never guess how unhappy Mrs. Dieckmann was.

Ruth stopped chanting, then closed her mouth and stared inside Mrs. Dieckmann's brand-new VW station wagon. Ruth and Racinda watched Mrs. Dieckmann's face move from irritation to something so soft when Kurt opened the door.

When she saw Mrs. Dieckmann's perfect hand spread so warmly across Kurt's back, what struck Racinda wasn't that *he* held on to *her*, the rare boy unembarrassed—or so in need of the attention—to touch his mother in front of his peers. What struck her was that Mrs. Dieckmann stopped the car when there wasn't even a shoulder on the busy road, just to take a little too long to hug her son, cars veering around on the narrow town road, honking.

Racinda watched the hand lie still, then smooth back and forth, and she realized that Mrs. Dieckmann's hand was as beautiful and perfect and devoid of the Devil and disaster as Mrs. Dieckmann herself was: the anti-Ruth, the anti-Amandine, even. The woman who when her son on-purpose missed the bus not only noticed, but would come to get him and would hug him anyway.

When Mrs. Dieckmann looked up, she seemed surprised to see Ruth and Racinda staring at her.

"Girls, we can't give you a ride because he's an hour late to swim team," Mrs. Dieckmann said, her left turn signal clicking off the time as she eyed her way back into the line of afternoon cars, as Kurt slammed the door and refused to look at them.

"We—" but before Racinda could ask Mrs. Dieckmann to call their mother, to remind their mother of them, the car was shrinking away. The Volkswagen's brake lights pulsed a few times, rushing only to then decelerate for the stoplight ahead. Then hasten away.

* * *

The embossed metal of the plates that held together the splintering wood panels of the merry-go-round left art-deco stars on Racinda's legs. The metal shifted burgundy to deep silver, that iron force emanating from everything, winter insisting on itself one last time.

The elementary school had been empty when Ruth and Racinda got there—Ruth could spin the merry-go-round as fast as she wanted without having to shove anybody off first.

Racinda looked up from time to time to see her sister opening her mouth to the wind, singing something not a song: when Ruth's thumping steps winding faster gave way to wet panting, Ruth's hands, already raw from the metal, pushed their winter sweat into her worn-soft denim skirt as she leaned over dizzy. Then Ruth gave more before she hopped on it herself: *Faster.*

Racinda huddled her heart down to her knees, her arms loped over one of the pipe-axis bars, as close to the center of the merry-go-round, of her body, as possible. Ruth, by contrast, expanded like a ribbon—holding on with only her hands at the crux of the spinning wheel, her feet dangling free to the centrifuge's pull away, a pull that might shatter her out to the green-paved ground, or fling her into the tree above the baseball diamond, or disperse her parts to the sky.

Racinda was at home here, spinning, because Ruth, over the years, had forced her to be:

The ground written through a space between the metal and wood, and the splinters of red, of yellow paint needling into raw boards—Racinda limited her vision to this—the bolts on the bars that held it all together, the gray-cream toe of her sneaker.

But what she was looking at gave way, as Racinda closed her eyes, to Mrs. Dieckmann's lovely fingernails patting, scratching Kurt's back in reassurance when she pulled him to her; Mrs. Dieckmann's blond hair rushing her son's straight fortress. Her posture. The way the car was clean and didn't have wound-looking pockmarks on its ceiling like Amandine's did from when Ruth got hold of her brown-rose lipstick and wrote the word *genitalia* across it.

The smear of Ruth's laugh and an image of her curling features fought across Mrs. Dieckmann's face in Racinda's mind—Racinda forced it out and imagined Mrs. Dieckmann in a 1950s prom gown, looking supple and light. Amandine tried for that quiet blondness, but her cracks showed through—the way her mouth dropped each time Ruth moved too fast, or said something with even a tinge of rudeness to it. But Mrs. Dieckmann and Lindy Ellen—the girl Kurt would be kissing in a few days while Racinda watched—*really* had the blond.

When Racinda opened her eyes for just a flash—focusing on the ground through the hole in the wood—the nubby green-painted blacktop of the playground shot under her like water out of a faucet. A whirlpool.

She closed her eyes again fast.

She—Racinda, was forcing herself into Mrs. Dieckmann's prom dress—*she,* Racinda, would be the blonde one, the neat one, the safe one, the right one...

But:

She, (even in the imaginary version), Racinda, had hair sticking out all over the place, the familial lipstick problem, shoes too small for her feet, a hard time balancing. The dress drooped at the chest, and stretched tight across her little girl's belly.

Impossible.

Would never fit the glass slipper.

Racinda lifted her head to banish the sadness that filled her, opened her eyes:

Ruth's mouth, wide too, crying glee with the air spinning around them.

Ruth's hair spilling out past her, her feet lifted from the merry-go-round an inch or two, but just for a minute.

Trails of spit on Ruth's face.

Mess, insanity, *Creeeeeature!:* song.

And a mass of confusion hit Racinda, because while she wanted the stillness and the beauty of becoming Mrs. Dieckmann in shirred satin, she incomprehensibly, opaquely hated herself for even thinking it, and with a suddenness and a power wanted to be forever next to Ruth, who held on tight at the same time as she sailed free, with mess and singing.

Ashamed of not wanting her sister, terrified of losing her sister, Racinda curled further down onto her own body, closed her eyes, listened to the wind and Ruth's voice. Racinda thought of Kurt Dieckmann's face, then—a wild, beautiful, face—and grew herself a little crush on him nearly as bad as her sister's.

Racinda tried again, later, after the crossing guard at the high school—long done with work, but having hung around to smoke a J with Mr. Alperi the mechanic—told Amandine he'd seen the girls walking up Union and they had been fetched safely home. After Ruth fell asleep that night, Racinda tried again to imagine her own face as Mrs. Dieckmann in a prom gown.

She even smelled her/Mrs. Dieckmann's gardenia pinned onto the plump top curve of the strapless gown—but then he started up with her again, her night visitor.

The Devil, whose glowing face—mustached, not red, but pale and flinty—became more solid in her mind the more she prayed not to think of him.

Hmmmm, he said. And laughed. And just waited, bent his fingers and stared at the nails, checked his watch, leaned on a wall. *I know you*—he said, not opening his mouth.

She tried to think of Kurt Dieckmann, arriving to banish the suave demon, but Kurt's rough, wind-chapped features just smoothed into Satan's grin.

The Devil traced a narrow hand across the air, leaving her name hanging there in glowing aquamarine. *Racinda. I know you.* He was telling the truth—he knew her well. He ran his top lip over his teeth and looked sideways toward the corner of the sky.

So she scrambled out of blankets, easily without waking her sister, and knocked on her mother's door, but of course Amandine, like Ruth, slept hard. Racinda knocked there, then looked to her father's door—her parents hadn't shared a bedroom since Ruth returned to live with them.

Without Ruth to provide a little slice of him, he showed up full-scale in Racinda's nighttime mind.

Racinda sucked in air, gave up on the notion of human assistance when Amandine didn't answer. *I will not think about—*

But as Racinda turned, the Devil turned behind her, as she stepped forward he circled her, as she tensed her stomach, her thighs, her lips into a hard shell to block him he became a creak on the stairs in the night—he entered her ears as a sound made by the wood of the house itself.

He always returned, that Devil, and more than his wan face it was the feeling around him that the worst was yet to come, worse than Racinda could imagine, and that she just had to repeat what Amandine taught her—*I rebuke thee Satan and I command thee to wither and die*—to put the turmoil or the endless nauseated aloneness off awhile longer.

He was after her worse, tonight, for wanting that mean boy her sister wanted so badly. Because the truth of it was this: Racinda had started claiming Kurt as her own, in the same indefensible, kamikaze-sweet way her sister did.

Even then, at seven, she knew that telling the Devil to leave prolonged his visit somehow, yet she suspected that if she didn't rebuke him, if she fell asleep and eventually got distracted by dreams or by breakfast or by avoiding Ruth or by cartoons, he would nab her, wrench his snaky hand behind her heart and snap his fingers on her soul, shattering it, dispersing it, irreparably, inside her.

Wasn't he winning if you forgot about him?

This was what Amandine told her. Yet the opposite seemed true. It felt like he was winning, like she was courting him, when she repeated till the words lost meaning *I rebuke thee.*

She conjured his face that way. By denying him she made his vapor solid.

She ended up that night where she always did—next to Ruth, praying for the Devil to leave her alone.

And when the Devil turned to her, his long face so familiar and peaceful, his hand so feminine, when he reached out to wipe her sweaty hair out of her eyes, she squeezed noiseless tears from herself, wept into the pillow and finally slept hard.

Did he stay with her into her dreams? Perhaps—if so he changed form and she couldn't recognize him, he wooed her close with dreamscape and a big messiness not tolerated in the daytime world, her Christian world, the world named by men who have lost something, men who have seen Eve in the garden and gotten that creeping feeling in their stomachs before they thanked God they now knew whom to blame.

How to banish the Devil? How to lure her sister's crush? How to repel her sister but keep her sister's love?—Racinda twisted herself into knots in her sleep, ground her baby teeth down, sharp. At least *awake*, having to pay such close, physical attention to Ruth, Racinda was distracted enough not to wear herself to the bone on the big worries.

I rebuke thee, she'd repeat, heart quickening into sleep.

Never once suspecting that Devil himself might be the one who could loosen her binds, who could dissipate the worries with a little breath, a little pleasure, a little faith.

*　　　*　　　*

What really no one knew about the Dieckmanns was that since before she'd even been coming to church at the Dells', Mrs. Dieckmann had been batting away the truth each night with two or three too many shots of sweet liquor—bourbon, rum—and an occasional Valium (occasional, like at breakfast and then again at lunch). The truth was that her husband, Dirk Dieckmann, was away too often, selling high-end Oriental rugs in far-flung suburban showrooms. It wasn't that she missed him so—Jenny Dieckmann was actually fairly sick of him and drank a few even when he was home more regularly, just to convince herself he still moved in some way that made her want him. More, it was that *without* him there for her to monitor for grouchy, meal-ruining outbursts, for swearing around Kurt and his older brother, Matty, for knocking Matty with the backs of his knuckles when Matty came in late (this lateness a completely unnoticed offense when just Jenny was around), Jenny got anxious and bored. The boys were as whipped as she was—Matty hid his drug use, and Kurt, until he was about eleven, went out of his way to stay quiet, to keep playing video games, to conceal any trouble he was in in order to avoid setting his father into fury and his mother silently pressing her nails into her palms or her mouth or her hair.

That week in January when she didn't sleep, though, changed everything. Dirk Dieckmann had been back for a solid week for the holidays, and Jenny's simultaneous glee of the job of having him around collided with her terror when he and Matty screamed for two hours before throwing each others' stereos from the deck onto the concrete by the pool. The specter of this collision kept her up nights, even after Dirk left for Wilmette on January third.

So she crocheted.

She plowed through two baby blankets for friends, oblivious of time, then started in on a black, lacy tablecloth for the round table in the upstairs hallway whose walls she'd had painted red for an ornate, Italian look.

For days it brought a sort of vision to her she didn't want to let go of, that tablecloth: something idolatrous, a barren hill; that tablecloth like a grandmother's shawl; a man's face—a grandson's? her lover's? such crazy images, such crazy stories murky beneath—a face that held wind and sorrow, a face whose light yellow-splashed eyes hesitated just past ochre skin, black edges; something primal, something in him that could always laugh, and some familial power to set the dog at the throat of the enemy; someplace alone, someplace beyond rules and language and what was expected of her; someplace before the Christians; idle, but waiting to spring; powers she knew nothing of; repeating in her mind: sex, some idol.

Crazy.

What kind of nut job am I becoming, she wondered, but this did not stop her.

Getting hungry, Matty finally took forty bucks from her wallet and bought himself and Kurt some 7-11 subs, bread, peanut butter, cold cuts, Pepsi, microwave popcorn, and Skittles. When Jenny's tears started, but came out dry, she just sat there, still, trying to hang on to her vision by playing Matty's cassette of John Lee Hooker he left in his old walkman, John Lee Hooker whose old, spare chords conjured for her another angle on the same stark, warm, death-facing scene. The earphones grew hot against her head.

But in the end, that stopped working, and she just had to rip the table-cloth out to perpetuate the landscape it brought to her, coiling each loosened stitch perfectly, cleanly, back into a ball then beginning it again, conjuring these threads of her vision into a lover and a life and a distant history in her mind.

The fire that happened in the microwave from Kurt heating Poptarts without removing the foil wrapper did not phase her (he put it out him-self, she didn't notice until afterwards, only got a vague sense of the screaming and the hot-plastic, scorched-sugar odor); the puddles of pot smoke coming out of Matty's closed, then, by the fifth day, shamelessly open bedroom door didn't rouse her; Kurt's tries at reverting to calling her Mommy instead of Mom even did little—she replied with a very sweet *honey*, but then poured more Diet Coke and rum into her rim-crusting cut-glass tumbler, returned her concentration to her black yarn.

Kurt felt something like an insect buzzing in him. He veered around the house and smoked weed twice with Matty and played Atari and jumped on all the beds, slamming his hands into the low stucco suburban ceiling. He ate too many Skittles and then, just to escape the long awful pull of boredom, managed to get himself on the bus to school when it started up the next week of January.

The insect in him quieted down back at school with the reassurance that he was the boss: the sadist behind the bus driver's back, mysteriously forcing the other boys to lower their eyes around him if they knew what was good for them. But by the next day Kurt's buzzing was louder, irre-pressible—the energy of wings moving so fast they became translucent—and he couldn't resist calling a timid, sad-eyed working-class girl something scatological and sexual in a louder-than-conversational tone during a spelling quiz. By the third visit to the principal in so many days, the call his mother got at one in the afternoon woke her from her reverie. After she fastened off the final row, she went in for the talk at school then slept until two days later and vowed—though she still kept a few bottles of Pimm's in a bedroom closet—to shape herself and her younger son, at least, into normalcy: Matty, perhaps, was a lost cause. But Kurt's detentions and even a suspension within two weeks, endless warning notes, failing grades, continued, so she took the advice of Linda Dell across the street and took the boy to the home church services in the Dells' living room.

Kurt wouldn't lean his head on her shoulder, watching TV, anymore, and he wouldn't wrap his arms around her waist after school and let her muss then straighten his hair. Increasingly it seemed like she didn't want to, either. The high shivering inside him kept him in constant motion, impulsive unless exhausted or stoned because he could feel the cracks starting between his parents and in Matty and under the house itself and the feeling was too strong if he stayed still.

As long as he kept moving, it felt like he could leap over any chasm.

When he would kick big dents in the antique-glazed storm door, when Jenny routinely started finding the Pimm's a few fingers down Sunday mornings, she stopped even wanting, at all, really, that touch her baby now held from her. She brought her arms and hips closer to herself in his presence, she began to be afraid of what was uncoiling inside her son because she believed she would never be able to contain it.

Three.

By March, both sisters were tensed and quietly desperate for a Kurt sighting, for something to happen. Ruth and Racinda waited, as always, outside the high school for Amandine to come get them, this time joined by Ruth's older friend Aimey Frank who did the easiest thing she could to be punk rock and put safety pins in her ears. Aimey Frank slept with college boys—with her auntie's ex-boyfriends, even older; she had a certain gravity in her face, and a fast, too-loud, don't-touch-me laugh.

"These boys wouldn't know what hit them," Aimey Frank spoke of herself, when a group of them, her age, passed her by without looking. "These boys don't know what a clitoris is," Aimey said, and she laughed with such volume that the weakest boy struggled to resist glancing behind him to see what stupid thing he'd done now.

Aimey's dark, loose-curly hair came short to her round face—she tried to harden its soft circles by bleaching strands and gelling them to spiky, but the curls always returned. Her lips, her cheeks, her stone-circle eyes: nothing of her body was as angular as she wanted, as the pins or the plaid skirts or the boots with square toes and pilgrim buckles or as the ripped fishnet stockings she had to put on in the gas station bathroom after school because they wouldn't let her wear them to classes all torn like that.

Aimey Frank befriended Ruth even though Ruth was an untouch-able—in special ed classes ever since her accident at the Dells' and the hospitalization last year—because Aimey Frank wanted Ruth's hard-ness. (Not that Aimey Frank was *so* far from untouchable herself.) Ruth put up with Aimey Frank because Aimey was as soft as Racinda, with the added benefit that Aimey didn't know Ruth so well, so didn't circumvent or dilute or dampen the intensity of Ruth's responses to things like Racinda did.

"Oh my God," Aimey said, "Look who's with *that* trampy thing," she said, lighting up a cigarette from the last match of the pack. She had her knees bent, her heels propped up sitting on the yellowish brick wall—just erected a decade previous; that cheap, Nixon-era architecture—next to the parking lot.

Kurt was walking across the asphalt with his hand in Lindy Ellen's.

"Look," Aimey said, and got Ruth's attention, "Kurt Dieckmann."

"He's not doing it to her," Ruth said nonchalantly. "He's a Christian. He's not allowed to."

That Aimey's laugh came so often at anything sexual was another big selling point to Ruth.

"He's not allowed to stick it in! Yeah right. Even Jesus was friends with whores, Ruthie!" Aimey said in a fast, high pitch, spitting, doubling.

"Shut up," Ruth said. "Go see what they're doing."

But Aimey just kept laughing.

"Like *watch* him fuck her? Pervert, " Aimey said when she caught her breath.

"He's not going to fuck her. She's a Catholic," Ruth murmured coolly.

But Ruth's eyes were on Kurt and Lindy Ellen's backs, their hands pressed together, fingers curled. She could feel the beginnings of sweat in the circles of their palms. She could feel how they were walking kind of fast to get to the woods behind the bus garage. She knew Lindy Ellen thrived on everyone else's view of her straight, long, blond hair, switching down her back with the rhythm of a chanted taunt.

"Oh yeah right that's what he's really going to be thinking about, this is a *Catholic* vagina, ha *ha*," Aimey said.

Aimey went to light a cigarette and realized she'd still got one in her mouth. She stared despondently at the new one in her fist.

"Why do you have to say *vagina*, you freak," Ruth said, but didn't turn her face to her friend. Ruth's expression dimmed, got liquidy and mean.

"Just because you're fifteen and have been to health class you think you can just say *vagina vagina vagina*," Ruth said, her lips sharper, her chin angled stiff.

The force Aimey's laughter provided to expand her features disappeared, and Aimey's face settled down to its natural, broken weight. An intolerably sad defeat rose up Aimey fast, whenever her showy laughter wore off.

"I don't know why you have to be so upset all the time," Aimey said.

She let the half-finished cigarette drop from her mouth and lit the slightly crumpled one from her fist.

"Bye," she said, very softly, leaving, as if she hadn't been standing around with Ruth all afternoon just for the company.

Though it was still cold out—still the end of winter—Ruth had forgotten her jacket in the bathroom and was out there in short sleeves, a little striped t-shirt that skimmed her pink-white arms and new breasts. The wind sparked against her skin but she didn't feel its chill, didn't rub her hands on her arms to warm them as she waited for Racinda to arrive from the elementary school up the road.

*   *   *

It was always a bargain between the two of them. Racinda accepted Ruth's force on the condition that Ruth put up with Racinda's insistence on keeping silent and removed.

"He's back there in the woods with *Lindy Ellen*," Ruth said.

"So."

"Go watch."

Ruth's white eyelashes pointed torture at her sister.

Racinda twisted one ankle behind the other and looked to the street.

"You can just watch them yourself through the trees, probably—" Racinda said, scanning their barren early-March trunks.

"Creature," Ruth said, "Creature how *much* do I have to hurt you?"

So Racinda never once looked in her sister's eyes as she descended to the black-gray woods.

"Come on," Kurt said, as if he were trying to get Lindy Ellen to move. His hands mapping her breasts, swimming through her hair, the cold nicking skin white, her shirt unbuttoned to the bottom.

She sat there.

She kissed him—opened her mouth for him—but she didn't really move her body. She focused anywhere but her mouth, because all the spit there grossed her out and she didn't know what else to do. She put her hands on his back and shifted them up and down on his flannel shirt.

Kurt could tell that something was missing from her, and when he felt this mysterious lack most clearly, it excited him even more.

"Come on," he said, his anger building as he pushed his chest onto hers.

When Racinda got there, her thighs tired from the walk up the hill behind the garages, Kurt's mouth was on Lindy's neck, and Lindy's mouth was a slight, fazed smile.

"Whoa," Lindy said. "Who're you?" The smile flattened, and the rest of Lindy's face was precisely still. Lindy took Kurt's wrist and removed it from underneath her skirt cleanly, without rush or embarrassment, even, in the same calm manner that she might remove a toy from her toddler brother's grip when it was time for him to eat.

It took Kurt a minute to get off Lindy. His lips crossed his harsh teeth, he sat next to Lindy on the bench without touching her.

"Oh god," he exhaled, abandoning his mean-boy persona.

Racinda could tell he wasn't just taking the Lord's name in vain. Kurt's eyes turned down a little at the corners and he winced automatically at the thought of the principal's office.

But it wasn't *really* the threat of being busted, because Racinda would never tell and even if she did he could deny it. Nobody really cared anyway. He squinted and hated the trees in front of him and they were the whole problem and Racinda was the whole problem but really, he kind of knew it but was getting more and more distant from the mess of it, it was the sorrow of being pulled away from Lindy's body and the sorrow he felt when his mother's confusion turned into a hardening the *last* time he got suspended. It almost overcame his studied toughness out here in the woods, but he held a hate for the trees in front of him and that mess did seem to go away.

He exhaled and stared at the ground and ran his tongue to the corner of his mouth which had started the day chapped and was now nearly raw red.

Racinda ran.

Kurt chased her, and tackled her.

"Do not *tell*. Don't tell anyone."

His mouth was slicked with saliva. There was sweat at his temples. His mother's face held at the back of his mind and he tried to bash it in with curses at this little girl.

He grabbed her fingers but didn't know how to bend them back as fast as Ruth did, so Racinda was able to wriggle her wrist away from him.

"You better not," he said. The warmth of Racinda under him brought on thick water in his throat.

Racinda knew to be still. She lay motionless under him.

She was younger, she was small, her eyes did not flinch from the sky behind his ear.

"Look at me," he said, but she wouldn't.

The buzzing started in him and he shoved at her from his knees.

She could smell his tongue. She could feel that his thighs were sharp.

She didn't move because she wanted him to keep pinning her down here on the dirty, half-decayed leaves, partly because he didn't know how to hurt her as bad as Ruth did, but partly because in this one moment she possessed what Ruth wanted. The feeling of it was like having stars inside her heart.

"That wasn't happening, got it?" Kurt said, focused, wanting a result from her, honing his skills as a bully.

Racinda smiled at him, her fear transforming into tense pleasure, just the tiniest smile, not flat like Lindy Ellen's but mischievous, devilish: Ruth couldn't take this from her.

"It *wasn't*," Kurt said, and slammed his chest into her, pushing the ground hard, fast, with his feet to do it. They could both feel he was about to get up and run, then walk the three miles home, leaving Lindy Ellen on her own, if she was still up there.

"Jesus saw you, you know," Racinda said, so brave, just to keep him there. Manipulative. "Just because no one else did doesn't mean He didn't."

Kurt's wheat-colored skin got pinker and the water in his throat pulsed and the sound of the word *Jesus* made him want the Dells' living room so much, the warm air there, the women singing.

"She's the only pretty girl who likes me," he said, forcing back tears. "All the other ones are dogs and sluts."

And then the stars were gone from Racinda, because she knew which of these categories she never had a hope of being in.

"Say you didn't see it," he said quashing the tears, quashing the want, summoning the sadist. "You didn't and I'll let you go. But I'll keep watching you."

But she knew he wouldn't.

He was so tall, and he moved like he couldn't care less who was watching *him*, and he shouted when he felt like it and he had coiled his stomach against Lindy Ellen like he coiled now against Racinda, kind of, and Racinda wanted to marry him, wanted him to save her from a burning house, from her own house burning. If *only* Kurt would be watching her: he'd gather her in his arms, he'd carry her someplace decent.

"It wasn't happening," he said, his mouth an inch from hers.

Was it his teeth that looked so sharp? Was it his tongue? The angle of black wedged in his throat?

"I've got my eye on you," he said.

Racinda heard Ruth's forceful, uneven feet tramping up the hill behind them.

"It wasn't happening," Racinda said, the liar, and was up and running to her sister before Ruth saw a thing.

*   *   *

"They left," Racinda lied some more. "They left when I got there. They're gone. They ran to the road."

"Did she have her shirt off?" Ruth said.

Racinda shook her head. "Just kissing. And she was just smiling, not even moving. Just he was kissing her, she just sat there like wood."

"Stupid bitch," Ruth said.

For the next week, Racinda could feel herself in Ruth's dreams—or maybe Ruth in *hers*? Sleeping, Racinda smashed her fist into Lindy Ellen's nose under cover of jumping twelve-year old girls, hair flying, under cover of the basketball's fleet trajectory, the dusty light of the gym filling her like air, days before Ruth actually did make the blond girl's nose crooked that way and got away with it as an accident.

Racinda felt blood—her hand like a cup, waiting for it—, sticky on her knuckles and fingernails, and the Devil said *hmmmm, I know.*

*   *   *

When her mind said: *The Devil the Devil*, she thought:
   I am not going to think about the Devil—
   And so there he was.

The line from his cheek to his chin like an almond, his eyes bright, thick flecks turned fast so she could never see them clearly, his mouth the same silvery smudge.

I am not going to.

His fingers, reflective, vaporous, came to her heart.

It was too much then—the Devil couldn't resist. He'd tried to talk to her before, in that slippery, androgynous voice Racinda imagined for him, but this time, it was something more real—a woman's voice.

The deep edge of treble, and soothing, and kind.

Honey, don't worry, she heard the Devil say, and in that music of the Devil's voice Racinda saw Ruth's hair spinning into brightness and the green spills of life out in the fields, in Button's garden, *honey, don't worry*, the Devil said, and Racinda knew just then, just for a second that the Devil was not what she'd thought, Racinda just for that one second knew it was something other than the Devil, and that this voice was actually for real, this voice was actually trying to soothe her.

But Amandine had trained her well, and when that second finished she convinced herself that voice was him, poor baby, she thought the touch of a smooth hand on her chin was something to cower from.

Hi, the woman's voice said.

Racinda felt the Devil's girly hand in that voice, she felt a giant, empty, new space where her sister misbehaved, where *rebuke thee* meant nothing, came out as jumbled syllables, where the words to real things were unformed yet, still tones and melodies, colors, the feeling of walking into a cloud.

Something shifted at the edge of the hill in her mind, where the road curved away to her mother's house—Racinda turned her head fast, expecting to see an animal scuttling off. But it was nothing, just shadows. A boy's face, and a man's face, that she'd never seen but would know in time.

Hi. The Devil? A sweet, feminine voice. How could it be so terrifying, and so close, and so full of adoration?

*   *   *

Kurt—Ruth wrote his name with a Sharpie on the bottoms of her feet, anywhere Amandine wouldn't notice: on the inside of beams in the basement, in the Burger King bathroom, on hairspray cans and mirrors and five separate Master locks in the junior high girls' locker room.

"Racinda," Kurt said from the last seat on the bus on one of the rare days they all rode it.

Racinda froze, just one more instance where the metallic, dusty, linoleum-vinyl smell of the school bus became impossible to associate with anything but humiliation and doom. She had known that Kurt was on the bus, but felt safe because except for the sisters and Kurt's posse the bus was empty except for an easier victim, Kevin Truesdale, who wore what were almost surely his sister's hand me downs, and whose parents wouldn't buy a television.

"Racinda how's your fat retard sister?" Kurt said.

Ruth, miraculously, hadn't sensed his presence until now. She had gotten her hands on a packet of loose tobacco and rolling papers and was making cigarette after cigarette under a makeshift tent of Racinda and Aimey's jackets.

She emerged from the pile of wool and polyester and turned around slowly, a strange combination of eager-to-please and surly on her face.

"Who wants to know?" Ruth said, licking the edge of a nearly-done cigarette and wiping the few pieces of loose tobacco from her lips.

"Come here," Kurt said. His three friends loomed behind him, smiling, bored, stoned.

Ruth, smiling in defiance, her heart holding its own monsters, and wide open to him, wiggled out of her seat and walked back, expertly, on the little strip of black rubber between the two rows of high green seats.

"Go get her," Aimey Frank whispered, pushing Racinda too hard on the shoulder.

But Racinda froze, terrified of the exponential damage she was in for with Ruth and Kurt located in the same three square feet.

The bus driver, long past breaking up any fights before they involved bloodshed, adjusted the volume on his walkman.

Aimey bit her lip, closed her book bag, adjusted its strap in her fist, nervously checked to make sure her safety pins were straight in her ears.

"Go—" Aimey said, "She won't listen to me."

But she wouldn't listen to Racinda either.

Kurt's urge to fuck things up was in a sort of holding pattern, these days—he'd gone back to the easy targets everyone just expected to get made fun of or beat up, back under the radar of teachers and bus drivers. There were troubles just behind Kurt's heart, but most afternoons, like now, he was easily able to hide them back there and not let them seep out.

In the past month, Kurt's recreational marijuana use had blossomed into an addiction. It was then that he stopped God, for the most part, though he still went to church. The weed numbed down how strongly he felt his mother's absence. Things had gone so well, so early, with Lindy Ellen that he was now brave enough to cheat on her with this girl in his home-ec class. He kept on cheating, less for the thrill than to abate his boredom with Lindy Ellen. He became a little fascinated by how his cheating transformed Lindy from her easy, graceful, nonchalance, her pretty girl's sense of entitlement, to a much more interesting teary, confused anger he could disdain and walk away from, hooked on the power, his movement away from her possessed of a time-extending pleasure, as if the stale hallway air were clear and cold and in his control:

In this way, this late winter, this sunny early spring of 1981, his thirteenth year, Kurt became what passes for a man.

"So," Ruth said, leaning her hip against the green vinyl of the seat in front of Kurt, "What?"

Kurt's eyes were so heavy-lidded as he paused. In the front of the bus, the nerd in his sister's old Lees made a barely audible squeak from the tension.

"So what do you want?" Ruth said, a little sweetly, to Kurt.

"Who's your new girlfriend, Laimey?" said Reginald Skrim, one of Kurt's cohort.

"Fuck off Reginald," Aimey said, chewing her lip.

"This is between me and you, Dieckmann," Ruth said, her smile swallowing up the tiny edge of menace in her.

"I—" Kurt said, and his head turned, so stoned, to look at the web of just-budding branches flying by out the window.

But then he turned back to Ruth and smirked lazily.

"I just wanted to know what it's like being in Special Ed. Being like the queen of the retards."

"Princess Retarded," Reginald Skrim laughed before petering out to stare at the amazing, rushing winter tree branches himself.

Aimey gasped. Racinda just held her breath. Nobody ever talked about Ruth's being in special ed. It was completely forbidden. Ruth had serenely taken her fork out of the school cafeteria shepherd's pie, and put it squarely in the calf of the last girl who had dared say anything. Ruth severed a tendon, completely got away with it, and that was a year ago. The girl smartened up, stuck to her story of tripping and falling into her cafeteria tray, bad luck.

But now, hurt crossed Ruth's features, she was naked, wide open to those boys. But then something else took over her face, a womanly expression, sexual and full of determination. She dropped her arms to her sides and just stared at him.

It unnerved Kurt Dieckmann. His stoner's distraction couldn't get him out of the powerful effects of Ruth's desire. So he leaned his neck over the seat in front of him, pointing his eyes at Racinda.

"Is God watching me, Racinda?" Kurt said and mustered a mean, boy laugh.

Racinda frowned.

But Ruth was still there, right in front of him, there was no escaping her, there was no escaping the fact that her unafraid stare was making him feel warmer, was making him want to grab her, and do—what?

"Fucking freak," Reginald Skrim said.

And with that the bus slowed suddenly, in front of the entrance to Kurt's subdevelopment.

"Come on."

Ruth didn't move as Kurt walked past her—he barreled by, brushed up against her and she didn't budge. She stepped aside when the other three followed him. Reginald Skrim and the other two walked directly up Kurt's driveway, but Kurt planted himself in a patch of just-out crocuses, squinting meanly at Ruth through the window, until well after the bus pulled off.

What was it in Kurt's eyes then? Racinda couldn't be sure—it wasn't just that thrill at the power Ruth was handing him, that charge of treating a person like so much dogshit on your shoe. A pale light washed over his eyes—green as the shoots starting out of the brown fields—and faded. Racinda didn't know what it was, that moment—something vulnerable, something he didn't have a handle on—and as the years march forward she will understand less and less that light. Racinda will forget that green wash—though evidence of it will cross her path daily, it will take her a long time to notice again that the king needs the condemned to exist, that the soap needs the dirt, that the mad burn propelling time forward is what the rules and the tidiness and the tries at perfection are fighting against, feeding on: that the rules that look so solid are actually quite simple to get rid of—drunken into a blur, etiquette snapped easily in two—but the fires on the edges, the furnace on the bottom of it all, whatever it was that pushed Ruth and whatever was just past Kurt's green-washed eyes is indelible.

And Kurt, Kurt stood there in the first batch of March blooms until the bus disappeared over the hill between his subdivision and Ruth and Racinda's farmhouse. Kurt held every muscle tighter to try to pin something down that was shivering across him, shivering across the seams of him.

Four.   *April 1981*

As the crocuses and the daffodils came and went, as the April tulips took hold against greening fields, Racinda turned that look in Kurt's eyes over and over behind her own. During Sunday worship at the Dells' she marveled at Kurt's relative docility around his mother, around these singing women. Racinda watched and considered his every reaction to the women, to Ruth's continuing stares. Later, after everything exploded and nobody could quite glue together the story of that day, Racinda couldn't tell which pieces she had imagined and what she actually knew for real.

What Racinda *didn't* fabricate in her imagination about the Sunday Ruth followed Kurt out of the Dells' light blue living room was that she'd known *something* would shatter. Racinda could feel it before anything actually happened. Kurt, who once whispered shyly in his mother's ear when he wanted something at the Dells' now walked up to Jenny Dieckmann and freely announced he'd be outdoors for the rest of the afternoon. Ruth sneaked—just picked up her faded satchel with the red embroidered star on its flap and left while Amandine was—quite ingenuously, quite happily, quite authentically—clapping and singing and smiling and even sweating (a *little*).

When Ruth followed him outside during a chorus—*the joi-oy of the Loo-oo-oo-oord is my strength*—Racinda paused mid-line—jealous!— anxious less for her sister's well-being than for her own inability to access Kurt.

The absolute brokenness on Racinda's face was so marked that it got Tracy Dell's attention immediately, and Tracy, dutiful Dell daughter, kind soul, not even a year older than Ruth, but determined to act a grown-up, pulled Racinda in front of her, resting her forearms sweetly on Racinda's collarbone. Swaying with Tracy, the attention and love of it, made Racinda forget to be worrying about Ruth's access to Kurt. Delight filled her instead with warmth and song coursing the room. Racinda found herself laughing and singing at once, her heart linked to the others in the room with tiny, powerful filaments.

Since she wasn't attuned to it, Racinda couldn't imagine the wash of desire curving like waves through the pool of Kurt's body just minutes before his teeth would be razed. She just thought he hated Ruth as plainly as the rest of the world seemed to. As he coursed down the road so slowly, nudging a basketball at his feet like kicking a rock forward, he was full of the sounds of the ball's textured surface pressing pavement, the low-wind *rrrrr* of Route One to the north. Because he'd been up all night smoking with Matty, Kurt's hyperactivity was drenched to stillness, fatigue. The quiet outside noises were just enough to occupy him, where the rowdiness of church had jangled.

Kurt's mind meandered to Lindy, but just for a minute, and then on to Ruth's stomach, pink and curved elegantly, he'd noticed, when she raised her hands to shake the tambourine and her shirt lifted above the waistband of her corduroys. The way Ruth's shiny eyes jabbed him—like poking someone in the ribs—when she caught his stare. There was a conversation, there was a two-step, there was a battle there that had not finished, and, even exhausted, Kurt was curious.

So it was like a wish granted he'd never officially even made when her footsteps gathered behind him and she called him, *Dieckmann*.

The buzzing, flying feeling in him started from the electricity of her nearby.

"What?" he said, not looking.

"Are you going to smoke me out?" Ruth said.

Kurt could hear that the words came through a smile.

"It's all gone," he said, exhaling. "We smoked all Matty's last night."

He turned to her then, he felt calmer, he felt grateful for the company. Her whitish hair looked neat and pretty back off her face.

Ruth wobbled and fidgeted in her sneakers, unsure of what to say next.

Shy, now that his eyes were on her, she crammed her hands down into her pants pockets and found the scrap of headline she'd torn out from one of Linda Dell's magazines a year before.

"Look!" Ruth said, nervousness exploding, and she handed Kurt the tattered bit of magazine—lightened folds from months in her pocket running through it like veins in a leaf.

Kurt looked at the paper scrap, curled slightly, like a shell, in his palm:

"'Is God Dead,'" he read, "So what?"

But the insect in him stilled, blinked, its great eyelids pausing halfway shut, sadly, its head tumbling onto its hair-thin front legs in sudden slumber. Kurt felt the blank, awful space in himself—a space that had been yawning wider for awhile now, but which finally, here, became undeniably real.

He slammed the side of a white-striped Adidas against the basketball at his feet with a surprising force, causing it to fly in a solid arc across the Dells' front yard, landing among the line of rhododendrons with a shivering of branches. This question had been on his mind lately. He'd sensed it, somehow, this death of God, back there on the bench with Lindy—not the day Racinda found him, but a bit earlier. Lindy had even started moving when he kissed her, but his desire for her was gone, making out with her was just an option of recreation after school—less appealing, suddenly, than playing Atari alone or even eating ice cream and watching the women cry about men on TV at three o'clock with his mother, who would pat him on the forearm, then move to the far end of the buttery leather couch, avoiding him.

Until recently, Kurt felt something at night when he prayed—an activity hidden into moments when Matty was certain not to find him—kneeling as his mother had taught him to ever since he was small. But, starting that January week when his mother didn't sleep, when the Skittles exploded in the microwave, he'd sensed a kind of non-response, as if God and his mother had caught the same strange head cold that was making them both a bit deaf. The absence of God was only even thinkable because of the absence of his mother. This deafness on both of their parts expanded—Kurt felt it in himself toward his mother, even in church at the Dells' house, where previously, free from Matty's and his father's judgments, Kurt had been able to enjoy the singing and this enjoyment had been a secret he only shared with her. His mother could hear him, God could hear him, but then she went kind of crazy and now the deafness that had started in the Dieckmann house was busy spreading to the Dells', even. Not all the time, but usually, like today, which was actually why Kurt came outside in the first place.

"So why do you go to church if you know that?" Ruth said, "If you're so smart about that? About Dead God?"

When Kurt looked up from the chalky gray road he noticed how red her cheeks were and it excited him. She somehow made him look directly into her eyes, and he felt a mix of fury at her and greed for her.

Her lips were wet, her eyes didn't flinch from his.

"What do you know," he said, unconvincingly, when he broke the glare.

"I know that you're sleeping with that stupid girl," Ruth said.

At any other moment Kurt would have scooped the desire that formed Ruth's last phrase right out of her and annihilated the hope behind it. But now, he couldn't. He felt himself sitting down on the grass, he felt himself leaning back onto his hands.

He felt his mother not wanting to touch him, he felt the absence of the whirring, slicing insect in him, and he desperately wanted God to be judging him now for what he'd done with Lindy, because if God weren't judging him for that, the shiny flat endless square of nothing in him would keep expanding like this, and all he could see above him was the seared-white sky and Ruth's cheeks like white dogwood petals with pink splashing up from within.

He leaned back as Ruth lowered her knees around his and when her mouth was just an inch from his face, waiting, dark, pink, and he could see that in that moment Ruth's mouth could stop the nothing square from expanding, Ruth's mouth not like Lindy Ellen's, which he felt he owned, really, Lindy's mouth something he could direct as if with a remote control. He could see that Ruth's mouth was a new possibility and that it promised even newer possibilities and delights and expansion of something solid, laughter, something real, something he could feel with his skin like he could feel his mother's absence, his mother repulsed by him, his mother weeping and he could feel the blackness inside his house that never lightened except from the television, the zings of asteroids on the Atari so like the insect inside him. So from just underneath the delight at this surprising mouth of Ruth's crept the feeling of his own gray-roaring house, and he knew, he understood that Ruth had one too, the grayest-black house, beyond that mouth, beyond the insides of her warm knees pressing just above his own, she had an empty expanding space and it made something shake down his legs and it woke up the insect who started and sped to a blind, screeching course through his body.

"Get off of me," he heard himself saying as his legs pitched up from under Ruth. Twisting.

And he heard her fumbling, and he heard the heavy triangle of metal slam first above his teeth, and he heard her saying *don't fuck with my head, Dieckmann*, sort of like somebody on TV would say, a man on TV would say: so the blows came.

Three times, four, and the jagged white flash of pain split through his chin. He felt the root of an incisor separate halfway from his jaw and he felt a back tooth snap, he felt the tip float off a canine as when a child in a bubble-bath blows so much foam off a peak of foam. The white, torn-skin feeling mended its edges but expanded—wrenching, heavy—from his hairline to his chest to his fingertips. And so Kurt didn't even see her, didn't see the force Ruth used decimating her own mouth, didn't see her surprise that it *hurt*, didn't see the blood she brought from herself. Kurt was running so fast, the insect flying and landing and stinging and flying and landing and stinging the insides of his veins, the cabinets of his heart, the gummy pinkness of the reverse side of his skin. The pain yowled through him, beyond him, and something already stiffening inside him cemented.

*   *   *

In the seconds and minutes and hour after Ruth attacked him, his slashed gums pulsing, Kurt wept in a decidedly feminine manner: bloody, shrieking, fierce, waving an arm at Ruth, trying to point but unable to, gesturing instead as if he were flinging water onto her. He was furious the adults thought he was responsible for all the pain and mayhem but he couldn't speak between giant gasps of air and tears and blood to express otherwise, and he was right in assuming that if he didn't clear it up now he would never be able to. It took several minutes before they got him to lie down and several more before it was determined the blood was still flowing and he needed to go to the ER.

When Ruth managed to become quiet for a minute, Racinda got a good look at her and saw that besides the tears and the blood there was an air of having won something quite important on her face. So Kurt Dieckmann lost, but what exactly beyond teeth he lost Racinda couldn't imagine. So much noise coming out of Kurt—it was surprising not just to Racinda, but to the Christian women as well. They looked on, but, busy fussing over Ruth, none came near him—only his mother did, and oddly, tentatively.

Racinda leaned her wide cheeks, her sharp chin against the wall, wrapped a piece of her long unremarkable honey-brown hair around her tongue and, chewing on it, watched Mrs. Dieckmann's hands.

Mrs. Dieckmann—her ash-blond hair pulled back into a thin grosgrain ribbon, creating a sort of a flowing pillow around her face, the rings on her fingers thick and round, nothing to catch a sweater—didn't pull her damaged son to her, but sat him back on the couch and put a cold compress on his jaw. There was a stiffness, a hesitation between them—she didn't pull his hair from his eyes, didn't touch him.

That she leaned a bit away from him, attached only by ice, seemed strange to Racinda.

Despite his injuries, Kurt Dieckmann got whipped with a belt later, by Dirk Dieckmann, his father, who, like most fathers, never came to church but who believed spare-the-rod anyway. Ruth's sharp-tasting, broken lips oozed blood onto her white-yellow skin like coolaid on a tablecloth while the women's heavy arms tended to her—lifted her up and cradled her. As Amandine shook imperceptibly, her hand covering her mouth, in the corner. As Racinda, all of seven years old, held Amandine's hem like she—Racinda—needed the support when really she was trying to keep Amandine from toppling the other direction.

On the way to the hospital, holding her broken but victorious sister's hand, Racinda got the sense that Kurt had used up all his crying, his screaming, on that day. From now on, she thought, he would be quiet. Crueler and colder. And she was right—he froze after that. The sobs and even the outbursts stuck in his throat, then lower. He learned to quiet the protest, he learned to push it outward, he learned to control himself and he learned to control whomever else seemed worth it.

*   *   *

"Well, don't be so queer, Lyman," Button, Lyman's stepmother, had said when he stood outside his bloody, disturbed daughter's hospital room door. "I knew Harts were queer but if I'd known *how* queer I wouldn't have married your father," she said, the sadness ringing the corners of her mouth belying the worry under all that annoyance.

"Right," Lyman had said then.

After Button gave him a sturdy push on the back to get him in there, he stood, with a blank face, blank hands, by Ruth's bedside. He managed to squeeze her fingers after she'd stared up at him so expectantly for what seemed like eons. Waiting for Daddy to make it okay--he could see that. But besides installing himself by the bed for a spell, with a bit of a chill, squeezing her hand, he had no idea what to do.

Simply had *no idea* how to proceed with his family: Amandine somehow claimed dominion over the girls. In his own childhood, his father had shown him a man's world of tractors, of work gloves, of building a low stone wall down by the creek. Had showed him the endless rhythms and varieties of the wildness still in the woods, and of the tamed stuff on what had then still been a partially working farm—just corn, summer vegetables—and the orchards.

It had been a family of two pairs: Elmer and Lyman, Elmer and Button. Not three. Button and Lyman had always kept each other just outside reach, both painstakingly guarding against the possibility of her trying to take the place of his dead mother, Violetta.

So with Amandine summoning and holding the girls under her own umbrella, Lyman didn't know how to get them under his, even for an afternoon. Lyman didn't know if he even *had* an umbrella for them to join him under.

"Well, *do* things with them," Amandine had said when his befuddled face broke through a defensive posture after they'd fought over it.

"What?" Lyman said.

And, yes, *what* would he do with them? They'd just chatter if he had them watch football on TV with him weekend afternoons—he didn't want the annoyance. And in his wood-working shop, in the basement, the girls would be nothing but a hazard to themselves—certainly unsafe to have them down there if he was going to get anything done, and how long could he really give them lessons on a bevel, on a sander, on carving tools, even if by some stroke of genetics they *were* interested? He couldn't imagine it.

"What would I *do* with them?" Lyman asked, the thought of Ruth damaging his tools, trying to scream over the sound of the hacksaw bringing back the irritation to the lines around his mouth.

Amandine looked very tired then, he noticed, as she customarily did before one of the migraines that would cause her to lock herself in a silenced room until the next day.

"I don't know, Lyman. Take them to the circus, or to the *movies*, or—just *talk* to them," she said, her voice trailing into a whisper as a hand began covering her eyes from the suddenly dangerous light.

But he didn't know how to talk to them, and the idea of a smelly, crowded circus, somewhere in Philadelphia, or past it, farther north—because the circus didn't come around nearby Wilmington, Delaware, anymore—brought a tightening to his chest. Just—the hassle of getting there, and what if Ruth had an episode in the car? Where would he bring her if they were on I-95, how would they get to the hospital? Where were the hospitals up there anyway? How would he continue to drive on roads he didn't know very well, to an unknown destination, full of crowds which Ruth would certainly be prone to lose herself in, not to *mention* the wild animals in cages, heavy equipment, and if she could do thousands of dollars of damage to herself with a *trowel* . . .

(Lyman knew what had happened with the Dieckmann boy. Never once *said* as much, publicly played the protective father of girl attacked by the class hoodlum when his own father or Button or Amandine wanted him to, but he knew which one had been the aggressor.)

Just *talk* to the girls, Amandine would say. Lyman had known how to talk to Amandine when she had a lighter quality to her, when she giggled a little bit too much at what he said, and often at the wrong times. But now that that girlishness was gone from her, and now that migraines trembled behind her older eyes, and now that the umbrella of her care didn't have room for him with the girls herded under it, Lyman had somehow lost the ability to talk to his wife, too.

"The circus is too much of a hassle, it's a *hassle*—" he said.

He wanted to explain it to his wife, he wanted her to understand why that idea was not going to fix the problem. He wanted her to want to laugh at his jokes. He wanted his wife to understand that he was expertly thinking very carefully through the options of how to repair Ruth.

"Lyman," she said, turning away from him, one hand covering her eyes as she headed to the darkened room, the other hand behind her, low, sort of waving to him, sort of shooing him away.

So here he stood now, in his own home, outside Ruth's door again. Ruth's mouth, and her brain chemistry, had stabilized enough in the last few days for her to be released from the hospital earlier today. He stood here, useless, unwilling to enter his daughters' room. Stunned and immobile. He summoned the memory of Button's earlier push between his shoulder blades, and stepped inside.

"Well," Lyman, said, "Well, Ruth, now. . ."

He stared at his smashed daughter, set his hand lightly on her messy white-blond hair.

The intensity of Ruth's eyes nailed to him caught his breath.

(The circus was *not* going to fix this, neither was show and tell in the basement workshop.)

He was the drink of water and she was parched.

Lyman coughed, he squeezed her hand tighter, warmer, with this desperate love that swarmed him then, and then he froze again, the unassailable need in his daughter absolutely terrifying him.

He was fading already. You could practically see the wall through his torso, the doorknob through his hand. He was everything to these girls, except he was everything as an *absence*. His not being there occupied huge swathes of their hearts, his not-being-there was the precious thing each daughter clung to until it was wrinkled, deadened, stained, but in her jeans pocket forever, impossible to toss to the curb.

So, though Lyman would be with them a few years more, he was already for most purposes gone. Mattered, already, mostly in the lack of him.

He chose to exist as the empty space between women.

He watched television. He withdrew from the chatter of his daughters. He both took from his life and gave himself new life by retreating to that woodshop in the basement where he sawed and hammered and carved and glued and stained and sealed plain, unnecessary, everyday items that piled up in the corners before he could think what to do with them.

"Well, Ruth, now don't go off without a *group* of children," he said standing next to the girls' bed, trying to banish the pain in Ruth from himself. Ruth scooted her face on her pillow closer to him, though he was already stepping away.

The corners of his eyes turned down. And the eyes sharp, urgent, held a sadness that gave Ruth so much of what she wanted from him. His face reddening, terrified for her, loving her.

"Okay, Daddy," Ruth said in a tiny, babytalk voice, "I won't do it no more."

Lyman exhaled. He backed into the doorway, the hall light behind him rendering his face dark.

"Goodnight, Daddy."

And when he left, the coddling, the sweet warmth Ruth had sucked in from his panic evaporated, leaving the room dryer, colder than before.

"See, Creature, they *don't* know," Ruth said with a slap to her sister's shoulder when she heard the noises downstairs that indicated Lyman was preparing a drink. Racinda turned her eyes away from Ruth's, but not quickly enough. Racinda held her breath at the exact moment Ruth's sure fingers began twisting the skin on Racinda's waist in a hard hard pinch.

It was better this way: if Ruth was hurting her, Racinda wouldn't think about the Devil who Amandine had taught her was always hovering at her back, and she wouldn't have to fight him in her mind.

Racinda didn't scream, and didn't scream, and didn't breathe.

"Getting tougher," Ruth said, slipping her powdery fingers back to her own side, and she was right. Racinda could hold her breath now until Ruth got bored, and only then let something go in a spitty exhale deep in her pillow's musty center.

*   *   *

Button, too, knew who was the criminal with the trowel. When Button noticed it was missing early that Sunday morning from her tool shed she just poked around instead of starting seedlings in the makeshift greenhouse, letting herself forget how behind she was in that department. Why would she think anything of it? She figured she misplaced it. She puttered in the shed—sorted the black-tipped violet tulips from the ivory ones: the bulbs had become jumbled but she could tell them apart by feel.

Could Ruth feel the difference between bulbs like this, if I taught her? Button wondered later. Did the girl just feel pain differently from the rest of us? The doctors had said that during the frenzied times, the mania, she could possibly not feel much of anything, but that such a state might change at some point into extreme sensitivity. Who knew. Button conjured the dolorous, abandoned, purple face of the child in a hospital bed then shuddered her old bones to forget it.

Soon after Ruth got out of the hospital, Button's trowel reappeared in her tool shed—exactly where Ruth had managed to hide it temporarily after the attack was a mystery. The thing was wiped clean of blood but smeared with oily whorls from a child's hands. Button just dropped it in the trash bin and drove to the hardware store in town with the purpose of buying a new one: green, enamel intact, less sinister. When the girls came across the field to her house late the next week for dinner and Ruth wrapped her arms around Button's waist, Button didn't doubt the veracity of the tears, didn't stiffen, didn't retreat into her body.

"Honey," she said, "That boy didn't mean it."

And Ruth wrapped her fists in Button's overalls, tightening the denim at the waist so it was hard for Button to breathe. Now that she was off the painkillers, entirely new parts of Ruth's jaw were still emerging in different degrees and varieties of pain—prickly, heavy, sneaky, swirling, sweating, damp—and she pressed her teeth together harder and harder until all the sensation converged in her throat and she cried as Kurt Dieckmann had. Button pulled her tighter, forgoing air for a moment to quiet the girl. But Ruth pushed away then, without meeting Button's eyes, and sliced through the house looking for her sister, who had locked herself in the basement, with a flashlight and a book, where neither the Devil nor her sister could get her.

*   *   *

Amandine and her girls kept going to the Dells', Sundays, after the signs were gone from Ruth's body. After her purple jaw returned to normal, after the Novocain finally took and dentistry was accomplished on her, after a certain dosage of medication was found, for the most part, to tone down her mania. When Ruth would have days of nonstop talking, nights of wide-eyes and torturing her sister till dawn, Amandine knew not to bring her to the Dells' home church, but when Amandine consulted the doctors they couldn't tell her much more than that: keep the girl out of situations that have exacerbated the behavior in the past. Medicate. Things calmed down, but with a sharpness underneath, waiting to slice the peace: the days of chattering would certainly start again.

As it got warmer, Racinda and Ruth would go to Button's after church at the Dells, where they would get to drink minted iced tea and eat chocolate chips from a bowl by the handful and the dinner wasn't so boiled and spare as it was at home with Amandine. Their grandpa, Elmer, would let them each sit in front of him on the riding mower, and when Ruth was so almost-normal like this she could even rest quietly on the old davenport in Button's TV den and braid Racinda's hair nicely, not pulling, just listening to Elmer's Pepsi fizzling against ice, listening to the melodic pings of the shiny pale green, silver-rimmed game show when someone guessed a right letter.

If there was something to be done in the garden by the fishpond, and it wasn't too rainy (these were the warmish, wet, near-May days, these were when summer just begins to say hi once in awhile, in this part of the world), Button would take them both with her to help get the seedlings in or to weed or to rig netting around the beginnings of Bibb lettuces to protect them from deer. Almost superstitiously, Button had bought two additional trowels on her trip to the hardware store—so that there was one for each of the three of them, to prevent any disagreements, maybe, but more as an effort to banish shame and violence and secrecy from the tool, more as a way to reinstate it as something useful and good, not weird and Born-Again and tongue-speaking and unpredictable.

Button and Ruth, digging: Button was determined to get rid of the tenacious mint root that grew back each year, the sweat almost bluish on her brow; Ruth happily, carefully was carving rows for the new pansies and Johnny-jump-ups to go in. Racinda lay still, on her stomach, her flat, brown-in-places, blond-in-places braids loosely flopped into a link at the back of her neck, her hands on her chin, leaning her little white nose over the fishpond, waiting patiently for Button's enormous, mysterious gold-fish to greet her.

Since the Devil hadn't been on her tail since Ruth got back, Racinda slept fine at night. Although she knew the grayness would return and that Ruth's hyper days would someday expand into weeks and that hospitals would in fact become a standard landscape as she grew up—though she suspected all this Racinda also knew to contain her awareness of it in a corner and just let herself feel the covers—not pinches—at night, feel the sweetness of her sister's hands sorting out her hair, her scalp, feel the quiet around a peanut-butter sandwich, feel the quiet around Button's morning toast pressed flat with butter, looking out the window at the finches and the robins hopping, circling Elmer's tall Lucite bird-feeder. The calm, the warmth grew in Racinda those weeks—it expanded like light in her, like melody where before there had been only a plain rhythm: cautious, spare, existing only for survival.

Every once in awhile, those days, Racinda would get to do something for *so* long without being interrupted that she would actually seek Ruth out. At first Racinda was able to convince herself she was making sure Ruth was okay, but after enough times of okay Racinda knew she just craved the old excitement, even though it had involved such torment. At the Dells', Ruth sang blankly. Suddenly, with Ruth's drama pacified, Racinda saw not just joy but the treacle of the songs, and the death in the way she and Tracy Dell and little Moab Dell all just did as they were told all the time, the way they were so interested in being such good girls. Racinda started to annoy her self with her own timidity. She found herself, not intentionally, at first, imagining Ruth in a rage, popping Tracy in the ear with a Bible, imagining Ruth and Aimey Frank forcing a perfect sing-song Dell daughter, under threat of a cigarette burn on the forearm, to say *motherfucker*.

Still, with Ruth okay like this, things were going so well for Racinda that even her own mean mental transgressions didn't call guilt and Satan to her heart. Underneath the momentary calm, though, he lurked.

Racinda knew she hadn't seen the last of him.

But here, waiting for signs of pond life, sometimes rolling onto her back in order to feel the beautiful stretch in her neck, Racinda's gaze always downward in order not to miss her favorite—a white-yellow fish with deep violet eyes—here, puddling the warm sun on her belly:

Here, occasionally like this Racinda's calmness was pure, and was enough to know that in spite of her worries the Devil couldn't destroy *everything* she loved,

and the warmth gained its voice, started pooling into her, whispering that there was always going to be enough, that help would always arrive, that she would be taken care of in the end, but

Racinda sat up, clenched her knees to her chest, tried to close away this expanding delight.

And because she didn't know who it was, she thought it was the voice of that Devil, refusing to leave her be.

She needed the warmth of that voice, she needed it now, still young, before the world and her mother and her sister would demand such toughness from her, such shutting-out.

Before Ruth drinks too much diet soda and knocks her serotonin back into hiding, conjuring flat grayness from Amandine, from Amandine's house, from her father in the basement, conjuring grayness and not death itself in Racinda, but the terror of it, and loneliness.

By then, the locks will have clicked and it will take a mirror-faced man showing up later to undo enough to let delight through, to unleash her heart.

Yes: before Racinda's drop back into constant fear and wariness and a sticky weight in the back of the throat burdens her and she avoids this warm hand completely, thinking it is the Devil's,

Before the grid of the world sets in, she needs this—this warmth, this bright pool of hope. Now: the moment to secure in her the sense that home exists, that rest exists, that somebody intelligent and kind and full of pleasure is watching.

2

THE FIRST GIRL

1968

Button

I'm the one who finally named her. Her parents let Ruth go blank for the first month of her life, distracted by their own childish pastimes. The baby's brassy, reddish brown hair swirled into a few tufty points and a watery sheen coated her eyes as if tears were always about to form in their corners. Lines trailed across her palms and the bottoms of her feet, mapping things out for her early. She filled up any little space you gave her, then, quietly. The noise around the house didn't bother her—a long, sunny cold snap began with her birth and it blew at the windows and doors with thuds, curled in the clear air outside with high-up whimpers. She sucked on blankets, fingers, her feet eventually; her eyes followed squares of light that the windows threw onto her nursery walls, bright patches trailing on through the day.

I thought she was a remarkable child, as I suppose is natural. Her expressions seemed so complex, her responses indicated so much—each shift, each opening and closing of the fist seemed calculated to communicate worlds to me.

I'd never had one of my own. I was almost fifty-eight that year.

She seemed to recognize the sound of her father Lyman's steps returning from work each day across the porch—when she heard his noise she wouldn't catch my gaze as she usually did, but would crane her head in his direction until it hurt her—I could tell—though she never cried from this. He had spent two weeks doting on Amandine, and when she dozed off he would sneak away into the nursery to stare at the baby, to hold her tentatively and make conversation. But he grew weary, and when he went back to work that willingness to take care of his wife and get to know his child waned. When they first came home, though, Lyman would hold Ruth, stare at her and talk to her and tell her about things—the way a cylinder works in an engine, say. He would hold her up to the window and point out the stream that crossed back in the woods, the bridge he and Elmer had built over it with yellow stones.

As the weeks passed and Amandine stayed in her bed, demanded more and more of him, he would head for the basement more quickly, shear minutes each day off his time upstairs. In the nursery, the absence of Amandine pointed to the absence of his own mother, and the mahogany crib the baby slept in was the same one Lyman's mother had had made especially for him. I could see the gap, the missing space of his mother, written on his face, so strong it might as well have been words hovering there: GONE. Looking down at his girl in his crib, he couldn't help seeing through the eyes of his own mother looking down on him, only to see his daughter there, the parent and the child at once, the declining and the just-budding intertwined.

Not me, I could feel him thinking, the *mother*—the mother is the one who is meant to be attached. And both mothers—his own and his child's—were missing. His own in body, his child's in mind and spirit.

Lyman would still stare at the baby and pick her up and even ask to feed her if formula was ready right when he got home from work. He cooed to her, and she coaxed him into a habit of being a notch friendlier than civil to me at these times. She didn't fidget when he held her, and she clung to him tightly but didn't cry when he set her down to go work on his hobbies in the basement or on the Plymouth in the garage. I would leave him leftovers from the dinner I made for Amandine and Elmer in the fridge, and would only hear his footsteps and the whooshy noise of the refrigerator door opening late at night, hours after the rest of us turned in. When I woke in the morning (well, after I woke for real, not just for feeding the girl) he was always already gone.

I don't think it was Ruth that Lyman was avoiding. It was me, the woman who he thought took his mother away, and it was Amandine, too, who was having such a hard time after the birth.

*   *   *

It had been five days already she'd stayed in the maternity ward and the doc said still a few more, Amandine's not doing so hot.

"Well for gad's sake!" I said, "What's wrong with her?"

The lights in the hospital made Lyman's hangdog expression even worse, like he was lit from within by the sick greenish bulb of a swimming pool at night.

"Postpartum depression," the doctor said in a low voice. Blah blah blah. He went on about the pills she should take, which ones not together and which ones how often. Elmer, Lyman and I stood in a tidy circle around this doctor in the corner of Amandine's hospital room that was farthest away from her bed. I looked at Elmer with raised eyebrows and a little devilishness in the downturn of my mouth, but he wouldn't indulge me. He focused on Lyman, who shifted his head slowly—smitten, his cheeks hollowed out from almost a week of skipped meals—to regard his wife. Back then he thought she was just so lovely, he thought she was more than he deserved. Ha! She was like a stretched-out doll baby, shades of paleness on top of each other, apparently asleep yet I had the clearest sense she could hear every word we said. Postpartum depression! More likely she just enjoyed the high-living of breakfast, lunch, and dinner in bed every day, the gluttony and sloth of it. The baby, the doctor said, should stay in the hospital as long as its mother did.

So left in Amandine's empty house, I waited for the child to come home, and I waited for the cold to break so I could plant. I hadn't got my tulips in before the frost because of being up in New York, visiting the few people who remained from my previous life, (those people I walked away from such a nervous wreck decades ago, but can go to now for something like solace.) Anyhow, tulips are the most expensive flowers I grow, the only ones I special order from catalogues. I had no intention on letting the bulbs rot out down the cellar till next autumn, but I was in New York when they should have gone in, and then it got too cold. This was an especially harsh first week of November: the temperature had been far under normal—freezing or below—since Halloween. I could just see myself, trying to chip away at the frozen earth, one palm getting filthy leaning on icy sod, my rear sticking up in the air, my arm thrashing at the ground like a piston not attached to my body, stabbing and stabbing like Norman Bates, with flecks of dirt flying away from the trowel and quickening around me in a squall. I knew better than to try it.

I waited.

*   *   *

When Amandine came out of the hospital, she took too many painkillers and stayed in bed for weeks, making loud efforts at lifting the pages of wallpaper sample books, huge heavy squares. Lyman fawned on her for awhile, hoisting the books up onto the breakfast tray that spanned her legs as if a bridge, Amandine a dull, slow, silent river—murky. Every few hours she would say, *water* or *tissue* or *pills* (meaning a codeine or later, a Demerol) or *saltine*, all she would eat. She would lift the pages of the huge square books and run her limp white hands up and down their textures as if her wrists were broken.

When she was silent, she seemed to be whining. And when she spoke, something bigger than her voice seemed to be shattering. Something of the finest crystal, smashing apart: *Pills. Water. Tissue.*

She would doze off within minutes of Lyman propping the wallpaper book up for her, and start snoring so obnoxiously—something Lyman swore she had never done before, even in those last heavy months of her pregnancy—that Lyman hurried to lift the book off of her and leave the room just to get away from the noise. When she woke up again, she would call him to her from anywhere he happened to be in the house by swiping her hand across the bedside table, knocking prescription bottles and often her lamp and a glass of water tumbling into a racket against the wall. Reckless. I winced every time I heard Lyman's feet run to this.

Sometimes I would bring the baby into her room for a visit. Amandine gave the impression of being a sort of a zombie, sleeping propped upright on a pile of satin pillows, looking like she was awake but just playing a joke with her loud heaving. I hated going into that room, and left Amandine's care up to Lyman. Without makeup, she didn't look so hoity-toity anymore, she seemed washed out and exhausted. The mess droned out of her. For the first week home, Amandine would keep on snoring, despite me nearly shoving her off the bed in trying to wake her up. The baby, who kept a normal baby schedule, waking every few hours for a feeding during the night, going about its business of stretching and flexing and staring up at me and the mobile and empty space, was undisturbed by her mother's ruckus. The baby navigated the crass noises without noticing the difference.

As the baby settled in on her sleeping mother's belly, I tapped gently on Amandine's shoulder, then nudged, harder, then started flicking Amandine's white cheek with my middle finger propelled off my thumb.

Amandine's eyes hovered slightly, opened a tiny bit as her voice stumbled.

"Pill!" she said, "Pain pill!" wakening but still muddled, "Where's Lyman?"

"Amandine, Lyman went back to work," I lied. "Look—it's your daughter on you."

A streak of horror crossed Amandine's pinched, mousy little face as she turned—scared stark white—to look at me:

"Are you going to take care of me?"

"Oh just say hello to your daughter," I said. "Lyman doesn't go back till tomorrow. And he's getting you a nurse. Just say hello."

Amandine leaned back into the mounds of smooth pillows, before starting, as if she just then felt the nine pounds of baby on her lap. She looked over to me for guidance.

"Just give her your finger for gad's sake. Like this."

I unfurled Amandine's hand—clenched so tight the yellow skin on her knuckles was blanching itself—and placed the tip of her smallest finger into the baby's pink fist.

Amandine tensed, made a wavering sound, high-pitched but quick, then seemed to settle in. The baby stretched itself out then contracted, again and again, as if trying to climb up to see her mother's face better. Amandine stared down, but didn't pull the child to her. For a minute I thought Amandine was softening, and about to make some normal, mothery gesture, but I had too high of hopes: the snores started again. Trying to move herself like an inchworm up her mother, the baby reached pitifully.

*　　*　　*

When they had first come home, two weeks after the baby was born, I carried her into the house, and put her down in her crib. The doctor knew to pass her on to me when, leaving the maternity ward. Amandine had refused her, just stared at the automatic door beginning to slide past her face and gripped the wheelchair's arms. The sky outside the hospital was white like with snow, though we never got any. Lyman rolled Amandine to the car, lifted her into it, while Elmer folded up the wheelchair, stashed it in the trunk—Amandine had insisted on bringing one home, to get her from the driveway to the front door. (She acted like she thought she was half-dead). From the front door, Lyman carried her to her bed where she stayed, except for her long trips to the bathroom, which she somehow managed to take all by herself just fine:

These lavatory trips gave me the incentive to try to rouse her, seeing as she was at least sometimes capable.

I did hear her talking in full sentences, one time, to Lyman before he went back to work. I heard her call me a hillbilly, among other things. He expected me to take care of her, she wouldn't even hold her baby, never mind nurse it, and she had the nerve to call me trailer trash? I might've liked to ask her, Who just held her own in New York City?

"Don't leave me with her!" I heard Amandine sobbing to Lyman, "She'll kill me off!" She was really crying, sloppy wet heaves, loud as her snoring, so I don't know who she thought she was fooling. I hadn't been trying to do her in at that point, but being accused of it and of the other sure might have done the trick. Might have set me thinking on it, if I was such trash as she claimed.

But then, Amandine's never been too clever.

*　　*　　*

After the nurse came, Amandine stopped knocking her prescriptions and the lamp off the bedside table whenever she needed something. Mrs. Townsend started the Monday morning Lyman had to go back to work, and she provided Amandine with a tiny silver bell to ring at her whim. (For all my beef with Lyman, I have to say his dedication to his ailing wife impressed me. Two years worth of vacation time he wasted just setting pills onto her pink cat-tongue and fetching glass after glass of water for her to fling to the carpet.)

A big woman—but one whose weighty arms and legs and hands seemed to be flat, not fleshy, just strong planes—Mrs. Townsend had the appearance and the steady demeanor of the family she came from—Hoopeses of Landemberg. Her mother, Rosalie, had gone to church with mine, so we had known each other as girls, though she was a good eight years older than I and always a little stand-offish. When I greeted her in Amandine's overdone foyer by saying, "Well, hello, Annie," she paused and looked at me so strangely that I thought there was something wrong with her, thought she was angry to be here, until she said, "Hello, Mrs. Hart," instead of "Hello, Button," and I remembered how formal a Hoopes is. *Mrs. Townsend* she liked to be called, nothing else.

She wore a white lab coat over her navy flannel dress, and a folded white hat, whose red cross flashed on its front panel like a badge. Her gray pin curls wound perfect and tight across her head. The same pale blue vein that had run under Rosalie Hoopes's ruddy skin between her left eye and her temple coursed there on Mrs. Townsend's face too.

"Mrs. Townsend, Amandine's right upstairs," I said to her. "Let me show you around downstairs first, then we can go introduce you."

I cringed as I walked through each room, the ridiculousness of Amandine's boastful house seeming so much more awful by virtue of a second set of eyes there with me. It must have seemed to Mrs. Townsend that a different overbudgeted person was responsible for doing up each room— anybody actually planning the full effect would clearly have to be some breed of lunatic. But if she did think anything of it, she didn't say: Lake Placid, was what I thought when I looked at her face. Nothing could ripple on her she didn't want to show you.

As we climbed the stairs, I turned my head back to Mrs. Townsend, sorry to have to unleash on her the beast Lyman married, and embarrassed about the house.

"Mrs. Townsend, we don't need you to dress up. You can just come here in regular clothes, if you like."

I said it because I knew how happy it would make Amandine if this woman wore a little hat for her. And maybe I was irritated at the thought of being judged by someone from our little clapboard church out in Landemberg for marrying into a certain amount of money, a little piqued about hearing in my head the rumors that would fly there about me ending up in such a crazy ward of a house, where clearly every kind of sick excess short of perversion was going on daily. I knew the nurse would get at me that way and I wanted to get at her first, give her some orders.

And then I knew I was wrong to say it by Mrs. Townsend's face—she blanked out on me in the same way she had done when I called her Annie.

As I opened the door to the bedroom, Amandine's head was tilted off her neck at almost a right angle. Drool forming at her mouth oozed onto a pillowcase with each snore. When she was on the upswing—an inhale— I grabbed her shoulders with both of my hands and pushed, hard. Her head—deadweight, like I always said!—knocked lightly into the whitewashed Mexican headboard she'd had sent from California after she saw one like it in a picture of Natalie Wood's bedroom in *Architectural Digest*. Her arms flew up strangely, tangling for a second into the swooping lace canopy curtain that hung from the ceiling and framed the mottled wood.

"Wake up! Meet your nurse!" I said, still shaking her but a little more careful now.

Amandine's eyes flicked open, and she closed her mouth while a stream of saliva made its way down her chin. Mrs. Townsend instinctively reached for a tissue from the bedside table and aimed it at the line of drool, but hesitated a few inches from Amandine's face—not yet having been introduced—then backed up and arranged it gently in Amandine's hand instead.

"Amandine, this is your nurse, *Mrs. Townsend*," I said, speaking in the loud, slow voice you use when you think somebody is deaf or stupid.

"Hello, Mrs. Hart," Mrs. Townsend said.

"It's going to be confusing around here with two Mrs. Harts," I said, "Why don't you just call her Amandine?"

"Oh, well, then hello, Amandine," Mrs. Townsend said, giving in because Amandine was so much younger than the two of us: I commanded the greater respect, though I could tell even then not by much margin. Mrs. Townsend said Amandine the way I had just demonstrated for her, that is, with a hard, nasally *A*, as in *banana*, or in the sound children make when they sing *nah-nah* to tease each other.

"It's *Ah*-mahn-dine," Amandine's voice crackled out, "*Ah*."

Mrs. Townsend nodded and straightened one of the black bobby pins securing her hat to her tidy pin curls.

"As in *al-mond*, " I said, "The *nut*."

The awkwardness was so heavy you could have bumped your forehead on it.

"You know," I said, "like in the candy bar."

They both stared at me. They were puzzled and I was getting on each of their last nerves. I thought I saw Mrs. Townsend's eye-to-temple vein give a soft throb.

"Almond *Joy*, " I said.

I sang the first line of the jingle to them from the TV, the one where there's a candy bar for if you feel wild and one for when you don't.

Amandine snarled her face up at me, and Mrs. Townsend did too, just for a second.

I continued, happy I knew the tune from the television commercial. I laughed, still singing, as I left the two women alone together. My skirt seemed to swish in time as I moved away from them.

"Ah-mandine," I heard Mrs. Townsend say.

I hummed down the hall to go check on the nursery. Then I heard the bell, tinkling its way through the house, prissy, fluctuating in volume as if on shifts of air. Almond Joy ringing and ringing and ringing it forever. Demanding more and more and never getting enough.

*   *   *

It was the first warm day—extreme, springlike—that thawed the ground out fast. Puddles clumped into strange patterns in the fields. This was my chance to get tulips planted, since Amandine was in high spirits from Mrs. Townsend and the silvery threads of sound her tiny bell wove through the house. Mrs. Townsend wasn't on as the baby's nurse—they had my free labor for that—and was busy fixing Amandine a hot lunch in the kitchen before she set to vacuuming (Lyman had hired her on for cleaning, too, as she was cheaper than his regular help) but I figured the mother could stand to watch her own baby while I went on my walk and got the bulbs in the ground around the fish pond. My routine was to walk through the orchards each morning, about three miles, but I hadn't got out to do it since the baby came home. Usually I was only about an hour, but if I chanced on something I wanted to look at, or think about, I could be gone for more than two.

Amandine had to learn how sometime, I figured.

I wheeled the baby in the small bassinet into Amandine's room while both of them were sleeping. I had warmed some formula and wrapped two bottles in blankets to keep it heated up. I pushed Amandine's perfume bottles and mother-of-pearl inlaid brush set and imitation gold-filigreed tissue box off to the side of her glass-topped vanity, and I laid out wet wipes and cornstarch and plastic diapers in their places. I lugged in the covered plastic trash bin for dirty pampers and set it next to Amandine's delicate wicker one. Amandine's snores were the noise you think should go along with bad breath—something deep and monstrous that needs to be scrubbed away. But the scent in Amandine's room was flowery, and not in a way to cover up sick stink like some public bathroom, but a true, green, light smell that surprised me. It was new since Mrs. Townsend had arrived.

"Wake up, sleeping beauty," I said, and pulled the sheets off her. Her lips barely fluttered as she puffed out a snore in response. She held her chin—even in sleep—perfectly level and centered, yet her face seemed crooked, off somehow. Her feet stuck out of a lacy cotton nightgown lifeless, limp like she lost all her bones.

"You have a visitor this morning, Almond Joy," I said loudly—almost shouting—and moved to her bedside. I shook her shoulder lightly. Her snore diminished, but she was still sleeping.

"Get up!" I yelled, leaning into her ear. But no response, just her breathy sound that meant she was about to begin another snore.

"Wake up!" I yelled. My nose was almost touching hers. The snore started to come out of her low and rumbling.

"Amandine, WHAT AILS YOU?" I yelled, my lips gracing her ear again with my holler.

She tottered her head and trembled open her eyes.

"What?" she mumbled

"WHAT ails you?" I said.

She rolled her eyes up at me, surly. Her hand shot out for her silver bell, but mine got it first. I put it in my pocket, careful not to let it chime.

"What is that smell?" she said, enunciating each word. She pulled the sheets back up.

"Amandine, you seem to be doing better lately so I'm going to have you take care of the baby for a little while," I said.

She twisted her thin lips into a frown.

"I need to work outside and go for my walk," I said.

I waited, but I got no response.

"You need to start sometime, Amandine," I said.

The baby began waking up, crying softly, huffing a bit. Amandine seemed more alert at the noise, on her guard, quickly aware of her daughter's presence.

"What did we hire a nurse for then?" Amandine said. She shut her eyes like looking at me was just too much work for her and she wasn't going to do it anymore.

"Amandine, you have a fine color in your cheeks today and this baby will perk you up even more," I said.

I could smell the baby's diaper. She kept crying, with more urgency—Amandine winced at the little blasts.

"You know how to feed her and hold her, I saw you in the hospital," I said. "Now get out of bed."

I picked up the baby and carried her over toward the bed and rocked her till she quieted.

"You know I can't get out of bed," Amandine said.

She nestled back into her neat mountain of pillows, eyes still shut, and seemed happy to be dreamy and leaving me. But then she wrinkled up her nose.

"That smell..." she said, opening her eyes, "what's that awful... Oh... it's awful, what is it?"

Her back shot up straight from its crouch and her eyes scanned the room. She no longer seemed weak and faint but ready to bolt up and dash away. I had had about enough. I laid the baby down in the bassinet again.

"If you don't get out of that bed right now I am sending Annie Townsend back to Landemberg where she came from. I put out the things to change your baby on your vanity, so you come over here and do something for once in your life," I said.

She stared at the wall.

"UP."

I yanked the sheets back down and grabbed her arm tightly.

"Alright!" she said.

She dragged her legs slowly and gingerly to hang off the side of the bed, moving sluggishly, as if she were tiptoeing and didn't want someone to hear her coming. She lowered her feet to the floor and after shutting her damn eyes again for near an entire minute, she rose herself up, gripping the ugly-as-sin bed frame for support.

She stood there awhile and sighed a few times.

I looked at my watch, I cocked my hip out.

When I finally barked another "UP!" at her she began shuffling on over to the vanity. She leaned both hands on its glass and exhaled loudly again—quite a show. She was lucky I can be a patient woman when I need to. As I set the baby down on the makeshift changing table, Amandine's eyes lit for a second—just a hint of interest in them for her girl before the weariness came back over her. She readjusted her hands on the glass and left two vague prints there.

The thought of the business at hand soothed me from all this. I set a palm on the baby's pink stomach—she squirmed a bit before relaxing.

"These are your fresh pair of pampers, Amandine," I started. "This is the back of the pampers and this is the front of the pampers. You put the back down here on the table like so, next to the baby. This is your cornstarch, these are your wet wipes. Any questions so far?" I said.

"I—" Amandine said.

She looked about to throw up.

" I think I'm fainting. What if I pass out?" Amandine said. She leaned her body and smeared her hands across the glass top.

"You faint and I send Mrs. Townsend home. For good," I said.

Amandine snuffled her nose, a bit snippy but trying to act like the victim at the same time.

"Now," I continued, "You take the tabs apart on each side and then *slide* the dirty diaper OUT from under the baby's bottom, like this—"

The baby had made quite a mess. This one always finished her whole bottle and it went through her fast. A sound that was a high-pitched version of her snores came out of Amandine—she fluttered her eyelids, and wrapped both arms around the bedpost like she was trying to dance with it.

"I *am* going to pass out," she said.

"No, you're not," I said. "This is your daughter, Amandine, what ails you? You need to take care of her."

I got Amandine up on two feet, dumped the soiled diaper, finished the demonstration, and put the quieted baby back in the bassinet.

"You had better mind her for the hour I'm gone," I said.

I tried to look back at her menacingly as I headed for the door

Amandine stood in the middle of the room, a little off-center and a funny shape from her flounced nightgown, like a hollow angel set crooked on top of the Christmas tree. She looked unsteady, as if by just sneezing, or shutting the door a bit too hard on my way out, I could knock her over into a hard fall.

"How can you do this to a sick woman?" she said. Pathetic. She appeared to be leaning on something that was not really there. Her dark pits of eyes were the only solid part of her: menacing, sure of themselves, full to bursting with her mean spirit.

*   *   *

It wasn't sunny, but it was warm, close to fifty. Dark clouds bunched in groups against the pale gray sky. Looked like rain. If I'd had any brains in my head, I'd have got the tulips in first, to beat the showers that seemed certain, but Amandine's asylum-styled household must have worked all the sense out of me in just a few weeks there. I wanted to walk. Something about one foot after the other, that rhythm, calms me like nothing else. So I set out. Not back toward my own house, but further out to where our fields give on a patch of woods that separates our land from the old Du-Pont estate.

My boots were barely muddy by the time I started having a strange feeling—a kind of fuzziness in my hands and feet, and a weight in my stomach. The hard look in Amandine's eyes stayed with me. I shouldn't have left her there alone with the baby, I thought to myself, maybe she really can't get out of bed too easy. But I kept going, my hand in my pocket on the silver bell I had kept with me, to prevent Amandine from giving in to her cowardice and getting Mrs. Townsend to do her work for her. The bell couldn't ring in the small pocket, the clapper just made a light thud with each step I took. That denseness in my stomach, like the pit in the middle of a fruit, had me feeling a little cruel. Or maybe it was the cruelty already in me that formed this tough spot. It ached. I continued a long ways through the yellow weeds of the fields with big, carved-out steps that turned me into a giant, lowering each boot on city after city of grass and sod.

The rows of elm that signal the start of the woods ran ragged across my vision—you could see where disease spread in black splotches across their trunks and limbs. Up high in one of the tallest there were yellow smears of hay, birds' nests that had crumbled in weather and dispersed among the rakish branches. I slowed down, hesitated before going into the woods. The wind sped itself into a bawl and I could almost see it swirling up fiercely into gray circles of air around the houses when I turned my head back to look at them.

I paused there, frozen solid for a moment, and I felt stopped, sure I had been foolish to leave Amandine alone. The bulky raindrops, colder than I had expected, started lighting on my forehead and arms then, sparsely, and woke me up. I turned on my heel and scampered back toward Amandine's house as fast as I thought I could.

My heels flung deep divots of wet earth up into arcs as I walked back through the sleeping fields. I was prepared for the worst. As I moved along the spongy turf, I imagined my course of action if I were to find Amandine with her head in the oven on my return, or if she put the baby in there to burn and choke on gas and then strangled the poor nurse. Or any other number of awful possibilities—I thought up every grisly one I could, as if to prevent from happening what I could picture first.

I was ready to take on anything I could conjure, but what I would find wasn't horrific, but was more odd, off, different, from what I would ever expect. I tried to pick up my gait. My feet stuck a bit with each step in the deepening mud, my hair and clothing grew heavy with rain.

From the edge of the yard I could hear the vacuum cleaner sucking at the wall-to-wall—its whirry roar was too loud. I should not have been able to hear that noise from my distance.

Then I looked up at the house.

The bathroom window was wide open, its curtain blowing across it occasionally with the effect of a flat white eyelid opening then shutting off and on, blocking the interior from view. Amandine was standing with her naked, scrawny back to the window. Only her torso, her backside, the tops of her thighs were visible. Her head was obscured, cut off by the window. Her arms were raised. The white curtain whipped back and forth with a snapping noise, turning Amandine into some kind of strip tease: now you see her, now you don't. I could hear the baby crying.

I bet that an old lady running so fast is not something many people have seen. I bolted. I charged, threw open the front door without bothering to close it, gasped some syllable at Annie Townsend who turned around quick, astonished, with one great defensive swing of the vacuum's hose before she recognized me. The vacuum blocked the sound of the baby's cries completely here in the house. I heard that machine wind its noise down to a hum and then on to nothing as I took the stairs two at a time. There was still some sort of a buzzing going on, though, alongside my own labored breath and the terrifying baby noises from Amandine's room.

And there she was, the tiny girl, her blankets, her doll-size pajamas, the coppery nest on her head soaking wet with milk from her bottle. Shivering and shivering, her skin alarmingly cold to the touch. Not unlike me, still rain-drenched at that point. Her right foot was bare, and its booty was not in the crib. I found it later far across the room, behind the bedside table, a mystery I never solved. The rest of the room was tidier than when I had left it—Amandine's bed neatly made, corners pulled tight, the diaper-changing gear nowhere to be seen, except the trash bucket, which had been pushed into a corner, the filigreed tissue box and brush-and-comb set placed squarely on the vanity.

A silence emerged for the briefest moment and hovered. Before it filled in—like water pouring into a glass from a pitcher—with the sound of wind rushing past outside, the baby caught my glance and stopped me in my tracks. I could almost see an adult face in her, and she knew what I had done, that I had left her. She was my judge and my jury. My stomach turned.

The baby screamed. Even then she possessed great strength and a sort of violent accuracy. She kicked the empty, leaking bottle next to her with her bare foot and it rolled in a neat arc around her, the few last drops of its formula spilling gently. I snatched up the cashmere throw on the foot of Amandine's bed and wrapped the baby in it, held her to me, and took her down the hall toward the nursery.

I could hear the cadences of language in the girl's crying—the rhythm of a broken, disappointed reprimand, and I imagined the syllables the word *betrayal* in the sobs. She wouldn't look up at me, but kept her glare sideways. The lower lip inflated? A pout, I thought, she just taught herself. I have always hated a pouter and when her crying then rose in pitch so that it became a shriek and a wail and a demand and an indictment I felt the anger grow in me—I am an old woman, this is too much for one old woman, this girl has two young parents where are they now to be cried at? Just for a second that anger bloomed before I shamed it down—a feeling that glowed then turned to a quick pain in my stomach then disappeared as I stopped for a moment in the hallway and stared at the wallpaper's cabbage-rose pattern thrown against a dull ochre background. Who was I to think such evil and selfish thoughts. Guilt, terror at my quick readiness to snap. Cabbage rose. Her sweet face and the wreckage of her sharp sobbing: *honey, honey, honey,* I said to her, I sang to her. The poor thing.

Her weeping—you wouldn't normally call it that from an infant but it's what she was doing—intensified as a few rivulets of formula dripped down her red face. She tried to wipe at them with her toy-looking fingers but couldn't quite do the job. Her heaving was tearing me right up, the worse for my guilt at hating that bottom lip I thought I had seen protruding. I talked to her, *baby girl, baby girl,* I sang it, and I smoothed the wet streams off her with a dry corner of her mother's expensive, bisque-colored throw.

I dried her off with that cashmere thing, and I couldn't find the wet wipes so I used it for diaper duty as well. She fell asleep while I was putting a fresh pair of pampers on her.

With the baby set down—exhausted, happy to sleep in her crib warm and dry, out of that wet bassinet—I went to Amandine.

From just outside the bathroom door, I could see through the window to where I had been standing—between the two poplars at the edge of the yard—and I could see the rain coming down densely in gray needles, long close slivers. I had to turn my head to see Amandine.

She was naked.

And.

And she was bald.

Bald!

Her perfect blond hair sat next to a jar of rubber cement on the sink's Formica faux-marble counter.

Bald but for little patchy bits of fuzz coming off her like a few lonely clumps of grass in an unwatered droughty lawn.

What in hell was she doing with that stinky glue?

There was an empty round space beneath the blond arc and arches of her wig. I looked back to her head and I was breathless. My thoughts ran amok and I wondered if there was a soft spot to it like the baby's—I wanted to stare at that tender thing, wanted to peer close and see the veins that might run under the scalp's translucent skin.

I did stare at it. I couldn't help myself.

Amandine's baldness was a great cap for her mousy face—its heft made her seem foreign and new, it crowded her eyes and her thin, pursed lips and her doll-small nose—these features that once seemed to be her center—into just the lower part of her head. I noticed that the forehead and the upper regions actually took up most of her space, but you could never tell with the wig on.

She was painting her head with that glue. Gluing her hair on.

Amandine sucked her breath in at the cold air from the open window, and she traced the stiff brush of the rubber cement lid carefully around her ear. Her breasts were full with milk, but still had a dour triangular shape to them as small breasts sometimes do—the tips were conical—and this fullness was the only sign she had just had a baby: the rest of her was angular, the tops of the thighs not touching, the hips lacking roundness. It was awful to me to see a body so flat and joyless. I said a quick prayer for the baby to develop a figure like Lyman's mother's before I set my mind on coming up with something to say to bare naked Amandine. But I just stared—Amandine hummed a tune I couldn't recognize, more absorbed in painting her head with glue than I had seen her in anything.

It had never occurred to me that the hair was a wig.

When she sensed I was there with her, she stopped her song, gripped the counter, paused for a long moment before she turned around. She moved as if she had always known this moment would happen.

She considered being embarrassed for a second, there was that hesitation, but she couldn't let me win so easily. She was backed into a corner. I could see her make a decision to let something fly up out of her, something black-winged and vicious she'd been keeping in a cage.

"You old bitty," she said, her voice gaining volume and strength. "You old bitch," she said, and paused, pleased with herself.

"From hell!" she said with a deeper voice than I'd heard from her before.

Amandine smiled a little bit at this and lit into more insults with an energetic breath before I could think of what to do:

"You scumbag!" she screamed.

It surprised my own anger back down into me, scared it into a hoarse rattle unable to emerge from my throat.

Amandine kicked the baseboard heater under the sink's cupboards and it clattered a second. Her face was twisted up into something extraordinary. I noticed a sharpness to her teeth I hadn't seen before. She looked frailer, yes, with no hair, but in another moment she would seem fierce, too, dangerous. There was a strength to her, a beauty of the unfettered sort she would never know about, never be able to see in herself or in another. Delirious almost, she moved quickly, the very opposite of the doped-up princess in her bed for the past weeks.

"For Christ's sake, Amandine, calm down," I said.

She moved with a new vigor, she moved not at all like the supposedly polite lady her wig transformed her into. She trundled around, stood with her back to me as if that would make me go away, then she returned. She jabbed the brush near my face, much as her nurse had waved the vacuum hose. Invisible fumes streamed past me in slow motion after the bristles did, like thunder following lightning.

"You old evil thing from hell!" she whispered.

What a ruckus! She threw her hands down in a gesture of frustration, then shook them excitedly as if to dry them off. But they weren't wet so far as I could tell. She couldn't contain herself, a child who has just discovered a new injustice and can't stop himself from fretting and hollering.

It seemed so obvious now: how perfect the hair had looked throughout her sickness, shiny and buoyant, presentable when the rest of her had bought a one-way ticket to Ugly.

"YOU COCKSUCKER BUTTON!" she said.

I felt myself blink. I should have slapped her by now.

She slammed the lid-brush back onto the big jar of rubber cement and both clattered into the bowl of the sink. I would have laughed, but I was frozen as I had been in the field when it began to rain. A noise in the sink turned my attention there, where a slow tongue of the amber fixative began a crawl from its brown glass jar to the drain.

I heard Annie Townsend's feet climb the first few stairs.

"Mrs. Hart?" She called up for me in a nursely, concerned tone as the steps creaked.

Amandine rushed, a blur of pale limbs, to get the blond crown onto her head and stash the glue under the sink. She mouthed the word *no* to me a few times, silently, but with the force of screaming. The wig tilted leftwards and down on her forehead.

Mrs. Townsend called up again.

"Just a minute, Mrs. Townsend," I said. I could hear the discord of the banister when the nurse paused there.

Amandine tried to force the spilled rubber cement down the drain with her hand.

"Nobody can know, do you understand," Amandine whispered to me urgently. "LYMAN can't know."

Lyman *didn't* know?

When she lifted her hand from the sink she realized the cement had coated each finger.

"Oh, God!" she whisper-yelled. She looked at her fingers, brought them together, tugged them apart. Then she got frantic again, frustrated, and she looked up at me with that fierceness and a hollow quality that had to be fear.

"You hillbilly! You golddigging old slut."

She slammed her sticky hand down on the counter. She spit a big blob of saliva into the sink; it remained separate from the rubber cement, floated on it like a yolk.

I felt the formula that had leaked all over the baby now curdling on my blouse.

I thought about Amandine's smart, beautiful girl she hadn't even bothered to name, and raised my eyebrows a second before I turned my face in the direction of the stairs.

"Mrs. Townsend, come on up here and give us a hand," I called.

I smirked at Amandine, naked, pathetic, but it was just a habitual gesture, devoid of the triumph I meant it to convey.

Amandine seemed to be condensing herself, compressing all her bitterness into a hard mean expression on her face. She glared at me and I felt my heart skip a beat.

I lunged at her. Just my foot, my knee, and I stopped myself before I swung. I gasped, froze, suddenly became aware of the raindrops hitting the sill and tumbling onto the floor tile, their pittery noise, the intermittent bursts of the white curtain up onto sheets of wind.

We could hear the pine boards of the stairs creaking again.

"Is Mrs. Hart all right, Mrs. Hart?" Mrs. Townsend asked, a little out of breath, coming up the last few stairs.

It was then, that moment, when I knew this: the adult face I had seen superimposed on the baby's had been her mother's.

My body somehow leaned out the door and shut it behind me as much as it could.

"Mrs. Townsend, you just give us a second here," I said.

The nurse looked confused, her broad face too big for her mouth that hung open waiting for her words of protest. I popped back inside the bathroom and locked us in there.

As I tried to ignore the queasiness in my gut, as I took a thick brown towel off the chrome rack and wrapped it around my naked crazy stepdaughter-in-law, I couldn't help thinking how useless the little red cross on Annie Townsend's neatly folded hat was going to be for this patient.

"Fix your wig," I whispered, "It's slipping."

Amandine pivoted slowly to look at herself in the mirror. Though she must have already sensed the wig sliding down so low it touched her left eyebrow, she looked surprised to see it that way. She peeled the blond edge up—it made a sound like tape coming off—and replaced it further back on what would have been her hairline if she'd had one. There seemed to be a ridge in the hairpiece now, a bump where it didn't attach to her scalp just right. But I wouldn't have noticed this the day before, when I had been still innocent of her fraud.

The mean, giddy rage and the brokenness were gone from Amandine—she was just empty. She looked up at me, squinted, sighed.

"Don't you ever leave her again like that," I said.

I couldn't look at her. I straightened the soap dish on the sink.

With her last shred of energy, of fight, before she pushed past me and went back to her bedroom to fade in and out of sleep for days, more and more pain pills surging through her, never quite waking, somehow convincing the nurse the narcotics were the cure for her troubles, Amandine mustered a stance and a glassy, tough expression and an exhausted, bored, condescension and said:

"*Don't you.*"

*   *   *

So that was that. I knew, Amandine proved, that she couldn't take care of her girl.

That night, I took a chicken out of the deep freeze as the rain slowed down and finally stopped. The storm had left a stuffiness in the house that made me have to open up the storm windows. The air was humid, remembering summer or else looking forward to it, and it convinced me to set up for the evening meal on the screened-in porch off the kitchen. I moved the girl from her crib to the laundry basket I had rigged up with blankets for her and she slept, she didn't make a noise all afternoon. The basket rested on the kitchen table while I chopped onions there, but the clicking of my knife on the cutting board and the teary smell didn't budge her.

I diced some shallots and some leeks and put them in the broil pan with the chicken and broth. I layered French-sliced green beans from the can with tuna and crushed potato chips in my little casserole dish I brought from my own house. I took Amandine's frilly parfait glasses down from the dining room china cabinet and rinsed them in hot water before I mixed a bit of red food coloring in one batch of cool whip and blue and green in other batches, before I dollied some Hershey's in the bottom of the parfait glasses then layered the cool whip—sea foam green, then Easter egg blue, then pink—between scoops of vanilla and mint chip and soft pastelly brown chocolate ice cream. I put the finished sundaes in the freezer, its frozen air puffing out at me like a breath that's been held in too long. They crystallize in there, the glasses, they get a nice frost on the outside and the different fillings converge into a whole inside the dark and cold of the icebox.

I only made two—Lyman never ate the desserts I left for him in the fridge and Amandine still maintained her no-sugar diet she'd had since before the baby. Just me and Elmer for dinner, as usual. He didn't mind eating at Amandine's house instead of our own. Mrs. Townsend stayed until eight but took her meals at odd times, alone.

I had to open more windows while the chicken was roasting because it got so hot. In December! I started searching through Amandine's downstairs closet for a fan—her kitchen didn't have much in the way of ventilation—and I ran into a cardboard box with one of those plastic-punch labels on it that said "X-MAS DECOR."

After I set up the fan I went back and wrestled that box out of the closet—I thumped it around and another thump from upstairs responded to me—Amandine got up her gall to worry about me messing with her house. She banged the floorboards and dropped something dense that rolled.

I stood up and whipped around in anger, as if readying to hit someone who thought she was sneaking up on me.

I knew I had to keep moving so I fetched a utility knife from the kitchen tool drawer and set on opening the Christmas box. A trail of sweat snaked down my collarbone.

The sound of slashing apart cardboard satisfied me.

*   *   *

The little white Christmas lights flashed on and off like so many flirts—they gave the screen porch a sort of café feeling. The late afternoon's strange warm wind had died down and the night was balmy and I had completed some mysterious, secret cycle when I delivered two plates heavy with hot, simple food to the cast iron table between the pair of matching padded lawn chairs.

The vinyl-covered cushion made a sighing noise when I sat down on it. Elmer poured me a glass of iced tea from a pitcher.

"Get your bulbs in?" he said.

I shrugged. "Not yet."

I was too tired to explain it to him, but he could tell I'd had a bad day and certainly didn't take offense. He got up from the table—an unusual thing for him to do, as I still liked to take care of him at the end of the day. But I didn't click my tongue at him, didn't budge this time.

He brought a bottle of sherry and two fancy-cut glasses back with him, pouring something like a double for me before I could say no.

"Thank you," I said. Why protest?

Steam was rising off the chicken and the casserole. I took bite after bite and each one was heavy, the weight on my tongue, the swallow like of the feeling of those two loaded plates in my hands the moment I set them down on the little lawn table—a satisfaction of weight and contact. I didn't touch the applesauce or the peas.

The little one in her basket at my feet was crying before I finished, so I packed her up into the crook of my arm and went to warm her a bottle while Elmer ate. When I came back my sherry glass was full and the Scrabble board was set up.

"Oh for gad's sake!" I said, "Elmer I can't think straight after two glasses!"

He flipped the pale tile over in his palm to show me his pick: W.

"I guess you go first," he said.

He held the girl while I got myself situated. She fell asleep with her bottle still in her mouth, as she always did with her grandpa.

"I hope you didn't bring that dictionary," I whispered to him as he lay her back in her basket. I was prone to fishing for words and he knew I didn't want the temptation.

He tapped his fingers on its worn jacket, Merriam Webster, sitting there on his side table.

"Elmer!"

I reached into the little black bag to see what I could come up with. I love the luck of the draw—you make do with what you get. It is random. The letters come to you and you make some sense out of them through practice and imagination and luck and sheer will and the limits of your abilities.

As needed in the case of the rack I picked just then: H U Z G RV T. Not much I could do there.

"Oh! You go first! I pass," I said.

He smiled at me and tried to hand me the dictionary, but I wouldn't take it. He turned back to his rack.

"Mrs. Hart?"

It was the nurse at the doorway between the screen porch and the kitchen.

"Yes?" I couldn't turn to look at her. I tapped my fingers in two quick trills on the dictionary. Elmer looked up at her for a second with an eyebrow arched to put her in her place.

"Mrs. Hart wants to know what the flashing light is. She's worked up, worried that you messed around in her storage," she said.

Annie Townsend looked tentative in the doorway. There was something she was about to say but it couldn't pass her lips, and she couldn't bring herself to cross the threshold of the porch.

"I told her of course you wouldn't do that," Annie said. Her voice got unsure.

I was angry. I couldn't look at her.

H U Z G RV T: I tried to figure a decent combination of so many consonants instead. I could get a three-letter, GUT or something, HUT, RUT,
but even as bad as I was at the game I wanted to hold out for four. I didn't
play for points, then, I cared more about putting down something interesting than getting a double word score.

H U Z G RV T

"I told her we all respect that she is the woman of the house, and that
settled her a bit, but she said she wanted to hear it from you," Annie said.

On the surface her voice was asking some kind of permission of her
employer, but underneath she was trying to call the shots.

"You tell Amandine she can straight to hell on the evening express," I
said.

Z R U G T H V

G R V U H T Z

I always hated the Hoopeses. The Hoopes women were always sweet
sweet but trying to get something from you. Amandine could have been
one herself.

My husband turned and stared at me like I had just turned into a frog
right there, with green shiny legs propped up on the ottoman.

"I don't . . . I—" the nurse said.

"Oh for crying out loud, Annie, tell her I'll put everything back like I
found it, just perfect, tomorrow morning and we'll have a bare naked
Christmas this year if that will make her happy."

H U Z G RV T. H U Z G RV T. H U Z G RV T. I still wouldn't look up.

When I had set the heavy hot plates down on the table earlier, I got that
feeling of completion you get when a meal is all cooked, a family is gathered and ready. The plates were heavy, full. I wanted that feeling again—a
whole thing. One thing done—the cooking—, then the easier thing, the
eating, begun. But now the plates were messed, scattered with the ends,
the uneaten and the smeared parts of the meal, peas tuna bones apple
pulp. Now the only feeling those plates gave me was the sadness of needing to clean up. I wanted the feeling of a neat, completed cycle but here I
was right back in the middle of *mess*—of hating the poor baby's mother
with a strength and a passion that had earlier delivered the hate into something more tender. The baby and Amandine and I were woven together
through air and matter and space.

So of course just as these thoughts occurred to me Amandine crashed
upstairs, apparently reverting to her habit of hurling her bedside table
against the wall. The baby woke with a string of tiny sobs.

"I'll be going," the nurse said, pointing upwards. I didn't look to the door until her back was turned and she was well on her way.

I picked up the girl, cooing to her, making a noise that was separate, a sugary melody far above my low, driving anger at her mother at first. But the cooing then became real, fell into the anger, wove itself into the anger so that the love and the care I felt for the girl formed a complex fugue with my bile for Amandine. I stared at the baby and I kissed her little forehead and I knew that I would take care of her and that Amandine wouldn't.

And I knew that the key to my sanity was to remember the mother was just as weak as this infant. To remember.

Elmer clicked his tiles down across the center of the board: INGOT.

"Ingot. . ." I said.

He made a gesture for me to hand the baby to him so I did.

R V T G U H Z

I finished the glass of sherry. I poured another one but I knew I wouldn't touch it. I listened to the three of us breathing: an old man, an old woman, a young girl.

R U G V Z T H

"Oh, forget it," I said.

The dictionary was worn and red, a comfort under my fingers. Too tipsy to be picky, I would take a four letter word, anything, even though I usually liked to keep it to five. I scanned a fingernail down the thin pages, over the tiny impossible print.

In the R's—there it was. My word, and the way for her, and for me, to remember what we would need forever to handle Amandine. Definition: "Compassion for the misery of another."

RUTH.

3

RUTH'S INTERLUDE

1972

Ruth is carrying a pot of petunias to Button and the bugs are going; Ruth doesn't mind them in her ears so much but she is afraid of mosquito bites because she always scratches herself till she bleeds, can never resist the itch. And then she picks the scabs. Ruth is almost four. The humidity in the air is so thick it could be bugs, the bugs could be vapor condensing into liquid and squirting themselves around. There is a buzz. The sky is a nice grayblue that doesn't make her squint and Button's hair has flown up around her head; it looks funny, stuck to her forehead in white strips.

Ruth giggles. She looks at the petunia in her hands and she wants to crush its velvety petals between her fingers. But Button would be mad—Ruth knows she can't do this. Ruth sits down and runs her hands through the June grass. Backs of hands, fronts of hands. Wrists flopping. *It is like funny fur. It is like a short green haircut.* Her calves are chubby and pink—she hasn't got any bug bites there yet but she pokes the skin above a knee with a soft fingernail. A little white mark. She draws the fingernail in a line to see more white. Again, again. Three white lines on her pink leg. She digs her fingers into the dirt under the grass.

Button is really her mommy—she wishes Button would stop calling Amandine that: *your mommy, your daddy*, meaning Amandine and Lyman when these words should mean her and Elmer.

Button's hair looks strange across her forehead and she's working hard. Sweaty and puffing. Ruth can feel Button right next to her, her soft skin, even though they are sitting yards apart.

Button's straw hat is yellow and round and her eyes are blue and round.

Button is digging holes in the dirt to put the petunias in. Ruth's job is to bring her each petunia plant in its pot from the porch where the pots wait for her. When Ruth brings them to her she turns the pot upside down— *oh no!*, she says the first time—but she catches the flower's dirt, spreads its roots out gently before planting it in the ground, mixing its soil with the earth's.

She is digging in the dirt and Button is digging in the dirt, they are outside their house where they live with Elmer, they are working together.

"Button?" Ruth says. She has made two little holes at her sides.

"Yes, Ruthie?" Button says. She doesn't look up at her but keeps digging.

"Button?" Ruth says again.

"What is it, sugar," Button says. She looks at Ruth this time. Button sees the holes in the lawn but isn't mad even though she's told Ruth not to dig in the grass before.

"Nothing," Ruth says. This is one of Ruth's favorite games.

Button smiles at her and shakes her head, like she might say *silly girl* and come tickle her. Ruth starts flopping her hands in the grass again.

But then Ruth feels something awful coming down the hill; she feels it like a mean thunderstorm, a bee about to sting. It's not any of these though, it's more specific and it is much much worse:

Amandine is about to get upset.

Amandine: relaxed and on top of things, but it will not hold. She can see Button and Ruth here at the bottom of the hill, she can see Button's garden from her own garden.

Amandine is on the hill above them, sweeping outside her house. Everything is almost perfect. She is sweeping the flagstone patio her new topiary surrounds, and then it will be done: perfect.

Birds and animals made of bushes. Ruth doesn't like to look at them because she has almost seen them crawling around—their leaves like so many stretching, sauntering muscles—in the middle of the night.

Almost there. Amandine just has to finish sweeping. Just has to sweep.

Ruth almost starts the nothing game again, just to block Amandine, but Ruth is too scared to speak.

Amandine's house has had enough additions built onto it, and the paint matches the rugs in every room, and each inch of soil outside is hidden with groundcover or flowers, and both floors of the house have just been spring-cleaned, and a complete new set of dishes is in the pantry, unused yet, and Mr. Taylor has just trimmed the topiary animals to shapeliness, and Amandine herself has weeded out the unfashionable items from her wardrobe and donated them to Goodwill, and a just-dusted room for Ruth has been painted apricot and filled with white bedding and dolls.

Lyman's started eating dinner late, after Amandine has already gone to bed. He withdraws to his basement woodshop until his meal—leftovers, sandwiches, macaroni and cheese, a fried egg.

Amandine is desperate for company, craving her child.

The night she couldn't stop from weeping, and then couldn't weep silently, couldn't stop the sobbing noises she was making, Lyman came upstairs. He sat with her and stroked her hands with his as if to keep them warm. But when he took her out to dinner the next night she couldn't stop from snapping— "What?" . . . "What?"—at his silence, couldn't take his hand on her back, settling her into her chair, the car.

She knew then that his nights away from her downstairs would resume quickly, because she knew she actually probably preferred it that way.

The soot from the flagstones disappears into the neatly-cut edge of grass. The stones are flat and clean. Amandine puts the broom in the garage before returning to the patio. She sighs.

Everything is done.

Amandine wants Ruth back now.

Amandine is dark red and sharp bursts—Ruth can feel it.

Amandine sits on the marble bench, under the nose of a leaping porpoise that Ruth has seen swimming just above the fields when everyone else isn't looking.

Amandine sighs again. It seems to her like years since she has breathed so much. Her domain is perfect, so she can use her lungs now. She inhales. She is ready for Ruth, now that things are tidy and done.

And Amandine is ready to hate Ruth for ruining the perfection. Ruth knows this but she doesn't let herself think about it.

Petunias, soil, fingernails: loud enough to silence her mother.

Ruth is rubbing her hands hard against the grass, staining them brown and green.

Amandine lets herself lie down on the bench and feel this one perfect moment.

Amandine doesn't need to look at her things to know they are all in order.

"Button?" Ruth says.

"Yes, honey?" Button almost sings it. She knows the game.

But Ruth doesn't say anything. She scurries over to Button and rests against Button's side—crouching like Button is crouching, but leaning into her.

"Well what's the matter, Ruthie?"

Button always says everything like she loves her.

Ruth hugs Button's leg and sticks her dirty fingers in her mouth. She sucks hard. Button turns Ruth so she can look at her face.

Ruth resists: looks up the hill.

Amandine is trying to walk down it elegantly. She is so skinny; she is wearing a white dress, flared at the bottom, with a narrow gold belt that catches sun.

Button stands up and dusts her hands off on her overalls. Ruth holds on tighter to her leg. Ruth presses her fingers in until there are surely white marks on Button underneath the denim.

Mommy: tall blond hair and walking trying to look like she is gliding.

"Ruthie, go check on those petunias back on the porch," Button says.

Amandine didn't want Ruth before, and now she thinks she does but she doesn't: Ruth steps so quietly over to the porch.

Mommy. Talking to Button in tough whispers, Amandine's gold belt throwing out sparks. Button putting a hand on her hip. Button shaking the trowel with just a tiny bit of threat at Amandine.

Amandine's old anger comes into Ruth's veins then: it starts as a thudding black explosion near Amandine's heart, then dashes through Ruth's vessels' lacework, turning red runners dark, marking up the organs in patches, leaving silty hate in her little liver. This hate comes to her through the air from Amandine. Is it for her or is it for Button or is it from Amandine to everyone in the world and it just concentrates itself into purity for Ruth's small limbs?

Ruth turns that anger back onto her mother, and this jolts Amandine into sadness.

Ruth runs to Button and grabs right back onto her leg, now just wrinkling the pant leg into her fist.

"You don't want me," Ruth whispers, her face toward her mother but her eyes away on the horizon.

Amandine's mouth dry, open, empty.

"And I don't want you," Ruth says, pulling back from Button.

Looking her mother in the eye.

Amandine still, stunned.

Tears and fury bead in Ruth's eyes, her face tightens as she picks up some dirt and throws it at Amandine's dress. It lands high, at the hip; looks like a brown rainstorm across the wide white skirt.

Amandine reaches a hand down toward Ruth's head but Ruth wails, then quiets and clenches harder onto Button. Ruth looks up again at her mother for a second and Amandine seems like she might cry but Ruth doesn't care, Ruth looks back down at the petunias and rubs her eyes with her dirty brown fingers.

Amandine ignores the mess on her skirt.

Ruth doesn't let herself think that this mommy hand might actually want to take care of *her* more than this mommy wants to brush the dirt off the dress. Even if that's true, it won't last: Ruth knows. Ruth holds tight where she is.

It is all too much. There could be thunder and lightning between Amandine's hand and Ruth. Ruth isn't even tempted to cry any more: she just sucks in more and more air.

"I would, ah, I would leave her be if I were you, Amandine," Button says.

Ruth's face is red and hot. Button smoothes the strips of white hair off her own wet forehead and pats them down into the rest of her hairdo.

Amandine turns around and tries to breathe again. Ruth removes Amandine's anger, Amandine's blood from herself. She gives up on her mother and she tries to feel instead everything that is in Button, but Button is sad too, now, so Ruth just rips the head off of one of the petunias and smashes it up hard with her fingers into her palm. Purple messing into brown and green. She rips the head off another one before Button takes her hand and calmly closes her own around it. Button steps behind Ruth and starts to walk toward the porch: with Button's force pushing, Ruth moves.

Just before the screen door shuts behind Ruth and seals her into the house, Ruth hears Amandine, still out there, make a noise that is not words, but Ruth doesn't know what it means.

Ruth doesn't know Amandine anymore. Ruth can't feel her anymore. It stopped.

4

CHAR

1973

In the foyer of the A&P, she can't get the thumbtack out of the wall. The corkboard it is stuck into is the tough, tight kind, and this blond woman named Amandine is trying to wedge the nail of her index finger under the tack. She has a desperate look to her. She feels a sneeze coming on, and this feeling—shaky, anticipatory, irritated—overwhelms her. Instead of taking a minute for this sneeze, she forces her nail under the tack until the nail bleeds a little around the top rim. Then sneezes. Almost swears, but catches herself. Shoves the bloody fingernail hand into her white purse, which has been designed in such a way that it holds much more than it appears to be able to, and pulls out a crumpled tissue to touch to her nose for propriety's sake. What she really needs is a big, snotty blow of it, but she has rules against doing this in public. The fullness in her sinuses feels urgent, though, so she just tears the flyer down, ripping it at the corners.

> CHAR
> Psychic-Healer-Advisor

Other women's feet patter along the ridged black mats behind the metal wheels of shopping carts, causing the automatic doors to swoosh open, shut, open again, on either side of her. Ladies in, ladies out. She stares at the phone number and name she is holding. Char. There might be a realer psychic up there, someone who can actually tell her what to do. She thinks, maybe an Esmeralda or an Artemesia or something continental or gypsyish, short and smoky, like that. Her eyes scan the bulletin board, but the rest of the flyers are only for handymen or cake decorators or babysitters or seamstresses.

Linda, Amandine's neighbor, wheels her metal cart through the automatic door. She proceeds unthinking, spaced-out, toward the second set of doors, but she notices Amandine out of the corner of her eye. Well, she thinks she notices Amandine out of the corner of her eye, but she in fact has some kind of ESP herself and feels Amandine there without knowing that this feeling is anything different from physically seeing. Linda says something, *hello*, and Amandine jumps a little when she turns to see who it is, *oh, hello*, she replies, but she is thinking, this dumb church woman with her big boobs and her potbelly is just another sign of why I should be living someplace more elegant, like Paris, France.

How are you? Amandine says.

The wet-cardboard smell of the produce aisle wafts through the interior doors as the hot cement smell follows the ladies in from outside. The odors mix in this entryway, a space surrounded by wire-hatched glass and cheap advertising, tempera on posterboard.

Linda actually could be quite striking, Amandine thinks, if she would just lose thirty pounds and get her hair done.

Just fine, just fine. And how are your husband and daughter doing? Linda asks, maneuvering her metal cart sideways a bit out of the flow of traffic, her ESP evidently not working anymore, because when she sees Amandine bite her lip and crumple the piece of paper in her hands into a little ball and turn a bit paler, even, she realizes this simplest of questions was somehow the wrong one to ask.

Fine, Amandine says. Amandine digs under a fingernail with her thumb. She is so pale.

Linda thinks, Is Amandine about to cry?

Well, okay then, God bless, Linda says, and goes on her way. Linda picks up on something more than just the obvious—that Amandine is a disturbed woman; Linda feels implicated somehow, she feels responsible for the poor thing. But just as Linda is exiting the entryway, worried, feeling guilty she didn't talk longer, she notices a big pink sign with cute magic-marker drawings done by a teenage employee saying the strawberries are half the price they were last week, and she welcomes the chance to think about something nicer than her crazy sad neighbor.

Amandine scans the bulletin board one more time for an authentic gypsy name. As Linda wheels away, an odd thought enters Amandine's mind—*I am a fool to think another woman can save me*. And she *is* a fool to think this, but it will almost happen to her, three times, and the seeds for these occurrences are right there in the cardboard- and oil-smelling, light-filled entrance to the supermarket, the doors opening, then shutting, then opening again, with small, reassuring noises.

Amandine crinkles the advertisement even tighter in her hand on the way to the car; the sweat from her palms—it is 85 degrees and humid, closer to 100 just above the asphalt—slightly blurs the lines on the erasable typing paper.

The inside of her car is also sweltering, the steering wheel too hot to touch. She gets in and lets the skin above her lip bead with sweat. She can feel it in her armpits and the backs of her knees, the small of her back. The heat eases the weight in her sinuses, but she takes a tissue from her purse and snuffles into it, delicately. Shutting the door with just enough force to keep the awful ajar noise from beeping, she thinks she could just sit like this, in the heat of the car interior forever, or for a certain amount of time, a long enough period of time for the things outside the heat of the car to change for the better. Or at least they will seem that way once she gets out again, at least *she* will be under the impression that everything is just fine at home, that she doesn't feel chaos and vermin edging in on her every night after she shuts the lights off and gets into bed alone and doesn't even know in the mornings if her husband has come to bed at all or if he stayed in the basement all night.

And the heat of the inside of a car in June might be enough of something to make it so that she at least cares if her husband has been there or not. And the heat of the inside of a car in June might make her daughter come home to her and it might make Button go away.

So many things to think about that she'd rather not. The heat swirls amid dust in front of her eyes, eddies up off the dash. She reaches for the glove compartment, snaps it open quickly before the surface can scald her, and removes a pair of short white gloves with an edging of baby blue embroidery. With these on she can handle the steering wheel, she can drive away. She starts the ignition, but then just puts her hands in the gloves on the wheel and holds tight. She watches the ladies pass behind full shopping carts, they are rushing in the heat to get the ice cream and the milk home, they are fussing with toddlers and with infants, they are imperfect and robust and most of them could stand to think about a new style of shoe and a different cut to their dresses.

But they are breathing, measuring air with their bodies, they seem to have an easy time out there breathing, Amandine thinks—for her it is just as hard to breathe out there as it is here in this hot car. It occurs to her to roll down a window, but she doesn't follow through. The containment in a small hot space, the uncomfortable feeling she usually has is somehow cancelled out by the nasty heat. Pebbles fly from the gray asphalt into the hosiery covering the ladies' calves. The ladies stop to chat in pairs or threes or fours. Amandine can feel sweat almost everywhere on herself now, like thin puddles shifting over the terrain of her body. She grips the steering wheel and bites down on her teeth, flexing somewhat at her temple.

But I have worked so hard! she thinks.

The women laugh and they gossip. One touches another's forearm in a gesture of comfort. They pick up each others' babies, they raise the boys to the sky and pucker their lips at these boys, they make noises like birds. They put their hands on their hips, the older ones dab at their foreheads with handkerchiefs, they make small, understood excuses to each other about needing to move along and they do, toward the automatic doors or toward their cars, and they talk to their toddlers and their toddlers talk to them and there is a mixture of happiness and irritation with the heat and an eagerness to purchase something in the children and in the mothers.

Amandine looks down at the crinkly paper:

CHAR.

Amandine finally rolls her window down, as if she has come up with a reason not to melt herself away right this minute. She sighs when the outside but now cool-seeming air reaches the wet planes of her face, and is so eager for this air that she reaches all the way across the seat and rolls down the other window as well, exposing her back above her skirt if anyone were watching, but she almost doesn't care anymore about that.

After stopping at the bank to withdraw money, she uses the pay phone outside, waiting through thirteen rings and wilting along with the bank's neatly mulched pansies and snapdragons in beds bordering the parking lot, thinking that snapdragons are really too. . . suggestive? And that she won't plant any of her own next year, that she will put nasturtium or geraniums or something else decent in their place.

Finally, she gets an answer on the phone. There is time open for a psychic consultation in thirty minutes, which is just about what it will take her to get to the location seven miles south of the Pennsylvania/Delaware border, actually the Mason-Dixon line, though almost nobody thinks about that anymore when they cross it. Just the old racist paranoid cranks do, mostly.

As she drives along with the windows down, she relaxes a little bit. She feels more certain that this psychic will be able to tell her what to do—the sign said "advisor," too. And Amandine will learn how to be one of those women in pink and yellow dresses, with a bright child grabbing onto her.

She wants the psychic to tell her how to get Ruth back from Button.

Once Amandine steers the car off the 141 onto Newark, she starts looking for the dirt road through a cornfield—the directions she got over the phone said it would be hard to find, but Amandine knows the road right away, it might as well be lit up like Las Vegas for how clearly it stands out to her, even though its mouth is shrouded in clumps of long grass, blades slouching to the ground.

The deep blueness of the shaded cornfield settles Amandine even more as her car bumps through it on the rough road, toward the woods at the field's opposite edge. Gravel flies up and makes shattery noises as it hits the oil pan, creating a noise that has a shape like a tail of a comet, widening in its span of particles at the end.

It's not really even a road, she says aloud. Then she thinks, really it's just two long tire ruts with some grass in between.

The shadow of the forest cools the air coming into the car and casts a more flattering light onto Amandine. Her eyes adjust as she pulls up to the little white house, parks. The surfaces inside the car, now under the deep shade of ancient oak and maple, feel almost cool to the touch. As Amandine puts on some lipstick, she feels a tiny shiver zigzag across her belly. When she shuts the car door behind her, the sound of it is so heavy and monumental amid the quiet and far-up chirping of birds that it might even be echoing itself for just a second or two.

Before taking in the overall appearance of the house, she rings the doorbell quickly, but she has a sense the dwelling is ramshackle, not quite set on right angles, in need of paint. And when she steps back to check, she sees she is right. The house does need paint, and the wild vines and heavy drooping ferns fill what in a sunnier place would be flowerbeds and badly want tending. A wind chime, caught on some unnoticeable breeze, rings once above her head. She looks up to see a green-patinaed Buddha with two metal strips dangling below him on wires. She doesn't know what the statue of the smiling fat man is. His contented slovenliness tells her that the psychic is clearly not of the Eastern European sort, but is aligned with some countercultural movement. She rings the doorbell again—the solid, decent-sounding doorbell—and, scared now, she has to bolster herself. Her eyes fix on an inch-wide strip where the white paint has peeled to gray and knocks once, quickly, cooing, "Helloo?" as she turns the knob and pushes inwards.

The house is dark inside, and smells earthy, more like outside than inside, but with a sweetness to it, and a layer of tobacco smoke somewhere in the mix. Newspapers crowd the living room—piled neatly here and there in little stacks. There are ashtrays. Spider plants hang from the ceiling in slings and perch—ready to expand and conquer more space—in the center of the heavy wooden coffee table.

"Helloo? Anybody home?" Amandine says. She traces a finger through dust on top of a stereo speaker, but doesn't look at it, just smears it off into her other palm and thinks about dirt and leaving.

That's when I stub my joint out on the doorjamb around back and come inside through the kitchen to greet her.

*   *   *

She's relieved when I appear in the living room that I am younger than she is. This way if I'm wrong or if I tell her something she doesn't want to hear she can deny me. She is relieved as well that I am not beautiful—that my nose is too pointy and I have a pallor to my complexion that she thinks has something to do with drugs. She might not be too far off the mark on that one, though I don't think the weed is responsible, probably it was the other stuff I used to do before I kind of settled down.

"Hi, I'm Char," I say.

"Char?" she says, like those four letters haven't been superimposed on every stop sign and taillight and cloud she's encountered in the last half hour.

"It's short for Charlotte," I reassure her, "It's my middle name. Naomi Charlotte."

She suddenly looks upset, well, more upset than she did before. She isn't as clear to me now that she is here—her high-strung mannerisms blur my sense of her. I pick up on her now, not as a pull-you-right-along story, but in distinct images that come and go. It's up to me now to string them together into some kind of sense, and, well, suddenly I'm not feeling so motivated as all that.

"Come sit in my reading room," I tell her.

I take my cigarettes out of my pocket—I need to burn her edge off me. She grimaces behind me as I light one and follows me to the corner of the dining room I have rigged up as a sort of a parlor. As I settle into my seat, with my back to the picture windows, and concentrate on her as she adjusts herself across from me, I see a filmy wash of treetops in back of her, like the ghost of a slide show on my wall there. Behind me she sees the actual trunks of trees through the window—grayish brown lines, thick, nubby. What I see behind her moves and is transparent, as if the shifting leafy bursts are a film projection.

This is odd. What I see is usually not physical like that, I mean usually I see it in my head. Not on walls, for sure.

I rip the filter off my Lucky and suck deeply. The treetops fade and I catch a glimpse of her current, most superficial thought, the things folks are generally wrong to fear psychics can read, because we so rarely catch these little ripply flashes. What we do pick up on are the deeper currents, the water so far down in the ocean of people's selves that the fish there don't have eyes.

But right now, I can tell she is thinking: How and why did this woman, *Char*, dye two potato sacks black and make them into a dress?

She thinks she's sly, thinks she seems like a *polite* person.

I want her to calm down. I put out my cigarette and I ask her what she would like to know about, what seems to be the problem.

She takes a little breath even though she wants a big, full one. She surprises me:

"I want to know how to get my daughter back," she says.

Her eyes look flat and clear and ready.

"All right," I say. I tap another cigarette out of the pack, light it, then set it on the ashtray while I get out my cards.

"A three-card reading is five, would you like to start there?" I ask. I don't know how much money she has on her. I am useless for money readings. If I got so much as hunches in that department I wouldn't be sitting here right now.

"What else do you have?" she says. She wants to spend more.

"There's the full spread for fifteen, that'll take twenty minutes," I say. I cross my legs and bounce the top one so that my sandal slaps my heel over and over.

"That one," she says, "The full,"

She reaches into her handbag to reassure herself of something. I fixate on this purse and don't respond to her. It needs an oil streak on it, needs a pen or a lipstick to drop across it and mar its perfect white leatherness. It makes me think of a visual clue in a movie—the rest of the furniture, the clothes in the room, the paint on the walls, the sky, complexions, all go together, and you *know*, watching, that one little object's color is off. But maybe your knowing isn't' conscious. Maybe you just sense it—but you don't think, "Oh, the color scheme is off." That's what her purse is like in my house.

"Okay," I say. I can't help a big sigh and almost rolling my eyes.

Maybe I smoked too much weed—I can feel myself detaching from her, I don't want to do this reading and I don't want to re-open the portal that lets her story come pouring through me so that she can listen to it being told.

In my mind I see hands fumbling with locks. I see gusts of wind banging a screen door wide.

"Shuffle the cards and spread them out when you feel satisfied," I say. I edge the deck over toward her.

There is a curiosity to her as she picks them up. Not even asking permission, she flips the deck over and looks at the faces of the cards. The multitude of the images overwhelms her—she wants to look at each one carefully and she knows she can't, that there isn't time. There is no guilt to her, little fear, just that sheer excitement of taking a quick peek at herself. Then she shuffles with the faces down.

Two men. Dirt and quiet. Quiet. The handle of a chrome electric coffee pot, its woven cord. A woman who could help is out and the door is locked. The pictures come to me as her hand leads the cards out on the table. The series of pictures is as horrible as it gets—a ceiling fan spinning to a stop, a pet chewing its leg bloody in the yard, the "accident," coming soon, sooner, that will leave her broken in that way—only the details of these harshest lives are ever different and that somehow makes it worse.

I feel the pain in my neck that comes at such moments. My hand clamps there.

"Amandine," I say. Of course she is surprised that I know her name. "Amandine, give me a minute."

I stumble a little as I get up. The hot shattering at the top of my spine shifts once I am on my little concrete stoop out back. As I take a joint out of my pocket, light it up, the darkness from Amandine increases, there is a low ominous note of music, it picks up power, and on my first hit the searing knot loosens. With the exhale it is gone. Amandine's past recedes into the forest, rushing backwards so quickly I imagine it made of dense matter, its velocity and weight strong enough to knock a hole in the side of a development house across the thick woods, strong enough to splinter siding and drywall and two by fours.

I used to try to rush the sad cases with pills, speed myself through them so fast I couldn't remember or repeat anything, quicken myself through the deep-down and then up, back across much, much surface. But now, smoking out works just fine—weed tempers the stories, mixes them up with impressions from my other senses, tosses in wild cards, unrelated, sort of like commercial-breaks to pause the process, dilute it. Dampen its effects on me. I become simply the teller—the story doesn't leave an impression on my body.

Okay.

Her daughter. A young girl—separate from this woman. I close my eyes and try to find a way in. But—there is nothing there, just the woods and the afternoon light and the sound of the bugs in the grass. I stand up and for a second I think I see two little girls, but then they move together, four translucent arms blurring into one pair, one set of legs submerged in the other.

"Which daughter?" I ask her when I sit back down in the parlor.

"I have a daughter," she says. She almost stammers. "My daughter, Ruth."

"Oh," I say. I pick up the cards and I start to lay them out.

This is you. This is what crosses you. This is what crowns you. This is your immediate past. This is your deep past. This card represents your near future.

She can tell that the Tower is not a cake and ice cream party, her eyes widen a bit.

This card is your distant future. This card is the base of your problem. This card is the influence of family and close friends. This card is your deepest hopes and fears. This card is the final outcome.

She isn't ready to hear what this spread wants me to tell her.

*   *   *

The Jesus on our wall belongs to my husband, Lucas. His auntie gave it to him, and he won't ever take it down. He sits above the dining room table and would close His eyes, I imagined, squinting, when I used to smoke pot in front of Him—He couldn't help but peek, though, I saw Him. That's why I now almost always go outside for anything stronger than cigarettes. My husband keeps smiling at me when I complain about Jesus up there, when I say, "Well tell old Jesus to come down here and pack a bowl if He's so freaking curious." My husband gets on my case about smoking too much everything, winks and says, maybe *He* can help you with those bad stories. My husband is no Jesus-freak, though, almost never goes to church, has his own personal religion of trees, sky, and a convertible; he just likes to nudge me about this, get a rise out of me, like a brother. Part of his religion, too, is that if something simple annoys you so much, it's probably you and not that *other* thing that's got the problem. Me, I don't have my own religion yet, I'm too high-strung still, but when I get one, I'm going to incorporate that last idea so that I can say it back to Lucas, see how he likes it from that angle.

So Jesus is setting up there above Amandine's head, and sometimes I like to imagine Him doing what I wish my response could be in a given situation. Like now, with this prissy groomed mouse desperate for help but too superioristic to admit it here in my living room, Jesus might strike His forehead like he was in the Mafia, roll His eyes, make a sour, tongue-out face. When He does this I mind His constant staring at me and Lucas a *lot* less, believe me. He's just not my kind of deity, I guess, although I know His universal love policy is a good one. He always gets that much in my book.

Anyway, there we are, me, Amandine, and the Jesus that Auntie Racinda gave Lucas one Christmas. We all knew she stole it from the church basement out of spite for some questionable comments the preacher's girlfriend made to her involving the nutritious value of lemon bars verses oatmeal cookies. My husband saw the empty, clean square on the wall behind the urinal in the men's room during Christmas Eve services with his family. I never go with them to church, just barely make it through holiday meals at some auntie or other's table. I'm not so popular with them—I agree with the preacher's wife on the lemon bar thing, for example, but of course I'm not dumb enough to speak up on that. They can tell though. They know.

"Honey, you're all the Jesus I need," I told Lucas after Christmas dinner that year, once we were home again amid soft, colored beams thrown from the tree lights off wads of metallic wrapping paper scattered around. Jesus, irritatingly calm and underfed, folded His hands inside His frame, leaning on top of a pile of presents for my people I hadn't quite gotten around to mailing before the date.

Lucas's neck and shoulders were in knots from the Christmas tension of all the chatty women he grew up with. I showed him the Boat, the Cobra, the Bear—yoga poses that might help the muscle strain—but it only took one little look, one little smile from him to convince me to get his undershirt off him and push Tiger Balm into the gold-brown of his upper torso. Jesus watched—He, Jesus, didn't mind. . . although, Auntie Racinda—generally so free and easy with many of the commandments, herself—maybe would not have appreciated subjecting her gift to what we were enjoying so much.

Anyway.

"You've had a hard time," I say to Amandine. This is how I always begin. Why not? It's true for everyone on Planet Earth.

So I get into it with her. I tell her her own version, what she can handle, and I'll butter up and slip in a harsher truth now and then, once she's feeling good and right and can handle it. I tell her the older woman is helping her out by babysitting for awhile, not being mean, not edging in on Amandine's share of good stuff in the world, and I tell her to try to be thankful for this woman she doesn't like. I tell her she will have her daughter back soon enough. Which is only partially true.

"And you'll have another one," I say.

"But my husband. . .we don't really spend *time* together any—" she says.

"Look—it's important for you to have the next one! A girl, you need to have another daughter. She will bring Ruth back to you," I tell her.

And I see the double image, the four legs condensing into two.

Amandine is almost scowling at me now. Her disbelief and irritation bubble up and mar her face.

"There's another girl coming," I say to Amandine.

"That's impossible," she says, pleased I'm wrong, whitish lips turning up just so slightly.

Me and Jesus, old hat at these topics by now, both raise one eyebrow each at her.

"No, I mean it's impossible. I haven't—seen—my husband in months."

"Well, I'm not saying she's a *physical entity* yet—I'm saying she's zooming her way down to you through the ether as we speak."

I think Amandine's just a rock over there, but tears start coming, tears without sobs, just wetness.

"I just don't see how—"

"Don't worry. She's coming," I say.

Amandine's white purse slides off her lap, breaking the stillness, and she jumps. As she bends down to pick it up, she sees the big wads of dust and cat hair that collect in the corners of my house. She reels in her exclamation of disgust before it gets anywhere near out of her, but she forgets who she's dealing with here. She's pissing me off now.

So I'm not Betty Crocker. So what.

Jesus taps His forehead, closes then shields His eyes at her ingratitude, her judgment, and at my own.

"She's on her way," I say, "Another daughter. She's a sweet girl, a good girl." I light another Lucky and look at the door.

And again, I see two girls moving together to become one. I see them separating from one another. I see them turn to stare at each other and I don't see Amandine, their mother, anywhere near them.

"But what is most important," I hurry, "Is for you to treat yourself right." I pat her forearm twice. "And you need some good love, some real romantic, sweet love."

The irritation breaks and a sweet, childish hunger washes across her.

"Your husband," I say.

Amandine tightens her fingers on the purse, and aha!, I think, maybe the flaw will be five sharp fingernail crescents. Her eyes have intensified on me.

"This is what you need to do," I say. I give her my only love spell, which I got out of *Cosmo* a few years ago. I have heard that in the short term it often works.

"Go spend forty dollars on a haircut and something nice to wear. It has to be forty, no less. Then go home, take a bath, and put a tablespoon of the water in his dinner."

I *know* it is not *hygienic*, but neither are public bathrooms, and even Whitepurse Amandine uses those.

"You'll have another girl," I say.

It's time for the reading to end. But she just sits there and looks at me hopefully.

"It's very important," I say "... So ..."

She doesn't want to get up. She is halfway in love with me and wants me to walk with her through her days, wants to be allowed to call me at 3am when she can't sleep and is awake, blanched, chewing a horrible thought.

A dark cat wandering in circles, the thin-lipped man and his son. These images from her past start to seep into me and the intrusion is too irritating to bear.

I've done my job. I'm getting bored, getting petty.

I light a cigarette and don't worry anymore about not letting the smoke waft her way. I know that when I get my religion I will have an easier time with these things, but for now, there's not much I can do. I start to want a little fun, and I just can't resist.

"And it's crucial. . . " I say, exhaling smoke her way dramatically, "That you name her . . ."

Jesus gives me an eager nod—I start to giggle at myself but I cover it with a cough: you just can't name a girl Jesus. Sorry. I shake my head at him a little. Then I put on my best psychic-concentrating-on-the-nether-realms face, close my eyes, open them with a suddenness:

". . . that you name her Racinda."

Oh my.

"Racinda?" she says, dazed, her hand rising to her cheek and pushing the flesh there around a bit.

"R-A-C-I-N-D-A. *Very* important."

I suck on my cigarette till the filter's soggy and I can taste its fiberglass. I get frivolous and antsy with these girls.

"*Very* important." I clasp her hands in mine and look at her meaningfully.

If the child ends up anything close to my husband's wild Auntie it will do Amandine some good.

"Very," I say. I stare at the ceiling. I stare at my hands clumping up the tablecloth in rows. I look around the room quickly, as if she has already gone.

"Okay. . . okay. . . okay. . ." she says, then, staccato, "Thanks!" and tightens herself a bit, gathers her purse to her stomach, pushes herself from the table. A little giddiness seeps into her on the way to the porch.

In the doorway, with the smell of the trees streaming down to us on the afternoon shadows, she pays me ten bucks extra—a shock—but it doesn't take away my annoyance at her. I see her begin to sweat as she starts the car up, before she turns it around to leave.

The driveway's yellow dirt flies and redistributes itself around her car. Yuck. I'm still touched by her, she's still somehow contaminating me, but I can feel my world, my little house, strengthening already in her absence. Only half an hour till Lucas gets home and I haven't even thought about a meal. Some housewife. When I think about how bad I am at it I feel despondent, actually, just so doubtful that this house and Lucas will ever be able to hold me in.

Hamburger helper. In any case. Or tuna, I think, and I have some greens in the crisper. I light a cigarette, still in that doorway, the pale wood door thumping the wall every now and then on the breeze.

Somewhere in my limbs a leaden exhaustion pulls at me. It increases in weight until I have to go lie down on the living room sofa. I let the cigarette sit there in the ashtray and smoke itself out.

But I don't sleep. Prone, I am not immune to her details. They travel through me in clear relief. The trip to Wanamaker's and the comforting smell of the clay facial at the salon, the surprising rose she buys to finish off the forty bucks and the petals floating, wilting, sinking in the scalding bathwater, her skin reddening, desperately, then pruning itself up.

Her husband's surprise that she solicits his attention, warms to his touch. That she's back to giggling for him, that he can see the old girlishness emerging in her, pushing dewy through her laughter. And his surprise again—gullible this one—the next morning, to wake up alone, and to wake up to the sound of her vacuum not only revving, but slamming into the baseboards downstairs.

She'll be down there because sweetness of the truth, that he really *does* love her, will curdle in Amandine when she wakes up freezing *and* sweating, ceiling fan twisting slicing stopping, husband's lips thinning, a cat screaming, her memory of its yelps from her girlhood fading only with the devouring roar of the Hoover once she's dressed, downstairs, busy. The cold sweat somehow causing one awful moment of that good night last night with Lyman to expand in her memory—the moment Lyman forgot that she never allowed him to *touch* her hair, her ears. The cringe and the terror when his hand grabbed for her face, her wig—a treacherous near miss—overtakes and swallows, in Amandine's heart, the hours of kindness that have passed between them and she then knows she *cannot* remain in the bed next to him. She whips herself from under the covers in one lightening motion, like the crack of a belt, or a cord.

To vacuum up all the dirt, to make tidy, perfect, safe.

This gift is so horrible. I say this aloud to nobody but Jesus over there on the wall. He's ignoring me. I open my eyes. And then I go out back, to numb it all down.

5

JESUS MOMMY

1974

Amandine doesn't know until later how much she loves the constant pull into sleep.

The baby, Racinda, watches with wide eyes: her mother folding sheets one minute, curled in a moon shape on the linoleum the next, puffing out a snore. Polishing silver, heady from fumes, collapsing onto the kitchen table, her arms and legs spread out as if it is a last chance raft to balance on and cling to.

*   *   *

Amandine has been having dreams about the sea hag. They start in the shallow brown creek behind her house, these dreams, wading dreams, but then turn over and over in space to become a great ocean, a night, warmth, nowhere near the creek—Amandine hovers somewhere above it, distant from it yet she knows its parts, possesses a registry of the different textures and natures of the vast, distinct yet inseparable locations of the sea. Amandine understands the faraway spot where a tempest swarms underneath as well as the soft, choppy, playful waves in a patch to her left.

She feels a great peace when she finds in that sea a circle, moonlit, where round-edged diamonds of water and light merge into each other with great elegance, forming chains only to disperse a second later.

And then she sees the sea hag, moving from the horizon slowly, a few inches above the waves, and Amandine can't quite make out what it is—she knows, though, that she is terrified. She wriggles and tries to turn, but the soft invisible thing that keeps Amandine hovering might as well be rope on her wrists and ankles. The well mannered circle of diamonds in the sea feels the coming too—swoops itself into a tapered stream and juts off.

The water all near Amandine calms, quiets, shushes in fear, but at its far edges crashes and breaks; angry waves begin gathering, then strengthen themselves into bunches.

The hag leaves a wake. Her hair flies behind her, wild, blending at its ends into the night, and nearer the scalp forming an outline against the stars. Pale seaweed slime covers her face, but the bones there jut out in relief. The skin underneath has the texture of limestone.

The hag reaches out her arm and opens her hand to Amandine. The fingers are sharp, filed to points at the ends, and in seconds Amandine starts to feel their tips sinking into her belly, breaking her powdered skin and dipping into her dark, running insides.

*   *   *

But back in real life, we go to the supermarket.

Little Racinda, almost a month old, making fists inside her blanket, sits on Amandine's hip, sticking out a little and not leaned against the shoulder like she should be—Amandine doesn't like to hold the baby to her when she's dressed well and drool might ruin the day. Amandine had paused here a year ago, looking for a flyer on the bulletin board, looking for anyone selling anything she thought might help her out. Amandine lets her eyes move more slowly than last year, she isn't going to settle too quickly on one thing—this time, not because she's grown up and mellowed or anything like that, but because depressed people are sometimes lethargic like this and can't quite keep time with the rest.. She insists on darkness and on small degrees of movement—you can't blame her in this kind of weather, actually. It's a bizarre heat wave, complete with wrenching humidity, in April. The asphalt steams. Amandine's slowness is necessary as ice.

Necessary not just because of the strange, intolerable heat, but because she's still gathering her strength from the birth of her second child, three weeks ago. She moved this slowly even when the weather was still seasonal, normally cool for April—so slowly that Lyman barely hear her around the house. "Jesus," he yelled, jumping, twice when she said his name inches from his ear—he'd had no idea she was even in the room. She thought her presence was obvious to him.

Lyman is proud of this baby, though he sighs, as if tired or depressed, almost all throughout the day. He hopes, as Amandine does, that somehow this second daughter will bring Ruth home from her grandmother's house, too. He hopes this in the abstract, though, because the one baby is creating noise, havoc in the house. Though he doesn't understand the name—Racinda?—he puts the nail up to hang the needlepoint sampler with that on it, along with her birth date, time, weight. A gift from one of Button's Presbyterian friends. Lyman stands over the crib and smiles, though he sleeps through Amandine's baby nights—she's the one up every two hours. He does bring home a new stuffed toy every Friday, though, he lines them up on the built-in bookshelf in the nursery.

Amandine doesn't mind taking care of the girl herself—she warms to the duty. And she gets nervous if Lyman spends too much time over the crib, not to mention when he decides to start giving the baby her formula in the early evenings. Amandine shoos him away. She wants this one to herself.

Still, despite the little bursts of joy that the shape of her baby's mouth, or feet, or ears give her, Amandine still moves ghostly slow as a tiny roof-leak staining the ceiling over a period of weeks.

But the women keep buzzing by her and the shopping cart wheels clack clack a little more than last year and have more lint and more tiny specks of glass embedded in their rubber surfaces. The ladies in dresses and the ladies in jeans and the ladies in pantsuits (well, only a few of those), and the ladies in tennis skirts and the ladies in culottes lean on those reassuring metal carts, either about to fill themselves up to the top or else leaving the store having just done so, the ladies swish past Amandine and she still hasn't become one of them.

The sound of a cart stopping barely registers.

"Hello, Amandine."

Amandine starts, of course, and whips around. A string of saliva from the baby's mouth flies across Amandine's chest.

It's Linda, Amandine's neighbor, again, a church kind of a woman, and she's grown larger: seems taller than the last time Amandine saw her, her breasts and hands expanded, her hair longer and fuller. Her nose and eyes and mouth take up more space now. Linda looks giant, round-edged.

Amandine's head is tilted, she's quite off today, so Linda looks tilted too—a still from a B movie, something called "Anxiety!" or maybe "Bad Things About To Happen," well, you know what I mean, but Linda herself is out of place in such a movie, Linda radiates warmth that is intolerable and irresistible at once.

"Whatcha lookin' for up there?" Linda says.

Amandine shakes her head the tiniest bit. Linda ignores her.

"Oh look, Ray's church has got a flyer up, great!" Linda says, flicking it, the pink thing, with her finger, and smiling.

Linda's eyes are speckled with yellow and her hair is streaked with it too. She's holding a brown paper bag on each hip, and one still rests in the cart. Her hair is long, it snakes down into a curve under her shoulders.

Amandine shrugs. She's shaken.

She got caught looking for salvation at the supermarket.

"You wanna help me with these? I parked right up here near the store," Linda says.

Amandine doesn't think, well, why doesn't she just wheel them on out there? Instead, she nods and suddenly looks at Racinda.

"Oh, how is your little girl?" Linda says.

Amandine stutters, and instead of responding, ends up saying:

"Here, I'll help you," motioning to the sack of groceries left in Linda's cart.

Outside the A&P, on a cement slab next to newspaper racks and green-ribboned lawn chairs for sale, is a rickety row of gumball machines, bubbled and bubble-filled transparent heads standing alert on red metal necks. A little boy sitting on the curb leans his head on one palm, staring down at an anthill on the fading asphalt, preparing, with the free hand, to drop his candy turquoise globe onto the sand pyramid's only exit.

A little assassin.

But as Amandine and Linda pass him, venturing out into the dry, unnatural heat smell of the blacktop, carrying four bundles—one a girl—the boy is concentrating and quiet and they don't notice him. They do notice the false-start cicadas chewing or rubbing or whatever it is that makes that noise, and they do notice the sound of metal wheels dragging across the pavement.

Linda feels a surge of joy and says to herself, "Thank the Lord for this gorgeous day. Just look at how He painted those clouds and they aren't just one color but streaked with a million lights."

But Linda almost even knows that that's not what the joy is about, freaking Jesus, she almost senses that underneath the willful talking to herself there is something else, something about the feeling of the air on her skin and the smell of the paper bags she is carrying and the presence of a new, naïve friend, a person to tug around who isn't a child but isn't so different from a child that it feels uncomfortable or like effort to be with her.

And Amandine isn't really thinking, either. She is *kind of* thinking, but its less of a thought, actually, than just the river of vague worries that Amandine floats through her day on. Doesn't count. She's not thinking and she's doing her dumb, worried brain noises, but at the same time she is taking in every sound and taste in the air. Like the perspective of a peaceful animal or a pre-lingual child—flashes of perception so rich and unmarred but in snippets. A smell, pools of heat, particles flying past, waves of outlines of light—these things fade into and past Amandine.

An abandoned, completely rusted VW Bug is dying next to the lot, beyond the macadam. It gives her something to focus on, something beyond all the shifting things floating at her and through her in her daze.

Amandine aligns herself with the dead Bug as she walks. Strange, from this distance, but she can see inside it, the woven-texture of the plastic, the tooth-sized chunks of bluish glass tossed across the seat, the stray willows that have grown up inside the car then died, too, parched from green into white dead things in the sun.

As Linda opens the back of her station wagon, Amandine says, "huh!" She hands Linda the grocery bag and the baby and walks ahead, to look at the wrecked thing. Her feet measure perfectly equal steps, a straight line.

Willows have taken root and died in the swamp that pooled over the seats once. Lichen and moss cover the dash—rotted pages of a magazine have been molded in little gray spots and rings, mildewed to look burned and then yellowed by the sun, plastered to the glove compartment. Amandine sticks her hand in the window through a hole that looks as if it were made by a baseball—something small and hard and fast. In her mind Amandine replays the transformation—slowly growing loam and green puddles, a flourishing and a bloom, then the dying/drying out, the preservation; the quiet, still perfection of a desiccated swamp.

Linda approaches her softly—"Well I'll be," she says, "It's like a terrarium in there."

"Yes," Amandine says, "Yes it is."

Amandine looks up at the sky with that oblique, crazy angle, a triangle of sky, clouds on diagonals—anxious clouds—not a nice rectangle of blue at all. These angles have been feeding her manic energy for weeks but now her attention gets pulled away, to Linda, who is round and organic and grown up out of the earth at the edge of the parking lot, like dirt risen up and formed into the shape of a giant woman, lit with yellow eyes and covered in luminous skin.

"Amandine," Linda says, "Why don't you come over for dinner tonight?"

Amandine stares, her mouth open, wipes her hand across her chin, licks her lip corners with the tip of her tongue.

"The kids are to their grandma's—it's just me and Ray. We can use the company," Linda says.

Racinda squeaks a little, shimmies in her summer weight blanket. Linda strokes the baby's forehead, a vertical line just above the nose, before turning her eyes back to the mother.

"Yes?" Linda says.

"Sure—sure," Amandine says, "Now?"

"Well, don't you need to get groceries?" Linda laughs and she bounces the girl on her hip.

"No," Amandine says, "No I do not."

Linda smiles and squints in the light. Amandine can't stop herself from staring at the dark spots forming under Linda's arms.

Amandine feels sweaty, too, but dry inside at the same time. She feels too perfect and too edged; she feels as if she has forgotten some crucial part of herself when she dressed this morning—as if she overlooked not panties or deodorant but a femur, or her liver, or a couple of pints of blood.

*   *   *

Covering the floor of Linda's kitchen is a brick patterned linoleum—-red and brown and orangey-rust rectangles outlined in a sort of mortar color. They interlock.

Amandine follows Linda into the kitchen. It is quiet in there, and it is cool, twenty degrees, at least, under the outside temperature.

"Fans," Linda explains, "Fans always running and you keep the curtains closed all the time."

"Oh," Amandine says.

"And I do think without the girls here that's three less bodies to heat things up."

She calls them girls even though the second oldest is male

Amandine looks at Racinda in her arms and thinks oh there is heat coming from my girl too, heat on my hip here. Yes, much too much warmth.

"Can I—can I put her down somewhere?" Amandine says.

"Oh, now you just sit on down and relax yourself. I'll bring my baby's bassinet in here and get you something to snack on. There's Tab in the fridge."

As Linda picks up Racinda and pads down her hallway to find the girl a place to rest, Amandine settles into the painted bench that runs one length of the table. How many kids would sit here every night? She can't imagine the noise, the dirt of children in this murky, breezy room.

The whir of the fan feels like her own breathing.

So this is how it started, Amandine's warming. Before she ran into Linda she slogged through her days with the baby—largely ignored by Button and Lyman, tossed a little conversation now and then from Elmer, whose nature was to ignore people's faults unless those faults were an immediate threat. Elmer too thought Amandine was sometimes mean and small, but since Button complained about her so he was protected and freed up to be a kind; would bring her a basket of peaches or of berries, would stop by for just a few minutes to say hello, talk about the new highway bypass or something else innocuous. Amandine would rise from her magazines or the television or the crossword or a simple daze, pull herself together enough to form sentences, then shut the door behind him with a sweet relief.

As soon as he left and the peaches were forgotten on the table—where they would rot, since she only ate saltines and Lyman only ate cold-cut sandwiches—the exhaustion would erupt from inside her, cover her skin with such a weight that hours later the sound of the baby screaming would wake her from strange places—sitting on the living room floor, her torso draped along the marble coffee table; or on her back, on the couch, with her neck and head hanging off the arm so that when her eyes finally opened, having fought the baby cries for as long as possible, the upside

downness of the china cabinet confused her, the strangeness of the familiar plates floating downwards from shelves made her wonder what had
possibly gone so wrong.

She could spend hours dressing. She looked good—that was really all
she could manage. She would lay out three different outfits and try each
one, turning prettily, slowly, for Racinda as if asking an opinion. She
would put on one set of false eyelashes then tumble into bed, tired from
the precision and the toothpick and the glue, for another little nap before
she got up, hours later, as if uninterrupted, to affix the other.

She would freeze while changing the baby—stare dreamily out the
window at the perfect blossoming curves of her topiary, at the brightness
of the fields in sun for minutes at a time until the girl squawked, quietly,
just enough to bring her mother back from the place that is not here and
not elsewhere. The two had an understanding. Under this painful dream-
iness a love, not a mothering love with strength and all the necessaries,
but a love nonetheless for the girl and for what the girl could give her in
between the shit and the puke and the crying, was what worked her body
through her days. And while she sometimes hated the girl for trapping her
in the house, her body always capitulated and ran through the motions,
because she knew that outside the house it would feel the same way or
worse. There was not a question of her forgetting her second girl. The necessary chores, the morning chores and the feeding chores and the
excrement chores and the soft evening chores she hadn't even considered
accomplishing with Ruth she did on her own now, alone, from a willingness which, while she remained distant, detached, walled-up, belied this
warming action in her that started well before Linda came along again in
the postered glass foyer in that strange, too-warm April.

Because this time she was alone, because Button was busy mothering
Ruth and Lyman was so gone from her and Ruth had screamed at her *you
don't want me* and it wasn't that Amandine was trying to prove Ruth wrong
but it was that she *did* want Ruth and she tried to tell Ruth that through
her sister. When she could stay awake, that is.

Amandine sits silent while Linda starts work on the casserole. She stares
out the window that reminds her of her own kitchen window but there is
no chance that here Ruth will fly across the field followed by the bitch Button. Just hot grass. Then, natural as sighing or blinking her eyes, she gets
up and goes into the living room and lies down on the divan, face toward
its back, curling her belly around a pillow covered with a grandma's knit-

ted squares. As Amandine leaves the kitchen, Linda looks over her shoulder but just keeps chopping the onion, unconcerned.

Something about the softness of the couch—the places where the upholstery is worn to pliant and the easy, pummeled surfaces of the cushions—must be working on Amandine; that and the browning onion smell from the kitchen, the hymn Linda's voice is weaving into the air.

Because when the sea hag zooms in from the horizon, hovering inches above the waves, and opens her poky hand to Amandine, the pointed tips can't dig into Amandine's belly—the belly doesn't give way to holes this time.

The fingers stroke Amandine's torso—the hag's dark eyes seem blind, the hag explores Amandine without vision, by touch. The binding force of clouds still holds Amandine, but her terror is gone. Amandine studies the hag's arches—lacquery eyebrows, cheekbones, the dramatic slope of her lips. She listens to the seaweed hair hanging off this creature, shifting in the breeze, she lets her eyes grace the starlight on the water. The sea hag's skin is mosaicked, fish-scaly with deep blue tesserae—it reflects purples and greens. The eyelashes seem fake—so curled, so tilted up at the edges they wink without blinking. Her lips—malachite—are translucent and shiny at once. The bottom one is full and tapers at the corners—the top one swoops down from a high middle with the drama of archy, plucked eyebrows.

It never occurs to Amandine to think of her as a mermaid.

The fingers aren't soft, but they don't scratch or cut Amandine. The hag traces Amandine's ear, runs her finger down Amandine's jaw line, her shoulder, her arms as if to soothe. The hag's eyes now follow her hand's path; her head, blue at its edges, tilts in a gesture of gentle curiosity.

Amandine feels the cage of her body melt off; she feels the ocean's elegant patch of liquid diamonds swirl into her, calmly, creating the sensation of stepping into a perfectly warm bath, and she knows this is the hag moving into her, filling her up, comforting her with the force of water rushing a vessel.

Two.

She wakes to Linda's hand coolly crossing her forehead. Amandine flipped over in her sleep, so now the pillow pressed at the small of her back and Linda's wide hips fill the empty space her belly frames softly.

"Hi Amandine, sleep well?" Linda says this gently, in a beautiful voice.

Amandine nods, wordless, not yet willing to realign her body to its familiar right angles and leave behind the shifting murky world, her dreams of seaweed dripping, though the images rush away from her so quickly all she can remember is the rough salt air in her throat.

Linda looks confused.

"Do you need to call your husband and invite him over too?" she asks.

Amandine shakes her head.

"Well, don't you need to—" Linda pauses, cautious to stay polite, "let him know what he's to do for dinner?"

Amandine wills herself into the world of speech long enough to mumble something about this being Lyman's night to play poker and eat sandwiches out. But then drops back into softness and dreams for a minute more, long enough to forget the reality—that she and her husband never eat together anymore, that after he gives Racinda her bottle he goes down to sand, to slice wood, gone.

"Dinner's almost ready and Ray will be home soon—I fed Racinda and she's back to sleep. Why don't you get cleaned up in the powder room and come help me set the table?" Linda says.

The feeling of Linda's hand across her head is like patterns of sun hitting you through a car window on a morning when you are just starting out for someplace wonderful, a fall morning maybe, promising mittens and puffy air and a big sky and a picnic table. The pleated plastic shade on a bronze colored standing lamp throws Linda's wide features into a theatrical glow that Amandine almost takes for supernatural until she sits up.

"Yes, of course," Amandine says, patting her hair back toward her ears. "The baby took what kind of formula? Usually she's so picky."

"Oh I just gave her some milk," Linda says.

Amandine remains quiet when Ray comes home and as they sit down to eat. She hasn't, she realizes, had a real conversation since Racinda was born. She's been so drawn into her awful farmhouse life that she can't tolerate the pastel talks with her old secretary friends—now mostly married too but shimmering in the surfaces of that life, not pulled down to crazy.

"Fathuh," Ray says—he drops the r—"fathuh," just the tiniest bit, and you can feel the South in him, a Southern pull to him but no twang and you wouldn't maybe notice it unless you were feeling quiet and paying attention like Amandine is. He's a small, slight man, with a head like a bird's—round at the pate tightening into a pointy chin—but with thick arms and legs, blockish limbs.

"Father, we thank you for this day—"

The three of them hold hands—the two women beside each other on the bench, Ray leaning across the string beans and the blue and white casserole dish to grip both of the women and form a circle.

"We thank you for the power of your love to lighten the burden of the enemy's deception and destruction,

"We thank you for cleansing us, for making us pure in your son's blood,

"We thank you for nourishing our bodies tonight,

"Help us to obey you with open hearts in the nights and days to come,

"Amen."

Ray and Linda say the last word as one voice slightly tripped up on itself, a voice jarred a bit as if put through some recording device and spit back out doubled.

Ray opens his eyes. Amandine's have been wide the whole prayer, a streak of rebellion poking out—she is certain the two would be eyes shut but she wanted to check, anyway, although she knows she doesn't need to, she knows these two obey the rules.

Ray raises his head. He removes his hand from his wife's and joins it with his other around Amandine's.

"'The Lord is thy keeper: the Lord is thy shade upon thy right hand,'" he says, naming the one he is clenching. He tries to lock her gaze—she catches him for a minute but runs her eyes up and down the diagonals, the blue squares on the tablecloth.

Ray just keeps at it. Amandine hasn't been looked at that for-real in a long time. In fact never. Never has someone been so intent on getting her to stare back at them. Certainly not Lyman. Maybe Ruth before she went away came close. She lets her eyes peer far up enough just to glimpse his mouth—the flat wide lips, the bottoms of benign teeth, perched.

Ray smiles, gives Amandine's hand one last, tighter squeeze before he looks over at Linda and says:

"Honey, let's chow."

*　　　*　　　*

"We started our ministry outside Miami, Florida," Linda says.

"Hialeah, you know it?" Ray says.

Amandine shakes her head, embarrassed at the huge piece of bread filling her mouth. She takes a sip of iced tea.

"I got my calling—the Lord said 'You go and do it now,' and so I started my own church," Ray rubs his lips against each other like he were spreading Chapstick. She focuses on his suit—a loden green, almost brown, gabardine—focuses on the almost-transparent nylon-silky material of the white-collared shirt underneath, probably short-sleeved the way it bunches. On the tie—a perfect, distinguished tie. A senator's tie.

"We're just starting our own ministry here, but for now Ray is running the social programs over to the Lutherans," Linda says.

"There's always a ministry, if you keep your eyes open," Ray says.

"Oh, yes," Linda says, "More beans?"

Amandine helps herself to another half a plateful, making sure she gets lots of the cheese and breadcrumbs on top.

"May I have some more casserole, as well, please?"

Amandine is surprised to find herself saying this.

As Linda fills the rest of Amandine's plate with the tuna and twisted noodles and sweet onions, she repeats her husband:

"Oh yes, there's a ministry everywhere. Alls you have to do is open your address book," Linda says and smiles, pushes a lock of hair from her breast to behind her shoulder.

"Even in the least likely places there's a ministry," Ray says.

"You know, especially there," Linda says, looking intently at her husband.

There is a pause—chewing, swallowing, the buzz of large appliances and fans, the little metal wall clock zooming its second hand around in a smooth circle, evening meal smells and crickets beginning.

"Can I have some milk?" Amandine asks.

"Well, certainly," Linda says, "We certainly have enough milk to share in this house."

There are two supermarket gallons and two dairy bottles of it on the top shelf of the icebox. Linda gets a tall, heavy glass from above the sink and fills it almost full with the dairy milk—a little cream floats near the rim. The old-fashioned bottle with its red foily cardboard cap is close to empty.

"Thank you," Amandine says with a hint of a sigh. She is getting tired from all the work her jaw is doing, from all the swallowing, but is still so famished it feels like she has barely taken one bite.

Ray pauses in his feeding to talk some more:

"Why, yes, I mean, Linda's right—folks can find a witness in the strangest of places."

"Yes," Linda says.

So the clock's hand keeps spinning but now it is a little sad and you can see that in the way the couple is looking at each other, in the paused angle of Linda's hands holding her flatware at the sides of her plate, in one side of Linda's mouth turning down and her eyes turning up at her husband.

"You're thinking of Sandra," Linda says. She runs a pinkie down the edge of her mouth to try to tame her fading lipstick.

"Yes, I am," Ray says. Pushing his plate away he spreads his hands outward on the tablecloth, as if to create a space for his story to play out in miniature in front of them:

"This was a woman in Miami, Florida, who was at the end of any rope she could find. No family, no friends, no husband, a boyfriend who was a drug-running gangster and beat her bloody. She had a hundred-dollar-a-day heroin habit. She had overdosed two or three times and nearly asphyxiated herself on her own vomit, sold her body on the streets, but here in a Miami, Florida, jail cell with no one to use her one dime on, one of our dear sisters, a warden in the jail, served as God's witness and delivered this woman into His sweet arms. He didn't care that she smelled like urine and excrement, that scars ran over her body, that she let herself become defiled. Now Sandra knows the Heavenly Father, now she has taken Jesus as her personal savior and has traded the wages of sin for eternal life. She has been sanctified by grace, God and Jesus."

And when Ray says "grace," Amandine sees her out there, out the kitchen window, the whore. Sandra from Miami, Florida. She is a thin woman—nearly naked, hipbones protruding, a little fleshy in the ass, narrow and slightly rounded muscles in her legs and calves—with wild ratted hair so covered in dirt that Amandine can't discern its color. Blood and piss and shit and vomit and semen cover her but she just stands there, monstrous, quiet, transported from a years-ago jail cell in Miami, Florida, to here, where she is all alone on a lawn and has no place to sit down. And she looks *tired*. Her eyes are buggy and ringed in black and stare straight at Amandine without asking anything of her.

Amandine feels that she should cough, or smile politely, or nudge her eyes to indicate the scene outside, but she just can't manage it, and knows that it's only she who can see Sandra now. So she sops up some oil and sauce with a chunk of yellowy bread at the end of her fork. And watches.

Even though maybe, just maybe she is starting to get full—and even now Amandine is primed to become alarmed at the slightest sensation of heaviness—she lifts another piece of the thick potato bread out of its dish-toweled basket and smears its entire surface with a quarter-inch of butter. The butter is salted and soft—this is the kind of household that always leaves a double-size stick of it out on the counter in a dish the shape of a black and white cow—the kind of butter you'd always find somebody else's toast crumbs or jelly bits in.

"Do you know what the wages of sin is, Amandine?" Ray says.

She thinks she sees Sandra shiver out there. The sun has shifted into that horizontal afternoon gold light but it probably hasn't cooled down outside at all.

Her eyes rimmed in black don't ask anything
Smeared in shit and worse
Her breasts are round and bare over a narrow ribcage
She doesn't ask anything and
Amandine can look at her
She is only wearing panties and a garter belt and crusted stockings.
Amandine can look.

"The wages of sin is death," Ray says, "But—"

Sandra, out there, seems to sigh, then starts to breathe evidently, heavily, with effort. Amandine watches the skin and debris shift over her ribs.

"But there is a way—" Ray says

Amandine, transfixed, exhausted, leans her cheek on her hand, squishing her face unattractively.

"—to eternal life."

Shutting her eyes tight as if she's had enough, Sandra exhales everything and sits down on the lawn. She leans back on her hands for a minute, then starts fussing with her garter. Her head is bent down in concentration and her hair takes on a greater wildness, all bunched and snaky. Her at-once thin and meaty legs sprawl at strange angles.

"Amandine," Ray says, "Do you want to take the Way to eternal life? The way that can absolve death which means to say every moment of guilt or sadness or loneliness or hatred or anger or pain or sin?

"Do you want the *Son* of *God* to touch *you*?"

And then she sees Him. He enters the window frame from the left and says something to Sandra. As Sandra, nearly reeling, greets Him, she lightens, loosens, is comforted—just by looking, by returning His look. Seeing. Amandine finds herself wondering how she, Amandine, is so sure its Him, Jesus—well, He does have that beard, those eyes. The wash of kindness that filled the trees and the sky and the whore when He showed up probably is a big tip-off too. Anyway. He's not wearing his usual robe—He's got on the most comfy-looking jeans, the kind a girl would want—sweetly—to steal for herself from her boyfriend's pile on the floor, and a gray tee shirt. Amandine can't nod to Ray to cover her wonder. She stares. She's almost *out* there with them.

It isn't that he is so beautiful, it is that—

He stands there completely still and his chest is tan and his short beard isn't too full but it is a couple different lit-up shades of brown and chestnut and straw. What he embodies is *ease.*

"Do you want to be delivered by His love, Amandine?"

Jesus kneels down and starts helping Sandra with her stockings. He's got such a mother-love to him, He touches her like you would touch a child. Sandra doesn't seem to want to cover herself at all. She raises her head up and looks at Him, like she isn't sure about all this, but then eases back on her elbows, swaying her fingers through the grass, slowly. He pauses to arrange locks of her hair—sweaty, or greasy—back off of her forehead. He edges his fingers gently under the tops of a stocking, at the band, and peels it down slowly, leaning in to inspect a run or a snag, lifting and smoothing the dirtied gossamer thing.

Amandine is in a daze again. She can feel the potato bread in her mouth and smell the onions and cheese and tunafish and even the milk and the iced tea but it can all fit in *her—so much.* So much can fit in her at this moment that she wouldn't have imagined could ever—the tastes and the smells and Ray's sermon and Jesus and Sandra the junkie whore. She holds all these things in her in this moment—nothing overflows her, pushes over her rim.

As Jesus works the second stocking off the belt, Sandra reclines, pressing her shoulders back onto the grass. She wiggles her toes and some formations of dirt flake off. There is a little breeze out there—the leaves turn to their ashy sides now and then at the edge of the yard. Shadows deepen there too, nearly blackening the creek that divides the property from the woods.

"Do you want the hand of the Holy Spirit to move things to right with you?" Ray says.

"I'm not—sure," Amandine says absentmindedly, before she returns her attention to what demands it. Her cheek has reddened from her hand's pressure.

He gets the second stocking loose and bends it downward, pulling part of the color off of Sandra's leg. Sandra shivers, and sits up—where he'd separated the nylon from a wound, fresh blood appears.

"If you ask Him to come into your life, Amandine, He will," Ray says.

"Mm," Amandine says.

"Well, who's ready for some dessert?" Linda says, lifting Amandine's nearly empty plate, setting the fork more steadily in the middle of the pile of breadcrumbs there.

Outside, the breeze picks up and a lilac branch waves across the window, snagging on something, blocking its lower half. Amandine stands.

"Oh, now don't you look exhausted and you're trying to help clear. Just sit down and I'll take care of it, honey," Linda says.

It is quiet in the kitchen for quite some time.

Once Jesus has them both off her, he carries the squalid things to the creek, down the yard's small incline. Sandra slumps onto her side, facing the house, and sleeps. As Jesus' torso, then head, finally disappear from view, Amandine looks over at Ray, meets his eyes, finally.

He grabs her hand across the table, and the wool of his suit brushes her wrist, scratchy, surprising. He thinks she is looking at him for real.

"Yes?" Ray says with his mouth full.

"Nothing!" Amandine says, "What's for dessert?"

She is aware of the split in her—one part capable of holding this conversation and chewing adequately and the other part seeing Jesus out the window, and aware that strangely enough this Jesus part was the same part of her also tasting the food and listening to the amazing noises of Linda clanking glassware in the sink and nudging up against the soft gray of the coming twilight and suddenly, profoundly, exhausted.

"Do you want a big piece of cobbler for dessert or a little piece, hon?" Linda asks her, holding out two plates of it.

Amandine yawns—just barely remembering to cover her mouth, and says:

"If you'll excuse me, I need to go lie down on the couch again. . ."

*   *   *

When she awakens it is dark out and her surroundings shock her. She settles in a second when she sees Racinda in the bassinet on the floor next to her.

She inhales, exhales, feels quiet and unconcerned. She rolls over and half-sleeps that is, she is aware of the noises Racinda makes in breathing and of the crickets and of the light breeze outside but she tumbles into dreams at the same time—

"Do you want a big piece or a little piece," Linda says, holding up the two plates of dessert.

"Big," Amandine says, "Very, very big. Bigger than that, for sure."

Linda happily gets her a second piece and puts the double-duty plate down in front of her guest.

Ray starts talking about God again, but before the words come into themselves as words, when they are still rivers of undifferentiated tones and rhythms and songs, Amandine says:

"Ray—Ray just give me a minute here. I just need a minute."

Even in her dream, Ray and Linda can't see Jesus and the whore, but Ray is sweet and polite enough—he smiles and even laughs a little. He nods decisively and shuts up, eats a big bite of cobbler, grins widely.

There is a lot of butter in the crust and the cherries are hot inside— blackest red Bings. Amandine smashes the crust against the roof of her mouth with her tongue and lets the hot fruit run between tooth and cheek.

*   *   *

Sandra seems to be napping out there in the dwindling light when the Son of God, the Son of Man, whichever you prefer, returns. He is only in boxer shorts now, has taken His t-shirt and jeans off, and drapes one clean, damp stocking over each shoulder. In one hand He carries a bucket and in the other a soft-looking cloth.

He bathes her. At first Sandra shivers when He squeezes water down her arm, but then she just relaxes back down into the grass. He is on one knee, staining it. Long muscles throw narrow shadows onto His back; shorter ones in His arms round and flatten as He soaks her then wipes her off then finally rinses her—as the water runs down her sides, she giggles, then starts shaking in laughter. He pokes at her sides a little, still gently, and the tickles push her further into mirth.

He steps back from her, grinning, and rolls each stocking onto an arm, sexy, joking. He admires them, sleeks them from tip to elbow like fancy gloves, cocks His head at a flirty angle. Overly gracefully, producing little giddies from Sandra, He swoops Himself downward and upward—into a handstand, and begins to parade for her. He lifts and points His fingers like a hot babe in serious heels, He purses His lips and shakes.

Shimmies His ass up there in the air like a girl's.

At which point Amandine notices that Ray and Linda are gone and the rest of the dishes are clean except for her plate still in front of her and Amandine is alone in the kitchen still eating cobbler, still noticing the salt taste in the butter and the brown sugar in the crust and the cinnamon somewhere in between the two.

But this all soon disappears, and she feels the baby's breathing time itself with her own and she feels the crickets and the stars fixed above her and the little light from the moon coming through the curtains so she sits up on the couch and realizes she has to go home. There is nothing of Jesus in the room, there is just dark.

*   *   *

Back in her own kitchen, standing at the sink, running a dish under the faucet and forgetting about the soap, Amandine looks for Him and for Sandra, but really she just wants Him. Her kitchen window is cleaner than the Dells': maybe He likes the murk, prefers their translucent glass to her perfectly clear window. Her movements even feel robotic to her. She goes through things but doesn't feel anything.

If there were a person around to notice, that person might think that everything deleted from Amandine—everything the omission of which turns her into this robot—would rise up at once in an extreme gesture or act. A break down or a blow up—one direction or the other. Something strained and ugly and painful.

Slants of light cross the lawn into sections, but He is not hiding in the shady ones, nor can she spot Him among the lined-up tree trunks down by the creek. She lets the tap water course over her hand, it deflects off the gems in her rings, and she forgets why she is standing there.

It's just curiosity, she thinks, I just want to know what *happens* with Him and that woman.

But that isn't really true.

She grips the edge of the sink and looks out there awhile longer.

She wants him and she wants to trace the outline of his beard with her finger. She wants to sit out on the lawn with him and inch together a little by a little—slow, dense movement—she wants a feeling of him curling up in the nook of her belly her lap and she wants the feeling of crawling into his space there.

But she can't find him. Can't call him, woo him, will him, force him.

She lets the plate drop, slowly, without drama.

Anger swells in her limbs, rushes tingly to the curve under her fingernails. Those fucking church freaks—she swears in her mind—Fuck those fuckers. It has been so long since her veneer has mattered, so long that she has been out here just past the edge of suburbia, on what is really a *farm*, or was one, her powder blue suits and pearls, no mirrors of ladies to reflect her, no windows to pass her two dimensional self in primly, so long out here that she is struck now with the glee of the crass words in a way that has never occurred to her before. Motherfuckers, she thinks, JESUS MOTHER FUCKERS. Cocksuckers! She thinks, they *are*, and *He* is— she thinks Jesus' first letters big in her mind then she thinks no, no he's out there on the lawn with that filthy girl why does he get big letters? Capitals. She giggles, but the anger stays. Why does he get capitals?

And from then on he gets small ones with her.

"Oh God dammit."

And she realizes it is dinnertime again; the Dells are probably there with all their kids and he is there with them and she hates him because how can he take care of that trashy whore on the lawn but not come here to her, Amandine?

And she sits at the kitchen table to weep softly.

And she decides, as she often does in such moments, to go wake up the baby, who cries out and spits at first, but settles quickly when her eyes focus on her mother. Racinda exhales, shifts. She has only been down fifteen minutes but she is so easy—not at first but she has learned quickly— and Amandine can tell the girl wants to be lifted and held.

As Amandine pulls the baby up, the rush of comfort swarms her like she knew it would.

"Little girl," she says and she coos to her girl and she squeezes the girl a little and fits the girl to her chest and forgets for a minute all about the Dells and Jesus and that she ever knew any swear words or what they sound like or the shapes her mouth makes on them.

And a sadness that is beyond her own washes down her body. This pure bliss of her baby pressed to her ribcage is something Lyman wants but she won't let him have—so sad, his locking himself down in the basement, or his not coming home from work until late, when he just can't take any more sawdust. Before her tears can start, though, Amandine remembers that even if Lyman *did* stay upstairs, did get tender with her, that he'd always, *always*, disappear again. She hardens.

Stay away. So what?

So.

What.

As the light shifts down, warming into its eight o'clock burst before evening, she thinks of the lawn again and of Jesus and that thick spark of desire and thinks I don't need *Jesus*, I've got the love of my family. This little girl loves me unconditionally, you hear that, boy, you hear that, Jesus? She gives me what you won't and so you can just stay over at their house and eat chicken with the fat churchwoman and her skinny husband.

Three.

The very next chance she gets, however, Amandine herself goes over for chicken. She doesn't call Linda of course—Linda shows up at Amandine's house, three days later, with heavy warm biscuits wrapped in a tea towel, a heavy warm hug for Amandine, a hug devoid of anything to do with church. Amandine goes over there for ribs, too, for spaghetti, for a sandwich picnic by the creek, each time surrounded by the children, the *girls*, the eldest of whom watches Racinda so well that Amandine gets jealous and a bit cranky. The church part remains peripheral—the Dells know from experience to go slow with her type, and Jesus is less than peripheral, never even leaning in from the corners of vision, though Amandine, super-alert and disappointed, *does* wait for him. They get her laughing a bit, though, the Dells, and she doesn't automatically wrench her face to a stiff blankness all the time anymore.

So the next time the kids are at their grandma's and Linda asks Amandine over to take advantage of the last bit of the heat wave, have a girly day, a beauty-tips-eyebrow-wax kind of day, Amandine feels herself as so much lighter, more used to eating, suddenly capable of leaving Racinda for more than an hour in day care, as she makes her way to the Dells' cool brown linoleum-brick kitchen.

*   *   *

"So I mixed up a big batch of it—it's honey and yogurt and egg whites."

Amandine looks at the enormous pot of white goop on the stove.

"Is it hot?"

"No, I just set it out there on the stove to cool," Linda says.

"I ah—I don't think I'd better. I have sensitive skin on my face."

"Well, that's okay—I made enough for whole body treatments—legs and arms, you know?"

"Oh."

"We'll just make sure not to get any on our bikinis—I don't think it'll stain, but it might get sticky," Linda says. She laughs.

"I'm so glad you were able to find a sitter," Linda says.

"Oh, well, this girl's quite dependable."

"I just send mine off to Ray's mother's once in awhile. Sometimes I feel a little bad, but I think she enjoys it."

"Hmmm," Amandine is getting drifty, wanting to go out in the sun.

Amandine nestles herself into the deck chair on the grass and watches the trees. The grass is dry underneath her, and Amandine can feel it tickling her through the woven green acrylic straps of the low lawn chair. She remembers the wide oval sunglasses in her purse when she starts having to squint.

"Do you think we should do our fronts or our backs first?" Linda says as she walks down the lawn carrying a tray with iced tea and sandwiches.

"I don't know," Amandine says.

"Well, let me think. If I do your back then I guess it might get messy if you did mine then, so maybe we could switch off. I could do your back and then I could do my front."

"That seems fine," Amandine says. Her voice drifts off. As the slow, distant buzz of a jet engine weaves down through the thick air, she remembers suddenly to look for Jesus—she had forgotten up to this point. Her eyes scan the edge of the yard slowly. But when Linda starts to talk again, Amandine's eyes fall on her wide rose-brown cheeks, the browbone that pushes out in a delicate, horizontal stretch waving S-shape. You can hear the insects flitting by now and then, you can hear the creek's purr down the low hill, so it isn't silent, though it seems that way.

"Well, Amandine, you better stop chattering so much or I'm gonna have to send you home!" Linda says. Forgetting her coating, she smoothes her fingers at the corners of her mouth, then has to pat the white stuff back into place.

"What? Oh. Yes, well, I'm sorry, I guess I'm just sort of a quiet person," Amandine says.

Amandine looks down at her arm and brushes something imaginary off it with a swoop of her fingers, cringes back into herself out of habit, though in reality she feels happy to be so noticed. A smile cracks in her, but she only lets it cross her face for a second. She rolls over onto her stomach.

Linda dips a wide, wooden spatula into the mixture and smears it across Amandine's back, avoiding the rust-colored bathing suit strap. Amandine shifts a little when she feels the surprise of the coolness. The mixture is a bit sticky, but the yogurt in it smoothes it out.

"Oh shucks, its just getting all over the place on this thing," Linda says. She shakes remaining globs off the spatula then lets it fall to the deck.

She dips her hand in the pot and cups a bit, smearing the mixture onto the small of Amandine's back. Amandine tenses, then, self-conscious, takes a breath in and holds it, stretches herself flatter into the lawn chair. She stares at the creek through a gap in the pool's cherry-stained latticework even though she now knows she won't see him today. When Amandine finally exhales it is almost a little moan.

"Linda," Amandine says.

"Yes, hon?"

"Do you ever—*see*—Jesus?"

"Well, sure, I see Him in my mind when I talk to Him, or you know, go out for a stroll and feel like He's there," Linda says.

"Oh."

Linda drips the mixture onto the backs of Amandine's thighs, just a few cold spots, inching in from the sides.

"Ow!" Amandine says, and gives a little nervous laugh. The sensation of the stuff dripping inwards makes her want to cry out again. She can feel a runny puddle of it forming where her legs are clenched together.

"Oh now I know it doesn't *hurt*!" Linda says. Her voice is light and fluttery.

Linda refills her palms and lets larger splotches of yogurt and honey trickle on the white skin just below the edge of Amandine's bikini.

"Don't worry, I'll keep it clean," Linda says. Her fingers spread out over Amandine's skin, following the mixture as it drips down the curves, scooping it up again, rubbing it in. Amandine spreads out, takes up more space on the chair.

The bushes down by the creek reflect darkness, catch and play with the shade of the heavy oaks and ash trees that protect the water—dark green and black twist and shift there. Amandine wants to see Jesus so badly now that she tries to conjure his face in these shadowy patterns. But he would not be hidden there—he is hay-colored, a tickly beard, sun-colored hands.

Her eyes close and she doesn't have to work to see him now, his golden face that she can look at and not have to turn her eyes from. In her version he would radiate pools of tawny light onto the blue-green lawn, he would reach out to her and she would let him grab her around the waist, throw her over his shoulders like he did with Sandra's stockings. By gripping the sides of her thighs, he would balance her; would adjust his hands constantly as he carried her down the lawn, nearly stumbling on the rough turf; to avoid losing her has to wrap each enormous hand fully around a leg.

"But you don't see him with your eyes."

"Well, no," Linda says, "No I don't, but I know some people have been fortunate enough to have a sort of vision like that."

Linda looks up to the sky, at the white puffs speeding by on a wind the women can't feel down where they are. She pulls her wide, coated hands up, spreads the fingers out as if to dry them. She leans her head a little and tries to get the explanation just right:

"The way it works is you just feel Him—He just is there with you and sometimes at the beginning it's hard to open yourself to Him but with time, things you thought were just 'happy' or 'peace' or 'joy' or 'comfort' you now have a name for and that name is J-E-S-U-S," Linda says.

The breeze blows across Amandine's legs and she feels she might weep from the sudden lack of another person's skin.

"If you get baptized, then what happens?"

"You feel Him inside you,"

"All the time?"

"When you need Him, when you remember you want Him, His sweet love,"

"He is with you but then he goes away when he feels like it?"

"He would, He does stay in you all the time—He does. It's only sometime you—I—forget He's there."

The yogurt and honey and egg whites stiffen on them—the two women, newly strange, covered in pale peaks and ridges. The whiteness edges onto Linda's sunglasses—she is a huge confection, her face and pliant belly whipped with it, her white cottony bikini completing the solid field. She is a cake, but under that fluff there is an honesty to her, a strength that Amandine can feel strongly now. Some level of her is like worn stone, something solid, but not unforgiving—like a stone fashioned into a cup, strength with room to hold what comes to it. It's like the thickness of the air and the moment—Amandine's sense of her own presence here—the smell of the grass and the heat, the shifting vapor in the sky, the noises of terribly confused, jumpstarted insects and the twinkling of the creek at the edge of the yard, her own breathing, are only real to her, can only be taken in because of the stone cup inside Linda. Without Linda there, Amandine knows the denseness of the false, early heat and humidity, of her breath, of sensation, would be unavailable—she would be left with just one thing, the one thing she knows is her own, the thin awful buzzing line of her thoughts, just one thing, just one dimension.

"But before you get baptized, you need to accept Him as your personal savior," Linda says.

"Oh."

"And he will give you eternal life," Linda's voice rings with something primmer than usual, she turns her head and this false earnestness comes over her. The icing on her belly cracks like parched earth as she leans up on an elbow to face Amandine.

"Are you ready to do that, Amandine?"

"Maybe," Amandine says, "Maybe soon. I—I'm—I don't know."

Amandine, a sliver of desperation in her mousy face, turns slightly to Linda. There is—this pressured feeling she had before in the kitchen she had blamed on Ray, not on her friend.

Linda's features look panicked, don't they?

"It's eternal life," Linda says, with great pity and grabs the arm of the lounge chair tightly.

Amandine's eyes seem to dim, sadness overtakes her and she suddenly knows she'll be alone at her clean kitchen window forever.

"Oh hon," Linda says, furrowing her S-shaped brow, jutting her lower lip out in concern, "Oh, hon, you take your time. I didn't *know* when I accepted him. I just jumped. Didn't *believe*, but he caught me. You take your time, sweetie."

And then there is nothing to say; they quiet themselves, and Amandine's old weight, the sleep, drags her down despite the heat.

This time Amandine remembers the dream. The hag doesn't approach slowly across the water, but waits there for Amandine and appears next to her as soon as Amandine falls asleep and feels the whirling, crawling surf under her. The hag's face is larger now, taking up more than half the world of the dream, curious, gently tilted to one side.

Amandine rolls over and the cloud binds, but then this time, releases her. She sits up, fresh and just born, in the air above the water, above the calm elegant patch of strung together diamonds, who are now dancing, flirting, merging and separating in mirth.

The two stare at each other for a long while, then the hag reclines. Extends her arms ahead of her, rolls to her side, bends one leg to lean on, and sleeps. Amandine notices for the first time, as if her eyes are just now adjusting to the darkness, the line of blood creeping from the hag's lip to her chin, running again down her thigh, smeared.

Amandine wakes again to Linda's hand brushing her hair.

"Come on, we're all dried out. Let's go down to the creek," Linda says. "I know the water is still cold, but wow, I mean how refreshing!"

Linda's enormous round sunglasses—strange, ghostly, focused—are impassable, two holes on her white plastered face.

Amandine's nylon thongs click her heels as she follows Linda down the little hill to the creek. The same stream crosses Amandine's yard too, but here it is wide and deep enough to swim in—Ray and Linda's kids have constructed a rickety ash-wood dock and tied a rope up in the big oak tree whose limbs lean halfway across the water from the other side.

Linda sits on the flat stone at the banks, heat scaling off its dry gray surface, and lets her calves sway in the water. Behind her, Amandine stands transfixed, staring across at the moist looking tree trunks. Linda's hair swoops out into a fan shape on a rock as she reclines. A breeze blows up now and then from the water but it is definitely getting warmer out, even here in the shade.

"Boy, it really takes it out of you, doesn't it?" Linda says.

Upside down, Linda's features recombine strangely. Her mouth, Amandine notices, seems fine from this angle, self-contained, gentle at the edges, a few creases but wide and drawn out in the same comforting curve as her brow. The body mask is cracked all over now, the most skin showing in the space between her breasts, but pinkish runners thread under her belly button, radiate on each of her sides, at the waistline. Amandine sits down next to her, lies back next to her. The stuff flakes off her back, her narrow thigh touches Linda's generous one.

Linda sits up and removes her sunglasses. As she leans over to fill her hands with water, her foot flexes to anchor her, her fleshy stomach curls inward under the dappled light. With each splash to her face, she sighs a little, the mask gets moist and rinses milky onto the pebbly bank.

"Much better!" Linda says, stretching the muscles in her face. Rivulets stream down around the round high spots on her cheeks.

"Now for the rest of us."

She sinks a toe, a calf in, then the other leg, breaking the water with small noises, shivery at the creek's unwillingness to be convinced by the air's untimely heat. Circles layer and expand behind her as she wades knee deep, waist deep, further until the black surface skirts the lower curve of her breasts.

"Ooh—it's nice. Come in," she says.

She splashes water onto her arms and shoulders, trails her fingers down, rubs. The stuff still covers her chest above the bikini top, her collarbone, her neck, though runnels stream down there, fading the whiteness in lines, melting it off in little rivers. On its underside, the bikini top darkens, soaking up shade. As Linda twirls around, slowly, sweetly, with a girlish fascination of movement, the tie around her neck seems to release a bit, lowering, and the material expands, slackening at the sides.

"Come in!" Linda says, smiling at Amandine, "Come on, you get used to it!" The light tumbles down on the water and on Linda, who seems to grow, to amplify herself in the creek.

Amandine slides off the rock and shivers as the coolness travels up her legs. She moves slowly, her arms and legs clearing through the water, strengthening as she becomes accustomed to its still-icy force. Further in, Linda starts spilling water on her neck and chest, rinsing its rarefied film onto her bathing suit.

"Oh my," she says, looking down, "I'm making a huge mess."

She looks back up and her eye catches on Amandine, lights with something unrestrained at the sight of her friend approaching. She holds her gaze. Amandine circles around her, exploring the smooth stones and soot below with her toes. She stops just past Linda, nearer the far bank, but in a shallower part, and lets her feet sink in—the smearing, encompassing feeling starts there but she can feel its echo in her stomach, under her arms. She steps deeper, up to her waistline.

Let me do your back," Linda pushes over, each thigh splitting water. She lets streams tickle down Amandine. Amandine feels looser now that the water contains her, safer and less naked. Amandine steps forward, leading them into deeper places, water to her waist, Linda traces her hands over Amandine's back. They giggle, swim, their feet lift off, they are floating now, into and around each other, Linda laughs a little, while Amandine has become languorous. Amandine can feel the tears in her throat and her belly, a nervous, slippery presence wanting to break, wanting succor.

"I want to accept him," she says, "I want to."

"Then accept Him," Linda says, a little breathless. Her eyes are closed and she strokes Amandine's head, "Say: I accept Jesus Christ as my—"

And then Linda sucks in a little, pursed breath.

Stunned, Amandine realizes only the water touches her, she has been pushed away, and the creek that had bolstered her feels weak, thinned out—useless to hold her, suddenly.

She only notices the sound of the car engine—it could be a million miles away, space feels so padded—when Linda says, "Ray, Ray's home."

"I—I—" Amandine says, she reaches her arm out across the water to Linda, who is looking down at her bathing suit, fixing the tie around her neck. Linda looks up, breathes deeper now, takes a sweetness on in her voice that isn't totally from inside herself, but is at least partly from there. Her eyes look bigger and a little glossy, her mouth soft but very strong.

"Say: *I accept Jesus Christ as my personal Lord and Savior*," Linda says each word slowly, carefully, holding Amandine with her stare as if with distant, locked-straight arms.

Amandine listens to the wind in the high branches, the thick summer air down here just barely disturbed, and she sees the shallow water at the banks edging around oval stones, around clumps of sedge and soil. As she says it, she knows it won't be true for a while but that someday it will be true. She notices the darkening shape on the lawn, Ray's shadow, the black space, once green, now inhabited by his old-fashioned hat with a tiny feather sewn into the band, a cheap suit leaving the ankles in bare relief, hands sticking out from thin, uncovered wrists, approaching and lengthening across the lawn.

6

SING PRAISES

1980

What happened the year *before* she attacked Kurt Dieckmann with a trowel, what sent Ruth to the children's ward for a month, what made Amandine and Racinda and Button finally have to admit there was something wrong with her erupted at the Dells' home church services one Sunday in 1980. Before that Ruth's symptoms were always justifiable; strange, but not indicating a sickness. After that—

After that, before that. Before a line was drawn and after: *before we knew and after we knew.*

It was spring. I stretched and breathed in the wet greenness of it. I curled with the leaves out of their buds. I nudged into a green roundness, slowly, what had been a landscape of the arching crags of bare branches against gray dirt, gray sky, gray air.

Button didn't like that Amandine took the girls to this strange church. It was bad enough in her book that both the girls *lived* with Amandine. Well, it had been years: when Racinda was two, Ruth got jealous enough, curious enough, at eight, that she decided to go back and live with her sister, her mother, her father. Ruth came over to Button's a lot now, still, even going on twelve—it gave Racinda a brief peace when Ruth would go alone.

But when both girls came over, by that point, in 1980, Button had a tendency to get snippy when too much evidence of their mother's influence manifested.

Button would start sweeping loudly or making a roast loudly or singing to herself whenever Racinda would mention church, would ask Button if she took the Lord as her personal savior. So Racinda stopped asking, but even if church came up in a roundabout way, like *what are you going to wear to church*, between the girls, Button stiffened, then slammed a variety of utensils around, started chopping gherkins, say, sweet peppers, celery to pickle to make chow chow relish.

Amandine and her two daughters usually got home late in the afternoon on Sundays, with groceries, which they unloaded from the car over their father's head—the kitchen located directly over his basement workshop—without his help. By then Lyman was in love with wood. From time to time, he heard the girls say "at church' or "at the Dells" or "when we sang 'Nearer My God'" but he didn't really listen, didn't notice, didn't try to piece it together. He just figured they went to the store on Sundays, that it took many hours. When he woke up, they were gone, and it didn't occur to him to question for how long. And when he did, from time to time, understand they'd also been to church, he assumed it was Button's Presbyterian church, the one he'd been raised in, the one that was less a site of spiritual access than a locus for the small-town's Northern-Protestant morality and social structure, though, by 1980, clearly, that church was less central than it had been when he was a child. He didn't quite notice this fact either—with his isolation in his job and his woodshop, he failed to see that the generation he'd grown up with in the church had also largely left the town or farms for housing developments, for cocktails and slightly more open minds, for a certain, sporty quickness with their own small families.

His ability to close his eyes—quietly, down in that woodshop—was nearly superhuman. Although his wife had grown up two hours away, and had told him she hadn't gone to church at all as a child, and though he had never even met any of her people (her close family all having died when she was young), he assumed church meant the same thing to Amandine as it did to him. He thought it meant his father's and Button's church from thirty years previous, from before the decades that tore family after family from the pews.

He thought he was unique in his drift from faith, he thought it was because he was smarter than the rest of them.

But it wasn't Button's or his father's church.

It was the Dells' living room, it was a place where people spoke in tongues, it was light blue, there were children in the other room, there were teenage babysitters, there was Bible study after church, before lunch, there was saran wrap covering cupcakes and wooden salad bowls, there were containers from each woman, each mommy, present, holding food, there were utensils that had been given on wedding days, there was Tupperware, there was ambrosia, there were meringue kiss cookies, there were cold cuts, there were big finger swoops in the icing which the not-so-docile teenage babysitter finally blamed on one of the eight-year-old boys, though you could see the elegant indentation of a long fake fingernail where the milky coating had been removed way above his reach.

There was love there, I'll give the Christians that much, they loved those kids right along with keeping those kids in line with their God.

"I don't think so," Ruth said when Tracy Dell, the long-nailed babysitter was trying to pass the cake-swiping off on her. "I think it was Brandon," and so the eight-year-old got sent to the room of one of the boy Dells, where after stewing a bit he just fell asleep, lungs full and warm with the golden, roast-chicken air.

"Yes, it was Brandon," Tracy said even after he'd been nabbed for it and banished.

The adults believed, the adults just believed her.

"I saw him," Tracy said, "I was teaching Ruth first aid."

Ruth nodded, a roll of scotch tape in one hand, torn-edged handfuls of magazine pictures in the other. Linda Dell's eyes narrowed at Ruth, at her daughter Tracy, then rested when she saw how Ruth was taping a square photo of a rich man in a too-tight tie to her forearm like a bandage.

"Well, good. Tracy, get your sister ready," Linda said, wiping her palms against her hips before she went back to the adults in the living room.

Ruth frowned at the babysitter, who was only a year and a half older than she was.

"You're a lucky duck," Tracy said. "Those are her *Ladies Home Journals*. And my Daddy's *Time* magazines. Stop cutting those."

"I thought you weren't allowed to say 'lucky'," Ruth said, ripping the picture off her arm.

Tracy looked to the side, not so tough as her painter pants, her rouge. Ruth was right. The Dells thought the word *lucky* implied superstitiousness, which was Satanic.

"Blessed. You are a blessed duck." Tracy shook her head a little bit and stopped being annoyed, by amplifying the age difference in her head and thinking of Ruth as a much younger child. As Tracy absentmindedly, sweetly put her hand in Ruth's hair, Ruth slammed Tracy's wrist against the wall, knocking down the worn yellow telephone that hung there. Its cord—tangled Ruth's foot and she kicked at it.

"What?" Tracy said, "Ow," putting the phone back on the receiver.

"Don't touch me," Ruth said.

Ruth went back to trimming away the uneven rips around her photos. She was bare-armed, wearing a thin cotton vest instead of a sweater—it was much too cold for it, but she'd insisted. The vest was cheap, gimmicky, but Ruth loved it—six small pockets perched on its front, each with a silvery buckle to fuss with.

As Tracy, on her way out to the family room, passed little Racinda, who was sitting under the table, stacking Legos in the most simple tower, one on top of another, in a regular pattern of colors, she knelt down.

"You okay, honey?" Tracy said, brushing her bangs out of her eyes. She meant it—she was a good-natured girl, really, the nastiness of adolescence was actually almost done racing through her already.

Racinda looked up at her and grinned, wanting the hand on her own hair.

When Racinda crawled over to her for a hug, Tracy held onto her tight, the two of them just under the heavy-legged, black-painted kitchen table. When Tracy closed her eyes, little black flecks of her cheap mascara landed on the low pink curve of her cheeks.

"Oh, honey," she said, detaching herself, holding Racinda by the shoulders for a second, looking at her closely, before leaving to find her own little sister.

Racinda felt Tracy's hair, the edge of it, swoop her face and then Tracy was gone. The Legos under the table were orderly, this was obvious. Blue green red white blue green red white blue green red white. Tracy Dell's brothers had taken all the black and gray ones for their military plane projects, and Racinda didn't like the yellow ones. Racinda was seven. Ruth had been living with her and Amandine for two years now, though when Amandine got really tired or Ruth got very angry Ruth would go back to stay with Button and Elmer, where Ruth had lived until she was ten and decided to come stay across the fields with her sister, her mother, her father. If Racinda sat with these blocks under the table, Ruth seemed to be leaving her alone. Blue green red white blue green red white bluegreenredwhite. Greasy snaps together, plastic nubs into plastic holes expanding plastic edges bluegreenredwhite. Women's legs in panty hose clicked or thudded by her and the women didn't notice her. The smaller children were in the dingy brown family room—just Racinda and Ruth stayed in the kitchen, not wanting the mess of babies.

Ruth was obsessed, doing something with the magazines Racinda wasn't brave enough to figure out, but which involved a lot of slamming over pages and ripping them out

Here under the table, though, in the Dells' house, she was safe. The Devil just stayed away without her putting any effort into it. And at the Dells' Ruth couldn't injure Racinda because the other mothers, or Tracy, would notice where Amandine was oblivious. And even to Amandine Ruth's transgressions were more obvious in the public setting of the Dells crackling home as a point of humiliation to her, to the family. Here, Amandine saw what was going on, if only in the frame of managing her reputation. Her protective urge didn't manifest as a curiosity to examine the weave of what was actually going on between her girls, rather as an awareness of the primary importance of shutting them up fast.

Blue green red white Legos, and ladies' legs, and Tracy's scraggly line of hair crossing Racinda's cheek as Tracy left her gave her enough distraction—warm distraction, not worried distraction like at home when she had to try to keep Ruth quiet so her mother wouldn't leave her at Ruth's mercies—enough colors pinging through the air, enough voices, enough breathing that she could be grateful for the Devil's absence without beckoning him.

Thank you, God, for all your love and that the Devil is leaving me alone did not bait her hook for him here. Here, it turned into a certain fascination with the feeling her bare feet made as she rolled their sides and heels on the linoleum, it turned to a dreamy knowledge of the paprika-skinned chickens in the oven, to the reliable sharpness of the edge of her Lego column when run up and down her arm, to the watery conversation of women in the other room becoming more solid and staccato as chairs were being arranged in a horseshoe around the piano, around the rickety, shiny music stand that functioned as a pulpit when Ray Dell placed his leather-bound folder on it.

And so it was time to worship. Racinda had been waiting—she loved the singing, she disappeared into chords, into choruses, into hands clapping. She would get to work the tambourine, Tracy would smile at her, her mother would be busy, and Ruth would maybe even get happy for a little while.

"All God's children to the living room," Linda called to them, not meaning *all* of God's children. Only Tracy, Racinda, Ruth, Moab Dell—just a bit younger than Racinda—and Brandon the banished, who that day slept through it till dinner, were old enough to come in to worship.

Praise the Lord! and *Hallelujah!* the elders interjected into the piano's rolling chords. The elders were a bunch of senior citizens from the Friends' Home including the Dells' grandparents, all women except Grandpa Dell. Each one, even the Grandpa, wore a pink t-shirt that said "Sing Praises!" in a shiny white script.

Ray Dell stood at the front of the room and told a story about God's Chosen People wandering in the desert. Then he told a joke:

"Tracy," he said, "If men say 'Ay-men,' at the end of their prayers, what do women say?"

Tracy shrugged, just barely resisting rolling her eyes.

"They say 'Ahhh, men!'," he said, and he beamed. Tracy giggled along with the rest of them and shook the tambourine for punctuation. She let Racinda jangle it for awhile, even though Racinda inevitably hit the wrong beats.

So Ray's God, while He still thought spare-the-rod, and women obey their husbands and all that, didn't mind these kinds of jokes. The Dells didn't know the God Amandine had taught her girls to worship. Amandine's God felt like peeing your bed or kids on the school bus spitting on you: a secret, some knife at your insides during a bad time about to go worse. Racinda and Amandine prayed to Him to keep Him from getting too active. Amandine's God created Ruth, and Amandine begged Him to hold her in.

Amandine was leaning over Linda at the piano, turning her pages. Tracy stuck herself right up there with them, shaking the tambourine happily, almost forgetting that last wave of surly rebellion, her long thighs and long, split-end ponytail jerking back and forth against the rhythm. Racinda mixed in with Moab, but Ruth resisted it all, hating the lightness, hating the other children for giving Racinda a refuge. Ruth found herself a new corner to curl herself in and frown, rearranging the magazine tearings into different pockets of her vest, closing the pockets' flaps—the little strips of fabric woven through simple aluminum buckles—then opening them, then closing.

The notes started and built on each other and flowed out of the piano like water. Ruth scowled in the corner through the first few songs, until her mother whispered something to Linda and she lit into "He's Got The Whole World In His Hands," Ruth's favorite. With all the clapping and the smiling, Ruth couldn't resist. She came and stood next to Racinda and her voice carried over Racinda's and Moab's. Racinda could see Ruth's words lift up and float out the window, fly across the fields, cause interference with their dad's buzz saw, or with the reception of the football game on his TV. The words would drag themselves across the fifty-yard line like a banner behind a plane: H-E-'S G-O-T T-H-E W-H-O-L-E W-O-R-L-D and so on.

But oh, I felt sad closing in on just Racinda here. The joy of the piano—and it was real joy, even if in word what purpose Ray serves is in service of joylessness—that piano's joy couldn't even reach Racinda because she felt, across the room, Ruth's fingers starting to work the buckles on her vest faster and faster, checking, smoothing each one as they all sang. *No, no, it's okay*, Racinda thought, her eyes to the ceiling, *Ruth—don't*. And Racinda imagined Button's garden for her sister, hoping the rough green of new shoots and the still-white, still-winter sun on their foreheads would seep through to Ruth, but Ruth's anxiety and excitement in the song were fortresses against Racinda's ESP. Ruth did stop patting her buckles—not because of anything her sister attempted—and Ruth started really singing, hands in fists at her side, chin and neck urging up, as if trying to grow herself in order to become louder.

So they all sang, and the verses went on and on in this song. *All* the different folks *in His hands*. He's got the whole world.

Racinda stepped back toward Moab, who linked arms very sweetly and swayed. Racinda retreated there to Moab's side, swam through this innocent world where Moab's white tights floated beneath the yellow cotton bell of her dress. Racinda squished the wall-to-wall carpet between her toes, still unsure, still paced to whatever was growing in Ruth that would make them lose their cover with the Dells and the elders, still watching Amandine's nervous clapping—so loud and too-fast in a misguided try to hide her off-key voice even after years singing with these people who loved her anyway.

Ray in his mind kept an anchor of propriety while the sea of notes and eyes and clapping swarmed the room in something sweaty and uncontrolled. All for God, sweaty for God, this use of their bodies for God. Ray's anchor reminded them that each moment they spun their bodies out away from secular, logical, materialist America here in this living room was completely and only in the service of the Lord.

They could only have this closeness to the juicy parts of their God—so the story rumbling beneath the Christians' surfaces went—if they agreed not to adulterate or abort or swear or disobey their husbands.

They thought they could only receive my rush through them if they punished themselves for wanting me.

I coursed between them anyway, the women in this room, the girls, the old ladies, Grandpa Dell and Ray, both of whose fingers were so long, with the same flat, oval nails like mirrors.

He's got the whole world—sure he does. Sure, they are right about that—it just depends on exactly what you're talking about when you say *Him.*

I rippled the elders' pink T-shirts and rounded the cracks in their voices to honey. I even got Racinda's feet moving on the third verse, got her white fingers, tight with Moab's, swinging her arm so that with my rhythm she forgot to hold the garden in her mind and forgot even her sister in this room now and just felt the swing and the song.

Except that—

Exactly when Racinda forgot about Ruth, Ruth's noises started. I had Ruth dancing and spinning, so gleeful, it even got a rain shower of a warm smile from Amandine before Amandine wised up and got nervous then plunged back into the obliviousness she was so comfy in.

Turning pages.

A thin, unconvincing smile at the end of each verse.

It stemmed from me but it took on its own velocity in Ruth's chemistry, this squeal that came out of her when her cells sped up, when heat floated through her and burgeoned.

At first the elders didn't really notice it. When Linda turned her head, concerned, eyes lowered to Ruth who by now was kneeling on the floor, the *eeeeee* coming from her as if all her muscles from the chest up were cinched together forcing out her air, she quieted her fingers on the keys and the chords slowed and softened and decreased.

Eeeeeee.

Racinda couldn't tell if it was pain or pleasure, but she could see the torn-out headline in Ruth's fist: Is God Dead?, it asked in a strapping red font on an outer-space background. Racinda bit her lip harder, and Ruth, slowly, determinedly, balled the blasphemy up and wedged it back into a vest pocket, but it wasn't a gesture any of the others noticed, because the other parts of Ruth were moving and the noises were still coming from her. And after a little while that seemed much longer than it was, everyone stopped singing.

As Amandine began to move to her, Ruth fell to the floor. Linda kept playing the piano, but nobody sang anymore. The elders were completely perplexed—their hands leaned on their metal chairs, some of them tried not to stare, their pink t-shirts buzzed along with the tense air in the room.

A painted Jesus looked at them all from his light-blue frame on a light-blue wall, full of forgiveness, sure to send the Holy Ghost down soon, Racinda told herself. The Holy Ghost would ignite pockets of flames above all their heads, scorch them with understanding and compassion for her sister.

As Racinda dropped Moab's hand, Ruth lay down, mouth on the carpet, spotting it dark with saliva, still squeaking. Linda started into a calm, anonymous hymn while everyone just gave in and stared.

Xxxxxxx, Ruth said, blurry, when Amandine's hand touched her shoulder. Zzzzz, she said, before she made herself hatefully still.

Tracy, somehow, knew to grab Moab's hand and lead her and Racinda, all barefoot, out through the kitchen to the yard.

*   *   *

"What is it?" Racinda said, "What's happening?" in the driveway, too cold in spring to be without shoes. Moab shrugged. Tracy looked across the hedge toward a hollowed-out viny bush, the prickly, green Sunday cloister.

"Let's go get the jump rope," Tracy said to her sister, clamping onto the tiny girl's wrist in order to drag her.

"What is it?" Racinda asked Tracy again, following too, wedging herself between the two Dells as they walked.

It was clear Tracy was excited, her arched hazel eyes in their darkened lashes avoiding Racinda's, Tracy's determined choppy stomps a way to focus her illicit energy into muscles.

"What," Racinda said, grabbing Tracy's arm.

Tracy looked down at Racinda, who became steely for just this moment, steely only when Ruth was threatened. Tracy's white cheeks and delicate, almost-woman chin tilted to the side and she said, quietly, matter-of-factly, "Casting out demons. They have to cast out her demons."

Since Racinda wouldn't play, Tracy tied an end of the rope to the railing next to the walkway and turned it alone while Moab tried to jump. Racinda waited through games, through rhymes, until Tracy got frustrated with Moab's messy steps over the easy low swoop of the rope and had to dive in and boss her. Then Racinda sneaked back into the house, inching the heavy storm door quietly shut against her weight.

She did not see Ruth, in the living room, holding her breath, red-faced, still lying on the floor. She did not see the elders, Linda, her mother, speaking in tongues and rocking themselves, eyes closed, though she knew all this was happening. What she noticed was the hazy blue light, like mist, and the sounds of the voices feeding it. *I rebuke you and command you to wither and die*, Ray said gently, kneeling above Ruth and resting his hands on her shoulder. *Satan, be cast out of this child. I command you to wither and die.*

It was clear Ruth had held her breath until she passed out, something Racinda tried but never managed to accomplish out of willful vengeance—she could only be scared into it. Awhile after Ray set Ruth, sweaty, down in the corner, Moab and Tracy reappeared and took their posts near Amandine. They joined in, holding hands, blind and swaying, God's gibberish flowing out of their mouths and swirling into the mixed-up alphabet the adults had painted the air that blue angel color with in their absence.

Everyone was reeling, their eyes were all closed.

Should I creep back into them now? I wondered. They wanted me to, but they knew from the stony floors of their stomachs that I was outside somewhere.

Well, outside *them*. Just with the girls. And about to be outside the house again.

When they pull this shit and lob some poor thing on the head with their nasty, outdated, pseudo-morality I leave them and they hate it. But they don't get that they thrive on the long, gray, shadow-flecked expanse of guilt that drowns them when I go. Without the guilt, I would be too sinful for them, these Christians. Because if there could be so much as there is when we are together, then everything they've been told—not just by "Him" but by *them*—is nullified. And then what?

So I leave the Christians, but the Christians always win me back.

I've never managed a grudge.

I've tried, believe me, but something always sneaks a laugh out of me and I forget how annoying they're capable of being.

It's just my nature.

Racinda knelt quietly next to Ruth and stared at Ray again, trying to hate him but still, like the rest of the planet, halfway in love with any father who acted like one. He caught her looking, and made a move to comfort her, his hand out to touch her arm or her head. Racinda smiled at him, affecting innocence, terrified she would be next in line for rebuking. As his not-large, not-small, but still masculine fingers, their perfect nails, came to her, she forced herself not to shrink back. *I rebuke thee, I command thee to wither and die . . . RAY*, she found herself repeating the words silently.

She gasped when he touched her—she realized her grave sin—thinking this good father was the Devil. Racinda sped up the language in her head: *I rebuke thee* not with Ray in mind but with the Devil. *Forgive me*, she alternated, for blaspheming Ray, Ray who was an instrument of God, though paint peeled inside her stomach from the echo of his hand moving to her face.

Forgive. Rebuke. *Forgive*.

But the words coming out of the Christians weren't so clear—tongues fretting and layering on top of each other, meaning nothing and meaning too much.

Racinda felt something very familiar to her, which was that everyone else in the room knew something she didn't, and they were about to find her out, *oust* her. Laugh. *Wither her.*

Racinda's eyes went from face to face and in a few minutes she starting speaking tongues with them—just making it up at first, just to pass, as if she were singing any old made-up child's song.

But soon her syllables carried her toward something else. Later it will occur to Racinda, several years from now, thinking of this moment, that the reason she never knew what she was praying for in tongues was that maybe she was praying to the wrong god. *Maybe I am a Taoist*, she will think, *and belong to the world of Ten Thousand Things*. Maybe she was actually a Hindu—someone just forgot to tell her—and to punish her misdirected faith the luminous elephant Ganesh or the mad wrecker Kali would keep something crucial from her forever.

Ruth licked Racinda's knee to let her know she'd awakened. Something in her seemed missing, but it didn't seem like just Satan was gone. Now, Ruth did not blink. Racinda led her out of the house, to the field while they all were still praying. Ruth's cheeks glowed brighter in the air that cut into Racinda's lungs, and soon it was Ruth leading the way, pulling Racinda. Racinda, watchful, followed her, sat on the grass after she did, lay down when she did.

In a few minutes, Ruth wrapped her arms across her chest and started to sing, softly at first, so that Racinda couldn't hear, but then so sweetly:

This little light of mine, I'm gonna let it shine.

She would pause and roll over between lines, then sigh into the next one, like she was bringing herself back.

This little light of mine . . . I'm gonna let it shine.

They could have been singing the same song right at that moment in the light-blue room, Racinda thought, the temperature would be rising from their spirits' heat.

But the song set itself free outside, with just Ruth singing it, her voice's clarity in the cold but about-to-bloom air dulling my memory of the piano's last petrifying chords, fading their decline. As if all the adults' voices, Tracy and Moab following their parents, had just been so many bars keeping a song in its cage.

Ruth was pure as bells: *Let it shine, let it shine, let it shine.* I could hear her breath, and could no longer imagine she would bite Racinda or scare her in the dark, she was that clean and dewy with the grass.

Before I knew it, she grabbed Racinda's hand and pulled her running to the brush at the far side of the field. They entered their cloistered girls cove, they slid through the thick, descending cords carefully, avoiding the prickers. The green, thistley tendons bent over and around them in a dome, shining and lit up at the top.

And when I curled into Ruth's eyes and loved her and restored her she felt the gleeful *eees* coming on again, but Ruth remembered the response they wanted from her in that room and it was too strong for me—there was nothing I could do to stop her. She spun herself through the cove's far side off the ledge beyond it, her feet shifting on nonexistent steps as she fell the five feet to the creek, body turning fully in wet cold air before she hit.

*   *   *

Ruth had sung herself back into her own joy that was a defiance of her mother's prim shackles. That such defiance was so clearly necessary for Ruth's song—too messy, too weird for her mother and even for the Dells—to happen at all was what finally pushed her over into such damaging chemistry, I think, if anything did. For really, now her joy was just a little girl's song, that's all, it was innocent and it was simple—that's what she really wanted to get to, this sweetness had been just under the veering wildness she conjured on the Dells' light blue wall-to-wall. Ruth's song's indoor intensity would have been fine if it were less unconventional to the Christians, if it had been, say, two suburban siblings fighting over some sugar issue in the cereal aisle, if it had been those low looks girls give to excoriate their outcasts' insides, if it had been boys punching each other broken behind the car wash: certain power was allowed in certain places. The same power in the wrong place, though, Ray and Amandine and the rest of the Christians named supernaturally wrong.

With each episode, what grew in Ruth was Eve's naughty grasp, the black juice just beneath the clean line of hemmed hedges, licking out from the dirt, catching your eye as you turn away, cringing your throat when you say the wrong thing, moving from state to state, penniless, dark, lips opening over a mouth, no consequences until the guillotine drops, masculine and feminine, irresistible—messy sweaty bloody and so necessary to the hard edges and the numbers and the banks and the marriages and the highways and the clocks but in certain ratios and in certain situations only allowed to go unpunished—in others, or with the least bit of bad luck, always punished, scorned with the hate that flows inside them all and keeps their above-ground edges so sharp, the pavement so smooth, the numbers so effusive and "reliable."

So not Eve alone, but the speed of response in the very specific world Ruth landed in, I think, pushed Ruth's chemistry from wild to dark, to knotted, to fog, curdled that rebellion to madness. Ruth knew that she had to steal her motion, her intensity, her voice before they could convince (or medicate) these things out of her. Cold winds rose at Ruth's edges— quite like her sister's Devil but without form, just a feeling.

But Ruth—Ruth, always, could grab the joy of her song as well, on its tail end—joy that left as quickly as it came, the lit, pale greenness of it pulsing warm, then shrinking against the sun, before the gray winds caught her.

*   *   *

To get past the vines Racinda had to dive low, smearing dirt across her knees and palms. Though she'd heard the splash she needed to *see* before she ran for help. Bloodied, but breathing, and Ruth's head was not under or near the water.

Racinda tore her calves on prickers the way back through and ran to the house to find the speaking tongues still filling it with their buzz like an odor. Her mother's eyes were closed in the living room, palms open near her face like she was waiting for God to beam something into them. *Hallelujah*, Racinda could discern, *Hallelujah*, something rough coming through Amandine, something wet but without weeping, something dark and guilty. Racinda dialed the zero on the telephone in the kitchen and asked the operator to please call an ambulance.

Racinda imagined, despite the rebuking, that Ruth wanted Ray to be down there at the edge of his family's field when the medics pulled her, bloody and in shock, from the rocks. But it was just Racinda and Amandine under the ambulance's red light that fell in a dependable rhythm from the driveway. The rest stayed in the room and prayed, tongues; though their syllables were empty and drear, they hoped, hoped for the shift that brought acceptance or relief or even just tears, though none came:

I was so pissed at them, I didn't go near them for three weeks: they mourned without knowing it. They saw gray. They didn't sleep.

It seemed to Racinda that without her own small fingers dialing the phone, Amandine would have taken no action, would have let Ruth spin herself right off the planet. Not to let her achieve the freedom of clouds that Ruth was set on, but to keep herself—Amandine—blind, innocent, and immobile.

Ruth knew Racinda put her in the hospital, and her meanness came after Racinda faster and sharper during the nights once the medication stopped working. Racinda was Ruth's mirror. Ruth hunted her.

*   *   *

I leaned onto my hill and I wept but not so you could see. She was gone gone gone and Racinda's face lengthened and paled into a small girl-child version of that sad, flat, untouchable Devil who Racinda hoped would come around less now that her sister was in the hospital. But who didn't—who kept up his terrifying visits to her bed. And Button still planted but wasn't thinking about planting. She was thinking about calling the doctors for an update, for a release date, for the re-spelling of the medicine's name so she could check it in the library.

I felt myself drifting then, less rooted to the place, and that was when Lyman first visited Atlantic City in his dreams, that was when Button first felt the heavy infinity of stars pulling her off in hers: I was at the bar, I was in the ocean, I was at the craps table, I was in icy places I had no business being. So that's when the real trouble started.

After her cuts were bandaged, no concussion diagnosed, when the regular nurse noticed how fast the sedative wore off of Ruth, a psychiatric nurse who happened to be filling in this Sunday morning examined her and admitted her. There were different diagnoses that would shift every few years from then on. Ruth never fit just one, and Amandine held tight to each new name for her daughter's problems, each new drug. Some worked, then they didn't.

From that first visit, whenever her sister was in the hospital, Racinda imagined Ruth in a sterile room with a hundred replications of herself. Each one had a different shade of hair, not just brown or black or auburn, but scarlet, aqua, silver and gold. Even their eyelashes glittered with these colors. The Ruths were spinning and would keep at it until they grew old. Eyes so wide. Twirling like tops and roaming into themselves, each one's sharp edges would brush another's soft places, slicing skin open, sending jubilant drops of blood onto the mean white plane of the hospital floor.

7

FALL AWAY

1982

Button sensed something was going to go very wrong that June, but her garden was looking so lovely, and she was so full of delight with the small details of her life that she didn't want to think about it. When she and Elmer returned in May from their big vacation, they looked like far more typical senior citizens than they actually were. Bags and bags of trinkets for the girls, nouveau-practical footwear, and slideshows that, so unlike them, they actually enforced on Amandine and Lyman, even made Racinda, even *Ruth* sit through, the air conditioning rattling, causing Elmer to have to nearly shout the boring details of each cathedral, each mispronunciation of Italian and French foods, the name of each nook of coastline. Button beamed at him, and it was clear that the traveling had done them both good, their faces flushed with a temporary absence of worries over Ruth—now going on fourteen—,over the depressed distance of Lyman, over Amandine's religious resolve, over strange, quiet little Racinda whose haunted expression caught them by surprise in moments when the rest of the family wasn't hogging all the attention.

And so the weeks after their vacation were almost as delicious as their vacation itself, with Ruth behaving relatively well, Lyman lured out of his basement, even, by the perfect, not-too-humid June, the heavy peonies and snapdragons and line of hanging fuchsias Button drenched her little patio with so appealing to him, such a respite from his wife's creepy topiary, he'd come over with the girls, who would quietly bat a tennis ball back and forth in the newly paved driveway, while Elmer made a point of showing off his mowing tractor, zooming across the impossibly green lawn carved out of field grasses, the lawn the heat shimmered off, the lawn the mosquitoes and butterflies and crickets and dragonflies and bumblebees adorned the bushy edge of, down by the creek.

"Like this," Lyman said, demonstrating to Racinda how to swing the tennis racket in a way that was less like defending herself from winged invaders.

She tried it his way.

"*Nice,*" Ruth said. "That didn't even—where did the ball go?"

"Come on, now, Ruth," Lyman said, "You're a natural, Racinda!" he said, "Amandine, we've got a natural athlete on our hands."

Well, Racinda *was* improving slightly. For an eight-year-old without any previous lessons she actually wasn't too bad.

Amandine smiled her most relaxed half smile. Took a nice sip of her iced tea and opened up the Sunday paper sitting on a wrought-iron patio table. Amandine eyed Ruth briefly, but ascertained that she wasn't getting jealous of her sister—just frustrated at never getting a ball back within hitting vicinity.

"Serve it up, Ruth," Lyman said, "Let's see what Racinda can do now that she's had a lesson!"

As he patted Racinda's back, stepped away, he noticed the determination and—what was it?—intelligence? watchfulness? in his younger daughter's face, waiting for Ruth's tenacious serve.

For Lyman, moments like this, soaking in the girls' adoration of him, made it seem as if he didn't actually spend most of his time hiding from them in various ways. Made it seem as if moments like these were the norm. But once he followed that perception to the next logical step—why *didn't* he have more moments like this with the girls? What could he do about that?—a slight anxiety started drifting into his jaw, his chest, and he had to stop thinking along that line to keep enjoying it all. In this way, these June times remained rare.

Breakfasts and lunches were especially delicious those weeks, with Button and Elmer's tastier foreign coffee, and the cigarette they'd share after each meal if the girls weren't visiting, a weird adolescent-geriatric secret, a delightful burst of rebellion, Button's wrinkled ankles strong poking out from her soft yellow a-line skirt, white dotted lines tracing across it as a sort of homage to the bees, Elmer always in his medium-faded dungarees, John Deere cap, thin blue or yellow or pink even short sleeved collared shirt, t-shirt underneath even in the most humid weather.

By July they were up to two cigarettes each on the patio by the fishpond.

It wasn't the cigarettes' fault that the heart attack happened, and Button knew it. Still, when the deep grinding noise caught her attention and Button first turned her head up from the *Daily Local* to see her husband strangely stopped on top of the tractor at a tree, not moving his hands from the wheel, the first thing she did on her way to him was to drop the entire ashtray into the fish pond, shove the pack of cigarettes—fast, deep—in the large garbage can for yard waste.

Without even understanding that her feet were in charge she stopped in the middle of the field, out of breath, about to run back to the house to the phone, but somewhere under the drone, in a voice not a voice, Elmer said, *come here, I want to see you again,* just like he had when she returned to him after he married someone else so many decades previous, that stupid Violetta, Lyman's mother. Halfway between the house and the accident, she was unsure whether to run all the way to him or to run to the phone first. She was reminded of that drenching day when Ruth's cries under a vacuum cleaner's droning called her to the other house, the tractor now doing the droning, the bees flying in the rushes by the creek, the bees zooming into her yellow skirt.

I want to see you again, he said, so she went to him again now, after they had managed a life together despite all that confusion at the beginning, and she lifted him off the steering wheel that he was lying on. *She came on over to me,* was how he'd always start the story of their marriage if anyone asked, *twice,* and he said it now, lips still, *three times,* as she wedged her shoulders under his to lift him. The tractor made so much noise, so she twisted her arm out from under him to shut the ignition.

She looked at his kind, kind face for one second before putting her cheek against his so that she got to feel his last minutes but didn't have to watch him die.

She knew it was over when his hand fell from her back and hung awkwardly past her side. With a great howl she bent in half and then became very still, very silent, lowering herself to the ground, lying on her back, and willing herself into sleep, where she managed to say goodbye to him in dreams.

Kind of.

At the funeral, Button alternated between a faraway daze not unlike many of Amandine's finer moments and a quiet weeping, and a strict attention to both of the girls. Button moved their hair out of their faces, traced flat solid circles on their backs with her palm. Lyman's depression returned and cemented, color disappeared from his face, a certain force of breath drained from his words. The girls and Amandine wept and stood together, the battles and the abandonments and the terror of each other melted together into something purer, love leaning on each other, Racinda's arm on her mother's hip, Amandine's arm around Ruth's shoulders, Amandine's palm across the back of Racinda's neck.

Button only lasted halfway through the public memorial after the funeral, half the town questioning her safety in driving home as she stumbled leaving the Masonic hall.

She *was* half asleep. She could hear Elmer still talking to her, *come along to me* and she wanted to go. Once asleep, she was fully with him again, in hours of conversation they hadn't had much need to bother with for decades.

So she napped as Amandine had napped before Ruth was born, constantly, to the point that Amandine and Lyman would go over and shake her awake and force her to eat dinner with them and the girls. Her eyelids drooped. She didn't want to be here. She wanted to keep talking to her husband. She shoveled the food into her mouth, though, as Amandine made a point of obtaining mass-produced versions of Button's favorite foods from the new, huge, multidepartmental grocery store in Avondale—salami sandwiches for dinner, always a cherry pie with hard sugar dancing across the top for dessert, usually a devil's food cake or some sort of tart as well. Because the food just sedated Button more, the pleasure washing across her face, the lids closing. She was eating and napping at once. When finished, Button would open her eyes with a bit of a jolt and excuse herself to her TV shows.

Amandine and Lyman would leave Racinda with her those times, when Button was supposed to be watching Wheel of Fortune or Peter Jennings or whomever, but Racinda didn't have it in her to tell her parents that Button just *slept* there, not even waking to say goodnight, leaving Racinda happily free to switch the cable box over to MTV. It was the happiest place in any of the two houses, at any time of day: Button well fed and sleeping with the most relaxed smile on her face you'll ever imagine.

After three weeks, and the addition of about fifteen pounds, Button's face mooning out to a younger profile, her hips widened with food and lack of nervous energy, lack of fretting at her granddaughters, lack of criticizing Amandine and Lyman, lack of speeding on walks through the fields and the woods, she was ready to give up.

She looked ten years younger, and she was ready to die. She wanted to be with him. It was getting into the last week of August, and those lush, shortening days before school starts were as convincing a time as any for an exit.

Ruth knew—she came back for dinner that night even though she'd had a watertight excuse to go smoke pot with Kurt Dieckmann's older brother Matty—(tonight was the school band's first rehearsal for their homecoming concert and Ruth, about to start her freshman year, was signed up as third clarinetist) Racinda didn't understand why Ruth was back until Ruth held her sleeping grandmother's hand through Wheel of Fortune, through the mindless sitcoms, held her hand so quietly, so passively, completely focused in that house. Racinda couldn't figure it out: Ruth loved Button, but this was unheard of when Matty Dieckmann was in the mood to bestow social graces.

"Why are you back here?" Racinda said, rinsing a plate without bothering to soap it first. Button was already asleep in the TV room.

"Whatever, Creech," Ruth said, rolling her eyes. "Here—" and Ruth squirted a stream of bright turquoise dish detergent across the "clean" plates drying on the dish rack.

"Jeez, Ruth!" Racinda said.

"I need a cigarette," Ruth said. Left.

Racinda's shoulders sunk, she retreated back into herself faced with redoing her entire endeavor. She filled up the sink for another rinsing.

"Here, Creech," Ruth said when she came back in. "I'll finish them. You go in and sit with her."

Ruth, with strange, poised affection, stroked the hair back out of her sister's dubious face.

"No really, Racinda—go," Ruth said, and pushed up her sleeves.

By 8:30 Ruth's affections were so gentle, so lilting, that Racinda was nearly shaking, holding her grandmother's hand, so alert she felt Button pulse slow a bit and she got it:

Button was planning on dying, and Ruth had known all along.

Racinda glared at Ruth, who ignored her. Ruth just watched television like a normal person—no tapping or gnawing of the fingernails, no constant readjustments on the couch—and in her fury Racinda began coughing, coughing, running out for a glass of water, returning to see both of them, Button and Ruth, with ridiculously calm expressions on their faces. Racinda could feel the bottom about to drop out, Racinda could imagine what would happen to her and to Ruth if they were left to their mother's, their father's supposed supervision. She was furious at Ruth for getting to be so reckless about it all. But to say *Ruth, make her stop*, to name something so wrong, would make it real. If Racinda kept quiet, perhaps it would not actually be happening. Perhaps it was nothing. Perhaps it was three people watching television in America. Perhaps Button would not leave them.

"Jesus Creature, have some respect," Ruth said, slapping her near-choking sister on the back.

Racinda gasped in air.

"Fuck you!" Racinda managed to whisper. "Ruth you know what she's doing. Stop her."

"Racinda there's nothing we can do." Ruth looked so beatific that Racinda, always the one to flee from a fight, tackled her. Ruth was so sedate, though, that Racinda could barely keep it up and broke down weeping in the corner as Ruth crawled back to Button's side.

"Oh for gad's sake!"

The words came out of Button's mouth mid-snore, though her eyes were still shut.

Racinda stood up and started hacking, gasping again.

And, eyes still shut, Button picked up the tissue box, tugged one out and presented it to her stunned, breathless granddaughter.

"Cover your mouth, sweetie," Button said, and opened her eyes, which were back to a fierce stare, the muddiness gone. She wasn't half here. She was all here.

All of her.

Button looked down at her newly plump legs as if someone had glued them onto her while she slept.

"Well, I'll be!" she said, the dreamy slowness completely gone

"Button?" Ruth said, leaning back from her."

"What? Stop looking at me like I'm a ghost, Ruthie!"

Button drank in the shape of her granddaughters' faces, the same pink wash on both their faces, the same straight, flattish nose. She knew she couldn't leave them. Ruth's cheeks rounder, white-blond hair explosive by this point in the day, Racinda's hair dark in this light, straighter, long.

But even then Button had a hunch—she could do a day shift here, a night shift there with Elmer, maybe? Who knew?

Tears came down Racinda's cheeks, her face reddening.

"What's the matter sweetie?" Button asked.

Racinda crossed her arms in front of her chest and looked down.

Button repeated the question.

Racinda let out her held breath in more coughing.

"You guys," Racinda said, choking on drainage at the back of her throat, "have to stop leaving me."

Button held Racinda then, tried to soothe her, and Button felt how deep Racinda's tears ran, and how impossible it was for her to take the pain away from this child. But she was going to try, Button was going to tell herself that she could. She held Racinda away at the shoulders to look at her, *honey*, and Racinda's dark eyes, so heavy, pinned themselves downward, her jaw set and tense, holding back sobs, before Button drew her back to her chest.

"What do you want, sweetie?" Button said.

"I want—" Racinda hacked, sobbed, "I want some peanut M&Ms and Sixlets."

Ruth and Button stared at her sweetly.

"The big bag kind of M&Ms and Sixlets," Racinda said, looking away, sucking in some of the moisture coming out of her face.

So after Ruth got back from Wawa with the candy and some ice cream for good measure, Button jostled the girls into laughter with her old-lady sarcastic responses to the sit-com that seemed to go on forever.

After more dessert and some mint tea, Button sent the girls back across the field with a flashlight, eased herself into a bath, so fascinated and determined about her new commuting solution that she thought about it too much, and the strangeness of her plan to live in both places upset her. She ran lotion all over her newly plush legs and arms, the vacation tan now faded from all the recent hours under covers.

"For gad's sake, who *are* you?" she said, a hand on her thickened middle. "Commuting!"

Except—it *did* seem a little tiring. After all, when would she *rest*? She smiled at her smoother face, more lush, in the mirror then.

But she knew her age.

In fact, if she really thought about it she was dumbfounded as to how one person might pull off such intense daily travel.

"How many people do you think you are?" she said to the mirror.

But she relaxed, a bit giddy, thinking of that *other* realm where her husband remained with her, and it again seemed completely *right* to her that she could go back and forth: take care of the girls until they were grown, but then visit her husband at night. Of course. Why not?

When Elmer's hand, his *come along to me*, reached her just as she settled under her blankets, though, she saw Racinda's coughing, death-smacked face in the TV room and she knew that it was true—at *some* point, the girl was going to have to feel that terror, unmitigated by her, Button. At *some* point there would be nothing Button could do to help.

Oh my, she thought, *commuting* isn't *going to. . . fix. . . it . . .*

And she dozed.

And Elmer's heart grew denser with love for her at that moment, pulling her more completely to where he was.

What happened, physically, at that moment was this: the shift that Button's heart could maneuver with grace and nerve proved to be too much for Button's tough, earthy brain. A vessel there, fissured from the cheap oils in the bakery pies Amandine was buying, snapped, leaving Button in a blurrier twilight.

*　　*　　*

The stroke was severe and left her only the use of half her body. It left her no speech. When she stabilized in mid September, she was able to communicate through squeezing hands once for yes, twice for no. Racinda taught her Morse Code in a day, and this way, even a week before she regained the ability to write, Button was able to begin to sort out her affairs while she was still clearly of sound mind, giving power of attorney to the lawyer son of an old friend of the family, creating a trust for Ruth's care that Amandine and Lyman could oversee, and that the lawyer, Johnson, would take over should anything happen to Lyman and Amandine. She also kept the land away from Lyman, whose recent disturbing money-burning habits she'd learned of from his friend Rolo's auntie at the Presbyterian church rummage sale. The land wasn't to be sold until Button's death, at which point what would happen to it was a secret between her and the young lawyer.

Button kept the world vivid and clear for as long as she needed to, then she let its colors bleed into its sounds, let go of the girls, floated off to El-mer. She stopped squeezing yes or no, seemed to become senile and unresponsive as October began and descended into crushed, wet foliage grounded off of skeleton trees. When the girls needed her they could sometimes feel her there beyond just her body—thinner, with parched skin more pleated looking, duller in the hospital light. Her left eye would fly open as if to chide or even to comfort them, the left hand would almost seem to squeeze, though they weren't completely *sure* that she knew they were there. Sometimes she did, sometimes she didn't—it turned out halfway was all she could do, and without leaving them behind completely, Button tipped the scales hard to the other side.

*   *   *

"What is wrong with you people? It's freezing in her room! It's like six degrees. Is the bill for this place all about air-conditioning? Like we're paying you to freeze her brain like Walt Disney's!" Ruth said, barging out of Button's private room, giving an empty wheelchair a solid shove into the nurse's station.

"Miss, you're going to have to keep it down," the very cute male psychiatric nurse said to Ruth.

"I'm calling *Johnson*," Ruth hissed before spinning on her heel and heading out the door. "You will be hearing from my lawyer," she lied.

Ruth, so calm when she thought Button was dying, couldn't stand seeing her in the nursing home, and couldn't stand *not* seeing her. Would go visit only to storm out past the nurses, into the yellow light of October, then disappear overnight. The first few times this had happened—earlier in the spring, before Elmer or Button left them—the cops put a small amount of effort into calming Amandine and cruising the usual places—parking lots, the reservoir, the woods behind the high school—for Ruth. By the fifth time it happened they told Amandine there was nothing they could do unless Ruth got in trouble with them while she was out there. Ruth would return the next day, refusing to say where she'd been, hair wild, and Amandine would drive her into school.

So in this way, their nerves were already stretched taut before the summer, before that October after Button disappeared into her bedridden body: that spring, Amandine had already chewed a small chunk out of the inside of her lip, Racinda did extra homework to block out the chaos, and Lyman, down in his lair, started a series of intricate children's letter-number blocks, but stopped when he got to K, because that was when his old high-school friend Rolo called him for that first weekend trip to Atlantic City.

In the car on the way there, the gray April rain insistent and soothing, Lyman knew what the casino would be like, and he knew it would carry him away. He saw the curling, blinking lights, the showgirls, their breasts waiting patiently under soft white feathers, under flashing gold trim. He saw long legs in old-fashioned can-can ruffles streaming pink over red over black over orange, he saw his hand reaching out to touch though he didn't even need to—just staring at them filled him as much as playing the slots would fill him and then when that stopped doing the trick, craps did it then blackjack then roulette and he'd start over again—girls to slots to blackjack to roulette. His gambling continued on as the spring buds burst into leaves, and then when Elmer died Lyman intensified this spiral one each trip to try to make himself feel like he was still somehow tied to this earth, to make himself feel anything at all.

Amandine believed him when he said he was traveling for work.

He'd walk out of the casino in the early morning light—Jersey, dull-lit, sand like the moon—seagulls and boardwalk and trash and water and sky just barely varying shades of gray, and then the asphalt and the exhaust and the misty smog around the highway on the way home just as gray, only the emergent spring green of the rural southern counties, the bright patches of fruit stands proof that the world hadn't been turned to ash. By the time, months later, that he realized he'd managed to lose the portion of his yearly salary that he was supposed to be saving for the girls' educations, he vowed to swear the trips off for a month or so. He came straight home after work for three weeks, launched into those sweet, tennis-playing June afternoons with the girls. He told himself he'd wait six months before going again. If he could wait six months, he'd know he was in control of it.

"Well," he said to Amandine once he was officially on the wagon, "If there's anything you want done around the house, let me know."

She tilted her head, too surprised to hide how much this perplexed her.

"Well, you know," Lyman said, ears reddening. "Thank goodness all those business trips are done with!"

Amandine nodded, her eyes still confused and tentative. He added even more earnestness to his expression as irritation burgeoned in hers.

He resisted temptation all summer, through his father's death, through Button's stroke and hospitalization into the fall, and was proud of himself. Lyman's wood blocks got more and more obsessive, detailed, with each letter. He worked steadily in the evenings, but in a few months only managed to finish up through letter P of blocks, his pace had been so slowed by his increasing interest in tinier and tinier elements.

After Button seemed to fade, however, in early October, Lyman couldn't see the reason for declining Rolo's invitations anymore. He had a serious financial cushion since his father's will had been distributed, and that was only even going to be necessary for a worst-case scenario that wouldn't even happen—it had been *four* months, certainly his previous loss of control had just been a phase.

His anguish over trying to keep himself from the casinos produced an exquisite, intricate few letters—on P he managed a lazy platypus, eyes beneficent, tail strong, lolling in vines and roses. He was gearing up happily to make Q as delicate and inspired when he ran into Ruth in the kitchen and slowed for a little break, leaning against the formica counter to chat.

"Hi Daddy," Ruth said, the only one in the house pleased to see him, the only one not nervous to be near him. She spun herself to the refrigerator, stood at its gaping door, mouth slack, before finding the last soda in the back of the bottom shelf and spinning back again to face her father.

Her hair was a funny, pale coppery orange. He wondered if Amandine had told her she could dye it, but decided against asking anything that might provoke an outburst.

"Well, Ruth, what's going on?" he said. His voice sounded just a touch over-inflated.

"Freaking clarinet. Freaking clarinet is *going on*. All I do, run up and down, up and down the scales," she said, sighing.

"Well you're getting better at it. Practice—" he said, but then realized he'd yet to hear her actually play a note.

"Look, I need money for the band trip," she said, pulling the tab back from her Coke, dropping the ring on the floor, kicking it under the cabinets, out of view. She took a long sip then belched as loudly as she could manage.

He had given her money last week for the same thing, and hadn't mentioned it when Amandine said she got a note saying Ruth had been dropped at virtually the beginning of the school year from the band for lack of attendance.

Lyman sighed, and got out his wallet.

"Thanks, Daddy," she said, but she still didn't hug him. She pocketed the twenty and walked out the back door, not bothering to close it. He closed it after her, let his hand linger on the old, green-enameled knob. His mind moved slowly these days—depressed—and it didn't occur to him to wonder where Ruth was going, or who might be picking her up, or when she might be home.

His good fortune—he was thinking about luck a lot lately—had taken a turn for the worse, it seemed, what with Ruth's lies and her vast screaming when he or Amandine tried to talk to her about her problems at school, or about such impossible, violent behavior at home. Amandine had started indicating that they might want to send Ruth to some sort of school that could handle her, but Lyman just walked out of the room once this sort of hinting began.

Rotten luck.

So when Rolo called ten minutes later, about to leave, spur of the moment, for the casinos, Lyman didn't put up a fight. Sometimes, he'd discovered, down the shore, his luck switched for awhile. As he folded a shirt into his briefcase and wrote out a note to Amandine, he forgot all about the Q block. Four months without the lights, the feathers, the dulled spinning and rolling and flipping sounds of the gaming tables. Close enough, he figured, and he sighed, exhausted, willing to go wherever Rolo took him.

Amandine hadn't much minded back in the spring that her husband was gone on the weekends. It wasn't different, really, from his being down in the basement. Calmer, actually, as she could step a little heavier on the floor and still not touch him.

But after Ruth's disappearing nights started happening twice weekly, and by early October when she got kicked out of the last public school in the area for biting another girl's cheek so badly it required plastic surgery, it became clear to Amandine that she simply did not possess the force of will required to contain her daughter, nor the knowledge required to ease Ruth into behaving, and that all the doctors and meds weren't really helping either.

Lyman was not helping, Button was not around, so Amandine had to do something.

Amandine stared at the phone, at the name and number of a place up north of Philly that a woman from her church—the Dells' church—recommended. She plied her cuticles with the folded corner of an envelope.

She hated that she wanted to talk to Button more than anything, wanted to ask Button what to do. But she remembered instead what it was taking her so long to learn in church, and she asked Jesus.

Take care of your girls, was what he said to her. *Find the best place for Ruth. Do something.*

So even though her hands were shaking and she didn't know what was the right thing to do and she didn't know even how to begin inquiring about this sort of thing and she didn't want the nurse on the other end, the nurse or secretary or whatever at a place that was both mental ward and boarding school, to know that she, Amandine Hart, had failed her daughter, she dialed. Didn't want the voice on the other end of the phone, a person she didn't know from Adam, for whom she was not responsible in any way, to know that she, Amandine Hart, had such a blight on her person as a crazy daughter, yes, but also that she, Amandine Hart, was unable to do anything to make her daughter better. Even the phone call was almost too much action to take on her daughter's behalf. But since Lyman refused to admit there was anything *that* wrong with Ruth, since Ruth had always been his favorite, since Ruth still knew how to get Lyman to laugh where Amandine and Racinda could barely get him talking, since *he* wasn't the one who had to figure out what to do with Ruth during the day now that she wasn't in school, Amandine did it. Called. Nobody else was going to.

By the week after Ruth's fourteenth birthday in November, on the day Ruth was scheduled to be picked up by the Oak Acres van, Ruth was gone again. The weeks leading up to the departure date had been turbulent—Amandine, finally giving up all the *turn the other cheek* Christianity she'd been dressing her fury up in, started throwing the plates *back* at Ruth when Ruth sent them flying. Racinda started hiding in the basement more often. Racinda went into the first bend of rooms right off the stairs, and knew that while lately he wasn't around much, her father would at some point be working just through the locked door to his woodshop again. Would be next to her, not bothering her, but *there*, providing something that passed for safety.

After Ruth returned from her night missing, Amandine cornered her in the bedroom, tried to explain once more how Oak Acres was a *wonderful* place, with art classes, and that there were lots of boys there, but of course her feeble attempts got her nowhere. Ruth held her breath until she passed out, a trick Amandine thought had gone by the wayside for other habits, like smoking and god knows what else. Amandine hardened to her daughter after that—the embarrassment in front of the Oak Acres people had done it. There was no questioning the school—if either of the girls brought it up, Amandine changed the subject cheerfully. And when Ruth found a filthy plate under the bed and threw it, Amandine simply left the house.

"Do you think you could, just once, just this *last* bit of it, stay up and try to keep her from sneaking out?"

"Just lock the door," Lyman said, yawning.

"Oh, I hadn't really thought of that," Amandine said and rolled her eyes at him. "It's *got* to be a window she's getting out."

"Well," Lyman said, "Now, there," he stroked his wife's upper arm. "I'm sure she'll calm down, tire herself out—another phase. I'm really beat, time to turn in."

Had there been any plates within reach, Amandine would have taken a cue from her daughter and frisbeed one at Lyman's head as he walked away from her.

Amandine dead-bolted the doors from the inside—lying on top of the key—and blocked Ruth's bedroom door by leaning a bookshelf against it in the hallway. Amandine stayed up all night, weeping a little, talking to JC when she remembered to, listening ferociously for the tiniest pressure on a windowsill, for the smallest metal whoosh of a screen coming out. But her escape artist daughter beat her once again.

Ruth was gone when Amandine went to check on her at three am.

Amandine called the school at dawn, before the van would have a chance to start out, and they *were* wonderful at Oak Acres, said just to call when Ruth turned up.

By seven am, though, the cops happened into a sleeping Ruth, acting possibly a little drunk when she woke, though she didn't smell of any alcohol, on the merry-go-round at the elementary school. They cuffed her this time. The van from Oak Acres School set off again from its post across the river from Trenton, NJ, and was coming up the Hart's driveway, inching its way through their old fields, just before noon.

Lyman and Racinda said their good-byes to her, but when Amandine went to hug Ruth, Ruth glared, spit on the ground, missing Amandine's low navy pump by an inch.

The van eased to the front of the house and the two friendly young men in khakis and navy polo shirts sedated Ruth—a shot in the arm—before she got in. They knew Ruth's calm, pliant act, her gentle loading of her own bags into the back of the van, was a ruse. They knew her type:

The type that wrenched doors open and ran at stoplights.

The type that grabbed steering wheels in traffic.

It occurred to Racinda that maybe Ruth had met her match in this school, and though Racinda didn't ever voice an actual complaint, so that it seemed as if her silence could result from simple sadness, she didn't speak a word to her parents for a week and a half. She found herself in the basement even without Ruth chasing her there, even without her father through the wall. Ruth didn't come home, three weeks later, for Thanksgiving.

* * *

Ruth did, however, come home for Christmas. It was a sad time—they all went to bed early after Christmas dinner once they somberly thanked each other for presents. Ruth left the next day for a trip with the Oak Acres school band, which she convinced Lyman and Amandine was really exciting for her, but which Racinda knew did not actually exist. Lyman went back to work right away—was not around for some time. Racinda and Amandine resumed their quiet schedules, talked to each other only when necessary. Racinda would go sit in the basement and fall asleep, only occasionally wondering when her father would start his wood projects up again.

On the mail table, in between red and green and silver and blue envelopes of still unopened Christmas cards, the thick blue-gray script of the Oak Acres return address sat in the corner of expensive gray envelopes like a bruise. Like the rest of the mail, the letters from Oak Acres piled up—why wasn't Lyman picking up the mail these days, Amandine wondered. When it was already nearing the end of January and she realized she actually hadn't *seen* him in two weeks, that the noise she heard in the basement the other night wasn't him but heat, mice, Racinda, whatever, she stopped in the middle of the downstairs hallway, just a little after noon, and her hand slowly reached for the wall, but she was dead center and support was a foot away. She brought her arm in and smoothed her skirt, checked her lipstick in the mirror, discarding the worry almost as soon as she knew it existed.

When he hadn't left a note last weekend before his business trip, she'd assumed the change in habit was simply because the weekend leavings *were* so habitual by now.

But here there were five letters from Oak Acres, unopened, and even with these letters pulled from the mail, the pile was four or five times as large as Amandine had ever seen it.

Amandine had noticed the Oak Acres letters, but hadn't opened them after the first one, which she'd thought might be some note regarding Ruth's progress, or Ruth's grades, or Ruth's test scores, but was just a reminder to Lyman to pay the bill, he was a month late. The amount shocked Amandine that time, but she justified it with the knowledge that Lyman could easily afford now, what with his inheritance from Elmer. And besides, even though Button hadn't anticipated as much as the school actually cost, there was a trust set up for Ruth's medical needs that would cover it. But of course it would never come to that, Amandine thought, as she tucked her blouse in more neatly.

Amandine ignored the rest of the mail, and shoved the five Oak Acres letters underneath the base of the lamp on the mail table, holding her shoulders higher, her back straighter, each of the numerous times she passed by throughout the day. By the time the Oak Acres financial affairs secretary called later that day, Amandine's neck was already shot through with a tough, dull pain. After assuring the school's secretary the amount would be wired by the next morning (not understanding that she needed an account number to wire it *to*, and so hanging up in the middle of the secretary's attempt to give that to her) Amandine got in her station wagon and drove herself to the recently built office complex down in Newark, Delaware, where Lyman's company had moved six months previous.

She knew from the look on *this* secretary's face that what was happening was beyond the beyond.

But *this* secretary was a great secretary, had been with the company ten years, and was primed to smoothing things over before she even understood there was anything wrong. This secretary laughed, and said, "Oh Mrs. Hart, did you forget that Lyman doesn't work here anymore! Well how are the girls?"

In the secretary's and her own chirping, Amandine was able to save herself, for the moment, with an excuse about being shopping in the neighborhood and needing to use the rest room, which turned out to be corporate and dark and gray, with smoky-looking plastic magazine shelves above the toilet paper holding *Time* and *Newsweek* and yesterday's *Wall Street Journal*. On the toilet, she stared at her hands, symmetrically gripping her knees, and when she noticed how perfect her fingernails were, she remembered when she, Amandine, had been a secretary herself, without a husband, and had had to save her laundry quarters for a manicure—it was either line-drying the clothes across her tiny kitchenette and living room, or raggedy-looking polish and cuticles. She had always picked the private indignity, when given a choice.

Air escaped her chest then in a silent gasp. She didn't get that *she* was the one breathing strangely until she stood up and looked in the mirror and started to understand that now it wasn't just her own fingernails and her own late-night misery she had to combat, but that now there were two other girls she was going to somehow have to make presentable, move around, manage the possessions of, *feed*, and that one of them was terrifyingly difficult, lately, to keep safe and alive.

Jesus, she said, aloud, *Jesus*, and all he could come up with for her just then was *okay, okay, okay*. Okay. The smile she gave the secretary on her way out was fake as spray cheese but she walked, and she drove, and she repeated it to herself, *okay*.

*   *   *

Even when, tearing through Lyman's closet, she found the cardboard box addressed to Ruth at Oak Acres that contained two boxes of salt water taffy and two Atlantic City ashtrays—*ashtrays!*—even then Amandine thought it was a mistress. Not business trips, but weekends at the shore with. . . not *that* secretary? But another one? And sending mementos of it to a daughter—she felt as if he and Ruth were in collusion. But there were no signs of it. There was no feminine feeling to his left-behind things, no speedy disarray, nothing tossed on top of a pile of dirty shirts to cover a lipstick stain, no alien perfume. There were poker chips, in the corner of the drawer, between the flashlight and the shoehorn, under the pile of grayblack socks, but that was normal, leftover from his weekly hobbyist-poker sandwich night with Rolo and some other men.

It wasn't until the next day, after Amandine carefully checked the balance in the grocery account—which she did awkwardly, never having asked the bank teller for the amount before, always, previously, assuming correctly that there was enough—to find only about thirty dollars left, she drove straight to the only pawnshop she'd ever passed by, in Wilmington, and got rid of her three hundred dollar earrings for a hundred fifty. The questions about where he was, exactly, when he would call, and whether or not there was another woman, these questions compressed inside her to a tough little stone she could easily ignore. She almost, *almost* didn't care anymore—she just wanted to be taken care of, she simply hated him for leaving her very possibly destitute. *Button* wouldn't even have left her destitute. What Button had left for Ruth's care had seemed like more than enough—really, when Lyman's salary would have covered it all easily. Button never would have *imagined* that the girls and Amandine wouldn't have Lyman's support. And Johnson, the young lawyer, was sweet, even babysat the girls one night when Amandine had a church event, but couldn't do anything now that Button wasn't talking, was barely conscious, was deep in dementia.

Before she called the lawyer, Amandine called Rolo, who mistook her voice for his school-marm auntie until the fourth time she repeated *where is he*, and Rolo just spit it out, *he's at the casino, he's at the beach.* Wouldn't say much more, except that there was *not* another woman and *I think it's pretty bad.*

What was bad? *Bad?*

She'd never been there, Atlantic City. They'd taken the girls to Ocean City once, and Linda had brought her along to Sea Isle, and she'd even braved seedy, packed Wildwood for a few evenings. Never Atlantic. What was the appeal, really, she'd always wondered.

No, *not* with a woman, Rolo said. No woman.

And it hadn't been a woman, and it still wasn't a woman. That was the truth. When Lyman lost nearly all the money his father had willed him, and, in trying to figure out how to get more, from the land, discovered that Button had circumvented him from doing so, he stopped going to work. He didn't go home, though—he remained in the permanent dusk of a seventh floor hotel room just off the beach, opening the windows only in the early morning, before motors started, before voices cracked the silence. He watched television. He wrote a letter of resignation. That he didn't call his wife or his daughters filled his stomach with something heavy, and he stopped eating. When a sliver of hunger hit him after the fifth evening, he made his way down to the bar and drank his way through a tab of three hours of Jim Beam, slow, not drunk. He ate two bowls of bar nuts and expended all his energy trying to block out the stale Christmas carols coming from somewhere he couldn't discern.

When the guy next to him, a noisy barfly wearing a pewter lariat, challenged him to a game of pool, Lyman ignored it, but as the drunk fake cowboy escalated and jabbed him in the ribs, as if joking, Lyman had no choice—he had to play the man. Because if he just slunk out of there, a man who had ruined everything for his family, run out on them, lost all his money, and lost all feeling for the world couldn't handle this basic, pri-

mal, challenge, then there was no man left in him. He might as well drink
Jim Beam here in silence until his blood turned that warm ochre color,
might as well wander out after nightfall into the waves. Just another shade
of moonlight. He might as well let himself fall away completely.

And though he moved his arms through the game as if underwater already, Lyman's night changed. And the drunk Jersey cowboy was good.
But something pulled Lyman's cue down the exact vector it needed to follow, so that he won two games of three so easily that his spirits followed
his luck back into the light of day. When the cowboy wanted a fight Lyman
gave it to him—a showy fight, punches thrown wide and loud but not actually that hard. A little blood on both of them but no real damage—the
opposite, in fact: both men were buoyed by the nearly painless show of
bright tail feathers. That extra vitality as well as the bright green felt of the
billiards somehow got Lyman back into the casino, and his last hundred
bucks turned into just enough to cover his bar tab, his hotel bill. He drove
himself away the next morning, unable to swear off the casino forever,
but able to promise himself to keep the brakes on his habit, nudging his
lost inheritance to the back of his mind.

As he pulled his Buick into the headquarters of his former employer's
main competitor, the man who Lyman had been just the day before—yesterday's bleached casing of a man, near-dead on a barstool, unable even to
meet the most basic challenge, his most basic responsibility—seemed like
another person altogether. Lyman developed a sort of a swagger. His new
exterior strength toughened him, took risks, pushed him harder at work
and on the betting floor.

This bravado, his self-imposed limits, a decent measure of luck that
kept him breaking not *miles* under even for quite some time—as well as
his new, better-paying job—kept Lyman just skimming the bottom, never
landing. A trip back to see the family lost to him now would have pointed
out the space gone soft in him, never shaped into any action, still sitting
lost at the bar. A trip back to Pennsylvania would have pointed out to him
the version of himself, Lyman Hart, that was mainly this: orphaned, his
mother then his father then even Button lost to him; would have pointed
out this gray expanse which had been expanding its acreage in his chest
weekly. But his risks at work paid off, his rules regarding not crossing the
Delaware River, not setting foot west of Jersey, kept him from this knowledge, and gave him a different life. His jokes got fouler. His cars got fancier.
There was a Saab convertible. The aging, masculine shell grew tougher

and more baroque. Yes: a series of younger girlfriends and a series of coups at work over the years sharpened his barbs.

He knew Amandine wouldn't ask him for a divorce—she'd never want the disgrace of it. He'd known her when she'd had no money, and he knew she'd take the stoic path. She wouldn't want to admit to needing to come after him.

Thoughts of his daughters, or that exquisite, unfinished Q block, even, emerged, early in the morning, out of the gray loss that was gaining on him, but the memories and the loss had no chance as long as he was in control.

The buried loss propelled him, and the newly brash shell protected him, occupied him. The part of Lyman that used to at least try to address his true responsibilities was blank, gone since that late December day he didn't come home. There was only swagger and dead space now where there should have been a man. It was so much easier this way.

*   *   *

January's routine of darting in and out of the A&P at 7 in the morning to avoid other mothers got old fast for Amandine, as did looking for temporary secretarial work forty minutes away so she wouldn't suffer supervision by any of Lyman's former associates she'd met before at cocktail parties or the occasional PTA meeting. She let Racinda do pretty much as she wished, since it wasn't in Racinda—yet—to run wild. She preferred to let other mothers pick Racinda up and drop her off when necessary, to spare herself the embarrassment of explaining she had to stay at the office until 5:30.

Only her church group was a relief—there she could weep and be assured it all would work out, she would be taken care of. But these women weren't exactly from her same station in life, and while she was greedy for their affections, their soothing—and even, many weeks, their gifts of casseroles and cobblers—a deep repulsion for them began quietly in her and, when the lack of money did not just let up, as Amandine had hoped it somehow, magically, might, she feared more and more becoming one of them: becoming fat, poor-ish, hassled, and plain.

Instead of rich-enough, aloof, and pretty. Pretty was turning out to be a little trickier without cash.

Before Lyman left, Amandine had begun to grow a bit more robust of spirit. The grief over losing Button made Amandine a bit more loving, a bit less shrill with Racinda, a bit easier to get to laugh in moments the sadness lifted. Less frozen.

But now, shaken further to the root, she reverted to what had always worked: distance, superiority, judgment, an insistence on the finer things, and an imagined, aristocratic pride where ordinary, pedestrian comfort and imperfect connection would have done her good. Winter. Amandine still talked to Jesus, and to Linda, who, being the preacher's wife, was good enough for her. Despite her reliance, still on Jesus, the rest of the Christians, though, suddenly seemed inappropriate to Amandine as a social milieu.

So, just before February began, when Ray Dell offered to fix Amandine up with a job as the church secretary for a small Lutheran denomination some Born-Again friends of his had revitalized out in California—a church with a *building*, not just a living room, a church that also owned a little two-bedroom house down the block it would rent below market rate to Amandine—she nodded for three full minutes, bursting into little giggles. Her snob's heart was at the root of her journey out, her escape from dependency on *these* Christians.

But, as Jesus kept telling her, annoyingly enough, when she cried to him at night—this trouble was opening her heart past its fear, past its snobbishness. *The joy of the Lord is my strength*, she thought, nodding at Ray, unaware she was doing so, until he, giggling as well, nodded back at her in time.

Was it Amandine's imagination? When the Oak Acres van brought Ruth back up the driveway in the February snow, through the fields, the two young men in navy shirts and tan pants looked considerably more tired than they had a few months previous. Amandine had promised Oak Acres, nearly weekly, to send along the tuition she owed them, but finally they put the head of Financial Affairs on the phone and told her Ruth was not welcome any longer.

Amandine looked more tired, too, but there was a new sense of efficacy about her as she wrapped Violetta's china and lowered it into boxes, as she ran out for more packing material, as she called the movers again just to make sure the insurance policy was comprehensive. One evening, in the thick of the mess and the rush, she realized, regarding cardboard and dust and the screaming sound of cellophane packing tape coming off the roll, that enough was enough and ordered the girls a pizza and actually sat with them, actually ate with them, actually remained in one place for more than two minutes and even laughed once or twice at the white-trash-centric sitcom Ruth insisted on.

Ruth was calm when she came home from Oak Acres. The sight of her mother actually doing things in the world calmed Ruth, and she settled down—after the initial period of raging at her father, she put everything into helping pack, talked about getting a job, even, bolstered her sister with stories of what would happen to them on the road. Racinda followed along as usual, her mood determined by her mother's and her sister's.

When Amandine had sat Ruth down, that day Ruth returned, and explained as clearly as she could that Lyman had lost his money and left, Ruth, exhausted, stared at her for a minute, her lips chapped.

"Didn't he *say* anything?" Ruth said. "Where he was *going*?"

"Well there was. . ." Amandine said, and she looked straight into her daughters eyes and couldn't finish the sentence.

"What?" Ruth said, and held the glance—such a long one was not usual from her mother. It was new—Amandine was new.

But still, Amandine shook her head and didn't say any more.

So, dependably, Ruth slammed out of the house and walked the three full miles into town. She was back by dinner though, and she ate her mother's boiled chicken and tasteless frozen vegetables without so much as a sneer. The moods still came, and she still went after Racinda, but in his absence her father was her main target. Even Ruth knew when the time came to hang on to what she'd got left. She helped Amandine pack during the days when Racinda was at school. She swept up each room once its contents had been condensed inside of a zillion cardboard cubes. She brought her mother glasses of water, but she also dropped so many dishes trying to help out that Amandine boxed the regular plates up sooner than she needed to, had them eating off paper ones fast.

Amandine: busy, with so much at stake, could finally manage to stare Ruth down. Finally had enough important things to do in the packing and the planning. The monstrosity that Ruth's illness—her *being* even—had taken on in Amandine's mind had no spare anxiety to feed on.

But that new ability to look straight at Ruth stayed with Amandine. She thought more carefully than usual about how Ruth might feel about her father's leaving, really tried to think through what she could do for Ruth to ease the pain of it.

She decided to stop protecting Ruth from him, him—in his absence—from Ruth. She decided to give Ruth exactly what Lyman had left for her. She decided to leave the taffy and the ashtrays one evening, in their little box, outside Ruth's bedroom door. Ruth promptly took the gift down to her father's workshop and filled both painted-glass tchotckes with two packs of cigarette butts over the course of the evening. She brought her boom box down there and blasted a Zeppelin mix tape Matty Dieckmann had given her. She chewed each pastel piece of taffy into a pulp and let it drop, trailing syrupy thick lines of saliva, onto his perfectly carved letter-blocks. Her tongue sore, pocked with smoke and sugar, she remained quiet as she threw the contents of the ashtray over the project, transfixed by the wood's transformation into sweet, ashy refuse. The music fed her smoke, then her chewing, then the blocks after she slammed them apart, finally, with a hammer. *Heartbreaker*—that song—*Heartbreaker*, but Ruth didn't pay attention to any of the words. Ruth ripped the workbench counter off the wall with a crowbar and a hammer, she drilled holes in the *blades* of the two nicest handsaws, she cracked the window of each silvery level and let the blue liquid, the red bauble flow away.

Racinda, hearing the frightening, mystical guitar-testosterone—convinced by the Dells' church it was Satanic—left the house even before the smashing started. Walked herself over to a tree at the edge of Amandine's now-unrecognizable topiary—unconvincing blobs, not-scary monsters now instead of animals—and sat there with a book and a flashlight until she saw the basement light turn out around midnight.

Amandine stayed though—crammed tissues in her ears and let Ruth do what she needed to do. Left the mess where it lay. Didn't say a word about the smoke or the devastated basement. Had the hired housekeepers deal with it as best they could the day after they left.

After Ruth won the fight to sit up front, after Amandine put the kitchen trash into the dented silver can in the driveway, after Racinda dug her missing mitten out from behind the radiator even though she knew she wouldn't be needing it in Sacramento, after all four car doors were shut tight and Amandine sighed and started the engine, Racinda noticed the basement light on—glossy yellow against the gray stone of the house's foundation, against the gray winter light. Amandine had left it on for the housecleaners, but to Racinda, it was as close to a message from Lyman as she could conjure: his hiding place completely separate from hers even back in that basement, when just a wall kept them apart. As Racinda dug into her parka, rested her plush hood against the headrest, she imagined that wherever he was hiding now he was somehow just as close to her: Daddy's hiding just through the wall.

Ruth chattered, making up a new soap opera in each state, characters named after the most exciting words on each exit ramp's sign. Amandine managed something closer and closer to a smile with each sign they passed announcing passage into a new county, a new city, over a bridge. Racinda let herself be lulled into the narcotic effect of the wheels' rhythm, lulled into a goodbye to everything she knew, lulled into a goodbye to Button, her worries a bit quieted by what she'd heard Amandine complain about on the phone—that Button owned the land and nobody could rent the house, even.

As Lyman faded into the parched lights, the stale surfaces and carpets of Atlantic City, into his little one-bedroom bungalow on a new cul-de-sac outside Cherry Hill, as Button chased Elmer through the twilight, as Amandine nudged herself inch by painful inch westward, inch by inch out of her sedated comfort, the girls moved forward on their own.

The girls moved into the world together and then diverged. Ruth leading with her thighs and her hips, her hair flying behind her, her face turned with a quick smile or sneer at the slightest comment. Racinda more tentatively, washing up against the sides of life, chin lowered, eyes up, steady, hidden, eyes pinned on the horizon to spot the next threat.

8

CRAZYSITTER

SACRAMENTO, 1984

Max

When she came there, it was like a dream, that whole night. Starting at twilight. That whole night came in crisp pulses when Ruth was in my house to baby-sit me and her sister Racinda. Both our mothers were off at a Born Again revival.

Watching, I was always watching, and I did that to her for awhile that night. But with Ruth I finally stepped *in* to things, you know, for a night or so I wasn't just watching the movie, I was a part of it.

It was that night that tipped them off to all the stuff that was wrong with her, and they sent her to a hospital for awhile. I don't know what happened after that but she ended up in one of those things for good. I never asked her sister about it again. I'm not the type of person to bring it up.

*   *   *

When Ruth first walked in the door it was just starting to get dark out, just graying and cooling in the distance. The first thing you'd notice is her strange hair, kinky and sort of metallic brown underneath, but blonder and blonder toward the frizzy ends, and then you'd see the way her cheeks were so round and always a little flushed, real apples. She was thin but her skin coated her like a layer of soft dough, plumping her, in a nice way though. It looked pink in some light, dead white in others, shifting, the way certain shells do.

Her little sister followed her like a mute. Her mother, Amandine, took the soda my mom got her and stayed away, on the couch, squeezing the lemon wedge into her Tab.

My mom was leading Ruth around the house in a sort of a tour of all the things she worried about.

"This is where all the phone numbers are. There's the fire extinguisher. The casserole for dinner is in the fridge and there's otter pops," etcetera.

Ruth kept her back real straight and smiled a tiny girl smile, nodded like she was taking everything in, but she made sure I saw her pinch Racinda's side—twist the skin hard—a couple times when mom's back was turned. Racinda just took it like a pussy, blindly attached to her sister. Amandine sat on the couch smiling wider when Ruth, my mom and Racinda passed by to inspect some other crucial detail. When Amandine saw the three streaming by in the hall, it was like a breeze swooped past her eyes and she posed to look happy. Not to convince someone else, more like for herself. Otherwise, she just sipped her Tab. I saw her lick the lemon off her fingers in a greedy way after she rested it on the rim.

When our moms were driving off, my mom yelled, "Praise the Lord!" out the window of Amandine's car, and Ruth actually said it back to them, loudly, enthusiastically.

My mom was just recently, like a year, into this Christian shit, and I would sort of go along with it when she wanted me to, but I thought it was stupid. I was still at that age when I would do things like that for my mom. I would like rub her feet at night after work, and I would like let her tell me how she felt bad and lonely about the losers she dated. A couple years later, by fourteen, I was pretty annoyed at her and started blowing her off completely, like walking away when she would say, *Max, I'm so sad*, keep walking when she would say *Maxy, how could you do this to me, why are you being so mean to your Mama?* But I just didn't want to hear how the men were being so bad to her anymore. I had girls of my own, by then, to be kinda bad to. But this night, at age ten, I still hadn't gotten pissed off yet.

Racinda seemed to inch away from her sister when Ruth sang out "Praise the Lord!", but I got closer, hovering across the linoleum, fascinated with whether Ruth was fooling or not. I could see the windows of

Amandine's Dasher lowering—a little vertical movement gobbled up in the horizontal of the car slipping down the driveway.

"Jeez, they are so fruity," Ruth said.

Racinda and I stared up at her—both of us were pretty short, and we somehow got younger than ten with Ruth as the adult.

"Jesus fruity Christ," Ruth said, pulling the screen door wide to let it go dramatically, to hear that bangy wood on wood slamming noise.

"Praise the fucking fruity Lord," she said.

She made me and Racinda go upstairs and watch TV in my mom's room, as she looked for a radio station on the stereo, she told us she had things to do.

*   *   *

I remembered Ruth and Racinda's mother Amandine from when I woke up late one Sunday morning to clapping and singing. I thought it was just my mom playing music while she cleaned, but it turned out to be live, about seven or eight ladies down there praying and whooping it up. The skewed feeling of everything from them was more than that they were ferociously off key, it was a wild, buzzing energy that pushed some notes up to wrong noises, noises like a child lets out practicing the recorder or the violin.

I came to the landing on the stairs and as soon as I turned to take the next little flight down I saw them. They weren't dressed as weird as the people my mom used to hang around before then, these crazy hippies who would get stoned and chant—but it was like there was something even worse, as if these women were truly on the edge, like the thin wire in a light bulb right before it burns apart.

I remember that Sunday morning when I was around nine, it was October so not too cold yet, I came downstairs and as soon as I hit the landing, before the second flight, I saw them there, the women praying in my living room, a circle of them wearing pale flower colors. My mom wasn't playing the piano any more, and they weren't exactly singing. Coming out of them were watery noises, noises like waves and gurgling words—some slower and deeper underneath the others and some chirpier ones eddying on top. Their eyes were closed. Speaking tongues. I held the railing in one hand and stared.

As if she knew I was there, my mom opened her eyes. She kept her mouth moving though, like an invitation; she was calling me, I knew it, and we just stared at each other till I flinched.

*   *   *

"You're getting crumbs on the bed," Racinda said.

"I don't give a fuck," I said back to her, and I bounced my leg so the milk sloshed onto the tray some.

"Oh I am so impressed," she said, but it sounded like she was just imitating her sister as much as I was. For a second I wanted to smash her face in with one of the old round stones on my mom's dresser.

I clicked through the scrambled porn channels slow like I always did—I left it on the last one, you could hear the music and the people moaning and breathing, when I asked her what she wanted to watch.

"Whatever," she said, "What-ever," playing with the word in a little song, sort of.

We each took half the bed, on our stomachs and elbows, she dipped her cookies into the soda and kept eating till they were all gone. The light outside turned bluer and became indistinguishable from the TV's pulse. Fine baby hairs ringed Racinda's face, I noticed in this light—the electron glow from the TV turned them shiny white against her hair pulled back in silver, glinting barrettes.

After awhile we switched to Miami Vice, and the sound of the guns and the yelling, the blare of the commercials wove through the quiet between us, but didn't cover it up. The quiet between us felt like air, a pressure, a force.

The music that had been low downstairs got louder and I had to turn up the TV.

The reason the music got louder was it was coming up not just through the floorboards but out the open front door into the night and back in through the upstairs windows. With the music, the night seemed to pour in too, to touch us more directly. The house got thinner, less convincing as shelter.

And I think Racinda picked up on Ruth's voice singing along just after I did—her head sort of leaned to one side, she panicked but she acted like it was normal or whatever, like she didn't care or notice her sister's screechy voice running with the right notes but then careening up, or down into a crawl.

It was that Prince song—*little red Corvette*—

I heard Ruth's high voice—higher now than before—off key but in time with the song.

"I'm cold," Racinda said. "Will you shut that window?"

I tried to get it but it was stuck open, the paint probably melted in the months of heat.

Cars zoomed by, people on their way out to parties and bars, some real loud with bad mufflers and some just quick streams whining by. Their rhythm was almost dependable, though you never knew when the muffler bombs would happen, when the occasional backfire would almost take your breath.

One of the whooshing cars slowed down—though we were both fixed on the TV I could feel Racinda hearing and sensing it all as I did, second by second. The car idled, it turned over strangely, clearly stopping in our yard by the porch.

There was this noise of crickets and it was almost like you could hear the sky way up there, like if you were to let a drop of water go, it would tumble *up* to the dense black night, following gravity to the heaviest thing, that darkness, and make a long and barely hearable rumble.

At the window I could feel more coolness on my face, smell the dirt settling in, and I could see Ruth down there, leaning one hip on the railing, craning her eyes up at the white lacquered beams on the porch ceiling, swinging a foot so her dirty Keds sneaker banged into the slatted wood. I could feel Racinda getting more annoyed with me each second I stared at Ruth's pretty arms hugging herself across the chest.

The pickup truck had pulled up onto the yard crookedly—on a diagonal.

It was tuned to the same radio station as the stereo downstairs, so now another stream of the Prince song came to us in the bedroom. I couldn't see the man's face inside the truck, but I could smell the smoke from his cigarette, I could see its red tip circle in the dark. It dangled from his mouth when he spoke, sometimes he lifted it out to ash.

"You live here?" he said. He seemed kind of unsure of whether to be talking to her, but I could tell he was a moth to her light as much as me and Racinda were. He just saw her sitting out there on the porch and he couldn't not stop.

"I'm just here today," Ruth said.

"Oh yeah," he said. Even though he was unsure of himself, he was like a tough guy, he wasn't some hippie or something. He didn't know if he was supposed to be there but he wanted her and he wasn't going to hide it.

"God I love this part," she said, throwing her arms out from her chest and standing up. She started to sing along again, to the line where Prince is squealing and screaming and all freaking out.

She shook her head from side to side and her teenage stab at cool wasn't fooling anyone, it was embarrassing, but even so I wanted her to think *I* was cool I wanted to be near her all the time, I wanted to be down there and protect her from this guy, I wanted her to want to talk to me. The way I wanted her felt so pure, so like, right or something, like she was going to fix things for me, fix things for me that I couldn't fix and my parents couldn't fix. She had this thing—she shook her head from side to side and her teeth looked fierce like a baby wolf's—fierce in a way no other woman I'd ever seen had had. Fierce in a way I wanted my mom to be against the guys she dated. Fierce like I wanted to be to them. And then Ruth giggled and bent over in her laughing, one bra strap slipped off her shoulder and her hand looked like a little bird when she fixed it, it moved so precisely and not like anyone else's I'd ever seen. But her teeth were still so sharp, and her tongue was dark red when she stuck it out at the man then.

"Sit down, Max, quit spying," Racinda hissed at me, but there was nothing that was going to get me away from Ruth then. Nothing ever happened in my stupid life except my stupid parents' problems. I was usually so ho-hum, whatever, never really *wanted* anything, just sort of went along and watched TV or videogames or tried to look like I was kind of paying attention in school. With Ruth, though all I did was *want*, and it felt like the difference between being alive and dead.

The man laughed at Ruth's tongue.

"You better pull that back in or someone might steal it from you," he said, and I could see by the way his jaw moved he was still pretty young.

She just kept singing, grabbing her jean skirt and pulling it out to emphasize the words, shifting her hips to the song. Light grabbed her neck and her mouth was so heavy, open, and she looked him straight in the eye, and she was too much, it was like too much to look at, too embarrassing, but I wanted it too, and I kept watching.

She'd sort of grin up at him and giggle some more.

Ruth was so young to that guy, she was acting so young, if you weren't in love with her like me and the guy in the truck you would think she was being silly, stupid, innocuous in the way only a girl could be. A boy could *never* be that fragile, that light, that silly as her little grin and her giggles. Meaningless, you know? And I wanted to be, in a way, that light sometimes, but I was just starting to really learn how *not* to be at *all* like that, you know, at eleven, twelve, you learn how to sound solid, like a real guy. I could just begin to imagine a man wanting that playful childish thing, that girlish thing he couldn't ever really have, that girly thing that would always mock him and lure him too, I could imagine wanting to pin that thing down and bruise it a little just to try for a hold on it.

"That's quite a number you've got," the man said.

I could see a shallow outline of his face now—he wasn't young but he wasn't old either; some straight, longish hair ringed his face and even though he was sneering slightly there was a gentleness or a shock in his face. He looked a little familiar but I couldn't see clearly enough to tell.

"Thanks. I *love* Prince," Ruth said.

She plopped down on the wicker chair and put her feet up on the railing, leaning herself backwards on the two rear legs.

The man mumbled something I couldn't hear.

The two of them faced each other without looking at each other for a while that seemed longer than it really was, the headlights filled the space between them with a thick yellow-white, revealing the night's rich exhaust and bugs you just couldn't always see, Racinda and I were held together by breath and the warmth of our skins and the way she was now grabbing so hard on to the windowsill next to me, immobile, watching.

The man mumbled something else.

"No, I don't know that song," Ruth said, eyes up, lips in a frown, buying time.

She sounded breathless. The man extended his hand, arm leaning just out the window of the pickup, lazily brushing something off the top of the side mirror, but the rest of him remained still and toward Ruth.

"I never heard it, that one," she said, a little higher-toned, a little nervous, talking just to fill up the space.

The man didn't say anything.

It was like there were all these little threads tying him and her together, and those threads were all about sex, all about their bodies. I knew it, Racinda knew it. Invisible ties in the air, sex and weirdness we didn't understand yet.

Ruth put the chair back on all four legs and pushed her hand down her thigh hard, like she was trying to get blood to flow to her knee. She took her hair down and smoothed it back with her hands.

"And I want to go with you but I am supposed to be here now so I can't go," Ruth said.

He tapped his fingers against the chrome, sarcastically, like *we both know you're gonna come, so get in already.*

Ruth scoffed.

"Okay? I can't—I told you. I'm not coming with you. So goodbye," Ruth said.

I could see now that his face was also doughy and young, also familiar in some way to me. He seemed sad at what she just said to him, like the rejection really stung him. He looked away from her, up into the distance, to try to get away from her for a second, to try to think of what to do next.

He decided to get cocky again, he tilted his head, ran two fingers along the top of the steering wheel.

"Shoot," he said, "You better hop on in before somebody meaner than me snatches you right off this porch."

He smiled, looking older, more sure of himself, like he was in control. Then he squinted, aiming for menace but not quite getting there. He got halfway there, though, he got close enough.

So low I could barely hear, she said:

"Get out of here. . ."

Her features hidden, her head lowered.

Her voice small, defenseless.

The corners of his mouth stayed up, a sort of victory, he kept running his hands over the leather-wrapped steering wheel while puffs of monoxide drifted past him, past Ruth, up to us on the dense night air.

But then she spoke again.

"Get the fuck out of here, *Davey Maye*,"

By the time she said his name—I knew who he was now—her tone had roughened, got surly, mocking, insulting, coated with that snotty, high-pitched, impenetrable thing that only teenage girls have, that snotty thing that they can only muster because they own those five or six years of that perfect skin and arms and breasts. Ruth had it and she was trying to lord it over him. Ruth hadn't yet started to die at all. Ruth knew everybody hates girls for how much power their prettiness has over men, Ruth knew everybody wants a piece of that chirpy girl thing to prevent or put off their own dying. Like to prove they can own that girl's little song and softness and stupid, pretty laugh.

It's so ugly, when girls use that voice to mock how much we want that stuff from them, but they've got us there, they've got us by the balls on that point. When they use that voice they are risking sounding stupid and worthless and dumb, but they've got us—if they don't share themselves with us, that mocking voice to us like crushes us, like makes us worth nothing. We're cut off from them, we're all loveless. They've got us by the balls on that one.

Except—

Except that they don't.

Except that the root of it is always the tiny "get out of here" Ruth started with, a peep I could smash with my fist, or yell at, or just ignore, even, till it fades into nothing at all. What girls are worth can turn on a dime. You call her a bitch and that song you wanted so bad turns into a fat old lady song, a dirty whore song, an ugly girl song, not something pretty and rare and delicious.

What I was learning: Just call her a bitch and you win.

Ruth kept her eyes up at him, daring him, silent.

He lowered his hands inside the vehicle, shifted his eyes off her.

Ruth's lips were wet, and her powdery skin shone in the night in a creamy way that made me and the man want to grab onto her. You wanted to like bite into her like fruit. Her shoulders were stuck out, her breasts stuck out, she was defiant but when she moved her foot her shoulders shook a little, reminded me and Davey she was soft too. I was completely in love with her. I think he was too. I have only felt that kind of heavy, heavy wanting for a woman in small flashes since then—nobody was as beautiful as Ruth to me. Nobody was as strong, nobody was ever so obviously as in love with the air on her skin, the night giving her a deep starry background, the arcs and dips and kisses of her own voice as Ruth was. Nobody took so much pleasure as she did. And *fierce*.

Racinda pushed me aside at the window. She leaned on me. I left my side against her, with some weight there, didn't move away from touching, and neither did she.

"Oh, c'mon hon-ay," Davey Maye, said, sounding way desperate all of a sudden.

Ruth stuck her neck out—the lights hit her skin and made it shine a little, as if she were sweating. An ugly expression crossed her face, and if he had been closer I swear she would have hit him.

"You can just hop in here and take the party on the road, don't be so fussy, sweetie," he said.

"Oh jeez," I heard Racinda whisper, "Jeez."

She pulled back from the window.

"Are you going to go down there?" I asked her.

She didn't say anything: she sat on the floor and sort of grabbed her knees to herself.

Racinda's bangs fell from the barrette into her eyes and she left them there, fixing her eyes anyway on the window so intently it seemed like she was trying to will herself out through it. It was like there was a stand-off between her still concentration and the murmur of the engine outside.

"Oh *God!*" Ruth said, loud, scoffing, completely disgusted, angry. "I can't believe you would even *think* I would do that."

She stood up.

"You're—" she was so angry now that the words were getting stuck in her and coming out funny "you—" she twisted the bottom of her tee shirt in a fist, "You *fucker!*"

He was still smiling. I would not have been smiling, if I were him. I would not, even though I've had my fair share of hysterical women yelling at me since then, and in those situations, I had to laugh too. It's not that that sort of thing isn't funny, it is, but with Ruth it was that there was really something wrong with her, she went from just angry to something really wrong. She was shaking and all that pleasure in the details of the night turned into this yelling that could go a bunch of different ugly places.

Racinda wrapped her fingers around my forearm. I let her dig her nails in and didn't say anything about the pain.

"Come on, sugar," he said, in a voice like you would use to coax a dog or a horse, "We can hop in the truck and go see the sights."

Ruth's face no longer looked like a girl's, even, her face was so tensed up and angry, red around the sides, snarled into an ugly mess.

I can't believe what she did next. She had no sense in the world, that girl. But to her credit, I will say that when she did it the front yard filled with stillness and the matter was somehow resolved, even though a lot more yelling followed. When she did it the night was held up and paused for a minute, everyone involved became a statue or a prop from a play that had ended with the audience already gone home.

"The sights are right here, asshole" Ruth said.

She pulled up her shirt.

She flashed him.

Her breasts looked powdery, soft like they were limestone, both soaking up and resisting the low-beams' glare, not as small as they'd looked under clothes. She'd done it so fast it hardly registered. No bra. The color of her tee shirt held up in front of her face faded into the wall of the house, and she was a chopped in half girl there, tits with no head. She was beautiful, like a statue, like the ideal girl. She let him get a real good look before she pulled it down again.

She threw her head back, whipped it back away from him, to avoid looking at him, and she did it so fast that a long line of saliva flew out over her shoulder. She was amazing to me, so fucking ballsy. But Davey didn't leave. He just stared her down from the truck, protected by all eight cylinders.

"Fuck you you cock sucking faggot!" Ruth yelled, backwards, refusing to acknowledge his invasion. But her little words did nothing. She let out a small blurry noise then that was trying to become a word but didn't make it.

*   *   *

It wasn't until a lot later, like years, eons, that I felt like that again, the way I felt around Ruth that night. It was like, anything could happen and the stars were more silvery in the sky, with Ruth around. The air was good, when Ruth was around—you noticed the *air*. It was like I was not ever gonna be bored again, ever trapped with my mom in the house. Even though Ruth was drinking and drinking, it was not like with my mom, it was not gray and boring drinking, Max bring me the paper drinking, Max get me some ice drinking, TV depressing and awful in the background. Everything was lit, with Ruth.

Things sort of changed for me after then—you know, you turn twelve, thirteen, you start messing around and fooling around with girls, you start getting tougher, working at getting harder edged and more sure of how far to keep yourself from people and more like you don't care about anything. You learn that. You learn to shut up. You learn only to say a few words that seem just right. So those years on from that night with Ruth and Racinda I dated girls and I, you know, got sick of them and had them calling me, or else wanted them and couldn't get them, but nobody shone the way Ruth shone for me then. Gripped me somehow. Lit me up.

Not until later, when I was eighteen, did I get that lit-feeling again and that, I guess *desire* is what you would call it, a want for something, a wanting that is like its own taste—the want is the taste in your mouth. That later want was for a bunch of things, a couple people, not just a girl. Racinda was around the second, later time too, incidentally, but that is all another story.

*   *   *

The truck pulled off just as Racinda and I got to the front door.

Ruth started crying and smashing around. It was scary and uncontrolled, she made the house seem flimsy again, even more of a sham.

I walked off the steps and in a circle on the lawn just to get that feeling off of, out of me.

Racinda stayed clear of her. Ruth sat down and bent herself over.

"Who does he think he fucking is?" Ruth said. "That fuck." Her voice thudded into the floor, her lips were inches from it.

"Ruth," Racinda said, her round face dotting a line in toward her sister, circling her from outside then zooming in, "They have HBO. I'll make you some macaroni and you can watch HBO upstairs."

"Fuck," Ruth kicked her foot into the wicker chair leg, hard, moving the whole thing, herself too. She gasped, surprised at her body's quick jump, and exhaled, started crying quietly.

"Come on," Racinda approached her slowly, touched her on the wrist and Ruth stood up. The traffic had died down, so it was quiet as I followed them back inside. I ran my hand over the forearm Racinda had held onto—there were four little white indentations, like crescent moons, in a line, but no blood.

*   *   *

Davey Maye had been the attendant at his dad's laundromat since the moment he could legally quit high school. I knew him cause we used to have to go there for laundry before we moved out of our apartment into this house. Tonight, he looked sadder and more confused than made sense to me. Even though he dressed like he was a greasy hesher and hung out with them, he had always been polite and jokey—his parents weren't trash but he was trying hard for it. He was the kind of person who would remember and practice stupid jokes on people, on people younger than him, and like forget the punch line and then tell it to you fifteen minutes later when you'd already forgotten what led up to it. He was sort of a little red faced and goofy, laughing sometimes before you'd understood what he said to you. But he looked depressed now, when he wasn't trying to be all dominating and get Ruth to leave with him.

I remember back at the laundry mat he would sometimes get real enthusiastic talking about something, something like how a glider works or what cars and television were going to be like in the Future to the point where it even embarrassed me, a little kid. Usually he would just hide his face in a newspaper there, though, surrounded by detergent and underwear swirling behind circles of glass, but he would also help fold sometimes, and carry bags out to your car. Now his eyes were red with crying, and his eyelashes seemed like a girl's—long and curled, the same weird ash color as his hair.

*   *   *

Racinda was the kind of person who cleaned while she cooked. Like compulsive. She had macaroni stewed up into a big orange heap in minutes while Ruth was upstairs.

"Get out the milk," she barked while she was looking around for bowls, "No not the skim, the real vitamin D kind. Where's the tablespoons? No the big ones. Don't you have real butter?"

When we got to the bedroom Ruth was all into my mom's clothes.

"Creature, look!" she said, "Look at these shoes!"

Ruth was wearing these giant platform clogs that my mom never ever wore but I had seen once during a yard sale. Ruth had put on long fake eyelashes and her lips were a pink color, shiny, so bright it was almost orange.

"You look pretty," Racinda said.

We all three sat on the bed, Ruth curled on her side, Racinda flat, and me sitting against the wall, we ate and watched more TV. There was something so nice about the slurpy, soft noises our mouths made on the food.

It wasn't long before Ruth dove back into the closet. She pulled out a purple dress—little filmy strings hanging off it in rows.

"It's so flapper," Racinda said to her and nodded like she approved.

Ruth stripped right in front of me, so I saw her tits for the second time. It was still exciting, but less than you'd think cause the scare of the first time was still in me. Racinda zipped her up, and Ruth climbed back in to the clogs.

"We should put on a show," Ruth said. She started sort of swinging herself around the room like a ballroom dance and the shoes banged the hell out of the floorboards. In a few seconds she was back at the closet.

"Racinda, there's gotta be something in here that would fit you," she said. "Look, try this."

She tossed this silky slip thing out.

"Oh jeez, look Max, you need something too!"

The purple dress on her was torn at the top of one of the lines of fringe, down on her ass, which was sticking straight up at us the way she was leaned in the closet.

She turned quick to face me and she held me in her pink shocking smile like she loved me the most of anything on planet earth.

"Max, do you want to dress up like a girl?" she said.

Racinda kicked me behind a pile of covers and I said okay sure Ruth, sounds good to me, cause I somehow knew however bad it would be it would be worse the other way.

*   *   *

I kept my eyes closed. Well I had to while she painted something across them, out the corners in curlicues, but for the rest of it, the hair and the all over the skin stuff, I didn't look either.

No, I said when I felt the hot pinch of an eyebrow coming out, *no fucking way*. I swung my hand behind me, aiming for Racinda, even though it was Ruth doing the torture in front of me. Racinda was the hair girl.

I heard Ruth laugh, I heard her wanting to rise to the challenge.

"You better not," Racinda said to her sister.

"Ouchy ouchy!" Ruth yelled at me. I didn't open my eyes, but she was close enough for me to feel her chocolatey breath on my nose.

"Oh it's okay," Ruth said, turning away, looking for something in the pile of makeup, "I'll just paint them on darker and we won't be able to tell they're a fucking rat's nest."

I couldn't tell who breathed first, me or Racinda, but there was a sigh then.

*   *   *

Ruth eyed me when I said I had to pee, but she let me go. In the bathroom, I took a look at myself in the mirror behind the john as I pissed. It didn't really freak me that bad, cause I didn't look like a girl, exactly, more like an old man trying real hard to be an old lady. White stuff was smeared and caked all over my skin. Black rings and whirls around my eyes, long fake lashes and the same orange pink lipstick Ruth had on, but outlined in a dark red, I guess to go for the look of a complete lunatic. On my head they put this little violet colored fabric hat with a circle of rhinestones in front. You couldn't see my hair at all, no natural hair on my head or my face, I noticed.

As I pissed, in the mirror behind the john, from the neck down I was a normal boy in normal underwear and jeans, I had a normal dick, I had a T-shirt that said "Drake Elementary Fighting Hens" on it, but my head got transferred there from the corpse of some old queen my mom could have been friends with back in her crazy San Francisco days.

*   *   *

Jerry. Jerry was the guy's name who would sometimes dress up when we went to stay in his apartment in San Francisco for the weekends. My mom's old friend. My mom and him would play all this like mambo music and dress him up and he would say, *Maxy, do my hair, wouldja* like some guido from New Jersey, that accent, and it was fun at first then got weird. He'd go out, and one of my mom's hippie boyfriends would come over and I would watch TV while they ate dinner. I would go to sleep and try not to hear them talking and kissing out there, try not to hear my mom talking about how hard it was to be alone with me and how much she hated my verbally abusive dad. Who I just don't feel like talking about right now.

I know now that you're totally not supposed to talk how my mom did about my dad around your kid, but she didn't know that then and she didn't know I was listening. Jerry the queen would like not come home until Sunday, and then usually my mom would complain to him about the hippie *and* my dad. *Jerry, you're the only man for me*, she'd say, and when I'd look up at her then she'd add in, *of course besides Maxy.* Jerry would pour her another mimosa and they'd play some more mambo, dancing together until we had to drive home at night. Sometimes he'd dance with me too, and it wasn't freaky or weird or anything, he was just being nice. *Oh come dance with your old Auntie Queenie, toots*, he'd say. It was a nice, fun place in that apartment when Jerry was back, the light inside and the feeling inside was all yellow and warm, and when he came back those Sunday mornings I never wanted to leave. But when it started getting into evening we had to. You could see the fog coming in from the ocean, breaking up the pink light of the sunset, breaking it in a way that made it even more beautiful.

*   *   *

"Oh my," Ruth said, "Looky here."

She pulled a bottle of wine and a bottle of tequila out from behind some shoe boxes in my mom's closet. We had a tea party. She only let us do the wine, she saved the tequila for herself, did a shot every twenty minutes or so.

I held myself back. I was still watching. Who knew what Ruth could do to me. I just moved and talked as much as I had to avoid her getting all freaked at me—I was good at this around drunk people from my mom. It was a tense sort of a thing to do, but it was actually kind of relaxing for me to do it because I understood how to. I pulled myself back away and made myself to be the kind of normal and the kind of unobtrusive she wanted.

But I wanted to go hug her, not even like sexual, quite, more just like I wanted to be as next to her, as close to her, as possible. I wanted her to cover me like a blanket. I wanted to put my fingers through her hair where its roots met the skin of her neck. But I stayed back.

"Some more, madam?" she would say to Racinda when Racinda's cup got empty and Racinda always nodded even though she winced with every sip. I hated wine, even then, but Ruth made me finish a cup of it. Of course, I almost puked, of course I almost did, but I held it in, and lifted my refill to my lips enough times for her to think I was really drinking.

"I want more," I would say, then when her back was turned pour it on the jade plant's dirt. After four times the holes in the bottom of the orange planter started to leak little rivulets of it out on the floor, so I faked a spill and hurried to clean it up before she could notice. I left the towel there to sop, it soaked up the stuff, thin purple blood, in big splotches that grew slower than she would ever notice.

Once Racinda passed out, some of the harshness left her sister, like she had less to prove somehow. Ruth sat on the floor with her dress lifted up over her thighs, ran a tumbling hand up and down her calves.

"Stubble," she said, "Ew."

I just looked at her. With Racinda gone I couldn't hide out so much. At all, really.

"Max, you would never date a girl with hairy legs, wouldja?"

I just shrugged. I pulled on some loose threads in the quilt and wouldn't look at her.

"Fuck it," she said. She took the tiny last sips of tequila from her teacup and stood. "I'm going to shave. It's just too nasty!"

With her first step she wavered, kind of like she was surfing the carpet. I hopped to it quick, got down there next to her and let her lean on me. But I was still hiding out, I was just aiding the drunken.

"Come on," I said. But I didn't know where to take her.

"Max, stopit," she said. She pulled herself off me, leaned in the doorway for a second, looking queasy as hell.

"Let's go downstairs," I said, "We can play my mom's old Zeppelin records."

"I'm shaving," Ruth said.

She grabbed the doorjamb tightly, solidly, then used it to push herself off from. Her pace to the bathroom didn't sway—she somehow didn't stumble. By the time I caught up with her she almost whacked my nose with the slam of the bathroom door.

But there was no lock.

I stood there and I thought maybe, maybe she will just pass out and maybe I will just be able to go downstairs and everything will be okay and normal and nothing more will happen in the screaming fight area. But then when I thought of just watching TV or playing Atari or just like reading old *Spidermans* I wanted to cry and this roaring feeling came up in my stomach and I knew I was not going to step away from Ruth. So then, then I stepped into it. Then. I stopped watching. I moved *in* to things.

I didn't say anything when I went in, and she just acted like I wasn't there, so, yes, I saw her tits for the third time. When she tossed the purple dress on the towel rack and got in the tub all she had on were her green and white striped panties. She set herself down quietly in the tub, didn't inch backwards when she turned the water on, even though it's always icy at first.

"Ew!" she said as she lifted the can of shaving cream off the porcelain tub edge. The bottom of it, the silver concave circle of its base, was grimed up. The white corner of the tub had all sorts of lint and stuff there.

She sprayed a line of it up each calf, slowly, so that it was a thicker thing snaking her leg and not a thinner one. It seemed strange to smell its limy, citrusy smell—something fluffy and creamy doesn't go with that smell, in my opinion. The shaving cream had a coconut and a lemon pictured on it, it was the men's kind, but I didn't even know that till later, till I had to start doing it myself.

Invisible drops of water flew up from the tub and made little holes, pockmarks, in the white foam on each shin.

Ruth let out a sound that was sort of a sigh, but had more song to it, and I knew the water was heating up. She leaned herself back and shut her eyes and I could feel the pleasure coming off her like heat. One of the stripes of shaving cream started to tumble apart, drip down her leg like an avalanche. Her underwear soaked up water and got clingy and see through.

When I heard her breathing slow down I shut off the faucet, slowly, so as not to wake her.

"Hold it," she said. The lips moved, but the eyes stayed shut.

She sat straight up. Her eyes were the most beautiful and terrifying ones I'd ever seen. Lit.

"You just hold it right there, *Max*," she said.

She turned the faucet back on.

"I'm not going to run around with a beard on my legs like some fucking French hippie," she said.

I shook my head slowly, like I was agreeing.

"Where are the new blades?" she asked me.

I got the packet of them, the neat little black and silver things in rows, out of the cabinet. The way I moved my body when I was around Ruth was different than usual—I kept my arms closer in, I walked more as if through a tunnel, avoiding the walls, compacting myself.

"Why doesn't your mom use the women's kind? The normal pink ones?" she said.

I shrugged.

I want to say that once she snapped the blade on the razor it glinted in the light and she laughed maniacally like Vincent Price, but it wasn't like that, even though it felt that way. She just hummed a song—a gentle, off key, made up, rambling song like a little girl would sing—rubbed the shaving cream into a thin coating, and began.

This was not television. Her legs had these amazing curves to me, the curve at the ankle and at the calf and then when she bent her knee. She caught me staring and sort of smiled when I looked away and maybe turned a little redfaced.

She edged back in the tub, away from the water. The pipes clanked a couple times, but other than that the only noises were that stream pouring out and hitting the drain, Ruth's little song, and my own breathing rustling through my nose.

The razor moved up each calf like a tiny silver lawnmower, clearing a thin path through the foam, then another, widening the clearing, so that more and more pink skin showed through.

I watched that blade shiver in her hand, my eyes fixed on it. The paths of skin snaked sideways in places, jagged lines that ran up against the into foam, ate into it.

By the time she got to the second leg, she was bleeding on the first one, in a couple spots, but just a bit, normal nicks. These spots, the origins of a few tiny circles of red and one narrow drip, seemed okay. Like they were the little tremors that happen when the earth lets off steam gradually, making the big one less likely or at least farther off in the future.

It took her a long time to finish. She sat very still as she did it.

*   *   *

I know I am a quiet person but that just doesn't help, knowing that. I sit there silent all the time and I wish I were one of these dudes who could come up with a lot to say but I am not that way. I'm the guy those guys befriend cause I'm like a vacation, a day sitting at some lake drinking beer and throwing a weighted, baited piece of nylon string into the water. I'm that water, and their thoughts and words and antics bounce off me like am radio signals, dopplering out and up. But what no one knows, I mean I barely even know it, is that sometimes I just soak it all up, the shit talk and the movement: everyone's drama sinks down there with the night crawlers and bothers the fish so much they lose their appetite. Like my mom, for one, makes me lose my appetite. But Ruth—Ruth made me understand how much I was starving all that time.

*   *   *

Disgustingness. Repulsiveness. Female revulsion, like when my mom's got nipple showing through her shirt. But also—that air around her body is something beautiful. And also—I wanted that thing as strongly as it pushed me far away.

*   *   *

When she leaned over to get the back of her calf I could see the little hollow on the inside of her thigh, right above the real meaty part. Strange—her little girl song and the way tiny dots of sweat were amassing above her lip and her forehead.

"Max I can't get the back of this ankle—will you do it?" she said.

As she lifted her leg over the side of the tub she slipped—I heard the wind escape her lungs—but she recovered by clawing the tub with her arms at crooked angles.

The way she looked up at me, I would have done anything, anything she asked, so I took the razor when she'd settled, handed it to me. I proceeded, carefully over the gullies where the tendon is, around and over the bone sticking out like something on a bird—a hard little wing down there.

I didn't nick her once.

"Do a little above, in back, too, right on, like the spine of it," she said.

She leaned back and shut her eyes.

So I had to hold her foot in my hand—lift the leg up to get to that part. She wiggled. As I turned the razor and aimed at the leaf-shaped smear of black specks, I saw, down in the tub, blood pooling, darker and more than just droplets.

I shifted my eyes back to the razor, hovering just under her Achilles tendon, before she noticed I was stunned.

"What?" Ruth said, "Are you going to shave it or are you going to stand around?"

"*Wait*," I said.

I turned, robotic, sped out of that bathroom with the silver razor in my hand and held it up, totally forgetting it, when I shook Racinda awake.

She was bleary and muddled still drunk but her eyes widened at the thing in my hand, and, I realized, the faggy makeup still all over my face. I lowered the razor to my side, and said:

"You gotta come, there's something wrong with Ruth." I was whining a little as I spoke.

She just stayed put.

"Come on!" I said. When I got frustrated and raised my voice I sounded a lot younger, I felt like a deaf person, or a person with an ear infection. My voice lost edges, sounds lost their sounds and blurred.

*   *   *

Curling, diffusing like smoke, the red mixed with the inch or so of water in the tub. It widened when she adjusted her leg on the rim. Some dappled her underwear, and that space on her thigh: half a Rorschach.

*   *   *

Ruth was concentrating hard on the water pouring into the tub. She let the slow stream fill her hands, then tumble to the drain with a thud. A filling, a release, repeating itself.

"Ruth, what are you doing?" Racinda said, slowing down her words at the end like she was trying not to seem drunk. The towel rack, this cheap aluminum thing, wobbled when she gripped it for balance.

Ruth's back was to her. Her feet were propped up by the spigot. She turned her head.

"Max was just helping me shave, you little fucking prude," she said.

Ruth was practically naked, and soaked, but the expression on her face—a sneer, but something less pointed than that, too—was dangerous.

"You're on the *rag*," Racinda hissed, then in a normal voice, "Ruth—come on."

Reaching her hand out to the toilet tank for support, Racinda stumbled, missed, leaned instead on the box of Kleenex, which slipped around on the porcelain. She opened her eyes and pinballed off the sink.

"I have to—" Racinda said, "I have—"

Racinda looked pretty, standing there nauseous. The sweat on her forehead had stuck slips of hair across it, and her face was softer. Her face had given up the fight, looked sort of helpless and overwhelmed, like a much littler girl's, or, well, like a little girl her own age, which was something she before now had been working so hard not to seem like.

Ruth back up at the faucet, filling her hands up, emptying them, silent.

Me just standing in the door, until I followed Racinda, defeated, back to the bedroom.

*   *   *

I couldn't sleep, not because there was a female in the bed who I wasn't related to, but because of that earlier feeling I had of the house being flimsy.

Just waiting for the wolf to come huff and puff at it. I had to stay awake to make sure this didn't happen.

I got up to check on Ruth, she had turned the water off right after we left her, but the window was still open.

She was lying in the tub, curled up, passed out. Before I shut the window I leaned in to hear her breathe, slow and quiet. I covered her with two of my mom's oversize beach towels from the cabinet behind the door. I ran up some suds of Ivory soap in my hands and got all the crap off my face until my eyes were stinging and teary.

Racinda, on the bed, was curled the same way, facing her sister from another room, bookends across space. I couldn't take it, the feeling brewing up in there, like magnetic revulsion between those two—pushing them that distance but also holding them there, keeping them from spinning away from each other—so I left. I put on a sweatshirt and my dad's old watch cap and got out of there.

*   *   *

I started leaving when I was real little and she would bring the hippies over, wearing their fringe and sometimes cowboy hats, and it continued through the tattooed face people, the man and woman from an island who would come over and chant with her, through the TM guy and the no white sugar no white flower no dairy nothing fermented dietician who cooked up big plates of spelt spaghetti and asparagus. I remember the smell of dust coming out of the old screen door as I leaned into it, the air forcing that dust through the metal pores up at my nose, and then the clean blue air outside, the grass dark with the first few rains, the color of my moms macrobiotic greens we always ate for awhile there, the dirt under the grass sometimes still evidently parched in places, though the two tire ruts had dirt that was darkened, dirt that could hope to be mud soon.

When I kicked the old wood fence post, dark brown strips chipped off, leaving raw pink strands, the guts underneath. I would kick and kick that thing, I did some real damage. An indentation. The sky would be gray when I started, metal and cold, a string of black birds would pin that grim sheet up there, I could hear the wind starting low and ending on a high, thin note.

*   *   *

Trying to leave those two drunk Christian girls, trying to breathe, I jabbed the back door with my elbow and pulled myself out into the oily light from the porch lamp. The shadows of moths flitted by, dividing it in sections against the darkness. The glazed cement landing all slippery under my feet. The night was deep and broad, cold, almost intolerable. I didn't want to kick that fencepost, so once my eyes adjusted to the dark I walked up the hill, just a bit, not far enough to really hear the coyotes. You could hear dulled howls, like echoes, almost, but they were distant, past the next bloated rise in the earth, not on this one.

I made my way to this crotchety old tree that in the summer stands black and gnarled, alone, against the honey-colored hill. Now it wasn't so impressive, now that things had greened.

Then I got to thinking about something weird.

I got to thinking about one of the hippie visitors, this guy Daniel, who had a bald head and a full beard. He would always lean down to me and talk some stupid shit—I must've been about six or seven when he came around—and his eyes were bright and moved around a lot.

It was a similar kind of feeling with me, that night back then, as now—shaky and unsure and in need of protection.

That night he was over, I was lying on my bed, watching the headlights from outside cross my dark walls, dragging shadows of the toys on my dresser from tiny shapes into huge, dissipated, gray masses. I could hear them downstairs, him and my mom, finishing their dinner, then touching their wine glasses together again and again. I could hear my mother's roaming laughter and Daniel's voice with all the mean supposedly gone from it, boiled out of it, you know, those hippie new age men who talk all soft. I flipped over and flipped over, got the covers near knots, and finally sat up, eyes restless, my hands stretching out the cuffs of Tom and Jerry long johns.

So I got up and snuck down the stairs, again stopped on the landing by what I saw.

My mother, her hair swarmed around a little, messy, unlocked her eyes from Daniel's twitchy ones and got off the couch to clear the dishes from the coffee table. As she bent over to pile the casserole dish on the serving tray, I saw him staring at her ass, just plain ogling it, the softness in his voice totally busted, like when you find out the Wizard of Oz is just a loser with a big amp.

Except I never had such high hopes for Daniel as Dorothy and her crew did for the Wizard.

My mom worked slow, with her ass sticking out like that, dropped a fork cause she was tipsy, and I started to sense that she knew he was looking.

Time slowed then, when he put his hand between her thighs, moved it up and down. I didn't know what to do. I noticed the smile under his thick moustache and it sickened me. I felt creepy all over my skin and in my stomach. She paused, stopped cleaning up, then pushed herself, just slightly, back against him.

I had to close my eyes. I couldn't move until they went into the kitchen, then I tiptoed.

It's like, my mom had said this guy Daniel was nice and not verbally abusive like my dad was to her before he left. This guy cried in front of me once, then said, "I'm glad you were able to share that with me, Max." And sure, this guy was like all soft spoken and touchy touchy and vegetarian and shit, but he made my mom cry eventually too. And he was lecherous, I saw it. *Typical*, my mom said, when she stopped crying over that guy. *Your typical male*, she said, blowing her nose.

He didn't swear like my dad or watch sports, but his niceness and sensitiveness were phony. I mean, if you're going to end up an asshole anyway you might as well act like a guy, not a pussy.

*   *   *

When I woke up—I don't think I was out very long—the coyotes were closer, melodic, so I walked real fast back to the house. What also kept my pace up was that all the house's downstairs lights were brighting up my path. The way out here had been dark.

The light surrounding the house looked watery, and I could see the bedroom through the upstairs window, I could see that on the dark quilt Racinda seemed drenched, floating, the cloudy, lacy nightgown she'd somehow tugged out of her overnight bag and stumbled her body into spread around her like a flower on a pond, her head leaning on a pillow, mouth open, dark hair against the black material of the quilt, straggly and spread out, just waiting there, just waiting for someone to drive by and roam the house for her, climb the stairs and pull her out of the water, dry her off and put her in a vase or flatten her in a frame. I thought I saw Ruth's hand, balled into a white fist, stuck across the bed from the left side of the window, but it turns out I just imagined that. Two drunk sisters, two girls, two drunk Christian girls passed out and floating was what I thought I saw, but it turns out I was wrong.

Just past our fence I heard my mom's old Zeppelin records going in the house, the scratches on the vinyl popping out into the night as if on an invisible, electric web. Davey Maye's truck was pulled into the driveway.

By the time I stepped onto the cement landing I smelled the weed and the cigarettes.

The screen door was opened wide, and I could see Ruth standing, leaned on the back of the couch in the living room, smoking. She was in the purple dress again. Her hair was wet on the ends, sticking out.

The left strap of the dress was broken now—its top edge slipped down her breast and showed crooked cleavage.

"How many times do I have to tell you, Davey?" Ruth said, she was all pissed.

Davey was pretty drunk, leaning in the doorway, smiling at her, real generous, not taking her angry voice serious.

They just stood that way, and you could feel that they wanted to just put their bodies together and start kissing, it was like vapor in the air, like water vapor that's about to collect on a cold glass.

Nothing to be done.

Ruth's posture got less stiff, more flirty. She hummed along to that Jimmy Page riff that is so famous, the one that seems to fall slow of Bonham's drums but then comes up to speed, sort of dancing with the drums and running from the drums at once.

"Ruth, where are we gonna go now?" Davey said. His words came out of his mouth like they were coated in peanut butter. Drunk.

"I dunno," Ruth said, her voice light and girly. She wasn't even looking at him. She was looking out the window at the shadows of shrubs shifting under the porch.

"I feel like I *know* you," he said. It made him wonder, you could see it.

Ruth swirled the tiny bit of honey colored tequila in her glass, held out in front of her awkwardly, like she forgot it, like she didn't want to touch it, like him looking at her so nice was too much. She set her glass in the windowsill.

"Yeah, well, you want some tequila?" she asked.

He started tickling her and they both started laughing then, *stop! stop!* she said, but she was laughing laughing, they were rolling around and some magazines fell off a side table and Ruth was squealing, so happy, giggling, but then when she saw the magazines on the floor she said *stop stop it*, but it wasn't like a normal person would say that anymore, it was like she switched, *get off me get off me get off me stop fuck fuck fuck* and suddenly it was just him down there, she was straight up like a daisy stem, and she flew around the living room suddenly, dusting off the surfaces with the bottom of her T-shirt, slamming into the kitchen and when she saw me hiding there she just whispered *oh hi Max*, and kept going, cleaning a dish and then flying back into the living room. She moved the turntable's needle to hear Black Dog again, but she lowered the volume, as if to indulge me, the spy hiding in the kitchen, so I could hear all of what was to come.

When she saw Davey on the couch there she got reminded of something and started going off.

You guys all just think I'm such a slut, and *I'm not and this place is going to be so so so so so so clean when they get back*, and *I am fucking responsible*, slamming her hand on some little smudge on the dining room table when she said *fucking*, and *they are not going to get rid of me by calling me an irresponsible slut, this place is going to be fucking organized.*

Davey just stared at her like he wasn't sure if all this had to do with him, the guy sitting on the couch, or not.

She started pulling the books off one of the shelves in the living room and started re-sorting them, alphabetizing maybe. *And you, you just think you can come on in here and. . .*

"What, girl?" Davey said, getting a little more annoyed.

"Here," she said, slamming a glass in front of him, "Have some more tequila. Nobody is going to say I'm rude and messy and not a good hostess."

Even the liquor seemed to run faster than it should have.

"Thanks." He settled in and read a magazine and sipped at it. She started tugging the furniture around in the dining room, rearranging.

"You need some. . . help?" he said, after about ten minutes of her shoving and swearing at the table, at the dresser that held the placemats and shit.

As he stood up he realized how drunk he was. He just stood there awhile. He'd say: "Oh. . . whoa. . ." He'd stop a few seconds then start again. So he sat back down and fell asleep.

Once Ruth had gotten all the furniture in the middle of the dining room, she told me she needed a little break, *okay Maxy*? she said loudly as she went over to sleeping Davey in the living room and got a joint out from the pocket of his cheap motorcycle jacket.

"Thanks, sweetie," she said. She patted him on the arm and, though she didn't notice for heading to the other couch, this seemed to bring him back from catatonia.

She put her feet up on my mom's glass-topped coffee table and lit the joint—she sucked in a long time but never coughed. She banged her leg against the side of the table over and over again, then stopped and slammed her free hand that way, not in *time* to the Zeppelin that was still on, but with her own ideas about rhythm.

Davey started talking, eyes sort of googling out then kind of settling into a daze in Ruth's direction.

"Ruth, you're so . . . little," he said, "So pretty. . . "

"Yeah, well, fucking thanks, Davey," Ruth said. Rolled her eyes.

"You are so little, so little and—" he said.

He tried to lean toward her and he knocked his tequila to the floor. It made a big stain on the white area rug.

"Fucking watch it, would you?" Ruth said.

Davey lifted his pudgy face to her.

"Ruth—" he said. He said it like a retarded person—earnest, with the vowels all stretched out and the consonants not quite finishing. So actually:

"Roo-oooth," is more like what he said.

But she wasn't having it. She snatched up the glass fast and stood up.

"You think you can just come in here all drunk and just make it look like I'm some huge mess, don't you," Ruth said, bending to stab out the joint. "You just think I'm like some little slut you can just—oh god, some little whore. You can just come in here and do what you like. I'm getting some towels. Fuck you."

She slammed back into the kitchen and grabbed like six feet of paper towels off the roll like I wasn't even there.

"Some little slut is what you think," she said to the spill—ignoring Davey—as she wiped it up. "Yeah, well forget you, Davey."

He was totally confused. He just stared at her as she patted the spill for like three whole minutes, hitting it and hitting it with one paper towel after another. She was kneeling on the floor, bent over, her back round like a turtle's, her face an inch from the spill.

He could see there was something wrong with her now. He got up to go over to help her clean. Big mistake.

As he took two steps over to her the plates stacked way over on the dining room table shook—he was a big guy.

"I'm sorry I spilled it," he said.

Tears were coming from him now, seeping down and into the corners of his mouth.

He wobbled, and had to feel his way along the back of the couch like a blind person, eyes focused nowhere in particular. Stooping, he patted the upholstery carefully, like the couch was a tiny pet.

I thought Ruth didn't even notice him, but then she twisted around fast to make an evil face at him.

"You touch me and I'll call 911 you motherfucking child molester," Ruth yelled, still on her knees.

He looked at her, thoughtful, even though he hardly seemed to be able to focus. Then he got back to work, tapping his way along the slipcover.

He stood above her and looked at her like she was the most beautiful thing he'd ever seen.

"You are so little and so . . . pink. . ." he said.

She turned up to him more slowly now, but still with that evil-Ruth face.

"What?" she said, but her nasty tone was about to crack.

"Just so pink," he said, "So—"

And she stuck her chin out, the curve of her cheek so perfect and white, her neck, and she knew she looked strong and beautiful but she started to cry then, her eyes weakening, her mouth tightening to try to stop it, but it was useless. The sobs took her over and she bent into herself some, melted, tried to right herself by getting mad at Davey again: *you just think I'm a slut, my mom just thinks I'm a—*

But it was no use. She closed her eyes and sobbed and sort of hugged her knees up to herself and cried and cried.

And after a minute, that's when he decided to lean in the three feet, above her, above the coffee table, that's when he tried awkwardly to hug her and make her feel better.

When she opened her eyes, all she saw was this huge drunk guy coming at her and she screamed in a tone that made me understand what someone means when they say "blood-curdling": it really does heat up your molecules, boil the juices of your body into something else for a minute.

"Max! Max--Max call 911! Rape! You—"

But I didn't. He wasn't trying to hurt her and nothing was going to happen. He was just trying to be nice to her, his thick arms, like low tree branches, reaching out, swaying:

And he tripped over the foot of the coffee table and started to fall on top of her. She screamed a long string of something that wasn't words and pushed him backwards, he kept falling, just that other direction, backwards, it felt like it took such a long time, every inch took an hour.

The corner of the glass coffee table was just waiting for him, waiting for the arrival of his soft temple.

Davey's arms knocked the Bible my mom had out, the maroon vase with twigs in it, off the table's glass top, into the wall, with a crash, but he couldn't grab onto anything for balance. He fell.

The look on his face before he hit was flat like the second before something catches fire.

She said words in her shrill voice but I don't know what they were.

Who could tell.

I heard my own breath, not just a whisper but with voice to it, rushing into me.

She turned to my high sound and didn't see him hit.

He gurgled, fell backwards and to the side. It was like a click, and then there was blood.

*   *   *

Head wounds really bleed. Head wounds bleed a lot.

The side of the coffee table and the corner of the area rug were getting expanded on by redness. The music was still going.

Ruth went around the coffee table the other way, avoiding him, storming, and acted totally unsurprised to see me there in the kitchen.

"You took off your makeup," she said, like she was calm.

A click in my throat.

"We're leaving," she said, "*Now.* Get the car keys," she said.

I could feel air all around my body and I could feel my stomach and other guts heavy in me and she knew all of this.

"GET THEM!"

It wasn't another curdle, but it was loud, riled up.

I just looked over at the basket on the microwave. That's all I did. After she saw them too, she jingled them into her fist and disappeared, hurling herself up the stairs.

Before I looked at Davey I turned the record off, lifted that old needle and stuck it back in its little forked holder. I watched, like always, to make sure the black vinyl stopped, stilled itself. Its stopping punctuated the night, somehow—I didn't want to lift my eyes from it because I knew the next phase was starting its engines and there was jack shit I could do about it.

Not real great, but he was breathing. I leaned down above him and could smell the old smoke and liquor odor coming out of him in slow pulses. Blood was coming off his rounded cheek into his mouth. His body was melded into the rug like it was glued there.

"My babysitter's friend fell," I whispered to the 911 lady, "He's bleeding bad from his head."

"Okay hon," 911 said, "You just hold tight. We've got your address here but what's your name?"

I told her.

"Is he going to make it?" I asked her. But then I had to hang up, because Ruth was coming down the stairs. There was a silence then, except for the stairs creaking one by one, slowly, and I asked again, in my head, *is he going to make it?* The 911 lady, fuzzy gray grandma-hair lady chewed her pencil and just stared at me in my head.

Ruth had an old suit jacket on over the dress, and Racinda folded over her shoulder. It took her awhile to come down the stairs, but on flat ground she moved like she had no extra weight on her—she moved like carrying her sack of potatoes sister was what she always did. She had no problem getting around the traffic jam of disorganized furniture blocking the way through the dining room.

She managed to grab the tequila with her free hand on our way out the door.

After I got adjusted in the backseat next to corpselike Racinda, I looked behind us at the house, and even though every single light was still on, it seemed dim and faded, muted, sinking into the night as the sound of the tires going on asphalt somehow propelled us away.

*　　　*　　　*

Ruth told stories. They merged into one long, intricate knot in your shoe-laces or hair, one elaborate thing I stopped following. With the radio off, there was just her voice and the rushing water sound of the car moving through the air.

We were in the desert, going east.

The stories had Vikings in them, is what I mostly remember, but the Vikings made it to Broadway and put on a magic show, and then joined the merchant marines. The chieftain and his girl chased each other from country to country on their ships, which sounded a lot like little speed boats when she told it but they were supposed to be big wood things with oars and sails. The ships, like some Texas Cadillacs, had bullhorns wired to the front.

She was one crazy bitch. I just wanted to watch her mouth move as she talked, I wanted to be up there next to her, my hand under hers on the wheel.

The story ended, well, just faded, then, with the Viking couple in their boat, headed for Atlantic City, New Jersey—Ruth just left it there, her voice softened as the chieftain explained to his lady about their budget—and her hands fell to the lowest curve of the steering wheel, as if to keep them up any higher required effort she no longer could put out. Her eyes flickered, but she forced them unnaturally wide open. She sighed.

As we passed a sign that said Reno, 47 miles, Racinda stretched her legs out so hard they locked at the knees—this was the first movement from her—and then she tried to curl herself into a little bug shape but woke up when the seat belt wouldn't let her. Her feet bumped me as she adjusted herself—she pushed off me for strength.

She almost said something as soon as she figured out we were moving, but then—

"Ruth, I have to pee," Racinda said. She was sitting up, mostly, now, but still leaning, floppy, into the door. Her hair splayed up against the window. But she knew exactly what she was doing. I could see it, feel the determination underneath the act.

Ruth seemed about to fall asleep. She took a breath like it put her out so much to take in the oxygen to respond, and said in a nasty voice:

"Well you should of thought of that before we left the house, shouldn't you?"

She accelerated and took a swig of tequila, holding the bottle between her legs to unscrew and rescrew the cap.

Racinda looked straight ahead at the passenger seat in front of her, kept her eyes level and still. It was creepy as hell, how unmoving all the parts of her were.

We kept going.

Ruth's chin would droop and then whip up again, and she would hum a little song to distract herself.

Racinda turned her head fast toward her sister:

"I want to ride up front."

The whine in her voice was something new that seemed brewed up from her hangover.

"Fuck you, Racinda," Ruth said, then, super sweet:

"Max, do you want to come up here?"

When I caught her glance, Racinda nudged her chin, just slightly, fast, toward Ruth.

"Okay," I said. I undid my seatbelt and scrambled over the high seat back.

The smell of my mom's closet and of shaving cream curling off Ruth made me want to sit right next to her, in the middle seat, and things were so weird anyway I might have done it, Ruth would've let me, just to piss Racinda off. But something repelled me from her, too, and it wasn't just the danger of her, her unknowable tides of nice and evil. I wanted to punish her, to push her away. To make her have to reel me in to her.

But she didn't. All she did was say,

"Hand me that Cuervo, sweetie."

Up front, I could see the dotted yellow line, metallic, reflecting our headlights in its own Morse code, before we passed it by and left it all alone behind us. I could see what was ahead of us: yes, the same.

Up there I could see the stars and so I said the word twinkle to myself over and over again, till it became some other word I don't really remember.

Twinkle. What does that mean, even?

She swerved.

Her head dropped and didn't rise right away and we sailed into the other lane. Racinda screamed a second before our car crossed the line, though, and there was no one else anywhere, no other headlights to indicate life in the desert besides us three.

Ruth noticed and straightened us out.

"Well, shit, Racinda, don't wig," Ruth said. The muscles in her arms popped up a little as she steadied herself against the steering wheel.

In the rear view I could see that same frozen face on Racinda back there, except now her eyes were wet. She ran a hand under her nose when she was sure Ruth wasn't looking—I heard the sniffle but Ruth didn't, I'm sure.

And then finally, Ruth started giving in to sleep.

We both felt it coming, me and Racinda, when Racinda sneezed back there and Ruth did hear it that time and rolled up her window. She'd softened. The tide was going out again.

A lullaby began—it was the same kind of girly song Ruth sang in the bathroom, twirling through different keys, I think, and not finishing itself. This song was a different color, though—muted, less flirting. I could feel Racinda wedging her foot under my seat. I could smell the sand in the air.

I looked over at Ruth and she was so beautiful—the night with its thousand light-specks behind her head was her perfect back drop.

My seatbelt came unlatched silently, and I leaned over against her. Now her song was to me too. The strings of the purple dress wiggled against my face when I adjusted myself, touching her.

Terrified to move, I stared at the radio knobs for the longest time. My head was against her side, under her arm. I could hear her song inside her, through her bones and skin.

It slowed. Everything. The song and the car and time. When I felt her body shift into dreaming I sat up and knocked her thigh, gently, off the gas before she could veer us leftward. Then I took the wheel and was surprised at how strong it was, how much resistance it put out to me as I directed us sideways into the shoulder's gradual ditch.

*   *   *

Racinda and I slept next to each other, on top of each other, stuck to each other, my sweatshirt covering us for warmth.

"What about Ruth?" I said. It was somehow colder than when we were driving.

"Touch her," Racinda said, and Ruth's skin was hot.

The sky could have eaten us, the sand could have. We slept but I woke up when Racinda did, thirsty, and she woke when I did, and we got through the night that way, sipping at the tequila which did no good for the thirst, dozing again. With the gray dawn sunrise, the cop leaned in and Ruth, barely awake, hummed her songs, her stories, up and down musical scales she made up herself. The cop's harsh words chopped and chopped at her music, and my fingers bound Racinda's as hard as hers did mine, both terrified of losing that song, of losing Ruth's link to the night air.

We've got three juveniles in a vehicle here thirty miles east of Truckee. The crackling and sputtering, the wet sparks of his radio broke up Ruth's talk, and as she rubbed her eyes and let the cop carry her out of the car she quieted down. We gasped, breathless without her.

BOOK TWO

There aren't any roots. . . so they lived cutting off the complicated and replacing it with the simple till there was little left.

ZELDA FITZGERALD

9

THANG

SACRAMENTO, 1991-1992

Racinda

It started in the shadow world of the bathroom. It started with lipstick. With a new dark lipstick, with leaning just slightly over the filthy sink, with the green watery light like something polluted. The portal, that bathroom. But then, it also started with Max. And it's always started, and ended, with Ruth.

"Is that lipstick, like coated in rubber?" Lisa said. Her hair was ratty and had dark roots. Her own lipstick was trying for the color I possessed, but it suddenly paled. It was a cheap imitation of mine.

"Yeah, it's rubber," I said. I had been looking at her in the mirror but I had to turn my eyes down.

"What kind is it?"

She didn't look at me either. She leaned over the sink, in closer to her reflection, licked her thick violet kohl pencil and dragged it across a lid.

I told her.

"I got it in the city the other weekend—all their stuff is rubberized." I said. I remembered to put it on—my hand had been paused between my face and the mirror. I fixed my eyes at the crux of my top lip.

She turned to me—I watched the reflection of the airy bones at the base of her neck, her shoulders sharp enough to cut the space open for her to move through. Her bra straps showed from her tank top and I could see the red lines from where they dug in to her before she'd shifted them.

"Can I see it?" she said. I gave it to her. What else could I have done. She didn't bother to wipe her own lipstick off, just covered it over with the redder, blacker, better version that I possessed, moving gloss across her lips like a curtain consuming a blank movie screen at the end of the show.

"Thanks," she said, handing it back to me, and she walked out.

My big plaid shirt was unbuttoned far enough for me to sling it back on my shoulders—they were so much rounder than hers, I am so much shorter than she is. My hair is not blonde and not brown, my face is fine but plain. Not extreme, not lush, not striking. The stuff on my lips made my skin seem ruddy now despite the greening factor of the light. I mean, on her it looked gorgeous in a slutty, dramatic way, even though all that clear skin was from a bottle, was pasty, really. Still. Its rubber case that had seemed so rock star now looked like a little plastic party favor, the kind you get eight of for a dollar.

What got me through it was caffeine, I think, three-dollar coffee drinks as meals, the sugar more than the caffeine, and the cigarettes that gave me a reason to stay alive another twenty minutes. At least I had a craving to satisfy.

All high schools are vortexes, and maybe I was a vortex too, incapable of seeing or finding anything interesting in the dry, suburban, Californian world. The pickup trucks, the flat stomachs, the white push-up bras, the yellow and blue bumper stickers from some radio station. The teams. The lockers. The drinking games that involved bouncing an object into a cup. I had one realm inside of myself, and then the regular world that I lived in. These never converged. I tried, but gave up early, retreating: silence being infinitely preferable to awkwardness, rejection, desperate boredeom.

Don't get me wrong, I was picking up some things in books, and I was pretty close to gleeful, actually, while shoplifting. Thank god that clothing yourself, being able to tell the difference between "foxtrot" brown lipstick and "luminesce" brown lipstick and "gnarly" brown lipstick, this sort of thing, can take up so much energy. They dump all that on girls, that sweet need to preen, the intricate, endless, colorful, dramatic creative labyrinth of getting to pretty, so that the howling underneath our lives doesn't turn us into a true public health hazard. Or whatever.

The beginning, the portal—the lipstick in the mirror. The push up bras that happened later kept me sane at my job at the copy store and at home. The new sense of thinner, tighter clothing. The thicker heels and platforms and straps edging up my ankles on shoes. New things. I learned not to underestimate that. She taught me.

*　　　*　　　*

The silence in my house, ever since my sister disappeared, has had a light blue feeling to it, purplish, cool on the skin. My mother is always lurking, in this pale light, and I can feel her eyes and her prayers—ineffectual, except in her ability to cling so tightly to me. In response, I go red, loud, whatever. I go choppy, I work in bursts and fits, jagged movements. I leave and I return loudly, quickly, often, stomping my greasy motorcycle boots in black streaks across the white linoleum kitchen floor.

"You just don't look at the positive," my mother says. She says things like this to me. She is polishing silver and watching a Lassie rerun, which always makes her cry. Her favorite movies, as well, always feature some sort of animal hero.

"You can find a black cloud in any lining, can't you?" she says. Then she hugs me, like there is nothing wrong, like my father and my sister, half of us, aren't gone.

"That is so *not true*," I say, and I lapse into the bily teenage litany—I know how it sounds when other teenage girls venomize at their mothers, and I know how awful it is, but I still can't help but indulge. It's ugly, but I do hate her so viciously that most days I can't let a lobotomized comment like that one fly. I spew dark, spiky words at her, I hit her soft spots, she yells at me, starts crying, and goes to her car for some dumb, toxic errand.

This is how it always goes.

"That is so not true," I say "If you haven't noticed, there *is* some kind of black cloud going on here, Mom. Ruth and Dad got away and I am here stuck with you because I am, well I don't fucking know what I am, it's not cause I like this Jesus crap or anything. You gloss over this shit and blame it on me and expect me to take care of you."

"You have no respect for me," she says between breaths, her eyes focused away from me.

My jaw drops in indignation before I light into her again:

"How can I respect someone who tells me 'you see a black cloud? That's not helping me. There are bigger problems here than my bad attitude . . . '"

"I've had enough of your abusive language," she says, "I have people who respect me and know how wonderful I really am," she says.

And then she leaves, gets in her Toyota and drives to the Circle K for a chipwich and a diet raspberry ginger ale before she cruises around a long time.

It can't be helped. It is this way, there's nothing to be done. Or, at the very least, I can't think of what else to do.

I turn on the television and eat some of the diet cookies she keeps on hand before it's all too depressing and I have to go outside and smoke seven cigarettes.

She comes home at 6pm when I am bolstered in my room, on the bed, wrapped up in my blanket, feeling the window lights and streetlights shivering out in the night, seeping into such a comfortable sparkling black sleep that comes in waves and then, once, shudders just a bit when the front door locks.

*   *   *

"I studied for chem at Dylan Reed's last night," Marie said.

My supposed friend Marie was leaning on the pole next to my locker.

"Rad." I said. I was throwing binders onto a pile of black sweaters I kept bringing to school and taking off in the middle of the day and forgetting about.

"Fine, Miss Grumpalot. Whatever," she said. "You don't have to be jealous. There's nothing going to happen."

She was right on the second count, and she knew it, but wrong about me being jealous. I looked up at her, at the button down shirt shoved into a pair of khakis, and her hair that no product could help, and the uneven spread of pink blood that formed continents, ugly continents, under the her wide round cheeks.

"Sorry. It is rad. That's cool," I said.

She was nice to me and she was all I had even though I thought she was the most boring girl in the world. I looked at the amazing poster of Sinead O'Connor in my locker, the amazing poster of Chuck D and I held my breath for one second and I said please. Please get me to my world soon.

And then, very soon after that, it started.

Max and I barely said hello in the hallways. We did, though. We knew the old things about each other, and at certain moments the tenor of the *hi* was a barrier to this knowledge, a necessary defense in the harsh hallway, the treacherous high school hallway, where to show a crack meant trouble. Marked you succulent, juicy bait: never went unnoticed. A glance always caught you. But once in awhile—in a carnival moment, something different when the usual rules were disintegrated and shifted—a fire drill, say—I'd get a lithe relaxing in my voice or my eyes. I'd sigh, "Hi Max," with a tone that said, God, I'm so weary from all this stupid shit, not to mention a crazy mother, and I know you've got one at home too. A fire drill. Or at the jock parties my dull friend Marie would bring me to—she was the manager of the football team and the lacrosse team—Max and I could sometimes drum up a little friendlier conversation, one of the few I'd have before walking home by myself or maybe being driven by some retarded but socially and chemically useful friend of Marie's.

So one day when Marie and I stopped for Diet Coke at the 7-11 on the way home from school, I saw Max hanging out in the parking lot. Marie waited in the car.

"Racinda," he said, rolling a Drum, not even looking at me, "We're going to hear this band tonight, Ally's friend Shit is playing McAbernathy's tonight, so if you want to come with—"

He was leaning against the wall, and his skin was perfect, white and olive and smooth like a girl's, pale as if the sun here that drives me so crazy somehow can't get near him. He is a good looking boy, if not well groomed, and that always surprises me, the good-looking part I mean. He hunches over himself like girls do, trying to hide their breasts at the same time their $10.99 midriff shirt is trying to show them off. Except all he's trying to show off is his ability to not talk too much and to smoke a lot. The skin of his face—white with violets and blues underneath—and his brownish hair and his icicle eyes remind me of winters in Pennsylvania, the grays of the sky and the stark trees and the way it seems you can go without words for days. Not like here, where I am always squinting at the glare, sweating a little but not so much that I have to sit down, here where there isn't any silence that moves between people.

But I don't like to think about Max like that. It's weird to think of him any deeper than as someone I pass in the hall and know a few things about.

Max's friend Ally, who I knew had a thing for me thanks to Marie, who keeps her ear perked for anything that might energize me socially, appeared from around the side of the building. He didn't see me at first because he was buttoning his fly and doing his belt, which took him awhile to get the three little leather straps into their heavy chrome buckles. When he looked up he blushed.

"Oh—hi Raceeenda," he said.

He stuck his hand out so I had to shake it. I had tried to convince myself he was attractive a few times before, but then he always had to say my name like he was taking Spanish 101. It made me want to tell him to go back to metal shop.

"Hi."

"I like your leather jacket, those—what are those?—spiders? are rad," he said. He traced a finger up my side and smiled. I smiled back.

"They're embroidered," I said. "It was three dollars in a thrift store."

Ally was almost tall, not as tall as Max, though. He leaned his wheaty hair against the warm cobblestone stucco surface of the building, and the arc of his skin was golden, lit there. You could see how he would be cute if he cleaned himself up. My body suddenly felt uncontained—my skin wanted to be held with pressure, pushed by the light inside a boy. Not necessarily by him—something about night air and a little tipsy, that's what I wanted. The truth is that both of them were getting to me, this nice attention, and that's upsetting because Max was supposed to be this little boy to me.

"I asked her," Max said.

Ally leaned next to him on the 7-11, his body thicker, more like a grown man, making Max look skinny and young. Made Max shrink. Looked at me and then looked away.

"But she didn't say yes or no yet," Max said, his big long fingers neatening the Drum he was rolling.

"You should come with us," Ally said, his eyes all big in my face, "It's Shit—he's my old bud, but now he is doing all this weird-ass art rock shit. I mean, I think you'll like it. He's got this single released in England and so he's starting to gig around here."

He looked at me like he wanted to be gracious, like he wanted there to be a door to open for me, something he knew he could do that would be nice and would be appropriate.

"His name is *Shit*?" I said.

Ally nodded.

I looked away—at Marie in her Honda Civic. She was scrunching up her face, mouthing the words to a song on the radio and the sad thing was I could tell immediately which one. I could tell that in a verse and a half she would light a cigarette from the glee.

"Sure," I said, smoothing my jacket against my hips, feeling the red thread, the ivory dashes, of my spiders on my fingertips. I loved that jacket—dark blue leather, flared just a little over the hips. Too hot for it, really but its embroidered spiders up the side and around the back were so beautiful to me I was willing to sweat.

I got shy and sort of looked at the pavement, the flattened orbs of gum, blackened, making patterns there.

"Cool. I always thought you were the kind of girl that is into that *weird* stuff, I mean, not like weird weird but like *cool* weird," Ally said.

I was trying to ignore the image I was having of a surreal camera angle on Ally, the sense that he was so absurd he should have been the before example in a zit cream ad. He was sweet, I was trying to remember that, but instead I saw just this boy in a man's body, Ally, in the middle of the frame, silent, a puzzled and eager to please look on his face, a big red nasty pustule on the tip of his nose. Even though he had no zits either—he and Max, gorgeous skin twins, miraculously avoiding the pollutants that assailed them from their lungs, their pores, their intestines, their brains out here in the fumey parking lot all the time.

"We'll come get you at 9:30," Ally said.

"I'll meet you here," I said.

Max pushed himself off the ice machine—really like inertia was *such* a problem for him—and got in my face, all spazzy just to be spazzy.

"Moms want you to stay home and pray?" he said, in this near-mean tone, then sauntered inside the 7-11 to steal some more "food."

I just rolled my eyes.

Ally crisped his chin on one shoulder, glided it on a very masculine, alluring arc to look down toward the other one. The commercial-vision vanished, and I thought, *maybe.* His eyes had an avoidance that was just lovely, pulled me in like the word *no* even though it wasn't mindfucking, it was shyness. He was shy, and even though he was too rough for me— would dump some weeping, some drunk sad thing about his family on me probably, or some long litany about taking mushrooms at an Allman Brothers concert—*still*, the way just one of his bottom teeth was crooked and his cheeks were so gold too . . .

And I needed an opening. It had been hard for so long. I mean, I had mean little thoughts like Ally should have stayed in metal shop but I think I needed a sliver of light, even if its source was a cheesy ass disco strobe, a blacklight in some no-future stoner's bedroom, the centerpiece of a shrine to Aerosmith or Rush or Eddie Van Halen.

*   *   *

Abernathy's was so dark, except at the stage, that you could hardly walk without hitting a wobbly, tiny table or the ankle of someone you never saw. On the stage a fat woman in her late twenties was whipping a short tanned man with a guido haircut. He had little artificial-looking muscles on his arms and chest and looked out of place, like he could be selling car stereos, or designer ties at Nordstrom. His leather pants looked like they should be immobilizing, but didn't seem to be constraining him—he lunged away from the whip and toward the microphone alternately. His boots had platforms and heels, not unlike Prince's footwear, I noted. The woman's generous thighs showed above her boots—miraculous stilettos—and below her long corset. Stage-lights pushed a deep blue oil shine from her leather, and some kind of irregular disco ball, its mirrors smashed into jagged shards, lobbed cells of yellow-white around them in drunken ovals, a whiter light pulsing from behind.

All this light moved in and out of an industrial noise loop—banging metal, feedback, and Shit singing into the mike in a raspy low voice—he was saying *something* but there were no words I could make out. He would sort of run from the whip-woman, bounce away from her, but then for the longest time he lay on his stomach, screaming lyrics, lifting his head up off the edge of the stage to eye us all under the lights. I thought it must hurt his neck—but since he didn't flinch from the whip, even, I wasn't so worried.

There were videos playing on about seven old TV sets of different sizes; people were getting killed and blow jobs, people were getting fucked in the ass, people were screwing dogs. Women, were screwing dogs. And getting killed. And I wasn't even looking—I got this information from when I had to look around the room to see where I was going—I avoided the screens. It was supposed to be avant-garde or something. I let Ally bring me a whole bunch of Tom Collinses, which is what I order when I don't know what to order. I let him put his arm around me. I sipped quickly and I locked my eyes away from any of it but the whip.

The whip woman: a line of bangs hitting white skin, the dark lips in a false, showy-shy smile. Sometimes snaking her shoulders, opening her mouth *ahhhh* after she snapped the thing with a sharp downward cut of her arm, starting at her elbow: she was trying to look like she enjoyed it. Running her free hand from her hip to her breast. But she wasn't. She was window dressing, she was a doo-wop girl. Shit *was* enjoying it—not the whipping, really, not like in any sensual way—thrilled with every moment of the show, loving each place on the stage he had to run to next, loving each indecipherable lyric. The whip woman looked bored, but kept smiling, snaking, rubbing her thighs together by circling her hips.

I watched the whip's black length curl out and switch, I watched its splayed tip crack between momentum and inertia. An empty space, then a line, a snap, a hook, a retreat. Wherever he went, she whipped him.

But I couldn't look at her anymore. She was too fake, too embarrassing, too Vanna White. I cringed, and my eyes drifted to the stuff on the TVs. It seemed fake too, but not as immediately fake because it was removed, distant, not live—I didn't have to feel embarrassed for the person here in the room. And it was serious, it was scary. *Not* for Vanna. You could see the women screaming, faking, did they want to be having sex with these men? No, but who could tell the difference. The blonde's soft face, a close-up, turned around over her shoulder, on her knees, her mouth wide, saying *yes* but it is a lie. To a handheld camera, lower quality, men in khakis tying another man in khakis to a chair. To a birdlike woman, black hair feathered against her temples, her frail eyes looking up, amazed, open, then down, demure, scared, then up, so grateful at what he, an incarnation of the devil, can give her, as he drives his dick into the back of her throat. I moved away from Ally then, acting like I had to really search for my cigarettes, acting like I had to tie my boot, and I didn't let him lean in to me any more after that.

I sat in the ladies room for as long as I could without annoying anyone. I tried to think of something soothing, but the only thing was Button's garden, and it made me want to weep. Home, I thought, think of home, but avoiding the garden, avoiding Ruth, all I happened on was our living room here in Sacramento—it still seemed new though we'd been there years by now—, the couch, closing my eyes on that couch. If I opened them, in my head, all I saw was my mother's Jesus on the wall, not the big, gentle charcoal drawing of him but the smaller oil portrait, on the cross, saw the colors of the nails and the blood and the way you die from asphyxiation if they crucify you, the way you die from lack of air, actually, instead of all the flesh wounds.

"Dude, Benjy is a nut!" was what Ally was yelling at me three times before I heard him. Ally wasn't trying to act like he wasn't a part of it—he didn't need to like defend himself in that way, because it was like a foreign country to him, and that fact was as obvious as that he was speaking English. "Benjy is out of control," he said.

"Who's Benjy?" I said.

Max had his usual stunned, teary look. His eyes were just so big and naturally watery it always seemed there was a deep ocean in him, something sweet to him, but he always had this look, even moments when he was a gross macho slut like this, ogling the big mama in the corset. He didn't seem to notice the TVs.

"Shit. Shit's Benjy. Benjy's Shit. Me and Benjy both played on the championship soccer team. He graduated a couple years ago," Ally said.

Ally's voice was flush with the bar, the stage; he was bouncing with the heavy bass of the tape loop—his whole body would start to thrash around when the big clanging metal crashing noises shot up from the feedback.

I watched Max's eyes drift to a screen showing a mans hand shoving a woman's face and mouth up and down on what was supposed to be a penis but looked more like an arm. I watched him not react to it, but just glide his face back toward the stage, run his hand to the back of his neck, sort of work that place where the back of his head met his spine with his fingers, and I knew then that he was nervous, not bored, when he did that.

Benjy/Shit stood up after running his tongue around the knee of the whip woman, introduced himself as Shit, and after starting another loop on the synthesizer got himself and the whole room moving. The girls with something to prove stayed in the mosh pit as long as they could.

Ally and Max went in, I could see their heads, their arms once in awhile. One girl, then another, left the pit, ended up in a line with me between barstools against a long, tall table, almost a counter. I couldn't see so clearly when the pit really got going, and I didn't want to talk to these girls. A couple of them were deadened, like me, a couple looked eager and excited, like the whip woman: one, then another, went back into the pit only to be tossed out, hand on bruised cheek, gently cupping bruised forearm—*ow, ow,*—but unspoken. Circling the red plastic stick around the ice in a glass, smoking a cigarette.

The editing on the TVs got choppier as the show went on, faster, so I had more freedom to look around—mostly the TVs blurred in the background. A few shots registered with me, though: it *wasn't* just porn—there was weird docu-drama footage of men getting shot, of men getting eaten by rottweilers. Shaky, handheld, homevideos.

I was sober, and sweating, when it was done.

After the show Shit invited Ally to his place. Max glided his mom's old Chevrolet Special through the lanes of the freeway, so stoned that he was driving too slow and Ally had to keep telling him to speed up, the minimum was forty. I made Ally sit up front, supposedly just to do this sort of driving management. I tried to adjust my black pantyhose (you didn't think I was the type of girl to wear nude hose, did you?)—tugging all the way up the leg from the toe of my boot where they bunched. Max floated the car up the boulevards of a development called Miller's Ridge where the houses were worth at least a mil.

"Um, Max," I said, my nylons' waistband still sagging down uncomfortably on one side, "Where the fuck are you going?" I was agitated and I wanted a cigarette but I also wanted my underwear not to be bugging me.

"No, he's right," Ally said, "This is where Benjy lives."

Nobody was home, no lights were on at Shit's giant mansion, so we had beat him there, which made sense since he had all the TVs and that gear to load and the dominatrix to drive to Florin Road so she could get up for her job as a crossing guard in the a.m.

"I knew we should have got food before—I don't know where anything is out here," I said.

A pure and easy hatred of these awful houses, their bare silicon breasts of hills, carcinogenic drywall, water- and oil-sucking, right-wing voting inhabitants filled me so fast I barely felt the flip side, which had to do with the fact that in Pennsylvania, my memory of Pennsylvania, the people who lived in houses like this somehow did not get away with it and that there were trees and wet air and no depressing, desert swathes of brown dirt all over the place.

Ally, pleasantly stricken and worried, looked back at me. He was so hyper it was totally annoying me. I didn't know why I ever thought he was cute. I guessed it was cause he was one of the few boys who'd shown this much attention, dating attention not slut attention, to me before. His old girlfriend, Deanna, was kind of thick—definitely you know, *not* skinny, and definitely thicker than me—and everyone said he was so devoted to her.

He was a boyfriend type, clearly, but he was incredibly irritating already.

"Oh it's no big deal, I'm not going to starve or anything," I said. "Max, will you smoke me out?"

Max hesitated. Packed a tiny bowl with at least one stem I could see, the fucker. Fuck you Max.

"Did you see those video screens?" Max said, handing the bowl back to me without even looking at me. I held it up to a patch of light and sifted through the scrag to pull out the stem.

"That was some sick shit," Ally said. "Shit does some of that stuff himself, films some of that stuff."

They weren't talking like they really would be if I weren't there but they were still acting to some degree like I didn't exist.

"Films the porno?" Max said.

"Yeah, the porno, but not the other stuff. The stuff that's like fake violent."

"I don't think it was fake," I said.

"Like it was *Faces of Death*?" Ally said.

"That shit was fake," Max said. He cranked down the window and then rolled it back up again.

"I don't think it was. It was too random and shitty looking to be fake. I think they really killed those people. You never heard of snuff films?" I said.

"You weren't even watching it," Max said, smoothing his pant legs down, fidgeting with the steering wheel and the ashtray, "Hey, where's my bowl? Don't bogart the bowl."

"I haven't even lit it yet you fuck," I said, "Ally do you have a lighter?"

I could feel the green filling me, the lit green, burning like red burns but it's so *not* red, and then the release of black night filling me, expansion like the edges of the universe, billowing out. The feeling of oil spilling into clear ocean. I took about three giant hits just to get at Max, and I tuned the chattering boys out. I looked out the window at the hateful houses, their breakfast wings, their window seats, their atriums, their skylights, their gardens' hidden irrigation, their pools, their hoops, their invisible nighttime asphalt. The girls who lived in these houses—I hated them, but I could see myself, eleven years old, thirteen, trailing behind them, cut out of their row by their steps, by their nonresponses to whatever I said.

That stomach-wrenching anxiety I nestled into at every slumber party, after we moved here, after Ruth left. Just hoping they wouldn't make the underground humiliation in my aloneness obvious—a finally spoken truth about my sister's slutty habits, a lie about some humiliating, bathroom detail and me.

I wanted those girls but I hated those girls.

I didn't even like them, they had nothing I wanted except the fact that they didn't want me and they did want each other. It wasn't the same way I had chased after Ruth, who actually had the power of escape, the power of bringing color and story and sex and joy and movement and a scream that banished my mother's gray simmering to our stony house in Pennsylvania.

Ruth I wanted to understand. These girls, I just wanted to pass with.

I couldn't look at the night suburbs anymore, but I couldn't find anything else to look at besides the interior details of Max's stupid car, so I closed my eyes.

I saw Button. Her mouth was all flat and lonely. I felt so bad for not visiting her more often, but she was practically comatose now, and it's not like my mom had the money for a ticket. Button was the only normal one, of the whole bunch, I mean I guess Elmer was too but he was always quiet anyway, and we were all so tangled, my mom and Ruth and I, it wasn't like something a man in our family would ever really have been able to sort out. It was between the women, we couldn't tell who was crazy because it was like the three of us were all one person. My mom, though, it started with her craziness, that I was so furious at, that I swore and swore at in those stupid fights, and that I then hugged, tried to soothe away. But it was bigger than me, whatever it was that had happened to my mom, whatever it was that made her like that, so sad, so *apart* from everything, so frail and fragile and weak. She didn't have even like a real family growing up, just foster care, and the places she stayed the longest—from the bits she's told me—were not nice places.

Without Ruth, I could pull myself away from my mom enough to get myself to a bar watching snuff films, to get myself back to Max's mom's convertible, to get myself out into a lost night with boys who weren't borrowing a kidney or a lung or a heart from me, like my mom did, like Ruth did. That's what I could accomplish: *away*. For awhile, that was enough just to get by.

"Racinda, where the fuck is that bowl?" Max said.

I shoved it up at him, aiming for his temple. I felt the bowl hit him there and it was the most satisfying event on planet earth.

It was pure, shining luck that the Miller's Ridge security jeep didn't catch us, sweet smoke pouring out the cracked window, in that half hour or however long it was.

After Shit's van drove up, I followed Ally out of the car. We shuffled behind Shit up the flagstones and I noticed little un-native pansies nowhere near wilting, so watered, in neat little rows, well-mulched. These sorts of flowers are so stupid in dry California. I got another flash of Button, I felt her, and I had to quash it down, the giantness of her.

Standing on the porch, under the night-shadow of an ionic pillar, Ally complimented Shit on the video footage, and Shit said he'd had to go to Mexico on a special trip to buy the snuff films before he could edit them together with the porn at the cable company's public access station.

"They are real people being killed?" Ally said, "Like *Faces of Death* but worse?"

"Yeah—the public access people don't monitor if you edit at strange hours. You know, most snuff isn't actually porn, isn't sexual," Shit whispered.

I could see that Shit's hair was wet and gelled—he'd showered—from how it glinted in the halogen porch light. He was patting his pockets for keys.

"Really?" I said, not looking at him, my eyes completely seduced by the way even the welcome mat even screamed luxury—a deep teal color, sea of soft fibers.

Shit's nails were clean on his keychain, and he was wearing a fake Gucci watch. He had changed out of his leather pants which were now, I assumed, in the plastic garment bag slung over his shoulder. Instead, he had on a gray tee shirt tucked into manufacturer-faded blue jeans, tapered slightly like people did it back in the eighties.

"Shhh—" Shit said, looking for his key on the full ring, "You'll wake up my parents."

Stoned, I sat on a silky loveseat and moved the pages of a Spiegel catalog to see the creamy glare of the track lighting bend on the slicked-up print. Someone handed me a Rolling Rock that a) did nothing for my cottonmouth and b) was the definition of anticlimax at every sip. I started obsessing over wanting to take my boots off, my socks and twist my toes into the cottonball texture of the gleaming ivory rug that seemed huge, a tough cloud brought down to protect the virgin pine boards underneath.

The boys were sitting on the fake empire couches and chairs, talking as boys will, soundproofed from the hallway, a feature Shit's parents had insisted on when they built the house.

Shit's tour dates. The championship soccer team. Whether Sub-Pop was over, was selling out (Ally quiet there, clueless),

It wasn't Stockton in 89, it was Tulare. That goalie with the missing teeth was fucked up. . . you remember man how McAllister took that . . . Nah, it's not over. . . not just like that bad to some big conglomerate. Doesn't matter what those couple bands do. All those other dudes are still going to stay up there. . . . My moms lets me drive it, yeah, but it's not mine. . .just at night sometimes when she's like not paying attention I take it out. . . Yeah, the European tour should start in like July and then I'll be like, oh man, get me some Guinness, ha ha. . .

This was just another tiny shard in the mosaic of my nights spent listening to boys talk.

I was too stoned to think exactly straight, but as I was playing more halogen beams off some model's brown suede tunic and matching knee-length skirt, $1140 for the ensemble, it occurred to me I could list precisely my handful of ways into the conversation:

One: I could skirt the edges by agreeing when conversationally appropriate: "That's fucked up," or just an obviously place giggle, or a "yeah,"—in other words, keep running after them, nipping their pant legs in that way, asking them questions about soccer or asking them things I already knew about beer, because if I said what I thought they'd get all weird and defensive for me to be challenging them.

Or, I *could* disagree and have that discussion, but it would make them annoyed at me and I'd feel like a loser, like, *oh did I say something stupid?*, later.

Or, I could get drunker and giddy and start saying random, weird shit to get attention, which would give them something to do, taunt me, lead me along.

Or, I could face the depressing truth, and just say what was on my mind, and have them look at me like I'd just beamed down from another realm if they didn't get defensive first.

Or, I could say nothing, like I was doing now, and wait until one of them decided he wanted to fuck me—or at least to act to the others like he wanted to fuck me, which is really different from the kind of attention Ally was paying me at the beginning of the evening—at which point whoever wanted to fuck me would open himself up to an actual conversation, away from the other boys, that I could kind of sort of name some of the terms of, depending on how bad he wanted to fuck me vs. how much of a jerk he was.

I wasn't as confident as I sound here. Part of me giggled when I was supposed to, even a little genuinely, kept a blind upturned mouth.

You are probably thinking that I am hanging out with the wrong folks.

But I swear, there just were no other boys, all the boys were these kinds of boys, *these* boys, and the girls were worse. Besides school, my bedroom, the VCR, books, this was it. What else was there? Mountain biking? Coin collecting? Please.

"What do you do, Racinda?" Shit said.

"I go to high school." I said tearing my attention from Spiegel.

"Oh." Shit said. "You a senior?"

When Ally just couldn't resist Shit's invitation to learn to tune a guitar he looked guiltily at me, he looked at Shit next to him in the doorway to the basement stairs, backlit by the bare bulb reflecting off exposed insulation and two-by-fours. He was so excited, like a little kid, standing on the balls of his feet, but not wanting to be rude to me. He was a nice enough guy, really.

"Go," I said, "I need a smoke anyway."

I couldn't stop looking at the catalog as I set it on the yellow silk upholstery. I wanted to know and understand every page. But I finally got up and left it drooping across the cushion, glossy sheen on glossy sheen, glossed and sheened up some more by the diamond precision of track lighting.

Max: leaned over a planter of succulents, gripping the deck's cherry-stained railing. Bent in half like that, he was about my height. The air was wet and cold—you could only see a few lit-up trophy houses from here. When he wasn't smoking, Max would sometimes put his hand across his mouth, or grip the back of his neck and let his arm hang there. He would fidget and look like he was thinking, but I don't know if he was or what.

You could see black outlines of hills and smell something real. I hadn't realized how badly I'd wanted the air in the dry light of the living room. "You don't like Ally, huh?" Max said, after awhile, not even looking at me.

"Well, I'm not really looking for anyone right now," I said.

I could feel nervousness twist in my gut. I was surprised he asked me that. Out here, it was different from in the car. He wasn't so pissed at me. It didn't really make sense, except then I thought maybe he had been annoyed that I was taking Ally away from him. Maybe that was the reason.

We stayed quiet.

My belly, my sides, felt lean, shook some extra space between my skin and my clothes. Feeling thinner was the closest I came to power. I thought of my jacket's spiders, crawling down from their line beginning at my shoulder into a jumble of legs.

I shook my head and let the wind play there, I felt a tiny bit beautiful.

"How's your mom?" I finally said, pushing myself back off the railing a little.

It took him awhile to answer. He turned to lean his side against the beam, to face me.

"In RN school," he said, "Good. You know, nuts. Normal. Who you been hanging out with?"

"Nobody really," I said. I knew he wouldn't ask me about my sister, but I kind of wanted him to. He was the only person at my new school Ruth had ever tantalized besides me—he was the only one who knew anything about the other world, the Christian world, the dark, crazy person world I belonged to in private.

"You look nice tonight," he said, and looked back at the inky horizon, but that's all that happened. I mean after that Ally came out and Max drove us all home. I went to school the next day. It was almost November. I had no idea what was going to happen to me next, really.

My mother was a crazy person and my sister was a missing crazy person.

*　　　*　　　*

My mother thought my sister ran away and joined a cult. What really happened, about two years ago, was that when Ruth's favorite shrink left the assisted-living place she lived at, Ruth left too, went out into the world on her own, ended up on the streets. After you're eighteen, your parents can't really keep you in those places. Ruth tried for a long time to get Amandine to give her money, to give her some of the trust from Button to live with roommates in San Francisco, but we knew she was wacked out on coke and speed then and after awhile Amandine wouldn't do it. I gave her money once during that time and she ended up in rehab for a week, we got the call at 4am and had to go down there. I had to say no to her the next time, and then whenever I answered her phone calls after that she would scream at me too. The last time she called the house screaming was like a year ago.

But my mother just had to think it was some bigger plot, had to imagine that behind all her problems were actual Satanists with, you know, all the goth props and the infant sacrifice and the graveyard mass, instead of the true, navy-suit Republican satanists and their political war on the mentally ill. My mom *loved* those guys, of course.

My mom had a deprogrammer, this guy Rudy Mitchell, smacking his lips for the minute they found her—Ruth would provide a long term paycheck and he knew it. His flyer listed the cults he'd rescued people from: Hare Krishna, Branch Davidian, Apostles of Infinite Love, All One Voice, Aryan Nation, Sinful Messiah, Garbage Eaters, Children of God, Scientologists, Temple of Set, etc. etc., and that was just the first page of his list.

"Rudy better watch it," I said. I was pouring about half a cup of sugar on top of my Special K, which, in case you thought otherwise, has a lot of sugar in it anyway, "Those Scientologists don't take this sort of thing lightly. They'll send Tom Cruise right after you. I bet they're tapping our phone right now just for having this brochure in the house."

My mother was ignoring me.

"Or else the Church of Satan is, " I said. I paused. "Tapping our phone."

My mother sang her next sentence:

"I don't know what you're talking about, I'm eating my breakfast."

This was one of her strategies, like the way kids cover their ears and yell out "Mary Had A Little Lamb" when they don't want to listen to each other.

Her moisturizer was shiny all over her face. I never ate breakfast with her—this was a freak occurrence. I usually just saw her at the end of the day when she got home from her job at her cheesy church. She had missed rubbing the lotion in near her forehead, so there was a little white line of it there, just like pointing at her wig. She acted like Ruth and I never knew that she wore them, but I mean how could we not? Little kids like poking all over their mom, even a mom as neat as Amandine. But she'd never let me see her without it, and even though I was annoyed at her most of the time I didn't want to hurt her so badly that I'd actually like *say* anything about it. The Christian crap, however, was fair game. She'd had me hoodwinked all those years, until Ruth left for good when I was about thirteen and I finally really got over the whole Jesus thing.

"And *look*, '*Sinful* Messiah.' That's *definitely* the one Ruth's in. He's the Messiah. He's Sinful. Ooh, give me his number, I'll *date* him!"

"Racinda, I am trying to enjoy my breakfast and, and you never respect my space here. You always have to focus on the negative. You can't see the positives in a situation. You always have to make things bad."

"Hey—you left this pamphlet sitting out here. You knew I'd see it, so in fact you're the one who brought it up."

She started humming under her breath. She could do this *and* chew and be elegant in her way. It drove me nuts because I *knew* her ways so well—it was a church song she was humming, something off a tape of hers, probably some lyrics about the blood of the lamb, stuff like that, ew. She'd hum these songs when she got upset, or else she would speak tongues quietly, just her lips moving. She'd hum the songs when she was happy too, and do a little dance, shaking her shoulders—she thought they were really *catchy*, "make a joyful noise," all that. When she was happy and we were listening to her station on the car radio and I wasn't mad at her it was actually a little cute—in the second before it made me cringe—the way she'd get so excited at a simple, bouncy beat.

Usually she would speak tongues lightly in the car when she was driving and I had fallen asleep. No music on, just her whispering. I'd bolt up, half-aware she was doing it, and she'd quiet down fast, denying the whole thing in her silence. *I don't know what you're talking about*, she'd say—unspoken, understood between us—and she'd smile, like she was a kid getting away with something, like she just *loved* and was so *right* to drive me nuts, like she was Jesus or Ghandi and I was the tax man.

"I mean," I said, "I don't know why you'd think she'd be in a cult anyway. She was trying to get away from that sort of crap her whole life. It's not like you have any evidence. It's just that you're so paranoid of cults."

She just kept singing, looking out the window like there were birds there, even though the feeder had been empty for months.

"For your information," my mother said, not looking at me, "after she left the facility, the nurses *said* she had cult literature in her room."

I turned the flyer to page two.

"LOOK! *Rudy* rescued a whole bunch of people from *Born Agains*!" I said. "Well, his contacts there aren't going to be much help finding Ruth."

It always turned into me having a conversation with myself:

"Except maybe she took their sons' virginity and then got them to drive her over to the 'Temple of Set,'" I said, continuing on down the list.

A big frown emerged on my mother's face and she pushed her Special K, which she had sprinkled with two packets of NutraSweet, away from her.

"Sorry," I said.

"Rudy said those people were in Kentucky having themselves bitten by snakes, that's not what *Born* Agains do," she said, smiling like *I* was the idiot. She opened another packet of NutraSweet and put it in her tea.

"It doesn't say '*Snakebiters*,'" I said, "It says BORN AGAIN CHRIS-TIAN."

"Well," she said, "If you're not concerned about your sister I won't fill you in on the details. I mean how ignorant, Racinda, really, how ignorant can you be if you think being Born-Again is the same as a cult—those cult people worship *idols*."

The word *idol* has the same resonance with my mother that *heroin* or *parolee* have to other people's mothers.

"You think *Buddhists* worship idols, Mom."

"They do. They have lots of different idols. That's why it's not a true religion. Christianity is about what's *inside*, not some idol that's *outside*. It's about the *inner* relationship you have with God. The personal relationship with Jesus Christ."

"Um, and plowing down abortion doctors? And burning women at the stake?"

She stared, confused and angry, her hand tight on her spoon. I could see the sadness in her and I could see her about to say something nasty and off the point.

"You need to get a little more educated about this stuff, Mom, " I said. "You sound like a redneck."

I was ready for a battle, I wasn't tired of fighting this out with her, although she was so impossible to have a conversation with that it never went into any kind of logical, useful back and forth where even the most obvious things could get through to her. The words didn't *mean* anything to her—these fights were just about the little eddies of feelings that carried her away from any sort of actual conversation. Tug of war between us, between me wanting her to make some sort of sense and her wanting things to be okay without her having to do so much work to understand. I looked at the lines on her face, the way her frustrated mouth made an O shape but nothing came out of it.

"I am not a redneck," she said, like a little kid who that's all she can muster as a comeback. Her voice was shaky and wet.

And then she stood up, grabbing the table's edge and was going to cry, her little beige work jacket and tidy white blouse, her feminine watch, her nails, her hair blown dry, her delicate gem on a chain, her thinnish lips traced in coral, her packet of vitamins and the gelatin pills she took for her nails sitting there next to her glass of Crystal Light, and then I felt terrible, but I was still so mad at being born into this sort of nonparental situation so I drank the last bit of sugar milk out of my bowl like soup first until I couldn't stand it and I went up to her and I hugged her and I felt all her sadness and I didn't know what to do. Her sadness is so horrible and I hate it and I can't let it be there in the room, I have to go hug her and make it go away, but it doesn't go away it comes back. It comes back and it is so deep and bottomless, but it's not mine so I can't even see if it *is* actually deep and bottomless and eternal and impenetrable. It's *hers*, and so it's mine too, but not mine so much that I can crawl in there and swim around, prove to myself I can live without air in the water of that sad. Just a big, looming threat of the worst things in the world that I can never even contend with, *her* black cloud, not one I can even start to clear away for myself.

When I pulled away after too long a time, there was a thin band of lotion on my sweater from her neck. She was thinner than me, rubbery, sort of frail feeling. I was more substantial and stronger, designed to lug things around where she was designed to sit. When I pulled away from her, though, I didn't feel solid at all. I said *it's okay mom, she's probably fine. I would feel it if she were in trouble.* My mom nodded and put her hand on my shoulder. *Yes, you would, wouldn't you. You always know these things. You two really love each other, don't you?* I had made her feel better. I told her yeah, yeah we do.

A cigarette after crying, even somebody else's, or your own when it doesn't quite come out of you, makes the air seem more beautiful. Maybe it's clogging your tubes up with two kinds of congestion that does it, makes you appreciate, I don't know, but that sort of cigarette just kind of gives you a moment to kiss up to the air, feel the trees around you, take a peek at what the clouds are doing. After I left my mother there in the kitchen, swung my book bag around onto my hip and clomped away with a slight effort to clomp as lightly and politely as possible. I had a few seconds of thinking I was still in Pennsylvania, and that I could climb the tree down by the creek behind our old house there like I did when Ruth and I were little. I thought that's where I was headed and then the reality of the landscape set in when I rounded the corner and noticed that there was no leafy deciduous vegetation, that I was here in Dirtland. How embarrassing. So fuck it, I walked.

Parts of our neighborhood do have a lot of trees. I am desperate for these parts sometimes. I prefer to drive them, but as that isn't often an option, walking them is something I have come to. And then sometimes I sneak on in to a little patch of these trees and have a smoke by myself. This is the best.

I'll usually sit on a stump or a rock or a patch of grass and sort of shuffle the dirt around with my feet. This time I stacked sticks on top of each other then dumped some of my water bottle on little stones to shine them up, for the time being. Rocks, smooth rocks, are meant to be under water—it's where they stop being dull and they start showing off intricate, hidden colors; patterns they will only speak to you if you know their magic ingredient. This is what they must look like, underground, in the moist dirt.

With the peeled end of a stick, I wrote my name in the dirt. I have never met or heard of anyone with my name, and of course I used to hate this and wish for Jenny, for Karen, for Kimmy, for Diane, whatever, but now I am fairly happy with it although sometimes it makes me feel like a monster, the *least* feminine and attractive person in vicinity. Anyway, I wrote it, *Racinda*, and then I wrote *loves*, and then I thought who do I love? Who do you love? Do I love my family? I love my stupid mother, I love Button, I love Ruth, but these things are all so fucked up, they are fucked up by, respectively, craziness, the stroke, and craziness. Drugs. I don't think I love my father. I don't think he can get that from me anymore.

I dig in my bag, which now has streaks of dirt across it like early morning clouds, and I pull out my fabulously stolen, beautiful dull silver compact and a lipstick and I trace my lips a little bigger than normal, apparently going for a modified Joan Collins Dynasty-era look.

Racinda loves.

Ew. *Not* Max or Ally. *Not* Marie.

Then I write *loves Racinda*. As in _____ loves Racinda. And that is so depressing that I get up and go to the payphone.

*　　*　　*

Fingers and noses and lips have smeared the metal of the booth with iridescent whorls. I hold the receiver an inch from my mouth. The digits of my mother's calling card are no longer stored in my brain, just in my finger, speedy beyond me. I think: who is an operator anyway? Do I know anyone related to an operator?

"*Hart. H-A, not H-E-A,*" *I say, but there are no R's listed in the 415 or the 510 or the 818 or the 213. I can't find her. There are no Ruths.*

*   *   *

Another party, the following spring, 1992, like early May. A house with a wing for the kids, but ranchy and a little run down. A pool table and a wet bar and MTV cartoons going before boys start playing Sega. Bad pools of overhead lighting.

"Raceeenda."

Ally. Yellow hair, brown skin on a little man's body, that tooth.

"How's life treating you?"

"Good. How's Spanish One treating you?"

"I—I don't take Spanish One."

"Oh. Where's Max?"

Shit.

"He's out there helping this guy in the band load his gear."

"Such a nice boy."

Ally shifts in his Nikes.

"You--?"

"Sarcasm," I say.

"Oh. How's the spiders?"

An excuse to run that hand up my side.

"Hungry," I say, "They haven't eaten in weeks."

When I smile I know my teeth look little and sharp.

Tim Simms, the high school running back, who I fucked once, at a party last year, and who curves to the side like something they should invent a surgery for, is talking to Marie but won't look at me. He is nothing to me, but still, I can't shake a spreading sadness in my gut and a memory of tile marks on my neck that I walked back into the blacklight with that night. So I light a cigarette and walk around the perimeter, putting my awkwardness into making really distinct, careful footsteps.

None of these football players will really look at me. Marie has some sway with them because of her jocky big brother and because she is asexual and bland enough that everyone knows the rules: they know she doesn't expect them to flirt and everyone knows they will never even think of dating her. With me though, I just bring them closer to freakdom, and they ignore me.

When Marie moves on to chat with this kid Nick, I at least have someone to stand next to and act like I have something to say.

Nick is this boy who is not a nerd, plays baseball and stuff, but has a certain politeness to him. He will actually always tell the teachers in advance if he is going to be absent, that sort of thing. Sometimes he forgets himself and writes his name, or refers to himself in conversation as *Nicky*—you can almost hear his nice mom in his voice.

He is nothing special but I am finding myself wanting to lick his face.

I can overlook the homophobic slurs and shoves that erupt from these boys when one of them messes up—drunk and lovey dovey—and hugs a teammate with too much vigor. I can even overlook that they are death to talk to, because of the amazing curves of their necks and the quick boy flashes that move their bodies and mouths and voices and punctuate their deep thoughts about Pink Floyd. I can overlook the anorexics they so supposedly love to fuck. I can overlook my abysmal inadequacy with even the football team, abysmally inadequate themselves, because of these small moments when their bodies seem to hold such exploding beauty in a gesture they have no control over, a gesture that just *happens* for them and has so much power, so much movement in the world.

"Beer run. Beer run!" Nick starts going around saying to people, getting away from Marie and me as fast as he can—just protocol, even though he is nice and we are not *that* socially lame or anything, it's just party protocol, don't spend too much time with the girls who aren't top tier. He interrupts football conversations with his deep, normal, boy's sense of entitlement. He even asks Marie if she wants anything, but he skips right over me.

So I get in his face. I step up underneath him and look up at the shady side of that jaw line and poke him in the stomach to get his attention.

"*Nicky*," I say, "Get me a six of Mickeys wide mouths."

I hand him two dollars less than it costs. He is back within the half-hour and another half hour after that I've gone through three of them and feel a lot better. I wander away, I sway a little, I feel my feet in my boots.

On a couch, smoking, nobody talking to me, reading *Rolling Stone*. There are cheap, half-wall-size windows, bugs dead in the plaster sills, windows that frame wanderers and chatters and keg rats outside, underlit with the navy blue moisture of the night, the wet black-brown off the here and there trees. Marie coming back from the bathroom, looking like a piece of cake. There isn't an item of pink on her, yet she oozes that color.

"I got us an eighth," she says.

I am in a mood. The light is too bright in here. The couch is cheap and nubby brown orange-tan. This part of the large room, the size of two garages, has been deserted awhile. There are people at the pool table on the far end, but here it is empty.

"*You* got an eighth. I'm going to buy myself some with my good looks."

"Fine," she says. She is good natured, she knows I am broke. I haven't *had* to get a job so I just haven't done it. Shoplifting kind of works for me, if you know what I mean. Shoplifting, and in this particular moment, Mickey's wide mouths.

Marie is my dark side in that she is my pink side. She is nerdy and clued out and will be happy to stay in a cultural wasteland for the rest of her days, I think, or maybe she will be happy with like a normal job, like at a bank. She pulls her shiny blown-glass bowl, teal, white, swirled, out of her tan suede jacket. She packs it and offers some to me even though she knows I won't take it from her because I've been mooching too much lately.

"Max!"

I am so drawn to him. I am having a bad chemical storm—not electric, just a lot of showers, puddles, damp, dark—in my brain. He crosses into the emptiness. The way he walks up to us—I wonder what he will say to me, I know there is something that I want for him to say to me, something to lure me somewhere underground with him, somewhere realer than this party, somewhere older where things matter.

He sits down but he won't look at me. He is wearing a sweatshirt and army pants and has a thick chain-chain, hardware store chain, around his neck that I have never seen on him before.

"What's up," he says. He pushes his hands down his thighs as if to dry them.

He lights his bowl for me, generous this time, and though she's right next to me for several more minutes before she gets bored and goes to talk to jocks, Marie fades away into a little pink curlicue of ether—Tinkerbell—then nothing.

*　　　*　　　*

It's her, from that green underwater-feeling bathroom.

Lisa's face in front of me again, huge and inquisitive, squinting until she determines I'm not worth the effort to place.

"Hi Max," Lisa says. She ignores me. "Do you have any weed?" she says, even though she sees I have the bowl. Her legs have little shaving nicks on them, but they are the kind of legs peoples' mothers are sure will get them somewhere in life. They are very long legs, they are muscular but curvaceous. They are a little larger than life.

"Oh, hi," she says. Now it seems like she really just didn't notice me. She holds her hand out for me to give her the bowl, but she doesn't smile. She's looking annoyed.

"Have you seen fucking Joey, Maxalicious?" she says after she exhales.

"No, sorry," Max says.

"God, here I am in the middle of nowhere at this like, junior frat in training party and they aren't even here. Ugh."

I can't think of anything to say so I stay really quiet. Her hair is long and blond and clumped together—not quite dreadlocks, but snaky like that. Ratty, a little, but moving like there is a living force in it.

I instantly feel fatter with her around. Her face isn't perfect but she's beautiful anyway—the long straight nose seems at an off angle to the full cheeks, and her eyes are roundish, huge, there's a heaviness to them, a seriousness always, when her face is still, when she isn't laughing or angry. A sort of a deadpan heaviness, a heaviness like she's heard it all before and is not impressed. *What*, her face says, *So?*, it says.

Max moves to the far arm of the couch so that she fills the space in between us. She flops down, resigned, still frowning, and her legs splay bare in front of her.

It could be that hours pass as we smoke the bowl and are quiet.

"What time is it?" she finally says. Max and I are both fine just sitting there with her. She is enough, herself, to make an evening.

"I think it's like one," Max says.

"Fuck," she says.

She draws the toe of her platform boot back and slams it against the green-glass ashtray on the floor. The ashtray is two inches thick on the sides and bottom, cut to look nautical, with rope and portholes strung around it, probably like five pounds. Huge, heavy like a barbell, and it flies hard into the empty fooz ball machine, spilling butts everywhere.

Pure hate crosses Lisa's face, and for a second I think she is going to cry, but then it seems like I have only imagined that.

"Where the fuck did they *go*, motherfuckers," she says.

She smokes a cigarette so hard I can see from where I sit that the filter is all chewed, all soggy.

"God, I have got to get rid of this man. Fuck."

She taps her foot hard until she lights another cigarette. Max and I are terrified of her. She's nineteen, I know as a matter of public fact, and technically I guess a senior but actually completely removed from the high school stuff, totally beyond any social hierarchies there. She seems older.

"Max, can you take me home? I need a ride and I don't feel like dealing with any of the meatheads at the party."

"Sorry, I got dropped off," Max says.

"Fucking stupid whore of a boyfriend, out at a real party and leaving me here, totally inconsiderate and immature and ridiculous," Lisa says, crossing and uncrossing her legs, bobbing her foot furiously.

Those legs are the thing the world has to go through first to get to her. The second thing is makeup, and her hands materialize an eyeliner without seeming to go into her purse. Her face is different now, not drunk, exactly, but sweet.

"I saw you in the bathroom," she says, "You should maybe try it like this," she says, leaning her face to the side to get a little light on me.

I turn my chin up to her. She opens her mouth as she traces the black stuff across my lids, *go like this*, and even though my products are better than hers what appears in that mirror when she holds it to my face is a different girl than I was before.

"Wardrobe," she says. And she digs into her big messenger bag and draws out a little pile of black material.

"You can borrow this halter," she says, "Strip. Max close your eyes so she doesn't feel shy."

Why do I do it then? I'm not about to object. My spider jacket comes off, my t-shirt, *bra too*, she says, *it won't work with the straps*. And so I lean toward the couch and she hands me the halter top, it takes me a minute to figure out how the fabric crosses my breasts, goes up around my neck.

"You could put the jacket back on," she says, "if you're cold, but look."

The mirror. Something new in there.

I am silent. Her hands, strong and feminine, fit onto my shoulders and she smiles, lighting everything around me. She wipes a strand of hair from my face.

"You are *so* pretty," she says. Like she made it that way.

I am still not totally sure here. I don't trust her but I want to. I want to believe her. I can't think of anything to say. I don't want to think I was so bad before but I have to admit she has definitely done something.

We sit around and smoke more weed and the three of us, that way, become strangely comfortable. She has to pee, she stands up and when she leans over me and Max to reach for her cigarettes she is huge. Her hair shifts under the one track light that is working—honey, straw, ice white, it moves and it sings. As her legs move her away from us, Max and I lean forward, almost imperceptibly, praying that she will come back.

For a second, in all this darkness, my mother seeps into my brain. Does she know where I am? Does she know anything? My mother thinks I don't know what she does in the mornings, but how could I not. She wakes at 5 or 5:30 and she kneels in front of the charcoal sketch of Jesus holding a lamb that she has hung up in our living room. She never would have decorated with something so déclassé back home but she has changed. She has become a little bit more ready to laugh, to cry, but it's all through Jesus, and it's weird. She kneels in front of him and she speaks in tongues, quietly, whispering, for ten minutes, sometimes, fifteen, thirty, then she does her sit-ups and her leg lifts and something for her triceps with little five pound weights, little purple five pound dumbbells. She makes herself oatmeal with Equal, or some fat-free cereal. If she is really tired she'll make some Lipton tea, otherwise just water with lemon. She might have a piece of fruit. She maybe feels better this way: the control of this routine, and the help of her Jesus. The house feels as gray as the charcoal painting, my mother as treacly as the lamb, as weak as that, so far from Ruth, from light, from this kind of power that Lisa has, from lipstick, from boots, from the night sky, from freedom.

And my mother loves this routine, loves her tidiness, but look, I remind myself, I remind her, all she really cares about is searching for Ruth. In spite of her neatness, and all the rules of her church, and her own rules about being skinny and pretty and pleasant, all that she really wants is finding Ruth, is finding the one who will scream and will laugh too loud, all she wants is to find the one who writes *genetalia* across the ceiling of the car in lipstick, the one who spills daily, the one who seeks her pleasure and when she crashes, lets herself crash hard, carrying the obedient ones—Amandine, me—with her into the other, darker, shinier, more immediate world.

Marie is as obedient as my mother and I are, but Marie truly belongs to this above-ground world. Kind to me, but I can't stand anymore of it. I see Marie walking toward me here on the couch, but I am trying to bite into, to digest this blue-black feeling of Ruth that I've caught the scent of somewhere, that I feel somewhere in my ribcage, my windpipe. I close my eyes, wanting to feel Ruth's strength, teased into wanting this again from the taste of hope Lisa has given me.

"Racinda? Where—oh. Our ride is leaving."

Marie waves her hand in front of my face.

"Hello. Hello?"

I can't think of what to say.

"Hello?"

I see that Marie is scrunching her face up at the halter top slut outfit. She can't tell what it is, what I have done to myself. She is taking in the dull chalk glow of my hugely exposed skin.

"I think I'll be okay," I say. "I'm not ready yet."

I stretch an arm out conspicuously, for the feeling of its curves, but to ash my cigarette too.

"What are you talking about?" Marie says.

"I can get home," I say, "I'll talk to you later."

Marie stands there a minute before I see her thick legs, her white button-down shirt, the back of her curly brownish bob turning away from me, *bye*, the one nerdy football player, faggy, holding the door to the night open for her. Lisa accidentally brushes against Marie on her way back to the couch. Lisa is not going to say anything mean about Marie—it's my imagination that she even would, because Marie is so far from Lisa that I don't think Lisa knew another girl besides us was ever in the room.

I don't know who gets up first, Max or Lisa, but I am apparently following them outside, and we pass the plastic Chinese lanterns strung between a lamppost and a clothesline, we pass the puddly keg, we pass boys in jackets. We pass through the smoke of different joints. We pass through air that has sucked the darkness of this place into each molecule, air that feels sharpest and coldest right under your ears, on your neck.

"Do you want my sweatshirt?" Max says. It *is* cold. I don't know if he's asking me or her. Her. He looks at her. But she doesn't say anything so I say yeah and he has to stop and hand it to me and I put the huge thing on on top of my jacket. I can see what Max's t-shirt says now: it says, Jesus Is A Cunt. When did Max get so punk rock, I wonder.

In a second, he disappears into a straggling group of boys around a bong taller than he is and then I am following just Lisa. My steps are large and full of power until I see Nicky and Tim Simms are at the bong.

I try to hide from the yucky reality of their existence by leaning so that Lisa is blocking me from these football boys I've wanted and hated and I think no, she will leave me and go over to them too. Nicky raises his chin as he sees Lisa, her hair winding down her back, her bare thighs above tall boots, but she ignores him, grunts, *ew*, she grabs my hand and she says, "Come on, baby, let's go down here."

And it starts to grow in me, this idea that I can maybe have what she has, that I can maybe be beautiful, that I can maybe touch a boy without it making me grieve.

I feel my breath retreat for a second, terrified at the thought of this, but with a few more steps I stop thinking Max is betraying me by leaving me with her and it seems like my bad-ass outfit and the way my stride crunches the mud down, my boots falling on the earth, somehow make me more beautiful than those boys could ever be, somehow fade those boys and leave their space empty for less mean ones, less boring ones, more delicious ones. I gulp in air, terrified to believe it.

There is a path, I don't know how Lisa knows it, it's dusty, giant rocks on it once in awhile, and the grade is going down, at first so gently I don't notice, but then it becomes more steep and I realized it's been downward all the way.

I am shaking.

"It's a grotto," she says when she finally stops in a darker patch of night. She sits down on a rock. When my eyes adjust to the lack of light, I see that there are oak tress all around us, at the edge of the property, the only trees really around in this brown flat ranchland. But we are cloistered here. Spiky reed plants and purplish grass grow around the big rocks. We smoke, and we talk. At first it is like I am all closed off and acting like a goody-goody—this is what I do with new people—but then I start being a smart ass and showing her that I am funny and even rude.

I can feel it already, it is like with Ruth: she is the guitar and I am the bass line.

"So," she says after awhile, "Are you seeing anyone?"

"Uh, *no*. Of course not. Like there's anyone worth fucking around here anyway."

She lets my comment sit there for awhile, and she speaks really calmly, elegantly, when she responds.

"Of course there are people worth fucking," she says. "There almost always are."

"*Right*," I say, embarrassed, sarcastic.

She holds her gaze on me, I can feel it, and when I look up for a second she looks very sad.

"Hon, there are. Believe that."

I am starting to. But I know better than to believe that eyeliner can really make it so—I have always believed eyeliner was what might bring one to me, and it never did. Before.

But now Lisa is giving something to me. Something of hers, something like what Ruth used to have.

Lisa pulls a pint of Jim Beam out of her pocket, doesn't wince after the gulp she takes. She waits a minute before she squints over at me.

"It's not that you—it's not that you aren't—"

"What?" I say.

"Well you are just really *beautiful* like this," she says.

If I were really beautiful, I wouldn't have to go home to Amandine. If I were really beautiful, I wouldn't have had to fuck Tim Simms, and he would not have told Marie a week later that he thought I was the girl in his French class, which I wasn't. If I were really beautiful, I would not have considered sleeping with the friend of a pornographer named Shit. There would be a few dozen fewer handjobs in secret world history if I were really beautiful, a handful fewer blowjobs. If I were beautiful, there would be a feeling of singing and of home. And also, I think, though I partly know it is not true, there would be a sister, a mother, a father, if I were beautiful.

"Yeah, right," I say.

"It's that you don't want it, or that you act like you *do* want it and that scares people cause they know you really don't want it."

"I don't get it," I say.

"Me neither," she says, "Except that it's completely *true*. I just mean you have that sweet—thing . . ."

"Sweet *thang*," I say. "*Thang*."

"Thang, *sweet* thang," she says, "*sweet thang*. . ."

And she grabs my hands and catches my eyes with the pure excitement of a little girl, her purple-plum mouth in that triangle shape, stretched, not beautiful and not even strong, exactly, but full of a certain kind of power. She is bouncing and giddy and I am still and terrified of her, frozen and afraid it's all a huge trick—that all her friends will pop out of the edges, take pictures and laugh at me.

"Thaaaannng," she sings, "thang thang thang. . ."

When she pulls me up, I start jumping along, more and more convinced of something each time my feet leave the earth. I say the words. Moisture falls off the grass around us onto our ankles, the colors beyond the trees shift as we bounce.

She lets go of my arms for a second and with the words, sweet thang, still jumping, grabs her crotch, and the giggles come over us:

Sweet thang, sweet thang, sweet thang

We are laughing and we just can't stop it.

10

WHAT'S YOUR PASSION

1992

Max

seven-eleven:

The sun was glinting in my eyes in a way that made me feel it was my main problem. Like it was summer, and the glare off new pavement, the dried-up grass, trees, the fire hazard, was my only opponent. The weather stays shit hot like this in Sacramento sometimes right up until the rain in November, stays dry and brown right up until the spastic burst of green that will happen with the first shower. But the sun didn't get to keep its space in the Big Gripe category of my brain, cause now things were more complicated than the summer, now I had to deal with getting to homeroom every morning, then algebra, World Cultures, etc., fuck, whatever.

I hacked a butt outside 7-11 then went back in and played a few games of StreetFighter II against the machine before this guy Joey came in and kicked my ass. He always chooses the girl character, Chun-Li—lame. because her moves are relatively uncomplicated, and repetitive, but hard to get around. Joey is boring to play against. I beat him *once.* Anyone who always wins at anything is boring to play against, but you keep playing because for some reason you think you'll beat them, eventually. It's the concept behind Las Vegas, the lottery, you name it. Whatever—Joey's twenty-six, he has a head start. And it's good to know him, he's in this band called Bandolero that is about to make it. He gets me into his gigs past the bouncers and for free, so I always buy him a pint.

I just turned eighteen. This morning. And I'm sure you understand how that doesn't mean a whole lot. When they want to make an example of you, you're tried as an adult, etc. When they enlist you in the marines, you're an adult. Trying to buy a forty of St. Ides, you're a cheesy little shit with a fake ID.

I almost won the first round of our fourth game, but Joey got me in the end. Joey pays for games each time I see him even though he has no job to speak of and Bandolero doesn't earn more than beer money. I play the Blinka character—this huge green monster who bites your head off if he gets in close enough. Blood spurts everywhere. I had almost figured out how to out-move Chun-Li with this decapitation step when Joey's girl-friend, a blonde named Lisa who is kind of slutty looking and pretty loud, but nice to me at the gigs, came pounding in with a cigarette.

The security doorbell rang and the clerk looked up from his Star magazine. Lisa started scowling the second she saw us at the game. She looked like she hadn't showered in awhile—her bleached hair with brown roots gets all crusty-looking—and she was wearing one of the short, black, tight dresses she always wears to show off her body, even in the mornings, with motorcycle boots. I'm sure she sleeps in these dresses if she's not naked.

"Motherfucker, I'm waiting in the truck for you to bring me Advil and you're playing Atari?" she yelled, pointing the cigarette and shaking it even though the cherry was about to fall right off it onto either me or Joey. Even though she was unwashed, she still looked pretty good. She's got one of those little girl faces, with big cheeks, with round pink lips.

He obviously didn't want to, but Joey finally turned around, in the middle of his play. I took the opportunity to chomp on Chun-Li until she tumbled off the side of the screen and Blinka did his thumping victory dance, spitting out her blood and chunks of his green gelatinous body everywhere.

Lisa was standing there, and I was surprised to see that in this light she seemed kind of soft, kind of like a little kid.

"I'm almost done. Hold on, I'm about to beat this little man," Joey said, gearing up for the next round that would decide the game. Lisa calmed down and just smoked her cigarette inside the store. We kept playing: Joey kicked my ass again, there was no hope.

"Did you get the Advil?" Lisa asked him as Chun-Li celebrated with back-flips across the screen.

Joey grinned and looked up at the ceiling fan.

"Give me the money, I'll do it," she said.

He handed her seventy-five cents in quarters.

"Mother Fuck," Lisa said, kicking the Streetfighter II machine with her boot.

Advil costs at least three bucks in a convenience store—my mom makes me come get it for her here when she's got backache and her herbal stuff doesn't work.

She pushed him, surprisingly knocking him a little off-balance for all his thick chest muscles, then headed out the door with the three quarters.

Lisa was in the truck and locking the doors by the time we got out there. She moved fast. Joey just stood next to the ice machine, looking seriously pissed, daring her to drive off with his eyes. She did it. She screeched right out of the parking lot in two fast, jerky gearshifts. We both watched his mom's yellow pickup go down the road until you couldn't read all the Bandolero bumper stickers anymore.

In my high school at this moment they were all messing at their lockers, laughing, hurrying to the fight or the girl or the joint that would save them.

Joey yelled something like a crazy-person at his feet and kicked the curb. When he saw me staring, he got it together and acted like nothing happened.

"I guess it's you and me, buddy. You got a smoke?" Joey said.

I gave him one and lit it for him.

"Fuck it," Joey said. "Let's go to Little Otis's and we'll just run through the bongo tunes."

otis:

"The ladies—it's not about a salary, it's all about the dowry," Joey said as we stepped onto Little Otis's porch.

"Yep," I said, even though I had yet to learn this from my own experience. And in fact did not have a clue what he was talking about.

We knocked a bunch of times before Little Otis showed his sorry ass at the door. He rubbed at his eyes and coughed a minute before he got the chain undone.

"Max Planet, Max Planet, my man loves to slam it, with Janet, Max Planet, got fists made of granite, on the TV he hams it for ex-ams he crams it, Max Planet, Max Planet, Max Planet, " Otis said, then giggled, letting us in.

"What's up, dude," I said.

Joey and him started talking about the band, and then they practiced this sort of blues jam for awhile, Joey on the bongos and Little Otis picking along the bass player's Fender to a song that I now have memorized:

"They call me Little Otis, and I'm scratching my scrotus, if you sink I will float us, Stubing Gopher and boat-us," he sang.

That's just the chorus, but I won't burden you with the entirety of it. I sat pretty quiet on the couch, flipping through these comic books of Otis's, one of which was pornographic. I listened though, and Otis really sucks on the bass. He's the only one of the Bandoleros who sucks on an instrument, but he holds shit together in other ways, I guess. I am probably better even, on the guitar, than Little Otis.

"But if you ever need something, I will share you my Chun-king, I will call in the Navy, sip from my lotus, baby."

"You ready to pull some tubes, dude?" Joey said after way too many rounds of Otis's Love Boat song.

"Lemme brush my teeth," Otis said,

"Some front man," Joey said with a high laugh, "learn an instrument, dude, because the fur-on-the-teeth thing ain't earning you enough image points."

"Oh yeah," said Otis, "Well let me," and he laughed the same high raspy laugh, "Let me just go in here and change into my wifebeater and give me. . . give myself, mulletize myself while I'm at it," he said as he went through the curtain made out of a Winnie-the-Pooh sheet to his bathroom, which I had never got the courage to set foot in.

"Fuck you, college dropout asshole," Joey said.

Otis is such a freak, I thought, what kind of a freak brushes their teeth at a moment like this. Joey started packing the bowl to Otis's big old purple six-foot bong. I knew I could barely do one hit if I wanted to be able to hold any kind of conversation for the next few hours. I had to psych myself up for this giant bong. Joey knew I felt like an asshole, being with them, skipping World Cultures, but somehow liked taking me under his wing, liked that I needed his protection. Otis didn't care, would smell my fear and tear it out of me for public display in his shithole apartment.

I did alright, I did two massive bong hits without coughing and then I was set. I was sessed out, blissed out. I stared at Otis's Madonna Like A Prayer cardboard cut-out stolen from the Tower records that stood up off the floor like a real, half-dressed person.

"Madonna and Max, sittin' in a tree, K-I-S-S-I-N-G," Little Otis said in his little raspy way. I wasn't embarrassed, but I think I started blushing.

"Stop bugging the shorty, motherfucker," Joey said.

"What? What? I'm Otis and I'm butt. You hand me a brew, I sit it on my gut," Otis said before Joey tackled him. Joey had him pinned in about half a second, without even knocking anything over. Joey is real buff, and Otis is weak with a beer belly. I might turn out like Otis, a skinny guy with a stomach tire, if I'm not careful.

"What, what?" Otis said, looking around like a cartoon with his blue bug eyes popping as he smoothed his wrinkled shirt tails over his pants, "He don't mind, do you Max? You don't mind that Joey's not getting enough at home."

Joey smiled and rolled his eyes; now he was busy going through a pile of Otis's records, sliding the vinyl out of the sleeves.

It would be nice to look like Joey if you didn't have to work so hard at it in a gym. Right now I'm wiry so I don't have too much to worry about. Joey could deal with that scene, in some ways, he seemed like that's all he wanted, despite all the music stuff, was to be the high-school football star every cheerleader was dying to fuck.

Joey started playing the bongos again, and Otis picked along on the bass.

"What's your passion, Max Planet?" Otis asked me.

I shrugged. I had no idea. I was okay on the guitar, I had basic chords down and a few decent licks. But I don't think that counts as a passion. Maybe StreetFighter II. I don't know.

"Max doesn't have a passion," Otis said.

Joey kept playing.

"Joey got the Lisa passion," Otis said, still pissed about the tackle. "Lisa."

"My only passion, motherfucker," Joey said, "is for the beat." He lit into this crazy 7/8 shit to make a point. He left Otis way behind. Otis tried to keep up on the bass, would stop and look around like he was thinking something deep, but just finally started laughing at how bad he was.

"No, Max, buddy, what is it? You got a passion yet, Max?" Little Otis asked me, all trying to change the subject.

"I started playing the guitar, but I suck," I said. I lit up another smoke.

"Yeah man? The Max The Max The Max, he lacks, he's wack, he slacks," Otis said.

"Yeah," Joey said, pausing, smiling.

I nodded, and we said bye to Otis. Joey grabbed one of Otis's big Mexican hats on the way out the door, and we went all stoned back down to the parking lot at the 7-11. By this time my sweat started to stink in the heat, I could smell it from time to time mixed in with exhaust fumes coming off the nearby freeway. I wasn't embarrassed, I actually liked the smell. It reminded me of my dad before he took off when I was five, before I realized how useless he was, when my own sweat was still more like baby dew or something, and he was always shoveling, building. The dog would roll in his damp clothes by the hamper like they were a dead animal, his sweat was that powerful. All these crazy things I think about when I am stoned. I tried to shut my shit up and keep pace with Joey's strut. You could've framed us, started playing some creepy whistling western music behind us like we were about to go rob a bank, dust circling up from our footsteps.

birthday:

I don't want to, really, but I have to go see my dad because it is my birthday so I get one of Otis's friends to drop me off. I find my dad outside his place trying on his wader boots and wearing his fishing outfit that includes a sort of safari hat with a net.

"I was thinking it was some yay-hoo blasting that crap music and here it is my own birthday boy," my dad says. He grabs me and gives me a hug.

"Uh, Pops, I'm not up for fishing this weekend," I say.

"Fine, fine, Mr. Seventeen- and-I-Know-Everything," he says. He starts taking off the boots.

"Eighteen," I say, "We going to the Seafood Lover?"

He walks the boots up to the house and puts them inside the screen door. He's still got the hat on when he heads back toward me.

"Son, lets go to the Salt and Pepper. You still a wing fan?" he says.

I nod. We take off in his van to this bar, the Salt and Pepper Cocktail Lounge, where my dad tends to spend his free time. He's never brought me here before. Inside, it looks like Las Vegas. The waitresses all have lots of cleavage and long black nightgowns. I am feeling a little strange looking at women like this with my dad. I am feeling a little strange with women like this looking at me sitting with a man in an explorer's hat.

And where are we sitting? I will tell you: there's seats all around a sort of person-free hot-tub with a big flame coming out of the middle. A trashy waitress comes over to ask me what do I want to drink and I order a Red Hook, which of course they don't have. I snort but my dad and the waitress don't even notice. She has a tattoo on her breast that she has tried to cover up with orange makeup.

"Two Coors Lights," he says, and he winks at her. She seems pleased.

"Don't tell your mother, boy. I figure its okay, cause when I turned eighteen I could drink legal and hell, I'm no psycho killer. Just don't get anyone pregnant, you hear me, son?" he says.

I nod. I wonder if he talks to everybody like this, or just me.

"Now, Max, we have what I would call a generational gap. I like fishing. You like heavy metal," he goes.

"Uh," I say.

"Whatever," he says, waving his beer in the air in a quick circle. "Point is, I think we are both too old for our normal weekends. This weekend, I'm going fishing. You're welcome to come along," he says.

"Dad, " I say. I am trying to figure out if he has always been this way or if he was better when I was real little because back *then* he seemed okay to me. This happens every time I see him, and he talks too much for me to have time to find the answer.

"Now hear me out. I know you don't want to fish. So I have decided you and your buddies can have my pad until I get back Sunday. Just kick back, relax with the men. I know what it's like to have a woman like your mother looking over your shoulder all the time."

At this point, he winks at *me*, like we're picking up girls together or something. Then hands me his house key.

He knows he's hit the nail on the head, and given me the best present ever by finally just leaving me alone.

When we get back to his place I feel a little sick from the chicken wings even though I hardly ate any off my plate. He drags me into the living room. Next to his entertainment center is something wrapped up in black and white striped wrapping paper from The Good Guys. My father buys me something from The Good Guys, this stereo store where he knows people, every couple years, but never anything this big.

"Happy birthday, my boy," he says. I stand there and don't want to unwrap it, and he goes into the other room and keeps talking to me but I can't hear until he's back and I start opening it.

"You need role models," he says, "So let's leave this baby here, not take it back to your old woman's," he says, meaning my mom's. I figure whatever he bought at Good Guys, either he wants to use it himself or he doesn't want my mom to know. I'm sure he's not trying to keep me around for the company.

It's a home karaoke machine.

"Look," he goes, "They have all the karaoke classics here," and gestures to the thing kind of dramatically before going back through his tackle box.

He hands me the manual to the karaoke machine and leaves with all his lures and his poles and an inflatable mattress for the back of his van. I wait till he drives off then go check the liquor cabinet, and then I look if there's anywhere in the hall closet to stick the karaoke asshole machine, so fucking embarrassing if Bandolero is coming here later. Which would be cool. The liquor is pretty stocked, and my dad is probably actually a little guilty about bailing, so he won't say shit if I empty it by Sunday. It will be a whole new level to have a party here.

I find that my dad still has some decent herb stuck in a sweatsock next to a flimsy clay pipe with a half-busted screen. He goes through a quarter a month. I only go up into the bedroom now when Pops isn't here, otherwise I stick to the fold-out couch downstairs for someplace to crash. He would let me sleep up here in this bed while he took the floor next to it the first year I started visiting him, when I was twelve and too chicken to sleep downstairs by myself. The next year I started sleeping on the couch—thirteen—and after I got over being so proud to walk around with a *dad*, I started realizing people were laughing at him a lot, and I started real fast hating to be seen with him in public.

I flop onto the polyester blanket and look out onto all the towing companies and warehouses in this part of Sacramento.

You can still see the Michelin sign out the window from the bed, the Michelin Man made up of piled white tires, walking along all lit up from inside the sign like he's got something to smile about. Who ever heard of white tires? Does the Michelin Man wobble when he walks? Do the tires balance like magic or are they glued together somehow? When no one's looking, does he swing them around like so many hula hoops? At thirteen I would stay up and wonder these things and try not to think about whether or not it would piss my dad off by asking him. I still wonder some of the same things, only now the Michelin Man looks more like a mummy with a beer gut.

Like if you pulled on a part of him that stuck out he would unravel and unravel, get down to something less puffy. I don't know what that would be, I can't imagine it.

her lip:

It feels like some other day but I know it is the same one. Joey takes me driving with him in his sister's big old Nova after more Streetfighter 2 at the 7-11.

We get to the apartment building Lisa lives in, Joey gets out of the Nova and walks across the parking lot, looking like a badass in his 501's and his white shirt and the big stupid wicker sombrero he stole from Otis. He looks like he could do anything. You would buy whatever he tried to sell you, I swear. He tosses his cigarette on the ground before he goes up the concrete stairs that run along the outside of the building.

I watch the cigarette burning a little pile of dead grass around it, flames shooting up a few inches for half a second, like the devil is about to show up. Before I call out to Joey it extinguishes itself.

I can practically hear the fire tell me, "Shhhh, don't bug him," before it disappears.

The building's concrete stairs don't seem connected to each other. They are suspended along a wall one by one, separate hovering rectangles, that just happen to follow each other. Joey climbs them like a gunslinger and goes up to the first door.

"Leese," he says, "Leese," and then lowers his voice so I can't hear. It finally opens a little, but you can see the chain is still done.

It looks like I might be here awhile.

There's a burnt patch in the grass from his cigarette, but you'd never notice.

When I look up again the apartment's door is shut and I don't see Joey anywhere. I look at my own hair in the mirror, I try to think about what it would look like if I got it cut like Joey's and put on a pair of Ray-Bans; I fuck with it and make faces at myself in the mirror. Some *cholo* walking past me on the sidewalk—tall, gawky himself—starts pointing and laughing at me checking myself out. I straighten my back real slow like I don't see him.

Joey and Lisa start screaming, their voices all on top of each other, rising and rising. When the door flies open and Joey falls out onto his ass: I know it's serious. Joey's snare drum flies out after him and makes a crazy noise as it lands, echoing through the outdoor hallway that looks like a cheap motel. All you can see behind the door to the apartment is dark. Joey picks up his snare with one hand and dusts his jeans off with the other, heads for the steps.

A faint ring of smeared blood around one side of Lisa's mouth as she floats in the doorway. A half a halo of blood there.

She's staring Joey down, she's trying to lock a target.

She yells his name, desperate and sweet—at the edge of the asphalt he turns around.

What is she holding? It looks like a big silver serving fork.

It is, I think.

She hurls the fork through the air and it comes so close to Joey it almost spins his sombrero off center, but it doesn't really hit him. Joey just laughs and slides into the Nova.

The fork lands near some dry bushes. Its prongs stick into the dirt, standing it up: shimmering, vibrating.

"Bone out," Joey says, jiggling down the windshield wiper lever the way you have to do to get the ignition going, "Before she goes for the tires." He laughs.

For Joey I know I shouldn't, but I turn around in the back seat to watch Lisa as we peel out onto the road. Her head is leaning like it isn't held up by her neck, only by the doorframe. The white slip she is wearing is all lit up from the sun so you can see she is naked underneath, and behind her is nothing but black. Her bleached-out hair sticks out crazy now, ratty like usual, but all over the place, and a little blood is dripping down onto her collarbone.

*   *   *

My moms: she's a nose-mom, she can smell the beer on me. But like she would even say anything anymore—her boozing's been chill for a few months but it could start again at any time.

"Maxy?"

We need beer money.

"Hi."

"What do you want?"

"Um. . ." I go. I can see Joey outside in the Nova tapping the stereo and nodding his head in the car to whatever fat ass beat he's got on.

I can't stop a split second from crossing my face that tells my mom so much, so fucking much. I hate her for it. It tells her: I need twenty bucks, that is the only thing that is going to make it okay for me, and I need this guy out there to keep wanting me around because then I might have a hope of something, something. Something past *her*.

And I see, in her split second that crosses her face, that she is just as scared of me not having a hope past her. And then she covers that split up with a stupid fake hope that goes sort of like: Max is about to meet a nice hippie chick who will bring him *right* out of his shell.

"Who's that?" Moms asks.

"This dude," I say, "A friend."

She puts her hand on my cheek and it takes all my will not to shrink back from her.

She sighs and stares at me, thinking she loves me, whatever.

"Here, honey," she says, and she sighs, and she smiles, and she gets the cash out of her wallet, a twenty, and sticks it in the pocket of my t-shirt.

I know she'll stop with this crystal-rubbing phase she's been in since she quit nursing school in June and she'll start drinking again by Thanksgiving like every year. And when she starts again I can spend my free time at home, in peace, if I time it to when she passes out. I can play Sega till four in the morning and she won't notice.

As I leave, she just watches, leaning on the doorframe like the day is still hot and she is barefoot like Lisa was in the morning. Mom is in an old blue bathrobe, and her mouth isn't bloody or smiling, mostly just tired from yapping into an office phone all week. But for a second, before I turn my head forward and fix my sights on Joey and the car and something farther down the road, her mouth looks lonely and stone scared in a straight line.

*　　*　　*

The streetlights, the cars going by, the way the sub-woofer makes the windshield shake with bass as Joey swerves in and out of the two lanes, passing people he shouldn't pass, makes me feel like everything is going to work out, like there is nothing more beautiful than moving down these roads, like something wonderful could happen to me, like all the people I know might hide their faults all at the same time. I see myself at the edge of water, I don't know where, with Joey and Otis, a couple six-packs, and a girl I think, but nobody I know. I can't see a face.

the man:

Dude, karaoke, Joey says.

My dad's apartment never looked so small.

And I am in a haze and I realize with a delay, like thirty second delay, that I haven't covered up my dumbass birthday present with a sheet in time.

I rode in the back, almost finished with a forty of Crazy Horse, but I have two more in a bag from Safeway. In the car here, they were next to me, curled up like they were in heaven together. Lisa resting in Joey's arms, her legs all sprawled over both of us so that her calves rested on my knees, it was almost like the three of us were a family. Her legs all muscular but long, really nice, fairly pornographic just to look at them for even a second.

"Jo-Jo-Bo-Jo, Banana Fana Fo Fo , Me My Mo Mo, JO-JO," Otis sings looking through the karaoke options, "Whatcha got, here Max? Freaking Tony Bennett, you got, my man, you got some Elvis . . ." he whispers all gritty in a way that makes it impossible to tell if he thinks it's cool or not.

"Love me tender, mind-bender?" Otis says to no one in particular.

Joey unzips his pants on his way to the bathroom.

Lisa is standing and trying to figure out what to do. Her M.O. is to look pissed and too cool, but to sometimes smile sweetly. It's so fake though, even I can tell that much.

I chug half of my forty and she grabs it out of my mouth and some spews on her but I am not laughing.

On his way back, Joey grabs my Crazy Horse out of her hand, takes a huge sip, and hands it back to her, then starts messing with some cables behind the karaoke monitor.

Hey, she says, hey, hey, and then gets it that her time with him for the night's kinda done.

Her big, bored eyes look all heavy—pissed and sad. She rolls them at Joey, then turns slowly to look around the room before finding a good corner and passing out quietly. Her body encircles the bottle of Crazy Horse like a cat nursing kittens.

I am hardly here. I can't tell if everyone knows or not. I just sort of sit here and squish up my bottom lip between my fingers like I am trying to remember not to do all the time because it looks like some stupid-ass shit. Otis starts yelling, and it's a minute before I figure out he's talking to me.

"You're up, my man Max," Otis goes, and hands me the mike.

My dad's favorite Frank Sinatra bullshit starts upon the karaoke.

"*Regrets, I've had a few. . .*" Frank sings

I look at the mike and start to say the words, but nothing happens.

"*But then again, too few to mention . . .*" Frank goes.

Me, the mike, and: nothing.

Nothing.

I can't say anything. The lyrics are on the monitor, in front of a big fat Frank. I am being led right through them by this bobbling white dot, but I can't say anything. I feel like if I could come up with *something*, even some raspy high shit like Otis, everything would be fine: I can't even do that much. I freeze up the whole room.

Everybody is staring at me now.

All I can think is I need to leave this place and if I got a haircut, something like Joey's maybe, I'd at least be able to sing when I had to.

Joey jumps up and grabs the mike from me.

"I've traveled each, and every by-way," Joey goes, in this deep deep voice, right up there with Frank, right on Frank.

Joey looks way better than even a young Frank. His getting up there and singing is more than just being nice to me, saving me from my muteness. It's like he has been me before, a scared loser, and he hates me for reminding him of it, can't stand another second.

Lisa seems to be awake now, but barely, and is smoking my dad's weed by herself in the corner, so I go over to sit down by her, she hands me the bowl. I can't think of anything to say, so I try to keep my movements slow, try to let her know it's fine with me if she passes out in the corner of my dad's living room.

Joey is singing and singing, he does it so easily, it would never occur to him not to enjoy every fucking second of it.

Me and Lisa are gonna keep packing the bowl over and over again, I tell myself. Each time she hits then I hit it's like something real sad from her comes through my dad's pipe into my lungs. I don't know how Joey can take so much sad from this woman. I can't take it: she looks up at me when I leave and then flops back down to passing out. Like she was desperate for even me to hang out with her. It's more than I can stand.

Otis pours me a shot of my father's bourbon and I do it and one more without feeling a thing.

Joey is really hamming it up to Old Blue Eyes, shaking his ass a little. On and on. Extended version or some shit.

Can I hold my neck up?

My dad's things, his dumbbells in the corner, a fishing pole.

Joey's mouth is speaking the words I couldn't.

Bookshelves that still look temporary. A cardboard box in the corner.

I stand up and everything spins for a second. Something in me feels like it's going to break.

I work harder to stay standing

I do it my way, Joey sings, like bellows, for real, and then collapses on the couch and picks up the phone and is talking, bringing other girls over, I guess, leaving me and Otis and Lisa in the cold for the time being.

This is the point of the evening when I realize my head is no longer attached to my body.

"I'm crash out," I go, knowing I missed a word there but not sure which one, and head slowly for the stairs, almost there when—through the puke she's hurled all over the area rug—Lisa grabs my ankle in a death vise.

"Oh its just you," she says, and I imagine—I think—I see her eyes roll back to the whites before her forehead lands in a puddle, back into Crazy Horse coma.

I shake.

All I know for sure when I make it into my dad's bedroom is that the only light is coming from the Michelin Man outside.

There's no point in even trying to open the window with my scrawny arms.

As I rip the blanket off the bed I can't stop staring out.

The Michelin Man is up there like the man in the moon, staring down at me and daring me to do something.

The Michelin Man is storming over everything in his way, running people down with his giant white tires.

Who the hell is he under that Halloween costume? What the hell is down there?

I am standing and staring and holding the blanket like a little boy asking for a glass of water in the middle of the night. If you peel away all those tires, what's there, Michelin Man? I wonder.

I wrap the blanket around me. I'm so thin it goes around my middle three times even though it is small. If I kept drinking forty after forty and shot after shot and beat Joey and Little Otis and all of them put together, if I kicked Lisa for puking up my ankle with her desperate hand, if I kept going and going for days after they went down, passed out, booted and rallied, came back for more, if I was the biggest alcoholic in the whole world then my beer belly would look like this blanket around my middle and my arms would still be this weak. This is it, I think to myself, I'm eighteen now. I toss the blanket on the floor and lie down in my father's bed, leaning my head over the side, away from the lit up window, so if I do throw up it won't come back and choke me.

11

SHADOW MAMA

Racinda

So I started to think of her in my mind as Vagina Popcorn. The orange stuff on the popcorn would get on her fingernails and she would suck it off, somehow erasing all the residue from the perfect silk-wrap cuticle rim. They were talking about douching, the air in the kitchen was a milky turquoise, reflected from the floor I guess since the light flouncing through the high windows came yellow off the curtains.

Vagina Popcorn said she wasn't going to put a bunch of chemicals up in there.

If there was an odor, she said, she was just going to go to the clinic. That's what she believed was the right thing to do, she said. Lisa half-heartedly slapped her five, as if out of habit, and when their hands met, Vagina Popcorn's showed their age. Vagina Popcorn's sister, Lisa's Aunt Beesie, believed in douching. I didn't know if Aunt Beesie was Lisa's real aunt, or if Vagina Popcorn was her real mother, or what. Lisa didn't seem annoyed enough at Vagina for Vagina to really be her mother, they didn't seem to know each other's every breath like it seemed they should have.

I asked Lisa later and she said, "What does real mean anyway? Look at her nails. Look at her cheekbones."

Vagina Popcorn was the kind of person who got her boyfriends to pay for plastic surgery, but had roaches crawling under her peeling, jewelly linoleum. Even so, I liked the way Vagina Popcorn looked at me like she understood at least something; I liked the way she nodded at the right times, so you *knew* she was getting it.

I sort of sat in the corner, even though I was right at the table with them. Sipping my Diet Schweppes and eating popcorn until I got a piece with a huge bomb of orange cheese-chemical on it and had to stop. I tried to wash it down with the Schweppes but the bubbles just went up my sinuses and made it worse. I coughed.

Lisa stuck a napkin under my nose just as I was about to snarf it all out. I managed to grab the thing out from her hand before snot and spit got all over her. I only spit enough out that the napkin sufficed to hide it. The food and spit and soda didn't explode, it didn't go everywhere.

I wanted to run out of the apartment, though, I wanted to say, "I have to go," before they started hating me. But what did I have to run to? School that was pointless because I was going to have to go back in the fall for gym classes anyway even though I was supposed to graduate? My mother, her search for the cult-sister? Nothing. Nothing.

"She can't hold her liquor, can she?" Vagina Popcorn said, and giggled in a way that made my eyes shrink away from her, focus on the matte aluminum lid of my soda can.

I always have the effect in these sorts of situations of making the people I'm with study me. I hide myself so well that they have to stare at me and squinch their eyes and test out little comments, observations of me, to get a sense of what they're dealing with. I just don't want them to have to deal with anything. I just want to make it through the encounter intact.

"When I was with Allen," Vagina said, "He couldn't hold his liquor, *and* I had to go to the clinic all the time." She reached out and rubbed my arm to soothe me but it tensed me up. She kept doing it though, and I calmed down some.

We'd been sitting around and smoking , Vagina pouring rum into our Schweppes for us—a drink they called the "Tri-Delt" for the sorority since it was made with pink soda.

"Delta Delta Delta, can I helpya helpya helpya?" Vagina had said, taking her first swig.

After awhile Lisa started tapping her fingernails up and down the edge of the table, which I knew already meant she was getting bored. I didn't want her to leave—I didn't want to be alone with Vagina but I didn't want to leave Vagina. And it wasn't that Vagina was creepy talking about her sex life—it seemed totally normal, like between friends, not between family members—that Lisa wanted to go.

"You okay, sugar?" Vagina said to Lisa.

Lisa did look a little green.

"You can't hold it either all of a sudden, or what?" Vagina said, and rubbed Lisa's arm. Lisa didn't shrink or warm to the touch, she was indifferent. She did look queasy.

"I think it's just that pink soda," Lisa said, "Ugh, I think I need to go lie down." Lisa traced her hand on the top of her belly in small ovals, and closed her eyes, but didn't get up to leave.

Vagina raised her eyebrows at me and repeated the gesture—her hand rubbing a small circle underneath her own ribcage—but then looked away quickly, a little sadly. Dumb, I didn't understand until later what this meant.

But now Lisa's eyes were trailing the small rectangle window above the sink—like a basement window, really, even though we were on the third floor of the apartment complex.

"Well honey, now how is that man of yours?" Vagina asked Lisa. Vagina wasn't hungry to keep us there, but didn't mind chatting some more.

"Which one?" I ventured, my voice cracking. But I was just proud of myself for speaking.

They humored me and smiled a little, Lisa with a sweet snarl like teasing.

"Fucked up," she said, "But the band is doing real good. That meeting I was telling you about with the guy from the record company is going to happen, actually, this week. Otis says they're going to get a deal—I mean, whatever, it's *Otis*—but then it will be all about 'on the road' and groupies and all that shit."

Lisa stood and spread her arms the width of the kitchen, hands resting on the chrome of her chair and the speckly-white formica rim of the sink.

"All.That.Shit," she repeated.

She stretched that way for a minute and then crumpled up her empty Marlboro soft pack, whose cellophane wrapper she had already burned into nothing via cherry-sized holes, nothing but warped crispy string, browning, oxidized.

"Maybe you could be the manager," Vagina said dispassionately. "Maybe it's your ticket out of here, baby."

"Yeah," Lisa said, also dispassionately, but for just a second her eyes flashed over to Vagina as if to see if she were serious, if she were trying to leave us or force us out.

"Yeah, well, I think I'm going to run out for more cigarettes," Lisa said. "I'm not really sure when—you know, when I'll be back, so Racinda I'll see you later."

At the same moment, Vagina and I both pushed our fuller packs to her, our hands and their contents nearly coming together on the table like vectors on a grid, then stopping, hovering, embarrassed to find our motives in each other's fingertips at the meeting place.

But Lisa stepped away, after squinting at my full, orange mouth with disgust, slapping the walls with her broad palms, toward the hallway and her room.

"I should, um, I should go," I said. "I should get home."

But Vagina, as if she knew what was waiting for me there, wouldn't let me. She got out some pretzels then, and then some cheese and crackers, so after a little while the orange popcorn residue was gone from around my lips. I felt my laugh getting looser and more natural, I said things I was actually thinking.

Each time I hung out there, I resisted less and less the cozy feeling in that dumpy apartment that became like a beautiful, underwater world in its way. Vagina had painted all the walls different, rich shades of blue. It was the exact opposite of my mother's white and gray-feeling house. There was light and chatter here; even though it was in a California dingbat apartment building, dry and ugly, cinderblocks and a front door that opens onto an outside concrete landing like a hotel, there was water and humidity in this apartment thanks to Vagina's hard work.

The first night I'd slept over at Lisa's, strung out on Dexatrim and hung over from the gin and tonics Lisa got thirty-five year old salesmen to buy us at a dive-but-trying bar called the Cat Club, I woke to Vagina stroking my sweat- and gel-crusted hair off my forehead.

I had jumped once I was awake enough to know it wasn't a dream. I scooted back into the beige and scarlet pinstripe velour cushion.

"Oh here, honey, you look like you need some coffee," she said, suddenly away from me, and brought back a little blue teacup of it from the kitchen.

"Thank you," I said. I was still wiping sleep out of my eyes, scraping the soapy layer of film off my tongue with my teeth when she came back. I was trying to angle my body so that my braless chest didn't show itself through the holes in my plaid shirt. I rushed to bring the blanket that I'd shoved down by my feet up over my chest. I was embarrassed, desperate for Lisa to come back and save me. I didn't know what to say and it made me anxious and exhausted at once.

"I'm Virginia, precious," she said, and started patting my hair down again.

I told her my name.

"You look like you need a cigarette and some eggs," she said, still smoothing my hair back.

I did need those things, and I needed a shower and to blow my nose, too. I didn't get up for awhile though. With each touch of her hand I just got more and more used to it, used to how familiar she acted with me even though she didn't know me. So what? I felt like. There was something about it where I could just lean into her hand, and even though it wasn't really me she could see I smiled up at her and sunk back down in the cushion until she brought me a big, old towel and a washcloth, and said I could use her special shampoo. I never really had to say anything much to Vagina, and I was still unsure around her, but she took to me, I guess, and it felt so nice.

I ate pretzel after pretzel that day in the blue kitchen, I couldn't think of what to say, Vagina sighed, and I imagined that it was because I wasn't coming up with any conversation. Fortunately, the doorbell rang three times, and then a fourth as a sort of teaser.

"Oh that'd be Ernie," Vagina said, even though she looked puzzled. The front door had opened and shut, and a man's footsteps were coming down the hallway.

"Hi sugar!" Vagina yelled, but Ernie didn't respond.

"I said *hello honeybuns*," she yelled, then raised her eyebrows at me. Like my own mother's they were very tweezed, neat pencil lines.

*   *   *

Lisa hadn't made it to the store. I found her sitting on the floor of her bedroom, painting her toenails, her legs at the crazy angles you have to strike to do that—for her it wasn't unflattering though. A black stripe of panty showed between her legs, where her aqua-blue dress leaned back. Her belly leaned out, convex, just a little, like a little girl's.

A man—thin hips, tall, his broad back spread wide—stood in the doorway.

"You're about as bad as your mama, avoiding me like I've got the bubonic plague," he said, and twisted fast when he finally felt me there behind him. It was so dark in the hallway his face was murky to me.

Lisa's face held an everyday expression, an expression that had a plan in it, was grossed out, was pleased with herself, and didn't give a shit, all at once.

"Ernie?" I said, but it wasn't. It was Jordan.

"Jordan!" Vagina came screaming behind me.

"Now Ginny, you never said not to come back."

He was a bad man—it was so obvious. I could practically smell it. His cheekbones held his face wide open, and his eyes crinkled in laughter even when he was far from smiling, like now. His lips were frozen, didn't move much when he talked. And even if I couldn't smell how bad he was, I already knew that Vagina was so tolerant of shitty behavior from men that he would have had to have really done *something* for her to be so pissed at him.

"Get the hell out of here. How many times do I have to tell you?" Vagina said.

"One cup of tea," he said, and his eyes dropped the laughter, "I been needing to talk to you. Mama's—well she's. . ."

"Oh what now," she said.

"They have a diagnosis," he said.

He looked to the corner like he was trying to hide tears, or something.

"One cup," Vagina said, rolling her eyes like there was nothing she could do.

"With a eensy-weensy shot of bourbon," he said, his face back with the smile-sneer I'd only before seen on teen-age boys.

"Jordan," she said, slapping the wall as she turned toward the kitchen, "Jordan," like he was a great mystery of the universe, the one thing she couldn't figure out.

Jordan acted like I was in his way when he passed me, and soon I was alone there, staring at Lisa painting her toenails. She was ignoring me, Vagina was ignoring me. I had left my watch at home. I shifted from foot to foot and tried to force myself to speak the words, *well I should go*. But I couldn't. I couldn't remember if it was Tuesday or Wednesday, having unofficially given up on school for the year, since I had to repeat gym anyway.

When Lisa finished the big toe of her second foot she leaned over the gray office-style plastic trashcan and threw up a little, just one heavy mouthful. She wiped her mouth on the back of her hand, lit a cigarette

"You ready," she said to her own lips in the mirror, blotting her lipstick.

"*Are* you?" she said.

Sure, I nodded, *sure.*

Before we finally did go, though, she stood over the bin again, and more frothy, sweet-smelling vomit fell out of her, silently, with a little cough.

Fuck, she said, and she kicked the garbage can so it shivered, she wiped the string of saliva that ran from her cheek to a matted lock by her ear.

Fuck, softer, sadder, and I thought, oh god, I think she *is* pregnant.

I hugged her then, and her belly was already seeming high and tough, and she leaned into me, soft for a minute before she sniffled once and hardened

"Let's go, before Ginny gets pissed at him,"

I set the can out in the hallway so it didn't stink up her room. I figured Vagina would deal with it.

Joey's baby? I thought. *Whose?* But I was a girl who knew when to shut the fuck up.

*   *   *

So Jordan was Vagina's ex-boyfriend, the mean-streak one she couldn't get rid of, despite Ernie, her nice, current boyfriend who was away a lot due to his delivery job. We took Jordan's keys from his cheap leather bomber jacket on the hook in the hallway.

"The devil incarnate," Lisa said.

I nodded.

"His roommate isn't so bad, though," she said. "He'll help."

The sun was brighter than I could stand after that dark apartment, so once we were in his truck I put on a pair of aviator glasses—the mirrored, cop kind—that he had in his glove compartment. Even though she was driving Lisa said she didn't want them—she just squinted.

Taped to the inside of the glove compartment there was a picture of a woman's mostly-shaved crotch—the woman was a redhead—closeup and biological. I didn't say anything about this, but Lisa just said, "pig," like she would say, "stopsign," or "weird time for traffic," when we were driving. We would drive in the quiet a lot of the time and she would say these words like thinking out loud. This was just the beginning of the driving, though. There was a lot more to come.

"Ed, Jordan's roommate, got a DUI and Jordan said that if I ask Ed nice he'll let us use his car till he gets off home arrest or whatever the fuck he's on."

I found myself waiting in Jordan's shitty "in-law" apartment, with industrial carpet and bongwater stains on the walls: the basement under the feet of an old lady whose presence below here was only announced by the three little ovals of cross-stitching pictures of poodles she was surely responsible for. Their oval rims were a pale wood, held together with a little crank, and someone had glued loops of pink yarn around the wood to make it more than just the thing that holds the fabric while you sew—it became a sort of decorative frame. She either didn't smell what these men burned in pipes or she didn't recognize the odors.

We just walked right in, and Lisa went to the back bedroom where Ed, the boozy roommate, was playing a game on his computer. I never saw him. I just sat in the living room reading a magazine about photography that was really just soft porn—tits through wet t-shirts, vaguely complicatedly backlit by the Hawaiian sunsets. I didn't see why these two, Jordan and Ed the DUI, even bothered with faux-porn when they had piles of the full-on stuff all around.

Lisa and Ed were talking low in the other room, and then just Ed was. I stopped noticing, stopped listening. There was insulation coming out above the drywall next to the poodles. There was a golf magazine underneath some of the porn that I thought about tearing up and folding into origami. Instead I just burnt cigarette holes into some asshole's red face under a tam.

Ed didn't come out. He just said, "Three weeks—three weeks," from beyond the door.

Lisa said uh-huh, bye Ed.

"My court date is in three weeks. *Three weeks,*" with a hint of nervousness and a hint of knowing he was a giant dumbass for giving her the keys.

Lisa had the greatest way of storming out of a place, like she was wearing tall knee-high boots even if she was in two dollar flip-flops, like now. She paused for a second—couldn't see me there on the couch though I was practically right in front of her.. Then she jangled the keys, held together on a little leather keychain with something embossed on it, leaves and initials, fading, and smiled.

She shook her head a little when she did finally see me, rolled her eyes, mouthed the words *blow job* and stuck out her tongue.

*   *   *

Driving and driving and driving and driving and driving and driving but then

We got stuck in a thin line of traffic, out there in nowhere in the foothills. They were digging a huge ditch next to the road, dumping something from the hills into it; a slag pit.

She shrugged.

For about five minutes it was just all gold, all gold light, barely any green coming in, and the radio was off, and I didn't even want a cigarette. I felt so free from everything. And I didn't even have to worry about my life, as in how to get out of it, because with her there was just this moment and this truck, and it was adequately exciting still to be enough for me. This was about all I wanted, I guess, just that she liked me and would drag me around with her. That she could do things I couldn't do, like blow some guy to get his truck for three weeks—I knew I couldn't do these things.

*   *   *

At some far, far town's convenience store, fluorescent lights wheeled out their purple glow above me, despite the sun. I chewed my Combos, getting the cheese out of my teeth with my tongue.

The same sounds here as at our own: freeway like wind, and boy noises over by the payphone, across the asphalt.

I watched my straw flash from white to bright red whenever I sucked more cherry Slurpee.

"Hey," she said, edgy and loud.

I jumped up fast, surprised, didn't understand how she had gotten out of the store so quickly.

She blocked the sun from my face, purplish fluorescents ringed her forehead.

"I'm getting rid of it," she said. "I want to have it but I'd just end up killing it. He'd end up killing it," Lisa said.

Red Slurpee got stuck in my throat as I nodded to agree with her. A huge, painful gulp of the icy shocking liquid sputtered up from me, like the pink soda had, but darker, vivid, freezing cold.

My mouth hedged, tightened to block it, but it was no use. It dribbled out. I held my breath

And couldn't hold back; I coughed and spit it everywhere—bright, brightest red-fuchsia—and the boys over there howled—*she spits*—the cherry red stuff coming out of my nose and mouth.

Stunned, despondent, I just stood there, red sugar coating my white face and chest and hands.

But Lisa got in the store and back so fast with napkins, wiping me down, around the ears and under my nose.

"Here," she said as she got it from under my eyes, "Here, honey."

She stuffed the dirty ones in her cleavage as she readied another one. I could feel little bits of napkin sticking to the syrup that coated me now. Still, she dabbed and dabbed.

Her shadow on the wall caught my eye: her shadow was a skinny mama cleaning off a giant baby.

I laughed and coughed, laughed and spit, and the shadow kept working, kept working to take that stain from my skin.

The red got all over her, at the end of it.

When her tears started coming Lisa had no more clean napkins, just thin, squashed lumps stained the color of faded methiolate tincture on skin. She smeared the soft used mash of white and pink paper again against her own nose to wipe away the snot.

*   *   *

"I say let nature take its course. That's how it is with sex and that's how it is with consequences," Vagina said.

My eyebrows inched together, my mouth opened. Nothing emerged.

"Oh now, don't you worry Racinda. You're over here enough these days that you'll get used to a house with an open, healthy discussion of sex. I know your mama doesn't do that for you at home, but you'll get used to it here."

Lisa quiet, hovering over her hot water with lemon, her ashtray.

Lisa didn't say anything but I could see her agreeing with Vagina, wanting to keep it. *He is the first one I've wanted to keep around*, she'd say later. I wouldn't know if she was talking about Joey or about the baby. *With the others I got rid of it, when this happened, I didn't care. He is the first one I want so bad*, she would say.

The first one of them I want to keep.

But other than that Lisa kept quiet. I could see the two sides of the coin—life, death, as if as clear as that—play across her face. But she wouldn't talk to Vagina about it and she wouldn't talk to me about it and I don't think she told Joey she was pregnant at all.

"But if that's what you've got to do, that's what you've got to do. I'll call the clinic. I have a double shift at the SPCA so I can't take you. Racinda can't drive. Jordan's going to have to," Vagina said.

Lisa got a blank look, stayed silent, but Vagina took it as a yes, call the clinic. They seemed more distant than mother and daughter, these two, but here they did understand each other without speaking, without gesture, even.

Vagina dialed the phone.

"Jordan, I don't care. You're driving that girl," Vagina yelled into the phone, and hung up. But she called Ernie just in case, she called Ernie as backup.

Why even bother with Jordan, I wondered, if you've got Ernie lined up anyway?

Lisa scowled.

"That'll get rid of both of the men, good work," Lisa said, but Vagina didn't hear her. Vagina put more water on and wiped up the crumbs and the twist-ties from around the toaster.

"It's about time for a little quiet around here, wouldn't you say, hon?" Vagina said when she sat back down with us, arrangements made. Lisa avoided Vagina's eyes the rest of the night, always made sure I was in between them.

We smoked all night, we glued ourselves to movie after movie. When one of us napped the others fast forwarded the boring parts until sleep overcame us all three and we slept leaning against each other, side against side, arm over shoulders, a soft chain on the couch, gray-purple flickers from the end of the videotape crossing our faces like breathing, like moonlight.

*　　　*　　　*

It seemed then to me like our mothers want everything from us, and they leave us behind, our mothers. *At least yours didn't leave you when you were a baby, at least she doesn't have Jordans around all the time, year in, year out,* Lisa said once, and I thought, but wait, mine left Ruth, and she has Jesus around year in and year out, a Jesus who is orderly and is so far removed from the women singing when I was little. Jesus of the charts, I'd think to myself, Jesus of the accounting books, Jesus who makes sure the bathroom is clean enough, Jesus who monitors bedrooms for silence. Lisa would wheeze and cry, would curse and smoke, we'd both drink with Vagina, share lip balm and Jack Daniels, sleep with our heads on each others' necks, and this, this was so much closer to the women's hands on my back when I was little, this was so much closer to the tongues that would spill out of my mother when she was joyful with it and not psychotic with it, this was so much closer to Ruth's glee running across our fields, scrambling all clothed the first hot day into the creek. So much closer than that dead Jesus on our wall, that flat, medieval face, that man who had left us as long ago as my father had.

*   *   *

I had been spending a few days at home and Lisa just didn't call. That was it. It seemed like a fluke at first and then it didn't.

Gray and spiky and howling and cold is what it feels like if I imagine the lines, the vectors underneath the plastic forms of Amandine's furniture, the forms underneath my body and my mother's body. The grids that hold everything together that you could see if you peeled back the air: gray, spiky, howling, cold. What is it, whatever is under there? My mother, somehow, pins life on these shadows. I don't know how to do anything about it. I avoid, and I hug her when she cries, and sometimes I scream at her, and I think about leaving in whatever way I can, but I can't quite seem to come up with a plan to actually get out of here for good. I seemed destined to be homeless, devoid of comfort.

Give me Vagina Popcorn to my own mother any day.

The sight of my mother's perfect hairdo elicited Vagina's blond shag, Lisa's wild knots. I would remind myself—that all happened so fast so fast *so fast*.

That what I felt in Vagina's apartment didn't really belong to me, was only mine temporarily, made the tears rush harder.

The band had gotten back into town: the first day she disappeared. I wasn't going to hear from her until she and Joey stopped fucking and started fighting.

If ever.

I stopped leaving the house at all, sat under the tacky afghan Button had knitted for me when I was a baby and that Amandine had wanted me to get rid of.

"Well if you don't feel better soon then we'd better get you to the doctor," Amandine finally said one morning.

"Whatever," I said. My cornflakes turned my stomach so I pushed them away from me on the coffee table.

"You need. . .:" my mother said, "Racinda—" she said, shaky, scared for me, and scared to confront me.

"What," I didn't look at her.

"What is wrong, *honey*?" my mother said.

"Nothing."

"You have got to start *doing* something. I thought you needed. . . summer school?"

I shrugged.

"What am I going to do with you?" she said.

"I have to repeat it all in the fall anyway," I said.

"And what are you going to do after that? Are you just going to sit here on the couch?" she said.

"Maybe," I said. "I like the couch."

"You're going to have to get a job, young lady," she said. "You're going to have to do something. You're going to have to go to school or get a job. Support yourself. This isn't right."

The phone rang then and I answered it, the only effort I was generally willing to rouse.

"Cindy," Mr. Wills, my mom's boss and the church's pastor, said, "Cindy, this is Mr. Wills. Is your mama there? How are you doing today, Cindy."

I scowled and handed the phone to my mother without speaking.

"Oh, Cindy's fine, she's fine, just a little under the weather," my mom said to him, pivoting her hips away from me, swaying cheerfully as she zoomed into the kitchen, *no, I think just the two dozen will do it*, she said, *well, of course, well of course, yes, if you think—we'll do three, right, they* do *enjoy those pastries. Of course.* She found a palm-sized pad of lined paper, its coiled wire binding flattened and bent, and took notes cheerily, some determination in her, some feeling of giving ideas away to this man, of taking his ideas for her own. *Right, Mrs. Wills wants the yellow, okay, and then what about—are we going to have a sign up for that or—right, okay, I'll stop at Walgreen's on my way to the bank. Sure, no sure, I'm glad to. . .*

Sometimes he called me Lindy, sometimes Cindy, could never remember my name correctly, and she let him.

But more than for failing to correct him, I wanted to punch her in the face right then for being so happy. For her stupid little job that gave her so much pleasure, for the little details of donations and coffee brunches, for filing. The old Amandine had been useless like I was useless on this couch—doing nothing in the world, worrying about the finer points, the aesthetic points, the shapes of her topiary animals or the two tiny pills on the elbow of a sweater.

My mother leaned prettily into the antique mirror so out of place in our wan "foyer"—she hummed what was not a hymn, but one of these new-age church ditties as she traced her top lip in a bland rose.

"Oh! My sunglasses!" she said and she bustled—bustled! with me on the couch hating her so strongly!—back into the kitchen to retrieve them from the counter.

She had almost forgotten about me, and when her eyes passed over me on her way out the door the darkness fell across them just for a few seconds before she walked out.

"Suit yourself, Mrs. Oscar the Grouch," my mother said. "I'm going to work."

"Bye, *CINDY*," I said.

When I heard myself gasp once I knew that it was to fend off tears, but it worked and I just sat there.

Very actively *not crying*.

The TV, the noise of air coming through vents, that my feet were too cold out of the blanket all conspired to make me furious, to make my every breath an insult to the planet.

And so while Regis Philbin's crawly, asexual voice snapped and twisted in the empty static of the living room, all I could come up with to dream of was how morning television had seemed much more interesting smoking a joint with Vagina.

A brown delivery truck inched up to the house across the street. I imagined the pesticides evaporating up from the hedges like spirits to heaven. I held my breath as long as I could.

I leaned my elbow up onto the arm of the couch and stared back at Jesus on the wall for a long time. *How much have You brought to us and how much have You hurt us*, I kept thinking. Dude, I kept calling him, Dude. Less with the excited intonation of dude, as in *dude—you've gotta see this bong*, but more with the feeling of *dude* a boy would use when his friend was swerving between lanes near a known late-night speed trap, or going home with the town skank ho. *Dude, what are you fucking thinking*, was the tone, *Dude, I can't believe you*, was the tone, *Dude, were you raised in a Dodge Dart?*

And when the gasping happened again this time I knew it was me, but I couldn't tell what it was for.

What? I asked JC and I saw my father towing the guilt he must *must* have across the sky in my brain, and I saw the pastors—Ray, and Mr. Wills—the men Amandine had sold me up the river for.

Jordan—the one Vagina abandoned Lisa for.

And Lisa's Joey, whose face I'd never seen, who'd taken the aquarium-blue apartment away from me. Joey—an idea, not a person—an idea that Lisa hung me out to dry for.

Dude, I thought, and I think Jesus thought back to me then: *It wasn't a promise,* he said, *it was a phase. A phase. The promise comes from Amandine.*

I bit my cheek until I tasted blood.

I didn't leave you, he said, *look at who left you. Ruth left you. Not me, I've been here.*

Fuck off I thought back to him, *shut the fuck up shut the fuck up.*

The fury beyond words I felt at his blame was something I'd never thought belonged to me. It was Ruth's.

My skin froze, I remained still, pinned.

That something in me was untenable, that something couldn't hold was now obvious. I breathed as shallow as I *could* until the crying stopped and I fell asleep, hoping it was my life in this living room that was what was going to give.

*   *   *

So the morning when Lisa finally called I had almost gotten over expecting her to. I was staring at a glass of orange juice and a blank whole-wheat tortilla as I was shoving around a bunch of idiotic textbooks in my plaid vinyl book bag—the attendance woman Mrs. Ramirez had called and even though I was going to have to repeat in the fall, I guess I needed to start coming to school if I didn't want to get into legal trouble. California *uber alles.* I was so accustomed to doing things half-assed while looking at something else, so inept, so resigned to being frustrated that the impossible cram of calculus *and* geology *and* physics into my cheap pack from the ho store at the mall was taking me the better part of five minutes. When the phone rang I expected it to be Amandine, asking me to check the burners on the stove, her favorite thing to do in the morning, and so I answered with a huge whine.

I didn't know what to say to her, but it ended up not mattering, since Lisa was still drunk.

"Where are you?" I said.

"Joey's?" she said. "I miss you, baby, little Racindarama."

"Are you okay?"

"Mmmmmmm," in an inconclusive tone.

"So. . ." I said, and suddenly the ill-fitting calculus book was intolerable to me, I ripped it out of the bag and let it drop to the linoleum.

"There's a gig tonight—we want you to come. Joey and the guys want to meet you, I told them you were so smart, so smary-art, huggybear. . ."
It sounded like a guy tackled her, Joey I guess, and she dropped the phone, squealing, and then there was a dial tone.

She didn't call back.

The next day at 7am on my way to school I tried to act like I was hard and didn't care about them anymore. I was watching my boots fall one after the other, feeling their powerful steps and their globy steel toes and some hope of something to come.

Who knew what? Something. Some feeling like a relief, and a push into a new world. I could hear a church bell from god knows where and I could sense the green on the grass shifting browner and the moisture in the air wicking up and away.

I felt my feet scrape against each square of combed, neutral concrete. New warmth in the air snuck under my ears, between my fingers, coming from the west, rattling the leaves a little.

And I heard the thing—or I felt it somehow—driving up next to me.

"Need a ride, sweetie?" Vagina said, driving slow next to me, creeping a little, not looking at the road, her hair tied back in a bandanna like Axl Rose.

"No thanks, Gin," I said, "it's not like I don't need the exercise."

Vagina drove one of those old prototype Toyotas that never dies. Hers was a yellow that looked like it had gone through three or four stages of fading, and was now sort of a hip, soft, lemony shade.

"How about some breakfast, then? I just went to the store," she said, and I loved how she could drive and not look at the road and still not hit anything. I loved that the way her neck skin was going wrinkly and soft reminded me of Button. I got in. I forgot my geology book in the car, there, and couldn't remember for weeks where I had left it.

After two big plates of pancakes and three mimosas, I wasn't even capable of being vertical. Oh well. Let the state at me. Pete Wilson, I'm yours, I thought, shifting around uncomfortably, my gut working as a pivot. I was horizontal on the living room couch, staring at puddles of real maple syrup and crumbs and a sticky napkin when Vagina gave up on getting me to move anywhere anytime soon.

Vagina brought the fuzzy, deep turquoise acrylic blanket down. Turquoise like chocolate tastes. She spread it onto me as you would set out a beach towel: gently, aerodynamically, working with gravity. I could feel its beautiful movements—the drop, the edges puffing up on air, the corners trouncing down onto my expanded hips and knees and soft upper arms. When it settled on me I sank deeper into the couch. Its satin trim, the same color but with faded patches that traipsed across it like river light, ran up against my chin and smoothed my jaw line, my ear, so, so soft.

Vagina's delicate, buttery laugh tumbled to me through the air.

* * *

I woke alone inside the turquoise apartment. Was it noon? I stumbled toward the voices by the door to the outside world.

I could see gray silhouettes through the dusty, grim, immovable yellow curtain, the window was thick as a cake, dark glass. Dessicated black dots—the corpses of a few dead flies and gnats—rimmed the sill.

I wiped my eyes, swallowed, tried to elude my stupor.

Vagina's Angie Dickinson hair shook along with her cigarette, and Lisa was crying. Vagina sat up on the black guard railing, precarious two floors above the parking lot, rested her delicate heels on the lower bar.

I could hear the freeway and the wind, but not what their words were.

Lisa crumbled into a little ball, a quiet thing sitting on the concrete.

It wasn't noon, it was twilight.

"I had to work," Vagina said, "Who do you think pays the rent around here while you're out there doing whatever?"

"But—*Jordan*," Lisa said, still sobbing.

"Well *Ernie* picked you up at least," Vagina said. "*Ernie* picked you up."

It was almost eight pm.

Vagina had gone to work and returned.

Lisa had had the abortion and been driven back by Ernie.

I had slept all day and into the night.

The two of them fell onto the couch after their fight, both teary, and crawled under the blankets with me. Lisa shared some of her Vicodan with us. Vagina got up to check on the chicken she was roasting—the smells of the vegetables and the chicken fat streamed through the room, and an antiseptic smell covered another, messier, smell coming off Lisa. Lisa would sniffle from low crying every once in awhile, but I didn't look at her, didn't want to make it worse than it was. She would clamp her hands across the pain in her belly and bend double, her back like a turtle's, but the spine bony and tough, and the turquoise blanket would come off me and my knees would feel the harsh chill in the air conditioning.

"My *skin* hurts," she said.

"*Everything* hurts," she said, and she asked me the time about every fifteen minutes to see if she could take another Vicodan. She'd already doubled up what the doctor told her but didn't want to push it worse than that. She was scared of prescription drugs in a way she wasn't so much of the other kinds.

We watched four different old movies overlapping each other on some cable channels, Vagina at the remote, cruising black and white spectacles of South American nightclubs and highball glasses and one-engine seaplanes and alcoholic sidekicks and bloody pools of light from streetlamps. Their plots converged, veered, layered into and away from each other. The three of us overlapped, too, leaned on each other, slanted against each other, our legs crossing on the coffee table. I was happiest here, my story woven in to theirs, taking the pain from Lisa.

I felt slippery, like a child just after a bath. I stretched in the heat under the blanket, pushing the memory of being forsaken to Amandine's house to the back of my mind.

She is permanent, this is just a phase.

Shut up.

But I imagined this sofa as permanent, our limbs and Lisa's hair like snakes.

A phase, Jesus Christ himself said to me, and I hated him.

We three were snakes under the garden, snakes in the nest, curled around our eggs, coiled in the warm burrow, taking heat from the blanket and giving it to each other. *Not a snake pit like you would think, Mr. Dude— what looks like the devil for your sort is home to me,* I told him, and he nodded, he frowned.

I snapped my split tongue at him across black space.

The three of us curled in an ancient pattern. The three of us curled underground in a home that is right for our sort. The three of us enough, strength in the three of us, love, enough. We nested in each others' shed skins.

Our new skins: bright leaf green, thick; we coiled underground and spiraled across the sky at once. Indigo, black, vectors lit in starlight.

"Well Goddammit, Jordan, I don't—" Vagina said into the cordless, "I—" she giggled, "Okay."

Lisa's eyes grew sober. Wide.

"You're leaving?" I managed, my voice shaking.

Lisa's hands went to her stomach, lightly.

"Take the chicken out in half an hour, Racinda honey," Vagina said, pulling a pink mascara tube from her white purse on the floor.

"Where are you going now?" Lisa whispered, "Where now?"

"No lip, honey. No, I don't want any lip. I've just got to go over and take care of something. Don't you even think about it," she said, tracing a flat brush the length of a thumb up each cheekbone.

Temporary, Jesus, that fucker, said.

Snakes you don't understand, I said.

Who roasts chicken at midnight? he said.

The devil, I said, *the devil herself.*

Without Vagina at the remote, Lisa and I had to suffer the rude colors and screams of commercials—I wasn't fast enough at switching.

But the phone rang.

"No, okay," Lisa said into the cordless.

"Who is that?" I said. She ignored me.

"That's totally okay, come now," she said into the phone right before she threw up a little more into the blue-trimmed trash bin from the bathroom Vagina had placed next to the couch for this purpose.

"Who was that?" I said.

"Will you go get me some cigarettes," Lisa said clutching her abdomen, then pressing her forehead, fastening her eyelids shut and exhaling in discomfort, in weariness. She didn't hand me any money, but I drew my legs out from under hers, away. Up.

Hemming my mind in to just 7-11 and something approximating hope that I could return here, I walked out into the blank Sacramento night.

*　　　*　　　*

The 7-11 had cable too.

"More often than not," the psychologist on the late-night replay said to Jenny Jones, "the woman will choose the child-molesting boyfriend over custody of her child."

See, Jesus said, *they will sell you out every time,* he said, *I'm here for you, babe.*

As I bought one pack and stole another from the stoned graveyard clerk, I imagined the store doused in turquoise. I imagined that the strips of beef jerky, under the plastic, had scales.

*   *   *

Joey's eyes were light and I fixed on him hard that first time.

They'd shoved the beautiful blanket into a pile, layers like a ruined pastry at one end of the couch.

She was straddled across him, they were making out, his feet up on the glass table, a plate of chicken bones sucked dry there. But his eyes were open and they were on me, they followed me into the kitchen. She ignored me.

His shoulders were solid, thick, definitely across that line into *man* territory. Not a boy. I don't know what Montgomery Clift looks like, but his face was like that—old movie star, old-school male who knows just how to push a girl around. All this and his black-and-white movie hair, dark, made his white t-shirt, some logo Lisa was sprawled on top of, seem completely wrong. He should have been wearing a fedora.

The breast meat was gone, the wings were gone, only the tough little legs were left on the roast, and I hated leg meat. I stood just past his view, still in the kitchen, and tried to think of what to do, where to go. Where my book bag was. I could see her feet now trying to curl around his, and I could see their shadows thrown huge and shifting from the television light.

The magnificent shadow of her hair danced gray on that wall, huge like a closeup at a drive-in. It covered the still, hard shadow from his head— gobbling it, passing over, returning. I took a few steps toward them and stopped, my eyes averted.

But I knew he could see me now.

I wanted to will myself invisible, to vaporize.

If he didn't know she'd had the abortion today he should have known it from my scowl.

What? What, I thought, and I turned my head slowly to his. The back of Lisa's head—her hair like blond snakes out of a hole, moving in waves—staggered across the plane of his face and I could see her profile, where their mouths met.

Kissing, tongues moving like blood between them.

I switched my furious glare back to their shadows on the wall: to graphite, to twilight—avoiding the real. I froze. I hated them both.

I watched their shadow heads making out for minute after minute, absurd. I just didn't want to leave and cause a scene.

It was awkward. And then:

I saw the shadows of his hands creep up behind her, into the air, though they kept kissing.

The shadows of his fingers started dancing for me—both his hands crumpled into little balls, with the index and middle as ears.

Rabbit shadows hopping across the wall. Simple animals a child could have made, shadows throwing my fury into relief. They goofed, they raced, they were trying to crack my hard expression.

Then a dog, a butterfly flopping to some comical beat.

He was making fun of her, of her weird love for him.

I met the gaze of his actual face then, and he *winked* at me.

I held my breath:

his man-angled jaw whispered of intrigue in dining cars and cross-Atlantic steamers and slapping the hysterical starlet across the cheek. And I noticed:

The perfect girl-arc of her eyelash stayed closed against her petal cheek. Happiness. And behind it all, his hands curled, pink, male, to make shadows for me.

His open eye, independent of the hemorrhage at his lips: devilish, it smirked at me, pinning me down, beckoning me into something I would never really understand.

12

SIDEBURNS

Max

The sun is starting to heat things up in Joey's garage-conversion apartment, starting to reflect off the dull metal pans in the sink across the room from me, the four forks in a glass, the Nova's fender that is propped against a cheap dresser. Otis is still breathing above me on the couch and it takes me half a minute to figure things out. I see tree tops shifting in the mild freeway wind outside, through the muddy sliding glass door. What has woken me up is a dial tone coming through Joey's answering machine, here in this kitchen/living room room, over there in the kitchen part on the fake wood counter. Someone has called so early and hung up, except I notice that it is not early, it is noon on the microwave. I am about to go turn the answering machine off when Joey stumbles out of the bedroom door in a pair of those underwear that are long like boxers, swearing, and he hits the thing with a random swoop that turns it off. *Fuckin crazywoman,* he says and he disappears back into the bedroom with Lisa, who I can hear snoring but in a sexy, feminine way if you can believe that.

"MORNING," a woman's high voice starts coming from inside the house. Joey's mom Elaine has some trouble with the door but finally gets it and has a cup of coffee in each hand. She looks at me, she is normal-sized on the top but huge in the legs and hips in this particular way like she should be an old-style woman in a Renaissance-fair outfit, cooking for a medieval army, stirring a pot. In reality though, she's modern looking, with hair that is short and dyed blonde and she has a thin face with bug eyes that's all excited and happy and intense. She disappears into the bedroom. They talk in there in the dark, in low voices, her and Joey, sometimes Lisa makes a little noise but not too often. Then it's just the mom talking, I can't understand the words but I can tell that Joey is just waiting for his mom to get the hell out.

When she does she whispers, "Hi Max, I know you're awake, do you want some coffee?"

Her face is inches from mine, she has bent at her middle, and I say no thanks, Mrs. Sykes. And she leans over to Otis's ear and whispers it to him and he shudders and in his little rasp rolls away from her saying *no, no man, I mean, thank you no thank you ma'am.*

Fine! Lisa yells the minute Elaine's gone, and then stumbles out of the bedroom in a t-shirt and black underwear with pink V's across the ass like birds. She goes into the back studio and puts *A Love Supreme* on the stereo and this gets Joey, and then me, and then Otis up and moving and into the bathroom, one by one, this music, these airplane swoops of saxophone, these men chanting then shifting that chant into a deeper register. Otis is always stripping down to naked and changing right in front of you—girls, whoever, despite his beer gut—because his dick is huge. Joey changes in the bedroom with the door closed. We all move around each other—into the bathroom, out of the bathroom, to the sink for water, to empty an ashtray, to brush out ratted hair, to the concrete landing for a cigarette—*A Love Supreme*—Otis and Joey to the studio room to make a phone call, to play computer golf, to get away from Lisa, from me until Elaine Sykes calls us up to the house for some breakfast.

Things are getting bad between me and my own mom, so once in awhile I stay at Joey's. Sometimes it is Lisa in the bedroom, sometimes another girl.

*   *   *

I didn't see Joey all week and then we finally ran into each other in the 7-11 one day. He took me home for lunch with him, and his mom Elaine was going on and on, you know when a woman's voice gets all chattering and clinging and you can't listen anymore you just can't it's like it's barely English and so Joey just snuck us out to the taqueria while she was still going on in another room. He'd make an excuse later and be real sweet to her and it would be okay—I'd seen it happen before.

When I got back from washing my hands in the taqueria bathroom, Joey in his white perfect shirt was staring out the window of the taqueria, looking at a woman and her daughter trying to load a three foot tall box with the words HOULIHAN WEDDING—3-TIER VANILLA written on the side into the back of a pink van. He gave a quick, dry laugh at the daughter's expression when her mother left her holding the thing to bend over and do something to her shoe.

"It's not about the salary it's all about the dowry," he said, and I still didn't know what this meant.

He was stirring the table's little bowl of green salsa with the plastic spoon Taqueria provided.

"I hate these open containers," Joey said. "Anyone could put anything in there. What's wrong with putting the hot sauce in a mustard bottle?"

He ran his cigarettes across the brown ceramic table tiles. At some point he'd taken money from Elaine's wallet for our burritos.

"Le chuga" he said, he chuckled to himself. "*Call me Le Chuga.*"

When he had tried to order his food in Spanish, the server, a cute, teenage girl who at least acted like she didn't speak English, told him that was the word for lettuce.

I nodded.

"That's a cool gangster name," I said.

"Call me Lettuce," he said.

"*Le Chuga*, though, LE CHUGA," I said. "Has like a ring, you gotta admit."

It was quiet.

"These dudes," he said, and he gestured to the Mexican guys grilling steak on greasy metal, "They have real honor to them. I mean, fuck if I ever get trapped doing that shit again but still, it's got, well it's got something to it," he said. "Better than fucking prison," he said, and laughed.

I had this image of Joey like leaving me, walking out of Taqueria and me being stuck here mopping up, scraping low-grade beefsteak grease off the ceiling and I wanted instead to hide in the band's van, hide in the van until the band had to take me with them away from this bullshit. The thing curling in my throat was like shame, maybe, that I couldn't be him.

"Don't worry slugger," he said, and he slapped me on the arm, "we'll take you along. You don't run into much pussy in 7-11, that's for sure. Back when I was—well I was in high school, you know, those bitches wouldn't look at you anyway. But even if they did, I didn't see them in 7-11."

"Fuck," he said.

"Your blood sugar?" I said.

He smiled, "Yeah. You know me as well as my women do," he said, and laughed.

"Shit," I said, not knowing I really said it.

"What?" he said.

"I just—"

I couldn't breathe for a second there. I coughed. I wanted to walk out of the taqueria and walk the streets to the onramp to the freeway and not come back ever. But I also wanted to hang out with Joey, hang on to him, like a little kid to someone's leg. I didn't want to be some fucking taqueria worker. I wanted something better, something closer to the applause he was always getting.

"Forty-one!" one of the Mexican dudes behind the grill yelled, and Joey winced. We were 47.

"So your moms hassling you?" Joey said.

I looked down.

"Yeah," I finally said, "Yeah she's been drinking a lot again and she kinda flips out sometimes."

He kept looking at me, really listening. Waiting for me to talk more.

"It's like not. . ."

"Healthy," he said.

I knew that but somehow him saying it made it real and I felt a lot less . . . temporary, or something, a lot less blurry.

"Not healthy for you," he said, "Not good for you."

He trailed off and started watching the women outside, lifting smaller boxes now, their purses swinging against their asses, the muscles in the daughter's legs lifting.

I stared back at him, waiting for more explanation of my problems.

"And like?" I finally said.

"Huh?" he said.

"*Forty-seven!*" the guy yelled.

"Would you go get that? And napkins, and a glass of water? No ice," Joey said.

When I got back he was grinning, starved. *Maybe you will take me with you now*, I thought, so glad he was happy. *Keep grinning.* While we were eating I felt like he understood me.

"My moms isn't a *drunk*," he said after he finished his quesadilla, before he started on his fish tacos, "and she's awesome to the band, you know?" he said.

I nodded and drank my horchata.

"But some *times*," he said, "it's just like what do you want from me, woman? What do you want me to do for you anyway?"

He paused for a long time, the van and the mother-daughter pair outside were gone now but he kept looking.

"She always, always calls when I'm getting on with Lisa downstairs, no matter how quiet. ALWAYS. Through the answering machine: '*Joey, there's spanokopita! There's nachos!*'"

And he imitated her voice so well that I spit out a huge doughy bite of tortilla and guac onto my little paper french-fry boat they served burritos on.

He reached over the table and messed up the top of my head.

"Max-cot. You're like the band's mascot."

I shrugged. I looked down at the floor tiles which were just big, dull versions of the table's tiles.

"Well, you can crash on the couch once in awhile as long as you keep the woman off my back," he said, laughing. "You willing to do that?"

I nodded. I was pretty sure he meant his mother. I brushed the hair out of my eyes and some lingering burrito off my cheek and I looked at him and smiled like a pussy—a big, stupid, seventh-grade school photo puberty zit grin with taco in my teeth. But I didn't care. Fuck it. I was *in*, now.

"I'm going to get a job," I said, from where I don't know. I wasn't thinking that. It just came out.

"Yeah, you do that scooter," Joey said, burping, inhaling deep, pushing away from the table.

He exhaled, he smoothed his shirt over his thick chest.

"So I'll see you out there for a smoke," he said, and left. I was still eating.

The table was covered with his burrito trash all over the place, a couple napkins he'd ripped to shreds.

So I tried to pile his little baskets and napkins and his water glass on top of my own, but they fell on my way to the bin and I had to get on my knees a couple times, and it took extra napkins to get the spilled fish sauce and guacamole up off the floor. He was into his second smoke by the time I got our trash all cleaned up and met him out there.

*　　　*　　　*

I was still living with my mom then but a lot of nights I would just like sit out in Joey's garage and get high by myself when he was in SF or at some other far away gig. I didn't usually answer his phone, but someone kept calling and hanging up on the machine; like the ninth time of this, I picked it up.

"Max, dude," Joey said over the din of the bar, "I need you to come get us."

"I thought you were in San Francisco," I said.

"The Red Dragon," he said, this Chinese restaurant/Polynesian theme bar just outside my dad's old neighborhood.

"What the fuck?" I said.

"We took a detour," he said, "The keys to the Nova are next to the answering machine," he said, "Lisa's freaking out and won't drive me home---" he said, and then he put the phone away from his mouth and whooped, across the bar it sounded like, at someone.

"I—" I said, but I was tying my shoes already when he hung up.

When I got there Joey seemed very still and shining white in this shirt like ones I'd seen Elaine pressing for him before. It made him look European or Spanish or something, and he was so clean in it when everything else in the bar was dirty.

Even the girl he was talking to, short and with huge tits, looked a little smeared with ash compared.

The girl was flipping her long hair from side to side and pointing at her forehead.

"Yeah, it's a tattoo of a turtle. When I shave my head it shows up, but I haven't in years—" the girl was saying.

Her mouth was too small, she was too untouched looking for her to have a tattoo or a bald head or "years," but I guess maybe that's why she did it.

"Max, my man, we out," Joey said, interrupting her, "This is Victoria."

He grabbed my arm the whole way through the crowd—their mai tais, their pina coladas, their sexes on the beach—and let go when he was out the door, me inside still unable to get past the bouncer carding three college frat assholes.

"Max. Max!"

It was Lisa, sitting on a table, across the bar, and I almost yelled her name but Joey's arm emerged to drag me away from her red lips and voice *sorry* I mumbled.

Joey was slamming—the car door, his palm on the dash, the gear shift for me when I couldn't get it out of first, the glove when it flew open when I *did* manage to shift. His shirt was still perfect, not a speck on it. When he got really drunk he didn't slow down or slur his words—he just laughed more, talked louder, sang a little more. He seemed fine to drive, actually—but after two DUIs he knew better.

As I drove toward the stop sign in second, away from the bar, I could hear Lisa screaming, her heels attacking pavement behind us.

"Stop," Joey said.

"Go back? She's chasing our asses down to kill us, dude."

"Just stop."

"Do you have a lighter I could use," Victoria said.

I ignored her.

In our respective side mirrors, Joey and I were staring Lisa down.

"What does she want?" I said.

"Just keep going. Fuck it. But go slow," he laughed a little, it was so wrong to. "Let's see how far she follows."

I kept it in second, driving the bottom speed I could for second, the engine dogging itself a couple times, me not wanting to look like a pussy struggling to shift it back into first.

Victoria in the backseat turned to air, weighing nothing.

Lisa's shirt reflected white and her feet took steps across sidewalk and glass and rocks and holes.

"What?" Joey yelled out at her.

That's when a big old Caprice station wagon pulled up next to us.

The driver had reddish-brown hair that looked a little like Elvis, and then on top of that his skin was all red and pink, like he'd been drinking or embarrassed or sunburnt or a combo of those three. He was middle aged and sad looking and listening to Johnny Cash and staring slow at Lisa's walk.

"What are you looking at?" Joey said.

The guy turned back, stared out his windshield, not at us directly.

"A mighty fine woman back there," he said with a kind of old-school voice, like a 40s movie voice.

Black makeup around Lisa's eyes, night-black air around her head, she was eyeing Joey so hard eyes as if to *say you can drive as far as you want but you can't ever get away from me.*

She was trying to turn herself into a ghost.

"It's your lucky night," Joey said to the Elvis man, raising his voice so Lisa could hear him.

Joey might as well have announced he was offering her up for a blow job, was the tone in his voice.

The red-hair, red-face man kept his face forward, not a move, said:

"You don't say," so flat, so unexcited, I couldn't tell whether to be scared of him or not.

Red's sideburns weren't mutton chops, and they weren't the kind of hip ones like Joey had. They were the kind of sideburns my dad used to have before some girlfriend made him shave them off.

Let's be honest: Red's last girlfriend was probably so long ago she had to get him out of the leisure suit habit before she could get to work on the facial hair.

"What the fuck?" I said, but Joey didn't hear.

"Look man, she wants you," Joey said.

"You don't say," Red said.

Red Elvis's eyes would sorta crawl over to look at Lisa in the rear-view, then snap back, ashamed, to staring blank, motionless, in front of him.

Lisa was shivering, trying to stand up straight and keep her skirt from blowing in the breeze by planting her hands tight on the outsides of her thighs.

The Johnny Cash coming through Red's speakers surrounded both our cars heavy, murky.

"She's crazy, though," Joey said to the man, all cool and conversational now, "She had me fooled into thinking she wasn't until now but she's fucking insane, sir," he said.

"Much obliged," the man said, never once glancing our way.

Red didn't look behind him—just reversed the Caprice back to Lisa as if he'd known all his life where to the inch she would be.

"Go, Max."

I could see Lisa biting her lip, hunching over so her boobs didn't stick out so prominently.

Fuck.

"GO," Joey said.

And even though the traffic light wasn't green yet, I hit the accelerator and went through, somehow, the cross-traffic's honkings finally diminishing behind us.

Fuck.

It was a cinch to work the gears into third and fourth and overdrive.

I couldn't see her in the rearview anymore.

I did it. *Me.* I drove away. Not just because Joey told me to go but because I knew I couldn't do anything and I didn't want to see it. Right? What could I have done. Lisa would have shoved me away. Joey would have left us *both* there and she would have done some stupid shit with some creep anyway.

Right?

Victoria, the only one of us who looked through the back windshield as we drove off, said Lisa did climb into the wood-paneled station-wagon. *She got in the car.* Back at Joey's I went into Elaine's kitchen and borrowed Elaine's Wild Turkey until I borrowed it all. I slept fast and hard and then slow, till about two pm when Joey was already gone to the city, or wherever he returned that rich bitch Victoria with the supposed turtle under her hair.

*   *   *

I didn't stay over there for awhile and the next time I did, I woke up without remembering an ounce of the night before

The VCR said 303 pm. I remember Lisa giving me a ride the previous afternoon, but nothing after that. Lisa wasn't around, now, though, and Otis wasn't around, and I didn't hear anything but birds and freeway. I shut my eyes, and Joey's footsteps came.

My eyelashes were so crusty they stuck together. When I finally pulled one eye open a sliver, I saw Joey, not in his Calvin Kleins, but butt naked, staring at himself in the full length mirror that hung by the sink.

There was always something about Joey: you always wanted to be with him because he kept himself always a little away from you. A little ahead— you always keep grabbing after him. But here he was, hiding nothing. And I didn't want to be anywhere near him. But the crust on my eyes was so thick that to close them hurt bad.

Joey smoothed a hand across his puffed-up chest, and down his jaw line, through his hair.

From the other room the stereo started playing James Brown, "It's a Man's Man's Man's Man's World."

Yeah, Joey said softly, so as not to wake me, *hm!*

I needed to shut my eyes. It was all so wrong, he had no idea I was awake. I needed to throw up but I couldn't do that either. He looked older, decades away from me here at eighteen, and I wanted to stay that far from him. I shut my eyes anyway, despite the pain. I froze.

13

STARFUCKER

Racinda

And when the band is onstage, I am performing too, dancing, trying to be beautiful, and when they get off stage, afterwards, I am one that goes with the band, not one of these girls who just shows up at the afterparty, not one of these fans who signs up for the mailing list and flirts and wants to fuck the band and be the band. Joey uses his tickets to buy me drinks, Otis follows me around. I sit gracefully and I look as beautiful as I can, and when the need arises I give these endless groupie girls no attention, like they are not in the room, and when I need to I say something smarter or funnier or coarser than these nameless, endless girls can understand: the band laughs and gets it and smiles and know I am not just a regular girl.

Lisa taught me, but I'm getting the hang of this myself.

Not being a regular girl is the whole point of it. Being more than a girl is the point of it. Escaping whatever it is that regular girls are condemned to.

*　　*　　*

When Lisa said she wanted to go on a picnic, that day, the Fourth of July, the rolling, damp lawns of Pennsylvania came flooding my senses the way steam opens up your pores and works its way into you. I thought of my

grandmother, my sister, the drenching greens and reds of zinnias, of as-
ters, of rhododendrons in June, wet pollen swatting through blue air.
What I got was something else entirely. What I got had a lot to do with
dirt, among other things. What I got: a lot of thin yellowbrown California
cindery dirt in my teeth, a few red bumps on my ankles from a source I
never could fathom, and a couple bites of a ham sandwich slippery with
mayo.

"I so love a picnic," she said

"You do?" I said. "Since when do you love a picnic?"

I stared at her too long, noticing that one of her zits was covered up well
with makeup, but the other two looked like she'd been picking at them
since she put it on, they were red and pinched. She shot me a quick snarl
before facing back on the road.

"I *love* picnics. You know, I'm not as anti-nature as you people think I
am," she said.

You people, meaning I think me and Vagina.

"You hate the sun, even, Leese," I said.

"Well, not all the time, for example. Today I like the sun," she said,
squinting.

"Mm."

We just drove along in some Jeep whose owner I was unaware of, and I
realized the feeling I had with her now was so different than how I used to
feel in the car with her.

We drove longer than I thought we would. We drove to Contra Costa
County, practically to Berkeley, I think.

"Where are we going, anyway? Did you bring snacks? I just brought
lunch. Is there anything to eat now?" I said, a flurry after such silence.

"There's Doritos," she said, her hair whipping me in the ear as she
flipped her head around to change lanes. "And Gin helped me make egg
salad and ham sandwiches and deviled eggs—"

She sort of bounced like a good song was playing then even though the
radio was off. There was something missing—she didn't want a certain
sweetness from me right now. She was worried about something and acting fake and weird, and she wasn't stoned.

"I *hate eggs*," I said.

"And jello squares," she said, "And there's chips, and KoolAid, and I
brought diet soda and a dime bag."

"Right."

In all this daylight, without any boys, without doing my makeup, she wasn't so great to hang around. In all this daylight, the only things she gave me were things I was trying to get away from: bad snacks and unreadable moods. She sniffled and wiped her nose with her knuckles and she started just then to represent *tacky* where she once represented *free*.

We drove up and up these hills, around and around maybe, one big hill—I couldn't tell. She finally found this patch on a slope like any other that was good enough for our picnic, and when we got out of the jeep it was starting to turn a little cold, a little windy. I spread out the blanket, and in seconds small sheets of dirt were washing onto it on tides of air. Brown brown brown.

"It's so gorgeous out," she said.

Brown.

She was looking up the road. From where we were sitting you could see that the peak wasn't that distant. You could see a few cyclists and runners up there, little moving blots.

"Gorge," I said. But it was always gorgeous, in California: all summer. No rain. Absurd.

"What time is it?" she said, looking at her wrist even though of course she never wore a watch.

"I think it's like one."

"Mm."

I couldn't figure out why she kept looking up the hill.

"What is going *on*?" I said.

"Nothing, retard. We're having a picnic," she said.

She adjusted the dress she was wearing—ridiculous red gauzy rayon with white polka dots, short, baby doll, punk rock, but somehow not all the way. All she needed were white tights and little black mary janes and she could pass for Minnie Mouse, slut version. She tried to nestle herself down gracefully, not showing cha-cha, but her boots, unlaced above the ankle, their leather all warped from winter rain, seemed really uncomfortable for her to kneel onto. She just gave up and let her underwear show, legs straddling wide the crackling beige plastic grocery bags with trashy food in them.

"Well," I said, "let's eat?"

"No!" she said.

"Okay?"

"I just... We never *talk* anymore, Racin."

"Okay?" I said again.

So then she packed a bowl and we got stoned, and she kept giggling and snapping at my hand whenever I went for my lunch after I started craving, craving it. She let me eat the Doritos. Then in a frenzy, she decided to spread out the fiesta food.

"What is going *on*?" I said, and fell back onto the blanket with a giggle that got lost as I noticed all the clouds up there.

"What did *you* bring?" she said, going for my white deli bag.

"It's like pasta, and then there's this polenta with red peppers and scallions, and also some cookies. . .from this deli place . . starch. . ."

The sky was a blue that was really white. The blue—like a soft blanket—was faking it. I knew what was beyond it. I could feel my stoned stoned lungs working harder lying back like this.

Spandex cyclists and cutoff cyclists and the occasional runner had been plummeting by us every ten minutes or so, but this one, blockish, dark, stopped and stared. I could feel him there though I couldn't see him, and I could hear the pinkness, the redness, the spit in his breathing, so I sat up, open and girlish and smiling.

It was Joey. A big grin on his manly, angled face, but his eyes looked annoyed, sweat was inching into them from his temples, his eyebrows.

"What. . ." he said, unsnapping his helmet with a gesture like a slap.

"Surprise, honey!" Lisa said, "I thought you might be hungry after all that work going up the hill."

She waved her arm at the tupperware containers as if she were a combination tour guide/beauty queen.

Before I could stop myself I rolled my eyes. Joey just stood there looking confused—he couldn't figure it out, his mouth a little open, his brows brought together. His spandex biking clothes somehow didn't suit him—like if the president were starring in a drag show, like Gary Cooper got stuck in one of those senior-citizen nylon warmup suits. Kind of ridiculous like that. The shorts that were too tight for him, and a cheesy bright yellow cycling shirt with the name of a nutritional drink dragged across it in a font was supposed to look hip and angry.

"Hi," he said to me, looking relieved at my presence.

"Oh," I said. Of course. She never wanted to get up off the *couch* unless it involved him. "How's it going, Joey."

"Good. Sorry I didn't get to talk to you that night. Some introduction," he said, and his eyes crinkled up at me in a familiar, friendly way that made it hard to hate him as much as I was trying to.

"S'Okay," I said, reaching for my deli bag. What, they were going to have sex now and I was just going to talk to the trees or something? I caught the impulse to yell for help to the next cyclist going by—*save me!*—but he was going too fast.

"Well aren't you going to eat?" Lisa said, standing, scratching a calf with the other ankle, "Honey?"

He shot her a look that had something to do with me being there. If I weren't there it wouldn't have been just a look.

"Sure," he said, exhaling a little angrily, letting his bike—expensive-looking, with front and back shocks—drop to the road.

A car drove by, a little Jetta, too fast, and sprayed us all with pebbles and more dirt.

"What's that?" Joey said, bent over my polenta.

I raised my eyebrows and almost hit him.

"It's pasta," Lisa said. "I made it."

He'd already got a good quarter of it in his mouth in the first bite.

"Good," he said, nodding to Lisa, face full of my damn lunch.

She ran her hands up her sides, fidgety, then dropped down to sit.

"There's egg salad and devilled eggs over here," she said.

"What's that?" he said, going for more of my lunch.

I grabbed for it but before I got it:

"God, Racinda, he's *starving*, don't hog the food. Joey, that's pasta from the deli," she said, and she had this sickly, stupid, expectant smile on her face, like someone was going to put the Miss America sash over her shoulders any minute.

"*Sorry.*"

"That's okay," he said, and he handed the plastic container of it to me. "You go ahead."

"No, that's okay," I said, certain of unpleasant future ramifications if I did.

"Well here," he said, spinning the linguine on a fork and leaning across the blanket to hover it in front of my mouth, "Take the first bite at least."

How could I say no?

He didn't touch her food, and he hardly talked to her. Made small talk with me, mostly. I was too stoned to figure out what to do, so I just ate Doritos and Diet Coke. Lisa threw a ham sandwich into my lap and stared me down till I messed with the wet Saranwrap and took a bite. The bread, the meat, each layer felt like another tongue flapping in my mouth. It was all I could do not to spit it out onto the grass. One good thing—when Lisa beckoned him over to a tree for a little private chat, I managed to eat a cookie.

"Have another bite of this," he said to me, and again I couldn't refuse. His eyes locked on me as the fork went into my mouth.

They talked or fought or whatever for a few minutes by the tree.

Come on, he said loudly, to end it, *we can talk later, you're being rude to your friend.*

She stayed by the tree, digging in the dirt with a stick, her legs smeared with yellow brown streaks of it now, pissed, and he came back to torment me some more.

"Tuna salad?" I said.

"No thanks," he said, made an icky face. Even though he looked stocky, I could see now that his legs and ass were hard, almost narrow—just his shoulders, chest, bit of beer gut were wide. He had good calves—usually I don't like that much hair, but his was light enough, shiny, almost reddish but not too.

Should I feel guilty? I was just looking anyway. He was cheesy. He wore ankle socks and *spandex*. He lived in his mother's garage.

He wouldn't look at me, though, and I wanted him to. He lit a cigarette. He narrowed his eyes at the plastic sherbet container full of fluffy salmonella egg salad.

"You would think she could give me one damn day to myself. How much is that to ask?" he said.

"Well, I mean, I don't know you or anything but it's not like you've been the most *present* boyfriend lately," I said.

I immediately tried to effect something non-committal but sympathetic on my face—eyes wide open, head nodding off my neck and tilted, corners of the mouth turned down, but he wasn't looking at me.

"Yeah," he laughed, "What do you know about it."

"Way too much, actually," I said.

"Oh yeah? Too many details and I don't even know you?"

"I mean, no. I mean . . ." I could feel the red flowing to my cheeks.

"Shy!" he said, and he touched the blushing. "You're shy!"

With that she slammed herself between us.

"He needs his space," Lisa said, "He's all dehydrated and sweating."

"Yeah," I said, and I inched away, thinking about how the sweat was actually the nice-smelling sort, leaning my head into the scent when the wind brought it to me from the other side of her.

We ended up leaving most of Lisa's food out, uneaten, for the coyotes or ravens or that famous Californian Charles Manson or whatever. Lisa, of course, wanted to get out of there the second after Joey took off on his bike down the mountain, but I made her wait while I unwrapped every vile egg and damp sandwich, piled the wrapping into a Wonderbread bag to carry with us so it didn't choke the seagulls or, duh, not the seagulls, but the whatever, the hawks.

When we passed him coming back down the hill, I was actually concerned that she would veer the Jeep to swat him off his bike. He made only the tiniest gesture of his fingers off the handlebars when she honked.

"Cocksucker," was all she said after she passed him. "I could have any man I wanted."

"So go get them."

"I don't want them."

"What about those guys at the Luna Club, Leese?"

"Fuck," she said, her fingers scratching at her zits like mosquito bites even though she needed that hand to downshift, the Jeep was about to stall as she braked on a curve, "Fuck I don't *really.*"

"You've totally walked away from them before," I said. "That's, like, what you *do.* Just walk away from him."

"I can't."

"He wears *spandex,* Lisa."

"That is not the point. That offends me—you're such a snob. He's a huge, huge talent," she said after she put us into second gear, finally, to take us around a curve without the engine falling out.

I exhaled loudly. Blood from two of her zits was now trailing down her cheek. I took a crumpled napkin out of the plastic bag that was holding our trash and wiped it for her and wiped her tears that started then, too, but once she got sad all I could think about was that I was sick of hanging out with her alone.

I wanted him around now. I wanted a party. I wanted what boys could give me. I wanted the taste of their sweat and whatever it was they were doing that got them so dripping in it.

*   *   *

The moment I think I started to know: he is walking up the path to my mother's house. I can see the van behind him and the fragile twilit outline of Lisa's profile on the passenger side. But it all fades to just him, approaching my mother's tinny door, useless against his force. He is wearing pants this time, dressed half-decently for the gig. Nice dark green-brown pants, tailored to him, and these old-school leather suspenders, very nice—make me want to rub the straps between two fingers, feel the oil on them. Finally, the clothes fit him. The light is starting to fade, and the coolness of night, curling down with mercy from the sky and the hills, seems to rush toward the house right behind him, bringing me some promise I can't decipher.

I don't know it yet, but this is the last time I will see him with Lisa and not cringe.

He doesn't need to ring. I wait there in the doorway sipping a lime soda from a coffee mug. We just stand there staring at each other through the screen, a few seconds that take on extra weight, extra dimensions, deepen. Then at the same instant that his grin breaks onto me, at the instant before I can doubt this deepening, the smile that has its roots in my gut, my thighs, blossoms out from me. I feel like I am something good to eat. I feel like my body has been rearranged around my lips; glossed, luscious, finally ready to speak.

When he starts the van up I see Lisa's hair, her snakes, and my heart instantly, deliberately forgets that underground home I once lived in with Vagina and her. As the ribbon of the road speeds, fills the windshield down the freeway through the night, I know why Lisa and Vagina kept leaving me. The road, the man, the being-carried-away. Irresistible. That adventure I never even thought to want before now. What he could give me: speed down this road, not in circles that lead back to Vagina's underwater apartment, but in a line, away, to the new.

*　　*　　*　　*

"You look pretty in that shirt," Joey said after a gig a few days later.

I bit my bottom lip and looked down, looked over to the ladies room where Lisa had just gone.

His finger curled from my cheek to my jaw line to the back of my neck.

"Don't blush," he said, "silly," and there was not enough space between us, until—

Until a blur of a pink sweater barreled into him and started hugging him and another woman started babbling:

"Oh my god, you were so great," this slutty forty-year-old secretary type was gushing.

"This is my sister, Monica"—the pink sweater—"and her friend—"

"Stacy," the slutty secretary said.

"Stacy," he said.

While Joey's sister babbled and cooed over him for too long, Stacy tried to wedge me away from him. She gradually moved so that I was directly behind her, so that she was between me and Joey.

But he reached around her to grab my arm. He pulled me to him and wrapped his arm around my shoulders and thanked her and said we needed to go now, turned me away from her like he was leading me in a dance.

"She's your number one fan," I said.

"Oh that's funny, I thought you were my number one fan," he said.

"Fan?"

He looked at me dead on. I couldn't hold his gaze. I jumped when the bathroom door opened.

But it wasn't Lisa.

I bit my lip.

"Yeah, you're a little too smart for that aren't you?" he said.

He gestured over to Stacy who was busy dropping a shot of tequila into a glass of light beer.

"You're never too smart to be a fan," I said, smiling up at him, leaning in the tiniest bit, and he pulled me closer to him.

"You're never too old to blush," he said.

His side surprising, tighter against mine.

"I'm not blushing!" I said, again unable to look at him, stealing glances at the Ladies door.

"Pretty girls always blush," he said, and when he nudged my cheek with his nose his lips graced there too.

Lisa swung the Ladies' door open, but she didn't look up until after he'd let me go, turned, had been to all appearances packing up his drum kit the whole time.

"Otis, man, where's my drink tickets?" he yelled, and then Lisa was the one fuming when five Sac State girls in jeans and t-shirts, wanting autographs, ringed Joey like a coven.

*   *   *

The way I had gotten money for incidentals up to that month was this: I would just go into my mother's purse, the pink thing with its delicate, archaic snap. It wasn't stealing—we had an understanding because neither of us wanted to admit I needed anything from her. We both wanted to believe I was just fine on my own. Didn't need money. Was easy. She just left me fifty bucks a week in her little pink purse. She actually used another wallet, mostly, a navy blue one with a velcro fastening, but she always planted some cash for me in the pink one. Before it stopped appearing, I noticed the Sacramento Bee left lying around for three days, open to a banal story on teenage entrepreneurs; noticed her careful fingers raising the TV's volume when those computer-tech institute ads came on in the morning before work.

It *might* have had something to do with the fact that I failed to graduate in June.

One day there was no money in the pink purse. That first week I veered fast to her real navy wallet to get some, but soon after that I felt guilty and figured I better just go get a job.

"Well, I hope you have some sort of plan for after you graduate in December," my mom said the morning I decided to start looking.

"Trust me, Mom, I know what I'm doing. It's not like I'm going to run right out and marry someone like you did with *Dad*, or anything. . ." I said.

But she was becoming immune to my shit talk. She was getting a little tougher, like she had a filter to remove the insults and swear words from my sentences.

"Right, you know what you're doing, that's why you sit around the house watching television all day and all night."

"For your information, Mrs. Critical, *I have* a job," I said.

"You *do*?"

"Yes."

"Where?"

"Well, I don't want to say, until, you know, the final answer on my salary comes down from the manager, you know, I don't want to *jinx* it, but you might just be a little surprised."

How this giant pile of lies came out of my mouth I have no idea.

"Well, I'll believe it when I see it for myself," she said.

I ignored her. She stood up to get her things together and I saw her remove her navy wallet out from behind the television—a new hiding place. It *was* time to get a job. This was not a depressing fact—now that I wasn't so hooked on Lisa's house. Now that the band stuff and all this attention from boys and indirectly from their groupies was happening, a little customer-service time was not so odious to me.

So I ended up at Pinko's, which is this kinda sorta alternative copy making store run by former socialists. Its fumes gave me a sort of a high that made the time passable. Toner, fax, white out, blueprints. All these things I was learning I could not transmit to you now in words because of the fumes in that place. When I was there, I knew how to go through the motions and make it all work, more or less. The thing about these places, copyshops, that you often wonder as a customer but are sure of as an employee is that the lack of service means it's totally okay to "steal" copies, to pay for half of what you made, to walk out unnoticed after hogging the color copier for an hour. Like the employees care. Yes: you are doing them a favor when you rip them off.

Anyway, I fucked up about half the orders. I have no capacity for the physical patience you need to get corners, staples, borders straight. If I had started working there a year earlier, I would have befriended almost any of my coworkers to get away from Marie. Now, though, the faces of my coworkers were as much a blur as my attempts to enlarge photos. Who cared? I was just waiting for Thursday nights when Lisa and Joey would pick me up. I was just waiting to put on some slutty shoes and get some free drinks from the band.

"Looky here," I said the morning after I got my first paycheck, trying to snap it under Amandine's nose but just sort of waving it instead.

"Very nice, honey," she said, but she was balancing her checkbook.

"No Special K today?" I said, waving the check around the kitchen as I looked for some kind of bagel or something.

"What—no, honey. Can you—"

I waited.

"Can I what? *What?*" I leaned into her and gave her a loud smack on her cheek.

"Can—Racinda. *Sit down*," she said.

"Yeee-es?" I said, spazzy, bouncy—there was a gig tonight, the manager was going to be away from Pinko's today, I was a happy, happy girl. I sat on the chair across from her and stared at her grinning.

"Yeee-es, missy?" I said.

But when she looked up she wasn't just standard-issue annoyed at all this hyperness. Her eyes were red from a bit of crying—not a major breakdown, her makeup was fine, but a long-suffering slow weeping, an up-all night weeping, a worrying, planning weeping.

"What?" I said, dragged into grayness, into dread with her.

"Well, remember Mr. Mitchell I mentioned?"

"No."

"Rudy Mitchell?"

I caught a glimpse of a brochure underneath her agenda book.

"Rudy Mitchell—*Cult Deprogrammer?*" I said.

"Yes. Now don't be sarcastic, it isn't attractive and this is serious."

"*Right,*" I said, Pinko's and my mother both seeming so unendurable right now. Attractiveness being necessary for anything serious in my mother's world. I craved escape, I craved sugar, I craved a cigarette, "So what about *Mr. Mitchell?*"

"We don't really have the funds, even with Button's account for Ruth, to pay him full price but he's agreed to take on our case."

"Mom, she's *not* in a cult. She isn't. She has *other* problems but the Magnum P.I. of Scientologists is *not* going to help her."

The quavering, the terror in her was on her face as clear as her lipstick.

"Okay, so what if he finds her and she's *not* in a cult?" I said.

"Well, then we'll be able to get her back into another facility. But I really think she is in a cult and he knows how to handle these things."

I'd seen Ruth "handled" before, and nobody could do it, and the more they *thought* they could do it, the worse and more violent her reactions were.

"If she's not in a cult do I get to help you figure out what to do with her?"

My mother nodded and wiped at her nose with a tissue.

"She'll listen to you," my mother said.

"Yeah," I said, wetness coming into my own chest, because that wasn't true. Ruth *wouldn't* really listen to me anymore, not after I had to do the tough love thing the last time when she was all strung out.

Ruth's voice strung out was a voice I did not recognize and a voice that could rob our house while we slept, a voice I secretly wanted to disappear from the planet: I hated myself for this.

I could feel the thing sinking in my abdomen that seemed like it should have been buried, six hundred feet under by now, it had sunk so often at bad news about Ruth, at the terror and love for my sister, terror and love that never existed one without the other.

"So you are going to hire Rudy," I said, spacing out, imagining myself walking out the door, walking the dry streets to Pinko's, getting the college kid geek coworker who had a little crush on me to smoke me out. "So what does it have to do with me? Why are you even asking me?"

"Well, he wants to talk to you," she said, that fragile weepy look fading from her at the thought of this man coming in to fix things, to get things on more solid ground.

"Fine," I said, my particles and electrons and nuclei already dissipating from this place, leading me through the day, leading me to the night when some other men wanted to talk to me, too.

*   *   *

The giant, spinning sign above me echoes exactly the color of the lit green rectangles on the dash. BP, it says, and I think, Be Prepared.

Joey and Ted the bassist get out to pump the gas.

The place is deserted except for a huge biker guy—black leather head to toe, a giant round helmet—who squeals his Harley to a stop by the pay phone. I turn away from the window then, before he takes off his helmet, terrified he has no face.

I am slumping, slumping against Otis, and even though we both are certain I will not end up going home with him again he's still trying stupidly to impress me. He is holding in his stomach.

Lisa crawls in back with us and takes a few hits. She gives me a little hug. I take a few hits. Max takes a hit and stares vapidly out the filthy window. Lisa's arms are the brightest thing back here.

Suddenly, those pale arms fly to the door, wrangle with its tricky, stuck lever.

"Ted let me out!" she says.

"Ted you fucking co-conspirator," she says.

She is banging and banging. Ted is squeezing the gas nozzle out there, flopping the hose around a little.

"Sadist!" Lisa says.

The Harley guy must have finished his call, have just put his helmet back on, but he quiets his engine, peels the robot-bug head off his own once more in order to watch her go.

Joey is talking to two high school chicks who have just driven up in a Miata. He stands behind one of them, encircling her in his arms, and holds her hands while she bangs a pen and what looks like a makeup brush on the car door. He is teaching her to play drums. Her tits have to be fake—so weird! so young so huge—I can see the way his arms, and hers, maneuver around them awkwardly. The other girl, still sitting in the car, has an idiotic expression of joy on her face, her eyes focused upwards at them; she giggles.

None of them notices Lisa hurling her condensed body into the night air, unfolding herself fast, stormily, into her full height. She slams one bare thigh after the other across the gas station. When she gets there, Joey and the girls look up at her like children at gifts, full of expectation.

Joey keeps the girl's hands going in something syncopated, some complicated, woven beat, smiles at Lisa, doesn't hesitate.

I push away from Otis and lean out of the van. I want to go listen so badly, but instead I just somehow, so drunk and stoned, make it over to the soda machine several feet away and fumble for a dollar.

Fake Tits at Sixteen smiles self righteously, not even trying for shame or apologetic sweetness. Lisa yanks Joey's arms off her and the girl twists on her ankle, her night-time shoe giving way.

But Joey doesn't notice her yelp: he moves off to the edge of the crystalline pavement to be bitched out by his girlfriend.

Joey is a horrible, bloody accident, a scab I have to rip off—I am so repulsed by his ankle socks, by his power, by how unaware he is of his own stupidity. I can't stand how the world somehow misses out on his cheesy details and gives him tons of attention anyway. I give him attention anyway.

I want his finger across my cheek, the life-plus feeling I get when his side is next to mine. He and those Miata girls were in love, all three of them, for those ten minutes—their magic, their joy, was so obvious. I hate him for it, and I don't:

I barely know him but I know I am now shackled to figuring out how he finds that magic everywhere.

He is off by the waxy shrubbery screaming quietly at Lisa, whose face is mauled with her anger and with alcohol, screaming back at him. I can only hear their curses, I can't hear accusations.

The Diet Coke sending off steam in my hand, so cold. My breath in my throat, the rest of me still.

The Harley guy smirking, watching it all.

Lisa then smacks Joey so hard in the head with her square green purse that for the briefest instant I imagine I see his feet lift off the ground. By the time he knows what happens she is back leaning on the side of van that's facing me, I can hear her breathing, crying, spitting out air.

She looks up at me standing with a Diet Coke.

She knows that I am that girl, I am the girl who was playing the drums. Breasts and hands and his grown man chest. I feel my breath escaping me like a kick to the stomach.

The Diet Coke falls to the ground, my hand still curled around its negative space in the night air.

The can spins and spins, a hole punched somewhere releasing the stuff, spirals of soda forming across the white ground, arcs of brown fizz appearing intermittently across my ankles. The noise is deafening to me, a hiss that blocks out all else.

I follow Joey to the van, and when he starts the engine, Lisa steps in front, blocks our way.

"You getting in? Or what? Get in now or don't come back," Joey says.

She spits on the windshield and wanders off.

The man on the Harley taps his foot once, looks at his watch, grins at Lisa.

Shit.

I yell—"Leese—come on, come with us," I say it so loudly, but she ignores me.

I am swooning, I am spinning, too stoned.

"Leese—honey—"I bang on the inside of the van to get her back but it is pointless.

The huge Harley man turns and his hair is not greasy hesher stuff falling down his back as I expect: it's cut expensively, he is some kind of yuppie—little round glasses and I see a pale yellow collared shirt under his biker jacket.

Lisa turns to me and her grin is half as wide as the biker's back, her little wave—a girl's—crisp and joyful.

"She'll be back," Joey says, revving the engine.

I hear the Harley's rev drown ours out—unmistakable, loud—a second later.

Lisa's hair thicker and longer and wilder seeming as it bounces up and down, a nod, a yes to an invitation, still bouncing as she swings one leg over the Harley and lifts the other from the ground.

*   *   *

So when Joey showed up at my job the next Tuesday morning, I didn't quite know what to do.

Not just from the Pinko's chemical brain fog. I was partly embarrassed of him, and afraid he would do something loud and drunken—I had barely ever seen him before twilight. Except for Fourth of July, he could have been a special kind of nighttime poltergeist for all I knew. I felt scared of him, since something slipped out from under me. Something I didn't expect. Going to the gigs, getting all the attention was fun, but let's face it, I thought I was better than him. I thought he was a little cheesy. I didn't take his seriousness about his drums, his art, seriously. But I still wanted him. Jeez. And here I was, searing the membranes of braincells beyond parched, storming right through them for just over minimum wage at a job I hated—like I was so great myself.

When he showed up there, way under all my surface distaste for him, way under my effort to be polite if he said something embarrassing, this *other* part of me was smiling sweetly, like my mother, or some relatively normal facsimile of her, might have once been smiling on a porch after some boy put a corsage on her wrist.

I wanted to drive off with him and not come back.

There was also just something about a real boy—a man, I think he passes for a man—dropping by to see me. That never really happened to me before. I wasn't the kind of girl boys ever wanted in that way. Not even Otis—I mean, if he had stopped by my work I probably would have gone for it, I swear. Like this one really wants me. And *this* one was Lisa's, I knew that, but it didn't even matter. He wasn't Lisa's—I found out later: the person he was with Lisa was so different from who he was with me— he didn't even look the same. To me, without her, I could see the boy in him, that he needed my approval, I could see the twelve year old who thinks anyone with breasts is a goddess, could see that warping, milky stream of sex flowing through his brain at twelve and now still, and I could see how smart he was—the way he was always three steps ahead, and be- cause Lisa was a whining, screaming child, his three steps beyond seemed manipulative from the outside with *her*. With me, it was just relaxing to be around someone so quick. Even when he drove—he just knew when someone was going to cut him off, the same way I could tell these things. Thank god—I could rest. He was the kind of rare person who, when the radio turns fuzzy stopped at a stoplight, inches the car up further to get better reception. Usually, I just sit, quietly annoyed, telling myself to be more tolerant and not have such high expectations when someone just lets the static fly or tries to change the station at this point. But he knew what to do.

He knew each moment at the best angles.

But I didn't know all of that yet. I just felt weird, like why are you com- ing to my job?

He was shy and wearing a neat, gray t-shirt, some thick, nice material, tucked into long, corduroy shorts, and his usual embarrassing footwear. He was wondering if I wanted to come to lunch with him.

And then I looked around me, at the sad older women who worked there, and the skeevy men who had that nasty salesman vibe even though for this job they didn't need it, and I thought, god, I should just leave with him right now.

But my mother's empty purse—a funny, hovering pink rectangle, tucked into curves at its soft leather corners—burst into my mind and I got myself in check.

"Where's Lisa?" I said. "I haven't heard from her in a week. Vagina says she's taking a breather, whatever that means."

He was grinning at me. It took me a while to figure out it's cause I called Virginia Vagina in public, out loud.

I was blushing a little again. I shook my head at him, like *well?*

"We broke up," he said, looking right past me, at the blueprint machine. He rested his wrist on the little purple plastic wall that separated the pay line from the service line, tapped his fingers fast next to a pile of brochures about making a calendar from snapshots of your pets.

Before I could even get out a sympathetic nod, he said:

"Taqueria?"

"I can't," I said, leaning my head and rolling my eyes back at the pit of buzzing machines behind the counter.

"I have a gig in the city tonight," he said, "and I was wondering—if you like jazz—*if* you might like to join me."

I was starting to be able to tell the different types of buzzing apart—the computers lining the far wall verses the rattling, useless fans in the ceiling verses the old black and white xerox machines verses the new ones, sort of like how my grandmother Button could tell you what birds were making different noises and why. Right now, the color printers were dominating, a sound like a cheap clock radio going off under a blanket far across the house. The noise fueled my surreal, defeated sense that Joey was just another Ally, with some cheesy idea of me being a smart girl, some dumb fantasy like that Van Halen video where the school librarian strips to bra and panties and humps the oak table for a bunch of hesher 80s teenagers.

Behind Joey's head, I could see Francis, my red-headed coworker who had zits, a filmy try at a moustache, and lots of other traits that made him seem trashy even though he was a Star Trek boy who was going to linguistic college in September. Francis was waving me down, pointing frantically at a color machine in the pit that I'd left on and was now on its seventh inch of copies of the same photo.

I sighed, *sure*, I said, and when Joey walked out I noticed that his Doc Martens had been polished, but that there was a flaw in the back, an inky streak of goop swiped down, marring lighter-colored rubber of the sole.

I felt my head tilting to the side and an idiotic, but irresistible expression crossing my face: he polished his *shoes* for me.

"Help?" Francis said, the stack a foot high now, and I beamed and the fumes, and Lisa, did not touch me for weeks.

*   *   *

"I used to work at this pizza place with him," Joey was saying in the car on the way down there, explaining how he got to know his friend Trey, who was on house arrest for a DUI now. "We would make up new combinations all the time. We were the first in Sac to have Hawaiian, but that's so stale now."

"Hawaiian pizza is disgusting," I said.

"Corn! Corn pizza is the next phase. You just wait. I should patent it."

"You can't patent pizza," I said, letting the very particular sweeps of clouds sink into my brain, letting the air rushing into the car rush into me too.

We were past Davis, past all the shit on the 5 that makes it so ugly. Now the hills were brown and suggestive, open, a tree craggy like a Joshua tree standing here or there, alone, black, arching, reminding me of the gothic trees coming out of the purple-red winter ground on Button's land, but these California trees shrunken, gnarled, turning in on themselves, designed for lack of water. I could feel my cells puffing up, free of ink fumes, full of fresh wind.

"What's this place like?" I asked him, "where you're playing?"

"It's cool—it's a little fake, some of the people, you know, but the music's good. It's a really cool place, actually, I think you'll like it."

We complained about our fathers. This somehow made it a date. Distant, abandoning, unaware of our best features. His left his mother when he was fifteen. He was a good man, I think, from what Joey said. He moved up above Humboldt County and was doing something called "downmarketing" ecological building materials.

"Was he a hippie?"

"He is sort of more World War Two. You would never guess he's into all that stuff."

"Do you hate him?"

"Do you hate yours?"

"I think mine is too lame to hate. I asked first."

"I don't hate him. My mom does so much for me though, and she hates him, so, you know, I go along with it."

The telephone wires whipped up and down through the window, a background full of motion for his head, which I was completely focused on. By the time we got to the Bay Bridge, it was dark and I was a little stoned off the pipe he kept in his sister's glove compartment.

I caught the corner of the Bay Bridge's lights, linking, traipsing a triangle's edge of bright-spots across the corner of the windshield. There was no question but to shrink down in the seat and lean my head back to catch them all, wide, swooping narrow at the towers. Some music on the stereo was playing, some kind of angelic strings with a blues lyric underneath, a dance beat, bass. I looked over at him and he was oblivious, but in a good way, his straight nose aligned with the road, his brow folded a bit thinking about the gig, something going on in that head, something as fast as what was going on in mine usually. But now, mine was slow, just taking in the miracle of these animated lights on the bridge cables, just taking in the tiny, outside edge bits of him that I could understand.

So after the Café du Nord, its red velvety wallpaper and me sitting on his knee afterwards, these older people surrounding us, me the youngest person in there, in there only because I was with him, the bouncer forgave my lack of ID, I knew this was finally something I wanted. Finally something I wanted a part of. He knew it too, was so kind and brought me drinks and shifted me so gently back onto him when he returned. I sat at the table of musicians. The old—like senior citizen—guitar player who supposedly played with James Brown back in the day told me I had child-bearing hips, but it was a compliment. "If you and your lady," the handsome upright bassist said to Joey, nodding in my direction, "want to come to the after party. . ." But my eyes locked his and we knew we wanted to leave soon, we knew without saying that other people, even *these* people, were getting in the way of what we really wanted right then.

We drove the river roads instead of the five back to Sacramento, even though it takes so much longer, because he had already had a DUI and even though he wasn't drunk there was zero tolerance, he said. He explained the town of Locke to me, I imagined the paint un-peeling, reversing time on those moonlit white porches, the sleeping people in them surrounded again by their gone-on families. I imagined the roads as dirt. And when he stopped so we could look at the marsh and the moon, when he made me get out I was afraid, because that is how I was trained.

But he made me, and he could tell I was tense so he wrapped his arms around me from behind and said he would not ever let me tumble into the delta, down the wet grasses and muck. Then back in the car, I knew something was up when he wouldn't start it, wouldn't go into the night, it was 3am, we were pretty much sober, and he told me he was falling in love with me. I could feel something in him transfer onto the same part in me, like a decal God is applying with his thumbnail. I thought, this is it, this is what it means to be in love with somebody, in that second before he kissed me, this magic is—and I kept kissing him and it felt like the whole night was blowing up into swirling, starry shards between layers of my skin I hadn't even known existed.

*   *   *

So when I wake up, Joey is not next to me. I know that he hasn't left me—am not panicking as I have in other situations when this has happened—I still feel like I have given him a gift, like I have stepped down from my public self, my critical self, to love him. I pull myself to the bathroom and wash between my legs with wet toilet paper, draw his toothbrush across my tongue, put on lipstick. A cheap, home depot door leads to outside from that tiny bathroom, and as the wind rattles it I feel tied in to air like never before. I want to eat breakfast in an entirely new way—I want to really taste everything. The day is wide open, an ocean of a day even just at dawn, a great wide shell of a day, a day that I think maybe I will ride with him in his car and notice every single thing. Heat, smoke, the scents that emanate off upholstery and freeway and his neck.

I can feel my shirt against my stomach as I cross the cheap carpet to the sliding glass door. He is sitting outside, past the shady cement landing where his weight bench sits, on a folding chair, in his tight, bikershort style underwear, smoking a cigarette, reading the paper. His bronze stomach pushes past the tops of the shorts, it is not all muscle, it is fat from beer, but its bulk is smooth and hard somehow.

I can feel the old girl in me turn from him, I can feel her ghost say ew, he isn't really that cute, oh my god, did you see his. . . , I can feel her say that— gray, gravelly under the frilly surface—to the other frozen, critical, motionless girls.

But she whisks off, up, into vapor, disappears behind me.

His skin is so brown, so lovely, and his eyes crinkle and there are lines around them—a man's. He puts down the paper and the coffee on a wood bin next to him. We both squint in the sun, it surrounds us so heavily, warm as water.

I walk up to him and I put one leg on either side of his, kiss him on the neck, smile quietly. This is a new girl in me, everything feels different. On the previous side that has just been drawn in my life, I thought resisting all but the most polished and perfect and impenetrable gave me power. Now I can feel the rush of beauty that comes with stepping past that, with literally stepping over it—I can enter into this world, I can feel him against my ear, I can run him through my fingers and toes like sand.

"You are pretty amazing to come out here and not be disgusted by my fat gut," he says, shocking me, holding my smile with his.

I shake my head, a smile somewhere between a mother's and a statue's and a child's, and I run my hand up his jaw line.

Our smiles still melt between us, we've got the sweetest secret, and I know what to do, I know not to push it.

"I've got work, I have to get going," I say.

As I get up off him, the distance we need emerges, but under it there is a certainty that the other person's stomach will flip around, jubilant, later as much as your own, manufacture annoying grins to everyone around you all day, sneaking a mouthful of candy in your mind as you go about filling the toner or opening the door or biting your nails. I want to stay with him but my body, trained to avoid devouring what it wants, carries me away, protects me from my appetite.

Yet, I did not make it to work. I couldn't resist the smell of him still in my hair, couldn't resist the opiate of clean sheets Amandine had made me put on my bed the morning before, the air coming warm through the cracked window. In the twenty minutes I took to fall asleep in my own bed, alone, the memory of him and imagination of him took me halfway to the drunken feeling of being next to him. Sleep then hit me with the satisfaction of the first morning cigarette.

Funny: in just a few minutes, I was about to get to smoke the *second* first cigarette of the day, because Amandine came stomping in and screaming at me.

"Blah blah blah blah he's here and blah and you told me you'd be blah blah ready blurrrr blurrrr almost a word almost not nonsense something something," she said.

"Who?" I said when I peeled my tongue off the roof of my mouth and my upper eyelashes apart from the bottom ones' crusted makeup.

"Rudy's here! Get up! You told me you were going to be ready for this breakfast and you wanted to help find your sister, now move it. I'm not putting up with this from you job or no job, Missy."

"What . . . Mom . . . Stop . . . Wait . . . Okay . . ."

And she yanked the sheets off me and threw the window shades open and a towel in my face. She was actually quite impressive this angry. Her eyes seemed strong instead of vague—pinning me down, demanding something useful from me instead of looking at me with sadness, confusion, and a desperate plea that I somehow save myself from the terrors of the world that nipped so close to her skin.

"Fine. . . ." I said as I moved in slow motion, half-blind without contacts, to the shower.

"In at nine in the morning!" she said.

"FINE," I said.

"Cream?" Rudy said to me, pouring half and half (since *when* did my mother buy half and half?) out of a little pitcher (since *when* did my mother use Violetta's china?) into my too-small too-delicate teacup before I said yes.

I swear, I think that just because he had a brochure, Rudy was *famous* to my mom. The cream for the coffee was her version of starfucking.

He was graying at the temples but was still kind of attractive. My mother had clearly buzzed around him already to figure out his every need before he said anything. His posture was very straight—military—but there was a softness on his face, this willingness to understand and to listen to you and to really *look* at you, the appearance of seeming so of course being his job. He wasn't totally evil, but I believed in our situation he would only *cause* evil: anyone going out to try to corral Ruth inevitably made it worse. We'd learned that. She was out on the street and I hated to think about it but whenever Amandine tried to go after her it just got worse.

"Mr. Mitchell wants to know—" my mother started, from her perch leaning on the counter, but he interrupted her.

"Hi Racinda, I'm Rudy Mitchell, you can call me Rudy," he said, offering me his hand, so male, so strange in our house of two women, so rough above the dotted and vined white porcelain tea set.

"Hi Rudy," I said, trying to fit the too-big teaspoon into the little opening of the sugar jar.

"Your mother's told me wonderful things about you," he said, "Racinda."

"Well she should, I'm the only thing that keeps her afloat," I said, but then felt bad, the force of my mother over there getting sadder and sadder.

"Amandine, could you—" he said, and made a shooing gesture with his hand.

"Certainly," she said, beaming, the hurt gone—just that crumb of attention, even just to dismiss her, was enough for my mother.

"Now, Racinda, you know why I'm here. Your mother told me you're not convinced that Ruth is in a cult."

"Right. Because she's not."

"But how do you know that? Ruth is manic—she gets ideas in her head and then runs with them to degrees other people never would. You know that."

"Yeah, but only if they're *her* ideas," I said. "Only if she can find a way to do it her way. She's not going to just bow down and worship someone's mystical cult juju." I wrapped one hand around my neck, exhaled less forcefully than I wanted to. "She's not calm enough for that."

"These groups find ways of attracting lost souls, even ones as powerful as your sister."

"Right," I said, I sighed. "Look, what do you want from me, here?"

"I want to know if you've kept anything from your mother to protect Ruth. I know you don't agree with your mother's religious beliefs," he said.

"Right. Do *you*?"

"Those aren't my particular personal beliefs."

"What *are* your beliefs, *Rudy*, if you don't mind my asking?" I said.

"I'm an agnostic," he said.

"Meaning. . . ."

"You know what that means," he said.

I gave him the blankest look I have and shrugged.

"I think I just don't know," Rudy said. "I believe in science, in reason, in evolution, in the order of nature, but I just don't proclaim to know whether or not there is anything *behind* it all."

"Okay, fine, *whatever*, but I can't tell you more than Amandine can, Rudy."

He leaned forward and stuck his hand out like he was going to grab my arm but he didn't.

"Look, Racinda. I know you don't go for your mother's Christianity, and I've just told you I don't either." His awkward hand gestured strangely in the air between us. "I'm an educated man. I believe in science. I believe in the real world. And in the real world your very sick sister might be in a lot of trouble with people who don't care about her at all, who are using her for their own goals, who are using her as a servant to their demented false gods, who are using her as a concubine, worse. Even if she isn't involved with one of these groups, she is out on the streets with no protection, doing God knows what with God knows who. I'm offering your mother some help, at a discount, I might add, to try to ease her considerable pain and torment over your sister."

I bit one side, then the other, of my tongue to keep the tears *in* my eyes, to keep them from spilling, but it didn't work.

"Now I know you want to get your sister back in a facility that works for her, and I know she told you more than she told your mother before she stopped calling here a year ago. I'm not here to try to get Ruth back with the Christians."

"They're the fucking cause of it," I found myself saying, and then I found myself sobbing. "Didn't Amandine ever tell you about *casting out spirits?* Didn't Amandine tell you they thought Ruth was the Devil?"

I clamped my forearm over my mouth and turned to the side, as if him only being able to see me in profile might make it all less real.

"Right," he said, "I could see how that might exacerbate—"

"Exacerbate!" I bent over double crying, so pissed that Ruth was taking away my best night ever, that my mother and this stupid man were ruining that shiny night, ruining perfection.

"Racinda, I don't believe in it either," he said, his voice low. "I believe in science and the real world just the same as you," he said.

But I didn't believe in science and the real world. I believed that the curve of the trumpet around the red walls of the Café last night was the sound of my sister's voice on a good day, was the smell of Button's lilacs and tomato vines and bee balm in July and I believed in the smell of little-kid-hair and of grown-man sweat at the nape of Joey's neck. I believed in the hands of women at those prayer meetings my mother took us to even though I hated them—I knew there was something there, and Ruth knew it, and this man was missing the point if he thought these people in cults, these Born Agains, were making a big brouhaha about *nothing*. There *was* something there, it's just that the Christians beat the shit out of you when they brought the something to you. And at Joey's last night I had just gotten a dose of the same woozy love—without the stupid preachers, without the no-sex, without the bullshit misogyny, without the self-righteous missionary stance. That same something from just beyond the skrim had come seeping in from the night, from air, from streetlamps, from taillights, from the sound of the Nova's wheels on the river road, from his mouth, and it was too much to stand, too much to think about, certainly too much to explain to *Rudy*. I sucked in air and sucked in air until the tears in me and the ancient trouble re-buried themselves.

"Okay," I said, "Okay, Rudy, just don't randomly like *deprogram* her. Just make sure she gets into a *place* if there isn't a cult involved."

"You got it, hon," and his *hon* was so sweet, so fatherly, so perfectly placed that it almost set me off again.

"Whaddaya got?" he said.

"Well," I said, "Well . . ." and as soon as I clamped the weeping down I told him:

"Ruth had this roommate who called herself Pandora whose real name was Cynthia and whose last name I have no clue of and who was in some kind of graduate school but was also on meth and was totally insane. But I think they were fighting and I'm sure that either one killed the other or they are very far apart right now."

He wrote these things down. I blew my nose on my napkin and cleared my throat.

"Do you know where?"

"She *was* in San Francisco. I mean, someplace cheap? Dumpy? Aren't you the fake PI here?"

"You don't know where?"

"She said she could see the downtown skyline from her window, and she said, and she said the landlord was 'Chinese trash' and she got a lot of attention from black guys in her neighborhood, and that's all I have for you."

"Do you have her old phone numbers?"

"Didn't my mom give you those?"

Rudy looked at his coffee and then at me, shrugged, and I knew Amandine had lost them.

"Yeah, I've got them. They're old though. She moved a lot and she was homeless a lot and it's going to be hard to find her. Don't think this is like easy."

"Right," he said.

"And Rudy, you don't know what you are dealing with with my sister. She will fuck you *right* up. She's like. . . "

"She's a very powerful woman," Rudy said.

"She's the *original* powerful woman," I said, "And every time Amandine finds some man or program who wants to chase her and quiet her down and get her 'functioning' and give her some shit job and get her off drugs she goes apocalyptic. She will *injure* you, Rudy," I said.

I really meant it. I was starting to like him. I didn't want him to go at her the wrong way, them both to get maimed.

"Right," he said, and he smiled, and I smiled, and he punched me on the arm like *you're a trouper.* He poured me some more coffee, his big hands clumsy on the antique, non-ergonomic teapot handle. Not one of his fingers would fit through the space between the arc of it and the side of the pot. He had to pinch.

"While you're at it," I said, "Why don't you save my mom from her Jesus-cult, there Rudy?" I smiled at him almost flirtatiously.

He sighed and set his chin down on his fist wearily.

"Thanks, dear," he said, straightening up, standing, patting me on the shoulders, circling between them to soothe me, "You've been a great help."

"No problem," I said, and I went outside for a smoke.

Sitting on the plastic lawn chair on our small deck, in the still-morning light, I tried to dig my fingers as far as possible under my ribs. I tried to inhale and exhale. I wanted to call Joey, but it was too soon. It was 11 am.

I wanted to call Joey and tell him all about Ruth and get him to drive me around and show me how to do whatever the fuck I want, like Lisa, like Ruth, like him. I wanted out of here so bad. But it was too soon. I'd just left him. I closed my eyes and imagined Ruth, then Button, holding onto me, wrapping their arms around me like mine were wrapped around me right now. But I saw Joey's face instead of theirs, and I breathed harder, panicky, terrified that Ruth and Button would hate me for finding something, finally, that I wanted as much as I wanted them. The grass was a little bit wet, and the smell of it, the sweet and rough dust smell, the also not-sweet juice smell of it slammed me from Ruth to Button to the fish pond by myself in Button's garden and the secret conversations I would have there with the sky—beyond Jesus and my mother's and Ruth's and even Button's grasp—to the space between Joey's jaw and his ear, to the amazing night that brought me to that sky-talk, to that city with red velvet wallpaper you could taste like chocolate, like the sound of a trumpet, to Joey's drums giving up a rhythm that had always been there but was now manifest, the rhythm that was always there like my mothers tongue-speaking lips were always there the second she was alone, like now, now that Rudy had left the room. I could see through my mother's living-room window, could see the nice portrait of Jesus, the big charcoal portrait. In it, He's holding a lamb, actually beautiful, beyond kitsch, and I found my-self imagining His arms around me then, and He was all of them: Joey, Ruth, Button, Amandine, the sky, the red wallpaper, the rhythm that is always there that only other people—my mother, Joey, Ruth—can re-mind me of.

You may imagine that I shuddered, then, to be feeling so fond of JC.

It's okay, though, because last night it became clear that there is future ahead of me.

And the future is Joey.

And he is in love with me.

Except.

I saw Lisa. I saw groupies. I saw Joey's hand on the back of his sister's secretary slut friend.

Except.

Except shit what if he was just saying all that to *convince* me to have sex with him and it's not true?

But that couldn't be, because I—because he was *pursuing* me, because he wears *ankle* socks. If I feel this way about *him* then it's like got to be the real deal, if I can look past the ankle socks and the living in the mother's garage and . . .

It wasn't like that. It wasn't. They don't *always* leave you. They can't possibly all *always* leave me, forever.

Ruth left you. Your dad.

Shut up, JC. Who fucking needs it.

I didn't leave you.

Shut up. SHUT UP.

It wasn't like that, like Joey was trying to convince me for a cheap thrill.

The drums beyond speaking, and other rhythms beyond speaking, the glances, the kisses, were *real*. Meant something.

It's okay.

Breathe.

Fuck you Jesus.

Fuck you Rudy.

Fuck you Ruth, for making us come after you again.

When Rudy had left the room—for the bathroom, I assumed—my mother soon crossed into the kitchen with the lightest step I've seen on her ever and whipped a lipstick out from her sleeve—must have been hiding it, for commando lipsticking at just this moment?—and puckered, touched up in front of the mirror by the sink.

She composed herself in a pretty posture, legs crossed at the ankle, back straight, but Rudy was too long in the bathroom, and my mother got antsy.

She folded her hands, she looked up at Jesus on the wall, and then her lips started moving—I could lip-read for tongue-speaking from here, easily, after all these years. I mean, it was obvious when she was doing it: lips moving with no pause between syllables, words, sentences: no stops, no rests.

"What's she saying?" I asked Jesus in my head.

No response.

"Come on, JC, what's she *saying?*"

She was saying, in her tongues-talk, in whatever language combo's she was getting at—Hungarian, Japanese, Urdu, whatever—she was saying, looking at her man Jesus on the wall, waiting for his replacement, she was saying:

He's gonna leave you. Don't even think he's gonna love you.

Breathing got difficult. It was like I was trying harder but I couldn't get any air in. I tried to slow my breaths, inhale from my stomach but it got worse. I let my cigarette drop and felt lightheaded when I moved to smudge it out with my foot.

When Rudy returned he offered Amandine his hand to help her stand up. It was the sweetest gesture, simple, easy, respectful—not on a thigh, not on the back.

The air left my stomach, my lungs completely then and I could not lure it in.

Of course, it was the same old story. Joey was not going to call, blah blah.

I was stuck out here in the yard again, smoking my second cigarette.

_____Loves Racinda.

I was inhaling and inhaling and trying and, actually, fully hyperventilating and when Rudy turned he saw me through the window—confusion then decisive action filled him.

In seconds he was patting me on the back.

"She's hyperventilating," he said, my mother, still smiling too much, coming onto the scene slower, behind him.

My mother stood apart, not sure of what to do with me spitting, puffing, bent over, turning red faced. When Rudy disappeared back into the house, and, after he returned with a paper bag for me to breathe into.

Once his back was to her, her lips moved once more into silent tongues without breaks.

What is she saying, Jesus? I managed in my mind, despite lack of oxygen, or too much or whatever was going on.

Who else wants a savior? my mother was saying, *not just me, babe. You too.*

Starfucker, I said back without hesitation, wanting to slap my mothers face: *the original groupie.*

But my mom stopped when Rudy could see her, and she moved closer to me when he got me settled down, she stroked my hair when my panting turned less terrifyingly inhuman.

"Thanks," I said, the tears puddling the shoplifted makeup on my face, and when Rudy hugged me I let him, even though he was going to have to be just another motherfucking savior to resist.

*   *   *

But by a few days before September, there is a shimmer on the ground from the rain. I feel full of all the details, fuller than I've ever been, now that everything has changed. Like my whole life I was in one movie theater, but finally, drowning in sleepiness, I dragged myself out to buy a soda and wandered back in to a different dark room to find a film that suits me, to find that film whose drenched colors and monstrous heads and sweet, spinning dances are so familiar, so gnawing, that in minutes I recognize these frames as the contents of my heart, the stories whose telling was secret, inscrutable until now.

Lisa has not returned. Gone. I don't miss her, don't think of her. I called Vagina, though, once, and she wouldn't say where Lisa was.

Joey did keep wanting me, he loves me now.

It's been a month.

When I asked Joey he said Lisa hadn't called, and neither of us has mentioned her otherwise.

Otis has just run upstairs to find a knife to open the box. The UPS truck is pulling away, and I think how different those trucks used to seem, back when I was stuck in the living room battling my mother. How now UPS trucks are a miracle, lit with magic. Joey is talking to Ted, the bass player, under a tree whose leaves are brightest pale green ovals, falling in bunches like a garment for a ceremony, a summoning.

Joey leans his hand out onto Ted's van, and I see the outline where it shifts the dew. I see his brown arm, how thick it is. I see the way he and Ted the bassist talk with little fight under it, but not in a bad way, just in that male way. So different from women, so above ground with something hard and selfish. They are talking about the way the rhythm tracks were mixed, Joey insisting in a really obvious way that the drums should have been louder. Except he's not saying louder, he's saying things like "more sophisticatedly," and "with a more resonant timbre." It's all about timbre, he says, then repeats, and it's something he says often and I am coming to agree with though at first I thought the statement was meaningless. I can see now how it applies to everything— what is the timbre of the moment? What is its color that is not a color but is a sound, a smell, a hunch? I am smoking a cigarette, feeling the lipstick perfect around my lips, feeling the way my calves touch each other and the edge of the porch step I'm sitting on.

Otis can't cut the box open right, so Joey steps in. Ted just rolls a cigarette and looks around like he wants to go. Joey makes a little show of opening the box, it's very cute, it's a big moment for them, and he inserts his hand like a surgeon to bring out the tape, surrounded in aquamarine bubblepack.

He manages to lift the tape so carefully, without ripping it, and he looks over his shoulder to me, says here Peanut, give you something to pick at, and hands me the packing stuff to pop. But I don't pop it. I keep watching them, I keep quiet, they have their backs to me, as Otis uses his skinny arms to hurl open the sticky door of the van, as Joey hops in the driver's seat, as Ted hesitates and becomes the passenger.

It's the remix. The club remix has arrived, sent from the DJ in New York who took a liking to them and fixed it up.

The song bounces, bounces through the open panel and the doors swung wide like awkward wings. Noises like bubbles from a fish's mouth, rhythmic more than melodic, transparent more than liquidy, pop in the middle high ground. Something like a siren on Quaaludes swells and ebbs in the bass. The drums have been slowed down not quite to narcotic, but to a few tequila shots speed. Otis's voice bobs, "Sip from my lo, sip from my lo, sip from my lotus, baby."

It rocks. It's obvious. It's a song for the summer, which of course here lasts well into October, so there is still time. You can imagine it coming out of every car stereo on every day trip, you can imagine teenagers lighting joints to it under strobe lights. It's a sound that is a promise.

And I look at these boys, and I am a part of what they are a part of, they are mine, and it is not a job or a stupid college fraternity or some atrocious church. I am not a groupie. Through Joey, I am onstage too, in a way, I am part of something that all the women, all the boys even in the audience know the words to, but something their voices can't be heard over. Something they want more than a good night's sleep, more than a clear morning, more than school more than squeezing in a workout more than their family more than skipping town—they want the notes and the beats and the beer buzz and the hope of it all—the beat the beat the beat that holds them together, dancing, sweating, ready to fuck, wanting Joey, wanting Otis, wanting Ted and wanting me too, in that way.

These boys, these musicians made this thing in the world, this band: they crack the people open, and the people pay for it, want more than anything to all know the same words and the same oldest rhythms and oldest desires. We are linked, through this wanting, we are tied to the beat that has been there since the first stars pulsed light down to us, since the first stick hit the first rock, to the beat under the freeways under the xerox machines under the bad perms under the plastic moldings under the waistbands under the insurance policies under the little tense moments that mean nothing. The beat that is tied to the whisper you most want on your pillow, the touch you most want on your stomach, the assurance you most want that something exists—the beat, the bass, the harmony—beyond what you can see.

The beat that everyone in the room possesses when the band is on stage, but which those little sluts in the front row nonetheless always want to find a way to steal—to steal what the men and what I, the girlfriend, possess.

14

VAMPING ROMEO

Lisa

She is going to have a fine life, she will own a dishwasher. Racinda is aboveboard, above ground, a well-lit apartment with hardwood floors. I know that I'm a basement in-law, shadowy. Renter's carpet. Well, fine, so that's it. That's what I am. I am the unrescued one, staying down here in Joey's darkness. I'm happy to. I'm living on the red splatters of anger he feeds me.

*   *   *

So the guy on the Harley that night when I left turned out to be the new head of A&R for the band's label in town to visit his mother, secretly stopping by the gig without anyone noticing. He is actually halfway impressed with the band. I make the mistake of letting him hear the tape of them in my purse and he is now talking to Otis all the time, helping them get more promotion from the record company. But we don't talk about the band. AJ flies me to LA from Thursdays to Mondays, every week, he takes me shopping in the boutiques of hotels. He buys me underwear that costs as much as me and Virginia's rent two apartments ago. By the fourth Tuesday back in Sacramento, I have so many hundred-dollar panties I start handing them off to Virginia fully wrapped and ribboned in the box.

I keep a low profile.

He likes. . . things. . . He likes me to stay in the hotel room all day, all night except when he's with me. Mornings he'll take my clothes with him in such a male, stinking gym bag that he has to buy me more later. He leaves me with nothing—no bra, just rabbit fur slippers, three different thicknesses of bathrobe, a hundred satellite channels and Mortal Kombat III on the Super Nintendo, fake-looking body parts littering the screen. Well, sometimes a little coke or other snacks, always in an engraved Tibetan sacred box or some shit that his wife gave him when they reaffirmed their vows.

This situation felt perfect to me, answer to something I'd always somehow forgotten to ask for, until a few weeks into it when I was just dying, dying to walk on pavement, to just pass by someone other than him or the bellboy or even his rich friends in restaurants at night. Normal people, young people, people with an edge on them that wasn't just an edge for talking money and fucking money.

When he got the bill the next day from the escape clothes I had ordered up through room service—you know you've gotten yourself somewhere when you can order jeans and stilettos and someone in a uniform brings them to your door inside a half hour—I was truly stuck, he put a ban on me ordering anything but food and videos. And you know, my little strolls too far down Sunset weren't even all that. The first few minutes out of the cab were a rush, but then the dirty heshers, hair hopelessly teased, leather pants worn gray at the thighs, really didn't do much for me. I craved the suits. I craved the martinis. I craved the $500 bottles of Scotch, the weed that didn't once leave a hangover. I knew nothing about this shit a month previous, when I was happy drinking a six of Mickey's wide mouths, anything above 20/20.

My flesh grows raspberries, hot blushes where I can see it, maybe bruises where I can't.

A flame, tattooed in reds and blacks, wriggles, writhes, snaps under his belly button. It makes me hate my own sad, thorny rose, so uninspired, done when I was thirteen, on my ankle. Already fading. He tells me his wife's intuitive instructed him on a focus, and then this flame came to him in a dream, strangely coincidental with the sex/money chakra. Whatever. It always just looks like a cunt, though, to me, churning half open on his hard skin.

I turn over and over in my mind: what could my plain rose become? I bring my stained ankle just inches from my eyes and imagine on it faces, landscapes, symbols from a language that never existed, but whatever I come up with, I know that cheap flower will not let itself hide.

*   *   *

The waitress looks like me, except that her teeth are straight, no gaps, and her skin is much, much more expensive than mine. You can read in her face that she's been to college and that the sapphires in her earlobes are real, but that she also knows how to screw and that she's willing to do it to get closer to being worshipped.

I could open her throat with my fishbone.

She acts like she isn't overhearing the men talking about points and units and bidding wars over unknown fifteen-year-olds in baggy jeans and expensive choreography, she turns back toward the kitchen right as one of the men is going to stage-whisper secret slime about somebody famous, but I see how slowly she walks, I see how she is gathering the information with those rich, sensitive ears. She is the only friendly waitress in the place, it's not expected of them, and she works this friendly into the ground. Her heels are too high and thin to wait tables on.

When I ask for the crabcakes with roasted pepper *coulis* she smiles like she's hiding something then demonstrates with a sneer how to pronounce that sauce correctly.

I drink some more wine and though it's sharp it covers my pink mouth like the sunlight I miss. With these people, two of AJ's smarmy colleagues and their girlfriends, who may or may not be hookers, who, if they're not, are definitely in my category, which is not *hooker* but not so far from it either. I don't get wild when I drink here, I don't get loud, I stay very quiet and dig my fingernails into my leg above the hemline.

"Mmmm, that's a good one, the best choice all night. . ." the waitress says when AJ tells her what the third bottle of wine will be, and she knows what she is talking about.

When she brings the bottle to him he holds on to it, and she doesn't let go, either.

Back in the room, AJ takes a shower instead of fucking me instantly, and I know it is so close to being all over. I have called Joey every day since I got here this time around, and he can tell that the click is mine, although other people, men and women, call him and hang up all the time. I barely even have to pick up the phone—Joey can't possibly imagine where I am, but he knows every minute when I am wanting him back so much. No phone necessary. I leave him messages every few days and tell him to call me at Virginia's, but he hasn't tried there either. He is screening, he is avoiding me.

AJ is hard getting out of the shower, and even though the lame future is whispering to me again, I can't just throw a fit and walk out of there like I know I should. I can't seem to dump them first, anymore. Not since Joey.

Fuck.

Joey shattered my hard girl into bits—ever since I've been with him I want every other guy to stay a little longer than he wants to. It never happened before. Thank God with these other guys I seem to be able to—but now only *after* the first humiliation—whip myself up and get over it fast. Whereas with Joey I just dive deeper and deeper into such watery *baby baby* bullshit.

The only time I was a vampire chick like this *ever*, before Joey, was when I was a little girl. A flower-yellow dress that fanned out so sweetly on me. Virginia's first boyfriend I remember. When I called him *Daddy* Virginia slapped my mouth so my teeth cut my lip and I bled. We left the next morning. Ronald. McDonald—I don't know his last name. Ronald. And I stuck myself onto his leg and wouldn't leave, *daddy, daddy* and Virginia stood out there by the car, her face tight as the Nevada heat—*he is NOT your Daddy*, her Tennessee twang returning whenever she got upset—and I knew she would have really done it, really left me there so I had to choose her. Because even then I knew that he couldn't make dinner, he couldn't take me to the men's room if I needed to pee in a restaurant. But I wanted him more than I wanted her—daddy, daddy, daddy, though he wasn't mine, or anyone's, and didn't act it. I fell asleep thinking about his face for the next five years until—. . .

Just this man, around, you call him daddy. It seems like he is the one holding it all together. Even though the mommy, taking out the trash, even, sucking the dick of the mechanic to get the car functional. But the Daddy—what protection is there without him? You want one so so badly. You want one like you want good clothes and money and to say smart things in school. You want one like you want your mother's eyes on you not the TV. And not on him.

And when the very bad shit went down with the sixth boyfriend, when I was eight, I stopped wanting even the first one, Ronald, back. It was as if Ronald did all the shit to me that the very bad one did. The faces blurred, the hate blurred. And then when I started fucking boys my own age a few years later it was like after they fucked me—whoever, whatever boy—it was like underneath it they were the very bad one and I had no problem walking away.

The best part was walking away. Even better if you did it before it *occurred* to them to take their dick out of your mouth.

Daddy—everything in you wants to stay with him, until that switch clicks off and your boots are made for walking and walking and walking and walking. But—there's something under—there's something—even in the fucking, just in the fucking. Maybe I was a vampire chick as bad, for all of them, though I never called them and hung up, though I never acted like I knew them when I shook the hand of their girlfriend minutes after my hand had been in their mouth, had scratched their ribs, palmed their balls in some closet at a party. Maybe just the fucking, and that moment— I was a vampire all along but I had it under control, or at least under ground, until now.

I think it was when the band started taking off that I couldn't tear myself from Joey.

I hadn't had to walk from him before because I didn't think I wanted him so bad. He seemed, I don't know, kind of convenient? I was tired? Who knows why I stayed. He adored me then because he was still in his head a fat band geek who came the second his hand was on your thigh. And then with Bandolero and all these groupies, all these uncouth vampire chicks surrounding him—god even Racinda was flirting with him and she thinks he's an uncultured idiot—somehow I grew fangs too.

What does the vampire chick want? What is the blood she steals needed for? Some kind of hope? I think: she needs some kind of hope of going someplace else. Needs to say *Daddy*. Needs revenge. Needs to beat out that little girl who thinks the man is such hot shit even though all he does is watch ESPN and eat Chex Mix and stack up empty Coors Light cans.

But fuck if I know.

Virginia taught me there was always a man around the corner, always another one there. I believed it until Joey. There was something in the music, not just the starfucking, I wanted.

If it was just starfucking, AJ would have replaced him.

The other thing Virginia taught me, by the way, that most women seem not to know is that if you have a problem with booze or a problem with being a slut, you can keep it a lot quieter than if you eat too much to make yourself feel better. You still look good, drinking and fucking, you don't get fat. No one can tell, at least not for awhile.

*   *   *

When AJ starts running his hands up and down, up and down my sides, my hips, there is a different thing propelling me than money and bad urges and fingernails and drugs. His no to me, his fantasy in the shower about the waitress, makes me crave him and want to bury him in my stomach, wrap him in me and not leave him.

But at the same time I want my nails honed enough to pierce his jugular.

And as we go on and get wet and sweat and the sheets fly from the mattress I can feel other water, tears coming from me and I am pounded away from AJ and I am weeping for Joey with each impact and you will not believe it, I see cakes.

Cakes everywhere.

Cakes in different rooms and for different years, but mostly in the living room, Joey's mom's house, and Elaine, his mom, is posing by the cakes and her hips are half the massive size they are now and she has a neat headband holding back her shining, flipped hair, in every dull sheened squarish photo, scalloped seventies trim.

And then in 1977 we went back to sugar instead of honey and he wanted the shape of an airplane so I made the mold myself.

Pulled back by that voice I see her standing there, now, same Sacramento living room, same black lacquered dining room table, *now*, this moment, now, dishes done, everybody full, Joey smoking a cigarette in the garage apartment, considering going to sleep he is so stuffed with paella but also feeling lured out by the night, and Elaine is showing the photos of her cakes, the cakes she baked for her son, to a girl, and the girl coos and is freaked out and steps back a little but is so in love with Joey that she wants to see all the cakes, the cake of every year, she wants to know what Joey looks like and imagine what he feels like in every photograph, at every party.

And AJ is about to come and I am about to come and usually I don't care when he comes in me but this time I start screaming and weeping because I know that this girl lets Joey come in her too and that this girl is Racinda. She is smiling so sweetly there, swinging her legs absentmindedly against the chair's support--where I just walked out after the fat lady's first cake— she is nodding and smiling and is what everyone wants a girl to be, just this plain little nice thing who does what you want, who listens to your stupid pride in your cakes, Elaine you sad fat woman who should be ashamed to even utter the word cake. And Elaine looks down at this girl and the edges of her eyes tighten up into a smile and she hugs Racinda and Racinda goes downstairs and wraps those same arms around Joey from behind and they go to bed early, easy, and don't go out to the bars, don't answer the phone even when Elaine's voice comes screeching through the speaker of Joey's answering machine, or, later, when I hang up on it and the click turns sour into a dial tone for almost a full minute before the thing turns itself off.

*   *   *

A month of hotel clothes curls in a sickening pile by the door when I twist myself out of bed at ten the next morning to answer the phone. Before my head is off the pillow, I can smell the locker room leather now woven into the clothes from way over there. The front desk politely reminds me that checkout is in one hour.

Do they usually do that? How do I know. Maybe once again, I'm so special.

AJ hasn't left me a plane ticket, nothing but this pile that I sort through by kicking at it with luxury toes, rich beige polish. I want to bring all the clothes with me, every gorgeous stitch, fuck the gym-bag smell, but there is no bag to put it all in. I wrap the near-vinyl catsuit into a huge scarf I wore once as a skirt. The catsuit's flared gothic sleeves and pointy collars, its deep v-neck, its detailed cuffs all get crinkled up sadly. It's the outfit Racinda will hate me most for being able to wear well. I toss all the bras and panties in there I can find, a leather bustier, and some soft, elegant silk pajamas. I tie the skirt scarf up like a hobo bag, hook a finger onto the knot. Any refined-looking stuff that isn't just for the bedroom—the light blue and purple suits and the draping, classy, suggestive wrap dresses—I leave.

The tip AJ left for the maid is just enough for a greyhound ticket and a Pepsi, but the cab to the bus station I have to pay for in another way.

*   *   *

He looked me in the eye a few minutes ago.

Night blocks Joey's way so he is hanging a plastic-caged flashlight on a hook above the gaping engine of his sister's Nova. He just keeps walking back between the little fake kitchen that opens onto sliding doors and the car, bringing out heavy tools, oiled metal shrinking in the night.

Since he lives in the converted three-car garage (which is too big for the house but he always has luck like this), the cars live in the driveway.

I am shivering, staring at him, barefoot and blistered, the untamed pair of Demeulemeester boots I wore out of the hotel now dangling from my tight fist, my scarf-wrapped tramp bundle on the ground next to me. I felt safe before he hung that lantern up, but now I'm sure my dirt is showing and that the outline of my thighs is coming through the white skirt.

AJ Morton, huh? he says, smearing a rag around something in the engine, striping it a rusty oil color.

I just stare

How was he?

Shut the fuck up.

You should tell Virginia to be more careful with your pimps' names.

Unscrewing the cap of a plastic tank, setting it carefully on the lawn table.

Oh I'm sorry, he says, *I mean your customers.*

His hands brace above, between the headlights, he's staring down at the metal edge between the inside and the outside of the motor.

I bet you didn't put in a single word for us. Your mouth was full, huh? You fucking distracted him from us, huh? Nobody works when Lisa comes over.

A sound comes out of the back of my mouth, but I catch it and just stare.

So you're fucking the A&R department.

So you're fucking the world.

This makes him smile, but I can see the meanness under it. He keeps his head under the hood, then leads it with the mild smile to the dry creek bed at the edge of the yard. His eyes squint.

His face is shaped like home.

I guess you think you're above me now, he says. The moon plays down to us.

Baby I say. I reach for him. I don't tell him it's over with AJ. I don't tell him I know about Racinda, even though the strand of hair he will brush off the pillow can only be hers.

You think you can just leave me and I don't care, he says. And I bend and break under him and apologize and I cry. But then when the phone rings, right after we are done, and he fucking answers it, sets the base of it on my bare ass, I want to wrench around and scream and tear the phone away—

how could he care so little after the tender thing that just happened between us?

But he is waiting for me to do this. He is waiting for me to scream. He wants something easier, he wants a girl his mother can show pictures of cakes to.

If I scream, I lose.

I turn to him fast but then the silence I know I need to win him back catches my words and I flop back down, I doze. Furious. Grateful.

*   *   *

I don't know where Elaine gets pants to fit her—billowy, turquoise, size of a beach umbrella ripped off the spokes, inch-thick ties to be knotted or bowed. Sweatpants tarted up to wear to the office, a favorite style of the morbidly obese, I've noticed. Not that she's that. She's completely normal looking above the hips, like a size eight on top, even a six. Who knows.

Elaine brings him a pile of pancakes and then sits down with her own stack before she laughs, cheeks widening at the realization of totally having forgotten me.

She doesn't say anything. I fume facially at Joey and he ignores me too. I can see myself stomping out of here but I remember that I am trying not to be that girl anymore.

"Um, can I have some pancakes too?"

"Well, there are some burnt ones on the bottom that Joey probably won't want."

I swear, she says this.

The small pancakes left are each near-black on at least one side.

She pushes the fake margarine spread over to me when Joey is putting a half-inch of butter on each flour slab. I ignore her. I wait for the real thing, after she takes it. I cover each and every black little hockey puck with butter then don't eat a bite.

I smirk hard but nobody notices.

"Joey always loved breakfast for breakfast, lunch or dinner," she says, to him. "Do you want me to cook up some of that turkey sausage too?"

His mouth is too busy to speak, so he snorts no. He isn't looking at either of us, he is reading the paper.

"Hey Elaine," I say, "When are you going to show me the cake book?"

For a second they both look up at me like I told them I wanted to start masturbating on the table, between the butter and the OJ.

"Joey, when you go to the gig in San Francisco next weekend I thought Mrs. Frey and I would come down extra early, so if you want to go out to eat in the city before hand—" Elaine says.

He is back at the paper now.

"The A&R guy is coming up then. I can't do it. I've gotta shuck and jive," he says.

"He is?" I say. But I drop it.

"What's going on with the A&R?" Elaine says. Her voice is a combination of sweet girl-child and shrill, angry, starving person, left for a lifetime out of the group. Her voice is the aging queen in Snow White faking it as Betty Crocker.

"AJ's really into them," I say. "I talked to him a ton about it in LA and he thinks that the band will fill out the spectrum of the label's current acts," I say. "He thinks that—"

"Not *AJ*, stupid," Elaine says, "*A and R*,"

You sad woman. You think he owes you something, you think he is going to give you something. But he's just going to keep taking, shunting up fake promises to get you to shell out for beer and cymbals.

Joey tosses the paper onto the floor and pushes away his plate. We both, me and Elaine, are so desperate for him to stay that we actually lean in and stare up at him. I pick the paper up off the floor and start folding it neatly.

"Do you need any money?" Elaine says.

"I'm cool," he says, not annoyed, just like it's absurd he'd need any money.

Something becomes clear to me.

He is embarrassed about this in front of me now in a way he was not before.

This, somehow, this is my trump card. I don't know what to do with it yet. Before now I would have screamed it back at him in a fight. Now, stakes higher, I need something more subtle.

I slip out somehow through the tiny space between the back of Elaine's chair and the wall. I fall into the huge lazyboy she usually sits in in the living room, and a silence wedges its way around the house, a quiet. I can hear the freeway tumble like water, I can feel my stomach acid breaking down the flour and the syrup and the fat.

"You know, my shoes have holes where the sole meets the leather," he says to her when he's forgotten that he hasn't heard my feet clomping back out to his garage.

"Your good shoes?" she says, "They were such high-quality! I didn't think they'd do that!"

"Yeah, well. . ." he says waiting for the offer.

"We'll have to go to the mall," she says, "what about this evening?"

"They don't have them at the mall, only in San Francisco," he says.

"Oh well we'll make a day of it!" she says. She claps.

"I have rehearsals and gigs, I don't think I'll have the time. That's okay," he says, "I can just duct-tape them and hope that when we meet with A—the A & R guy he won't look down. Mom—really, no sweat."

"Don't be ridiculous," she says, and I can hear her purse open, her wallet. I can hear the bills slide across the formica.

*   *   *

In those weeks through September, the frenzy of the band still building, when Joey doesn't want me around every night, or even every other, I act like it doesn't occur to me there is another girl involved. Racinda calls while we are in bed but the machine is carefully turned down. When Joey puts face-time in with Elaine I sneak back out to the garage and listen to Racinda's message. The first one is open and girlish. The next phone call has an inch of guardedness in it, and the one after that the tone of someone counting the hours before she can hit redial without total humiliation. But now her voice is in green fields, her voice has the kind of sweet, lamby, baby-girl dreams I've heard of but never really believed in until now.

There is also a message from AJ, looking for me. *Joey, my man, I thought you said last time I called you'd let me know when you see Miss Lisa*, he says, *I haven't heard from you. Call me—I think I have been able to work something out on a publicity budget but I can't do it without that girl, if you know what I mean.*

My stomach twists. Though I run to the bathroom to throw up there is nothing in me.

*   *   *

But then Otis's birthday party the last day of September, held in Joey's little garage apartment, is my excuse for wearing the catsuit.

"To the left to the left," Otis says as he sets up stacks of paper cups, fascinated as a boy.

I am on top of Joey's couch in my big boots and vinyl outfit, trying to hammer a tack into a flashing strand of Christmas lights, fuck it if I hit the wire.

"You know," Otis says, then his raspy laugh, "I was thinking more of swooping the lights rather than lining them with the ceiling."

I put my boot on his dumb plaid shoulder and shove, surprised that he crumples back a few steps.

When the lights are all up, Joey hands me a big, ugly card—like an Easter card more than a birthday—of a barely-dry cartoon chick coming out of a pink and purple-ringed crystallized egg.

"Put it up in the middle, right where everyone will see it."

"What the fuck?" I say, taking the pen out of my mouth.

There is one main yellow chick in the middle, emerging fat from its glitter-overlaid egg, and two little ones on the side, their shells already gone. It is an extra-extra-large size card, the size of three human heads lined up.

"It's from Elaine."

"It's from the Dollar Store. I don't want to get blamed for that ugly thing," I say.

"Jesus, Lisa," Joey says, and gets all thoughtful looking back out through the sliding doors, down at the creek.

I reel my fury in.

"Sure honey," I say, and I say, "Hey, did you lose weight, those jeans look hella loose on you."

But Joey is ignoring me, just looking for rats to shoot—rats run across Elaine's clothesline and he takes them out with his dad's old .22 nights he doesn't go drinking or have rehearsals or gigs.

"It's actually a *really* pretty card," I say. But he's watching the rats, mouth wide.

"*I said*, this card is so cute, actually," I say.

"She's doing something really nice and you just can't admit that," he says, not looking at me.

"I know, you're right, I'm sorry. Hon—I'm sorry," I say, and this panic unwinds in my stomach when he just walks away from me then.

Elaine's eyes are in that chick's dark sockets, looking back all starletty over its bare baby duck-flipped ass, and will be watching her boy bounce between me and R all night. I know. Elaine wants to be up there with the best view.

So I hit the tack hard, put it right through the bird's feathery, yellow heart.

I check to make sure Joey isn't looking and—he'll never notice—I draw little fangs hanging off the beak of the fat one, the big fat chick who wants to be the star of the party.

Racinda's footsteps in the doorway behind me ring clear as freeway buzz in the morning. As I hit that tack one more time it breaks, its plastic head smashing into slivers that float down onto the top of the couch, I understand that I have just killed that place inside me that would let Racinda know I know she is screwing my true love.

Killed it, I think forever. Just like that:

Because I had to kill it, because I have missed her. Virginia is jealous of my panties and my plane trips—she's being mean again. I missed my little girl, my little R whose head I used to stroke until she fell asleep in my lap. Because I wanted to tell her, the way a murderer has to tell the boys at the bar, the traveler in the next seat, his brother—I wanted to move my lips in the shape of my secret: that I knew what she wanted and that there was no way I was going to let her get it. But if I told her, it would no longer be true. She'd run to Joey and he'd banish me. So I killed that part of me that wanted to peep.

Slam, slam, tack in wall, done. Risk of fuckup all finished. Eliminated. Dead to me. Don't have to worry about her. Just him. Just worry about him waiting to tell me it's over, to throw me out the moment I slip up and get the least bit angry. *I will not get angry.* I will be the girl surrounded by a mother's cakes.

"Sweetie," I say, I turn to Racinda, and my hug gives as much love as you can while clenching a thumbtack in your fist, as much warmth as you can through vinyl.

*   *   *

"Leese—AJ call you? What did he say this week, my cat woman birthday girl?" Otis says and gives his gurgle that passes for a laugh.

Joey's eyes wedge to slate.

"Whoa, Joey Joey bo-boey," Otis says.

"Fuck, hasn't this rhyming phase stopped yet?" Joey says.

"Sorry dude. And sorry about AJ, I know it must be hard to have someone with a real job steal your lady."

"At least I got ladies to steal. . ." Joey says low.

"Or a *couple* of them," Otis whispers.

They've all been acting like Otis rather than Joey is going out with Racinda kinda sorta since I got back. Not one of those fuckers—not even

Ted the bassist, the most human of the bunch—has felt the need to mention to me that Joey had another official girlfriend for the month of August when I was gone. Or that she was still in our midst.

Fucking Otis. I hate that motherfucker. The way he is all over Racinda—I can feel her stomach turn each time he palms her. And then I can see her resist his sloppy fingers and drunker comments and try to make Joey jealous with it. Pathetic.

But Little R, she just wants what I want; she just wants a ticket out of here and just wants—

I slam the tack in my palm *into* my palm, dead center, to remind myself what I decided. She *doesn't* need him. She has other things.

Because what do I have? My own blood on my hands, is all. I can feel it puddling up, can feel its redness.

"Anyone need smokes?" I say. "Joey, come with me to the store."

Those eyes get hard again.

"I'm gonna wait here for AJ's call," Joey says.

"I need a fucking escort," I say, "It's dark. You can't even hear the ringer in here anyway."

He ignores me.

Racinda is snuffling as she exits the bathroom.

"I'll loan you some smokes," she says, and I try to choke all compassion down further--even though I am safe, you know, just for good measure--and I go out there with her, take the one decent bottle of wine from Joey's "apartment" and sit my ass down on the cement for a chat.

Sometimes, staring in Racinda's face is like staring up at the clouds while you are hugging just the right person.

And it keeps on being like this—I get all pale blue with her, but only so deep as my secret that I have killed all chance of telling her. We smoke cigarettes until hers will eventually run out too, and then even before that happens this nasty burst of hate washes over me and I dismember her in my mind, suckle her on nails, on this ash and cinders feeling in me.

I tell her about AJ out there, but lies mostly, like how he was so in love with my vampire pussy that the only reason I'm not with him right now is that he had to put some face time in with his wife before he left her for me.

She tiptoes around what is plain as day—won't say anything about Joey. My quiet kindness is pure subterfuge—it will get back to Joey, every word, every mellow, insipid thing that comes from me, and Racinda is still impressed with me enough that she will believe me, add convincingness where Joey would smell bullshit if he heard my words.

I curlicue and preen up AJ's passion in my telling.

I give Racinda another hug.

And imagining Joey's whisper to her—*just do it for now, just fake it like you're with Otis till she helps us sign our deal*—I can feel the tack rip in my palm—my blood, my skin scissoring apart—and my promise to myself. Thank god for the sixty dollar bottle of wine Otis's mom sent up for his birthday—I am having a hard time descending to cheap shit the way I am going to need to to survive back here. So I drink it straight from the bottle, to get used to things. It feels different over your lips that way.

"Have a sip," I say, and she washes it down quick without even noticing it isn't Gallo.

I notice how her eyes fix on his rats running down the clothesline: she is learning to think the way Joey does about nailing a moving target.

*   *   *

Racinda is so sad, just lugging herself around, not really drinking, staring at Otis like he is talking to her in Swahili, cracking a smile only when he is very funny, and also cracking tears so that she has to run to the bathroom, butting in the front of the line which the overgrown crowd lets her do since she is so OG now with the band.

Light blue, then a blackish fire in me. It is like watching TV—the predictable plot strings you along, you watch it more for comfort than for surprise.

I am very close to eliminating her. I'm not sure---I'm not--

She tries to signal Joey into the bathroom to bitch at him—he hasn't gone near her all night, and she is bored as all shit on top of being depressed—I leave for cigarettes, real quietly, so that no one will really notice, but before I go to the store I stop beneath the viny trellis that covers the bathroom window, lit shadows of the bougainvillea twisting in the breeze.

"Don't fucking push me away. Let's just go down by the creek and talk a little," she says.

I hear her hand brush the shirt I gave him. I hear him pout.

"Honey," she says.

"This is my *work*," he snaps.

Him saying that utter shit, to *her*, not me—it makes me grin. I squish my feet into the wet dirt, wedge them in in half circles. I brush the fluffy petals of the bougainvillea off my neckline.

"This is my *career*," he says.

I hear the soggy pause. *Career*, Jesus Christ. I can't help it—I peer inside and see the rage on him.

"Getting shitfaced with Otis is your career? Well does it come with good benefits? Do you get executive parking with that?"

She grabs him by the shoulders and the second she pushes him his hands throw her off of him and he slaps her, just grazes her because she is very fast in dodging him, but still it is a hit. She gasps.

My girl. That blackeyed bird on the wall can't do anything to either of us when I am grinning like this and a sea of palest blue envelops us, the two young starfuckers fighting for someone who isn't even in the sky yet. I glide to the 7-11 lit and hearing music in my head.

By the time I get back, Racinda is shut in the bedroom, which is more than I can stand, her in there. You can't hear her crying unless you are listening for it.

I shove the door but I have to do it a bunch of times before I can get it open—she is leaning on it slumped.

She stuffs something in her bag real quick and acts guilty.

"Sorry—I was just tired. I just happened in here—" she says.

Coke in her bag? I think, then, *no*. What is she hiding? I can feel the hate crystallizing in me, I want to strike her. But I am so close. I am so close to keeping him.

"Don't worry, sweetie," I say, brushing the hair from her eyes.

She makes a smile that is like an embarrassed curtsy and hurries out.

And the stupid girl leaves her bag.

(I can still hear her gasp when he hit her).

Get this—but get this. It isn't drugs or anything she is hiding so fast in her purse. It is a book—a thin little thing, as odd at this party as the giant hatchling card on the wall. Its tall, thin, eighties lettering, across bands of color deciding down the cover, spells out *Signs of Living With An Alcoholic*.

That's it.

Signs of Living With an Alcoholic.

He'll dump her the second he *sees* that.

Her cat is *so* out of the bag.

I catch a glimpse of just my left eye in the mirror—still pretty, still okay after all this booze time—and I hear something from my stomach tell me—*he's yours, sweetie.*

I look pale. A little, victorious fang would not surprise me, poking over my grin.

She's set to ruin herself with him as sure as the blue held me to her soft as candles all night between the patches of hate.

All I have to do now is wait.

I am home free, and there is this joy but there is also this absence in me. Because what--because blankness.

Because what—what have I what have I got. What have I got now?

(You could tell, when he slapped her, that he wanted to make a fist but had to make it seem open-handed, like in the movies).

I shut the light in the bedroom and carry the book out to the party. Joey is leaning over yet some other girl, and I see Racinda plotting and planning and making herself nice and not angry and I see myself standing in this doorway knowing she has lost and I see the fanged chick pinned up to the wall—Elaine, watching and waiting and wanting him.

We make him repeat his promises to us over and over because they mean that he is willing to go to the trouble of lying to us; that is the most we can hope for in this world.

I have won but I have won nothing. My baby girl--

There is nothing there except in the waiting for him to return.

What I have won: eternally waiting for him to return. I have beat her out but

I will still be waiting.

He wipes his nose on his wrist when the young little groupie he is flirting with isn't looking. He sucks in his stomach. He stands taller so that his dick feels bigger.

*   *   *

But this isn't even my big moment, is it? This isn't even my big return to him because was he really there, was he ever? He was there? He was there for seconds and minutes but then he was gone and all his promises of returns, the returning, there is nothing to return to because there was never anything really to leave.

All he is is leaving.

I am waiting for him to save me from his lies but his lies *are* him.

My winning is a dead thing, or many dead things—cremated then scattered in me.

It is like having walked off a cliff. What else is there to do? What world have I entered now?

*   *   *

More than the blue or anything else I know underneath it all I hate Racinda for getting free of all this. I can imagine her standing at her nice dishwasher, looking out on a terrace, drinking iced tea, traveling, sending her children to schools where they will never once duck a blow, and I see Joey turning me redder and redder and grayer and meaner through the years. I see myself desperate for decent wine, leering at the yuppie store sadly when Virginia takes us out to Safeway on a beer run.

But I have made my decision. And our fates are so determined. Keeping him is worse than losing him, though, so I will finish her off with a mean little crush of my spiky toe, the only pleasure left to me with this knowledge.

*   *   *

The scent of toxic, burning plastic sneaks out to me through the garage wall from inside Elaine's house just as the beer runs out and most of the freaks, everyone except the band and their closest hangers-on, leaves. It is the smell of a couch and drapes and wall-to-wall on fire.

Fuck it, I think, let Elaine's retarded house burn. I'm not running in there. A hush hits, a hush hits just in time for Joey to make another entrance—crowds always part for him, the bus is always waiting whenever he needs it. A hush hits, and I open the door at the sound of his footsteps through his mother's kitchen.

His voice blooms through the drywall, round as that wine I'd finished off and am dreaming of now.

"Happy birthday you fat fuck Otis. . ." Joey sings.

The house is *not* burning down—the plastic-fire smell is happening because Joey has melted the bottom of a table-candle onto the cap of a bottle of tequila. You can see where he burnt the lid to the base of the candle—the plastic warped up in little waves like a baby choppy sea, hardened to peaks. The silver ribbon pasted to the label is drooping and about to fall right off.

Racinda is propped on his bedroom door, her calves pressed back into the wood to keep her from falling asleep.

"Say thanks to my moms, you fucking old man," Joey says, and hits Otis so hard on the back that Otis can't hide a sputtery cough.

Then Joey and I are leaning like a gothic arch over Otis, whose wide face pushes up from his seat on the couch to blow out the flame. Our eyes fix Otis in that moment like a snapshot, his face white and separated from his dark body by the island of candlelight.

Otis cuts his palms on the burnt plastic, trying to open his tequila. Joey takes it from him and opens it with a t-shirt someone hands him, carefully swathing his precious fucking musician hands. Spurred by the applause when he gets it open, Joey doesn't hand the bottle to Otis, but puts it to his own lips and chugs away himself.

I see the phrase rambling across Racinda's mind, horizontal colors of her secret book's cover streaming up and down her screen like when you move the antenna around: *signs of living with an alcoholic*. Racinda is almost just a black outline, all hollowed out. *Oh,* she thinks, *oh, that's another sign . . .*

Her despair bolsters me and feeds me. I can't tell if it's my teeth that are sharper, or my tongue.

At the line of shot glasses, Joey is applauding and yelling for me to join. The gold stuff burns and doesn't burn, and I fix my eyes on the worm in the bottle as it bobs around, spins, shimmers each time Otis pours another one. First glass, second glass. Third. When I am on the fifth one, inching toward the lime, the salt coda, I see Racinda turn her face to me, her profile so stony, and, miraculously, just then, when the green fruit is smashed across my teeth and tongue, Joey bends me into his thick arms and spins me around, giddying me into shrieks and laughter.

"Look," I say to Ted quietly once Joey has put me down, "Look at this book Racinda is reading," and I write her name across its inside in block letters.

It makes its rounds at the party with perfect timing—people reading paragraphs defensively, so obvious they *are* fucking alcoholics, but the *so obvious* in their voices supposed to convince themselves they aren't.

Joey never does find out I was the one who started passing that around . . .

"Racinda found you out, dude!" Otis says, waving the alcoholism book at him, and Joey has lost so much face here that he takes the mock punch in the stomach and laughs lukewarmly.

Otis rips the cover from the book, pins it up with a tack above Joey's coffee pot. The word *alcoholic*, in everyone's increasing drunkenness, gets repeated and repeated and giggled at and howled at, finally loudest by

Joey, trying to shrug it off. Racinda huddles over a magazine, her face gray.

As soon as the door shuts behind me, an hour later, leaving to be driven home by Ted—I gracefully let Racinda have Joey for one more night, gave a peck on Joey's cheek, *I'm sleepy,* acted like I didn't notice that she had no ride, that she was the *only* person left there—I hear something slam, something fracture something roar apart some bass words he is breaking over her head and then such peaceful sleep comes to me in the passenger seat of the van, I doze so heavily and with such a grin that Ted can't bear to wake me, drives me around until sunrise, when I wrap my arms around him and scream in joy and hate.

15

WITNESS

Max

The yellow around me is a sort of oval, bounded by the mirror that hangs up against the thick white paint on the back of my bedroom door. The yellow comes from a poster behind me I've had since I was 12, of a devil on a Harley, with a giant halo of golden light behind him. I'm standing so that in the mirror that halo is mine. I don't really look at myself—just when I turn my head, out of the corner of my eyes. How can you really look at yourself in the mirror anyway? My mother is yelling down there, *Max, get down here don't you think you are going out again tonight, you're never here and you barely even live here anymore and I'm not running a hotel here you need to be a part of this family,* meaning me and her, *if you are going to live here I mean it I mean it Max god dammit* she drops a pan and shuts up and gets distracted in her cooking. It's six o'clock so she is already halfway drunk on margaritas that still seem kind of innocent. So sugary. She switched to them from box Chardonnay a while ago. She has red deep lines on her face. Her eyes are still huge and beautiful but everything else, except her arms, is fat and the men don't happen to her anymore. I'm the only one she's got left, and she can feel that I'm going to be out of here as soon as I can figure out a way.

I push my flat palm toward the mirror in a move that is sort of like judo, kind of passes for it, and I focus on my hand. How can you take more in than that, a hand, a wrist? I don't want to.

I pick up the ringing phone before she can even hear it, it rings in my room first, and it is Joey, coming right over to get me. Before I hang up, there is a horrible clanging noise, but not like metal, downstairs. It's like heavy rocks crashing into bowls. She starts screaming and I have had enough of this, this isn't anything unusual.

These red streaks and then light reflected off the devil's yellow. I have to lie down on the bed, I stare at the ceiling, I know, I know she is crying down there—this happens about every other day, I'd say, soft tears. I kick my pillow off the black quilt and it hits the dresser quietly, not enough for her to hear. I light a cigarette just to piss her off—it's time to go, I gotta wait for Joe outside.

Her cries get louder when she hears me coming on the steps, above her head—she is in the downstairs bathroom next to the kitchen

"What?" I say, "I'm going out."

"My foot!" she yells, "My fucking foot!"

I get really worried, a rush in my breath, but then she yells:

"Come help me you selfish asshole."

Right.

I round the corner and see the green bathroom door, like a dark sea color I always thought, flung open, which she does just to get at me—taking a piss with the door open even though I'm eighteen freaking years old. Her thighs hanging off the seat in a solid roll—I know to shut my eyes before it even registers.

But this time, she is on the ground, on her side, ass away from me thank god, one hand full of toilet paper, the other hand red, pushing up like a little crab off the floor, unable to lift her.

"You're going to stay in and help me?" she says.

I shake my head. Her margarita glass has rolled away from her. Her face, her face. Her mouth—what can I say about it, what can I say about her trying to reel me right back in.

"I think I broke my foot," she says and she starts crying again, her hair falling around her face in gray and brown lines. Behind her, light comes in through the white curtain.

A couple years ago maybe I would have been in there, helping her up, waiting outside till she wiped her ass, talking to her, watching TV with her. Making tea. Heating leftovers. Last month, maybe even I would have.

Sitting with her till she passed out. But since I started hanging out with Joey and the band it's at the opposite extreme and I can't *stand* her. I know I'm not the best son, but I just can't stand her anymore. It's not that I'm afraid I'll snap and start smacking her drunk ass around, split her skull, bloody her up—it's more this heavy, dead feeling I get, like anything I have to do with her is killing me.

"I'm out of here," I say.

"I could have you arrested for neglect," she says.

After I go to the kitchen to turn off the burner she left on on the stove and come back, leaning in the doorway, she freezes her face, staring up at me blank, like it could go to a smile or it could go to a scream, depending on what I do next.

I toss her the cordless phone, actually aiming for the bathmat, but she's taking up most of that space—it lands on the tile, clatters, but the battery doesn't even fall out.

She'll be fine.

"Call 911 if it's so bad," I say.

Her voice gets rough and steady, not weepy anymore, not screaming:

"Don't come back if you walk out that door."

I can hear Joey honking, so I leave. He gets out of the Nova to greet me, and when he smacks me on the arm *Max my man* I try to stand my shoulders as straight as his. I am a smaller guy but I try to make my chest large with air and posture. I punch him back on the arm harder and when his eyes crinkle up, his way of saying he can appreciate that I am tough but not thinking I am an asshole, I know I am doing the right thing to get away from the rock in my throat that is embarrassment about my mother and that is being trapped with my mother and that is wanting to stay very still and not move and not do anything so I don't hurt my mother and so that nobody else sees me to ask so much of me. When Joey hits me back one more time I know I am going to be okay. His specialty is getting away from crazy women. His specialty is doing what he wants and not being embarrassed. He can be my antidote.

*   *   *

Yeah, so it was another real long night of weed after that. When Lisa pulled me and her in the Nova up in front of my house at dawn the next day, Joey and Otis having crashed at Joey's mom's house, Lisa being the only one remotely okay to drive, the 24 hour locksmith was just stepping off my mom's front porch.

The yellow light of my mother's bedroom window closed then into darkness, the white curtain sucked into a flat black square.

My housekey felt heavy in my hand and I understood that it was just a meaningless cut of metal now. I turned back to Lisa, who was leaning over the steering wheel at a sleepy angle, her legs splayed strangely onto the pedals for lack of room in the Nova.

"I, um, I am going to need a place to crash for awhile," I said.

Lisa's face was blank and exhausted, her mouth open, her posture sucked. But she nodded. She looked behind her; the locksmith's van was paused at the stoplight, its motor a kind of warmth in the cold morning.

"Let's go back to Joey's, then, honey," she said, and I wanted to squeeze her, to curl into her like I did Ruth so long ago.

But I just sat there and smoked and wondered if my mom really did break her foot, and then cursed my mom out in my mind for being so drunk that she managed to fuck herself up so bad in the safety of the freaking john.

"She gets herself so fucked up she's horrible, mean," Joey once said about Lisa, "and then she blames you for being like this big male asshole for not wanting to be around her."

I was starting to understand this.

I jumped when Lisa reached across and stroked my hair.

"Max, honey, relax," she said. I would have got a boner but it was totally maternal of her.

Fuckin, another crazy woman wants me to feed her mom-food.

But her hand did something to my spine, to my stomach, made my guts relax and feel like crying at once. But I didn't, I didn't, cry, that is. I made my abs tense up and I took up more space. Fuck this.

"Your tits look nice in that shirt," I said, and her hand smacked me so hard I bumped my forehead on the windshield.

"You fucking asshole," she said.

And then she squinted her eyes up at me and said, "You poor little guy."

At Joey's, she covered me in two beach towels like blankets, a couple of t-shirts wadded up worked as a pillow fine on the floor with Otis on the couch above me.

As I fell asleep, I saw that square of light of my mom's bedroom turning out again and again, and the first few times I was overjoyed, free, flying into the randomness of dreams, into outer space—no gravity.

Then this question would show up: what do I *do* now? I can't just play videogames. Can I. Can I. No I can't. I have to get some kind of job. *Shut up. Go to sleep, stop being such a pussy.* And it worked, telling myself that. I'd feel free again, flying.

But later, every hour, I woke with a terrified jump, a pulse going through my body that was my own fear but was also like an electrical current that had nothing to do with me:

Dreams of working at Seven-Eleven. Dreams of being in a chain gang for holding up a Seven-Eleven. Dreams of begging broke in the parking lot of the Seven-Eleven. Until Joey came along to save me, and me and him ran and ran in the night to our jobs that were still unclear, but that was easy and fun, involved receiving a lot—*a lot*—of applause.

I sucked and sucked for breath and fell back asleep as soon as enough came.

*   *   *

Within a few hours that first day, Elaine provided a list of chores for me to do.

She had like all these metal trays and teacups and bowls and pourers out on the dining room table. She was sitting there behind the stuff, her arms outstretched to sort of frame it, white arms speckled with red dots and freckles and a few moles. Her watch was loose and baggy on her wrist, its face fell limp against the table and made a metallic noise against one of the trays when she started tapping her fingers to some song in her head.

She smiled at me as she listed the chores off, so happy that I had joined her.

"*And*, I need someone to keep me company when Joey is on the road," she said.

Fuck.

"Hey, though, he's our roadie too, aren't cha, Max?" Joey said, passing by in a towel from the garage to the shower.

But she went on explaining what she wanted done. I nodded, moved back in my chair, didn't look up. I was ready to walk out the door and not come back except there was nowhere, nowhere to go and I knew it. Seven-eleven, Max? Shit.

Elaine pushed the plate of biscuits over to me.

"Don't worry, Max," she said, "I won't coop you up."

"Mrs. Sykes I'm so stuffed," I said. "Thanks anyway."

"That's okay, there's more for later then. I think pot pie for dinner. Do you like pot pie, Max?" she said, and she tilted her head like a girl.

I nodded.

"Thanks. My mom only cooks microwave food these days," I said.

"Well, you're not there anymore," she said, trying to hide her disgust not to dis my mom too bad, "Joey told me. Here, Max, here we know how to treat you right."

And she squeezed my hand then to slip me a twenty. It was hard to look back in her face and smile but I did and it was important to.

"You have a home here as long as you want it," she said, and though that made me feel nervous it also made me feel warm, and tired in good way, tired like I drove all night and now I finally got to rest.

"So where do you want to start," she said, "polishing all this silver or doing the landscaping?"

Though I had only woken up a few hours ago, I wanted a nap. I picked up the little silver-polishing sponge and wanted to throw it across the room, but seven eleven? I couldn't just smoke cigarettes all day. I could try to *do* something. I could try it. There was a little thrill underneath that I noticed, a little thrill to be needed not just as a babysitter.

"Ummm. . ." I said, "I don't know, um—polishing or the *yard*. . . ."

Joey slapped me in the head on the way back, his hair slick and wet.

"Landscaping, dude!" he said, smiling down at me, holding the towel on his hips closed with one hand. "None of this pussy-ass shit for Max." He smacked the pink silver-polishing sponge off the table.

I grinned. Elaine grinned. He was right.

Joey taught me real quick how to use the mower and the weedwacker and I thought maybe I could get done enough of it in time to go with him and Otis into the city to put up flyers and hang out. But I was back there in the yard, trying not to cut myself apart at the ankles with Elaine's weedwacker when there was a roar out front, the Nova starting. I saw the Nova boom down the cul-de-sac, throwing dust into its trail of bass, the new mix to the title song. Joey and Otis honked on their way out, and I figured, well at least they did that. At least they honked, and at least I have a freaking place to stay. I don't know why I thought they would take me with them to the city anyway. So I freaking weed wacked. Forgetting was the best I could hope for. Forgetting and noise.

I got so into it I wacked too much, but that's okay. Like hair: it grows. I was into it. You just kinda gnaw away at the edges. I dug it. I would have done the whole yard with it, though, been happy to. And when Elaine brought me out an article about mulching and pointed out where she wanted some shrubs put in and where the raised beds of flowers were going to go I got kind of excited. We talked about color schemes on perennials and she put her arm around my shoulder and I felt useful for a minute there.

After I'd finished the edge-work I was exhausted but I didn't want to stop with the mower either—I was so *into* the mowing now. The lawn went back behind a creek and I still had a lot to do—my chest muscles would kill the next morning but I didn't care. The sun was lower in the sky and I zoomed around and around the yard. I covered certain patches two or three times. I almost ran over Racinda.

She shook her hands at me to wake me from my dreamishness and evidently she had been screaming at me over the drone of the mower for a few minutes.

"....AND WHERE IS JOEY?" came out of her right after I shut it off.

We both stepped back from the force of her voice without the power tool blocking it out.

"Where is he? I was supposed to come over and we were going to go for a bike ride, that fucker," she said, patting the pockets of her jeans for cigarettes.

"He went to San Francisco. It was a band thing," I said.

She looked hot in her tank top but she was annoying me.

"That fucker," she said.

"Whatever, dude, Racinda, he's got responsibilities for the band you know?" I said, "He can't like sit around and like baby-sit you and give you something to do all day," I said.

"Oh please Max, because now he's officially *your* sugar daddy?" she said. "And who are you, his fucking lawyer?"

"He's got important shit to do," I said. "You people like always want him just to hang out," I said, but even as I said it I knew it applied to me too.

The half-fooling, half-shocked face she made said: I am so appalled!

"Fuck you Max," she said, "You want to suck his dick just as bad as the rest of the groupies. Now he's got you doing fucking yard work? Who's the ho now?"

I raised my head and surveyed the perfect trim at the edges of the lawn, the perfect lawn-mower stripes that I had been really proud of before she had to show up and be such a bitch.

Her breasts were like little half-oranges under her tank top.

"Whatever man, some of us have to work for our money," I said, looking away.

The grin that crossed her face then was one that I remember seeing when she was little, ten, when Ruth would do something ridiculous. It was a teenager face, but she'd had it since she was a kid

"Yes, of course Max. You work *so* hard dontcha there? The man on the street doesn't understand how very *labor-intensive* serious shoplifting really is," she said.

She laughed and I wanted to smash her face in for a second like I did when I was little.

"I fucking mowed this whole lawn and did all the trim and I've only been up since 1pm," I said, trying to rush past the weird young crack in my voice as I said it. "Some of us do have to work for our money," I said, "You don't need to be such a bitch about it just because it's not like I'm some rock star like your fake boyfriend."

I knew I sounded like a little kid. I yanked the cord to start the mower to drown my weakness out fast.

Her face got a little softer, confused, less fake-tough for a minute before her mask came back.

"Yeah, *some* of us have to work for it. But not him," she said. "When did he say he was getting back?"

I shoved the mower past her, inches from her feet, and left her in the grassy dust of it. Bitch. I pushed it hard on a slant across the steep slope of the hill by the thin trickle of the creek. I felt the sweat pouring from my armpits and down my chest and I thought about all the bugs I was crushing to gray bug blood and all the sticks and rocks I was pulverizing, pounding into nothing to make the yard neat and clean and well kept and submissive. Fuck you Racinda. You go suck his dick. He's got fucking two of you to do it and you are keeping your fucking eyes closed to that fact, bitch. That mushy moment on her face snuck up on me though and I had to push her and also the spookiness of her big sister Ruth from my mind.

After I bagged all the yard trash that was piled down by the creek and broke up the downed tree into firewood size branches it was dark but still warm even though by now, October, winter was already coming and all around the hills it was getting green. I slouched back onto the frayed lawn chair and fell asleep there, *all* through the night, bugs creaking, wind hitting my ears and neck every so often.

In the morning Elaine laughed at me and gave me a toothbrush and a towel and explained how to work her weird shower knobs, and she said today she would show me how to mulch and how to put in the beds of lobelias, which, by the way, need to be watered by dusk every day, lots, since they are meant to grow out of a swamp, not dry soil like we have out here.

Back outside the sun was still hot and bright and instead of waking me up it made me squint. I lay down, noonish, on my back, on the grass, just to kind of get it together and I fell asleep *again*. Elaine must have seen me out there, but she let me. I woke up twisted around in troubled dreaming, with my face in some woodchips, my heart jumping in that moment after dreams when your truest or worst feelings can't be hidden: I heard Racinda saying *You want to suck his dick just as bad as the rest of the groupies.*

Shut up, Racinda. But I saw her little boobs in my mind and got mad at myself for even thinking about that—I knew I was tied to Racinda, I understood I still knew her and suddenly the details of the night with Ruth were clear as the soil now pressed under my nails.

Now he's got you doing fucking yard work?

Shut up, Racinda. But she wouldn't.

Who's the ho now?

And then she was a ten year old, and I was inches shorter, a ten year old, and we were pressed together for warmth in the dry Nevada night.

After Ruth fell asleep that night she was babysitting us, before the cops found us on the side of the desert road, cold but fine, Racinda and I slept next to each other, arms all on top of and around each other in the backseat, each other's only safety in the world for those hours—that night the only other one I'd spent under the stars until last night here in Elaine's yard. I wiped splinters of wood chips off my chin and tried to get back to *now*, to *yard*, but I couldn't stop thinking of it all.

The Nevada state trooper had knocked and looked in at us in the backseat of the convertible with his funny eighties glasses, kind of punk rock, strange, if you think about it, like an alien, and kind of a faggy thing to wear for a cop. Ruth was so out she didn't wake till he shook her, but Racinda sobbed—fast, like she wasn't in control of it and didn't know it was happening. We shared a blanket and a pillow on the cold clean floor of the police station, and then never talked about it again, after our moms came to get us. Ruth was somewhere else then, somewhere in another room, and I think they sedated her, she was woozy and spaced out so bad that I couldn't even imagine how much shit they'd had to force on Ruth to get her to the point where she was barely able to walk, this girl who a bottle of tequila could barely touch.

A red dent-line crossed Ruth's face when the officer, hardly older than her, brought her out of her cell—like she'd slept with her face on the corner of a kitchen counter. Her hair frizzed in places, matted down in others, tendrils poking down her back. And I wasn't scared, I wasn't, of her, of how crazy she had been, or of night. The stars above us as we slept in the Special were so wide and white. The desert smell had cracked my heart open and made me feel like I could do something to help, and I *did* do it. I waited for the right moment and I turned that wheel to the side and then let Racinda be next to me to make her feel calmer, and I let her do the same for me.

The cops were what scared me, the way they talked about how Ruth was fucked, *crazy fucking babysitter, mental, nice piece of ass but you shoulda heard her growl at me like an animal when I brought the doc in,* like we couldn't hear them, like we, Racinda and me under this cotton, dusty knit blanket, couldn't speak English. *This little piece almost killed her boyfriend back in Sacto!* they laughed The fluorescent lights and the cracking voices on the police radios and the smell in there, the bright light and the bright polyester cleaning products matted down dust smell. Tile smell. And when our moms showed up there was this pulling away motion—Ruth taken to the car first, then Racinda woken up and separated from me, our arms peeling apart from resting against each other like when you pull a Twizzler off the mass of Twizzlers, off the brick of Twizzlers at the movies.

That pulling away ended the night and made everything too bright and normal and ruled by cops. The lines on the road home weren't leading us anywhere, me and my mom.

It's a good thing you called 911, Maxy, my mom said, when she'd calmed down a lot, halfway home, *It could have been real serious for Davey otherwise.* The lines on the road were separating and tidy and kept the desert in order. I closed my eyes but missed the stars in my darkness.

I didn't see Racinda again until high school, where we couldn't find a way to ever speak about it.

How did I know to take the wheel that night when Ruth spun out into makeup and blood and stories? Somehow things had piled up on me since then and maybe I hadn't had an emergency to act in. I just had my everyday life, stupid school and hanging out and smoking out and videogames.

Walking around, driving around, getting yelled at, spending my mother's grocery and booze money on cartons.

There wasn't a wheel to take. What if there had been more wheels, I wondered. How would I be different now?

But what I did have in front of me: mulch. Where is the wheel? No wheel. Just dirt to sift through. Lobelias in crumbling rich soil that Elaine wanted put in raised beds. No wheel, but I had my hands. I had work to do. And this was a new development. Earth in my hands, soil—not like a wheel, not exactly. But maybe close. I turned my brain off and stuck my fists underground.

*   *   *

So I did all this landscaping as the weeks went along. I learned a lot. I made square spirals on the lawn when the time would come, with that greasy old mower Elaine told me only Joey and his dad had ever pushed besides me.

We had changed the garden so much since that first day. The raised beds were in and the last flash of the annuals were in just for Elaine's vanity and I was convincing her slowly she needed to get something cool, a fountain or some shit. I was reading up about how to install it.

"Max, my man," Joey said and made me jump when I was in the middle of my spiral action on the lawn, his hand on my shoulder.

"Hey dude," I said, quieting the mower.

I blew my nose on my shirt bottom, because Elaine would wash it for me, and since she bought me some new t-shirts I had enough to get by on for awhile. She got dark colors and white, none of that beige shit, pink shit that my own moms would try to push on me. The gasoline and grass and dirt smell mixed with my sweat and somehow got onto my tongue.

"Hurry up, Max, hop in the shower, we're driving to SF to go to this release party of another band on the label," he said, punching me in the arm.

I looked around the yard, the way the grass was bending all crazy and long down at the bottom of the hill, down by the creek, over by the flowerbeds, so tall the railroad ties were almost hidden.

"I told Elaine I'd finish up today and we were going to go over to Home Depot tonight," I said.

Joey looked confused then cross.

"Like maybe get a little water fountain or something, even? To put in," I said.

"What?" he said.

"I gotta finish up here," I said.

"Look Max, we need you to drive us," he said. "Also, I was thinking you might want to ease in to being a kinda temporary local manager for us," he said.

My heart grew a size just then. I was so proud of myself.

"Yeah?"

"Yeah. I mean, we'll have to go with someone professional sooner or later, but you know, you don't want to be doing this shit work forever," he said, and my heart shrank back down.

The muscles in my arms were thick from this shit work. The flowerbeds were plumb, and the fences were now too. But he was right—what was it really? Dirt. I would go back upstairs when I was done and drink one beer with Elaine and listen to her old stories and it would be nice for a little while but then it would start to feel lame. I could do that, I'd *been* doing that...

Or I could go out and drive Joey around and watch the girls flock around him and watch Racinda and Lisa act like they didn't know about each other.

Shit, I was fucking eighteen. Of course I wanted his life.

It was like a black, transparent curtain lowered across my eyes. Everything dark. I was stuck with sad Elaine and I wanted to go with him so bad, more than anything.

"You know what—I could come—I could just tell her—"

"Actually," Joey said, turning his face back to me after looking up at the sky for a minute to think, "I just remembered I was supposed to go get my friend Carlos anyway and so we won't have room. Now that I think of it. Yeah. That's okay dude, Lisa can drive, you do your thing here. Elaine's real happy with it."

And when he punched me on the arm it was like a nebulous space thing—all bad radiation rays—that grew up and out of my stomach and I just knew I was going to be fucking trapped with the women forever.

I aimed for fallen sticks, drank their horrible crunching breaking sound in like rain in the desert. I even slammed the mower into a tree, just for the weight of it, just to use my arms hard.

The sky etched itself with clouds, when I looked up, and I wondered what my moms thought I was even doing, if she even knew where I was, if she put out an APB. I bet not. I bet she was just crying and making a big deal and getting the neighbor ladies or the men from her church group to come feel sorry for her and not show them how many bottles there were in the recycling out back. I bet she made her face up every night and she was finding a new man to do all her shit for her. Someone was cooking for her. Especially if she *had* broken her foot or ankle or whatever. What did it matter. I'd be upstairs bringing shit to Elaine later anyway. I finished early and told Elaine I felt sick, went to sleep on the couch before it got dark.

"Max! Wake the fuck up."

It was Racinda.

"He left," I said.

"Fuck," she said and sat herself right down on the floor.

"Whatever," I said, as snotty sounding as I could manage.

She started crying.

"Racinda, what the fuck?" I said.

She took off her platform shoe and threw it at me but it hit so softly I hardly felt it.

Red-faced, snot. God I did not want to see this. Women crying all over the place.

"Racinda," I said, with the tone of a school principal: *stop this now, young lady.*

"You don't fucking know. It goes all deep between me and him and then he's fucking *gone.* Fuck. I can't take him any more but I can't do anything else."

"So leave him," I said, and she took of the other shoe but this time aimed and hit hard.

"Ow," I said.

I wanted to go put my arm around her and let her cry on me but I didn't dare, not because what if she pushed me away but because then fuck what if I started fucking caring and Joey kept talking about other girls' tits and Racinda's ass and how he wanted to fuck Lisa and Racinda at once. Then what. Then I'd have to fucking hit him. Scumball. He was all I had right now like he was all she had. I didn't want to stop wanting him, because then fucking what.

"Racinda," I said, and I sat down by her, and I let her sort of lean against me but I didn't put my arm around her or anything.

"Why do I have to love him, Max," she said.

She snuck under my shoulder so I *had* to put my arm around her.

"Shit, I don't know," I said, and I pulled back, I moved so there was space between our bodies.

"I don't want to be this much of a crazy person, believe me," she said, "And Lisa didn't want to be such a *bitch* when *she* was his girlfriend. But it's like he loves you so much and then you *have* so much more in this world that it seems okay to be here and then he goes and you have so much *less* than before. You have fucking boring muscle guys and to have to go to the DMV and some horrible job you hate but have to be happy to have at all and it is *worse* than before he showed up."

I stared at her and my head sort of wobbled or shook because she was talking so much.

"It feeds him!" she said, "His leaving me and my wanting him feeds him. Fuck. It *feeds* him that I get like this It *fucks* me. Fuck."

I stood. I kicked the leg of the coffee table back into place where it always comes out. I piled up the magazines into a neat stack. I flicked my Zippo open and closed, open and closed, hard, just standing there, not knowing what to do. I didn't want to talk to her anymore, I didn't want to be near her but at the same time, I knew I wasn't going to walk away. I stood looking at her and her little girl body—it was like I could remember when I was so small I didn't know the difference between girls and boys, I could have been a girl, I could have been stuck in a girl's body, been that unprotected, that fucked.

Max, don't be an asshole.

So I reached down for her hand.

"Come on, Elaine will give us dinner. We can watch a movie. Come on," I said.

She smiled, cried, then laughed, then cried, then laughed. I could hear it switching behind me on the way into the house.

*   *   *

When I felt all that old stuff about Racinda I *hated* her for having a body like all these other sexy women. I hated caring and knowing she was this body, these breasts. Hated her for being so easy to crush, this girl, this strong girl from a convertible in the desert. So easy to crush, just some other bitch, just some bitch with tits and ass. I hated caring about her and not being able to tell her we all knew—all the guys in the band—she was so easy to break, that Lisa too, that Elaine, was so easy to break. Not just some special information about *her*, Racinda, either: just that when I got to that root of me and her back in the Special in Nevada it started seeming fucking *criminal* not to tell her the shit men say when women aren't around: that shit men say seemed like it needed to be told to her, it seemed like she needed to know what Joey says about her when she isn't around because all the men, all the men, Joey and Otis and the band and all of them, were not ever ever going to tell her and she would never suspect. Though what men say is in women's faces—nobody goes to too much trouble to really hide it, in their actions, say, unless the bitch is a) screaming or b) about to give you some. It was all women men talk about like that, but it was just Racinda not knowing the secret—taking them at their word on what they said to her, not protecting herself from them—that bugged me.

One of those first mornings I'd been at Joey's, Racinda had walked out of Joey's bedroom in her underwear and a tank top and I jumped awake from the way she banged into the coffee table.

"What the fuck Max?" Racinda said, and ran in the bathroom real quick, locked the door as loud as she could.

"Close your eyes before I come out," she said.

"They are."

"I'm serious."

"Yes'm."

She kicked me in the thigh on her way past me and for that I watched her ass, halfway out of her black panties, shift her legs back into the bedroom. Her ass was thick on the outside, that round, cute thing. She was louder than Lisa, surprisingly, when they did it, and it took longer afterward, I could hear his voice then; I didn't really think twice about it at first but later I started putting a pillow over my head. During sex, he never made a sound. I went outside and smoked and waited for him to get rid of her so we could go to Taqueria, but I soon learned she ended up coming with half the time. They were all cutesy. She would pour the hot sauce on his burrito for him, her hands and rings working the tiny spoon across his tortilla, and laugh at him, tease him by telling him she saw someone *spit* in the open container. He would scoop hair past her ear with his fingers like it was running water, but then he'd start talking to me like normal, like she wasn't there, when he noticed me noticing so much.

*   *   *

The tub's faucet was dripping, a plinky noise, it left a brown stain on the porcelain.

"Max!" Joey yelled. It was the first time he'd been around since he ditched me a few days ago when he thought of someone else to drive him.

"In here," I said. I rushed and the toilet paper flew off the roll.

When I got out there Joey was bent over a tackle box, sorting through shit. What the fuck, I thought. Fishing?

"We're going fishing, Max," he said, "you ready?"

"Sure," I said.

Fishing is like the antichrist to me,

"Here, it's not great, but you can use this pole. Unless—do you have one at home we could snag?"

I shook my head. He was scooping his fingers through the boxes of lures, of hooks, and his hands came out without a scratch. He tossed me the keys to the Nova and sent me out to 7-11 for a case of beer.

I could just walk away. But I put thoughts of Lisa, who after a week had not called, out of my mind. Racinda had been around but he was getting antsy of her too, rolling his eyes when she wanted to hold hands with him when I was around, making excuses to get out of there and leave her with me. He even drove me to Home Depot to get away from her once. It was cool, it was fun to walk the aisles with him, he had me laughing and he asked me tons of questions about what kind of mulch, about what kind of irrigation system. For once I knew more than him.

During the Home Depot run I just put the shit with Lisa out of my mind.

There would be bars in whatever town we ended up in. There would be bars and there would be some adventure. There would be me and Joey, not me and Elaine, and suddenly fishing didn't look so bad. So I spent my own money at 7-11 on an expensive case, got us Anchor Steam to show him I appreciated him bringing me along.

"Ready, Max?" Racinda said, smacking the fishing poles in the drivers seat so they shivered—her voice greased in black irony, pissed *I* was coming along. The motor was running. Fuck. I ran into the house and grabbed a couple shirts, a toothbrush, then angled myself into the backseat and opened a beer.

I fell asleep almost right away, but when I woke up, far in the middle of nowhere, Joey and Racinda were talking like they thought I was out. I could smell their cigarettes, faintly, and the pure metal-piney air of whatever empty stretch we were traveling through. They were laughing and tender in a way I wasn't accustomed to. I never saw him that way with Lisa, and it hit me that this niceness was something Lisa and Elaine were always trying to tease out of him. The promise of it was always there from him. Maybe even for me.

They sang 99 bottles of beer on the wall down to 72, in different accents and sometimes like little kids. She took off her seatbelt—and Racinda was a seatbelt freak—and put her head oddly under his right arm—his shifting arm. I could see her looking up at the muscles in his biceps each time he downshifted going up a hill. Sometimes she would lick his arm there, and he would squeal like he was being tickled. He looked down at her, swept fingers through her hair when she nodded off.

When he got bored he started speeding, and when he jerked the Nova to pass a slow lumber truck, then had to switch back almost suicidally fast to avoid a construction lane, she woke, cranky and phlegmy, sort of crawled back into her seatbelt and fastened it. She was awake, though, and started rummaging through her messenger bag with the black ink stains.

She started reading some book.

"What are you reading?" Joey said.

"Just this thing," Racinda said, still sleepy, and smiled up at him like he was ice cream.

Joey started passing people crazier, even. When there wasn't anybody to pass, he would stay in the fast lane and run the tires over those little reflective tiles they put on the white line that make a clanking, annoying sound in case you have fallen asleep at the wheel.

"Quit!" Racinda said.

"Max, you up?" Joey said. She rolled her eyes and went back to her book. Then on second thought she checked her lipstick in the visor's mirror, ran a finger above her lips.

I acted sleeping. I'm perfect at this—it's my one ruse, the one lie I can do.

When they were both not paying attention I slit an eye open to see what the book was—something about *Addictive Personality and Codependency.*

She's crazy.

"Aren't you carsick yet? It's not good for you to read in the car," Joey asked her. Now he was flipping channels on the radio, nothing but country, and I know this annoyed him so I couldn't figure out why he was doing it.

Static, twang, static, twang, ad for a vacuum, static, hymn.

"Why are you always reading that stuff?" he said.

"I dunno," she said. She was so into her book she didn't even *notice* it was really pissing him off.

"I talked to Lisa yesterday," he finally said after he shut the radio.

"Why are you telling me this?" she said, her face suddenly reappearing, pointy, lips tight together.

I breathed heavy like a snore, smashed my cheek into the armrest, adjusted my hand and wrist in front of my face so I could see them better.

"Well *you're* better friends with her than me," and he laughed. And he looked to his other side.

"Fuck," she said, sighing, like *we're back to this again, are we?* She lit a cigarette and started reading.

"How come that's such a little book and you're such a smart girl and it's taking you so damn long to read it?" he said.

She shrugged.

"I guess I'm just thinking about it." Her voice sounded full of water.

He pulled his chin fast away to the left again, avoiding her, like he was talking to the fence and the fields and the air.

"I told you how I feel about those books," he said, "That was fucking embarrassing at Otis's party! I don't know why you think that is what is going on here. I'm *not* a fucking alcoholic. I like beer, fine, it's a free country but I could stop drinking it any time I want," he said.

"I know, honey," she said, "I love you so much, of course I don't think that."

"Then why are you reading it?"

"Well, it's like, well it's like some of the stuff *I* do maybe is like the bad stuff people who live with. . . do. . .Like all the stuff you get sick of, like me calling and wanting you to hang out when you have to work or have band time just want alone time or whatever. . . It's *my* bad pattern, I'm trying to get better for you."

What the fuck was she talking about.

"But you still think I am one, huh? That's great. I didn't drink for six months once," he said.

"What?" she said.

"But you think I fucking AM one," he said, and he smacked the dashboard so hard I felt the tremor in the back seat cushion."

"No, honey—" she said.

"Yeah well that's not what you said before," he said. He fumbled on the seat for a cigarette, smashed in the lighter, and looked ahead of him.

"Sorry," she said, she was trying to be sweet, reel him back in, she was stroking his arm and then his leg and making her voice soft, fuckable, "Honey it's me. *My* fault. I see that now. I was wrong, I'm sorry I said I'm sorry, it's not you, it's me that's doing those patterns."

He didn't lean into her, he didn't bend. You could smell the anger coming off him like nervous sweat.

Empty road, dusk starting, reflecting line on the blacktop gathering light to it.

Bone-etched moon starting off dead center in the sky.

No honey, no I was just—and she got smaller, little, and flopped her arms on him but he stayed straight and stiff. She tried that little voice they'd been singing in but it wasn't working on him. She curled her fingers on his ears, his shoulders, his neck, but he tossed her off with the slightest, subtlest motion, not even a shrug.

She thought it would pass, she thought he would come back, but still, so strong in her, to herself—I could practically fucking hear it—she was saying *yeah well maybe you are an alcoholic.* She didn't want to hear it, so I heard it for her, unspoken. I was sure there was no hiding anything then—sure that they both knew I was awake and that Joey knew what Racinda was thinking about his problem. But nothing happened—not even more of Joey's pissed-off percussion from the road reflectors. The drive was so smooth I actually did fall asleep so fast again I was confused that I had been asleep at all when the jerk of pulling off the freeway onto the winding hilly road woke me. We persisted, silent through darkness to the cabin.

*　　　*　　　*

I slept hard again once we got settled into the like very rustic bedrooms, and he woke me at 4am to start out for the lake. He had everything ready, I just rolled in the car next to him. He left her sleeping—I peered in the bedroom and she was lying with her arms and hands above her head like she was grabbing for something.

I didn't tell him my dad always forced me to fish as a kid, so I was able to just drink in the amazed compliments on my fishing brilliance when Joey thought he was teaching me about lures and bait so fast, so well.

After the orange wet sun turned yellow through the reeds, after we ate the first round of BLT sandwiches Elaine made, after the fish mostly had stopped biting and we were at this point still out in the little rowboat just for the beer was when we started talking more than five words an hour.

"Which one?" he said.

My back was to him and I expected him to be holding up two lures, two knots of feather and shine and dangling things to test me on what he thought he'd taught me. But he wasn't holding anything. He was just staring off at some twisting trees, some hills behind them.

"What?" I said.

"Which one? Max, if it was you, which woman would you want? You could have either of them."

"Not both?" I said, but he didn't laugh or even smile.

"Not both."

"I dunno. Lisa's pretty hot, but you guys have a sort of a stormy thing going on."

Air came out of him like a laugh but it wasn't, it had no tone to it.

"Racinda's—" he said after awhile, and I just looked at him.

"Racinda's too much work," he said, "Racinda's complicated."

"You guys seem pretty happy when you're not fighting," I said.

"Huh," he said, from his belly, and pushed just slightly on the wall of the boat. "It's not gonna last. It's not gonna hold."

"Racinda's really cool," I said.

He laughed.

"Yeah, she's cool, she's trouble," he said.

"How?"

"It's like she sees into me and she's right in what she says a lot but she's also *not* right. She's convincing about all this shit, even, that I'm an alcoholic, but shit, I'm not an alcoholic. And then it's like why would I want to be with someone who thinks that about me?" he said.

"Yeah," I said.

"And why would she want to be with someone she thinks that about?" he said.

"She said—she doesn't think tha—" I said, but I forgot I was supposed to have been asleep when I heard it but he didn't care.

"Yeah, I know she said she didn't think I was one in the car, but she totally does think that. Or even that she—even that she fucking *could* think that. . ."

"Maybe she just like really loves you," I said.

"Yeah, I mean, *yeah*," he said.

"Maybe she—" but I couldn't say maybe she's *right*. She wasn't right, he was not like some street-bum alcoholic, I mean obviously, but maybe that stuff did kind of cause him some problems with her? But I couldn't say that. I mean like I should talk, though I'd noticed I'd kind of been naturally cutting back with all the landscaping work tiring me all out. I couldn't side with Racinda, though, even for a second. Joey'd dump me in the water and leave me to swim.

A dragonfly landed in the puddle of lakewater next to the beer cooler and he swung at it with his foot. It touched on the lake briefly, then flew to me and I dodged it, spastic, like a pussy. In my panic, shielding my face from the bug's attack, I blurted:

"Racinda's really pretty and like *deep*."

Joey laughed at me and slapped me on the back so the boat rocked a little.

"You got your eye on my woman, there, Max? Yeah she's deep. Fucking *deep* deep, and Lisa's deep and sad deep and *pissed* deep."

"They're both cool though. Racinda's, she's like mature? Or something," I said.

"I could see why you'd think that, not really knowing her too well or for more than when we just like hang out at parties," he said, looking at me, thinking he was really taking my perspective. "But she needs me like a little kid."

I felt stupid for blabbing that stuff, so I blurted some more:

"Would Lisa even take you back, I mean, after you left her to that man to fuck?" A laugh escaped me.

But his seriousness, the weight on his face wasn't at my laugh.

"She does what she chooses," he said. He got this thoughtful look like a college professor, like an expert on TV.

"Being that fucked up and crazy was her choice," he said, "And letting that guy fuck her, if that's in fact what happened, who knows, was her choice. Not wearing underwear was her choice. Taking a poll of whose dick she wanted to suck in that bar was her choice. Yeah, *mature* is not that one's selling point. . . "

A second of heavy wind came over the boat and left a shiver in me, *you could shut up now*, the wind said, it made the water shimmer in diamonds, in hexagons.

What moved under Joey's face was closer to the surface again.

"Max, my man," he slapped me on the back and I didn't bend to it, "Fuck these women. Let me show you what will bring in the biggest fucking bass you ever saw," and his fingers ran through the tackle box, then worked, lifted something small to the hook.

*   *   *

Racinda wouldn't look at him when we came back. They fought quietly in the bedroom while I read an old *Time* magazine on the foldout couch in the fake kitchen area where I'd slept. Except for the stream of light from the dirty windows, the cabin was dark, under big trees. Moldy greens and browns was the decorating scheme.

"There was only room for two in the boat," he said.

"I've been telling you for two weeks I wanted some alone time with you," she said.

"I didn't think you wanted to be out there with us," he said. "I thought you just wanted to get away and. . ."

She shh'ed him and kept her voice to a whisper.

" . . . READ your BOOK," he said.

Silence.

"I need to clean the fish," he said, and that was the fight.

When I heard his feet moving down the little hallway, I acted like I was asleep because even if it was with Joey, cleaning fishes was not worth it to me. He stood above me staring, watching the fake-sleep drool fall out of my lips onto *Time* magazine's picture of the woman who cut her husband's dick off. When Racinda called for him, *Joey*, he left me, grabbed a beer from the fridge and went out to do the gross work.

But the smell of the fish kept me from sleeping, really, and I listed to each scratch of the knife across the scales, saw gray and that iridescent oily purple blue shine as I would start to doze. I wasn't sunburnt, but my edges were warm from the long day. I think I heard Racinda crying a little bit in the bedroom, and I heard her pen scraping the hell out of some paper. I imagined it burnt through with each letter, a thin stream of fire burning the words in.

I finally got up and watched him from the window. His white t-shirt was neatly folded and set onto his tackle box. He went at it hard and per-sistent, sweating—we'd gotten more fish than we could eat, he didn't throw any back, and he collected wood from a fire and poured some lighter fluid on it to start it up. Flames spiralled in a whoosh, then calmed, and only then did he sit on the log, and he sat for a long time.

I went and sat across from him on another log, but he didn't acknowl-edge me.

The flames spread quickly, like water running over the sticks, quicksil-ver streams following the liquid pattern of the butane. Joey's eyes fixed on the fire, and I thought of how in movies they show the flames reflected in somebody's pupils when they are about to sign the pact with the Dark One. Joey's were just black and blank, but something was going on in him. When the campfire puffed up into way too high of flames, he still didn't move, and it seemed like he was waking out of a dream when I asked him in my small voice what we should do about the fire. He shrugged.

The bass got overcooked, dry, but we ate them anyway, somehow the fire went out completely. When Joey and Racinda had too much beer already early for the drive to town, I had to drive the Nova. You could feel how annoyed they were at each other, trapped together, up in this noplace land. How did they get so annoyed? They'd seemed fine in the car one minute and bloodthirsty the next. That freakin' book.

You could smell the wood and the water and the leaves in the air.

The heaviness was gone from him, and the hum was back: he was singing random reggae lyrics again, in the front seat next to me, talking about this new album and that new album. She stewed behind him, kept her eyes and her nose and her chin and her lips pointed out the Nova's back window.

"So I think this is it," he said, running his hands against the grain on the old wood bar table, risking splinters and bad vibes from old love carvings.

There weren't too many people there yet, but more were arriving. Old hippies and shit.

Racinda and I, across from him, stared at him blankly. I was way slouched down, still tired, so my beer bottle blocked his mouth, I could only see from his nose up.

"You and me, like this," he said, holding his two index fingers up, together, in front of his nose, then moving them apart, as far as his wingspan could take them.

I sat up so I could see.

"What are you fucking talking about?" Racinda said.

"I want to break up. I want my freedom. I don't want to be in this anymore."

She smiled like she thought it was a joke. But then it wasn't a joke.

"Why are you telling me this here, at the freaking bar, in front of *him*?"

She shoved me.

"Ow," I said.

"It just became clear to me," Joey said.

"You fucking brought me up here to break up with me and you bring *Max* with you to protect yourself? What kind of psycho are you?" she said. "Max can't you go to the bathroom or something."

"Max, can do what he wants," Joey said.

"Well," she said, "Let's go back then. What am I supposed to do here. Fuck. Max can't you go to the bathroom?"

She wanted to cry and get pathetic, it crossed her face but then she couldn't do it because I was there.

She stared at him, less pissed than dumbstruck.

"God," she said, but it was a sob more than a word, "Why are you doing this?"

"I don't want to have some endless closure discussion. It's just done."

"Why?" she said. She made soppy choking noises.

He slapped the table and asked if anyone needed a beer, then went up to the bar.

Joey only stopped back to get his cigarettes, then he was gone again. She couldn't see, but I could, that he was talking up some rat-haired hippie redhead townie at the bar.

Free.

And I was staring at Racinda and she was getting redder and wetter and uglier, and the bar noise and the Dylan and Floyd and Journey coming off the juke was starting to drown her out.

She just kept saying the same things *over* and *over* and *over*.

If he loves me how can he do this to me? Why is he doing this here? If he loves me why won't he stop fucking drinking? I am so much more than all those freaking groupies. He's more than that, I know that, but then its like. . .

She asked me this shit like I had answers and I didn't. I was starting to get nervous, like Joey was going to kick me out of the house because I was siding with her for just *listening* to all this, but then she said:

He is such a fucking pussy, such a coward, letting you mop up his mess. Thanks, Max.

And at that moment I knew he wanted me *right* here. He wanted me to clean up his mess. She was right. I saw then now that he had planned it all very well—there was no way she was going freak out at him with me there.

Coward, she said.

I thought about that. And I saw Lisa back outside that other bar, her face turning from revenge to something close to terror, not quite terror, something edging up on it, but like Lisa couldn't quite admit that, her eyebrows lower to her eyes and her chin trying to force the face up, smears of red somehow across her lips, a scratch already on her neck, the redneck Elvis's truck in reverse.

Is this a wheel for me to take? I thought. What the hell kind of wheel is this? I thought. What do I do? Is this crap being offered to me as a chance to do something? What do I do?

And so I only left Racinda to go pour quarters into the jukebox when she asked me to, or to get more pitchers, cigarettes, and I listened to her till my drunk plummeted and started to wear off. I just tried not to let her merge into my mother complaining about some guy, I tried not to feel like that about it, because in truth Joey had done really lame things and I was going to sit here and try to make up for it, even if it was mostly because he wanted me to.

*   *   *

Racinda asked me for jukebox quarters and I gave them to her. I bought her more beer even though I thought this was hurting more than helping. She used the quarters to put on all the songs on the jukebox that would annoy him the most. She saw him there with the hippie, how could she not, and started fuming.

"Maxy, Maxy," she said, "Help me think of what to say when I walk over there and break a beer bottle across his face."

This childlike delight crossed her face at *that* idea, boy, but in half a second it vanished into an even worse sobbing than before.

By midnight she was determined to get up, do something, the bar was simmering down. I grabbed her forearm to stop her and she just said, "Max?" and I let go. She took off her jacket and was going around in the little tank top that showed cleavage. Within minutes this sort-of hippie, sort-of redneck thirty-five-year old guy wearing his flannel unbuttoned without a t-shirt underneath just to show his rock-body was leaning her over the pool table, acting like he was showing her how to break. There was a crowd of them, these men all around her, and there was laughter and it went in rhythms, and I was sober and smoking and trying to figure out what to do.

Joey looked at Racinda, then led the hippie lady in a slow dance.

Racinda let the pool player with the pecs show her how to shoot from behind her back.

I lit one cigarette before the previous one was done.

Angie, Angie, the jukebox played, *Angie, Angie.*

She couldn't believe Joey would dance to this music, nevermind with such an ugly woman. Joey *hated* classic rock. *When* Racinda played the Stones in the car he would smack her hand from the dial—it wasn't jazz, it wasn't soul, so it annoyed him. The redhead woman he was dancing with was wearing a long like hippie skirt, and her hair was all ratted-up like I said or else just frizzy naturally. Her eyes looked a little crooked, a little confused, but she seemed nice enough, her face seemed sweet. She was older than Joey, a little. Her face seemed drunk but her body wasn't swaying.

California, California, the songs kept coming.

It seemed clear that everyone but sweet-faced Rat-Hair knew Joey was very angry that the shirtless man playing pool with Racinda was ten years older than him and had perfect, perfect abs.

Wheel, I thought. This *is* one. I was at it, even, I was freaking driving already. But what could I do. It's not like I was going to drag Racinda *out* of there.

Then it occurred to me: Sometimes *waiting* for the right moment is doing something.

Racinda tripped onto the floor and two of the men had to help her up. They sequestered her back into a booth, and I couldn't see her anymore. I started up, I went to get Joey, but he was out the door.

Behind him, in the parking lot, I called his name, but he ignored me. He opened the redhead's Subaru's drivers side door and then closed it so politely for her—she was drunker than him, but he didn't want another DUI. As he entered the passenger side he looked back at me and I believe winked, though I couldn't be sure of that in the pitch night with no ambient pink suburban lights.

I still had the keys to the Nova. I wondered what it would look like tomorrow, leaving that place: me, Racinda, Joey in one car. I wondered if it would be just surface wounds or if there would be actual puddles of blood on the Nova's floormats.

*   *   *

Racinda was wrapped in Christmas tree lights. The three men had taken them off the moldings of the low ceiling and watched her spin until she was coiled in them. She was finishing the twirl—was all tied up—right as I got back inside, and her face looked different when she was this drunk.

"Time to go," I said after I'd made my way through pounds and pounds of these men's stares.

"Max, go home," she said, sticking her right hand out of the green wire in a shoo shoo motion from the wrist.

I wasn't thinking, just breathing and moving and talking.

"Racinda, let's go," I said, and then the three moved in:

"Let the lady do as she pleases," a hick said as he handed her a shot of whiskey.

"Last time I checked it was still a free country," one said.

"If there's going to be trouble we can take it outside," one said, while the fourth, a short one, his black hair a hard teardrop under his baseball cap, held the end of the lights, and Racinda spun herself out, arms gradually raising, like a corkscrew, next to the low-lit pool table. The string of bulbs fell to the floor when she was done, and he tried to whip them like a towel in a locker room, the trails of light distracting me for a second before I grabbed her arm again.

"Max!" she said, drunk eyes widening, "This is the song!" and another old Joni Mitchell thing, my mom's music, came on the juke, loud, speakers right next to us.

"We have to go," I said, grabbing her arm.

"Hold on," the black-haired one said and grabbed *me*, tore me off of her.

"What?" Racinda said, "WHAT?" and she reached back out for me.

Right as the shirtless one landed a punch on my chin.

When it hit I saw his teeth—like a child's teeth, squiggly and separated, as if his mother took some wrong medicine or snorted meth when she was pregnant.

That is what I saw—weird teeth—and then I woke up out front on the dark gravel. I sat, leaning against the steps to the front door, and waited for the waves of pain to pass. That people walked by me was the only way I could tell it wasn't too long since the KO punch, and that it was getting on to last call. I hadn't heard Racinda among those people though.

Confusion of all sorts filled me for a few minutes, and then it turned into despair of keeping something awful from happening to all of us.

Take the wheel, Max, I thought, though I didn't have any idea how to do this.

The ground gave off onto a sort of ravine not too far away, and I imagined luring the four men over there with Racinda wrapped in those lights, then pulling the cord and spinning her back to me as they fell into the ravine.

Keep thinking.

I wandered to the rear of the place, followed its chipped paint around to the back windows. If I went in there again I'd just end up bloody and unconscious, so I didn't do that either. *Smart guy*, I thought to myself, and when the despair thing caught up with me again I had to choke back a cough.

So I just looked through the window:

"Sing it again!" the redneck dudes were saying. Racinda was sitting on the counter-like surface of the juke box, her ass hanging half off of it, her hair a mess, her tank top shifted crooked so her stomach and her bra straps were showing. Her eyes and mouth closed and opened with her singing along with the juke as if it took all her effort.

She wasn't bad.

Fuck.

Enough. Enough. I stood up, back from the window. The bar had been emptying and it was obvious what was in store for her. I looked around, and laughed when I realized I was actually looking for a steering wheel— a little one, made of chain link bent hard into a circle, like what the *cholos* put on their cars instead of a normal one.

And then I thought: It's not going to be right in front of you. It's there, but you have to look a little. It's not going to be, from the start, *obvious*.

And once I got *that*, it *was* obvious:

I still had the lighter fluid in my jacket pocket from when Joey handed it to me at the campfire, and I got to thinking. And I got to running my hand on its metal curved corner and I knew what I needed to do.

Pouring it in a line, along the grass at the edge of the building, was easy, I did it without thinking, but I froze when I realized it was better just to dump it on the wall. To do it for real, not halfway.

But what if I just fucked it up like always? What if the fire got Racinda and not the men? I forced myself not to think about jail, about cops, and once I realized I wasn't afraid of that aspect I knew exactly what to do and I aimed right where I thought the rednecks' booth was, so fire would engulf these men. Shrivel their testicles to little ashy toasted raisins.

But there needed to be more. I ran back to the car and got Joey's bottle of Beam from the trunk, threw it in streaks against that wall. With the corner of my shirt I wiped my prints from the bottle, from my Zippo, from the lighter fluid and stepped back to look at my invisible creation, in the near black night, like an artist.

Before I even set my Zippo, its flame as high as it could go, against the wall my feet were backing me away.

My eyes, though, pinned hard and still on what was going on inside through the window:

One of the hicks went up and kissed Racinda, ran his hands up her back, and the others clapped. She leaned her head back, not in pleasure, but like she wanted to fall all the way down·

But she sprang up, singing along with the song on the speakers.

Something about darkness, something about the bar. I couldn't hear clearly at this point.

My fingers spun the little Zippo-wheel, my hands still wrapped in my shirt to keep it clean, and when I tossed it against the wall the flames seemed to just dance, so shallow, so surface, but then chewed deeper into the wall fast. Smoke filled my nose as flames followed the thin, greasy liquid. I backed off into the trees, and waited.

Then, as one by one the hicks smelled, then saw the wood getting eaten away, as the extinguisher failed, as the fire alarm sounded, as they tried to pull her, to pick her up off the juke box, she resisted. Little thing she was, she somehow gripped the flat surface and none of them budged her.

Her lips moved to the song, but I couldn't hear her voice out here.

The bar's smoke alarm shrieked.

But were there no other sirens?

The fire alarm stopped, I don't know why—smoke everywhere, gobbling up darkness—and then just one of the redneck men was in with Racinda. He wasn't trying to drag her out. She was still singing. He put his hands on her breasts and rubbed up against her leg.

But she just sang. He bent, coughing.

Smoke filled the window and I couldn't see her anymore, so I took the empty liquor bottle, bashed the window open, and hauled myself through, wrapping the sill with my army coat.

She was pushing out the words, her eyes closed, maybe some pocket of clean air around her just to let her do this one more line, I think I could hear the words but again they scrambled—drinking him, drinking him, the words just barely off her lips. I heard them and forgot.

I went to her and yelled, *come on*, in her ear, but nothing. She closed her eyes and mouthed words, I was choking on smoke, no one else was inside anymore, a ceiling beam came down by the front door, but I could see where there was a back door, around the bathroom corner, it was open, Racinda's mouth moving, then no more songs came and I could hear sirens now and beams cracking and I could feel myself passing out and I guess I did, because the next thing I know she was tugging me, her face clear through the heat, her face sober, now towing my arm and pulling me out into the night. I was leaning over her back, supported, but I was walking too, and once we were clear and out I fell on top of her then next to her into the wet grass.

She hauled me up again, got us somehow past the fire engine spraying stinking water onto the bar, past the men, past the cops, we walked behind them quiet as ghosts, and she put me into the driver's seat—my hands, her face, our clothes covered in ash—and I started the motor so quiet nobody's head turned at all.

BOOK THREE

And when she cannot find him and cannot conjure him even in her imagination, her disillusionment turns to rage and constellates the demonic.

MARION WOODMAN

16

ZOMBIE

It reminds me of something that happened to one of them at twelve. She has these feelings, these nighttime feelings about boys, and little juicy stories she tells herself, but then in the daytime she still acts with her girlfriends like boys are nasty.

Who knows, who knows what the others think about in their beds?

Anyway, it's like this: you are walking down the street, the gritty sidewalk in Pennsylvania, and you are chewing the pinkest, reddest gum or maybe eating a chocolate Sixlet every now and then, trying not to chew it down, trying to suck on it slowly, and the cars are going by, and the cars are occasionally honking as is the custom here, occasionally blaring a Philadelphia rock station or Latin groove, it is early spring and there is a feeling in the air, and maybe this is the first year you are wearing a miniskirt—they seemed too weird, too strange before, but now both that they are in fashion and that you are twelve conspire to get you to walk around in one, legs newly shaved, but still just a baby, just someone who watches a lot of television and who hates her mother for not being able to protect her anymore.

Pinks are starting to smear the tree limbs, you can smell exhaust fumes mixed in with the clean, wet air, and you are walking with Josette Hoopes, whose mean streak has dominated the life of every female in your grade since you were tiny girls. The water tank on top of the factory seems to hum precariously, its spindly supports about to give way any time, flood you, and as you pass the automated gate to the factory surprises you enough so you have to hide your little jump. You slow, you deliberate, making the car that is trying to get out, to get home, the car that precipitated the shock, wait for you and Josette and whatever third one is with you to move out of the way, girls in training, loping.

And with every car that honks at you three Josette says, riccans, which is the common slur wielded by white trash against the Puerto Ricans who have come here—mostly men, mostly without their families—to work in the fields, in the dark cinder block buildings where mushrooms are grown. Again and again, riccans, pervert riccans, says Josette, even if the culprit looks white as heat, and you and the other girl, less trashy, know better and don't say anything, although you are not extremely disturbed by her talk. Though you know she is wrong you are somehow protected by her unwillingness to be as quiet as you are willing to be about your own views. But for Josette it's not unwillingness—it just has never occurred to her to be so quiet. Sometimes she says riccans too loud and you are terrified that whoever she has accused will double back around, screech a U-turn in the middle of Union Street, oblivious of the oncomers, inch along with you and say things with their tongues, their fingers.

But this one time, when a black guy passes and honks, Josette doesn't turn her eyes up, surly, and say what you expect her to say—jig, a word you've only heard her use, never heard elsewhere. You wonder if she's made it up. She knows better than to speak the other word in public, though you've heard her mother and sister say it at their house, under the wall of vases and glass saved from the dump, behind the freestanding fish tank with the mechanized décor: the treasure box that opens and shuts, opens and shuts, the shiny diver who rises again, every time, pneumatic.

Is it his white Camaro? Is it the smile that could light you right up? Is it the way his shoulder muscles look cold as metal and cozy fire-warmed at once?

This time, this time, Josette preens her face over her shoulder, this time she waves, a tiny motion with her hand, nearly demure, this time when he doubles back she gets in with him, stopping traffic, adjusting her legs slowly and carefully into the low passenger seat, and leaves you there, bewildered, popping round bits of hard sugar into your mouth even after the Camaro disappears, creasing the road up the hill, past the high school, past the drug store, past the gas station, into the trees.

After that, for a little while, you will keep acting like you aren't interested: white boys, black boys, Puerto Rican, Italian. Why? Something about none of them being good enough for you, something about being scared of them. Later, the alcohol, the desire, the freedom and dread rushing around you will eliminate it all—that hesitance, that need to whisper about his zits or his cheap jeans or his crazy mother the police had to drive back from the A&P at three in the morning when she climbed naked onto the roof. That impossibility, that no. That need to stay in the home country and not go exploring will finally crack into a new song: this way, this now, is the way, I am sure of it. Then the man will loosen the moorings of your body and you will emerge on the other side, uncharted, unprepared, maybe broken, but new.

*   *   *

So after Joey acted as if he had forgotten Racinda, acted as if only his skin and not his heart and bones had been involved, she descended. For days after Max brought her to her mother's door, fresh from fire and those woods, cinders in her teeth, she moped, showered, slept. She could feel Joey forgetting, feel residue of her self across town rising from inside him to his skin, sweated out on his bike rides and during sex with other women.

At twilight of the fourth night of this, after coating each toenail in a too-thick peelable armor of grayish lavender polish, after shaving her calluses off to blood on one heel, after scouring her face and her elbows and her shins with handfuls of salt and sugar to remove the burnt smell she imagined still lingered, after putting lipstick and a little cash into a tiny pale purse, she drank a tall-enough glass of her mother's blackberry brandy and started the long walk across town to where Joey lived.

Joey's street was impossible to sneak onto: though pleasantly untidy, with bushes and bunches of grass and blooming vines tumbling onto crumpled pale gravel at the curb, it was nonetheless suburban, designed for cars. But which of the neighbors would spot her, and which would know to warn him? Of what, even? Of embarrassment and difficulty? Of having to look her in the eye?

Doesn't she know what is going to happen? Of course she does. Why does she go, then? Why is she nurturing hope when she knows it is false? She's not a dumb girl, by any stretch.

But:

Something other than her skin, her brain, is guiding her. Her blood, her bones are, for he is the portal. However excruciating it will be, she is determined to embed herself deeper into his betrayal: she can already see it, she already knows he will scream it at her, *the facts*, she will weep and not move until she is physically, forcibly removed, humiliated in front of witnesses, begging, pathetic, the witnesses being people who were once her friends and are now just his. Perhaps the stinging in her mutilated heel, the tiny sharp pebbles wedged in there, are a means to prepare her.

*　　　*　　　*

What *was* it he gave her that she wanted so badly? Easy: knowledge of how to walk into any bar and grab attention and create a sort of a family of men and their onlookers; delicious vulnerability when she prodded him about his mother that one time; a passport into the world of musicians; holding open doors for her without being apologetic; ignoring her just enough that she wanted him desperately; food for the starfucker in her. The dripping pleasure of waking at noon and driving around listening to Sonny Rollins and taking two hours to eat a fish taco and avocado salad. Her newfound inability to stomach nodding, predictable boys who had no taste for the undercurrent, the maneuverings—of what she could only categorize as any real *male* situation—beyond a convenience store parking lot. And, most importantly, he gave her a crisp awareness of what lay outside the grid, a crisp taste for his willingness, and her own, of doing exactly what he wanted.

This was his gift. They slapped him for it, hated him for it. He is the asshole in any fragment of a story you overhear between two women talking in the stalls of the ladies room while you are leaning over the sink, mouth open as if for a wafer, applying mascara.

You know who he is.

He is only an asshole if you stick around.

She could walk away. And why didn't *you*?

A taste for severity you always had but never knew you had.

A taste, like his, for doing exactly what you want to do. But you don't admit it, not here: this taste is hidden, certainly, in the powder-peach ladies room as you replace the mascara wand, as you smooth black specks from your cheekbones, as you give that smile that makes your face thinner, as you straighten your blouse over your waistband, hold your shoulders high and your neck carefully tall to prepare for reentry.

*　　　*　　　*

It was dark when Racinda arrived, and the lights weren't on on the side of Elaine's house, so she had to descend so slowly, carefully, in her big shoes, over rocks, test the ground with toes for holes and gullies. Each moment was a miracle she was still standing.

She saw lights and shadows down near the cement landing to the side door to Joey's apartment. She heard party laughing in there. She heard people dragging on cigarettes and passing a pipe. Funk. Bass. Four or five people besides him—few enough that their voices were separate, melodic.

She just stood in the doorway, her white dress rippling like a brook across her thighs.

How she lured Joey out there, looking so ashen and cold, is beyond me, but actually, I'd guess that he wanted to cement her inside him, remember the victory, memorialize his power to destroy. He wanted that ashen girl and he wanted to refuse her even then, as if refusing his own death. He knew that *he* had lured her down into her purple-gray-white state, had lured her eyes into the blank orbs that now stared at him.

"Yes? I've got people in there," he said.

People eyeing them from inside the windows, people whose ears were ready for the sound of a bloodletting.

She grabbed his hand tightly and swung it like a child would, leading him, in small steps to the tiny creek further down the slope.

He stopped. It took a gulp of air for him to look at her that seriously for one last time, it took a gulp of air and a feeling of armor in his chest for his awareness to linger on the wet curve of her eyelid, the straight-down line of her nose, the shell-edge jaw line. He was reminded that he knew the something in her for weeks, months of his life, better than he knew anyone's, then. That something being the pinkness in her? The life in her?

As the armor tightened across him, Racinda's features slipped away from familiarity, her features slipped closer and closer to any girl's.

"I can't just be running around having a garden party with you here. There's guests," he said, looking away.

"I'll take you back if you just say sorry," she said.

The suddenness, and that she turned her head from him when she said it surprised him. Then he began to laugh.

Joey *laughing*.

"I have to go back inside," he said. "Listen, lighten up," he said, and patted her shoulder as if to do so were gracious.

When he turned from her she didn't follow. She pinned her eyes on the irritating water in the creek that she wished would just *stop moving*, but when she heard the tiniest rustle of his shirt sleeves—formalish, that was him—the minute she heard that linen that his mother had bought him rustle away from her she spun herself around and curved in front of him and hit him so hard on the jaw that he felt it worse on the other side of his face—though the joint fell right back into place, he felt his jawbone distinctly pop out and back.

Then the screaming, the scene started. Limbs flew and they both landed in the mud, but the worst he did this time was aim the heel of his hands into her collarbones, spilling her into black water, punctuating her chest with purple dots for a week.

Ted the bass player, inside, told everyone else to stay put, but by the time he was in the yard Racinda was gone, she was in the street and he couldn't find her, she must have run, the bushes stood still when he reached the front and the road and he came back empty-handed. Before Joey and Otis and the party-sluts made some joking comment, before Joey showered, before he smoked too many cigarettes and fell asleep on the cement-perched lawn chair before the guests left, before all that, Elaine stuck her head out the door and asked Joey if he was okay. He nodded but didn't go inside that way, through Elaine's house. He walked up the side path, he stood in front of the house as if to guard it, as if to make sure Racinda was gone.

*   *   *

Racinda had been strong enough to save her mother from complete lovelessness, but she hadn't been toughened up. Abused, by Ruth, and even loved by Ruth. But Ruth's wasn't the necessary toughening. And the sort of devotion Amandine showed her left Racinda starving: it was not in itself the nourishment a fragile girl needs to survive. Her family never demanded that Racinda become useful to her own happiness—instead they kept her alone even with people, guarded, cut off from the world by her family while also totally vulnerable to intermittent attack. But this devotion was steady, if lean. And so, when she got another bit of devotion, from Joey, it frankly shocked her that it would even *occur* to him that it wasn't an ongoing thing. Disbelief, then desperate clawing. Waking in the night to find her fingernails gripping onto her own shoulder, her own neck, as if his. So in a white dress that ruffled above the knee, hair now streaked with mud, dark lips shivering, she managed to walk to the 7-11 looking not unlike a certain kind of high-fashion photo shoot, *still* not believing Joey at his word, still planning a return visit, still lolling over how kind and homey his mother had been to her these past months, still determined to possess him, not understanding that if she ever actually possessed him, sucked all the him out of him, she would no longer want him.

Still resisting surrender though she was already defeated: for now, dreams of and plans for that moment of convincing him back, and of then somehow *becoming* him, lifted her away from the beams of pain that ran through her infected heel, from the elbow that she had smashed on a rock trying to grab Joey's hair, from the two blackening fist-prints on the delicate, illuminated bone above her breast.

*   *   *

Her heart was split wide open, and it was about time. Something could come in. And, as they usually do, she fought this state with every step, every breath, every thought. But now that she was so tired, so beaten, this fight she knew well let up in her, and she just took the steps and the breaths without so much anxious consideration. Not by choice. Just because it hurt and the lights above her, halogen, sulfur, glowing, gave her something pretty to look at, and she remembered the old Jesus songs she and her sister used to hold hands and sing until the words made no sense and then swept the song and themselves into new territory and old territory, into the realm of the fields where their grandmother, old stubborn self-contained mistress of a hilly blotch of wet green land, grew peonies and wildflowers and clematis and turnips and carrots and tomatoes. A place I myself admired quite a bit. A place, thanks to their grandmother, where I could grow and lean back on one of those hills when I needed to, a place where the three of them—two small ones and one larger and wrinkled and fast—fed me with their hearts as they fed themselves.

*   *   *

Thing is, even when I think these girls are down as far as they will go, something weirder always happens. Takes me by surprise. Every time. I guess it has to—I love them so much that if I planned the entirety of their transformations I'd have them start rising again before all the seeds have time to germinate under the dark, frightening earth.

Racinda is defeated, and with every step she hovers between reaching back for Joey in her mind and giving in to the light and the pain around her. Miraculously making it across freeway-feeding boulevards, heading where she knows best to go, the 7-11. As she approaches Jimmer, a random acquaintance, but not *too* (he is ancient friends with Ally who brought Racinda back to Max a year ago)—Jimmer, the soft-spoken but excitable one, the sweet curly-haired half-metalhead one, the *only* one sitting out there tonight—the thought traipses across her mind that she wants Max to be there to plan and scheme and chase Joey with her.

With Jimmer, she can't show her full obsession: in this way he provides more dignity than she could otherwise possibly conjure right now.

Jimmer hands her a napkin and she holds it blankly in her hand until he explains.

"You have mud on your face. Here," he says, and without any kind of come-on, his sexuality ambiguous and hidden, he soaks an ice cube in a layer of napkins from his large cargo pockets and clears the harsh black streaks off her neck, her arms, her face, without messing her makeup.

She eases her body down, legs drawn to her chest, and Jimmer shares his joint, his cigarettes, and then, stupidly enough, a hit of acid, which Racinda puts under her tongue without thinking, as if chewing a straw or the inside of her cheek. He wraps his heavy army jacket around her. She falls asleep and wakes with a jolt an hour later, the speed leaping from neuron to neuron, cell to tissue, blood to brain. Each leaf in each breeze, each loose wrapper, each bent cigarette filter filled with meaning. Racinda pats around on the filthy ground, looking for her leather jacket, the beautiful blue-lined one with embroidered red and ivory spiders crawling up the sides. She could swear she has brought it with her tonight, but she hasn't—the air was warm, and it didn't go with her white dress so well anyway. Where, where are my spiders, she thinks.

"*Wood* spiders," Jimmer says.

"What!" she says.

"*Wood* spiders, *not* black widows, are the ones you gotta watch for out here. Fatal. Live in, well duh live in wood. It's worst in new houses—when you disturb lumber they come out—in old houses they just stay put if they're there at all but in new houses they'll crawl on out before they get settled in the walls and bite the baby."

"Only new houses?" she says.

Jimmer nods.

"Of course, there are exceptions. Like you put on an addition or something. Or you have bad luck or something, too."

Racinda can feel the spider waiting for her in her beams.

But she can't tell if she is an old house or a new house.

I mean, she thinks, a little less scared for the familiar syntax, the familiar tone of her speaking voice in her thoughts, *it's not like I'm hallucinating or something.*

It's just that she can feel the spider waiting for her.

She leans back into the building and Jimmer. He puts his arm around her, but it isn't an advance. She pushes and pushes on her feet, but she can't get her body any tighter against the wall of the 7-11.

"Jimmer," she says, but he took 3 hits and can't hear her anymore.

Every set of parking headlights that hits them punctuates an epoch; every suburbanite who strums keys on his way into 7-11 for milk or ice cream or a paper, every shift in the air of the night holds the spider.

Racinda closes her eyes, but knows the speed in the acid will prevent her from finding safety in sleep. Still, she does it, squinches up her face muscles. When her cheeks and her teeth start to hurt, she lets out the tension, gasps in air.

Racinda's is *not* a wood spider. It's the other kind.

Yeah right, she thinks, *it's not like I'm hallucinating or anything, Jesus.* And she gives in and she starts trying to breathe as calmly and deeply as possible, ease herself into whatever is going to hit her, but the tension of threat in every noise holds, doesn't break into something grander. A spider, waiting for her—she can almost smell it.

Racinda says: "Fine. Fine, come if you want. What are you gonna do to me? Bug."

And the spider, meandering slow, like an elephant—timid—peeks her head around a corner. Her black, fuzzy head, her big black body, soft with down, moves with great ease and great effort at once: she requires a huge force to move herself, yet manages to glide as if skating, as if wheels turn beneath her. She suggests the sweetness of a lovely, heavy woman, graceful, about to dance, a woman with strawberry lipstick, yellow hair, ruddy skin, a round, eye-sparkling woman at the moment she is ready to believe she will be loved for the great beauty she possesses.

When the spider catches Racinda's gaze, the spider lowers her own so shyly and with such gentleness—curled scoops of lashes hide Minnie-Mouse whites of eyes—that Racinda can feel an ancient sadness pooling into her chest, that ancient, constant loss of some sweetness, some hope she knew as a girl, some hope contained in Ruth.

Racinda wants to shake Jimmer to show him but it's no use.

Headlights swerve, blinding and clear, and in the next scene
the spider is no longer big and soft and dripping in love and loping—
she's spindly now, in a red vinyl chair, her narrow legs and arms bleeding.
The torso is elongated. *This* spider is arched and pointed, gothic, plucked;
with slick curve and crack. Black and shining. Lacquered. Weaponistic
and sexual, this spider is Lisa.

"Got you," the Lisa-spider says, and Racinda sees that she does: up in
the web, Racinda sees her own tiny body.

Jimmer's bright face appears.

"Joey," he says, and he's right. By their feet, a tiny man in a tiny pressed
white shirt.

"Joey!" Racinda says,

She grabs him by his pencil-lead leg and swings him up to her giant human face. Racinda lets him dangle there and delights at the terror in him
as she lowers him gracefully onto her red tongue, curls him into her dark
throat.

*   *   *

She's swallowed him. She finds herself back in front of the 7-11, the worst
of the hallucinations dissipated into haze from the lamplights and headlights and chrome reflecting car bumpers that transforms into a
geometrically angled doily between her and reality. It recedes and pushes
forward rhythmically, ocean-mist obfuscating distant waves.

Beneath her feet there is the smeared, crunched corpse of a fat blue spider, fresh blood, and she thinks, if it could be called blood, what is it in her
veins?

Lacy holes ripping through asphalt, dissolving, but when Racinda
turns her head the blacktop is solid again, though now the ghost of creek
water—sinewy bends—seems to course just under it.

Who else is going to give me what he gave? she thinks.

Creek water faster, nosing up in crests, outlines of gray fish swiveling,
flicking.

Ocean.

The faint image of the huge spider's elegant eyelashes graying, fading—that sweetness of girlhood—that sweetness of hoping someone just
might see you and pull you toward him—Racinda reaches her arm out but
there is nothing to grab, the ocean is gone.

Except not completely: Ruth's presence trails as gray memory, a ghost here too. Gray outlines—shattered, broken, dotted lines, like thinnest streams of airplane exhaust.

And the gray lines traipse into waves, into gulleys—the memory of a wildness behind the concrete.

Who else is going to give this to me, Racinda thinks.

The ghost of an ocean.

Who else?

Ruth.

She knows the answer the instant a fish leaps in a neat curve from the asphalt water.

Here, says Jimmer, and puts sixty bucks and the rest of the acid into her muddy purse.

Thank you, she says, hugs him goodbye. Each foot does what it needs to, somehow.

Wait, what? she thinks. The gray lines swirling beyond the 7-11 and the blacktop and the lit signs and the night pulse bright and disappear.

Foot, other foot, and she is off chasing the lost, wild sister who preceded her.

Except.

What?

Oh.

What was I looking for?

She draws a blank. But she knows she urgently needs to catch a train to go find whatever it was.

It all depends, I know it all depends on finding. . . on finding. . . this . . . what?

And maybe because I know what she is in for, when she gets to the train station she has just enough time to pee, drink a soda, sigh a few important sighs, wonder at the miraculous letters on the train board—D-E-P-A-R-T-U-R-E-S-A-R-R-I-V-A-L-S-E-M-E-R-Y-V-I-L-L-E-S-A-N-F-R-A-N-C-I-S-C-O-L-O-S-A-N-G-E-L-E-S—and the numbers, the numbers, flipping as fast and as wholly as she.

Does she notice that the stars puddle like the rainwater lying next to the tracks? Does she notice that the rainpuddle contains an ocean, a face, as do the stars up there? Does she know the night air is for her, this night is for her, does she know the wind calls to her her own imminent journey? No. But the shriek and pound of wheels bashing the tracks as the train arrives—she notices that.

Joey, she manages to think when she feels the rich pleasure of air in her lungs. He is the only ticket she ever recognized as one. But there are others—the one in her hand now, for instance, though for how she's seeing it it might as well have his name on it.

No adventure without the man, it seems.

Does she notice the other passengers—seven women—in the train car then? Does she notice the black-haired grandmother peek over her *Wall Street Journal* to make sure that the creep with his eye on hopelessly stoned Racinda keeps walking to the next car? Does she notice the conductor take her ticket so gently, does she notice the conductor—her face wide, harsh, kind, the green eyes slow and full of intelligence—explaining to the twin sisters in the back seat how far she's been with this job, how she's crossed each state hundreds of times? Does she hear same green-eyed conductor admire these twins' tupperware-container meal of roasted chicken, of boiled greens, of parsnips? Does she hear the conductor say *the best chicken I ever had—butter on your tongue, just tender enough— made by a man in New Orleans—now* that's *a train ride, but I wasn't a conductor then.* Does she hear the wide laugh from this conductor, does she hear the knowing *what <u>were</u> you then?* in unison from the ageless twins, does she hear the conductor say *those were my wild days. Not that these aren't wild*, the wide laugh, does she hear the wide laugh?

17

ALL THIS IS NOT NAMED HIM

Racinda

When I woke up there was a woman in a yellow smock trying to pass for a blouse rolling me over and sticking a needle in my ass. I yelled, and she said, "Well it's about time, sweet pea."

Everything hurt. When she rubbed my head, it felt like her whole *hand* was made of needles.

And when I remembered something besides walking to his house in my white dress and that I had lost him and that nothing made sense any more, I closed my eyes, not tight, just heavy, and tried to let my bones sink into the bed until I lost consciousness, but I didn't. The attendant in the yellow smock brought me a plate of food and I kept my eyes closed until her hand-needles attacked my shoulder, gently, and she said, eat. Everything was inedible, I just nibbled on it, except the chicken, which fed my memory and I remembered feeling like the power was in that white dress, in the twilight. I remembered that I traced the carpet wale on the wall of the Amtrak for two hours that seemed like days, that a man in a hat wanted to sit next to me and feel my ass until I summoned something outside myself in my glare and it made him go away.

I sort of lobbed the chicken around my mouth and dowsed it with water when its yucky industrial boiled taste became too clear to me, when the light from outside seemed to brighten somehow, making me wince. I remembered that a car softened me, somehow.

The nurse's nametag said Annette. Her shortish hair looked like she'd put curlers in it—these lush, wide rounds of curls, but she was obviously not that type. She was about thirty I think and had this pretty, funky brassy filigree metal necklace on that made her nurse outfit look less lame.

"Excuse me, Annette?" I said. "Annette? What is going on?"

"You took some bad acid," she said. "Did you ever see that Freddy Wiseman movie, *Hospital*, where the kid in the black turtleneck is explaining how he took a bunch of mushrooms in Central Park and then suddenly starts projectile vomiting all over the ER holding room?"

"Uh—" I say.

"That's why they have tile walls. Hose-able. Well that was what was happening to you, only it was all inside your brain. Like a lightshow in there, I'm sure," she said, folding up the blanket at the bottom of my bed. Its edges were frayed, and for a second I panicked and thought I was in some deep ward of a huge crazy hospital in a decaying northern city, like Detroit or Cincinnati, but when I looked out the window the landscaping and lawns were perfect, lush as hell despite the dry dirt, and the parking lot was full of SUVs. I could see the freeway coursing around some hills— it wasn't so nearby as to give off exhaust fumes, but the view of traffic was excellent.

"Just north of San Ho, honey. You lucked out because SF General was full. You'd be sharing a room with a pee-smelling street schizo there."

Everything hurt worse, suddenly, all over, and as I covered my eyes with my forearm I realized it was bandaged. I made a wailing sound—not intending to, but everything hurt in a way I didn't understand.

"I'll catch you later," Annette said, and padded out of the room on her little white square-toed nurse shoes.

There had been this wildness, the sound of a trumpet curving around a bus stop in the Mission in San Francisco, curving through neighborhoods to me here, curving through months from that night Joey first took me to the red-wallpaper café, curving even further back to things my sister howled—true things, false things, things I still didn't want to hear. If I stayed very still it stopped on my inhale, and after several minutes I was able to ponder the question of how I got here and it all came flooding back.

After the Amtrak station—where? Who knows? Oakland?—they put us on a bus and we crossed the Bay Bridge and I followed this older woman with a little-girl's pink backpack onto a bus and I didn't know where I was and the streetlight said 24th and the sounds were smells, etcetera the usual. But it was rich and milky, this night, and I believed every minute of my trip and I found myself staring at a stack of meat, a pyramid on a stick, gray and brown and red at once, spinning in a heat lamp in a window, grease on the pane mottling its colors and tenors even more, and after seeing epics in the swirls of fat in the meat it had occurred to me that this was the spider I had squashed, and that spider was Joey, so I was in an even worse boat: I had killed him. I longed, there in front of the pork, the beef, whatever it was, who could tell, to be back in my old mournful situation, in which he had betrayed me, forgotten me, because this—me killing him somehow when I was peaking, me killing the one thing that mattered— was so much worse.

You did it, creature. You're as bad as he was. Ruth's cracking voice, broken across the city's careening lavender clouds, faded into tinny pops, into static, and as she kept trying, but kept fading, it was this static I couldn't stand any longer—voice but no voice, her presence in absence, her presence through Joey and through the lack of him.

And I heard a shriek coming from me and heard sobbing and shrieking and sobbing, and my noise finally, finally was crazier than *hers*, louder, melody gobbling up her just-too-far radio signal, and I felt my dirty legs crossing each other, fast, and I felt the wind in my earrings and I knew I was running and then it was the street and there were four bright lights, two cars, coming at me on Mission and going fast in the night and I just stood there, I just stopped.

"You were lucky," Annette said. "You were bleeding a lot where the Honda scraped your leg but there were no serious injuries—we thought head injuries but they found the sheet of acid on you—some intense party *that* cop is going to have tonight—and you really, you really lucked out, you're scraped and bruised but nothing broke. The kid driving the Oldsmobile that *didn't* hit you followed the ambulance all the way here when they sent you down from the ER at SF General. You looked like death warmed over..." she said, "Or maybe like death microwaved..."

She looked out the window like she was trying to imagine what a clear visual of that would actually entail.

"But except for you having dusted your own brain beforehand, you were physically good considering," she said.

"Then why are there needles flying through the inside of my body?" I said.

Annette looked at me and frowned. She pushed the white pleated paper cup of pills to me.

"That's just whatever bad speed was in that acid talking, taking your emotions into your veins. It'll be out of your system in a few days," she said, waving to me without looking at me as she took meds to the next room.

After I somehow got all six pills past my tonsils I stared at the fakewood door as it remained so still, so lifeless once Annette had passed through it. My urge was to fall back onto the pillow, roll my eyes, but my body now worked in tight rubber band movements to keep me from doing these things that hurt so badly.

Once my emotions were out of my veins and back into my head or my heart or wherever they normally lived, it only got worse. I could taste each sip of beer on Joey's lips, each sip of beer that meant equally a drive through the night and a warm heat inside my hips as well as someone else's cheap good time, some little slut's cheap good time that kept me from that night, that warmth. Him. Those first days I watched the television in my room until I had fallen asleep to it then woken up deranged by it at least three times— only then did I manage the energy to turn it off, to press that button on the remote. Every show had at least one actress on it whose ass I strained to see for longer than the camera let me; wild with jealousy, obsessed, I needed to be in Joey's head and know if this was an ass he wanted.

Big enough?

Small enough?

The shape of it?

My eyes were transformed into my best approximation of his and though this psychovision exhausted me I did not want to stop using it and go back to my own.

I didn't even think my own eyes really existed any more, untinged by him. And I didn't want them to.

Because what would be in front of me then?:

Freeways. Boys in baseball hats turned backwards. Copy jobs and community college. Maybelline. My mother and Rudy. This surface, this endless reality of California that is empty and dry and hopeless to me without Joey to light its underbelly, without Joey to provide magic, hope, something underneath and beyond it all. I could just imagine my mother getting pissed at me, at first, for staying away too many nights. I could see her just sitting there, eating a lowfat yogurt for dinner, waiting for Rudy to call and pester her long enough that she'd have to tell him why she kept crying all the time. Rudy would shake his head slowly, think about what a sensible girl I was how it was such a shame, then mount a grand plan to get me back on the afternoon shift at Pinko's, get me into some dopey hellish course of study at Sac State.

But my mother was only partially a citizen of the freeway world, the huge-parking-lot world, the lowfat world, the pantyhose world. My mother could bring me, with a single glance, with a word before it escaped her lips, into something *else* underneath, into something like the whisper of my sister, *Creature*, that could still shake me, into the underside of this world the underside I did *not* want, the underside of my mother's weightless tears in dry air, the underside being those hills in Pennsylvania where the Devil whispered to me, the underside being those whispers I was maybe still running from.

That underbelly I was not interested in: where the green vines down by the creek could drench us and seem to speak in my sister's voice, Ruth's power slicking light off of icy black bone-trees between our house and Button's in winter, careening light and terror into our bedroom.

My best bet was to fend it off with the deep-sea world Joey gave me.

Fill me with him and the rest cannot get to me.

"Honey, why don't you come on out here and play Chinese Checkers with the folks after you eat?" Annette said.

"Right," I said. "I'm not fucking crazy," I said, and I started crying so hard it sounded like screaming again.

"Right," Annette said, but she wasn't being sarcastic. She ran her hand across my forehead and looked at me.

"Fuck," I said, and I shook her hand off.

"Well, you know where we are if you want us," she said.

But I didn't want her. When I tried to shift in the bed my legs felt heavy and broken even though they weren't broken. Bruised, they told me, plus the huge gash under a bandage the size of a small towel—I hadn't looked at that thigh yet. The rest of the leg purple as fuck—bruised was right. Bruised and bandaged.

Fuck this.

I got out of bed and by kind of cementing my jaw together it didn't hurt at all. I walked to the door and opened it *very* slowly and peered to see the crazies out there.

About five of them were sitting around a low coffee table eating their dinner in front of the TV. They all looked older than I knew they were. One was singing, one was picking her nose. Three were sitting silently— the men—but you just *knew* there was going to be some explosion of insanity the second they opened their mouths.

Creech.

Shut up.

Creech! Here you go, right at home, Ruth said to me

Shut up.

Right. Okay. I'll shut up. Because I can, because you must be the manic one now, Racinda.

Shut up.

One of the men over there was talking really fast to, then french-kissing, the heel of his hand.

Perfect, Ruth said and her voice dissipated. I tried to hear her laugh. Her laugh was mean but not mean—just really aware of the pitfalls, just able to keep chortling in the face of the nut-ward. I tried to hang on to Ruth's laugh here but her sound disappeared into the fuzz behind the nurses voices on the nurses station intercom.

I'm getting out of here, that's it.

(My sister's voice underneath calling me to her and I refused her, refused her world of the crazies and I managed to cram it outside myself and silence it and tell myself that I am all about velocity, I am all about *going* places).

But then when even Ruth was silent, came the next thought, the one that goes *where exactly am I going, exactly?* My teeth came unclenched and the pain rushed back into the outside of my calves and the inside of my thighs—like this heavy, heavy tiredness beyond tiredness—and I shut the door as slowly as I could and I fell onto my knees and I knew I had to stay here. There was nothing to go back to. I couldn't go back to Joey now. I remembered.

Later, somehow, it just stopped being so bad.

"See? What'd I tell you?" Annette said, pushing that little cup of meds, its piped rim, its Easter egg pills, across my tray.

"But I sort of don't feel anything. I just watch the TV."

"They'll have you in to groups soon, and you know, if the tube is rotting your brain, there's a rack of books out in the lobby. Why don't you get your ample ass on up and take a look while you wait for your appointment with Dr. T?"

I could feel the old me flopping back onto the pillow and rolling her eyes, but instead of doing that I found myself just saying, "Okay," and meaning it, and getting out of bed to leave the room for the first time in what felt like eons. *La la la*, it felt like, *whatever*, it felt like, but with a lightness to it—the hate was boiled out of me, and when Joey came into my mind I didn't cry, I just sort of diverted myself with whoever's face was in front of me—Annette's, a crazy's, Captain Stubing's on the tube. *What's the difference between them and him*, I'd wonder, and it would go kind of weirdly deep—like why did it have to be *Joey* I needed so bad and not whatever other person I walked past even *here*, they seemed nice enough, right?—and then it seemed like there *was* no difference between Annette and Joey or the night nurse who took Valium and Joey, and then the part of me that was doing my thinking for me on these meds was like, okay fine then, what's the big deal about missing him then? Big freaking whoop!

Why couldn't I just stay here? It was so simple! Ruth was leaving me alone now, Joey was fading. Things were feeling Okay. It occurred to me that my mother and Rudy were surely looking for me, trying to drag me back into the dry surfaces of California and then underneath back into that murk where I *was* Ruth and I *was* my mother and even maybe I was Button and even maybe I was all the old battles between all of us and I thought, *you know what, no thank you. I will take Annette, thank you.*

I clicked the channels on the remote—quickly, slowly, however I pleased—and I thought of how the TV was different from a radio, say, where you could get two stations at once, static. On this TV, with its crisp cable, everything was clear and I could click it as I chose to and the variables were something I could understand. Yes. Here. Good.

The waiting room was covered in gray industrial carpet—even on the wall up to my waist—then a glossy yellow paint took over. It was also, I understood, the group therapy room in the evenings, and was less of an actual room than this sort of open center that the nurses station looked on. The doors to the right had a big red X across them and you could only leave if the nurses buzzed you out. They were metal. On the other side of the nurses station, to the left, past the open area, were the men's residency rooms.

Somebody had superglued a red silk scarf embroidered with little pink swirls and spirals over the moldy foam coming out of a torn corner of one of the airport chairs—a nice touch I thought. It was kind of cheery, kind of happy, and it made me think again that I could stay here awhile.

"Hiya?" this voice said.

I put my book, *The Women of Dallas*, down, but nobody was there.

"Hi?" I said and went back to reading about Sue Ellen trying to get the visiting Middle-Eastern heiress executed gangland style. I shifted around, but ended up sitting in the one position that didn't put pressure on my bandaged, fucked leg.

"Hiya!" again and this tiny middle aged woman but with the blond soft hair of a child, a child's slight build, under five feet tall, hopped onto then rocked back and forth in the mustard-vinyl chair perpendicular to mine. She sang a little song. I listened for a minute and after that minute I kinda got it, that song. I could understand how it was comforting.

But I kept my arms across my chest, I took small forced breaths, I didn't want to get near her.

She had a *bow* in her hair.

"I'm Edda," she said when she was done, when she curtsied.

Her little girl's long wispy blond hair held back in a barrette with an aquamarine colored grosgrain bow glued onto it. I frowned.

But then she looked up at me with these voluminous liquidy eyes, and my shallow little breaths in and out to try to protect me from her stopped working—with the air, this cleaving affection for her came into me. Obviously, whatever it was that made her like this was like *not* her choice. Right? Whatever it was, all of a sudden—it was just *clear*—it was easier not to hate her for being crazy and weak.

"I'm Exene," I said, deeply pleased and thankful that I'd somehow had the prescience to give them this fake name, the name of a punk rock goddess, when I arrived here.

I kind of applauded her song then, very gently, and Edda seemed thrilled.

Understand this: I was getting used to it here way, way, way too fast.

A bald, brave beauty to how Edda blinked her elephantine eyes with such trust at me before she sat down a few chairs away. I thought of a sea turtle, slow and gorgeous, emerging low from surf, eyes bent on the peace of the dunes.

Right as I was about to get up, Edda leaned in and stared at me, quick as light.

"You don't like to put monkeys in jars, do you?"

I didn't breathe in fast. I didn't freeze for half a second.

"Never in my life would I do that," I said to her, and I grinned.

Edda grabbed my hand and swung it back and forth like a little girl.

Hers was softer than mine—pure and innocent and somehow untested by the world. A hand used only to put the hair ribbon in place, over and over and over and over.

"I hope you get to stay here with us. I think you're the cat's meow," Edda said and then her flat, thin smile unnerved me, just a little bit.

"Exene Cervenka?" Annette said.

I moved my lips around on my face.

"Somebody's happy," Annette said at the stupid, blissful smile I settled on to express the deep pleasure of hearing my new fake name and letting go of Edda's hand.

"Doctor's ready for you, babe," Annette said, shooing me into the office corridor with my file.

I looked back at Edda and she rolled her eyes and put her head on hands folded like a pillow, made a snoring noise. I dragged my feet until it hit me that this was how Edda walked, so when I actually entered the shrink's ice-blue room I had the posture of a yogi.

The shrink's hair was bleached way blond, and sort of shaggy over a headband tied dramatically, like a textbook illustration from the early eighties. She was tan, almost orangish, and before she spoke I could tell her voice was soft as pansies, rounded, even though she was a tough woman.

"Miss Cervenka, I'm Dr. T, why don't you tell me what's going on?"

"Um," I said.

I was going to have to lie and make up something about being homeless, etc. etc., and I just didn't want to lie to this woman. She wasn't some idiot, she wasn't some *guidance* counselor or anything, I could tell. So I just sat there and stared at her across her desk.

She didn't say anything, and the silence hung unpleasantly.

Hm.

"You seem high functioning enough, is what Annette says here," she finally said, looking up from my folder.

She was exuding peace and patience where a normal, untrained person would be staring at me with expectancy.

Shrink.

I didn't bite my lips, exactly, I just sort of folded them in under my teeth and let them roll back out. The big red naugahyde chair was making me sleepy—Edda was right.

"Don't fall asleep," Dr. T said.

She leaned across all the papers, right in my face, and clapped her hands about an inch from my nose.

I jumped.

"Look," she said, settling back into her chair, bracing her hands on her desk, exhaling loudly.

"I know you're not a runaway, street person. You have parents, a house, maybe even a car—no maybe not a car—" she said.

She squinted her eyes at me, trying to figure it out, like whether or not I owned a car was a detail, a freckle on my cheek, she might be able to read on my face if her eyesight was just good enough.

"Honestly," she said, "I'm just going to discharge you here and you are going to have to figure it out on your own or else be presumed a minor and get released to Social Services."

Some punk rocker newbie at Social Services would *definitely* know that my name was not really Exene Cervenka, and I'd end up back—

"I don't want to go home," I said.

Strange tears, like someone else's, came to my eyes again but didn't emerge—too dry. Then I just forgot about them and stared up at the ceiling and wished very, very hard that Dr. T would change her mind and let me stay.

She exhaled loudly.

"You can't even cry when you need to. These damn meds are just making you into a little vegetable there, aren't they?" she said.

"No," I said. "They're totally helping."

We just stared at each other.

Right, Creech, Ruth said, then faded, and I saw myself in my mother's living room, nauseated by all the various statics—morning TV, my mother's Christian radio smarm, every single immobilized electron of my own body, self-condemned to the couch. Frozen.

I knew then my mother was hunting for me and when she found me would not let go, I would not get out of Sacramento, I would not get out of my mother's living room and my job at Pinko's and the ugly freeways and the dry horrible air.

I understood that the bottom dropped from under me then, but it didn't feel so bad. I understood I needed to beg.

"Please please please please please," I said to Dr. Templeton, "Please do not make me go back out there right now. Please please please."

I looked at her.

"I need a rest."

No response.

"I'm desperate."

Pursed lips on her, a smile or not, indecipherable.

"My head is *not* together here, I need to get it—" I said.

She blinked.

"Doctor?" I said, "Please?"

She squinted again at me, long and hard, and I wanted to keep jammering and begging but I knew better, for once, I knew to shut the fuck up.

"Right," she said, nodding, like she finally got what she wanted from my desperate expression and now she was bored, "Right," like giving in, "Look. You can stay. I'll admit you. I'll officially 'believe' the homeless runaway malarkey from you for now here but you are getting off the meds, Exene."

"What?" I said. "I thought you guys like *lived* for the meds. They help."

A rock—speckled gray and gold, shiny in parts and shaped to fit in your hand—sat as a paperweight on Dr. T's desk. There was a word carved in it I couldn't read from here. Dr. T picked it up when she saw me staring at it, in that silence. She tidied some papers, set the thing back down. I couldn't read it.

"I think you're someone I think we can help without putting on meds. Look at yourself—you want to learn how to be an adult in *this* state?"

I realized I was sitting Indian style on the chair, my mouth wide open— mouth-breathing—maybe a minute and a half away from drooling.

I tried again to rearrange my legs but the bandage on my thigh, the soreness wouldn't let me.

Dr. T wrote something else in my file and seemed to be through with me.

My eyes closed and I felt myself napping, that swirl of dreams just starting to melt into the backs of my eyes.

"Yep, Dr. Robefield has you on way too much stuff. You don't need it. I'm going to put you in Nae's program, and we'll see if we can't get you balanced up in a month or so."

"A *month?*"

She got up and pulled me by the forearm out of the chair.

"I thought you *wanted* to stay, Exene," she said, smiling in a very annoying old-school feminine-sweet-seductive way.

"Who's Dr. Robefield?" I said—I'd never met him. "Who's Nae? And I'm sorry a *month?*"

"A month, maybe two months. Now scoot and tell Annette to send Edda in. She actually needs my attention."

I was so slow, opiate, that she had to guide me, press my shoulders toward the door. As I thought about a *month*, it looked like this: thirty blank white squares on a calendar, maybe *sixty* empty squares.

Okay, I thought, when at the sixty-first square I couldn't imagine anything else filling it at all. More blankness: fifty-eight, fifty-nine. I'll stay. Okay. Good.

*   *   *

"Alright tootsie pop," Annette said on her next am round, "no meds except the antibiotics is what it says here on your chart."

"Groovy," I said.

I was watching a get-thin infomercial. The TV buzzed hopefully even though its angle was precarious, suspended from the ceiling, right above Annette's head.

"Oh good," she said, "Dr. T says Nae's Plan so we'll get you started on that once she's back from vacation. I *thought* you'd be a good candidate. How are those bruises—yeah, they're looking pretty, looking delicate even I might say. I think you'll get off the antibiotics too, soon, especially if Nae has anything to say about it. . . ."

"What's Nae's Plan, may I ask you my darling?" I said and I blew her a smooch.

"Nae's plan, my sweet sweet thing, involves good hard work and getting off the institutional crap they're feeding you here."

Oh. Like cleaning *toilets* hard work? Like . . . ?

I got a vision of boot camp, of my face covered in mud and my feet lighting through rows of tires and having to propel myself up a blank wall. But like everything bad on these meds, this yicky idea passed and TV moment verged into TV moment and all was just *fine*.

"Does it work? Will it make me a productive member of society?" I said, improving my posture.

She sighed. I smiled.

I was this chipper, this silly, this *fine*. When I'd go to dinner sometimes—not in the main place but just with the few people who ate in front of the common area TV, the other crazy people kept their crazy smells and lists and wailing to themselves, and didn't touch me, didn't bother me, I wasn't really *one* of them BUT then:

one blurry day I woke up and the meds had finally worn off just before dawn, in the hour that is blue and empty and strong and blank, and I felt everything again and the wail that came out of *me* woke the night nurse from her Valium sleep and she came into the room and stroked my head with her wide red hands and looked down her wide pale face at me and said she'd have the doctors see me and I shut up, I said no I think I'm fine, and I thought *bitch* what are you doing for me what am I doing here? and when she left I started my wailing again, but quietly, into my blanket, into my big white sweater, into the curtains soggy between my teeth when I sat on the chair and looked out the window onto the freeway that could take me out of here take me back to him.

"Hello? Hello?" Edda said as she stuck her pale old-young head in my door.

Even the yellow bow that had joined Edda's aquamarine one at a crazy angle didn't get a smile out of me.

I tried not to, but I scowled at her. Edda jumped. Hid her face. Trotted off sadly with her light, barely-earthbound steps.

"Baby," Annette said on her visit, "baby, your new program will start soon. Honey," she said, and she stroked my hair but the sharp edges of everything pouring out of me made me push her away and say *sorry sorry sorry*. In a tiny voice between sobs I said, *thank you* just to get her to leave.

And then I said *fuck you*. And fuck all these crazies. And this is not where I belong. And I hate you Annette and I hate you Dr. T and I hate you all of you Edda and the droolers and the wailers and the television zombies and the nasty man who makes jerk-off noises during dinner time over the vile vile food.

In my tears, Joey's Corona, his Red Hook, his Anchor Steam appeared, I could taste them again, and the nettles and needles and broken teeth and glass shards in my veins started shaking and tearing at me each time I stopped crying so I cried until 3pm when I fell asleep like it was night time, I fell asleep real hard and I didn't dream a drop.

"Well. Do we *really* need an hour of silence again, Exene?" Dr. T said, nudging the rock paperweight and a stack of files over to the edge of the desk before sitting daintily in the armchair across from me.

I saw what the paperweight said. Are you ready? It said JESUS. Carved in perfect, deep, crisp letters.

Another one!

So we did need that hour of silence, and a couple more hours. Of glowering and hate from me. But then I just couldn't keep it up—Dr. T was not the same breed of Christian as my mother and her pals, this was obvious. Dr. T didn't mention Him and didn't even, like, *structurally*, let's say, think like a Christian. I finally started talking those days before I began the program—which I will get to in a minute here—and I kept talking my venom even once I started working my ass off for Nae. The things that flew out of my mouth at Dr. T were from like the lowest rung of vermin on the planet, well not like child molesters or executioners or corporate bigwigs but from the ungrateful, the whiny, the self-aggrandizing, deluded, cruel, petty folks, the Americans, the people who think they deserve to be in a magazine, the people who don't tip, the people who want to get away with things, the people who think it's fine for soda companies to provide logoed food-pyramid posters to elementary schools and take it as a tax write-off. I thought I was so fucking smart. It was painful to hear myself after the first five minutes of it. So smart. So sure. So *far* from the crazies and the meanies, so far from the ugly qualities of Joey, I was so sure, though then if he was so horrible and mean why did I want him *back*?

So far from how crazy my mother was and Ruth was. So far from the Devil. So far from the terror the Christians live under. So far from the stupid empty blankness of California, so far from the dryness. So critical: I saw it all. It was all so *not* me, I assured her.

Yeah, right. None of that had *anything* to do with me. It was all separate. That's why I couldn't get my fingernails out of the holes they dug on my forearm.

I was a cretin, a whiny, horrible cretin. It was very, very important. The ugliness stayed with me a long time, it seemed. I stopped brushing my teeth, I let the rot smell keep the nutbags away from me at dinner so I didn't have to say anything else mean to them. Dr. T smiled at me, each session, Dr. T waited.

Otherwise, in those days: sleeping and crying and taking two or three wet bites from a tray had blurred into each other, Annette's frowning face, flashes of sun and white cloud and too-dry California air through the window she kept opening.

My cretinhood and foul mood and indiscriminate bitchy fury expanded.

CLOSE THE WINDOW, ANNETTE. But she wouldn't. *Say please,* she'd say, and when I did she ignored me. The sun beat me down.

Joey is the only thing that matters. And I kept repeating that to myself, and I forced myself to believe it because the more complicated things underneath were gnawing at the barrier in my mind and these words were all I had to keep them from overtaking me in the night.

I begged her, Annette, for my meds, and she told me to hold up, hold up, Nae would be back tomorrow and I could start her program then. And I hated Annette for it all.

Nae's program.

How enticing.

I didn't want to stay here anymore.

Without meds: no fun. Let me warn you all: The Ward is no fun without meds.

I could hitchhike a ride. Surely somebody was going to Sac. My white dress and slut heels were still in the closet along with the smocks and fucked up Kmart clothes the hospital so kindly provided for my stay.

I hadn't smoked a cigarette since I'd gotten here. It occurred to me that I might like one now. It occurred to me that I might like to leave here now.

And I said: "I hate it here. It's not helping. I want you to let me go home now."

And Dr. T said: "Okay."

And I said: "I've got to go find him."

And she said: "Why?"

And I said: "I need to tell him how bad this feels."

And she said: "Why?"

And I said: "Because I need to tell him I can't stand it anymore."

And she said: "Meaning?"

And I said: "Meaning I can't take it. And he will listen to *that* if he ever cared about me. That I'd rather just *stop* than feel like this anymore. He will listen to that. He will listen to that. He will he will."

And she said: "*Stop*, meaning . . . ?"

And I said, "*Stop* meaning stop being here, stop fucking *being*."

And so apparently, if you are a threat to yourself, they can commit you, keep you against your will. That's what she did, and that's when I understood for real the meaning of the word *seething*. I understood wanting to put another person's eye out with an icepick or a hammer. I was more of a cretin than ever but the fury in me did not let me see this at the time. I looked out the window behind Dr. T's head and imagined I saw Ruth's face out there in the pearly clouds—*Yeah*, she said, *yeah, now you fucking get it.*

CLOSE THE WINDOW but Annette still wouldn't and the sun came in and I seethed and it burnt me and dried me out inside like the fire never did, I burnt until there was nothing but an ash skeleton inside of me and I wouldn't talk to Annette and I wouldn't talk to Dr. T and I wouldn't eat my dinner and I wasn't hungry and I didn't cry and that was that was that was that and I decided it was time to get out of here, committed or not. I sat very still on my bed and hardly had to get up for anything, not even for the bathroom since I hadn't sipped a drop and I just sat and sat and decided how I was going to do it.

"They're all fucking crazy. What the fuck was I supposed to do?" I said.

"So you became critical of them," Dr. T said.

"I mean, how could you not become critical of them?" I said. "Amandine speaks in tongues all the time. It's like *humming* to her. Like tapping your fingers."

"But there's something about that you miss, too, isn't there?" Dr. T said.

"Fuck you."

"I mean, *all* this despair at the regular world and wanting Joey to make it somehow more magical—maybe your mom made it magical. Surely Ruth did."

"Fuck you," I said, and as I strained to shut the door on my past.

But I could feel Ruth's hand grabbing for mine, Ruth's hand now so different: faultless and innocent, like Edda's. Ruth's hand free of cunning, free of maneuvers and convincing and struggle and taunts. Just another sad, crazy person at the mercy of fucked brain chemicals, at the mercy of history.

Ruth's hand swinging mine back and forth, harmless—ready, though, to snap me underground, ready to drag me through the fear of her nightscape.

Ruth would take me there, underneath and back, with a slight nod, a secret command from Dr. T.

I curled my lips together, tightened my eyes, stared at the floor.

Dr. T sighed.

"Fine, shut it off," she said, "That's what saved you from your childhood. That adolescent stance of shutting it all out. But it's not going to keep working. It's not going to save you from your womanhood."

"Whatever," I said, suddenly exhausted. I yawned hugely. I put my head on my shoulder and slept until the session was up.

The night nurse who took Valium was sweet, I didn't want to get her in trouble, but I knew she kept the keys in plain sight when she dozed, it would be so easy to turn the key in the metal plate in the wall and take off through the space where the two sides of the painted X separated.

Creature, I could hear Ruth whisper, and I even jumped when I thought of the Devil behind her voice—it still scared me. I couldn't muster sarcasm. *Creature*, she said, and my mother's head jolted up in her sleep in Sacramento before I got the TV screen in my head to sink down into a tiny blue dot.

I felt like a ghost in my room, putting on that white dress and the white shoes Joey'd crushed me into. *Escape*—the word like drugs on my tongue. My sister and mother passing into shadows. The lights from the parking lot outside reflected and sunk in through the window, lit me like my clothes were made of wax mixed with something to make it sparkle.

I would walk down to the road and hitchhike. I would smoke a cigarette. I would get someone to buy me a white Russian. I would get back to Joey and tell him how bad bad bad it all was inside me and he would come to his senses. It was so clear, so clear, everything so perfect in that dress.

He is the only thing that matters. I had said this to myself constantly. After hearing it in my head about three billion times, this phrase had begun to sound like the voice on the Nordstrom speaker while you are fake-shopping in luxury: the powdered, lipstick voice, full of quiet restraint, voice size 4, voice gooey, an anorexic with silicone implants, voice official, voice customer-service oriented, voice *Jane Smithfield, please meet your party at the Lancôme counter. Jane Smithfield.*

I knew from people who worked at Nordstrom that these announcements were often secret security codes. *He is the only thing that matters. Please meet your party in Women's Separates.*

Authoritative, calm, to disguise a transgression and its consequences.

And under the loudspeaker-pure voice, a hint of static? A hint of Ruth, underneath it all.

But the night nurse wasn't sleeping. She was on the phone just behind the front desk, beyond the safety glass. I could hear her talking, laughing, whispering at one point, before I even left my room. I held on tight to the door handle with one hand and smoothed the other hand up and down on the wall.

My leg had healed just enough.

I breathed, and nudged the door open. Thank God for the pool of darkness right outside my door.

But between me and the big doors to the outside world, the big doors with the X on them, there was wide light, there was no way to get there without her seeing.

I sat. I prayed. I thought *Valium, baby, what you need is a Valium* to see if I could urge the night nurse into a doze via ESP. My thirst for velocity had me jumpy but I forced myself to sit still.

He is all that matters, the voice came back, again and again and the words lost their meaning.

(That perfect, together-woman's voice. In a suit, in pumps, tiny, pretty. *She* was telling me what to believe: he is the only thing that matters.)

She—pink lips—is the authority.

And I started listening then for Ruth's background fuzz, her words focusing and unfocusing in background static, but it wasn't there.

I wanted it there. All that time running from it but—I wanted it there. I wanted Ruth's nastiness to mess up the hair of that pink-lipped woman, I wanted Ruth to smear that woman's Lancôme pink bullshit clear across her well-employed jaw line.

Ruth?

I called her in the dark.

But there was nothing, just the pool of black I sat in.

There was nothing to run from.

Sitting out here in the dark hallway forever seemed totally possible.

With no talk from Ruth, there was nothing even to run from.

This was *it*.

Looking into the pitch-drenched, institutional-tile corner, staying so still, I began to feel light pulsing around my body—the outline of me, the outline of a girl. As if another presence, but it was *me*.

Nothing to chase, and nothing to run from, and I sat on the tile floor of a mental ward.

My outline grew brighter, I closed my eyes and could feel it, I could feel myself sipping at the darkness, tasting what was exactly in front of me. The darkness had different qualities to it over the hours that passed. The darkness swirled purple and white in places when I stared hard enough.

Mine was bright gray, glassy. It was glorious, tensed. It transfixed me.

Soon enough, I saw another one, the outline of another girl. Ruth's: a snaky yellow color, burnished gold, swirling over to me, and I was so still so safe, somehow, in that darkness that when it decided to overlay mine, weave itself in, cover me, I didn't care.

Escape stopped mattering.

Ruth's gold thread wrapped around my gray one—roofed mine, hid it. Only one of my arms, one leg, was separate from her, flailing slightly, unsupported and confused.

Fine, gobble me up:

Home, safe, and far away from the daytime world, from corporate job prospects and architecture, from the loudspeaker woman, from community college and Pinko's.

But when the dull-shine yellow trail of my sister left me, *ow*. Ow

"What do you really want from her?" a woman's voice asked me.

I jumped but did not scream.

This voice was *not* in my head.

"Edda?"

"Ha. *Edda*. As if. No it's not Edda," she said. "It's me. Look, are you gonna bust out of here or what?"

I couldn't tell where the voice was.

"Fuck yeah," I lied.

"Follow me," she said, and she grabbed my wrist—she'd been standing above me—and tugged me to my feet.

A few steps into the bright hallway I saw her from behind—she was a real, slight, muscular woman, her dark hair back in a long braid, her steps symmetrical, her steps light and grounded at once. She pulled a key from her pocket and struggled to turn it in the panel, nodded back to the night nurse. She had a pretty face from the side, a flattish profile, I couldn't tell her age.

My free hand was shaking like it belonged to someone else and I bit my cheek until I tasted metal because that seemed like it might get my hand to stop.

Out in the main foyer of the hospital, under these bright fluorescents, the woman nodded at the pink-face security guard—I hadn't really thought about one of those being there when I hatched my escape. So much for *my* planning abilities.

A rush of electrons in me grew destitute, craving the added pulse of my sister, craved her outline threaded into mine as if led by a needle.

"Come on, sweetie," the braided woman said to me and squeezed my hand a little tighter.

The automatic doors to the parking lot opened for the woman normally, but I would have believed they weren't automatic, that they just let her pass like the guards had, I would have believed that the unadulterated way this woman was walking and the way she had just appeared in front of me in the dark like that gave her some freak power to open doors.

The night air was wetter than the fucked arid shit that flew around the hospital rooms even with the windows open.

"Come here," she said, and she swung left on a concrete path, leading us behind the ER wing of the hospital, back to an area facing away from the freeway. We approached a row of shrubbery—the slick, corporate kind, but as we got closer I noticed an archway between the fortressy waxy bushes, a trellis archway drenched, weighted with roses that looked gray, then turquoise, then blue-purple as veins.

"Are they blue?" I asked.

The only light came from behind us, the safety beams illuminating the parking lot, but it was enough to see her smile and nod.

And after we got in there she let my hand go and turned a corner and I couldn't find her. My hands were shaking shaking and in the dark I could feel my mother and Ruth very close to me but somehow kept at bay and I was breathing really fast, *slower*, I heard, and I breathed slower, and the smells here, the air, started to fill me where before there had just been panic.

The earth smelled damper out here in this night garden and as I adjusted my eyes to the darkness I could see there were rows and rows of vegetables growing in the middle, a sort of labyrinth of shrubs to one side of me and heaping, messy flowers behind me.

"Where are you?" I said, loud but not too loud.

"Here," and the voice could have been anywhere.

I thought about sitting, then no, decided to walk, and my feet followed each other, and I went in a circle around the vegetable rows, followed my feet, followed the dirt, let the air sink into my skin and into my chest.

And I knew then, foot after foot, step after step, understanding the braided woman was somewhere in that garden keeping my sister's demonic voice at bay, that if I had managed to sneak out to find Joey again I'd be so much more as lost and as wandering and as pointless as I was here on this path, in this nighttime garden. I'd *feel* like I had a mission—the coked-up edge of that shimmery word *escape*—but I would end up with nothing more than I'd already got—just emptier, burnt to ash inside.

Ruth's demonic voice.

But—

Her golden outline—nothing so comforting as that

I could hear the soft, homey thuds—or feel them, of the braided woman's light steps through the vegetable rows.

I could feel the dirt under me and in me, not California dirt, too wet, something older and loamier and richer than that. Something specific to me, my own dirt, and being here it didn't scare me so bad.

I started breathing really slowly, and I could feel my insides relaxing.

I stopped, right there on the path, and sat, and closed my eyes, and breathed in. The dirt smell filled me.

God, I thought it was all *Joey*. I thought the night and everything was all Him. I thought everything like this smell of dirt was Him.

When I opened my eyes, there the woman was in front of me, flat ovals of warm eyes, hair pulled back calmly and simply, a face who you knew was older than its lines. Smooth as the calla lily she pressed into my palm.

I turned the flower around in my hand—so many reasons to be annoyed at it, its pristine bridal veil for a petal, nothing pink or lush or explosive to it at all. A flower like a slick black and white glamour photo. Button wouldn't know what to make of it, this California bloom, looking something like what a leek would come up with if it tried to cross-dress.

But none of this bothered me: the calla lily was perfect.

"Thanks," I said.

"No problem," she said.

"Um, who are you?" I said, words wet and messy.

"I'm Nae."

I panicked briefly, but then got it that I wasn't, like *busted* or anything. A certain relief hit me, then, that this woman wasn't another patient.

"You're famous around here."

"Yeah, well," she said, "I do what I can."

I bent over my knees and sort of hugged myself again and she just sat there with me. It was a weird way to get introduced to someone, really, but I was beyond feeling awkward. It was like she knew just what I needed. She didn't say anything, but I could feel her saying to me *don't be afraid of them, they can't destroy you. Don't be afraid of them. You can touch them without being destroyed.* With this woman Nae sitting next to me somehow those unspoken words seemed true.

A gray-silver and an opaled-gold outline of a girl joined, separated, joined.

What? I said, but Ruth didn't respond.

Both the light-girls, me and her, flashed brighter, sucking light from the sodium streetlamps, then faded. The gold one pushed back, detached, then wound away in a sort of side stroke, swum off into the clouds. The gray hung there before slowly burning itself off like mist. I held that calla lily like it was a crucifix until Nae stood up and took my hand and led me back through the parking lot, the lobby, the metal doors, to my room.

With my hand on the door to my bedroom, suddenly everything felt more normal, but in a way that made me just want to cry some more: the smell in there—the blankets and the endless stupid television and the knowing each morning I was going to have to get up and be one with the crazies.

"Don't worry—" Nae said right before she tucked me in, "It'll come and it'll go. You're going to get better, hon."

I let her hug me then, even though I didn't believe her. I squeezed the calla lily so tight the stem crushed a darker green in the pattern of my fist. When I woke up the next morning it was snapped in two on the floor.

The next day a select group of us who had been determined "good candidates" began the introduction to Nae's Program.

"No caffeine, no sugar, no dairy, no red meat, no fake sugar/diet soda type stuff, no white flour, no ferments," Nae said to the nine of us packed into a little room behind the extra kitchen where we would be preparing all of this imaginary food.

"What does that leave?" said Ernest, who looked middle aged but could have been a teenager by how he held himself. He chewed on the heel of his hand, so his consonants were stunted with palm. You could see his nipples through his thin, cheap, sixties nerd shirt.

"Lots and lots, there, my friend," Nae said. "You can have whole grains—but not more than one serving per meal—and just a little *organic* tofu, and fish, and 3 parts vegetables to 1 part everything else at a meal, and free-range chicken for those of you who are carnivores. Any questions?"

I had no idea whether I was a carnivore or not, whether it was something that I had to choose or if it would be determined for me via an astrologer, and I didn't get this whole thing, the point of it all, and I'm sure nobody else did, but nobody asked anything in the silence, until Ernest piped back up.

"Whad aboud cocodud bik?" Ernest asked her, then took his hand out of his mouth, briefly, to smooth back his overgrown bangs. The gesture was quick and panicked, but he calmed once the heel of the hand was back between his teeth. For the glimpse I saw it it looked red and mauled, its edges soft and white like a dog-chewed toy.

"Coconut milk?" Nae said, and her face furrowed, again, so sweetly, really considering this stupid suggestion, "Well, I suppose that's just fine. Actually, yes, lots of tocotrionols, *very* hard to get elsewhere. And we don't have them budgeted into your supplements. Yet. Well, *thank* you, Ernest."

Ernest, still chewing, nodded happily, the four fingers pointing up at his nose, like a cage of his own flesh on his face.

When just then she said staying in the program was optional, that we could leave and go back on our meds any time, and nobody walked out, I started suspecting that the loud, wild schizos weren't "good candidates" and we were here just because all nine of us seemed depressed, wussy, and so easy to push around. The other eight people in the program were mostly older, more washed out, tough to talk to—they didn't all keep their hands in their mouths like Ernest, but some of them might as well have. Just tell the depressed ones what to do, that's all we want. Just *make* us.

I kept going to see Dr. Templeton, but other than that everything changed. Nae's program *was* sort of like my version of boot camp in that it required all these hours under the sun, weeding and hoeing and picking vegetables, and then cooking them. If we were tired or freaking out there was an allowance for that, but really, it was hard.

Nae's program also involved yoga. I hated this so much—everything in my whole body hurt again and when Nae would say *let your joints find their perfect spot* as we were twisted into the triangle or the knee-breaking forward bend on the stinky dust and sweat soaked yoga mats—supposedly easy stretches were all we were doing, but it hurt me so much. She just smiled when I told her I was certain she was a dentist her last lifetime around.

It's not spirit that is telling you to try to get your hand all the way to the floor—its ego, she'd say, and I'd manage not to scream at her. I wasn't *trying*.

I would just count the minutes, on my blue soft yoga pad, staring at Nae's perfectly spiritual alignment, until it would end and that soft, tingly skin feeling, tingly bone feeling would happen.

My fingernails turned brown and I couldn't get the dirt—excuse me, the *soil*—out. But on the days when it wasn't so hot, I'd be full of the sensation that Button was there when I was putting in seedlings or taking out weeds. Just the calm repetition and the smell of the soil there, as if there were something for *sure* on this earth. The cutting of seedling roots before putting them into the ground, writing carefully on the little signs *salvia broccoli fennel chard*.

I learned how to tie a do-rag so that the sweat wouldn't get in my eyes. I learned how to keep moles away from onions and other bulbs. I learned how to break up weeds so they possibly won't come back. And my sister and my mother, in my head, weren't bothering me so much. I was laughing more. Nae was nice. I was clearly not as crazy as the rest in the bunch but she didn't kick me out of the program. I hadn't had a cigarette since I'd been in here and I didn't want one anymore—that alone was enough to convince me all this California detox bullshit really worked.

Out here on the ground we were getting ready for late-fall planting (what would *Button* say about the unnatural length of this growing season?) I wiped my hand across my jeans and then rubbed my eye, but dirt still got in and stung and I squinted and blinked until it went away and I sat back from my weeder's squat, sat back and lay down and stared up at the clouds.

Creature? But I couldn't hear her. There was something besides Ruth with me now, there was this work that was fucking hard *work* but that was *something*, giving me some point.

And so I leaned back and ran my fingers through some empty soil and closed my eyes. No Ruth voice. No spooky sparkly outlines. Just birds, and breeze, and something like the sound of all that California light.

I was far from Ruth now. I kept breathing, waiting for her, all that empty white light noise surrounding me and quite nicely warming my skin, but there was nothing.

If I lost her, if I lost her totally from my heart then what?

You don't exist without me, she'd say, and I'd slam the door on her and get back to weeding—in other words, she'd be back, right? If I truly tried to get rid of her she'd be back? Right? It wouldn't really *work*, would it?

The white warm expanse stayed in me and Ruth didn't show up or necessarily seem gone for good, and I somehow got to feeling brave and curious:

There were puddles of darkness, trapdoors behind my heart I was starting to become aware of lately. Dark places of old hallways, of my mother, of the eighties. Without Ruth around, somehow it had become impossible to ignore these corners of me that I usually just rushed past, whistled past, shut my eyes tight at.

I found myself in my mind, walking through the old hallways of our house in Pennsylvania, and I wasn't so terrified of the Devil or of Ruth or of my mother doing something accidentally to hurt us all anymore. I could see it with some distance and I could see that I was alone. I could feel the wood under my bare feet and my breath coming in and out, a little girl, seven, and Ruth was about to leap out and terrorize me and my mother was asleep and Button didn't know, I was so silent, Button had her hands full worrying about Ruth, and pulling back from that hallway, seeing it from above, it was like I was just this teeny, tiny, thin, so-frail thing and my long hair made me look so pale and this look of sheer panic on my face hardened even at seven under an expression of *nothing is wrong don't look at me of course everything is fine*, a total girl-face, you know what I'm talking about, a polite face, no trouble, a face of *this is not happening, these dark tastes my mother is convinced are hunting us, watching our every move, are not really much of a problem at all really, I am seven but I am fine* and then, just then, the white-blue of the California sky somehow irritated my closed eye and—

Creature

(I called *her*. Creature—creature. . .)

but the breeze just jittered

Creature:

The girl with the face that is a lie

That is me: my lying face,

My lies.

I could sense the fury coming to me then as when you know you'll smell something burnt as soon as the match is lit.

Quiet—how odd.

Not Ruth's—

Mine.

Mine, it was my own pure hatred for my mother.

I sat up and slammed the trowel I had been snapping roots with into the dirt and I exhaled like I was about to start in on someone, start getting in someone's face but there was nobody there except the turnips.

The sky seemed to be losing oxygen, the air thinning. Dry hands, it felt like, thirst, and I was sure I could stand one more second of it but this fury—a wispy white-blue line of smoke rising from my heart, suffocating—continued, this fury continued.

I looked up, into the building, and just then, though it was not our wing, Dr. T and Annette were walking together. They saw me. They waved.

I eyed them down with dry sockets until Annette got silly, raised a fist in the air, kissed the glass and left a mark. I managed to uncurl my own pale fist into the cheapest little wave you can imagine.

These amazing people: I screamed and had fits on these mental ward people and they still not only put up with me, which they were of course paid to do, but they were nice about it.

"Come on, Exene," Nae said, tapping my shoulder, "lunch," she said, and I stood and I could feel that vicious white smoke—what I had thought was always not mine, what I had thought was always the voice of my sister—twisting down the trunk of my body, white smoke that had no name except fury. It was pure, it was clean, it denied everything else, and my hands started shaking again like they weren't mine. These people—Nae, Dr.T, Annette, all the nurses—were giving me so much and it hit me how that hadn't happened before—where was Button that whole time? Where was my fucking *mother*?—that hadn't happened to me before, people really watching out for me like that, and I was *pissed*.

So I called Joey collect from the pay phone.

"I'll accept."

"Max?"

"Yeah?"

"It's Racinda."

"Dude, Racinda, they think you're like dead or something. This guy Rudy just came over here with your mom because the cops are being useless. That dude, man—"

"Max is Joey there?"

"No. Dude, Racinda where *are* you?"

"I'm—well I'm okay."

"That's good. I heard you came by here and it got kinda ugly."

"Yeah. Do you know where he is?"

"No. I don't have any idea."

"Come on, Max," I whined, "Don't front for him!"

"I'm not! I don't *know*. He's probably in the city with Otis."

We were both quiet and I could hear the birds outside, the sounds of Joey's apartment. I wanted to say something but I would cry, so I stayed quiet, wanting *those* birds.

"But wait I mean, really, like you should tell me where you are," he said.

"Why?"

"Well, I mean—they're all really worried about you."

I could see it: my mother at her table, Jesus whispering. Waiting for Rudy's calls and waiting for mine. I could smell her hateful lotion, I could see the lines under her eyes. I shut the door on this sight in my mind.

She wanted me to save *her*. And the smoke rising from my heart billowed. Who was supposed to help that little girl in the dark hallway? Fuck my mother and Ruth. The smoke swirled purple and black behind my heart and I wanted to do anything, anything, to make the two of them go away.

"Max, is Joey worried about me?" I asked, this gross coy thing in my voice.

Max paused.

"Yeah—Joey is. He's pissed too, that guy Rudy was like really rude to him."

"Well he's not named Friendly now is he, Max?" I said, and my mother and Ruth faded for the minute with my brief cretinous glee at that sentence.

"Come on, Racinda—are you okay?"

"I'm in a mental ward, Max."

"...Oh."

"It's not like I'm crazy or anything."

"Right. I mean."

"I mean, *you're* fucking crazy still living at that asshole's house," I said, although we both knew I'd be doing it if I could.

"It's not like I have a lot of options here," he said.

He feels *guilty*, I thought. He feels like he's selling me out, I thought, and I got little prickly tears in my eyes from this fact.

"Right. Where would you go," I said.

He was quiet—even the freeway sounds, just slightly, I could hear through the phone.

"What mental ward?" he said.

"I don't want fucking Rudy on my tail, Max!"

"Right but shouldn't like *someone* know where you are? Just for like safety or something?"

Safety.

"Fuck," I said.

Max was quiet but then he said, "I'd come get you if you want."

"You don't even have a car!"

"I'd come get you. I'll drive wherever, I'll get there, I'll get you."

More of those tears came to me then but I covered them with a cough. The first second of them seemed to have to do with Joey but then it was so obvious just that it was that someone cared about me like that.

"Just—Max, just you can't," I was slurping, coughing, "you can't tell Rudy or my mom *where* if I tell you that," I said, and I coughed and coughed, my mother's pain at losing me *too*, my mother's quiet horrible lonely terrified mornings and artificial sweetener and little quiet alone prayers so clear in my mind.

"You can tell them I said I'm in a ward and that it's real fancy and high quality and that the state is paying for it but just tell them it's like in Oregon or something, you think, tell them I hinted it's real green and cold here."

"Sure," he said, "You—" I could hear the smile in his voice, the vowel coming out through widened grinning lips for a second, "So I guess it's *not* in Oregon? Where are you?"

"Max. . ." I said—what was it I needed to tell him? I had no idea. There were no words for it, and I just trailed off then, couldn't even be bothered to cough to cover up the crying.

He started to say my name but then he shut up and just listened to me wail and careen and snuffle until I finished.

"He's a fucking asshole," Max said, "He's a dick. Forget it," he said, and I told him the name of the hospital and that he should ask for Exene Cervenka.

"Um," he said, "I guess call if you need anything," he said, "And don't let the crazies steal your matches," he said and I restarted crying but it veered into laughing so hard when I said it:

"Arsonist!"

I thought I was going to need a paper bag again for hyperventilating I was laughing so hard. Where was Rudy when you needed him?

Nae taught us to breathe and to feel and basically felt sucky. I vacillated, but I was still pretty deep into acting like a cretin: snappy and shrewish and persecuted and bilious. Feeling fucked by the weirdness of my up-bringing and how alone I was now in the world, with just a mother only halfway on this planet, a missing sister, a cult deprogrammer and Max to my name. I knew that as an exceedingly fortunate member of the First World I had relatively little to complain about, but a lot of times knowing this doesn't help if you're as fucked-feeling, as useless-feeling as I was then.

I would spend whole days, it seemed, in that hallway of my childhood, my pale feet taking me down its knotted beams, each set of toes poking slowly out of the ghostly ruffle of my nightgown, moving me forward—to Ruth or away from her? I don't know where she is. I don't know if moving is worse than staying still. The hallway carries me from my mother's house to Button's, and here at Button's the moving is right, because I will make it to the basement, somehow, Ruth will forget to look there, I will sit there in that basement and ward off the acidic smell of the Devil, ward him off with Jesus, Jesus, Jesus, with begging, with eleventh-hour bargains, with my terror as a sort of peace offering.

"Did Jesus come to you then?" Dr. T asked when I explained those days.

I had to think about that. Maybe He showed up but He didn't make it any better.

"How could they let me fucking sit all those hours in a *basement*?" I said.

"They did the best they could," Dr. T said.

"What?" I said.

"I said they did the best they could."

The Devil himself rose in me then and I imagined Dr. T's face bashed in: I knew exactly what it would feel like to slam the JESUS paperweight up her nose and shatter her skull. The crumbling of cartilage. I imagined the smell if I, say, flew into the waiting room like an avenging ghost and vaporized the people waiting for their shrink appointments. The smell of agent orange crumbling Nae's garden.

It was like Dr. T knew all this. She had been waiting calmly.

"Putting yourself in the status of Innocent Victim gives you a blank check to avenge yourself by any violent means you wish. If you are all good and they are all bad. . . I'm just not so sure that's useful," she said.

"Um," I said, syllables sleety with determined chill, "I spent hours of every day in a basement fearing the apocalypse?"

She nodded, with raised eyebrows, but not in a sarcastic way. Waiting. And the white smoke of whatever pyre torched my heart could have become an equally blazing inferno of dry ice.

I refused her a word. Let her wait.

Ten minutes, fifteen.

Dr. T was drinking me in with her eyes that whole time.

"Exene, I do understand," she finally said, "I think I do understand. I think you are just very convinced that nobody *could* understand, that still nobody cares that you are in that basement," she said.

"Oh right. A victim is a victim. How is a little girl not one? Victims *exist*. You worship one, I might add," I said. "Jesus, the little girl you mail your prayers to, is just always going to be on the cross, right, that's the image all over the churches, he's always fucked, that's how the story goes."

Those eyebrows stayed up, but infuriatingly enough in a very *kind* way.

"Oh really," Dr. T said.

"That's funny," she continued, "because they way I always heard it He got down from the cross and moved on with His life at a certain point. . ."

Get down from the cross.

Right.

What could I say to that?

What could I—

And then the inside of me separated from the outside of me. The inside of me felt peeled up, as if a layer paint on an ancient wall curled away and left the lower layers clearer. I saw into what I was missing, and I felt Button's rough-soft hands on my head and my face when I was little and I felt the way Ruth's body and mine fit together, riding in the backseat of the car and taking naps and watching TV. And I felt the way my body also fit together with my mother's and that peeling away happened from all of them, Ruth, Button, Amandine. From one to the other.

Dr. Templeton's face was as real as her JESUS rock in front of me, but then not real at all.

I saw the fields behind the Dells' home church.

Soon the smudge-black hallway in our farmhouse reappeared, there was no stopping it, I was there I *am* there I have never left there, there is no protection my feet follow my feet follow my feet follow the other feet, white toes, pine boards, and all I can hear is my breathing—but its sound is just a promise of death.

The Devil's many hands are waiting for me in that hallway—he loves me and he wants to annihilate me—I can't escape the grasp of that Devil, I'm not just some normal girl, I can pass for one in school but not here, he wants me more, there's no getting out of it.

There are hands reaching out to me, hands on all sides of me, the Devil's I am sure and then suddenly I am not sure, I am not sure it is me walking down the hallway and not my mother, my poor, terrified mother.

Wooing the Devil. Failing to repel him, both of us. His scent is impossible to wash off.

I am following Amandine, her nightgown as death-lit as mine.

Two of us, two terrified girls, one right after the other.

The Devil's hands wrench and grab.

My mother is the terrified me who precedes me.

I stop walking and that girl—my broken mother—falters yet trembles forward, ruined, barely managing to shirk the hands of the Devil who will steal all comfort from her.

As the girl preceding me dissipates, shrinks, continuing into the darkness, one of the white hands, lit, swoops right in front of my face and stays there, stops

Others approach and my belly shrinks into itself to hide from their devouring grasp, afraid they will reach right into me but

Whatever is behind those hands says *no*, she says *don't be afraid* and that *one* hand right in front of my face reaches around my neck and cradles me into some force, something warm, something larger than me, all the hands do, setting me back, brushing hair out of my eyes, and *they have not been malicious all along*, I realize, and I breathe again, suck in and in and in, then release and when I open my eyes it is Dr. T holding a cup of water to my lips in the waiting room, Nae pulling my hair out of my sweaty eyes, Edda, tilting and rocking from the anguish of seeing me like this but still concerned, peering off the edge of her long neck and stroking her fingers along the chair next to me.

I breathe.

18

TRIP

Max

Fact is: they notice you shoplifting a lot more if you smell bad. I knew how to get food, I was an expert at this, but even *my* excellent technique started wearing thin after a couple weeks without a shower.

It was fucking cold at night.

I did things like bums did, except I didn't ever think of it like that. I thought of it like the old hoboes jumping on trains and having big adventures. So the newspaper stuffed into the jacket, the cardboard boxes piled up on me, the blanket I bought at the Sal Army, this all wasn't humiliating.

I wasn't going back to moms.

I wasn't going back to Joey.

I slept behind a freeway onramp that had never been completed, an onramp without a freeway.

But when they wouldn't let me in any of the 7-11s within walking distance anymore I had to start hitching to the mall and eating off peoples left-behind trays in the food court. This was better than out of the trash, which I would do in a pinch if I had to. Off the trays you could see whose leftovers you were getting, and it was really just kind of like that, like leftovers. Like recycling. Conservation of resources and shit.

Joey's moms Elaine owed me money but I wasn't fucking going back there.

You know, it's true also that you do stop being able to smell yourself when you stink so bad. I couldn't figure out why people were backing away from me until I ran into Ally and Jimmer outside Radio Shack and they laughed at my ass for my rank odor.

(There is only so much you can do to get clean in a McDonalds bathroom.)

I ended up back at the 7-11 downtown with Ally and Jim that day, though. They left the car windows open even though it was like freezing out. Ally started to understand what was going on and told me in a real low voice just to go to his moms house if I needed to shower, so that was cool, but his mom's place was real small, I couldn't stay there, I knew that. Ally and Jimmer shoplifted me a loaf of Wonderbread and some peanut butter and a burrito and they donated me two packs of reds and a dime bag but then they had to take off.

I was still full from the food court so I just put the bread and stuff in my bag, sat in front of the old 7-11 that somehow started the process that got me all homeless like this to begin with. Funny how you get thankful for getting out of a worse mess no matter how unbelievably lame your situation is: I was so fucking happy Ally and Jimmer didn't see me picking off other people's trays at the mall. But then it hit me that maybe they had seen that and just didn't say anything.

I smoked five cigarettes in half an hour, they made me so happy, and then even though I didn't want to waste my food on the munchies, I said fuck it and rolled a skinny joint.

"Share," she said.

I looked up and it was Lisa, staring all down her legs at me. I smiled real big and tried to lift up her skirt to fuck with her and maybe even succeed at getting a better view.

"Max!" she yelled, slapping my hand away, and then she squinted at me and started to look all sad.

"What?" I said, so goofy and happy to see her. I could have licked her face like a dog.

"Come on," she said, and she pulled me up. She put her hands on my shoulders, and though she held her breath real tight, she hugged me hard and for a long time. She tried not to make a P-U face but I could feel the muscles in her cheeks tighten up like that against my stinking neck.

*   *   *

I stayed at her mother's apartment for awhile, and it was cool. They fed me a lot and I didn't even care that I smelled like a girl using all Virginia's strawberry and grape-ass smelling soap and shampoo. But then this thing happened where Virginia insisted on giving me a motherfucking manicure. There was no way around it, she had been talking about it for a couple days and had that look in her eye and I just had to like give in because she was feeding me. And then that same day Joey came over.

"Well, Max, haven't seen hide nor hair of you," he said, all bellowy, daring me to mention the fire or what he left Racinda to up north or Lisa to that night at the bar.

"Yeah," I said, and I tucked my fingers down into my fists. The tips were all like white, Virginia actually painted the tips white. I didn't look at him.

"I quit smoking," he said, and he looked away from me.

"Good for you."

"Yeah, well, you know, someone around here's gotta have some discipline," he said. He looked over at Lisa who toasted him with her pink soda and vodka drink.

It was eleven in the morning.

"Max!" Virginia yelled from her bedroom, "Maxy, come on, it's time to reciprocate. I can't reach the bottle of topcoat and I'm not about to get this polish all ruined trying to cross the carpet."

I clenched my hands back into fists.

"You know," Joey said, smiling but not in an eat-shit kind of way, "We still have a lot of stuff that needs to get done in the yard. I heard you might be looking. . ."

He reached out and messed up my hair like I was a little kid.

Part of me wanted to thank him and part of me wanted to hit him. I told him yeah, I'd stop by later and see about that.

You know, Virginia had been real nice to me, real good to me. After Joey left, I put topcoat on her toenails for her, said thank you about four times and let her make me French toast, but then I walked my ass back to Joey's.

*   *   *

I hardly ever saw Joey, he never took me to gigs. Otis and those people weren't around, I didn't even care who was calling his answering machine. Lisa would come over and kind of try to act like my mommy or some shit and I would be a dick and she would leave. I put Joey out of my mind and did Elaine's yard work and got a little happy until I had to go back into Joey's space that wasn't my own. In the yard, though, I was fine. When Racinda called—I had only been back there less than a week I think—that threw me, I had to rush back outside and put another coat of stain on the fence, which fucked it up, it was too soon, but I didn't care, I just didn't want to be anywhere near Joey's things. The fumes helped me out, believe me.

But then one afternoon Lisa was over and I was watching TV with her and Elaine upstairs because Elaine couldn't find anything for me to do, and Elaine said I deserved a day off cause it was Saturday. What this meant, apparently, was that I didn't need to do anything in the yard but I did need to help her dye her hair. Whatever—what was I gonna do. Joey came in, late in the afternoon, having just woken up. He started laughing real hard, bent over double, actually, when he saw me sitting there pulling strands of Elaine's hair through a little plastic cap with a crochet needle thing.

"Come on, my little man," he said.

He stood up to look at me again and then bent over laughing again.

"Come on, we're taking you out of here," he said when he caught his breath.

Yeah, okay.

So I drove his Nova to his gig that night, which was not with Bandolero but which was with his friend Carlos's brother's wedding band. (Which is why Joey started drinking *before* the gig). I took the turns a little too hard. I passed even fast cars, yeah, a little recklessly. It was nice just to be going somewhere, the energy of the road and of driving and of that white dotted line flying past, flying past, dotdotdotdotdot.

"Wedding band, shit," he said.

I nodded.

"Pays the rent," he said, "Pays the rent."

"You pay rent?" I asked.

"Well, you know," he said. "Hey," he said, "Do you have a smoke?"

I squinted at him like what the fuck, man?

"You quit," I said.

"Five weeks, not bad," he said. "Gimme one. Don't tell Lisa. Or my moms."

"Fine," I said.

He closed his eyes, flared his nostrils, bent his head back in pleasure when he lit it.

"Like putting your dick in your wife," he said.

"Right," I said.

I remembered that not that long before this, I'd been massively hugely grateful for strangers' pizza crusts. Now, well-fed and clean and with people to talk to, I was just irritated again: even driving is not that satisfying when what you are trying to get away from at eighty miles an hour is sitting in the seat next to you, spouting such brilliant fucking wisdom.

*   *   *

The bride's hair was short and hard, kind of shellacked into place. The rest of her, her voice and her lace dress, seemed soft. She held her huge skirt up at her hips, kind of like you would hold a robe or a towel around you, as she bustled through the rental hall.

The rental hall was all corporate and temporary looking, but the stage and the dressing rooms seemed old, with peeling paint, as if they were the original structures and the rest of the building was built around them and nobody had bothered to try to hide the difference.

"Hey man," Joey stuck his hand straight out, like a divining rod, for the black guy at the table to shake. "Joey Sykes."

"Donald," he said.

He didn't look up from his crossword puzzle, although it was so obvious he saw Joey's hand.

Joey stood a little higher at the shoulders, dropped his hand to his side.

"You're the new percussionist," Joey said.

Donald didn't answer. Joey weighed—in seconds, fast, fast—what to do about such a dis.

"You the bongo player?" Joey said.

"I am the percussionist," Donald said. "Excuse me." His voice seemed deep without being all that deep.

Joey stared at Donald's back as he left.

"What's his problem?" I said.

"He doesn't like white musicians," Joey said, looking in the mirror, trying to get some of his hair to not stick out. He brushed dust or lint off of his chest.

"What?"

"He doesn't like white musicians. Most of these guys don't. It's like you have to be black to be a real jazz musician. I mean it's like they just don't want you honing in on their turf."

"Oh," I started looking around for an ashtray, but all I found was a no smoking sign.

"Here."

Joey tossed me an empty beer can that was sitting on a ledge.

"It says no smoking," I said.

"Fuckem."

I sat on the couch, ratty thing, and lit up, and Joey soon joined me, as usual, smoking mine.

Donald came back in, and I saw how tall he was, like six five, and that he was one of these real well groomed men, that his dreads, each the same exact thickness, thin dreads, were also trimmed, neat. He didn't look us in the eye, just went back to a duffel bag in the corner to look for something.

"No smoking in here," Donald said.

"Oh yeah, I thought that sign was about your girlfriend's blowjobs," Joey said.

"No smoking in here. How you going to play a show without oxygen?" Donald said, taking a clear small plastic zippered bag with what looked like lipstick and shit in it with him back into the hall.

He looked at me, like he wanted to know what I was doing there, but still not at Joey.

I put my smoke out, nodded to him like *it's cool man*, but Joey lit me another once Donald left.

"Mad," he said.

"Mad what?" I said.

"M-A-D. Musicians Against Discrimination. I should start a group for white jazz players. MAD. M-A-D. Fight the power," he said, then he got up to get a beer.

What the fuck am I doing here.

I put my cigarette out. I thought Donald was cool. Something about him. I could just tell.

"How old is that guy?" I said.

"Thirty-six," Joey said. "He's like an insurance salesman during the day, got kids."

"Oh."

"Tight-ass motherfucker. Uptight as shit. That whole family. I used to date his sister."

I wanted another cigarette but I didn't light one.

I waited till they were on the stage about half an hour later, and went out back by the dumpsters in the parking lot to smoke.

Two bridesmaids, not so pretty, in especially slutty looking dresses for a wedding, lavender with black lace down the low cut front, flirted with me. They were so drunk their makeup was smearing their eyes. One of them kept showing the other her engagement ring. Then she would forget and put her hand back down into her skirt and swoosh the material around until the ring caught it and we could all hear it tear.

The sky was big and blank, and I thought, what the hell does Joey have to complain about.

* * *

Donald blew Joey away. I only missed the first few songs, but by the third or so, when I was up there trying to avoid the boogying people in fancy clothes, trying to sit by myself at a red-papered table with purple flowers in a cheap vase wrapped in black lace, I could see Joey's frustration inching into his face in between beats—it pooled in him in those split seconds and fucked up the beat when he hit it. Anger building, too much fuel, he was a little too fast, his tempo was a little off. His features were a little red. There were seven guys in the band that day, all of them doing great except Joey.

Donald and the trumpet player—an old guy, a pale, balding guy who looked familiar to me, who could have been like a friend of Elaine's or something, a guy on the young end of grandpa—were stepping all over Joey's solos. I mean, who wants a drum solo at a wedding anyway? The old guy's trumpet would sneak in and start something catchy and Donald's tympanis would coast in in a few measures. Back and forth between those two—the audience loved it.

What am I doing here.

When they broke after the first set, Joey toweled off then headed back into the dressing room, but I didn't want to deal with his mood, so I went the other way.

The two bridesmaids followed me out for another cigarette, but I went beyond the dumpster, across mud they weren't nearly sober enough to cross, and sat by myself.

Me and the motherfucking bridesmaids.

Never a bride.

My feet were cold, so I started kind of wiggling my toes, and then my feet were kind of tingling like happens after you hit the breaks emergency-fast when you have nearly missed another car.

Emergency feet, tingly, like: this is the body part you need to use now.

Except in my case it was like: Time to walk away Max. Just leave all this shit and walk away.

The bridesmaids were a big purple blob of giggles and stupidness nobody would ever want. Of *course* it was me out here with them. They were looking over at me, desperate women who needed attention, but I wasn't gonna look at them, I wasn't gonna flirt with them. They were only a little older than me, but headed straight for, like, bored housewife-land, and not the foxy porno version of that, either. They were the losers, by the dumpsters, they were all three a little fat and not very pretty, no fucking way did I need any of that.

Walk.

Away.

Max.

And not just from the bridesmaids.

But I remembered my old cardboard bed by the freeway, the feel of it, actually kind of nice at the end of a wandering day but fuck not as nice as the couch at Joey's. I ran my hand through my really soft and clean hair and I told my feet to shut the fuck up. I shivered out there but stayed to finish the butt. I was thinking how stupid I was not to bring any weed with me.

Once I heard the sizzle of my cherry in the muck, I went inside to warm up and decided to retrieve my sweatshirt from the dressing room. But I got stuck—this posse of floral-dressed, all different prints of fabric women, like somebody's aunties, was blocking the only aisle between tables. I couldn't get through without having to ask some old person to scoot their fat ass further under the table, and I felt too rude, doing that, so I just stood there.

The aunts cooed. A baby was the reason for the traffic jam here.

Excuse me?

Nobody heard me. I just stood there. I couldn't see past them, the aunties' wide backs covered in vines and roses and ferns, mismatched, clashing.

Donald's rad-looking head and torso rose suddenly in front of the aunties, whose own faces turned up to him. He was holding a light brown little baby, not like a newborn but not like walking or anything.

"You need to get through?" Donald said.

"Yeah. Excuse me," I said.

But the aunts didn't move.

"Here," Donald said, "Go to mommy."

He handed the kid to his wife, I assumed, who was sitting next to him, putting on lipstick from the bag Donald had fetched in the dressing room. She was white, had straw-colored hair and a surprised, frequent smile.

"Awww," an aunt said.

"He loves his daddy," an aunt said.

"He loves his mama," an aunt said.

"What's his name?" I said.

I couldn't stop looking at his fat little legs, his sharp, precise tiny fingers.

"Dexter," Donald said.

Donald smiled at me, with a perplexed look, as if he was surprised I wasn't a big asshole like the company I kept. Donald took a thick, pale green cloth carefully off his shoulder and folded it exactly perfectly, but I only saw this out of the corner of my eye because I was looking at the baby. Dexter. Donald handed the cloth to his wife.

Dexter stuck out his tongue, and curled the tip up. He kept it that way, like he was tasting the air.

"Daddy better get up on the stage," an aunt said, pointing an orange fingernail to all the musicians eyeing the audience for the missing one.

Donald kissed the wife, he kissed the baby, and he left. The aunties stayed. Dexter's wife, Megan, patted the empty seat next to her and whispered "Get it before one of them does, they're driving me nuts." When she got out her boob to breast feed she was real careful that I didn't see it, but the aunties got a full view. I was surprised—even though they probably had gone through that themselves, they got out of there in seconds.

She strapped herself back up. Dexter started tasting the air again.

"He wasn't even hungry," she said.

She smiled, fast and full like someone had just told a sweet old joke. With her free hand she tapped the table in time with Joey's beat, kept smiling, rocked back and forth to give Dexter a little breeze.

When Megan went to the bathroom she gave Dexter to me to hold. I would have put him up close to me, but I didn't want the smoke on my clothes to bother him. I held him on a knee and bounced him there and he managed to smile while his tongue was still out, still hooked upwards. He stared at me and I mouthed his name in a little song, *Dexter! Dexter!* And he seemed pretty happy.

When the second set ended all the musicians except Joey came down to our table, and they took turns hold little Dex. The grandpa trumpet player swung him up in the air, then bounced him on his hip. Dexter giggled, it was so obviously a laugh. I realized I knew this old man trumpet guy—he was the pharmacist at the CVS my mom sent me to when she got sick and needed antibiotics, steroids for her lungs, freaking pain pills. If he recognized me he didn't say, didn't indicate. I had always imagined his life as boring in his little cage, handing out morphine and antibiotics and hemorrhoid cream, I always thought, I am not ever going to be in a cage like that, but when he spun Dexter over his head here the lights filtered down on him different and I saw that I had been really wrong. He had age spots—yellow ones, purple ones, brown—on his pink bald head but he was shining in the eyes, passing Dexter to some obvious relative of his, they looked so much alike, a young guy who looked like a frat boy and was probably going to go as bald as his father or grandpa or whoever the pharmacist-trumpet player was to him.

What I'm doing here is. . . what? I was going to go get my sweatshirt. . .

The aunties were back all at one end of the table and they wanted the baby, were staring down the baby, but the frat boy son was holding him, then passed him to the pharmacist.

"Dear Lord! Lordy!"

The auntie end of the table had dropped about a foot, and one auntie was covered, eyelashes to potbelly, in Pepsi.

The table had lurched downward where the aunties were leaning on it and whatever of the drinks and cakes that hadn't flew onto them was still sliding toward them. Drinks were swimming down the table cloth to the now-screaming aunties' laps.

A leg had given way.

I somehow got over there and held the table up with my back. Walter, the pharmacist guy, was next to me in a flash and, squatting down, introduced himself and said he recognized me from the CVS.

"You're a pretty fast kid," he said, "Now lemme get a look at this table leg here. . ."

The aunties had backed off and were calming down, so Megan let them hold Dex as a diversion tactic.

My back started to hurt real fast holding that table up, but I stayed and before you knew it Walter and his grandson Jed and I had the thing up and running. Well not running. Up and standing, whatever a table does.

Jed brought us each a tequila shot from the bar and they patted me on the back and I just sort of stood there.

"Well done, boys," Walter said.

I was shy so I kept looking at my feet while everyone talked and Walter once in awhile told someone I did a fine job fixing that table, and when I finally looked up it was at the two lavender bridesmaids, across the hall, who were staring at me.

They still looked drunk and a little messy, and my instinct was to not look at them, I don't want some loser sort of chubby girls on my ass. That was the last thing I needed, to be left high and dry with the lonely women one more time, yeah right, I thought. But then I kind of looked at them not directly and noticed that they had kind of fixed themselves up and they looked kind of pretty, not like my taste exactly but still pretty and they were giggling and seemed like really good people, good girls, you know, and I could see the sadness in them and that they were sort of scared and they didn't deserve the shitty treatment they surely got from whoever treated them so bad that they were reduced to making moon-eyes at *me*, and somehow when I noticed that I also noticed my feet tingling and kind of doing their thing again.

I had been going to get my sweatshirt.

My feet had been cold.

My feet had been tingling like, go Max, get out of here.

"Max here is going places," Walter said when an auntie came over to thank us for fixing the table, "If Max knows anything, he knows how to fix a table!"

And Walter patted me on the back and said, "Max, what's a fine young man like you got planned for his future?" even though he had seen me for a long time come and fill way too many pain prescriptions for my mom, and I mumbled something about landscaping and right then and there I knew it was time to leave. I told everyone it was nice to meet them, Megan and Walter and Jed and Donald and little Dex, I waved across the hall to the bridesmaids. My feet were tingling, talking, and I finally, finally listened.

The floors of the place were sticky like a movie theater now, with rainwater and wine and the goo from the yams, the glazed turkey. I pushed my way through the emptiest aisle I could find leading to the dressing room.

It was full of smoke, and weed smoke.

"And this little piggy went wee wee wee," Joey was saying when I got in there.

There was what looked like a tenth grader, barefoot, in his lap in the big chair.

"See you," I said. Sweatshirt in hand. Bag in other hand. Not looking at the no smoking sign.

She didn't giggle when she turned back to look at me. She could have been older than tenth grade—her face—but her body didn't look it. She stared me down with a smirk.

"This is Tracy," Joey said.

She wiggled her toes at me, she was all draped over the chair.

"Hi. I'll see you okay?" I said.

She waved at me with her cigarette and its smoke hung like a banner behind a plane.

"Bye-bye," she said.

"Hang on a minute, there," Joey said. "Honey, move a minute, kay?"

He tickled her ribs to get her off him. I kept feeling like she was going to squeal but she didn't. Her cheeks were pinkish orange in the heat. She moved slow.

Donald came in, coughing and coughing. He had to bend his head under the first beam to get into the room. Dexter was sitting in the bend of his dad's elbow.

"No fucking smoking, man," Donald said.

"Fuck off," Joey said, and all the happy he'd been brewing up to say goodbye to me left him.

He sat back on the chair, lit a cigarette, and motioned for Tracy to come back to him. She collapsed onto his thighs.

"Maybe if you quit drinking whiskey you'd be able to keep the motherfucking beat," Donald said, pushing an empty shot glass off the table so it landed in someone's jacket on the floor. "Now how am I supposed to keep the baby in here?" Donald said.

Donald stared Joey down, but Joey wouldn't look back.

"Where am I supposed to change him then, do you suggest?" Donald said, shoving a milk crate loudly to the side with his foot.

"Try the great outdoors where nature intended," Joey said.

Tracy looked up at the rain-pounded window, and then at Joey.

Donald was about to boot the milk crate in Joey's direction, but he just rolled his eyes, frowned with half his mouth, and took Dex out of there.

I sighed.

"Okay," I said.

Joey was smelling a thick strand of Tracy's hair, his face buried in her neck.

"Joey, bye," I said, "I'm leaving."

It had seemed, when I'd gone in there, that I'd needed to say more than that.

"I'm out," I said. It was enough.

"Bye," he finally said, and he stared out the smoky rainy window, and he didn't ask me where I was going or how I was planning on getting there. We both knew the score.

*   *   *

I learned how to hitchhike then almost as well as I already knew how to shoplift. The first days of it, all I did was sleep once I got picked up and settled into the cab. I didn't want to think about anything so I would just smoke too much weed, hitch a ride. I went in circles on the freeway— hitching rides north, south, north again. West, whatever. Around the loops of the overpasses. Then straight, barren hours. I slept through November downpours and cold frozen light. I slept until I woke and we were in the blank chute of the 5 going south and I got out of Ed's rig at a truck stop and felt the cold wind in my teeth and got a ride north with Jose. I slept day and night in the trucks. Whatever trucker, Jose or George or Ratty or Don would buy me a burger, would buy me fries, I lived in a world where another ride and another meal always came along. It was the strangest thing. I didn't want to speak. I just wanted to sleep.

*   *   *

I dreamt of the ocean. There was a man in there, throwing a baby up in the air and catching him every time. But it wasn't Donald, it was a white guy, long hair, but not a hippie. Tan and just this aging surfer guy. Dad! I would think, waking up, until I remembered that mine was more like Herb Tarleck from WKRP, bad hair, bad jacket, bad talker, loser. That there was nothing in that dream that I wanted except the wanting.

*   *   *

When I couldn't stand sleeping any more, I got back to Sacto because I remembered that Elaine owed me money. *Max, Max,* she whisper-yelled, *Max come help me move this chair.* I did it, the thing in place and I blurted out *I'm leaving.* Her cheeks were powdery and sad, her face then settled into something I recognized as love. She pulled me to her and I relaxed and I breathed heavy to hide crying of my own. She made me stand in the foyer until she went upstairs for something, which turned out to be four hundred dollars.

I bought some weed before I took back off on the road, and I made sure to donate some to the truckers. It was nice to be able to pay for my own meals once I got started again.

I almost didn't even get in the cab with the trucker I stayed with the longest of all of them. He was this giant tattooed Aryan nation-looking baldheaded hick with an inch-thick chain tattooed around his neck in a few different loops. I almost turned and ran but we were alone on the side of the road, and there was nowhere to run to, so I just got in. I was too nervous even to offer him a cigarette, my fare for safety, my exchange for food and civility. But he didn't smoke, and he actually made me wait till the next stop to get out and hack a butt.

We hadn't talked at first for a while, and when he first did speak to ask me not to smoke, his voice surprised me. I expected a Mike Tyson squeak or a bar-bouncer bark. But it was exactly the middle, normal. A slow voice, like he was really choosing his words.

"It bothers my allergies," he said, "That and molds—beer, mushrooms, mildew. Can't stand em."

"Sorry," I said.

I turned my head to watch the sparks of my cherry fly past the window, like they were moving so fast but maybe just the truck was, they were staying still, just dropping outside in the air.

I tried to fan air out the window with my hand but it didn't do much.

"Yeah, well, it's amazing what you start to notice once you can feel things," he said, and wiped his runny nose with his fist. "Fucking *allergies*!" he said, and he laughed.

I felt bad for making him sniffle—at first afraid he'd be all pissed but then just like that was so rude of me not to ask.

I tried not to stare at the three loops of tattooed chain around his neck, but I couldn't help it once in awhile. It looked like the chain dangled down, like maybe the whole rest of his body was locked up in it too.

He'd picked me up just before an off ramp in the top right corner of the state—beautiful land up there. I thought for a second, drive me east and get me away from this shit, further even from my home, whatever that meant but then it seemed like I stole that thought from him, or from someone in a Honda or a Cherokee so far beneath our perch. The sandy snow in icing sheaths of Lassen, the end-of-the-earth smell—even on the highway, even through the windshield—of Shasta.

He chewed gum, about half a pack of Trident every half hour. He would unwrap the miniscule rectangles with one hand, pile the bare gum on his leg, then pop them all in his mouth and chew till the glob just had to be a big stringy pile of nothing-taste.

"Where you going?" he asked me.

I just shrugged.

*   *   *

Dusk came earlier every night. If I wanted to I probably could have found a way to measure the time by this big-ass trucker's gum unwrapping, but I just stared out the window and fidgeted until I could smoke at the next piss stop. We were below Sacramento—when I saw the sign for Yolo County my guts twirled—well into the valley, below Modesto. After Turlock he took an off ramp but cruised onto regular non truck-life streets.

A craft store, a McDonalds, a taqueria in a shit-brown strip mall plaza. Clouds curling in gray from above that made all these things look impermanent, toylike, temporary. At a stop light, we were inches from the back of a full-sized van, where a brother had a sister by the hair and was digging his knuckles into her eye socket. Michael blew the horn and the boy jumped up, let go, unashamed, just so excited at the noise of it. He was obsessed, that little kid, and so he pulled his bent arm down in the universal request for a trucker to blow his horn, over and over and over. But Michael ignored him, he kept quiet until we turned into the parking lot of the YMCA, when he gave a honk that was sort of like an announcement of our arrival.

"Don't you wanna know where we're going?" he said, and he smoothed his hand over his bald head like he forgot he had shaved off all his hair.

"Whatever," I said. But I was nervous. I jangled my leg up and down, jangled change in my pocket.

Michael smiled—so weird that a scary looking guy when he wasn't smiling could turn into this warm face that just put you at ease instantly. Like he understood why I was nervous and thought it was kinda funny but still wanted to make me feel okay.

"Free dinner," he said. "Friday nights, before the AA meeting" He laughed. "You don't need to go to the meeting to get the dinner, but of course you're welcome to join us there too if you want. Tonight, they're having a, uh," he looked at his boots and smiled more shy, "a, uh, dance afterwards I think I'd like to stay for."

I nodded.

"Like, other truckers?" I said.

His neck tattoo moved up and down he was laughing so hard at that.

"No, just people from here. AA people from Turlock. I like to come to this particular meeting on Fridays when I can."

"Cool," I said, but I didn't know if I meant it. AA worked for like a month at a time on my mom but never really turned into anything different for her. "Cool."

"You'll probably have a hard time finding a ride back from here, actually," Michael said, and he looked concerned. His nose was red in the corners by his nostrils, and there were random marks above his eyes that sort of looked like a bird had pecked him there.

"It's okay," I said. I looked away.

"I'm going to be back on the road about, oh ten I think."

He pulled out a little appointment book—not a truckers log, but a thing from a stationery store, red snakeskin patterned leather and some shit, and he wrote in it with a thin silver pen that looked like an oversized needle in his huge hand.

"Sure, that's fine," I said.

I could see a bank of windows steamed up, the pool in there probably. Steamed up and iridescent with pink and lavenders of grease and humidity and greens of fluorescent lights. Squinting, I could see that the strange movement on the glass was a finger tracing a heart that said MT+AT, backwards to me, from here. The finger started to draw that arrow through the heart, but got distracted, I guess, forgot to finish it, disappeared.

*　　*　　*

At the dinner I got my pieces of Italian bread and meatloaf and felt warmed and terrified by all these people smiling at me so nice. I sort of hovered so that I could go sit alone in a corner—I waited till all the seats around Michael filled up with people, and then made my way quietly to the back. He looked around me, though and waved me over.

They made room for me, between Michael and this guy Stuart, who was tall and skinny with a big hooked nose and hair like auburn broom bristles coming off his eyebrows and his head and out of his ears. He signed himself like a Catholic and led a prayer I couldn't understand before we could eat anything.

"That's a fine freaking choice of a higher power, there, Stuart," this woman Earla said, rolling her eyes and crossing herself, too, in swooping, ironic moves.

Earla's eyes were like this shocking bright blue and her hair was dyed really red, her lipstick was bright red and it all looked even more lit-up because she was wearing this bright light green sweater. She was younger than my mom but older than Joey, like in her thirties I think. Her skin was pale and looked really pretty, even though her voice graveled, was all chewed up by years of cigarettes. You could tell her body was probably okay under that baggy sweater.

Earla stared at me, raising her eyebrows.

"Huh?" she said to me, "Huh?" and nodded, waiting for me to say something to agree with her.

I just sort of grimaced at her.

"Oh, well, cat got his tongue," Earla said and she wrapped her long red hair around her fist, "But even he knows the truth, Stuart."

"*Whatever*, Earla," Stuart whined. He started putting a ton of butter on a roll.

"Capitalism and Christianity just do wonders for the inner life there, huh Stu?" Earla continued.

Stuart ignored her, but seemed nervous. He bit into his roll really hard and chewed furiously. His hair was frizzy and seemed to get messed up just by the activity of sitting there at the table.

This big fat lady on the other side of Michael leaned over him.

"You'll have to excuse all this," the fat lady said, "I'm sorry—I'm Vanessa."

Even though she was so large, in this dress like a big tablecloth, all green vines on it, she was really pretty. Her hair was all soft and bleached blond like Marilyn Monroe's or some shit.

"Michael," Vanessa said, "Get her to stop needling him!"

But instead of saying *lay off Earla*, Michael just grabbed Earla's hand across the table, leaned over and whispered something in her ear.

"You rube!" Earla yelled, but I didn't know what that word meant.

Earla's pale face froze on me, her red lips were like this big childlike grin.

"It's a dummy," she explained in a baby voice, then harsher said "Like someone from Iowa—Idiots Out Walking Around."

Earla left me alone once I started eating. I ate everything but the boiled onions, the little teeny kind that have always grossed me out. I stared at the Girl Scout posters and the choking diagrams on the walls as they kept up all this talking.

"What's his problem?" Earla said when there was a lull.

She swirled her spoon in my direction like I was a baby and she was playing airplane.

"He's just quiet. He's got a lot going on in his head. Don'tcha Max," Michael said. I looked up at him and his head looked gigantic. I could see from this angle that on the left side of his neck, he'd had one of the chain link tattoos removed—a redness there, an absence and a blurry scar.

"Did that hurt, getting that tattoo removed?" I said, surprised at myself.

He thought a minute, and gave me a little nod.

Earla lit a long black cigarette off the candle in the middle of the table.

"Earla! This is no smoking!" Vanessa said, this expression of total shock on her face.

"Oh, she does this *every* week," Stuart said.

Michael sniffled but didn't say anything about his allergies. I could tell he was trying to stifle a cough.

Earla just smiled, straight at me, all devilish. Raised her eyebrows and exhaled a huge plume.

"Huh?" she said, nodding, grinning, like she was saying *how about that!* Like me and her were getting away with some serious fun while everyone else was having a freakout.

"*Every* week," Stuart said.

"Hello? Hello?" Vanessa said, "No smoking!"

She waved over one of the YMCA ladies—like school cafeteria lunch ladies, monitors—who made Earla take her smoking outside. Vanessa's chubby face looked less pretty when she got so angry, but with Earla away from her she started to relax and look okay again.

*   *   *

They invited me to their dance, but I didn't want to go. I mean, come on. They held it in the room next to the pool. Michael and the fat lady in the vines, Vanessa, talked to one of the YMCA ladies, like school lunch ladies, and got me a pair of swimming trunks, but I had to wait awhile for swim team to be over.

There was a line outside the pool—all of us showered, dripping, the concrete beneath our feet shining from the overhead lights and water dappled the hallway from previous swimmers.

No running, no running! the YMCA lady said when she opened the doors, but all the children were off carrying big floaty noodles and water wings and the adults and me walked in behind them, behind the splashing and the yelling and all those kids feet trying to halt themselves into steps that didn't run, didn't propel them from the ground.

Horrible hot air, chlorine air, though you always get used to that in an indoor pool.

But the water was hot too. It was stultifying, but then it became stultifying in a nice way. It was sleepy and warm. I sort of spun around the water in my generic shorts they hand out to strangers, here in Turlock. The black kids were playing water polo, one tried to get me to join but I said no thanks, man, thanks, and swam away, a fish.

After twenty minutes of swimming, when I came up for air this one time it was like there *was* no air. The hot air exactly the same as the hot water against my skin. I hopped up the ladder straight as a stem and crushed the ankles of my sneakers, barely making sure they were mine, and walked out into the hallway of the Y, the front doors wide open to the night getting cold, cold in November, cooling. And I was dripping and I breathed and I breathed. The lights outside looked ringed in rainbows from all the chlorine in my system, I could feel the redness in my whites, inside my nose. I breathed and I squinted and as my eyes narrowed the rainbow halos around streetlights, guiding the way back to the interstate, became ovaline, elliptical, then rounded again.

I breathed and breathed and the hot humid weight of the pool fell off of me so fast I became just as desperate to get back inside. The Y ladies in the lobby ignored me, dripping all over their carpet so old it was pressed into the cement beneath it.

I dove back in even though it was too shallow, my limbs moved through the aqua until I was feeling lightheaded from needing air. I came up and the screams were muted, then louder *look out man—over here over here—marco—polo—marco—polo—nofair—no running—no running* and the swish of a million tiny waves on the four edges of the pool.

This was their home, here in Turlock.

I had to get in a truck in half an hour.

I stood holding the edge, just deeper than where my feet could reach the bottom, I was constantly floating then touching down. Pushing back up with my toes.

What next.

I could hear the 70s funk coming from the cafeteria room where Michael and Earla and hairy Catholic Stuart and nice fat Vanessa were having their AA dance. Lassos of light reflecting from the water's surface cracked and flew across the cinderblock walls and the ceiling. The lifeguard was hot, brown haired with a ring in the middle of her nose but still hot in this sporty-looking suit, all the twelve year old boys and their fathers and me myself couldn't stop looking at her.

One dad, I couldn't tell if he was Latin or what, you know, Syrian or some shit, was holding his baby in the pool, just shallower than me. The kid was asleep, and the dad just kept staring at it. Does it only last while you're a baby? Or do some people not even look at you then?

I closed my eyes and tried to imagine mine in a pool with me, a baby, him just standing there thinking about how cool it was to have me around, but mine's eyes kept darting around in my mind, mine decided to hand me over to my mom and went to organize a water polo game for the adults, muscle the black kids off the equipment. When I looked around, back in the reality of Turlock, there were a bunch of other dads there too. The water curled around my chest and something inside me did the same. My own—the last time I'd seen him, the way he sat on the brown ruddy couch, his fifteen pound weights dark silver on the gray glass of the coffee table, *bye*, watching CNN like he hadn't seen the headline news bits four times in two hours, his new beagle Arthur staring at him like my dad was staring at the TV, *see you pop*, and he looked up shocked, jet lagged from his trip to sell something stupid he thought this time, this time would get him where he wanted to be *oh bye Max, see you next week*. Except I didn't come back, because after I turned 18 it wasn't required anymore. And I didn't return his calls. I just smoked and waited for Joey.

*   *   *

"The Earla bird gets the worm," Vanessa said to me. She sighed. She was big but was so pretty, she even had a beauty mark like Marilyn Monroe. Before now I would have kind of blown her off, but she was really so nice to me, I could see her good sides. Like for example, her arms moved in this extremely graceful way, her hands turning like a small, pointy-winged bird.

I didn't get it—why Vanessa seemed so upset—but then I saw Earla and Michael slow dancing. Earla was like swinging her hips all into Michael, and when she wasn't doing that she was like rubbing her hand all up and down his back. Tossing her long red hair so it got in his face. Earla was definitely more into it than Michael, but still, I felt bad for Vanessa.

Not cause she was fat, just cause the other girl was kind of getting the guy.

"Nah," I said, "He doesn't like her," and I looked over at them dancing. I patted Vanessa on the back and smiled at her real big and thought how beautiful she was and Vanessa actually smiled.

My hair was still dripping, I wiped water off of my neck with the back of my hand.

"How long does Earla have in the program, Stuart? Six months?" Vanessa said.

"Four," said Stuart. He was still chewing something, gum or a stick or something. He twisted some of his brown-red hair around a finger.

"Well!" Vanessa said, "We all know you're supposed to have a year in the program before you date!"

This official face now took over the smile I'd coaxed out of her, and she marched over to the DJ who faded whatever Air Supply song it was into James Brown, fast, right in the middle of a verse.

A cheap shot, but it worked. Vanessa was no dummy. Michael pulled himself away from Earla and, well he kind of like got the *spirit* or something. I never saw anything like it before. He like transformed.

It was like--Michael took up the space of *five* dancing people, and he didn't even notice any of us were around, he went on and on through Mother Popcorn and Funky Drummer and Brand New Bag, kicking his legs out and shuffling around and swinging his arms back and forth and making happy, funny faces to the music and he smiled and smiled and smiled and popped his head back and forth and wasn't embarrassed for a second. He moved in such a cool way that it was like you couldn't really see the chain tattoo around his neck anymore, even though it was in plain sight. He mouthed the words, he gestured on the beat, his hips led him, his shoulders led him, he was dancing for god, not for us, he was dancing for his higher power, whatever that was. A bassline, by the looks of it.

"Thanks a freaking lot, Vanessa," Earla said, snarling her red lipstick mouth, punching Vanessa obviously too hard on the upper arm.

When Earla lit a cigarette Vanessa punched her right back.

"Thank *you* a freaking lot for the second hand cancer," Vanessa said.

"Come *on*," Stuart said, with a panicky look in his eyes.

"She *knows* its against the rules," Vanessa said, pinning her eyes up to the ceiling.

Out there on the dance floor, Michael pushed his knees and pulled his shoulders and shimmied and twisted.

"Come on," Stuart said, pulling himself together, "Let's take a walk over there," he said, and he smoothed his hand over Vanessa's back and guided her to another corner of the room.

Michael beamed and glowed and danced some more.

I leaned against some kids posters on the wall—it was impossible not to, every inch was covered with collages and scribbly drawings—and watched Michael, this random trucker guy I just met, do his thing, the closest thing to complete happiness I'd seen since Joey's band. Only if I'd seen Michael do this to their music, I would have been joining in with everyone else there in feeling like Michael's blasting, huge happiness—strange with that weird chain on his neck, his bald, super-white head—was somehow not cool enough to enjoy, to really look at. I would have looked away fast, like I did with those bridesmaids. But here, it was like these AA people took a little goodness wherever they could get it.

I had to agree with them, you know, I really had to agree with their policy.

Sweating, grinning, Michael walked away when the next slow thing started. He patted Earla on the head when she looked up at him. It was loud, I couldn't hear much, but I could hear Earla snort and see her frown. He looked at his watch and nodded—Earla flipped her hair and crossed the room to smoke another cigarette, right next to Vanessa and Stuart.

But the black cigarette didn't bother Vanessa anymore, because Stuart was leading her out to the floor for the slow dance.

"You ready?" Michael said, and he looked at me like he could really see me. I thought about shrugging but instead I looked up at him looking at me and said yes. I could feel the beat still coursing through him—he was still grinning like all blissful and everything-is-perfect. Yes, I said, and I got not an idea, exactly, but a feeling about where I wanted to go.

*   *   *

Michael had this Talking Heads tape on in the cab, I could tell it was calming him down, he didn't have like 220 volts running through his legs and arms anymore.

"Where do you want to go?" he asked me.

Take Me to the River, was what the song was called.

"I don't know. Where you going?"

"South," he said.

"LA?" I said.

But I grimaced because that wasn't it, that wasn't what I was looking for.

"South Bay, then LA," he said.

He started unwrapping Trident. He did this without thinking, like shifting gears or checking mirrors before he changed lanes.

We were quiet for awhile. *Take Me to the River.*

"When are you going to want to go home?" Michael asked me.

"What's home?" I said.

"Oh," he said, his hand scooping up another batch of gum like a claw. Chewing.

When he got the gob under control he said, "I had a shitty home too."

"Who says it's shitty?" I said. "Who says it exists?"

"Gotcha," he said, "Gotcha."

We let the night seep between us for an hour or so.

"Where's your home?" I asked him.

"Here."

The truck.

"Not Turlock?" I said.

"Could be, but for now it's here." He looked out his side window and I thought how far he had to go, around his neck, to get the rest of the tattoos off.

I thought about a home that always moved, and I thought no that's not it.

Take Me to the River, the tape just kept playing over and over.

But I hated the river I always got taken to car-camping as a kid—in Guerneville, the Russian River, where I sat around and read BMX bike magazines and then walked the woods with other boys of single moms up there car camping and beat sticks till the bark should have been bloody, till we boys were pushed to the edge of the unspoken that we would do that to each other if anyone got out of line.

(If I saw Michael there, in Guerneville, I would have assumed he was Hell's Angel, a murderer.)

And why did we go to the river even though I begged for the ocean? Because with my father my mom had always gone to the beach at Santa Cruz, *Salt everywhere!* Maddening, was all my mom would ever say to me about it. They went there before I was born, *it had soured even by that point*, she would tell her friends while I spied from the kitchen and ran plastic car wheels over the plastic soles of my Nikes. She would pour her friends green tea or a mimosa or a whiskey sour or Kombucha depending on the phase and the time of day.

Salt everywhere, maddening, she said.

Maddening.

It wasn't like there was some great passion and it ran afoul of reality, she would always say to whatever-faced woman she trapped in a lunch. *It was just I thought that was all I could get, and really*, she would say, *what did I get beyond that?*

"I've never seen the ocean," I confessed, shrinking the pools of night.

"You haven't seen the ocean," he said.

"Just the river," I said, "You know, just rivers and creeks. A lake."

"You want to see it?" he said.

"Yeah, I think I do want to. I think I'd like to."

He let a smile pour light across the dash. "I've got a delivery down there, down east of Half Moon Bay, we could make a little stop for you, easy."

"Good," I said. "Good."

"The ocean's a very spiritual place," he said.

Coming from a guy with tattoos on his neck you don't think of a comment like that as too feminine.

"Yeah," I said, to be nice.

* * *

Michael said that a party that he was pretty sure started in Half Moon Bay in 1988 ended when he woke up one morning at seven at night, in 1990, in somebody's dirt yard in eastern Colorado, which was practically the Midwest—this was before he started trucking—and then and there he knew something had to change. That's before a bunch of relapses but that was when he first started getting clean, he explained.

"I had some very special chemistry," he explained.

"Have," he corrected himself.

He remembered getting the first half of the tattoo chain done, but not when it circled completely around his neck, and not when it dangled down around his bicep and shattered. He showed it to me.

"Like the Hulk," he said, and I had a vague idea, having seen the reruns.

In his blurry alcoholic dreams he was like the Hulk. In mine, I am just Max.

*   *   *

"So your home was around Half Moon Bay?" I asked him.

"For a time," he said.

"And in the beginning?" I said.

"All over, like now. I took inventory and the all over part was the part I wanted to keep."

I nodded and thought about this.

"What did you get rid of?" I said

He laughed, then looked at me with a half smile like *do you really want to know?*

"Yeah," I said.

He centered his fists and his gaze around the steering wheel and thought about it for so long that if I didn't know how he was by now I'd have thought he forgot. Many exits along, though, he said:

"The disrespect. I'd say the disrespect. Those who gave me love, even if they were crazy, I kept that and lost the disrespect for their flaws. Those who gave me disrespect and strung me along and were diseased themselves and never gave anyone any love, just gave bait like to a fish, those I got rid of."

I nodded. This was satisfying to me, and I realized how rare that was, for words to reach down into me and say something useful.

"There it is," Michael said, but it was so dark I couldn't see anything, just hills, it seemed.

He rolled down his window and the ocean air came in, sweet, something like a bakery to me, but salty and wet too. I could only hear the wind passing the sides of the truck, I couldn't hear the ocean itself, waving or crashing or whatever the fuck it does all the time.

It was way too cold to swim, like they always say. But I took off my boots and my socks and waded in to my ankles until I was numb to it. I closed my eyes and listened to the pulse of the waves cracking. I listened to it there for a long long time, and I just, like, smelled it. Inhaled.

How *much* is out there. Sky, too.

We crashed out in the cab next to the ocean, in a pull-off for trucks south of Half Moon Bay, land of the last party. But I only really got a few hours before dawn—up till then my mind wouldn't stop. What to keep and what to give away? Give away Elaine—but really, deep in me, I wanted to keep her. Keep Joey, but he was an asshole and I was done with him. Keep what about him? Keep that he wanted to do something, that he always had people around him, that it wasn't just video games and weed and silence, but music and talking to people when he was around. Give away Lisa's sadness but I wanted to keep the eyes Lisa turned on me when Joey wasn't around. Keep Racinda, I thought, keep Racinda, though part of me shook a little, afraid of crumbling at the thought of having to talk to her again, both of us having descended pretty low and neither one having any illusions about it.

Keep Racinda.

There were noises outside besides the lapping of the salt water—party noises of the truckers in the parking lot, men crashing bottles—but when they faded into quiet I slept, and when I woke up just before dawn, I knew what to do.

19

BACK

Amandine runs her bottom teeth over her top lip before taking in, very slowly, the last sip of tea. It's already ten-thirty, Monday morning, her breakfast is sitting, mush, in front of her. Untouched. She has called in sick for the first time in three years, and she's not sick. Amandine told the preacher she works for that she has a stomach flu.

Ruth left a frantic and giggly message the previous Friday evening. . . *thinking about coming home for a visit. . . busy this weekend, you know, a busy busy girl, that's me but I will call you Monday morning. . . I want to come home before I leave on my—*

Amandine stares straight in front of her and does not move. Waiting, on edge, once more for word of a daughter.

She hasn't had too many of these moments lately. Most of her free time has been taken up by Rudy, who is busy wooing her gently with dinners and lindy dancing once a week and movies starring animals—a new one out every month, it seems—the only kind of movie Amandine is sure to be comfortable watching with a man. When he isn't trying to impress her with his least indelicate war stories or getting her to laugh or complimenting her on her fancy footwork, he's got a bit of a new angle on where Ruth might be, or a new program for her, or later, an idea for the same for Racinda.

He'd brought it up Friday night at the Olive Garden when Amandine's eyes were starting to scan the room toward the end of a long tale—one of his favorites, he *had* told it before—involving a stolen canoe, three innocent privates from Tennessee, and a stolen pig.

". . . and right as they were approaching the banks, with *both* sides shooting at their little dinghy. . ." Rudy said, and when he noticed Amandine's finger rudely, uncharacteristically, fetch something from between her molars, he turned on a dime:

"Well, I think I found a good, stringent program for Racinda too," he said, blustering.

"Racinda needs a *program?*" Amandine said incredulously, hands folded back into her lap.

The quiver that came to her face when he brought up the subject of her daughters never failed to reassure Rudy that he wasn't *completely* tedious to her.

"Well, not one like Ruth needs," he explained. He'd been consulting a shrink friend of his from the war on this one, one of the best men in the country. "Ruth—Ruth needs the big guns."

"Oh!" Amandine said.

And her eyes shone so elegantly, full of something delicate and passionate that Rudy could scoop up for his own, that Rudy wanted to protect, that Rudy wanted to witness daily forever.

"Figuratively, dear," he said, and patted her arm just past platonically.

She nodded, and let him protect her from the possible fates of her daughters in that moment. But when she got home and the message on the voicemail—Ruth in a bar? On the street? Yelling, and noises like a siren or like rock music—all it took was one little gesture, her finger, Amandine's finger, on the 2 button, which meant *delete*.

Her thinking was this: if she erased the voicemail now, she wouldn't have to tell Rudy about it this weekend. Which she didn't. She wanted to be taken to dinner and the movies, she wanted the toe-heel toe-heel backstep and her skirt swishing around her calves and the hours of movement over parquet that felt like laughter, felt like it was giving her enough minutes of laughter to make up for the full years—*years*—when she hadn't laughed once.

And if she *told* him Ruth called, somehow, all that would not happen any more. At first she had been as gung ho as Rudy about finding and somehow saving Ruth. *More* even—"patience wins in the end," Rudy often said to her in those moments when a frustrated pout would emerge on her face at a lead that didn't pan out. But lately, that laughter feeling filled up her chest even when she wasn't laughing, lifted her steps as if she'd swallowed a helium balloon, and she didn't want to look for Ruth that badly, or for Racinda. She wanted to be twirled, she wanted to make up for lost time.

What kind of mother have I become? Then she'd have to crowd, expertly, those early, depressed months after Ruth's birth out of her mind.

Because she was weary. Each new lead on Ruth seemed to fizzle within the week. Amandine had been chasing Ruth for Ruth's whole life, and she had no better idea now what to do with Ruth at twenty-four than she'd had when Ruth was twelve and bashing in that poor boy's teeth.

The more determined and energetic and hopeful Rudy became about finding Ruth, the more Amandine's old daze came back. *Mmm-hm, okay, let's do that*, she'd say, and she'd let Rudy prattle on about bipolar disorder and former roommates and cheap bus rates between LA and San Francisco that he thought would be irresistible to Ruth. The daze like the old one, but now, switching easily back to laughter once Rudy finished his piece, relaxed, poured her a glass of chardonnay. Where she and Rudy had shared this early passion for brainstorming—*where* might Ruth have moved from San Francisco? To Vancouver? To LA?—and tracking of the most minute details, now she let him hold all the determination and eagerness.

The less worried energy she put into looking for Ruth, the more he did.

This suited her. Someone was taking care of it.

All she had to do was be sweet and enjoy herself, he was going to fix this for her, as if all it required was jumper cables.

But once Racinda disappeared, too, Amandine could feel an undertow, something drawing her away from Rudy—as much as she loved being with him. Without Racinda there to roll her eyes at the mention of his name (although, thinking back, even Racinda had been slowly getting fond of Rudy, ever since he stopped her hyperventilating with that bag), Amandine found herself stepping back, cutting their dates short, seeing him less, staying at home and praying more.

So, on this defeated Monday morning, having turned herself into a liar, Amandine pours more water from the pot over the withered teabag. She wants a fresh teabag, but doesn't want to move. As if moving will force her to admit she *exists*, which will force her to admit she is lying to Rudy by omission.

Rudy who is so kind to her. Whom she is starting to love. Whom she does not want to lose for anything.

But whose brochure for a new, rather extreme sort of program to cure Ruth is sitting right next to that weak cup of tea.

Amandine's seen a million of these brochures: cursive font, art-deco font, big nasty bold militaristically simple font like this one. She's gone *past* frustrated by dealing with finding the right treatment for Ruth. Which is why she turned to Rudy. Which is why *this* brochure, with its big bold capital letters, FOX HILL WELLNESS CENTER, is sitting on her table, which is why she wants to shut her eyes and imagine that FOX HILL WELLNESS CENTER is just like any of the other places Ruth's been to over the years.

She gulps the tea, lets the heat overtake her mouth, *then* shuts her eyes for a minute.

God, Amandine thinks, then berates herself quickly for taking the Lord's name in vain, *I know I always have to go if I drink two cups of tea.*

Her bladder is very full.

Why do I do this to myself?

But she doesn't want to move, because what if Ruth calls while she is in the bathroom and she misses it?

If you'd just told Rudy about this, she thinks, *he'd be here dealing with it and you'd be so much more. . . comfortable.*

She brings her thighs tighter together, but doesn't move otherwise.

Comfortable.

She stares at the phone. But no ring.

"FOX HILL WELLNESS CENTER uses innovative and traditional treatments to heal the resistant patient. At FOX HILL we employ up to the minute technology that. . ."

If she moves she will pee her pants.

She stares at the phone.

The phone sitting there.

What do they mean by WELLNESS, exactly. Or by CENTER. HILL. FOX.

Amandine winces her eyes shut.

If she gets up to pee, will Ruth call, will Ruth hang up, will Ruth disappear?

There was something else in Ruth's voice on that Friday message—not the same franticness that was always there before, not the fury that defined her.

Mom, I'm coming to see you, I think. I need money for a plane ticket, but I want to make—and a siren or something, it sounded like she was inside a nightclub, interrupted, but did she say peace? She wanted to make peace? And a few more syllables were garbled but then *before I take off on my journey.*

Click. Delete.

On my journey. . .

Something too final about that, something different.

Amandine knows this moment—Ruth's eyes have pinned her in this moment countless times. A test: will Amandine love enough the daughter she couldn't love at birth? Which action is the right one? A hug goodbye before school could be right one day, the next it would be a violation of freedom so acute as to set Ruth into a fury, enough to require a new windowpane, a new fruitbowl, a new remote control *and* a new garbage disposal.

But if Amandine wasn't paying attention *enough*? Bruises on Racinda's arms and legs the next day, or Ruth gone for three, and if Amandine was lucky, Ruth would call her collect from the other end of the state.

Ruth at fourteen, at fifteen, at sixteen, and Amandine learned to demure under Ruth's gaze, guess at which response her daughter might want.

Amandine knows now, with Ruth twenty-four, that these patterns are worn enough to cross time and space. She understands that if she makes one false move away from the phone that the consequence will not be as simple as Ruth sticking the remote control down the garbage disposal, smashing dishware.

Mr. Wills, the pastor whom Amandine works for, has told her stories about the Hindus, some of whom own a little grocery across the street from their church. The Hindu women of India, Mr. Wills says, are expected to set themselves on fire if their husbands die. The idolatrous women are expected to burn themselves to death.

Amandine has thought about this habit of the idolater widows more often than she'd readily admit. She's imagined it—her husband dying. What if Lyman had *died* rather than left her? What would her face have looked like before she poured the gasoline on herself? What would she be thinking before she lit the match?

If a woman were going to do that, she figured, the woman would be calm, would be unresisting, peaceful.

She imagined she could hear this same kind of ashen peace in Ruth's voice on that message.

Before I leave on my journey.

Amandine's thighs now locked together, one ankle twisted in a vise around the other, and she knows that if she gets up to pee. Ruth could throw lighter fluid on all three of them.

Love me enough: if not, a lit match.

Love me too much? Not let me fly? Pour on the kerosene, burn as I burn, a suicide whose main point is matricide.

Amandine cranes her neck, automatically, to be able to see herself in the mirror across the room. It's a small mirror, and it makes her head look smallish, pale, yet still put together, still attractive. She freezes herself in that glass, as if doing so will stop the progression.

But something is off in that reflection. The lines of her face seem different, suddenly, this morning. What is this! What has happened to her face? She's so concerned that she doesn't even try to take in the nature of the difference—it could even be an improvement, she can't tell yet. She leans forward, squints her eyes, and wouldn't you know it, leans forward just a little too far and ruins the perfect clamp-down position.

Runs, in her dainty slippers—massive footsteps thumping china against the cabinet—to the bathroom.

Ah.

Such relief!

And the phone doesn't ring!

So after she dries her hands on the clean peach towel she plants herself firmly in front of the wide, clean bathroom mirror, knowing now that she is capable of running for the phone—something her lackadaisical self of the weekend, of making Rudy go get the popcorn could never manage.

But what *is* this?:

The lines on Amandine's face—so familiar to her by now, at forty-five—have altered their course. She knows it, she can tell, she just can't decipher the effect. It's not that she looks any older, but what exactly *is* the quality these lines are giving her? She studies.

Yes, different since yesterday.

Yes—it's a positive difference, it seems, not fewer lines, and nothing anyone else would notice as such. They would just think, *Oh, Amandine is*

looking rather <u>capable</u> today. Or, Even though Amandine's got some trouble
with her daughters, she's looking, rather, happy, isn't she?

This has happened to her once before:

Nobody packed a house as fast and as perfectly as she packed up the
Pennsylvania farmhouse back in 1983. Nobody plotted an itinerary more
carefully to get her family across the country, on the northern route, in a
cold March. The farmer's almanac helped, and each morning, before
rousing the girls from their hotel bed, she checked the papers at the front
desk, and called the hotel chain's branches in the next three states, to get
the local forecasts there.

They had avoided two snowstorms this way.

Ruth had stopped being furious with her that trip. Ever since she got
back from Oak Acres to find Lyman gone, her mother busy and useful and
determined and decided, Ruth had started to believe that her mother was
capable, was worthy of respect.

Amandine barely looked at herself that trip. Enough to make sure that
she was presentable, enough to put on makeup, but she didn't really *look*.
Avoided mirrors in the rest stop bathrooms because any information they
would have provided her—that she was alone, that she was aging, that she
was lit by fluorescents, that she was in the middle of Nebraska—would be
nothing but depressing. She passed incidental mirrors—winter-dirty
panes of filling station offices, silver gas pumps throwing sun back onto
snow—without a thought as to her appearance. Her appearance didn't
matter. What mattered? Wheel tread on asphalt, missing the snowstorm,
knowing ahead of time the exit was from the left lane.

She understood that she finally had important things to do. She understood, in twilight moments, that she'd always had important things to do
but that there had been other people to do them for her.

So she didn't look in mirrors. She also didn't imagine forward, into
what sort of furnishings the house might have, how Ruth might excel in
some sport or other, what new friends Racinda might meet, nor backward
into painful stomach twists of wondering what she might have done differently to keep her husband around.

The challenge of it—unthinkable, months previous, that she, the one
who shrank, faded when Button simply came into a room, would be able
to get her two daughters across a continent—consumed all her attention.
Windshield, precipitation, defogger verses defroster, juice for the girls,

coffee for her, carefully timed meal stops planned out from the AAA guide, motel reservations double-checked each morning.

Awake, awake, awake.

She could have done sixteen, eighteen hours of driving in a day.

But what would more time in a sedan do to Ruth? Amandine stuck to six.

Awake, so planning, planning. Monitoring the oil gauge, the gas, the heat.

After beating a snowstorm, just getting out of Minnesota and into the eastern edge of South Dakota, the weather broke into spring. Nearing six o'clock they got to their little motel, with a huge field in back so lovely and muddy and breaking out of slow freeze that it didn't even creep little Racinda out that the place, the whole town, somehow, was in the shadow of an obvious prison, huge.

"We don't want to eat dinner!" Racinda said, jumping on the bed.

Amandine tensed—there were reservations somewhere, somewhere written in the tiny notebook in her purse.

"Girls, we eat dinner at six-thirty," she said.

"We don't want it!" Racinda yelled.

The happiness on this younger, grimmer daughter's face was too much to resist.

"Yeah, fuck dinner!" Ruth said.

Amandine rolled her eyes.

"Sorry," Ruth said, still temporarily fond of her mother, saving her hatred for Lyman these days.

"We want to go play outside!" Racinda squealed, slapping her upstretched palms against the stucco-lumpy ceiling as she jumped.

"Fine, go play in it," Amandine said, exhausted, happy, "Just wear your play clothes."

And the two ran, their feet tossing up behind them like those of that Indian widow Amandine would later imagine, the terrified but smart one, the one who refused to burn. Except her daughters' flew in glee—that great banisher of fear—at the sixty degree temperature, at the dusk that somehow had been convinced to hold off a little longer tonight.

Amandine lay back on the hotel bedspread for several minutes. It was the first time she'd had in days without at least one of girls—the car, the hotel rooms, the frigid air keeping them all glued together. Any deviation had seemed like a betrayal, but now with warmth in the sky there was room to wander.

She got up and shut the blinds almost completely, so that it seemed like dusk in the room. She removed her shoes, her neat skirt, her hose, her silk blouse and put them away neatly in the closet, reclining back in her pristine white half slip and bra. Knew she should snap on the pink nightcap that held her wig in place during sleep for this trip but decided not to. But even in the wig, she settled. She closed her eyes, then opened them in a panic—where was her purse? But there it was, right next to the television, the same place she put it in every hotel room.

An inch and a half of hundreds in the bottom of it—what she'd sold Lyman's wood carving tools and most of his mother's china for before she'd left.

Her eyes fluttered closed, flew open to check that purse—her stolen goods, right? Were they? Hadn't he stolen much more from *her*?

But then the quiet cradled her into immense solitude, and she navigated, in sleep, to its restless edge. Just out of her reach: a little rowboat, bobbing to and fro gently against a low bank. Roped to a dock. Birdsong, evergreen, clean dirt. She could hear, could smell, could see but could not will herself into this place.

She woke a little later, rose, bolstered by her girls' happiness, exhaled, went to the mirror.

Her hands on the glassy-smooth edge of the dresser, shoulders rounded, she looked, really looked, not in a rush, not in a blank, fast way, at her face, for the first time in more than a week, and the lines forming around her eyes were *different*. There was no denying. Before now, the lines had depressed her not because they aged her—no getting around age, she knew, she knew that in the right light she passed for twenty-six when she was now ten years older than that. Rather, her lines had always depressed her because they were the lines incurred by a woman who had spent every ounce of her being to do everything *right*. To do everything the way Lyman wanted, or the way that seemed presentable, acceptable, proper, publicly approvable, correct, classy without being showy.

All that effort, and here she was in a hotel room, a purse full of his pathetic money. Was it her money, rightly? She averted her eyes from the thing.

Used to be: lines earned by doing nothing. Path of least resistance lines. Could be anyone lines.

Lines on the face of the woman in the commercial selling soap, the woman who knows her husband's loyalties lie elsewhere—elsewhere than women—and keeps smiling, the woman who watches her figure, the dainty woman, the "attractive" woman, the complicit woman.

But now—

That new dip between lip and chin spoke of defiance. Spoke of surprising, hidden strength and ability come to light. Spoke of the beautiful rather than the pert.

She grinned.

The just-starting delta of shallow streams outside her eyes told of a woman who always got her girls dinner just after nightfall, a mother who knew how to take care of them, a woman who made decisions based on meteorological information, on her daughters moods, on when the oil needed to get changed or just replenished. A woman in charge, driving, squinting into a bright sunset that held the promise of a less terrified life.

(A laugh escaped Amandine then, as she could just *see* the soap lady in the commercial wash the makeup off—scrub it—as soon as possible after the director yells Cut. Amandine could see the bare-faced actress—in California, of course—hop in her convertible and drive until she gets to the road that links the mountains and the ocean, drive to a destination that is secret and indulgent and rare.)

So when Ruth and Racinda came barreling into the room, dripping in mud and rainwater, giddy and thrilled and all wound up from the breath of spring freedom, she let them hug her, and her perfect slip was soon as covered in dirt as they were. She jumped on the beds with them a few minutes before ordering them into the shower.

By the time everyone was done, the restaurant was closed.

"I'm not hungry anyway," Ruth said.

"Me either," Racinda said.

"We could try McDonalds, girls," Amandine said, but even that failed to catch their fancy.

Ruth whispered something to Racinda.

"Mom, we're not tired," Racinda said.

"Well, it's almost time for bed," Amandine said.

This phrase, miraculously, had worked thus far. It was as if both girls understood that everyone's survival meant keeping Ruth regular, routine, unmanic.

"We want to keep driving," Ruth said, her kinky white-blond hair blown crazy and unpredictable, stared straight into Amandine's eyes and gripped her forearms.

Amandine half-faked a soft, ineffectual expression to try to calm Ruth down.

But the breeze coming in the window did make it seem to Amandine like it was possible to keep going, like some great pleasure or adventure was to be had in a night of driving. The doctor had said, though, absolutely no variance: keeping Ruth to a routine was the best way to calm the banshee in her. The exacting schedule had somehow worked until now, and Amandine clung to it. They had already *paid* for this hotel room, obviously they weren't going to check out now, plus it was dangerous for a woman to be alone at night on the interstate, plus the girls would get hungry, and Amandine didn't have any reservations for them. She didn't know *when* they would get hungry, she didn't know where they would be, she didn't know if they would run out of gas.

"No, girls," Amandine said, moving her head to avoid Ruth's gaze. "We've got a plan and we're sticking to the plan."

That was the wrong answer. Ruth's eyes narrowed and she slammed into the bathroom, turned the shower on full blast, found something—what could it *possibly* be—to throw to the floor noisily every minute or so.

Amandine and Racinda sat on the bed in silence.

Amandine drew her knees to her chest.

It had not been the answer Ruth wanted to hear. But it was the right answer. Wasn't it? What the doctor said.

(Something *metal* Ruth was throwing to the tile.)

Amandine tightened her knees to her and closed her eyes, *Jesus, what is the answer here?*

But he wasn't showing up either.

She touched the corners of her eyes, the fine streams there, pulling toward her temples gently as she lowered her lids.

(The actress in California forgets her shoes in the car, leaves the top down, crosses a lawn barefoot as the ocean air licks off the last of the makeup, a path snakes across a ridge, high branches whistle and bend, a door opens.)

Amandine stood quickly, gently, and went to the sliding door that opened onto a small concrete patio. West, in the direction opposite the brightly-lit prison, the stars seemed dense as sugar crystals in a teaspoon, bright and wild.

"Pack up," Amandine said, "And go tell your sister. I'll be back in five minutes after I check out and I want you both *ready*."

*   *   *

At the same time that the hugeness of the night seemed to gobble them up, stars seemed to drench them in light. Westward in darkness strewn with white beams from above, ancient pale messages. When both girls were awake at once, it seemed as if the three of them were one person, out here, coming up on the badlands, deep carved rivers and gullies and plateaus and inlets, now empty, moonish, the ancient Dakota ocean no less beautiful for its age and loss of water.

For entire hours the three had free reign in the realm of each others' thoughts. And when one of the girls would fall asleep, or when Amandine would drift into her own world, out *here*, it didn't seem like a betrayal to anyone. Somehow, out here, there was enough space for the three of them to separate without becoming furious at her, at Amandine, there was enough room, enough light, enough darkness, enough lunar curves and nooks and dimeturns in the falling-back Dakota Badlands behind them for Amandine to zip into herself, to leave her girls for a minute or an hour or a good chunk of a night without Ruth or Racinda, in their loud and quiet ways, to become hellbent on matricide.

* * *

They canceled reservations, they detoured, they preferred to drive at night, they preferred to eat pancakes by starlight, singing to the AM stations, *Breakfast 24-Hours*, postponing laundry until California.

* * *

And Amandine remembers, now, nearly ten years later, here in her peach-painted Sacramento bathroom, now with the girls grown, the problems grown, the matricide repeated again and again in their vicious stares and their invectives, here in her own bathroom Amandine remembers later in 1983 when her face shifted back to its old lines, its predicted, proscribed path. They'd arrived in Sacramento, gotten all unpacked, washed all the Dakota mud from the girls jeans, broken down and recycled the cardboard boxes, revived a schedule, hung hooks for the dishtowels, curtains in the bathroom, prints in cheap frames, a few portraits of our savior in the living room. And Amandine got very good very fast at her job at the church, very accustomed to anticipating the daily, the hourly needs of the office, which is to say the needs of Mr. Wills, the preacher, and she cooed and she complied and she begged for forgiveness for her sins, these sins such great reminders to do as she was expected to do, and the lines on her face went back to those predictable ones. Tame ones. She found ways to forget about how depressing this was, and then she pretty much forgot the other lines ever happened. The struggle to survive—keep Ruth alive, keep the girls in jeans and carpool, keep herself in lotion and wigs—took over.

And so now, in this same bathroom that she'd witnessed her return to what was expected of her, she can tell that there has been some change.

She grins, but it's possibly just from the relief of not having such awful pressure still on her bladder.

What is it that's different? She sucks her cheeks in as is the habit of many women her age, but that just makes her smile and grin some more.

But then when it hits her the grin goes away completely:

Her face—now, *today*—is a face that doesn't have anyone to lean on. It's the face of that mother who knew how to get her girls across eleven states without the sick one having a breakdown, but the only way she gets to have those wrinkles, instead of her previous, cowardly ones, is by not doing as she's told.

It's the face of not having Button, Lyman, Elmer to fall back on, having no one.

In other words, it's the face of being shit out of luck.

That's the face, yes.

It's a face that doesn't have anyone to lean on.

As if her face itself has decided the choice she will make, so that she doesn't have to spend forever weighing the decision.

Shit out of luck.

She throws the peach towel to the floor.

The place Rudy wants to send Ruth to is *wrong*. For Ruth, for everyone. And Amandine knows it but—

She wants to keep laughing, she wants to keep dancing, she doesn't want to be locked in the house with Racinda, worrying about whether or when or how Ruth is going to die.

If Rudy is there to take care of Ruth, *he* can carry that load for her. But he doesn't even want to carry it—he wants to send Ruth to FOX HILL WELLNESS CENTER.

The problem is that short of that, this will keep going and going, Amandine will be put in this same position for the rest of her life—will Ruth live or will Ruth die. Panic stretches out in her throat.

She retches, coughs until tears bead her eyes.

Even Jesus, even Jesus can't seem to fix her girl, but she asks him for the millionth time anyway, for there is no way she can continue to carry this load, there is no way she can be the self-determined person that the new wrinkles on her face somehow think she has become.

She begs.

*   *   *

He's not coming to help her now

Help me Jesus help me Jesus help me Jesus help me Jesus help me.

Amandine holds the phone tight without picking it up—she can feel the ring shake her to her jaw, to the base of her spine.

Ruth?

Or Rudy?

Jesus please help me Lord.

She has unplugged the answering machine and she doesn't know what to do.

Rudy?

Ruth?

Ring.

She doesn't want to lose the lindy hop, or the way Rudy's funny gray sideburns tickle her cheek when he pecks her goodbye, or when he looks at her with a face that can only be thinking *what did I do to deserve such an angel?*

But what is she going to say about Ruth?

Rudy, you know, let's just call it off.

Or

Not that *place for Ruth, I don't think, do you?*

Certainly, certainly the lines on her face have made a mistake.

Oh Jesus help me.

She doesn't wait to make the decision, but as sure as the past of those Dakota badlands held a crushing weight of water, the lines on her face name her next move.

The lines tell a story of a woman at the mercy of her own volition—the lines have skipped ahead in the story, already told her she can't remain propped up on a man. She just doesn't know *how* the lines get there, and she has no idea what to do to get the present to match up to the future they've already told her.

427

She doesn't know what that next move is. She can't imagine herself making it.

Ring.

*   *   *

"Mom."

"Ruth. Honey—"

Amandine loses her words, averts her eyes determinedly from the brochure—pins her stare on the front door, tries to remember what Rudy told her, what strategies he mentioned for not scaring off Ruth, for getting Ruth to come in their direction rather than run straight away.

"So, hey, mom," Ruth says.

"Hi, honey," she sighs, relaxes a bit.

"How's it hanging, mom?"

"Good. How are you, dear?"

She tries to force the badlands back off her face, trying to get the porcelain perfect cracks back.

"Jeez, Mom," Ruth says, "How am I *ever* doing?"

How can I possibly take care of her? Amandine ducks for cover, she woos her old daze and it returns, cell by cell, slowly overcoming her.

Jesus help me Jesus help me Jesus—

No.

Rudy?

No.

Ly—

No.

"Just joshin, Ma," Ruth says, "I'm *actually* doing real well, I'm full of direction and zip and *enthusiasm* and energy and—"

"Mania."

Amandine says it.

This is *not* part of Rudy's strategy, she believes. His strategy has to do with never violating Ruth's ideas of herself until she's been wooed back under their control.

Control. Amandine's eyes crinkle in a dry sad smile. Right. Just *control* her.

"Jesus, Mom! Mom, look, I know you think that's the whole problem and you want me to come to the therapy first but there's some stuff I need to take *care* of here, like 300 bucks and then plane fare—"

"Ruth—"

"or a bus ticket, whatever. Whatever, that's fine, that's fine, that's cool."

"Ruth, where are you? I thought you were still in San Francisco."

"I'm in Philly."

"What?"

"I'm in Philly. I'm feeling—I don't want to take the bus. I want the plane."

"I don't—you want *how* much then? That's about six hundred dollars—"

"Seven would do it."

A skateboard, a motorcycle, a delivery truck go past the house.

"Mom?"

"Yes?" Amandine manages through a throatful of grief, of silence.

The refrigerator hums, the phone line hums.

"Ruth I've given you . . ."

". . . money. . ." Ruth says.

". . already. . ." Amandine says.

The two of them listening for a click, neither hanging up.

Given her so much. . .

But what have I really given her? Amandine wonders, and guilt ties the grief into knots. Just money, and I've given her that porcelain face. A soap commercial.

"Ruth—I can't just—We talked about this. I can't just give you money—you lost your trust with me when I gave it to you the last few times"

"Mom I'm not on speed anymore how many times do I have to tell you I stopped that crazy shit and now I just need to get back there to get some therapy and that will all be fine fine fine, god I can't believe you—"

Amandine takes a breath and leans into her new face tentatively, as if it is a mask someone is holding in front of her, ready to snug the elastic behind her ears, as if she is about to press her face into some *other* woman's decision.

"Tell me where to find you and I will bring you the money, Ruth. We will talk about it then and we will get you into some kind of therapy, something you want, and I will bring you back on the plane myself."

"God, I'm not like fucking twelve at the Oak Acres school mom, fucking trust me would you."

And Ruth hangs up.

And then the phone starts ringing again as soon as she sets it down.

Exhale.
Ruth?
Rudy?
Rudy.

"Are you ready for the good news?" he says.

"Mmmm," she says, and she tries to make it sound hopeful but that syllable obviously conceals tears.

"I think I found Racinda," he says.

The skateboarder returns, the delivery truck pulls away. There is no motorcycle.

Amandine can't think of anything to say. She wants to be sitting in the car next to him, she wants the smoothness of the drive when he shifts gears so expertly, but the brochure—not for Racinda, for Ruth, but still—

She doesn't want him near her girls anymore.

"Hello? Amandine."

"Yes."

"I mean—" Rudy gets flustered, "I'm almost certain I've *got* her."

The hum of the refrigerator. Or is it the heat.

"Amandine?"

"Really," Amandine says.

"Yes, well, I'm—fairly—certain," he says.

The hum is the heat.

"We—well if it doesn't pan out, it will be a nice drive down the peninsula, you and me, what do you say?" he says.

"Rudy—" and a little sob catches in her throat.

"Yes, dear?"

"That. That sounds. . . fine . . ."

But her voice is deadened, bored, unenthused, unbelieving.

"Is something—wrong?" he says, "something else?"

"No," she says.

"Well," he says.

Every time she suddenly seems a continent away from him, like now, he wonders what it is that he's done wrong? The lack of progress he's made finding her first daughter? The ensuing loss of the second one? Maybe she thinks he, Rudy, drove Racinda away? No, that's crazy. A pang, introducing the worse fear that he simply isn't up to her level, isn't equal to the beauty he sees as exquisite, or to her regal demeanor. The fear that Amandine is simply bored of him. He's tried to upgrade—to take her to a play, say, but she insisted instead on the movie about the St. Bernard again. No, it must just be that she knows he's not the best man for the investigative job anymore, that his glory days of wooing young people back from cults are over, that his connections have mostly retired or changed fields.

"Well. . . " he says again, but she remains silent.

The pang. He wants her back in conversation with him, wants her interest and her laughter.

"Well," he says, "even if it's not Racinda, on the other front, we've got some *very* good news on *Ruth* from my friend who works at that program I mentioned for her, Fox Hill. He said they've found a space for her, definitely, they can get her in as early as next week, should by some miracle we find her by then."

Shoot, he thinks, she could hear the pathetic eager beaver in my voice if I mailed that as a telegram.

Amandine pauses.

"We could get her into Fox Hill immediately," he says, "They can get right to work."

How can he *possibly* tell her the *bad* news about Ruth now?

But suddenly she sounds as if her face has widened, turned to him, full of nervous—no, excited, even *pleased* energy.

"Really?" she says with what he interprets as genuine excitement.

See, old dog, he says to himself, she just wants a man who can do his job. You've still got it. We'll find these girls. I'll just tell her the bad news a little *later*.

"Um, what about Racinda, what did you say about Racinda?" Amandine says, and emits a strange titter.

"Well, we can go see if it's Racinda down the peninsula today, if you'd like. I'll book us into a hotel and we can make a trip of it. But, you know, on the Ruth front—" and his voice drops a few notes.

"Where's Racinda?" Amandine says, "Let's talk about Racinda right now, Rudy. I want you to tell me everything you know. About Racinda."

Amandine packs fast, leaves the phone number of the bed and breakfast on her outgoing message, and when Rudy shows up at her door, an hour later, she hears the click of the lock behind her and, smart valise in one hand, purse hooked neatly over the other shoulder, tries not to think of how the lock's sound resembles, somehow, the striking of a match.

*   *   *

He doesn't tell her about Ruth until they get on to the 680, about an hour into the drive.

"Actually," he says finally, "I found some more information out about Ruth's activity recently."

"What," Amandine says, softly, not looking at him.

"Well," he says, "I'm not quite sure how to tell you this," he says, and her fingers grip the velour under her seat so hard that it separates just slightly from its molding.

"I talked to the old roommate," he says.

"Cynthia," she says, voice dreamy. Watching scenery turning winter green.

"Yes, Cynthia, who in general we know to be a bit unreliable because of the drugs, of course, but whenever there's money involved—Ruth owes her back rent—very easy to predict."

"Mm-hmm."

"So, she says that Ruth has become an acolyte of a mystic-claiming yoga guru. So, Amandine, your instincts were right—there is some sort of cult activity going on."

"I knew it," she says. She jumps slightly in her seat.

"There, there," he says, but she is wondering if the cult could be any worse, really, than the place Rudy wants to send Ruth.

"Wheeere's—" she says, groping for something, anything, to get him off the trail of her elder daughter, "Where's Racinda, exactly?"

"In a minute," he says, "And Ruth apparently wants to follow this guru to the third world."

"The third world?"

"India."

There is all of a sudden no air in the car, but Amandine has considerable practice faking it in this sort of situation. When oxygen seeps back in, minutes later, she's trying to hide the fact that she's twisting her hands so tightly together.

"There, there," Rudy says, taking her left hand in his right, cooling it, never taking his eyes from the road, "There, there, dear."

*   *   *

"We're here looking for Racinda Hart," Rudy says.

"And who might you be, there, sir?" Annette says, her eyes pitched up at him with a reproach that would be clear to anyone but a white man of a certain age.

"This is her mother."

Amandine nods.

"Well, I'm Annette. And you are?"

"Amandine."

"Amandine. Nice to meet you, and—"

"Rudy Mitchell, PI"

"P...I?"

"That's—"

"I know what that stands for. Hang on. Nae?" Annette says, looking over her shoulder.

Amandine shifts her weight onto Rudy, leaning against him like a teenager. She's still trying to distract him from Ruth, so she's got that franticness to her a little bit, but it's blooming into genuine hope that Racinda is here.

"Oh, she is getting on my last nerve," Annette says and clanks her new necklace (not my favorite of what she's made in her night class, actually) against her collarbone, "She was *right* here and then she always just disappears like a ghost. Her door's shut, let me try her line."

Amandine grips the counter, but otherwise her face, her body, are slack. Rudy stands up straighter, leans forward infinitesimally as Amandine slumps slightly.

"No, not answering. Oh," Annette says, taking in Amandine's weariness, "I can see—you really are her mother, aren't you," she laughs. "I can tell because you look like how *my* mother looked for awhile there. You can't tell if you're more scared for her or more furious at her. Well, I can't tell you if she *is* here without some documentation, but I can tell you if she *isn't* here—let me see if there's anyone here by that—there's no one I know of, someone could have come in though while I was off. . . spelled R-A-C-I-N-D-A?"

Amandine nods.

Annette shakes her head.

"No, nothing, so sorry. You know, you might try General up in the city."

"Look, I know she's here," Rudy says, "Is this the number of your pay phone?"

He shows her the circled collect call on Joey's phone bill. It had been sitting right on the dresser, in Joey's garage apartment, next to the phone, and that little Max didn't notice him slip it into the pocket of his sportcoat.

"Well, to be honest, I don't know *what* really goes on in that phone booth there," Annette says, biting her lip and wincing conspiratorially. "I stick to the desk myself. You can feel free to go check the number—I *think* it's on the phone—when Ernest is done."

Ernest, in a too-thick, too-tight argyle sweater and corduroys two sizes too big for him gestures emphatically with the hand that isn't gripping his face in there, talking, surely, to a dial tone, as is his habit.

Rudy folds up the Pac Bell bill in a way to demonstrate his hurry, but those two aren't going anywhere. He snugs his arm around thin old Amandine and guides her over to the waiting room chairs. They both sit down tentatively, not resting their backs for support, not leaning on the metal handles. Oh, the typical shyness of germs in a hospital but especially a mental ward.

Ridiculous. We know about Amandine and her proximity to the other-worldly and the deranged. And *Rudy*—what is a PI, anyway, if not a chaser of the craziness behind the heart? A spy in there behind the dark ventricles with an infrared scope, searching out everything we do that is so unfathomable, and so precedented. Rudy's life, before the cult-thing, was the life of a regular PI, tracking and fathoming and explaining and putting into a tidy file the man who rips out the throat of his beloved, the mother who sneaks out in the night with someone else's husband, the insurance salesman who has never gotten a speeding ticket but starts selling coke when some sociopath he meets in a bar suggests it might bring in enough extra cash for a jet-ski. A PI is a secret agent for the Rationals, endlessly chasing the inexhaustible Inexplicable.

Yeah, it takes one to know one.

Knock knock knock—

Ernest freezes.

Pound, pound.

"Look there, we just need in there for a minute. Sir, I have to ask that you come out right now," Rudy says.

Ernest hides behind his hands.

The phone dangles in a shadow. The dial tone starts blaring into an operator's recorded voice. Ernest presses himself up against the wall as if trying to disappear.

Which, as far as Ernest is concerned, works, because Rudy simply leans in, checks the number on the little white rectangle covered in plastic on the pay phone, then shuts the door again without even looking at Ernest's hidden face.

Ernest sweats in relief.

Rudy winks at Amandine.

"She's here?"

"You betcha! Same number, she's here, " Rudy says, and the blue eyes brim with success and vigor.

The wideness of that midnight Dakota sky in 1983 floods Amandine and she is too full of anything to make a peep, to cry, though it's a feeling like crying. Racinda, honey, Racinda is *here* and the undertow of that brochure FOXHILLWELLNESSCENTER noses in and demands to be dealt with but even that, even that can't take away from the joy of this.

Huge, huge sky, breakfast every hour.

"Miss—Annette! Annette!" Rudy yells as he strides over to the nurses station.

The sight of Rudy, a big, *sane* man bellowing through the ward is unusual.

"Miss Annette!"

Annette is bent under the desk picking up the rows of staples she just spilled, and takes her good time standing up.

"Mmmm," she says, the distaste for his Rudeness loud enough that even *he* can tell.

"She *is* here! She must be here under an alias. We have the missing persons report right here, and—Amandine?—here, she has a photograph. Amandine?"

Amandine doesn't need to hear *she's here*. She *knows* Racinda is near her now. And she smiles a little, despite the sadness in her chest, because that sadness is the good kind, the growing kind, the kind of sadness no love is without, and Amandine is reminded it is a sadness she can carry, a sadness that she in fact has carried quite often since that drive across cornfields and wheatfields and night fields of desperate interstate towns almost ten years ago, a sadness that does not keep her from stepping forward now to the nurses station, from opening her California fall white leather purse and sliding the blue-tinged photograph of Racinda last year--cigarette in hand, arms around her legs—across the formica counter to Annette.

"Oh, *Exene*!" Annette says. "She told us her name was Exene Cer—I always forget—Exene *Cervenka*."

"What?" Amandine says.

Rudy shrugs, points his face back at Annette whose dislike of him has by now gelled into the standard professional demeanor.

"Where is she? What sort of auspices are you holding her under here?" he says.

"Well,—we run an unusual sort of rehabilitation program here," Annette says, and Amandine's stomach drops four stories. "I'll ask Nae to give you the tour et cetera but here is some literature we give to families you can peruse while you wait in the waiting room."

*   *   *

Though she usually lets Rudy do it, Amandine introduces herself to this nurse who will explain things—*a bit strange*, Amandine thinks, *something a bit strange about this nurse Nae.* She's genteel, though the edge comes up quicker, nervous—this woman she is meeting, *Nae* Williams, the head of the rehabilitation program, seems familiar to her and irks her in the way someone who seems to see through you before you even have spoken with them can irk.

"So we've really enjoyed your daughter. She's made great progress with us."

"Let's get down to business," Rudy says. "What kind of program are you running here?"

"Well, it's a holistic program, for our more high-functioning patients. We stress life-skills as well as body-mind awareness."

"Yoga? Chanting?" Rudy says.

"Well, some of that."

Cult, Rudy is thinking, *definite cult.* He nods grimly and frowns. *Look at this woman*, he thinks, *Nae, is it? the faraway look to her and that smile that keeps coming up. Brainwashed. Here in a hospital!*

"Also, there's a rather intense physical detoxification and massage element, it goes along with working in the vegetable garden out back and preparing meals—a hard work component has been crucial to our successes."

Snort.

Yoga? Amandine is thinking. Yoga? To Amandine, that word is synonymous with *idol* with *adultery* with *pagan* with *Hell's Angel.*

The idolaters are going to burn up *both* her girls!

"I'm a bit concerned, I have to say, because Exene—Racinda, excuse me—still clearly needs a bit of time with us, but since she isn't actually a minor as she has been telling us, the funding to keep her here isn't going to remain available indefinitely."

"Lady, this is verging on mind control, and we're pulling her out as soon as you tell us where she is in here!" Rudy says.

Amandine nods determinedly.

"You know what, sir?"

Rudy feels a tinge bad—seeing a woman back away from him, seeing a nurse—even one he thinks is so misguided—shrink from him not in fear, exactly, but close enough, shames him adequately that he softens his features, becomes willing to negotiate.

"Yes, ma'am, I'm sorry if I got overdramatic there."

"Well, no problem. You know, though, that as she is legally an adult you have no say as to whether or not she stays or goes. She gets to choose herself whether she wants to stay as long as the funding lasts."

Amandine waits until the last minute then grabs a tissue from the box on the desk to keep the snot from running down onto her lip. She dabs daintily at the tears first. *Yoga?* She thinks, and sees her baby with six arms, shaking her belly like "I Dream Of Jeannie," skin blue like the cartoon-looking goddess at the Indian grocery across the street from the church. Blue skin charred black, peeling off bone in a pyre. . .

"But there isn't funding for her, so she's out?" Rudy says.

"Well, she's still got a few weeks left before her paperwork goes through, but then after that we'd really have to scramble to get any for her."

"Where is she, my baby?" Amandine says, that strong mother she provided her daughter in South Dakota shaking like jelly here in my office, thrown to bits by the new territory she thinks she's in of having *two* daughters in cults, this latest of which is, horrifyingly enough, medically sanctioned and state-funded.

Rudy stands, himself a little shaken just by Amandine's sadness and fear. He stands next to her, rubs a tender circle on her back.

"Nae," he says, "Just show us. Where's the girl?"

"I'll tell her you're here," I say, my eyes narrowing, his bluster starting to piss me off even though his wide, deep heart is underneath it all. "It's up to her whether she wants to see you or not."

This is all very wrong, this thing of me seeing Racinda and her mother so clearly. I have certain . . . *barriers* up, let's say, ever since I got divorced and Californized and name-changed and sober fifteen years ago, and these barriers have grown stronger even since then. But when I run into cases out of my past—even little piddly ones I totally forgot about, from my grocery-store psychic days—I can't ease out so automatically. And I get a little tempted, honestly, sometimes, to know the ends of the stories. Except by now it's way into the *beginnings* of so many other stories, these folk are from so long ago, and I get all spun around and out of whack and my energy gets taken away—fine, yes, *I* let it go that way—from the work at hand which is this clinic, this program. This is the worst case yet—I know better—Racinda is just *such* a piece of work, and Ruth! Ever since I figured out who'd popped in on me here the bits me behind my heart want to keep peeking in on them, and I just haven't been able to resist.

*   *   *

"Excuse me? Nae, what are you talking about! What? *WHAT?* Excuse me, but fuck that. Send them the fuck home," Racinda says.

"Honey, look, they can't make you do anything, *Racinda*," I eye her mock-accusatorily though I've known her real name for a while now. "Now that we know that you're a legal adult, they can't do anything."

"Fuck that, Nae. I'm not talking to them. Fuck her."

"Racinda," I say.

"No."

I avoid biting my lip as I'm trying to figure out what to do here. Fine, it's up to her. Hands off. But you know what, I don't really think she needs it here as bad as I said—I *hate* it when they use the protection of the hospital past the point when they need it. She's strong enough now, she's just hiding out. Regressing.

"Well, if you want to stay here you're going to have to talk to them, because your funding was dependent on you being a minor, toots. The only other option is transferring to General."

She's heard the horror stories. She goes pale. But still refuses:

"Sorry," she says.

"Suit yourself."

She doesn't notice that I swing the door wide so it catches and stays open as I leave, why should she.

"Sorry," I tell Amandine and Rudy back out in the hallway. "There's nothing I can do."

I wink at Amandine though.

"You might try our *other* exit, though, go out that way," and I shrug my head in the direction of the hallway containing Racinda's open door, "You'll get to see our gardens—I'm very proud of the work the patients do—on your way to the parking lot."

Amandine furrows her brown in confusion—I nod.

"It's a much better way to leave than how you came in. Trust me," I say, and Amandine is about to place my voice when Rudy distracts her, saying goodbye for both of them and leading her away.

*　　　*　　　*

"Fuck!" Racinda says.

Amandine and Rudy, middle-aged detectives, stop in front of her door and bend sideways at the waist, just slightly, in unison, to peek into her room.

"Fuck."

Rudy grimaces, Amandine's face quivers.

Racinda yields immediately to her mother's rushing hug.

"Fuck, I told them not to let you in," Racinda says over Amandine's shoulder.

"We just got lucky, I guess," Rudy says.

"Fuck I am *not* leaving here."

"No one said you were going anywhere, dear. Now Racinda," Rudy says. "I *know* you like tulips."

They are perfect for her—two dozen of them a lush, tremendous bunch, purple unto black. His fist barely fits around the fat bunch of stems. He must have set them in the waiting room during his little investigation of the phone booth—a miracle no one stole them.

When Amandine lets go of her, Racinda cranes her chin to see him arranging them in the water pitcher. She sighs, gives in.

"Thanks, Rudy."

"No problem. Now what are they feeding you in this joint? What do you say we go get a burger?" he says.

"Mom," she says, sniffling, trying to hide her own tears as Amandine hugs her the second time.

A girlish, giddy grin spreads across Amandine's face as she braces her hands on her daughter's shoulders.

"Look, Mom, I'm sorry I didn't call," she says, swallowing, biting her cheek.

"No problem, Racinda," Rudy says, and Amandine nods and giggles, hugging Racinda the third time.

"I don't *eat* burgers, Rudy."

"Pizza?" he says, eyes innocent and genuine, somehow. Racinda's skin seems softer, younger, as if it has soaked up rest and water, given away enough years to be the face of a thirteen-year-old.

Racinda sighs, closes her eyes. Breathes for a minute, and Rudy and Amandine exchange worried glances that give way to the irrepressible happiness of reunion once Racinda opens her eyes and has made a decision.

"Yes, sure. I would *love* to go get some lunch with you two nutcases," Racinda says and the awkward little pause on Rudy and Amandine's faces gives way fast to more of that irrepressible glee.

*   *   *

The rooms Amandine and Rudy have taken in the B&B in Hillsdale are overdone in a way more typical to the East Coast—frills, pink wallpaper with red fleurs-de-lis flying in delirious verticals, uncomfortable part-acrylic ruffles running the edges of every pillowcase. Racinda lowers her head, happily full after too many pieces of thin-crust pizza heavy with prosciutto and greens. That the outside input—even the strip malls and the traffic and the could-be-So-Cal landscape of Silicon Valley—was so welcome and calming and occasionally invigorating to her is—even she knows it—a sign that it is almost time to reemerge into the world. But she doesn't know how, or where, or for what purpose, so she ignores the question, just cruises on her body's thrill at nearly raw, thin-sliced red meat. Alone in Amandine's room, she zooms into a dreamy nap while Amandine and Rudy make Ruth-related phone calls from Rudy's room.

"What? You guys, I'm so asleep," Racinda says into the phone when it's become clear after about ten rings that whoever's calling isn't going to give up.

"Creature?"

"Ruth?"

"What are you doing there?"

"I'm—I"

"I figured this was like some Christian conference thingee Amandine was away at," Ruth said. "Did the Blood of the Lamb finally *getcha?*"

"No, Ruth. Fuck."

"So..."

"So."

"You never called me back, Creech."

"You were fucking strung out on speed."

"Well, sorry about that. You know. I was living with Cynthia, it was impossible to live there without being on speed."

"Right, it's not *your* fault or anything."

"Fuck you—I got off that shit. Do you know how hard that is to do?"

Silence.

"You *are* a feisty one lately aren't you."

"WELL, Ruth, now that you're not here to hog all the freak outs some of the rest of us get to have emotions as well."

"Oh ouch, you're just such the martyr, you never got *any* attention for being so perfect and quiet now did you?"

"Fuck you, Ruth."

"..."

"..."

"Creech—sorry."

"What?"

"Um, sorry."

"So where are you anyway, Ruth? Are you still in San Francisco?"

"Philly, baby."

"Philly!"

"Yeah, well you know—if I tell you this you can't tell Amandine."

"I won't."

"Yeah right, she's got you at her Christian *conference* with her! Sorry creach!"

"It's not a fucking conference."

"What is it then. It's a bed and breakfast, they said that when they answered. Are you like on a vacation with your *mommy*? Didn't you find a boyfriend yet?"

"Fuck you."

"Poor baby."

"Up yours. Why are you calling her? I thought she wasn't going to deal until you are sober."

"I *am* sober."

"You *are?*"

"Yes. Well I mean no speed or coke or whatever. I mean I smoke a little weed, you know, you know it's like calming but nothing harsh."

"Right."

"It's true. Believe what you want."

"I will."

"Fine."

"*Fine*," Racinda sings it and curls up into a little ball.

They listen to each other breathing.

"I really am, Creech."

"*Fine.*"

They listen to each other breathing some more.

"Ruth, wait, why are you calling her?"

"I talked to her this morning. I need money."

"Jeez."

"Not for drugs. Not for drugs."

"What for?"

"I can't tell you."

"Well what did you tell Amandine it was for?"

"I have to—pay this guy, and then a plane ticket."

"*Right.*"

"But its—I swear it's for something good I just can't tell her, she'll freak. She's such a fucking Puritan Born Again prude white girl."

"I don't think she'd disagree except for the 'fucking' part."

"So anyway, Creech honey, it is so amazing to talk to you sweetie honey, what happened with the boyfriend."

"Oh, God. Well," Racinda said, "I just today left the mental ward."

"You—"

"Yeah, I'm not lying. Except, I think I'm. . . going back."

"Which one?"

"Santa Clara Residences in—"

"Oh god, *Nae's* program!"

"What?"

"Yeah, I did that for like two weeks but then the funding ran out."

"I can't believe this. I can't even have my own *breakdown*."

"You went crazy, Creech?"

"Well, I took some bad acid, and then, yeah . . . I guess I sorta . . ."

"How's the yoga."

"Oh my god. I call her the Dentist it hurts so bad. I'm so happy mom sprung me from class, today, actually."

"I know. I *hated* that back then. I actually, Creech you're not going to believe it but I am very into that shit now."

"What?"

"I swear."

"Well don't tell Amandine—she thinks you're in a cult."

"What?"

"One of the nurses who is also a Born Again at the last. . . place you were before that evil crackhead roommate—she told Amandine she found quote cult materials in your room after you left. This nurse called like a *year* or something after you left there, said she just felt she *had* to. . .a Christian nurse."

"The JC Mafia!"

"I *know*. And so—wait, stop it—shut *up*, Ruth, listen to me—so Amandine has this guy Rudy who is a cult deprogrammer and they have been trying to find you for like all summer—while I was kind of having my breakdown."

"What?"

"A *cult* deprogrammer."

"Oh. My. Goddess."

"He's actually—he's actually kind of nice."

"Creature if you are on their side of this I am hanging up the phone right fucking now."

"I'm not—Ruth—I'm not but he's just—I mean I know he's wrong about it or whatever but he's not a bad guy, he's just like all military and shit."

"What-*ever*," Ruth sings. "I'm hanging up."

"Don't! Ruth, don't. She didn't tell me she talked to you. What is she telling you? I'd fucking watch it, it's a fucking trap. Oh my god, Ruth, I can't believe she's like trying to get me and then like also trying to trap you. Ruth I swear, I don't think Rudy is that bad but—I dunno, this *deprogrammer* literature—it's scary—I mean I'm sure you could handle them but—wait I think I saw his brochure in here, god Amandine's like practically dating him and she's still hauling around his brochure like he's in People magazine. Wait hang out let me go grab it--"

"She's *dating* him?"

"Well I don't know. What does that even mean? She's not even divorced from Dad really."

"Yes she is."

"Ruth—what?"

"She did it last year, Creech."

"How do you *know* that?"

"I have this friend who looked her up on the computer. It's in public records."

"Thanks, Mom, for the info."

"No shit."

"Let me go get his brochure, it's scary but it's also fucking hilar—"

". . ."

"Racinda?"

"I'm here. Holy. . . ."

"What. WHAT."

"It's not—Ruth it's not *Rudy's* brochure. It's this brochure for this place in Mendocino—it's *shock* therapy."

"What?"

"Shit—Fox Hill Wellness. . . something something. . . *'Electroconvulsive Therapy has been much maligned in recent years but for serious cases not showing improvement with more commonly used contemporary treatments it can provide. . .'* I don't know if they want it for you or for me."

"Obviously not you, Creech. . ."

"Ruth. . ."

". . ."

"Come on, Ruth."

". . ."

"I'm going to go, Creech," her voice is smaller now, sad, "I don't—I don't even *need* to get the money from her. There's this thing—"

"Don't go, Ruth please don't go."

"There's this thing. . ."

"What," Racinda asks, "What. Ruth, please?" She's crying now.

"Button's talking."

"WHAT?"

"Button's talking."

"Like in your head?"

"Fuck you, Creature."

"Shut up, what do you mean? How do you *know* she's talking? Did you go see her?"

"I called there. She picked up her *phone*. Like you just picked up the phone. I just sort of out of like. . . I just sort of like would call her sometimes, it never did anything but I just liked to call the place where she was, the people who were with her. . .*wishing* I could *talk* to her, you know?" Ruth chokes herself back, "But then this time I called the place and I said Button Hart and the receptionist chick put me through and *Button* answered."

"Was she—was she like *clear?*"

"Weeeelll, *kind* of. Kind of but not really but I mean it seems like maybe she might—is that your bread and bek—bed and breakfast *door* opening?"

"No!"

"Omigod, Creech, if you are *in* on this."

"I'm not—Ruth. I'm not—"

But it isn't the door—who knows what Ruth heard. The dial tone shows up fast and when Racinda star sixty-nines nothing happens—the hotel phone system prevents it from working.

"Fuck. Mom! MOM—..."

As she slams out into the vanilla-candle-scented hallway Racinda is overwhelmed with the sense memory of how her mother's thin skin shakes just perceptibly right before she breaks into tears, she is overwhelmed with layers of memory, with her mother spouting tongues like cheap affirmations.

The fury grows in Racinda, from something the size of a billiard ball behind her stomach to a thundering *what the fuck do you think you're doing* as she pounds on Rudy's door long and hard enough to leave a bruise on the length of her fist for a week, scaring Rudy enough that he excuses himself and practically tiptoes—for a big man, a feat—all the way down to the lobby.

Rudy nods to Amandine as he leaves, and though she clings to him for a second, she vows to look her daughter right in the eye when the screaming stops.

"Shock treatment?" Racinda says.

"What are you talking about Racinda?" Amandine says, but diverts her gaze to the cheap metal runner at the edge of the carpet.

"I saw the brochure, Mom."

Amandine looks at her daughter then, and the blond added to Racinda's long hair—growing out now—looks luminous where before Racinda had run away it seemed extreme, loud. Amandine is struck by the beauty that has somehow come to Racinda's features despite the scowling, despite the red nose and eyes.

"Racinda—" Amandine says.

"WELL?"

And the strength in her daughter—this drenching love overwhelms Amandine. How did this amazing creature come from such a mother,

Amandine wonders. Look how well your daughter can protect her sister, Amandine thinks, and reaches out to pull Racinda into her arms.

But Racinda swats Amandine's forearms away, rolls her eyes, scoffs. Stands in the doorway, facing her mother but not looking at her mother.

"Here, come in the room at least," Amandine says.

"Fine."

Amandine wedges herself between the small round table and the wall. Racinda sits on the bed, kicking her legs up and down alternately against the metal frame.

"What the fuck are you *thinking*, Mom," she says finally.

Amandine puts her chin in her hands, elbows on the table. She doesn't know what to do. She feels so confused. How could a mother suggest such a thing for her daughter as Fox Hill? She knew Racinda was going to be furious. But so then, what should be done for Ruth? That same drenching love she felt for Racinda floods her again as she sees Ruth's defiance in Racinda's thunderous kicking of the bed. That swooping, impossible love for Ruth fills Amandine, it aches. And she wants both her girls to be safe, both of them to be *alive*, to be as amazing and defiant and bright-haired and scowling and giggling and bed-kicking as Racinda is now, as they were in the night-drives and starry motels and breakfasts-every-hour of their trip out here so many years ago.

How could she think that she, Amandine, could possibly raise two such luminous creatures?

And Racinda's kicks get louder and more frequent, the bed clanging with the weight of her heavy shoes. And the expression on Racinda's face turns to a little girl's expression before a temper tantrum, a little girl's frustration and exhaustion.

The thought of shock therapy for Ruth scares Amandine, yes, and she ultimately doesn't trust it, but how can she alone possibly protect these delicate, astounding creatures who are her daughters? Didn't Rudy say the ECT was what experts recommended?

What does she, Amandine, know about taking care of Ruth anyway?

Racinda's bed-kicking intolerable to hear, now, loud and fast and childish.

Suddenly, Racinda appears at the table, cornering her mother on its other side.

"Give it up, Mom. What are you guys trying to do? She won't go there on her own."

Racinda wants to climb across the table and pin her mother to the wall by the throat.

Breathe, she hears me say, breathe.

Fuck you Nae.

Breathe.

And she does, and she steps back then, her eyes still dark and furious.

"Fuck, Mom. Ruth doesn't need *shock* therapy. Why are you even thinking about that?"

"It's a last resort," Amandine says, "Rudy knows people who deal with this sort of problem and when all the medications cease to work it's supposed to be a viable alternative, Racinda."

"I mean we don't even *know* the story, if she's off the drugs or what, you can't try to get her into that kind of a place. That kind of a place would kill her. And what the fuck does Rudy know? He's not part of our family."

"Rudy is trying to help. Rudy is the only chance we have got. *I* certainly can't do it, obviously. Don't you look at me like that, young lady! Rudy knows a lot more than you do, Mrs. Know-it-all. Rudy's got a few years on you there, if you haven't noticed, you're only eighteen and I don't know what I'm doing and Rudy *knows*."

The scowl that had looked so forceful and endearing now seems like a direct threat to Amandine. What had seemed passionate and strong in her daughter had now turned on her; Racinda seemed like a child playing with a gun, a child whose lack of supervision and control is about to ruin her, ruin all of them.

"Rudy!" Racinda shoves the table so it hits her mother in the stomach. "I'm sorry, but Rudy has not been here all these years. Ruth was okay at that place in Santa Barbara because she *liked* it. I mean maybe we just have to find something like that."

"I happen to have more information than you, young lady," Amandine says, switching to an almost smiling defiance, pushing herself away from the edge of the table, holding it away from her with taut forearms.

"Oh yeah?" Racinda said.

"Yes."

"She wants to go to *India*. She's trying to buy a ticket to go follow some roommate..."

"Cynthia? The crackhead? Ruth's not gonna follow that girl! You're so wrong."

"No—Cynthia's the one who told us about this. Ruth told Cynthia when she went back there to get her things.

"What other roommate *was* there? I'm sorry—India?"

"Oh I don't know. Someone Cynthia told Rudy was older, was an aco-lyte of some guru over there in . . . "

"India?"

"Yes."

"Huh," Racinda says, stumped.

She looks down for awhile, and is puzzled by her mother when she next looks up. Amandine summons all her strength to sit straight, to not weep, to be as strong as she can, and Racinda knows it, but Racinda doesn't want to see her mother trying. Racinda is as scared as Amandine about Ruth going far into a wild, unforgiving place where she might disappear for-ever.

Racinda remembers South Dakota, too, then, remembers terror bend-ing her in two as it is now doing on this hotel bed, remembers her mother's arm around her on the cement landing outside the hotel room on the hill a few miles from Mount Rushmore, remembers her mother soaking up her sadness and her terror of what was on the other side of the Western edge they were headed for. Remembers her mother walking out into the meadow past a mowed lawn at the motel in Wyoming, the sudden spring warmth, her mother beckoning with such a wide, sure gesture, *come on*, remembers the way Amandine's laughter bent into her own when they ducked the zooming dragonflies. The wild, unscheduled drive made Am-andine so much more convincing, so much more a provider of safety than she had ever been at home. God was on their side, doing this—it had been clear Amandine believed it completely, and by not hovering in sadness and night fear in the house in Pennsylvania a lightness, a sureness had come to Amandine for that emergency time of leaving, of resettling. Drag-onflies; laughter.

But here her mother is, paling again, shaking in front of her.

"Rudy thinks we have to get her before she gets the money together or we'll lose her," Amandine says, voice breaking. "It's just another of her manic delusions but this time we must control her or else."

Control her.

"I'm leaving," Racinda says, "I'm out of here, I'm not going to be a part of this."

And Amandine's eyes turn to a beggar's eyes there, the eyes—Racinda knows them well—of the other little ghost-girl stepping clear of the devil in the night hallway. But the ancient guilt that rises in Racinda gets screamed down by the thought of Ruth turned to a vegetable from shock treatment, or lost in a country without a safety net, without clean drinking water, where people can sell a kidney, or their girlfriend's kidney, for cash.

The sight of Amandine sitting there ineffectual, handing the responsibility to yet another bumbling man, twisting the delicate rings on her right hand nervously, looking for approval from a daughter is as infuriating to Racinda as ever.

Racinda slams away. Walks the mile and a half to a gourmet grocery store, full at this luxurious hour of the day with plush dreamy rich mommies with full purses, grocery bags, and jogger-strollers. Hitches a ride in that most ridiculous of vehicles, the Mercedes station wagon, back up to the hospital with a quite nice story about a sick sister and a lost wallet.

Her fury propels her back to me, her fury propels her back into the story of her mother.

*   *   *

The word is *lugubrious*. Racinda moping around her room and flopping on her bed and sighing and then the word is *anxious*, she's getting fifteen-minute passes from the desk and she's getting cigarettes from one of the older guys on the men's floor and she's *smoking again*. The anxiety twines up into a nasty knot. The anxiety twists into plans like a girl's hands playing cats cradle with a loop of string—a line here, crossing there, endlessly, until any possibility of her sister's safety becomes wrapped into hopeless tangles.

Racinda knows that her mother's electroshock idea is a sort of well-meaning last-ditch, desperado attempt to *make* Ruth's a once and for all situation. Yet—wouldn't it be nice—possible?—for that string to emerge as a perfect cat's cradle, a bridge, elegant and arched and strong and intricate between two hands? Or even just a bow, tight on a birthday gift. A simple freaking tied shoelace, is that too much to ask?

But that length of twine only seems to wind up into a tight, nervous ball in Racinda.

What if she just pulls the string of that ball of twine, pulls it hard and lets the ball roll away from her, walks, walks, holding the end she's got? Once and for all. Tidy. Neat. Clearly finished. Lets the end she's got drop from her hand as soon as it becomes less than slack. . .

Impossible.

Yes, what she wants is a tidy bow, a shoe-lace double knotted: it will remain neat, it will not come untied no matter what chaos a wild girl's feet put it through.

Her fifteen minute outdoor pass is up, and like almost all the patients she loves the rules with the kind of affection most people reserve for sugar and their credit cards. But she's storming in, the line of despair grows, tightens behind her heart.

I'm trying to glue a peeling piece of fake wood grain back onto the nurses station because the maintenance guy is on vacation.

Her elbow smacks me as she stomps past.

"Whoa," I say.

"Sorry, Nae," but she doesn't stop.

I turn, glue covering both my hands, and watch her slink so dramatically back into her room. God she is pissing me off. She *knows* better than to fester like this and not ask for help. I bring my fingers together then separate them for that satisfying sticky feeling before the tug apart as I'm trying to figure out what to do.

The wood grain piece is crooked on the counter, shows a dark crevasse between itself and the mainland, looks worse than if I had left it alone.

Glue all over my fingers.

Stuck together, pulled apart. Stuck together, pulled apart. The glue gets tackier, starts to dry.

"Is this a new kind of yoga, missy?" Annette says as she pushes a tray of meds down the hallway.

"Ha," I say.

But it is kind of meditative there.

Stick the fingers together. Pull the fingers apart. Such pleasure. So reliable.

"Is it working?" Annette asks, on her way back already. God, these hospital folks are so great to put up with me sometimes. I must have been standing here for twenty minutes trying to figure out what to do with Racinda when there's a grant proposal due in three days that will bring in funding for ten more patients if I polish it enough.

"Clearly, clearly," I say, "It is *not* working. Clearly it is not."

*   *   *

"Alright. What's going on?"

Racinda just rolls away from me.

The flat nose stoic, the teeth fierce under her pillowy girl's mouth.

"Honey," I say, "Tell me what happened."

She sighs, drama queen. When she rolls over to face me I sit on the bed next to her and brush the hair out of her eyes.

She shrugs my hand away and looks, well, *lugubrious.*

"I'm in here to be nice to you," I say. "I can go."

She just stares at me, thinking *nobody fucking understands this.*

"I think I *do* understand this better than you know, Racinda."

"Amandine wants to give her *shock* treatment. And then because Amandine is controlling the money that's like the only kind of therapy she could get. And I don't know what to fucking do, and Ruth now wants to go to *India*, I'm sure—you can imagine how well she'll play *there.* And I don't know what to do with myself, I shouldn't have to be worrying about these two. I've been worrying about these two my whole life. I mean, what am I going to do about *myself*?"

She sighs so heavily again and flops on her back on the bed. Then she sits up, furiouser and furiouser.

"Wouldn't it be nice if Amandine could act like a grown up and think for herself and like *do the right thing* for Ruth?" she says.

"Which is what exactly. In your esteemed opinion," I say.

"Well it's not fucking shock treatment thank you very much. I mean, I am so sick of taking care of both of them my whole life."

She presses her stomach with her fists.

The swirling dark old house, and her mother a small girl walking in front of her, so terrified, and Racinda terrified too, a tiny girl who wants to save her mother more than anything else. The only reason not to stop completely is to take that hounding darkness away from her mom, the sadness of the little ghost girl in front of her too much for Racinda to bear, she curls in on herself to avoid feeling it

Stop stop stop stop

Under *control*

and that ball of twine starts tightening again and the fury at Amandine for getting her begins and she sits up and says *fuck fuck fuck fuck fuck fuck fuck.*

"I just want her to be a fucking grownup. She is being such an idiot and Rudy means well but fuck he does *not* know what he is doing and fuck fuck fuck fuck fuck—"

"Okay. Stop it," I say. The glue on my fingers has dried, it's not tacky anymore, and it crumbles off, dust, with the least effort.

"What?" she says, so surly!

"Just stop it. Just let it go and just stop whining."

"Excuse me?"

"It's time. You're whining. You're past this. You know better than to just *blame* her."

"Excuse me?"

"You heard me?"

"I didn't have any role models."

"Oh my GOD, Racinda, what are you *talking* about?"

"Oh like Amandine is a role model?"

"I—" I stand up, back away from her, all professionalism evaporated from my little tiny brain.

"You actually think you *deserve* a role model?" I said. "You think *that* is what's keeping you hiding out in this hospital instead of moving forward?"

"Oh thank you, I'm such a horrible person all of a sudden *I* don't deserve a role model," Racinda says.

"No, I mean you seem to think you're *entitled* to one just kind of knocking on your door and saying, hi, I'm your perfect role-model-slash-eternal mommy and I'm here to make every single pain you feel go away easy as buying a candy bar."

"What is your problem?" she says, the tears starting. "I just don't know what to do."

"Well . . ." I say.

"Well!" she says.

"You have to *find* your role models, Racinda. Know why you need them, how to use them. Or even just *notice* them."

"Right," she says, tongue spitting nails, "like on *television*. Like, oh like Betty *Crocker*. Vanna White . . . some bitch selling freaking *laundry* detergent. Sandra Day fucking O'Connor?"

I slap my knee in a strange, violent, slightly country-western fashion that confuses both of us.

"You have *Button*! Do you even *know* what she did before she settled down with your grandfather?"

Racinda looks at me like I am out of my gourd.

"She was a nurse in, for the army or something," she says, defensive, "And then she worked in New York. I mean, I don't know exactly all that went on, I mean. No, I guess. No."

"That's right. You *don't*. Even not knowing all that stuff about her— which is pretty amazing stuff, and which would do you good—even *not* knowing that, you have more than most women get, let me tell you this much."

"So, um, *what* exactly does this after-school special spiel have to do with my mother and not knowing if Ruth is going to live or die or get lobotomized?"

Rolls her eyes and pats around to find her cigarettes, clearly bored of all this, clearly settling her bones comfortably into a passive, smelly muck.

"GOD, you—I have no idea how you got this whiny!" I say.

"What?" she says, disaffected, above it all, "I can't believe you are getting this abusive . . ."

Turns to me: the horror, the horror, her eyes say, the *outrage*!

And then I say:

"I can't believe you turned into a *whiner* all these years after I told your mother to name you after that old belligerent Auntie Racinda!"

My hand flies across my mouth.

But maybe I did mean to say that.

Racinda's brow furrows, her mouth drops, the face acquires severe stillness.

"*Exene*," I say, rolling my eyes, shaking my head. "*Very* nice. Exene Cervenka."

She is just *appalled*. I chuckle.

Well.

The cat is so far out of the bag that the SPCA has already put it to sleep. Clearly, it's time to fess up. Clearly.

So.

*   *   *

"Well, Racinda, I'm not quite sure where to start here. There's—there's a bit *to* all this. I met your mother the year before you were born, I was working as a psychic off Route 141 in Newark, that field—you've passed it many times, you loved driving past that field, where in the late afternoon the cornstalks look bright blue. Yes. Well, your mother came in and her sad tale seared me to the bone—I had to get out of that line of work soon after. It wasn't just her—there were scores of broken women over the years but she and a few others who came in right after that, well, I was just way *open* to them in a way I hadn't been before. I had a really wonderful husband back then and that true love he gave me was new to me and that love opened me up to other people's pain, but with my, gift—I just wasn't ready. For it, for him. Since then—since then I've trained and grown stronger and I choose not to use the gift so much, just little blips here and there, and then once in awhile when I'm real tempted and know I *can* know something, or sometimes, more rarely I just can't *help* but know something. It's funny, though, the knowing now doesn't happen for new folks—just folks I zoomed in on back in Newark, Delaware when I was wide open and nearly useless as a radio that gets all the stations in the world.

Your mother. Stop making that face, I know you're angry at her. You feel like you need to do something but you don't know what to do. You are stuck, hovering, confused. You *still* want something outside yourself to tell you what the clear path is—you want Joey to tell you, or Ruth, or even that little nic fit craving which will so kindly tell you the clear next step is obviously a cigarette.

Tie up the loose ends, or shout them down or shoot them or gas them or have them disappeared: not very democratic, eh?

Well you're going to have to sit in this gray, in this discomfort, and listen to me awhile. You're going to have to stop freezing yourself worse by searching out something to move you out of your frozenness. You're going to have to start reaching *in*, start reaching *back*.

You know that already.

Fine, make all the faces you want. Do you want me to continue?

Back, back, back, it was 1973, imagine that, and your mother's little white purse was an insult and an annoyance to me in my house. Your poor mother—she realized how badly she wanted Ruth back from Button and she was as frozen as you are here—a frozen girl, completely unclear on how to become anything beyond that, on how to act in any other way than *pretty*.

Oh please. You know Amandine's got more in her repertoire now. Well, jeez, this weeping desperation thing isn't just *pretty* now is it, and that's what you're so pissed at her for, right? Right. And besides that, she doesn't show it around you, but she's getting some other acts in her show as well.

Yes. I'll get there.

But look at Amandine now. She's in that hotel room—god, so tacky, and overpriced but you know, that area, I've always hated that part of the peninsula. Too *precious*. Amandine's as gray, as frozen as you are, but here's Rudy, knocking on the door, sauntering in, a big man. Your mom's trying to resist luxuriating in the reassurance that you can only get so quickly, so unearned, by having a big man look after you. Honestly Amandine isn't that much interested in his strength now. The little bit of her that *is*, however, grows each second he's so kind to her, bringing her tissues and not thinking for an *instant* that she isn't as pretty with her makeup smeared and her face all red. He thinks your mother is the most elegant creature in existence. But the undertow in her is thinking—*it's really between the three of us, it's really between the three of us*. And she knows she should send him out, face this storm alone, but she doesn't, she gets more and more still and gives easy, tiny nods as he pats her on the back and smoothes back her hair and starts talking about their grand scheme to catch you two.

She's become, again, as frozen as you are right now. You in your fury, and some confusion, and Amandine in *just* confusion, her fury so far away from her she still, *still* can't get to it.

I need to tell you why.

You need to hear why.

You know her parents died when she was young, but in fact she doesn't even know that that's true. What has she told you? Right—not much. In fact, virtually nothing.

Amandine was abandoned—her mother left the apartment and never came back—as a tiny baby, a neighbor called the police after what was maybe days of wailing. Messed all over herself, sores, cried and cried and then *wouldn't* cry after the pastor's wife of the neighbor's church took her in. It couldn't last forever, though, and by three she was in foster care, place to place to place until she was twelve, and she found the family that was willing to keep her. Her hair had always been wild and embarrassing—kinky, frizzy, yellowish and white like your sister's but not in any way *pretty*, as your sister's is if you're in the right mindset, and at this final home the mother hated Amandine enough that she used a hot iron to make it straighter, as was becoming the fashion at the time. Amandine hardly even felt the burns from that sadist, the mother: the worse stuff happening in that place had numbed Amandine, by thirteen. So the burns settled in, and soon the hair was falling out in little patches.

And so whatever it was that made Amandine finally bust out of there for good posed as *vanity*. She'd been able, since junior high's witch-hunt nastiness ended, to blend in on the sidelines, stay quiet and polite, grateful to no longer be the target of awful, active, determined teasing. But once the hair started coming out in visible patches, once the bald spots grew large enough to be hard to cover even with a hat, once even adults couldn't resist wondering at the sight of her, once other girls scoffed in the bathroom, once children had to be told not to stare in her presence, she decided.

She stole the money for the wig from the sadist mother's wallet. She knew she should pack first, but she went to the wig store right away, got what she'd had her eyes on for months. She hid the elegant, but believable, up-do blond wig before mother could report the theft to social services, but wasn't able to finish packing before the father came home a bad beating as punishment—*bad beating*, do you know what that feels like? It's not like what happened to you at Ruth's hands. That man had already taken from Amandine what she needed then for her mind, her heart to remain intact. She had split them apart from each other long ago, and then gone on to divide parts of her mind from other parts of her mind. So, bolstered by the wig, she set about, quite calmly, packing her things and finished before the social worker came. Headed straight for the bus depot, barely feeling the weight of her bag.

On that Greyhound ride down to Philly, Amandine dabbed the blood still coming from her gums and her nose, so daintily. She dabbed the blood, sucked it from where it collected at the roots of her teeth, and looked in her hand mirror. The blood oozing from the corner of her mouth, from her nostrils, even the bruises hardly registered to her wearing that shining wig singing to her like angels.

Rape isn't about sex, but it steals a woman's sexuality. Rape is about power, about asserting power over women in general through whichever one you can dominate enough to do it. That a woman's sexuality—among other things—is what gets stolen is also about power, Racinda. Your sexuality is *yours*, you get to choose who to share it with, who to just hint at it with, who to let really see you naked, which has nothing to do with whether or not you've got clothes on. If someone takes that whole category from you, that particular space to roam, they take away your power to feel your instincts, they divide you from your essence. They take away your power to meander safely in your mind, not to mention your heart. They take away your power to move inside yourself when you need to know what to do: inside your own head it is *deafening* after you have been raped. You should thank the heavens every day that it never happened to you. You can't be fierce when you need to be, because the possibility of doing so becomes too horribly sad, a reminder that ferocity didn't save you when you really needed it. You start to mutilate yourself. You would *never* belong to a club that would have you as a member. You look outside yourself.

You look for a savior, a Jesus. You are frozen, you have been convinced you are powerless, you are a victim and unless someone helps you out of seeing things that way you stay feeling like a victim, even making the smallest decisions can feel impossible. Gray, frozen, vaporous—dead, really, you are almost not there at all.

Every Monday and Wednesday, coming home from school, Amandine knew she was going to be raped by the father and his brother. Days the mother worked late. On schedule. After awhile Amandine just stopped trying to find school activities to go to these nights, because the mother, at the father's pressure, would insist that Amandine be there to make dinner and make sure the father "got to relax" after work. *Come here*, he would say, *slut*, he would say, *who's my baby* he would say, *who takes care of you?* he would say. He would bind her with electrical cords. He would rub her back until she fell asleep. When she awoke, she would clean up.

It's as if she brings out in Ruth and in you the fury she needed so badly.

Honey.

I don't know how—I don't know how to tell a person something like this, honey. But you need to know it, and Amandine—who knows how much she even remembers anymore.

Honey.

Yes. When you see a broken girl in her *that* is the kind of breaking we are talking about.

She hasn't. . . come *through* it exactly, but she is stronger. You have the Christians to thank for that much—they opened her heart, they loved her. Of course, of course at a certain price. That intense kind of Christianity preys on the most broken ones. But Linda, Ray, all those folks loved her and she got to trust a little and parts of her insides grew a little stronger, a little braver, a little freer.

And *Jesus*. Yes, he helped.

Stop looking at me like that. You know I'm not so into Him either, but . . .

He came to her as something older, something messier and bigger and feminine and more necessary than Him, but she, like so many, could only see that as Him. To get past the gray, struck, brutalized limbo she'd been in since she was twelve, she needed a new story—Jesus gave it to her.

Jeez, Racinda, *she* needed a role model—don't get me wrong, you do too but you've gotta dig for it. And she found hers—it doesn't matter that they call Jesus *Him*:

I mean *come on*, what a *woman*, up there, nails pushed through the palms!

Who else would they do that to but a woman?

After what she'd been through, how could Amandine, in the truest, secret places of her heart, *not* know He's a woman up there, His power stolen, pinned to the beams?

I mean, we *all* know the violent macho bullshit that religion has pulled for eons: even on their terms He's a giant, succulent, threatening, wild pussy.

And look at her *now*, your mother. Right. Well, I can. She's in that hotel room, she's asked Rudy to leave her alone awhile and she's talking to Him, to Jesus. She can't get through to Him though—the connection isn't working. Her sobs are messy and sliding everywhere and she doesn't know what to do about you—Racinda, do you understand that she believes, *believes* absolutely, that you are going to go to hell if you don't come around to JC? And Ruth too? She doesn't know how to fight for you. She knows it's futile to pressure you on that stuff—praying for you two is going to have to suffice. She is trying, in her way, to be a warrior, to fight for her girls. Here she goes, hoping you'll take Christ into your heart. Eternal damnation is something you can chuckle about but she is sure there is *no way out*. She's saying this: *Dear God, I've done what I can do about their coming to Christ. I give that struggle to you. Now I just need to know what to do about keeping them alive and not in cults or mental wards. Do I go chase Ruth, now, or Racinda? Thank you, Jesus, for sending Rudy to help me, thank you for that kindness.* As she veers into tongues there, she's keeping one ear on the door for signs of Rudy. She's whispering. Rudy has been so kind to her but she can't show him all this. I wonder . . .

But Jesus isn't answering. Her tongues get louder, she's starting to forget that Rudy has the key to the room, that he might come in any minute and then if he sees her doing this and freaks she'll be left really on her own. Except now it isn't so terrifying—this old, well *vision* I guess is what you'd call it, a vision that she's had before at different crucial times in her life is coming to her: the ancient black ocean, and the old woman hovering above it, a sea creature, a sea god, from way before Christ.

And Jesus comes then, really just a descendant of that old god, or a translation—the strength of that god in the body and voice of a man— that your mother can understand. She feels strength and the answer filling her—she has, by just opening herself to *something*, to Jesus, made herself open to the ancestral mother Jesus whom she needs in order to get herself down off her favorite cross of not knowing what to do about you two, her favorite cross of feeling frozen and alone and impossible to help.

Because honestly, Racinda, you have to look *back* to find that, and you have to look *in*. If you look around you, what do you find for a savior? You find the public face of Jesus, the one everyone ties to Jesse Helms and *love, honor and obey*—you don't find the one who loved the Magdalen, you don't find the one who turned the tables and fought the man. You find your secular savior: fucking nail polish, fucking soap commercials. You find tidiness and prettiness and *things* and you find the shell of Joeys, of Lymans to freebase like meth.

But look at her now! Amandine's standing up in that hotel room and she's taking off that custom-made wig and she's staring in the mirror, bald and weeping, she's telling herself she'll *know* what to do when she needs to do it. And she knows she needs to tell Rudy that Fox Hill electroshock torture is not going to happen, that they're going to have to figure something else out. And that maybe he will, being so strong-willed, disagree with her and leave her, but somehow, with a *breeze* crossing her bare-naked head quite pleasantly now, with the risk and the thrill of possibly being found out like this, it doesn't scare her as badly to have no one to lean on. It doesn't feel like that means she's shit out of luck.

Look. She's telling herself she can fight for you two. I wish you could see her . . . I wish you could see the *ferocity*: her little teeth look so sharp, and her mouth is redder as if remembering all those years ago on that Greyhound. If she spoke just this minute, to protect her daughters, she could rip someone in two.

Honey.

Your biggest problem is vastly underestimating what you can handle."

*　　*　　*

The light coming in from the eastern windows as dusk settles in has a milky, blue quality that Racinda will always associate with this knowledge of her mother's pain. She sits on the bed, her arms around her knees, her bare toes curled back, and she is frozen. Racinda starts to rock forwards, backwards, forwards, and as she forces herself to inhale more deeply than just to the top of her chest she can feel that this milky light is a light that has survived, a light that surely happens dozens of days a year and has happened for millions of years, a light that changes and bends into nightfall, a light that gives way from the bright cracking white of the high California day. And as she breathes in and starts to cry again her tears bend, at moments, away from the fucked-feeling victim tears she's been crying off and on for awhile here in the hospital, into the stronger kind of tears, into the kind that receive her own sadness and her mother's like the mountains to the east receive this evening's milky light.

She doesn't want to move from the bed, because if she goes out into the hallway, the common area, the nurses station, she knows she will feel like a ghost. She knows it is time to go.

But go where?

She holds on to feeling alone, she holds on to this burgeoning guilt about her mother's terrible early fate, she holds on to hating the fact that there is no one to show her the way. She pushes away any stirrings of desire for movement, remains stuck even as the light shows her the astounding beauty and power of acquiescence, of change, even as it lets darkness fall, even as the stars fly bright and fix themselves into the firmament.

* * *

When I knock on her door the next morning she opens it only a crack, sticks her flat little nose out.

"What, Nae?"

Whiny!!

"You have a visitor."

"Fucking Rudy?"

"Nope," I say.

"Who?"

"Trust me. Get dressed."

She's padding around in a pair of medical scrubs that she found in the back closet and that are very against the rules for mental patients to possess, but in her own room what's the problem, I figure.

"Fine."

"MAX!" She screams it at him and runs to him and hugs him and then steps back, both of them a little sheepish about all this display.

"Hey," he says, looking at the floor. *What* a cutie.

"Can I get a smoke pass?" she says.

I nod, try not to let the naughty grin crack until after they're out the door. He's too young still for her. He's going to take awhile. I'm just so thrilled to see her *lively* for a second.

White-light, no-heat day, chilly in November. Max is still a little be-fuddled having sat waiting with Ernest and Edda and their small crew of regulars playing Yahtzee in the common area.

"Why were they like all wearing weird hats and masks?"

"They like hats—holds their brains in," Racinda explains, "A lot of them are kind of manic like Ruth, you know like when your brain goes and goes and goes when you smoke too much ganja and you just can't get it to stop—I think it's like that. The hats kinda hold them in. They're left over from Halloween," Racinda says.

"Oh."

"It's always a holiday on the ward."

"Oh."

She sucks in the smoke like a movie star.

"So—when are you getting out of here?"

"Fuck, Max, I don't want to talk about that." She chases the movement and light and breeze and taste out of herself. Plants feet. Knees to chest. Closes down.

"Okay," he says, and he stares at her then. Somehow, with his eyes on her like that, unflinching, she can stop the dreary girl-habit of policing herself from the outside, can really go *in*.

"Fuck, Max, I don't know what to do."

She presses a set of knuckles steadily into her jaw line.

"What?"

Graciously, he stops gazing so hard when she looks back at him.

"Ruth is trying to go to *India*."

"India? Like the country?"

"Yeah."

"That's, like, not probably the best thing for her right?"

She looks at him as if to say *duh*, but then tears brim over onto those dark lines of lashes.

"Right," the word cracks and Max hugs her.

God, she thinks. She nestles her face into his neck and cries a little and then just smells him, it's a male smell but a boy smell, god, if only if only, if only this boy could take her over like Joey took her over, Max, come with me to Pennsylvania, you will be able to help me convince her that she should *not* go to India, that India is like the Nevada desert, a bad idea, if only you, Max you could help me Max can you fix this Max what do I do I don't know what to do I am frozen.

Max?

And she sees her mother, frozen, still, on the bed in the hotel before the sea hag came and Racinda wishes, one last time, for Joey, sees Joey driving her across Nevada, Nebraska, Michigan to go do what she needs to do.

God, I just want to love something, she thinks, and she starts feeling the organ chords, so kind and deep, of the love she has for Joey still, a sensual love, air on her skin and him in her mouth and night skies inside her lungs her heart her belly, and the organ chords long and low of the loss of that, and of the loss of Ruth, the loss of the wildness of both of them thrown into terrifying relief by the combed concrete and smell of corporate bark-chip landscaping and the tidy little shrubs that surround the bench she is sitting on, *I just want something to love like that* and she melts a little more and the vision of her unfrozen mother standing bald in the mirror comes to her and she looks up and sees *Max* sitting there, that night sky inside her stomach feeling, that feeling that any new thing could happen any amazing minute, warms her to standing and it becomes clear to her that she has to *go*.

Is she shaking again?

But it goes away.

She's shaking.

Poor Max really starts wondering if she *is* crazy.

Where do I go?

Look *back*, she hears me say, look *in*.

Button.

And she sits across from Max, still, now, but not frozen or trapped, she holds his shoulders.

He can't get me out of this.

But Max, maybe Max could give her a *ride*. Without the saving bit, just a ride.

"I need to get to Pennsylvania," she says.

"Yeah?" he says.

"Can you drive me?"

"I would, Racinda, but like with what?"

"How did you get here?"

The thumb, practiced and eloquent and adept.

"Fuck."

"Here," he says, "You could fly."

And he reaches into the pocket of his cargo pants and hands her the four hundred bucks from Elaine.

"Max?" she says.

"It's yours."

"Max!" she says, and hugs him, and fingers through the pile of cash, pulls out enough for Greyhound, slips the rest into his jacket pocket.

Max helps her roll up her socks, but is shy when she's folding up her panties, her bras—all of it bought for her from Kmart but now so precious to her. She's bopping around the room, she's fending of the fear with nervous energy. She leaves Max sitting in there watching One Life To Live when she comes to say goodbye to me.

"I'm going to check out."

"That was fast," I say, and I can feel the tears coming on already.

"Well, you know what, I've been here awhile."

She rolls her eyes with a soft, silly smile.

"Good for you, honey. I'll have Annette get your paperwork together while you go say goodbye to Dr. T," and I tell myself that when it's really time for her to go, when she walks out of this building with her suitcase in an hour or so, that I'll leave the story, drop my too-strong interest in the ending, resist spying through the ether. Wait for a postcard and a Christmas letter like a normal person would.

She makes the rounds, sweet and happy, nothing like the vexed, dark being hiding in her bedroom earlier that morning. She hugs Edda for a long time, then straightens Edda's hat. Blows a kiss from the nurses station when she's done signing her paperwork. She scribbles her mother's address on a prescription note and pins it on the bulletin board with an exhortation for everyone to write her.

"I'll definitely write," she says when she hugs me, "Definitely."

So I blink back my crying, and Annette and I hold hands as we wave to her, as Max carries her bag, as we all wait for the big metal doors to open and spill her out into the world.

When they close back up again, the stripe of outer lobby between them slimming to nothing, I know I've lied to myself. I *am* going to keep peeking in on this girl. Just from time to time. Just to check. To make sure she's okay. What harm, what harm can it do?

*   *   *

In the parking lot, the light is muted again, like twilight but it is just that it has gotten overcast. The bite in the wind and the gray, easy sky pleases Racinda but here she is saying goodbye to Max, *where are you going?* But he doesn't know. She gives him the name of Button's nursing home in Pennsylvania and tells him if he wants he can find her there. *Max you sprung me twice!* she says and they both smile goofy and try not to be sad and hug each other quickly when he says *okay then, bye* and grips her on the upper arm as if for strength, turns, walks down to the freeway.

She watches him saunter away more like a man than she remembers him walking, she lights a cigarette, waiting for the cab to the bus station. With each deep inhalation she can feel that old frozenness in herself, the wishing for Ruth or for Joey to drag her along and tell her what to do, to bring pleasure to her, to bring *life* to her, to bring change. She knows this bus will take her straight into chaos, straight into the impossible question of her sister. But she can imagine its forward speed already, the thrill at each new mile, the thrill of the rush of one unsure moment after another, no one to lean on, okay.

20

SPEAKING

Button:

Time is not happening, and then it is happening. When it is not happening it is like those layers of cellophane in different colors that stagehands put on theater lights. Thin films of color one atop the other. Yellow: my husband, waiting for me. Three distinct versions of him; one Elmer wrinkled and bent, gray hair, smoking a cigarette on vacation. Another Elmer: a grown man, watching me leave him behind. A third, his chest still whippet-lean, a boy's, lazy, turning his eyes from me, turning his eyes to what his friends think is the true prize. Cyan: the true prize that wasn't—Violetta: the white-pure girl who he married first, cyan the moment he takes that vow, cyan her murderous inability to stay alive, cyan the rows of slicing, perfect lilies banking her casket.

(Any fool knows when you layer all the cellophanes together you get pure white light. Death light, everything light. A shimmering, a brightness.)

Red cellophane, magenta—is it red?—the color I know. I knew red by the time I was seven, blood covering my father, covering the steer he's butchering, red on me helping him. Red twenty years later, the color of the tiny cross on my nurse's hat. White, red, one is murderous, pure, and the latter is the color of death before it settles, death ready, a stomach full, of stench, of life.

And the cellophane layers separate themselves, which they would never have to do if I had died. If I had come here for good. Goodbye for now, Elmer says, the wiry boy version and the thick manly farmer peeling away from the wizened, sweetened form Elmer took at the end. And the sheets of moments separate and fly apart like a stack of paper, now, like when a secretary trips over her heels, the cellophanes now more like her paper flying everywhere, blowing through an endless wax-dust tiled corridor. The moments must be restacked. Order reapplied. The corridor blows and sweats and expands. Breathes. But—a ringing, such ringing, ringing and ringing it jangles it irritates and I shift my hand away from my side—a hand. A real hand, that failure of bone and tendon, arthritis or now something worse tearing through each infinitesimal shift but even so. A hand. Not just the scrim of a hand, the memory of a hand, the cellophane of a hand—but my actual hand.

A body.

A hand. Its history more than ideas: packing-sausage hand, goodbye-hand, hand flying across clacka-clacka typewriter, hand through a man's intestines, a lamb's, hand through twists of her blond hair, her tiny hand on mine—until now it was just memory, just idea of hand.

Nothing!

No thrill, the idea of hand, nothing compared to one second of earthly hand, to even the worst of hand, now, shrill pain of hand inching toward nightstand. And ear: strange pain of a real raven cawing in winter, and the terrible, terrible sound of the arrival of the telephone, terrible cacophony of a call.

I lost Elmer two times before I finally married him. I lost him two times before he died. I was not about to lose him through the ether but there was really no choice, that telephone next to my bed rang and there was no choice a'tall.

One.

There were precious minutes when nobody knew I was awake. The view the window accorded was its own kind of heaven—ice webbing across the majestic black limbs of trees. I assumed it was the middle of January but later I learned it was still November. Strange freeze. Nincompoop weather, the whole month, it would turn out.

I could hear the ravens cawing. The more the wind swooped at them, the more they played, the faster they flew into its gusts. One by one. Such a game! Such glee! Difficult, frozen weather, ice on their wingtips, maybe, but they loved the wind, they played it.

I moved my tongue in the bed of my mouth, just slightly, and the languishing muscles, even there, in my mouth, burned. Still, I nearly started giggling from the new thrill of the old occupation of having a body.

When I tried to adjust my arms, though, I couldn't withstand that shattering feeling. I gasped, and I wondered, now that the otherworldly secretary had gathered those papers, ordered them for this world now that the secretary continued clicking her way down that infinite hallway, would I ever make it back to Elmer through the murk? Would I find him again? Would I lose him the third time? I tried to brush my fingertips along the edge of the blanket and the ripping feeling took the breath straight out of me.

Yes, take me back there, there is no point of me being here, tempted by these fast, smart-aleck ravens in trees. Probably never to get out of this bed. With no air—yes, the blankets of comfort of the other world. No earthly threat of loss. So silly! Of course. Leave this earth for good now! With no air—the decision clear. But—

Breath came rushing in, and with its exhale another came, and another, and—my room, its huge window—I could see that great black bird, its midnight wings shiny with swirls of oil, on the top of the tree. He dug his claws into the bark as the branch blew in a gust his *caw, caw* a celebration in the wind.

And ring, and ring, and ring, the telephone jangled, how to possibly answer it, I couldn't imagine, but after the while it took to get the receiver all the way to my ear, the voice asking *hellohellohello?*

"Hell-LO? You people need customer service training. Hello?" the voice said.

" . . ."

I'm looking for BUTTON HART," she said.

"Sperrr---erreeeeaking," I said.

"WHAT?"

I gurgled then. It was beginner's luck with that first word there. Other words weren't at hand immediately.

"Ssss. . . . speaking."

My throat was dry was the main problem. The racking itch.

"Button!"

It was Ruth.

"Yoooo—eeesssss---ssssss," I said.

Words through a long, narrow tunnel, distorted.

"Button!"

"Ye-ye--esss, deeeeeeeeearrrrrr-uh."

Hoot owl. Hoot owl and moose combined, that was the noise of me now. I would have laughed at the thought of it but it was too much effort.

"Why didn't they tell us you were better?"

I gurgled, the words failed me.

She talked for awhile anyway. I'd coo and warble and, oh I think I even grunted. Like a pet. But it was delightful.

"And then I left that that evil speed freak's household and I moved in with this woman Beatrix who has a little house on the water in Sausalito and sometimes you can see it and then if you walk around the bend the hill blocks it, I moved in here and I've been doing this really serious *pratyahara*—"

"What?" I said.

"Study of silence, Button, it's part of my practice."

My girl couldn't study silence for half a minute, I knew that much if I knew anything.

"Yoga," she said.

I imagined her and this Beatrix with turbans on their heads like Johnny Carson.

I croaked out a syllable.

"Relax, Button," she exhaled and I could hear the pitch rising in her, the irritation and the fury, "God did the stroke turn you into Amandine?" she said.

"Hmmph," I said.

It pleased me, though, that Ruth still knew how to get my goat.

"And then I was all set to go train in India, there's this ashram—"

"Ashram!"

"Chill, is this *Amandine*? Listen. There's this ashram, and it's like very cool there, and I think it would really help, I just have to get out of this place—"

"What plooooooo-ace?"

"This *country*. This place where it's like so. . . messed up spiritually and there's just—Button I just feel all these bad things here, these bad things just make themselves very clear to me here and I think there they don't have them or they do maybe, they have the same dark bad things, invisible things, but there they have people who talk to them and they talk directly to the good things that can keep the bad things in check. . . "

"Oh, dear," I said, when she finished.

She waited for me to weigh in, but I couldn't muster the words even if I'd known what to tell her. I gathered what saliva I could in my mouth.

"Button, I need to go over there," she said, tears in her voice. "I need money for a ticket and I think Amandine isn't going to help me and I need money for medication and I think Amandine is going to make me go to a horrible detention center hospital, I don't know what to do, I need a plane ticket though, I need to go over there. It's my home, I can feel it. The dark—the dark isn't going to be able to get me. The walls there, they paint the walls orange, they paint the doors blue to keep out—"

I struggled to sit up straighter in my bed, my back made noises like when you snap dry kindling. I half-expected dust to rise up from the cracking bones. The pain was becoming tolerable, but constant, and just these few minutes of it left me wanting a nap.

Ruth's voice, a clear thread despite the panic, a golden thread tying me to this world, her voice a twist a strong rope. I couldn't go back.

I formed the words carefully. . . I waited until I could say them exactly. . .

"What are you . . . talking . . . about, girl?" I said. "Ruth. . . what. . . is happening to you, dear?"

She trilled. She cried. She waited for the right words, too.

"Come here," I said. "Ruth, come visit, and weeeeeeeeeeee---ee—ee—" I stopped.

"We'll sort it out, come visit and we'll sort it out," I said, or at least I tried to. It was moosy, queer, but she understood.

Months or years, I don't know how long it was, weeks or days. Grays and lavenders and the flecked whites of hospital tile, and hot tea and little words strewn here and there and dull smiles or actual joy depending on the nurse at the fact that I'd mouthed "more" or "I'm done" or a frown, that I'd opened my eyes. My throat would grow dry, and I'd drink and drink water, as long as the nurse would stay and lift it to my lips. And then, in days? hours? months? I started lifting the cup by myself, pouring and lifting and drinking, and if I saved up my voice I could scare the night nurse now and then with a loud, fully-formed sentence.

I missed my husband. I wasn't able to find him during sleep—in my sleep I was too aware of this room, of the lack of a pulse in the building itself, the lack of a breeze. Whoever designed the ventilation here had no sense in his head. I would stare so long at those frozen trees outside that I didn't know if I was awake or dreaming them. When the confusion would shake off, I'd wonder, what's the point? Is Ruth even coming? I'd wonder how much longer I would last. I'd wonder if I could find my husband again or if this time, leaving my body for good, I'd end up in strange and unfamiliar company.

*   *   *

The ravens in the trees kept me company. They shirred their feathers, cocked their heads impatiently. On their frozen spikes of branches, on their hillside of black trees, they waited for a huge blast so much more powerful than the sum of its parts, for a wind barely negotiable by wings.

*   *   *

I felt her young, hot hand on mine.

I smelled Greyhound—it's not a dissimilar smell from what it was back in the seventies, last time I took it myself—a smell of carpet, of sweat, of breadcrumbs.

The hand felt like Ruth's—hot, too-tight. I smiled, because Ruth's hand didn't feel crazy. It didn't have Ruth's old will to deny reality, deny all of us. That hand made me think I was waking up to a less grim, less dire thing.

"Button, it's me, Racinda," she said.

I opened my eyes to find her delicate, sheer skin hovering inches from mine. She nearly crushed me with a hug and a kiss.

I made my old moosy sounds in my shock.

"You okay? Sorry!" Racinda said.

"Okay," I managed. "Water," I managed, and she held the cup to my lips.

I shook my head when the glass was empty, and showed her that I could pour it—it took me forever, so shaky, so infirm: *me*.

The round, white rim of the cup, glowing in the old blue late Chester County light. Quietness, this quiet joy to her, and to me too. Just taking her in. Refilling and refilling that cup so that I could water my voice enough to speak.

The good girl, she seemed truly impressed. I managed a grin at her between sips.

In the time it took me there to tune back in, I studied her face. Peeled my eyes wide so I'm sure I looked like a baby bird, long neck and wrinkly skin and bobbing throat. Wisps of hair.

This is just a fraction of me, I wanted to tell her, this is just the thinnest layer of me, girl, remember the stronger versions, remember the versions you don't even know.

(Layer on layer of color. Of time. Age equivalent to white light, then? This wrinkled shell, this pain, just the result of all the selves brought together?)

I never expected Racinda to have this kind of beauty. Her neck strong, pale, regal. An intricate metal necklace—sculptural, thick—sat heavy there, a choker dotted with round greenish stones like a constellation. If any of these girls, these nurses in here wore it, they'd seem cheap, or just odd.

I had thought she'd be scared and hunched into herself, her face tight with worry.

But here she was, bringing the cup to my lips now that I was tired again.

Hope took flight in my heart a raven finally receiving its breeze. Racinda, Racinda was grown and strong and—

Amazing! Certainly the trajectory she had been on so tightly as a child did not lead to this proud inhabiting of herself. Something must have intervened. How old was she now? Couldn't be over twenty, nineteen even. Her mother's frantic worry had left Racinda's eyes. Something calmer had taken hold. Something calm enough to *see* a situation, to watch long enough to make a capable decision. Not from panic, or not from avoiding hurting someone's feelings. Not from *manners* or whatever else Amandine's prettiness and her kook church tried to teach.

So our terrified mouse of a child would be the one person in the whole bunch to survive.

But then, the racking itch hit my throat. I hacked and Racinda held the cup as if waiting for me to be ready, as if waiting to help.

"Button?" Racinda asked.

When I shooed her away, trying to wind down the cough, a tremor of such sadness crossed her. Racinda looked away then, but not before a broken expression overwhelmed not only her face, but her posture, too, and not before pressing her tiny white hand to her neck. A feminine hand, a hand so pale, gesture exactly like her silly grandmother, Violetta, in the one photograph my husband kept of her.

That perfect white hand against the softest neck.

During my razored coughs, through the haze of pain each spasm thickened, I stared at her.

With her in profile like that, it all seemed instantly clear, that girlish weakness.

Racinda had Violetta's perfect white skin, and flat, almost geometric nose, and deep eyes. That fragile quality, the terrified silence that enveloped her when presented with any threat.

Yes. I could see it so clearly:

Violetta.

A quick hot stretch of jealousy in my heart. That white-pale soft-lily Violetta I'd never quite given up hating for taking Elmer from me the first half of my adulthood. Was Racinda doughy like Violetta was when you caught her in unflattering light? Sickly like Violetta? I couldn't tell, my eyes peeled back wide, I couldn't tell.

I'd never seen it before in her. She lifted the cup to my mouth and if I hadn't been so worn out by the pain I would have inched away from her. But I took the water, and it soothed me. She ran her hand—the pale, strange, hated hand of Elmer's first wife—but it wasn't Violetta, of course, it was Racinda. I had to tell myself that.

But my curiosity—sick, sick—got the best of me.

I sat up as best I could despite the pain and leaned in to inspect her features more closely. I just couldn't get over the resemblance. Violetta was the youngest and most beautiful of the five Cloud sisters. Rich. Pampered. Happy. Easy. All the things I had never been as a girl. A Cloud, right *in* Racinda—the blood of the two sisters who stole Elmer from me in quick succession.

First Vida Cloud stole him, then Violetta did.

Yes, I could see it. It was clear now—Racinda's newly-won strength was not going to be enough to counter the lily-white force of Cloud bloodline.

A matriline of fragility.

Elmer Elmer Elmer come here come here come here come here I'm here I'm here I'm here

Beautiful, pale, cowering, turning away: Violetta, and her sister Vida before her. Lips full of sugar, wishes fulfilled before they were even spoken. Rich daddy, beautiful mother. That whole family, right down the youngest one who became my husband's first wife, pure as driven snow, as the saying goes. Snow driven to death, more like, snow caving roofs in, snow in a desk-globe, snow covering a perfect domestic world, the Cloud house ornate as a baron's, a perfect, delicate world, perfect silks, perfect parties, perfect suitors that the rest of the girls in each Cloud daughter's school class peered in on. Victoria, Virginia, Vivica, Vida, Violetta. The rest of us girls in town were giants, and sandpaper-rough compared to them, we were real, we were monsters. Victoria, Virginia, Vivica, Vida, Violetta. Like dolls.

Violetta.

But Vida is where to start.

I had wanted to take Latin in the early afternoons my senior year—amazing they once offered this at a public high school, but they did. Only three girls were let in, however, and I was not among them, so I ended up in Sewing 101, along with Vida and her crew of not quite as rich, not quite as beautiful cronies. But prettier than I. And all of them better seamstresses, believe me, except for Vida. For whom it didn't matter, of course, with all her father's money.

I didn't speak to those girls. They'd giggle about me or as *if* about me, and I'd ignore them. Try to get my fat hands around the embroidery needle, try to get the damn flowers to replicate somebody's idea of a flower—certainly these embroidered things didn't resemble real flowers even when sewn on by an expert hand. And with *my* efforts, what were meant to be smooth green patches of leaves came out as knotted nubs. It was hopeless, but to avoid the awful trapped indoor feeling I went at it furiously, as I did everything in that time.

"Cute as a *button*," hissed those girls, hissed Vida, and week after week I ignored them. Vida would put a finger to her lips, as if saying *sshhh* to her less perfect friends, but only on the rare occasion when Miss McCracken noticed and got peeved enough to glare over.

Since Miss McCracken was truly single-minded about sewing, she rarely bothered to look up from whomever's project she was supervising, her eyes and ears locked into the small universe of the sewing machine. Oblivious. After a few weeks, Vida and her crew discovered, in a storage drawer, a trove of tiny, light buttons they could hurl through the air at me. They pitched the diminutive, annoying things—never big bold ones, always dainty, round, common—in my direction. Miss McCracken, so wifty, that woman, noticed none of it.

Each day would take me the entire two-mile walk back home to get my namesakes all out of my hair—my one good feature, my one vanity, long and light brown, tied tight into a bun and wrapped in cheesecloth when I worked afternoons and weekends in my father's butcher shop.

(But you never really get away from the smell of blood and of thick flesh, the smell of the moment right before decay, the moment where corpse turns to food.)

I wasn't the same sort of young girl as these tidy-stockinged ones who hissed at me. I had no suitors, I had few friends. I had an increasingly morose father whom I saw less and less of, somehow, and an awful great-aunt, Stephanie, who lived with us for the sole point of making my life miserable.

"Cute as a *button*," Vida's girls would hoot, somehow not tired of themselves already.

It got easier and easier not to hear it. But after everything changed in my life, I stopped ignoring them:

I had become so used to it, I guess I could tell when the buttons would hit me without even looking. One day, as if supernaturally, without looking up, I started catching their projectiles in my fist. A button so delicate, mother of pearl, the size of the nail on your pinky flew into my hand while my eyes were pinned on whatever ugly thing I was sewing. Only after a nice long pause did I raise my face to theirs.

The witches jumped, but Vida's expression did not change.

I rolled my eyes at them and grinned.

Then I dropped the tiny thing on my outstretched tongue, curled it back into my throat. Swallowed as I turned my eyes straight to Vida.

Well that shut them up for awhile.

I smiled, and rammed the embroidery needle in and out haphazardly, deliriously happy, regardless of those witches, because finally, a few weeks before, I *had* found a suitor.

As often happens, the best, most precious things in life have their root in a moment when you could never imagine things being less than dreary and awful. My Aunt Stephanie, lording over my few hours out of the butcher shop, in evenings, had decided that my hair was the hair of a harlot.

"Passionate hair," she'd say, "the downfall of Woman."

Compassion for Stephanie's deteriorating mental state was not in my repertoire then. It got worse, in my father's increasing absence.

"Harlot hair," she'd whisper over and over, then "The innards of Woman!"

I silenced my outbursts and my hatred for her—for I hated her, I had not one single drop of love for that poor, simple woman. Any tolerance I showed her was for the sake of my own survival and for love of my father, whose health and business were already failing, and whose nerves didn't need the additional burden of feminine domestic turmoil.

Thank god my father was still in the shop, that day, the slicing machinery shrilly buzzing at full speed when Stephanie finally got out the scissors.

It was a rare afternoon off for me. I dropped my pile of books on the bench outside my room, and quickly ran a brush through my hair to find any of the last projectiles from home economics class. I smiled, and I was pleased with what I saw in that mirror—a rare occurrence. Usually I looked plain, though it didn't bother me much.

I sensed something behind me, but as I was looking in the mirror I didn't worry, figured I was just imagining things.

But then I heard the metally *shrrrr-shrrrr*, the snipping sound of Aunt Stephanie's pinking shears, coming up fast behind me, so fast, as if flying.

I turned, raised my arm stiffly, hitting her forearm, sending the wolf-mouthed scissors tumbling over the bed, clattering into the dirty pipes under the steam radiator, just missing an heirloom mirror of my mother's. I came an inch from knocking Stephanie in her chin. My fist stopped somehow. I swore at her, instead, for what seemed like ten minutes. She shrunk back in horror, and just as her mouth tightened into judgment, into disdain, I blustered past her.

I walked all the miles from our shop in Toughkenamon halfway to West Chester, found a bare golden hill, winter-dead grass the color of my own hair. My expression as black as the end-of-winter tree trunks dotting the land. Then easing, easing as I got off the road and climbed that hill to the top, to the edge of someone's orchard, I didn't care whose.

I hoisted myself fast—these red-blood hands strong and good for the real rather than the art—into that tree and that's when Elmer showed up.

That tree—really not so far from where he put a fishpond in for me later.

"What did that tree ever do to you?" he asked me. I hadn't even noticed I was absentmindedly, furiously, kicking a patch of it down to the rose-brown meat under the bark.

Somewhere in the next hour, behind his dark dark lashes, Elmer's blue eyes seemed to go all swimmy at the sight of me.

It was night by the time we climbed down from that branch together—jumping at once, holding hands, tumbling—ha!—safely to ground. He walked me all the way home. Since that first moment, he has yet to say a single simple-minded or uninteresting word to me.

My father loved me, but had the stoic manner of his family and was reticent in showing his affection. Never had I known such pouring love, such kindness and attention as Elmer gave me. All of a sudden! Three mornings a week (when he didn't have to mind the cows) Elmer would walk out to Toughkenamon to escort me to school. Letters, hearts of sweets, sodas. A necklace I still have somewhere, the tinny, pretty thing. The moment of liking what I saw in the mirror expanded into weeks of feeling like that, mirror or no.

So the daily bombardment in sewing class dwindled to zip in the face of my good mood. I found myself smiling through most of it. I was impossible to irritate.

By day I swallowed the button—swallowed myself!—I was so sweet on Elmer, so happy, that I was completely out of the woods of caring if my defiance angered those Vida girls into some sort of smear campaign, some sort of turning even the teacher against me. I'd seen them do it time and time again to other girls who stood up to them. (They got poor Abby Miller kicked out of school for supposedly stealing, when everyone knew she was the best-behaved choirgirl of all the Presbyterians.) Vida's unnatural power at that school was why I remained quiet until Elmer came along, until Elmer had chased me and wooed me for three weeks, which seemed long enough to feel secure in his affections.

Well, I was *seventeen*.

Who cared what the sewing teacher thought I'd done? I had this fine boy waiting, out on the marbly steps, to carry my books home for me?

A big breath of a year, 1928, all the hope in the world, though for what, *exactly*, I hadn't yet pinned down. Vague adventures were awaiting me—this sense of a temporary *roaming* destiny had been with me since I was a girl. I saw my future as a sort of vision. I saw it very clearly: a woman, dressed in the old-fashioned bun, soft eyes, tiny-waist fashion of my mother's generation would one day cut the tether to the basket of my hot air balloon, and then the wide vistas of the world would be all I needed to stay afloat as long as I preferred. But by this point I knew it also involved Elmer. I knew I wanted that land under the apple tree and the boy in the tree with me.

That pearl button in my stomach, doing who knows what, but it didn't irk me as I left the school building that day—I had shocked the witches into silence, and my love was waiting for me. All sunshine, lightness, 1928.

But Elmer avoided my eye, out there on those steps. I could feel the weight of the tiny button inside me suddenly, the weight doubling, tripling with each passing second. The weight of my own arrogance, of my own reckless dive into hope.

He was with his friends, and that Vida Cloud wanted Elmer's attention had been made clear to every boy in the group. One shoved him, ever so slightly, in her direction and I stood there slack-mouthed—that button a pound of stone in my stomach now—watching as he carried *her* books home for her—headed *her* up Union Street, headed to the Cloud mansion right near the northwestern edge of town, headed to the insides of the snow-globe world so few were ever allowed to enter.

I didn't use Stephanie's pinking shears myself when I cut off all my hair later that night. I found my mother's good old scissors, inside a perfectly-embroidered sewing case in her closet, and hacked my one good feature into the slattern cousin of a bob. By pitching a fit in the vice principal's office—he was a shy man, easily embarrassed by such feminine excess—I managed a switch from sewing to typing, and the clacka-clacka noise from those keys kept the tears away until the bell rang, when I'd go to the ladies room, run the water loud, and weep.

I will admit it now: years later, when I heard of Vida's death—tuberculosis—I smiled. The corners of my lips turned up. I never told Elmer, and I don't like myself for it now, especially since I see his leaving me was so necessary, such a gift. But still. I hated her. Purely—not 99% pure, like Ivory soap, but all the way pure, white pure hate.

It only lasted a few weeks between Vida and him, but Elmer was too embarrassed afterwards, and I was too proud, for either of us to look at each other again. When my tears subsided, months later, suddenly I was all too aware of that *redness* of my hands, the red blushing splotches on my face. Time spent in the butcher shop no longer seemed precious to me for the help it provided my father—the blood was not leaving me and I despised it. Rendering *me*: unwanted, unrefined, un-beautiful, un-Cloud. Elmer's father was a farmer but on the gentlemanly side of that word— there was money and class in that family even though they looked so Irish and had dirt under their nails. I knew I couldn't compete.

I wanted *away*, and when my father died, right after graduation, it only got worse. So Stephanie went to darken her sister's home in Delaware, and I was free to go. I had a certain amount of money from the sale of the butcher shop to set me up. By August I was on a train to New York City.

I got myself a secretarial job, some connections, some fine clothing the linings of which I can still conjure on my skin. The shapes of the heels of the shoes—if I were an artist, that shape could take me years to explain, to get at on canvas. In this way, I began to measure up. I got myself some class, then I became so occupied with my work and the events and people in front of me in New York City that I stopped worrying about the trappings so much and by the time all that crazy money ran out—not even until the *middle* of the thirties where I worked, strange luck would have it—I had no problem facing death again: I got training and a job as a nurse.

I thought about going back to Pennsylvania then. A sudden barrage of love letters from Elmer set my mind churning on it, but I decided I just wasn't ready to go *back* after all this. I told myself Elmer had just been a childish fancy, that surely I'd feel the same way about someone else soon. Why would I return to the countryside to live with a farmer? I doted over my work at the hospital, I felt needed and useful, I felt that my unsqueamish, unfeminine nature was finally put to good use. I was essential, *crucial*. I was *not* ready to give up, for Elmer's sake, this blood I chose again. But then there were more and more swooning letters and a few phone calls. He phoned the hospital drunk and begging; it turned out he was calling from a bar on 13th street. I'd grown my hair out again, long enough to wrap twice around his hand as I negotiated his drunken mass down Seventh Avenue.

One thing let to another, and I decided to go back to him. I gave notice at work. I wriggled out of my lease. We set a date.

But then, after he'd gone back to Pennsylvania to wait for me, Violetta came along, the week before I was to move out of my walk-up on Perry Street. Maybe I had become a beauty in my own right with years in New York, maybe my fingers were fast from typing and suturing instead of scored and bloody and death-soaked from rendering. But I still had to work for it and the Clouds still didn't and though she was *nine years* our junior, Elmer's and mine, Violetta somehow managed to steal my home from me the second time.

Like sorcery—I to this day do not know how she seduced him. His love for me was so true, obvious and necessary as rain.

The details of this theft are something I have never had the heart to get exactly straight—all I know is, somehow, drunkenly, in a fit of cold feet, Elmer got Violetta pregnant, and with a father like hers, you better bet they announced a wedding date within days of knowing.

The second damn Cloud sister to ruin for me. This younger one, the most perfect of all five. As if my horrible Aunt Stephanie's god were working out the kinks of my reality via one spotless family, one spotless chain of daft girls.

I shipped out overseas, where I gave morphine. Overseas, I poured shots of whiskey for myself and for the living whose flesh was already maggot-gobbled. I lied with sugar in my voice. I stared at night instead of sleeping for a month here and there. I learned that a drink of water, a breath, can be enough. A wink can be enough. A smile. A needle. A bullet. Hope can be enough, and resignation can also be enough.

I sewed a man's ear back onto his head, using no anesthetic, while leading him in "The Battle Hymn of the Republic."

I dug graves.

Each great army worked in abstractions: lily-white at the top of the food chain. Lily-white and most vicious there, most vicious not in actual ripping of flesh, but in its coldness, and in its scope. In secret. White-death issued from the top. Clean and removed and keeping its power. For us—the tiny red cross on the white cap—it was a redder death. The loved-lamb embraced seconds before its mess—its body—turns to corpse. To food. Necessary, and honored by those like my father, who knew and admitted this bloody death was necessary and that he was—we were—responsible for it. It's only useless, vicious, heartless, wrong when the killer keeps his hands white and distant, when the killer insists that purity, innocence, is possible and that he, the vegetarian murderer, embodies purity's grace.

To live you kill. Any simpleton knows it. The Clouds of the world hand it off to the butchers of the world. To become a girl, which I never rightly achieved, I had tried fine leather heels and a tidy secretarial job. But then to become a woman, I became a nurse: I repaired the work of too many soldiers with my old, red heart, with my red, sullied hands of a butcher.

I came back in 1946 and didn't speak for two months. Violetta was already dead by then—my opposite: her fragility killed her, finally. Nervous exhaustion led to what finally put her under.

I lived then in the prim boarding house on Union Street, run by Miss McCracken's sister, Betty, another maiden lady. She and the other three residents seemed to understand that I would nod or shake my head, but never utter a sound. This silence somehow protected me, worked as a bandage to heal me of what I'd seen.

Two months of it. But then the small details of life came seeping into me and the blood of my childhood in the butchers, the death of money that I'd attended in New York, the bodies that decomposed in front of me finally became part of my past.

Elmer came calling for me the morning after he'd heard, at the barbershop, from the milkman, that I'd finally opened my mouth and talked six hours straight. (It was to Miss McCracken, who was as interested in cleaning as her sister had been in sewing, and who buffed every single armoire in the house to a piny-smelling glow that morning while I prattled and prattled and prattled on. Not about the war. About the clothes. The gloves and the stockings and the lingerie and the stoles.)

I hated Violetta for taking what I had once secretly maybe wanted most: safety. I can't quite explain this even now. I hated her because before I saw the things I saw in the war I maybe still wanted that Cloud safety she had. I hated her because her example proved that even in safety, even on the farm with Elmer, I was eventually going to die. Even after all I had seen in the war, it still seemed unendurable: the impossibility of the *hope*, even, of anyone's ever actually being as safe as I once thought a Cloud girl *had* to be.

You have to understand: the carcasses of steer, of baby lambs, of fat sows whose names I had given them as piglets had been familiar to me since I was four and my father kept watch over me in the shop, while he worked. Death protected me. Life *without* a focus on death terrified me— after the war, such a wide absence of death, the butcher shop long sold, peacetime yellow and sky blue and new babies everywhere. I was terrified.

This is all another story. This is not the story for right now.

Right now—this ancient body, my fingernails brownish and thick and my blood a hundred years old, a thousand. An old lady's bad breath.

Right now—screeching pain as I tried to turn back to Racinda to see if it were true, if she were, strange enough, the third in a line of Clouds to steal me from the man who is my home. That is to say, if coming back into these cranky bones was futile and hopeless for Ruth because the weakness was too strong in her sister, the only savior possible.

Yes. Futile.

Right now—the aching light of this place, winter light. Right now—Racinda grown, twenty? Violetta in her face, her white tiny chin.

Right now Racinda staring down at me waiting for me to talk more. Then starting to talk herself: mental hospital, boyfriend, oh what a jerk, what ailed him, that one. Ruth, Ruth Ruth, and me, drawn into her eyes and me, braying here, a grunt there.

I managed an *of course* that I thought sounded normal.

I said it before: I always knew the touch of the girls apart. Ruth scalding, tight, demanding. Racinda temperate: Racinda's hand gripping you tight only because she feared getting carried away by wolves, by devils if you let go.

Such exhaustion swarmed me, such despair. . . I let my eyes slip closed.

That hand, its abilities clearer and clearer through the grayness Elmer's hand yes, I reached mine out for it and I felt myself start to awaken on the other side.

Except it wasn't Elmer, it was Racinda. And I was still in the hospital room.

Honey colored hair.

I looked down and my hand was tight around my granddaughter's, and I understood:

Yes, she *was* mine as much as Violetta's and it was her hand that had somehow become capable and strong despite her bloodline.

"Button?"

"Dear. . ." I said, and I just smiled, I just lay back and smiled.

With that her tears began.

"Come here no come here—no, come here come here—" I said to her and I forced my absurd arms out into a hug, my pain banished somehow until she sat back down in the chair.

"Ruth wants to run away to India," Racinda blurted out.

I nodded, words stuck in my throat.

"I don't know, I don't know what to do about it," she said. "I mean, even if I find her what am I supposed to do."

She smoothed the skin of my forearm absentmindedly.

I cleared my throat with a sound like you'd make climbing a mountain, a sound like you'd make emerging from a cave.

"I need to tell you something here, young lady. I need to tell you something about your father, about your grandmother—"

"Violetta?"

"Yes. Now listen—"

And with that the door to the hallway flew open.

"Oh for gad's sake, don't tell me visiting hours are up?" I said, coughing something up into a tissue.

The door was open but I couldn't see faces.

"Well who's there?" I said.

"Oh, God," Racinda said, dropping my hand.

Two heads, murky, leaning in my doorway.

"Hello, dear," the male head said.

"Jesus. What are you two, anyway, Hospital Kojak?" Racinda said.

"Watch your mouth, young lady," the male head said, "Your mother's upset and you know she doesn't like it when you use the Lord's name in vain."

"Oh for Christ's sake," I said, "Amandine? Amandine?"

And she wasn't young anymore, and she wasn't fragile anymore. But how old was Amandine? Forty? Past it, of course, but the she still looked attractive as such. Why was I so surprised she smiled, honestly elated to see me awake? I had forgotten that we made a certain peace all those years after Ruth was born. Amandine had been so white-innocent, lame like Violetta Cloud, when she was in her twenties but now—something, something *else* to Amandine. . . .

The constant death-scares of Ruth, surely. Of course of course of course.

So when she came to me first—she and Racinda avoiding each other. I braced for the pain of movement and held Amandine tight to me.

Amandine turned to Racinda, but Racinda spoke first, with her eyes averted. Softly, kindly.

"Hey, Mom."

"Racinda, honey."

Amandine hesitated, looked confused and afraid, as if bearing bad news.

Racinda's face darkened, that softness gone from her voice.

"*What.*"

Racinda inched back from her mother, eyed the man suspiciously.

The confusion on Amandine's face turned to love, to a smile for her daughter. I couldn't tell if it was the same empty kook-church expression Amandine used to get when was with the Jesus freaks in the seventies, or if it was genuine.

A big-faced man, he was—not bald a'tall, so I don't know what Racinda meant by calling him Kojak—put his hand on Amandine's shoulder as if to brace her, as if Amandine's love and confusion could only make her unsteady.

"I think, Amandine, we might want to take this outside so as not to upset Button," he said.

"Kojak, who are you anyway?" I said. "How about an introduction?"

"Button, this is Rudy Mitchell," Amandine said.

"It's an honor," he said, and bowed in my direction, as if he knew how badly it would hurt me to shake hands.

Rudy—I liked him already.

"Button," Amandine said too loudly, as if I were deaf, then realized what she was doing and started talking normal again, "He's helping us find Ruth and. . . he's helping. . . her. . ."

Something dark on Amandine's face, a confusion that *was* unsteadying.

"Yeah, *right*," Racinda said.

"Let's—" he said, "Let's take this outside. Ma'am," he said to me with such a gracious, honorable expression on him, "If you'll just excuse the three of us for a moment."

"Well, no let's have it out in here, sir, I can handle it," I said. I struggled a bit but was able to lean forward and not rest my back on the raised bed.

Racinda's face was the color of ice.

"What!" Racinda barked, but in a near-whisper. "What happened to her!"

Amandine eased on in to her.

"Now honey—"

"What is fucking going on—"

"Now, Racinda, calm down. I just, I'm just going, I need to make this clear to you," Amandine said.

"Is she dead?"

"No, Racinda, she's not dead. She's not—not yet."

"*What.*"

"She's—it's just, Rudy and I really, really need to know, honey," and Amandine's hand went out to smooth the hair from Racinda's eyes, "We really need to know if you know anything about her, or where she might be, because we are very afraid for her if she goes out of the country—we just don't think in her manic state that she'll be able to take care of herself. We're. . ."

Racinda glared.

"We're very afraid she might—*she* might think she has not that long left, and that she might do things that could hasten. . ."

How could Amandine say these things in this calm, sure voice? The man, Rudy, was controlling it all. I had yet to be dead wrong on a first impression, but I wasn't sure I liked him so much now. Amandine was under a spell, acting not on her own. But then, when had she ever acted on her own, out of any clear idea of reality, out of any clear motivation?

I tried to say *that's enough*, but it came out as a gurgle.

Racinda inhaled, pulled her hand away from her mother. And sang a little song.

"Fuck you, fuck you fuck you," she sang, "you are a crazy lun-a-tiiiiic, I am going the bathroom." Then, "La. La. La," in a black, ironic tone I found distasteful.

La. La. La.

Left.

"For gad's sake," I managed, "Rudy, please get me some water—for gad's sake Amandine, what is wrong with you? Why are you going around scaring her like that? She's already scared. No need to make it worse. Hmmm."

"Button. . ." Amandine said.

"What?" I said, "Don't *Button* me and then shut up like that."

"Well, we *are* very worried about Ruth. We need to get her back in our care and make sure she's in a controlled environment," she looked to Rudy and nodded.

"So?"

"If you've heard from her, or know anything, we just really need to know. Time is of the essence," she said, and she got that soupy God-grin again and held my hand sick-sweetly.

"You know, Mrs. Hart," Rudy said to me, "Because of the trust you provided her we can get her to the right facility, the right place for her that will give her more control," Rudy said.

Amandine shot him—for the briefest second—her *own* glare.

But I'd already made my decision.

"Sure thing," I said, and my voice cracked into a wheeze, a cough. They seemed relieved.

I tried to remember that lawyer's number.

I couldn't even remember his name. The wires were crossed in my brain—wires into and out of the other realm, wires sparking into lost years, wires flying down Route One between here and State Street that, once I remembered, would take my phone call to the right man for the job.

Two.

Amandine decided that that was the last time she was going to feel guilty at the sight of her daughter's stomping out a room on her when she was in the middle of saying something. She was going to be very sure that she knew what ground she stood on, so that if Racinda stomped away in those awful boots again, Amandine would know she hadn't mortally failed her daughter.

Button dozed off before they could properly say goodbye, but Amandine planted a light kiss on the old woman's bony forehead, smoothed the cotton-tufts of hair down neatly

The two stood by the plate glass window in the waiting room and looked out at the fields, still patchy with snow on the edges, in gullies, and windy and gray at the heights of trees in the distance. It looked cold out, but in fact November's early freeze had given way to a sixty-five degree morning.

Amandine felt a little giddy—at least *one* thing was clear. She *had* to put her foot down about the shock therapy Fox Hill place. She was sure she was going to say something to Rudy. No question. So she inched herself closer in to Rudy's body, tried to imprint his side, his thick, practiced arm, into her memory, because she was *almost* sure that what she was about to say to him was going to drive him away and leave her to a painful, long, not even peaceful life of solitude.

"We're hot on her trail, I can feel it," he said.

"Rudy—" Amandine said.

"I can just—sometimes in this line of work you get what I like to call a 'gut' feeling."

Amandine knew the gray, windy landscape would feel strangely warm for the season once she was actually out in it, but she couldn't believe it from here, on the other side of the glass. She shivered. She leaned on him in the very quiet waiting room.

"Rudy," she said, finally, the imprint of his side against hers forever linked now to the vision of Racinda storming off, a furious shake of the teenage locks, furious back of the neck, of legs, disappearing through a door

Lowering herself onto the mustard-yellow cushion of an uncomfortable bench, she spoke, finally.

"Rudy what are we doing? I just explained that to Racinda, but I'm not even sure—I'm not even sure what the right thing is to do for Ruth once we get her. She's an adult. We can't kidnap her."

"Amandine, we've talked about—"

She stood, turned her head to him and took in his bewildered expression—one she'd seen snippets of before, but that he'd always quashed into forward-thinking determination and confidence and male bossiness.

"Talk, sure," she said, and she fluttered her hand across her cheek. "Talk, Rudy, we've talked, and I've talked to doctors, in circles for years, and I just don't really know, I mean, what can ever be done about her? Years of the same, years of not knowing. Losing her and getting her back and she manipulates and. . . "

"This new facility, the EST. . ." Rudy said, trailing off, whether into hope or doubt was unclear.

"Rudy—I just—"

"We're so close, Amandine! I can feel it—"

"Feel it. . . . ? Rudy?"

He wouldn't look at her. She stopped trying to get him to, and just stood there with him, her head just below his shoulder, nuzzled into him quietly.

Amandine sighed, steeling herself against cracking apart.

"Rudy, she's not going to the shock therapy place," she said, "I've decided.

Her voice fissured at the immensity of it, she didn't even reach into her purse for a tissue, just wiped her nose sloppily on her hand.

"A mother knows. This is not right for Ruth," she said.

Amandine turned the white cuff of her blouse over and blew her nose into it very gently. Bit her lip.

Would he leave her now for not following his careful plan?

Would *she* fire him now that his services had failed to succeed clearly with Ruth?

The fears of each one budded and blossomed and fell to ground, dried and decayed and molded into new earth in the silence that followed.

When she finally looked up at him, she was amazed. His face wasn't contorted in fury. It wasn't cold and avoidant. It *was* confused, though.

"Well. . ." he said. Hurt, but also curious.

She waited.

"Well," he said, "If you've found someplace, of course, with a more effective cure rate... I wasn't able to... locate..."

"No, we'll just have to find that place," she said. "I need your help."

He smiled, but his sad eyes mirrored Amandine's own: this confusion willing to stay the long haul, confusion with a good measure of humor in it.

And determination. Not the determination of a once-young man commanding an army, but the determination to stand right where he was, at Amandine's side, facing out at the shock of a thawing ground, facing the delight of the bare winter branches.

"Where are we going next, then?" Rudy asked.

"Good question," Amandine said.

"Well, we could still drive into Philadelphia and see if we might spot Ruth in there. The drive would give us some time to think," he said.

"True," Amandine said, a sudden ferocity coming to her at the specter of Philadelphia's small time sleazebags taking advantage of her beautiful daughter. These Philadelphia crooks raised her ire more, somehow, than their west coast counterparts, whose hippie, free-love glaze somehow made them less dangerous.

"Yes—maybe," Amandine said, "Okay," she said, "Let me, let me peer over there down that hallway and see if I can't get Racinda to say goodbye to me before we go."

But Racinda wasn't in the hallway, nor the ladies toilets cross from Button's room. Nor in the phone booth. Amandine sat down on the sweetly upholstered cushion of the empty pay phone and made a reservation in a Chadds Ford motel for Racinda. Amandine got an envelope from the nurses station and put all her wallet's cash plus a note about the hotel room in it. Button was still asleep when Amandine left the envelope—marked with two hearts and Racinda's name—under Button's water pitcher.

"So," Rudy said after they'd walked in silence to the car. "Philly—or—?"

"Let's have lunch first," Amandine decided, "Let's just eat. I'm starving. I'm starving."

*　　　*　　　*

Racinda wandered the hallways, blocking out the infirm and the crazy, the just plain old and the nurses who attended them, until she found a bathroom down a ways and settled into its emptiness.

She left the lights off, tried to figure out which stall to hide away in. Sun pooled in a few high windows but had the effect of coming into a basement. Warm, orange-flecked brown paint covered the stalls and the walls, the mirror was narrow, just showing Racinda's head, her neck. It looked like a cheap full-length mirror from Kmart tacked up horizontally in front of the old sinks. She peeked quickly under the stall doors for feet, and, finding none, nestled herself onto the closed toilet lid in the far stall.

Ruth could die: Racinda tried the words on for size but immediately wanted to eliminate all three of them from her repertoire.

On the bus on the way here it had hit Racinda much as it was hitting her right now.

At first the dip and line of the bus's chrome exterior had thrilled her. The air of San Jose had been fresh with the coldness of winter approaching. Hills greening. Racinda had sucked California through her teeth there at the Greyhound station, inhaling a certain glee at the vastness of possibility—a sense of adventure rushing into her, the adventure of going it alone. Not tugged along as the dragging anchor of someone else's unmoored boat—Joey's, Ruth's, Amandine's. That frozenness in her had cracked a little, had let spring rivulets of water up, had let her be carried to the next bend in the stream: ready to brave the next twist, to pitch around the banks, to take the bruise from rocks and branches in her path.

On the bus, Racinda tried to smile at the unaccompanied thirteen year old girl who sat next to her for most of the ride, but it didn't matter, the girl couldn't look her in the face. The girl put her canvas duffel up on the rack and wedged in next to Racinda, then doused herself in Love's Baby Soft, that eternal pink drugstore perfume, caramelized baby powder.

"Excuse me," Racinda said as she stumbled over Love's Baby before Love's Baby even knew what was going on. Racinda held a hand over her mouth and nearly ran to the bathroom in the back of the bus, jolted herself in with the metal lever that locked the door tight. The stench was different, worse, barely *earthly*, in there. But she stayed.

She gasped air in, she sucked to banish the dizzy nausea but the horrible fact underneath all the details filled her. There was no getting out of *breathing* now, was there? She thought *Ruth could die*, she felt herself dissipating, thinning out, watering down and she felt herself trapped with her sister's, with her mother's history, trapped with that terror, frozen. And she held her breath.

It kept the bathroom smell out.

It kept the Love's Baby Soft out.

It kept *everything* out.

But it was not going to show her anything. It was not going to show her anything at all about how to keep Ruth alive.

It seemed perfectly reasonable to crawl back to her seat. She almost did it, too, she almost fell to the ground after putting her weight on that bathroom door to open it, but the smell near the ground was clearly worse than the dizzy, sick effort to walk upright.

Just past the Ohio border into Pennsylvania, still hours from her home, sleep finally hit her like a second bottle of wine.

She went deep into it. The approach home registered in her dreams— the deep blacks and teals and blues of her mother's sea hag, the claws reaching into Racinda's belly now, the claws violating and stealing what was hers.

Just outside Lancaster, at dawn, Racinda twisted awake, sweating, the fear painted across the gray November horizon, the brown hills wet and shining in yellow, painterly light.

The sea hag reached out and grabbed Racinda's hand back into sleep and led her down, through the darkness of her dreams, down *into* Ruth, and Racinda could hear the voices Ruth heard, Racinda could feel the rage welling into muscles that had to pinch, had to scream obscenities, had to wipe out a boy's teeth with a trowel, had to smoke crystal meth until there was no money left and there was no buzzing left in those muscles, until there was a crash that was finally something like calm even in its excruciating clarity. *Go to India*—this voice wasn't Jesus, it wasn't Char.

Don't try to turn me off the voice said, *it's time to go to India. It's time to find what she promised you. It's time to make a clean breast. It's time to lose yourself.*

Ruth's voices.

As Racinda sucked in air and tears, the words faded, sleep faded. She kept her eyes closed and prayed, to whomever would listen, for the voice to go away.

Three.

Button:

The watery fuzz of half-sleep lifted and though I was alone in my room and not dimwitted enough—yet—to start talking to myself, somehow words were clearer in my throat. I could tell. I could feel them there, fully formed, free of lapses into moose noises. Thoughts were clearer. I sat up without bringing on sheer exhaustion. Racinda looked shaken on her return, confused—what ailed her? She'd left here drunk on plain anger, storming out on Amandine like that.

Well, I guessed it was time I ought to try to help clear things up.

"So, dear, what I was saying was. . ." I began.

"Yes," Racinda said.

"What I was saying was, your grandmother was fragile. Frail. Nervous. Thin-skinned," I said.

"Violetta," Racinda said, her brow still knitted.

"Well. . ." I managed, "Your grandmother came from a rich family. She was the last in a line of five perfect sisters. We all hated them—their birthday parties, the Sunday drives their father insisted on to show them off. You wanted—we, *we* wanted, the normal girls of the town, that is—wanted to believe their gaiety was a show, but it wasn't. They enjoyed their superior, sunny status. Beyond haughty. Beyond. All the money *didn't* isolate them. . . just the opposite. Suitors galore.

"But when she married your grandfather, when I was up in New York, Violetta had to give up the heavy cream of all that. Still worked little, but made meals for herself and your father, at least. And that's when. . . well, she started to get sick. The life started going out of her. Her beauty cracked and aged and without the whole of her (and a bunch of paid help's) attention going to her own vanity and sense of superiority. I do believe she *decided* to die.

"Even her son—your *father*, dear—wasn't enough to keep her here once the outside props of her self got unsturdy."

"Sad," Racinda said.

I looked at her. I felt a little betrayed for her saying it.

"Your father was only six when she died," I said. "He saw her not be able to handle the fact that Elmer couldn't pay a cleaning woman that year, that she had to mop her own floor. I always thought she died on him instead of cleaning her own house."

"Jeez," Racinda said finally.

"Your father—I think when he left," I said, and she started crying on me. "Dear, come here," I said, and my feeble hand stroked her hair, "Now your father, I always thought he had this same nitwit fragility. Always going for what was safest, what was tidiest. Like your mother, too—so perfect, and she kept everything up so perfect and tried to hold onto that so tightly. But then, of course, all that crushed the life right out of Lyman.

He just—I could see it growing in him before he left. He didn't know he already had it—he had to run away to find mess, to find life."

"Shoot, Button. Fucking—*he* isn't our problem right now," she said, leaning her head against me.

"Where did you get such a mouth?" I said. "No, he's not any more of a problem now than he's ever been but listen. They all convinced you, I did too, that you were as fragile as your father, as Violetta. As your mother."

"What are you talking about?"

"You hid in the basement. You ran from Ruth. But you didn't *always*, dear. You fought back sometimes, but we just—we all just bolstered this idea that you were the weak one even though she was sick. That you would cling, you would stay, that you needed your sister.

"I can see it so clearly, one day out by the orchard, this time of year exactly. Always getting the damn bulbs in late, the ground a little too tough."

My laugh radiated as pain and then something else—a dissolving, a shattering of time—through my extremities.

"And Ruth starts to get angry. Ruth stops digging the holes and instead starts swinging, spinning around with a branch six inches thick and taller than either of you. A dervish, sharp and dangerous and missing little you by inches with this limb off a tree. Ruthie, now stop, I say to her but she's caught up in the momentum of it and just before I get up to stop her—expecting you, the little one, just to bend to her, appease her, I notice something.

"I notice that you made a little dance of dodging her blows. And—blows, they weren't blows. You danced with her crazy spinning. You were laughing because she couldn't see you for all her wild twisting around to notice. You stepped in and out of her range just perfectly, and you tumbled to the ground right when Ruth was ready to stop. You kept it from becoming a . . . scene . . . an episode."

"Yeah," she said, voice thick and watery, "It was like my only point was to be her fire alarm."

Outside a raven pecked at a turkey vulture, got himself his high branch back and sent that vulture scooting away.

"But now you know it," I said, "Now you know all that."

The twilight murk of the room all around us, filling that moment with breath, expanding it.

Racinda's brows clenched together, thinking, dubious.

"You bought it hook line and sinker without me ever saying a word. You knew and believed me. It just seemed so real, this bloodline that ran from Violetta's peaches-and-cream skin to your father's watery eyes to your own hiding, your own hiding behind your sister and behind your mother."

"Yeah?" she said, defensive.

I sat straight up and she had to take her head off my arm.

"It's a damn lie that Violetta believed and was willing to die rather than get over. It's a lie that your father is probably still running from. And it's a lie that you are fragile, and it's a lie that you can't live without your sister. You've done it for years now already, look at you. I want to keep her alive as much as you do but if something did happen to her you would be fine."

"Now you *know*. You know. And that dance you did, it wasn't just *sad*. You didn't break—you knew exactly when to step, when to give yourself a laugh and how to corral her back in. You didn't always run for the basement. Dear—*look* at you!"

Her beauty was her own, not her grandmother's. She tilted her head like she was considering it—her own strength—for the first time. She bent one corner of her mouth down in the way she always had, as a girl, when she was secretly puzzling through something.

"Look at you."

She tilted her head and waited for my hand to smooth her hair—the gesture didn't hurt me a lick. I'd rarely seen her so peaceful and happy, to tell you the truth, so I hated to ruin it with what I was going to have to tell her next.

"Dear," I said.

"Hm," she said, her face sweet as kittens, at ease under my fingers.

"Racinda, dear I've gone ahead and. . ."

Oh, her features had that sweet-molasses set I just hated to ruin, but there was no choice.

"Well, Racinda, I've gone ahead and switched you to Ruth's legal guardian. Well—I'm going to as soon as what's-his-name the attorney gets his act together."

The lip twisted into a new, deeper frown.

"You will worry about her as much whether you're in charge of her trust or not. Competence is the only choice here. So—leaving it up to you, dear, you're the one who knows her the best."

"Button—" she said.

I widened my expression to welcome her complaint.

"And it will be worse for you to battle your mother *and* worry," I said.

"Button—" and looked to the floor. The window. The doorway.

"Well," I said, "Well, you're going to have to, or you're going to have to find someone else to do it for you. But you're going to have to step up to the plate here, Racinda."

"I'm eighteen years old!"

"Well, when I was a year younger than you are now I took a train to New York City on my own. I set myself up at the YWCA and found myself a job typing even though I was still useless at it for being lovesick all through typing class. All I knew how to do was render and butcher and season."

"This isn't exactly a two-hour train trip here."

"Who else is going to do it, Racinda?" I said.

She wadded her hand into a little spitball of a fist and stuck it in front of her mouth.

"It's not wrong just because it's not perfect," I said.

"Button—I just need to get some air for a minute."

The metal rail of my bed shook with her hand as she gripped it to stand up.

"Of course, dear," I said, and I could feel the strength and beauty of her shining face—even through the confusion, the essence of her lit onto my face like the sun lights the craggy old moon. She kissed me on the head and nearly ran out of the room.

Johnson. That's the lawyer's name. And amazing, really, that I remembered that young Johnson's phone number. He liked to died when his secretary finally put me through. Like to died.

Four.

Giving up the nice girl bit, Racinda haphazardly smacked the nursing home hallway's waffle-weave wallpaper on her way to hide in the bathroom again. Nobody noticed.

She understood Violetta completely. Wanting to crawl inside herself, get smaller and smaller, back into a dark, tight space, little air, no movement. She'd always been dragged back out before—by her sister, by life, by the daily exigencies of things. But here, she felt she could stay. Sink.

Would I rather die than deal with Ruth for the rest of my life?

Maybe if Racinda went back to Button's bedside and crawled in with her it would all be okay. Shrink down under the cottony, pilled white blanket, gnaw on its satin border as she had done as a girl. She backed into the stall as far as she could go against the dank, slightly smelly, slightly spacious, slightly disinfectant-sweet stall.

This is ridiculous, she thought.

Ruth can't die.

Of course Ruth will die.

I can't stand this, she thought. I have *got* to get out of here.

I am staring at my knees, locked in a bathroom.

The creak of the door jolted her—embarrassed her—to standing.

Something being wheeled in, each slow push intolerably slow. Dense, wheezing breaths.

Trying to sneak out of her stall, Racinda tried not to stare but the face of this tiny old woman on a walker wouldn't let her pass without looking.

The woman's face a pink, awful blur, something Racinda absolutely did not want to look at, but as if the moon itself had dropped low and hung in the women's room, it demanded attention.

Something—pale red, like tomato soup—smeared across the woman's face, saliva swabbed across her chin. Racinda hovered, ineffectual, unsure if she should offer to help or if that would be condescending. Or even dangerous.

"Hi?" Racinda managed.

The woman smiled.

Racinda smiled back, breath rushing into her as she touched the woman's arm.

The woman opened and closed her small mouth, slowly, as if trying to speak, but the opening quickened and breath paced through and in a minute she was shrieking, a bird's cries, screaming, swooping. Racinda stepped back. The woman's eyes tightened, the woman's eyes swam in fear. Her hands flew at Racinda, tangling in the long pretty hair

"I'm sorry—I'm sorry," Racinda said, offering her hand out in a stay-calm gesture as she backed away, but the woman's hand was caught, shaking and pulling, that tangle of Racinda's hair close to ripping out, and then the smell hit, something worse than a bathroom on a bus.

The woman's hand refusing to relax, Racinda's scalp beginning to sear at the tight point of roots, the stench unbearable—Racinda could see now that the woman's legs were covered in shit.

Racinda looked down at her own fingers, her white, soft hand—the hand precisely ready to pinch her own nostrils shut—and she at the same time saw Button's hand, covered in blood, in 1943, sewing a man's ear back onto his head, saw the black thread going in and out, tiny crosses in an arch across the side of the bloody skull. Heard the man's screams. Saw Button's flat, impassive face give no hint of fear. Saw Button's chest expand slightly, saw something in Button give way and not be walled off. Saw Button take in this man's pain, and the pain of hundreds more. Their deaths. Racinda looked back down at her white, soft hand, and the thought of holding it to her nose almost had her laughing. Useless.

Was it her own little white nose the hand would be holding, or was it Violetta's?

Or did it belong to her father, who had *left* them? *Left us.*

The rot swarmed her. The knot of pain on her scalp quickened, pitched.

The woman just panting now, no sound coming out, but the bizarrely strong hand tightening—Racinda's roots pulling away in a clump, blood coming,

"Hang on," Racinda said, her teeth so tight together she could barely speak.

As she touched the woman's face, Racinda's own pain faded. She smoothed the woman's delicate rings of hair pinned up in bobby pins.

"You're okay," Racinda's voice ancient and soothing and strong.

The woman exhaled and a trail of yellow vomit tumbled across Racinda's legs, her hips, a forearm.

In Racinda's mind: that prissy gesture, those two white, safe fingers about to pinch the nose *were* hers, and she understood now that she'd been doing it on and off her whole life. Some blue, ocean-deep sorrow pooled in her thighs and her stomach and her chest then, because she couldn't imagine the vastness of what she had stupidly lost, all along, day in and day out, by doing this. She wiped blood from the curve of her ear.

When the two orderlies got there to help carry the woman out, they found Racinda under the sinks, serene, covered in vomit and shit too now, her arm around the woman's back, her hand on the woman's forehead, the woman now breathing if not calmly, at least quietly, a thin clump of honey-colored hair in her fist.

Racinda wanted to wash the smell off, but it wasn't exactly *intolerable* any more. *Sad*, she thought, a sad smell, and the rot of it no longer nauseating. Racinda was surprised to find herself saying a quick prayer for the red-faced woman. A prayer to whom, she still didn't know, but this time that didn't matter.

Five.

Button:

I could smell something awful coming from the hallway, something on top of the smell of Greyhound and of Racinda. I could hear a demented woman's cries and I was grateful, so grateful for my earthly sanity. I had called Johnson the lawyer fast, while Racinda was out there and though my voice nearly shocked the pants off him he agreed to work up the documents and get some psychiatrists and MDs in here to prove I was of sound mind. And though I didn't think he really believed that's what they'd say, he humored me. Well, they'd believe it when they saw me.

I closed my eyes, rested, and it seemed clear—it was time to go.

The air and the time started to shatter into waves, like light and water in a lazy swimming pool, lapping and returning. Soon. The hand through the murk—but it was shimmering now, white, not so gray as before—that hand was definitely my husband's. It was the multitude of his hand—every moment of Elmer's hand in this world and that world and others. But that something. . . . something. . . *smelled?*

How irritating! I opened my eyes.

"Button?" Racinda said.

Racinda had a slight dazed look, but wasn't unhappy. She was covered in—what *was* it?

"What happened to you?" I said, and just as she opened her mouth, such sleepiness overwhelmed me.

*   *   *

Soon, soon. My own fingers pulsed. My eyes fluttered. That hand—Elmer's hand, superimposed on the light of the room, *flash*. Then my eyes shut—swimming pool light—safe, no harm, no movement, rest. Hours? Years? But my own hand stirred, awoke me again to the delirious adventure despite its pain. Racinda was gone. She'd nearly crushed me in a wet-haired hug when she got out of the shower, and after that I'd fallen asleep. My eyes reopened just in time to see the raven fly into a massive gust outside, wax-whorled wings the picture of delight. Air and time tumbling forward, Maybe soon. Maybe.

21

The Subaru salesmen smoked cigarettes and talked pussy, leaning against the plate-glass door of the dealership, bending spent filters into a sand-filled ashtray. Hopefully slick, the blue and white and orange and green and yellow pennants hung from a line, flapped in breeze, but there were no customers. There were no mommies to promise safety and all-wheel drive to. There was just asphalt and the whack and slip and crack of those pennants in the breeze. There was the mustard-colored Wendy's sign and green-arrow left turn signal and Hit or Miss women's clothing store and TJMaxx across Route One. There was the Radio Shack whose assistant manager promoted his cover band from his mother's former basement rec-room. Strip malls, asphalt. The promise that if you bought something, even just a double bacon cheeseburger, you could freeze the moment, you could be okay, you could be safe.

But no mommies were coming, that morning—the mess was too big in their houses, the mess was swarming, the mess swamped and pooled and felt like drowning. The beginning of flu season, middle of November, arrived with chapped lips and chapped bottoms and piles and piles of dishes, piles and piles of germs on the dishes.

Today it was warm, but the warmth arrived on the tail of an early, solid freeze. Creeks had already hardened, small ponds had iced over near to their middles. The warmer morning today cracked all the sickness well into the open. This morning, it swerved to the other side of seasonable—somewhere in the high sixties, bright sun, though ice still sparkled across the fields.

The Subaru salesmen edged their conversation in pure guy sureness and the pleasure of being terse. They pushed the missing mommies from their minds this way. One of them—-pink faced, not unkind, mustached, hair blown dry in a perplexing geometry if you looked at it closely—-felt the terseness give, though, felt the control of the man-conversation slip when a moment of silence descended onto Route One, no cars in either direction. Hush. Until.

Long wild tendrils of blond hair flying out the car window filled the emptiness something like a roar in reverse—a sucking-in of all noise. Just for a moment, just until the very loud car stereo got drowned out by this driving woman's voice. Just a regular mid-size rental, a white Ford Taurus, but inside and outside it felt like a convertible. Ruth, driving and still even as an adult perpetually too warm, had all the windows down where anyone else would have been a little chilly, despite the strange weather for November.

Did Kurt Dieckmann recognize Ruth when she shouted his name out the window that day, or did her voice just veer back into the taunt and crack of Mick Jagger's on the radio? Did Kurt Dieckmann swallow the sentence he had been ready to unleash on his Subaru cronies? Did he think of the different way their eyes would land on his wife's backside as she walked up to the buffet at the Christmas party, if they heard what he was just about to tell them? Did he feel mess encroaching? And excess? And a giddy laughter that made him nervous? And his wife's unequalled, delicate jaw line, the woozy drop in her voice right before she'd fall asleep? And the bloody scream of something perpetually beyond the edges of what he understood?

*   *   *

Racinda's stomach soured at the sight of the strip malls on either side of Route One. She had hitched a ride in yet another Mercedes station wagon, which, if you're a woman going it alone, is as good a bet as any. The sweet alto-voiced driver of this one preferred the tennis hair fashionable to the wealthy women of Delaware, and had the khaki shorts and pearls to match. A talker, she explained to Racinda the expanded hours at the new indoor courts in Greenville but Racinda didn't hear much of it. The woman didn't seem drunk, but there was a near-empty bottle of Budweiser hanging from a plastic drink-holder, like you'd buy from the automotive aisle in Kmart.

Where the Subaru dealership stood had once been a field whose sounds and patterns and grasses and smells Racinda knew intimately from her childhood. A meadow that had comforted her, that had given her enough space and the chattering of crickets when she'd needed it. A meadow she still visited in dreams, even, with woods behind it whose secret characters Racinda had understood clearly since she was a child.

Racinda found herself bending over her stomach, just slightly, as if to protect herself from the ugliness. As Racinda tried to take it all in, she discovered she was shrinking away from the fine leather interior of the Mercedes, from the tennis mom's concern.

"It's viral season," she said, and Racinda noticed the way the woman's two front teeth on top overlapped a little, nestled together like kittens, "The viral cloud descends, honey, don't let the weather hypnotize you into thinking you're safe."

Racinda's slight curling in on her chest seemed like what it used to be to her: an old, defensive gesture.

But now, it wasn't: Racinda was simply trying to hear something, cupping her body as you might cup an ear.

She closed her eyes and emptied her mind.

Ruth.

As the station wagon passed the new Subaru dealership, Racinda sat straight up. Somewhere in her peripheral vision—even as if before opening her eyes at all—she caught a quick glimpse of blonde hair, shimmering like light on water. Of course, it couldn't be. She bent in on herself some more, and heard the lyrics in her sister's breathy-rough mezzo-soprano— the darkest Stones song, she thought, this "Angie." Racinda looked fast over each shoulder. But nothing.

As the developed part of Route One gave onto the old, lushly frozen landscape, Racinda understood that the old chant—*what if Ruth dies*— was gone. Perhaps Racinda was a little numb. Definitely strangely *calm* in the new situation Button had just placed her in. But somehow, now that her role was clear, all the monstrous, endless worry seemed useless. There was nothing to do now, but find Ruth, or wait for Ruth, and deal with what needed to be dealt with then. No decision made now would make it any easier.

For a little while after she had showered and changed in Button's private bath, Racinda had staked out the hallway outside Button's room, and she imagined then that she could feel Ruth approach. Even when trying to hitch a ride out on 926, Racinda felt as if each next car might contain her sister. She had stuck out her thumb brashly, sweatily, hotly, more because she knew what Ruth would rush to than because she actually felt it.

She was almost right, out there on 926, because had she not hopped in the wagon with the tennis mom, it wasn't Ruth who would have passed her by next, but Amandine, returning, circuitously, from lunch.

"You know," Rudy said, "I could drive if you're tired."

"I know these roads, Rudy."

"I'm just saying, if you're tired, if you need a rest. It's been a rough morning."

"Thank you."

She took them up 52 all the way to West Chester, then back to Kennett on 842.

Just driving around.

"Where are we going?" he said.

"I've just got a feeling, Rudy. We just wait for what's next. That's all we do."

He furrowed his brow, but didn't complain—she looked so peacefully determined. He hadn't seen Amandine this still, ever. And her voice had never sounded so clear—her voice had the colors of spring in it, where its normal tones had always been the browns and the grays and the frosty edges of this season, this about to freeze season.

"Okay," Rudy said, shrugging amicably, and he settled in for a little nap, hoping very much that he would not drool on to his shirt, as seemed to happen whenever he slept on a full stomach. But his nap was short-lived.

They were on 82, headed south around the Brandywine's curves, when the rev and scoot and purr of oncoming, then fast departing, bass and speed and wild energy shook Rudy fast awake.

Amandine's hand flew to her mouth when she saw who was behind the wheel of the other car.

Amandine swerved but righted herself fast. The oncoming, identical white-bland rental car nearly missed hitting her head on. As she looked in the rear-view mirror at the other car speeding away, she became sure that she in fact *had* seen Ruth's shocked, tired face behind that other steering wheel.

"What in the bejeezus—" Rudy said, smoothing his sleeves and patting his mouth before a string of drool could land anywhere.

Amandine bit her lip, pulling the rental into the parking lot of the old paper mill that had once turned the Brandywine methiolate-red with its waste. Shhh, her lips mouthed, though no sound came.

"What was that?" Rudy said, once she got the car turned around, heading north.

"That's what's next," Amandine said, and she sped up.

*   *   *

"Thank you so much," Racinda said, and smiled at the tennis mommy who had so kindly gone out of her way to take her out to Button's empty farmhouse.

The woman, whose name Racinda never caught, toasted Racinda with the beer and took the last sip of it.

"No problem sugar. And if you want some lessons with that pro I'll be sure to put a word in," she said, patting Racinda on the arm.

But Racinda hadn't heard a word of it—on the way out here, the pluck and zoom of curving fields, had filled her with sound, with buzzing, with careening voices, with breath like panting after a run.

"Thanks," Racinda said.

"Are you. . . sure. . . this is where you wanna be? The development is just down the road, maybe that's where it is?" the mommy said.

"No, this is it. Thank you."

"Okay, sugar, well you be careful!" and the mommy winked.

The peeled paint on Button's porch became more intricate when the clouds gave way to a little sun; dappled light sashayed down through the overgrown oak branches that nearly touched the second story windows by now. The stairs to the porch leaned desperately; one step had completely collapsed.

The ground was muddy in a shallow way. Slippery, but still frozen underneath from the hard, cold November that preceded this moment. Each step erased a little more of the image of Button confined to a bed, filled Racinda more, instead, with the force of Button's story. Sun cracked the frozen brown grass into puddles. The slope of this hill that she had walked so many times as a child was as familiar to Racinda as the shape of her own waist, where her hand might naturally fall when resting, now as familiar to her as the lines starting around Joey's eyes.

She stopped, gasped softly, understanding then that she was not ever going to see Joey's eye-lines up close again. Before she knew it, her feet were running, and she barely felt the ground underneath them. Like flying. Airborne, into the future.

So fast, practically flying toward the house she grew up in

So whose. . . footsteps. . . were behind her?

Racinda stopped, twisted her head fast, but there was nothing. Just her breath had outpaced her body, that was all.

A trick of the mud.

Ruth, come on, she thought, Ruth, get here, come on, let's get this show on the road.

Her own house, the one she'd last seen from a backseat before she was even ten years old, the one Lyman had left them to, seemed small and wild. Vines wrapped around it like they were trying to grow it an exoskeleton, hold it up. Racinda stared at the many-paned living room windows, imagined her own face reflected from each of the twelve near-squares.

The smell of her own mud, her family's mud, filled her so much there was no need to be afraid, no need even to smile. The beauty of that ground was enough. She felt her hands hang by her side. She felt her tongue in her mouth. She felt the footsteps, real this time, approach her from behind.

"She's not here yet."

"I guess not," Racinda said. She turned around to face her mother.

The white silk blouse rippled across Amandine's arms and torso in the breeze. Amandine's smile perplexed Racinda for a minute—not tight and showy, not protective. There was sadness in Amandine's face, but she wasn't in any sort of *mood* Racinda was going to have to deal with. Racinda couldn't quite believe it.

"Well," Amandine said, putting her hands back into her pockets when she saw that Racinda was keeping her distance, "I saw her driving on 82. She'll be here."

"Yeah," Racinda said, "Yeah, she'll be here."

Gray clouds collapsed in a far corner of the sky, out toward Toughkenamon, but the rest hung blue, lit yellow.

Rudy was sleeping in the car. Racinda could see his head rolling slightly with low snores.

"What's he doing?" Racinda said.

"He's napping. He's going to let me deal with this one," Amandine said.

"Right."

Racinda stared at her mother's smile again, amazed that it wasn't prissy or careful.

"Maybe he has the right idea," Racinda said.

"Come on," Amandine said, hooking her arm for her daughter, "Let's walk over to the topiary and see if we can't clear off a bench."

Amandine didn't walk with the mincing steps that Racinda expected. How could she have forgotten that her mother had once walked across the fields almost every day to pick them up from Button's? When the ground got uneven, Amandine dropped Racinda's hand, strode ahead of her, comfortable leading the way even though she lost her footing a few times—the thin, melted layer of mud would have caused anyone to slip once or twice.

The topiary animals, with no shearing for a decade, had transformed themselves into beasts, unrecognizable.

Amandine's brow stiffened into a frown. Racinda dropped her eyes, waiting for the old brusque and dainty manner, the old self-righteous prettiness to return to her mother. Waited for a stale pronouncement, inflexible, on how to clean this overgrown mess up and make it behave *properly.*

But Amandine put her hands on her hips and laughed.

"Well, I guess that project went to seed!" Amandine said.

Suddenly, Racinda felt too tired to keep up the wariness. Whatever mood Amandine was going to veer into, it couldn't involve actual shit or vomit, so she figured she could handle it. She sat on a bench opposite what she thought had once been the dolphin.

Something was different—there wasn't going to be a veer into the screaming fight they both knew so well.

"They're like alien life forms now," Racinda said. "They evolved."

Amandine brushed a hand against the side of the pony whom she recognized as such only from its placement, tried to imagine its equine shape buried somewhere underneath the voluptuous branches.

On the bench, Racinda brought her legs to her chest and wrapped her arms around them, closed her eyes.

Ruth, come on, she prayed, *Ruth, we all love you and we're waiting for you and we want you to come back, come back.*

Ruth's blond tendrils billowed in the black night playing across Racinda's closed lids. But when she opened her eyes it was only a pile of yellow and orange leaves fluttering up into the air on the too-warm breeze.

Racinda looked at Amandine's softened face and couldn't muster any of her old fury at her mother.

"Mom," she said.

Amandine was standing, her own arms wrapped around her middle, her eyes closed.

"Mom, come sit."

Amandine opened her eyes.

"Okay."

Racinda brushed the dirt off the bench, and offered her hand for her mother to hold.

"You think she's really coming?"

Amandine's hand was hot, like Ruth's.

"Honey, I don't—I don't know. Maybe she was already here."

"Should one of us go back to Button's?"

"I told them to keep her there if she shows up there."

"What, like with the *cops*. Oh great, that'll work."

"I don't think that's going to be the case. I think she's coming here," Amandine said, scratching her nose with the side of a finger.

Racinda closed her eyes.

"Please, Dear God, Lord Jesus, bring her home to us," Amandine prayed, and Racinda didn't even wince. "Please, Dear God, Lord Jesus, keep her safe and loved."

Except for the breeze, they sat in silence and the home-smell of their own mud. Behind Racinda's closed eyes, those blond swirls of hair spun like ribbons off a maypole, schools of ocher leaves swam between. Racinda clung tight to her mothers hand, and the straightforward, matter-of-factness she'd felt since cleaning another woman's shit and vomit out of her own fingernails and ears receded, but did not fade. The fear of that stark old hallway, her mother a broken girl in front of her, opened like a mouth to swallow her.

Viny tendrils seemed to lean inward.

The old creek behind them surged a little faster over its rocks

The breeze coursed their hair warmly.

And a different rhythm appeared: a quieter one, somehow sweeter from weariness. The rhythm started in the creek that ran behind the house, the creek that linked their house with the Dells' old house down the road. Racinda could feel that old breathing, that beaten breathing, that wild breathing down there, in the water, she could feel something ancient and untamed and more than she ever thought she was allowed to have, a breathing that could endure but also a breathing that could sing. A breathing that expanded from the rhythm of the tiny Pennsylvania creek to an ocean wider than any earthly ocean, an ocean not far from the ocean that once covered that South Dakota motel room where Amandine had jumped on the bed, too, where driving all night became possible. An ocean that broke and twisted and destroyed in places, an ocean that frothed and played in places, an ocean that nearly gave up millions of times, but endured.

Racinda opened her eyes.

"Ruth!"

She was here. It was *her*.

It *was* Ruth, Racinda could see her. Ruth—the distance of a shout away. Ruth, here.

Slam of a car door.

Ruth. Just-emerged from the white rental car identical to Amandine's parked in front of it. Ruth. Throwing, maybe a little too hard, a cigarette into the gravel and stomping it out. Thin, jeans and jean jacket, the hair still wild but considerable kink pulled out of it by its length. But Racinda couldn't see her sister's face clearly from here.

"Ruth!"

Amandine jolted up when she saw, hand clinging so tightly to Racinda's that Racinda was suddenly standing, too, through no effort of her own.

Amandine screamed her daughter's name, the laugh and the cry tumbling together.

Ruth waved, seemed to smile. Racinda couldn't see, at first, the vestiges of the speed that left the skin under her sister's eyes purplish and lined. She *could* see how thin Ruth looked, the black scarf lanky and stripped down looking as well. And at first Racinda could see Ruth's face locked back onto her own, she could see hope on Ruth's face, she could see Ruth's skin and tell that it was still warm to the touch, could even see that Ruth's skin still looked like liquid rose gold was rushing underneath, pooling in the fields under the cheeks.

Ruth took a step forward, then stopped. And instead of walking toward them, Ruth turned toward the car again. Hunched over. Hiding? It looked like she was messing with the door handle, Racinda couldn't tell what she was doing, but she seemed irritated.

"Don't leave!" Amandine said.

"Shhh," Racinda said.

Ruth was pulling at, fretting with, her long skinny scarf, which she'd slammed in the car door.

But Ruth paused then, exhaled, braced herself, hands on thighs. She patted her jacket for cigarettes, lit one nervously, and started the walk over to the topiary.

Racinda could see how hard Ruth was working to walk toward her and Amandine. She could see Ruth biting her lip, could see Ruth clutching her hands into fists, then press them onto the side seams of her jeans as she walked. She could see that all Ruth wanted to do was run right back to the car and go find some weed, some anything, but that Ruth was pushing herself, working incredibly hard to keep that rose-gold in her skin, that hope in her expression. Ruth's thin legs seemed longer. Racinda could see the hollows in Ruth's cheeks, now, the way the face arced like a woman of thirty's starts to, so elegantly, though Ruth was only twenty-four.

Racinda could see now—how bad it still was. Ruth tossed aside the barely-smoked cigarette and lit another one, paused to suck in the first drag. Even though Ruth's eyes and skin were lit, as she got closer, the world-beaten cast in her eyes became undeniable—they darted too fast from trees to earth to sky—she refused, even, her ancient pleasure of staring Racinda down, her eyes both shadowed in fatigue and ringed in dark liner.

Panic set in. Amandine and Racinda both inched forward, in unison, and stopped. Racinda coughed, embarrassed. Her arms, Amandine's arms stayed by their sides, did not reach out then, but in their hearts they were running for Ruth, hugging her until she acquiesced, pinning her between them until they could get her someplace safe—a hospital room, a tiny place with a lock, a puffy white cloud somewhere away from this world that demonized Ruth and that Ruth demonized.

Nausea swam through Racinda's midsection, her throat. Her hand reached out, ever so slightly, and the beginning of some word started out of her mouth but then

Ruth stopped. As if she could feel them just *wanting* to grab for her, Ruth stopped. She bit her lip, and her gaze aimed no longer at her sister, but up into the trees.

"Ruth!" Amandine said, couldn't help it.

Ruth shivered, tapped imaginary ash frantically from the end of her cigarette, but did not move. She looked to each side, then over each shoulder.

Which is when she saw Rudy coming straight at her.

Loping quietly, yards and yards behind her. Even Racinda hadn't seen him get out of the car.

The big stomach, the big head, long legs, the khaki pants and too-dressy shoes taking determined strides, toward her.

His hand outstretched for Ruth to shake it, despite the distance still between them.

Ruth's eyes got darker, even, as she folded her hands across her chest.

"Ruth," Rudy nearly yelled over to her as he approached, each word slow and with generous space around it, "Ruth, you must be Ruth. Well what a pleasure to meet you. I'm Rudy Mitchell, I'm a friend of your mother and sister's."

Ruth made herself still as a rabbit, eyes wide, still as something whose blood prepares it well for the minute it is about to become prey. And when Rudy's outstretched arm—his wide fingers ready for a friendly handshake—got a few feet from her, his shadow falling full across her before him in the afternoon light, she backed up slowly, then braced into a run, fleet as that rabbit, to the rental car.

It was then that Racinda felt that bright, hopeful constellation of the three of them finally die, all predictions of ease and victory now off.

"Ruth!" Amandine said, dropping Racinda's hand, ready to take off running.

Racinda's arm blocked the run, though. Flew out across her mother's chest as if a car had lurched to a halt when exactly the opposite was happening—-gravel pitched, tires squealed as Ruth peeled away.

Grief distorted Amandine's face as she slumped down onto a bench. She bent over her knees. Then bolted straight, wailing clear across the fields. Rudy had the good sense to go back to the car, Racinda noticed, and wanted to hug him for it. And Amandine bawled, and bawled. And rocked, her daughter's arm tight across her back, her daughter rocking with her, under the kind old eyes of the feral trees.

"Come on, let's walk to the creek," Racinda said.

Racinda brushed off the two big flat sitting stones that endured where the little dock had rotted and been carried away.

When Amandine raised her head and looked at the water, another cry nearly came out of her, but melted a little, into a sighing, more, as the creek's movement thickened and shimmered under the thinnest ice possible around the edges. In the center it flowed fast.

Racinda, from her own rock, kept her arm around her mother, rubbed circles on her mother's back. She stared at the water rushing and tried not to think of previous versions of this creek, tried not to remember Ruth falling in. Tried to forget her early visions of spinning Ruth, many colors of Ruth, in the sterile hospital rooms that she knew by now nearly as well as she knew this creek. She stared at the water and felt the rip of air and moisture filling her mother with pain and she wished, in that moment, for other water. She wished for Button's goldfish pond, she wished precisely for that day when she was eight and Ruth was quiet and everything was okay and something out by that pond told her yes, you are going to have enough, you are going to be enough, you are going to be able to handle anything that comes along and the world is not always going to feel this dark. *It will be beautiful, it is beautiful.* She wished for the pure flash of those goldfish tails then, she wished for the way Button pressed her sweaty temples trying to figure out how to pattern the petunias.

But now Amandine's face—in a twist of features recognizable universally as a mother who has lost her young—pushed Racinda into old grayness, into dread. *Stop. Stop.* There was nothing to do but give in and listen to the awful sound of her mother crying. So she listened.

Doing so, Racinda noticed the tendrilly, flaky patterns on the ice of the creek—at least five different grays right there—, and the strange way the breeze felt warmer down here though down here was where you could still see patches of snow.

Racinda stopped holding her breath then and she listened, really listened to her mother and she held her mother to her, and she understood then that she was not being a mother to her mother, but a daughter to her mother.

The icy creek edges melted into its rough-running center and the devastating beauty of this water threw Racinda deeper into her mother's cry.

She saw herself in it:

A broken girl, a piggy girl. A hateful girl, a filthy girl, a burnt girl, a bleeding girl, an ugly girl, a weakling, a messy girl, an always-passed-by girl, a fat girl, a deluded girl, a useless girl, an embarrassing girl, a too-much girl, a naïve girl, a starved girl, a buck-toothed girl, a scorned girl, a failing girl, a girl who is a joke an awful-haircut girl a mutilated girl a blotchy-skin girl an armless girl a mommy a pointless girl a gluttonous girl a left-out girl a polite, secret fascist, a selfish girl, an immolated and immolating girl, a protected girl, a wet girl in a ripped dress who deserved it, a frozen girl a pathetic girl a terrified girl an abandoned girl Jesus a scummy girl a silly ineffectual girl a famished girl, an underground girl, a cancerous girl, a contagious girl, a devouring girl, a wanting a savior girl a wanting a ride girl a whore an exhausted girl a blank girl a removed girl a miserable girl a running girl a dying girl, a violent and impassable girl, lost to pretty, then broken.

Amandine hadn't wanted to start speaking tongues in front of Racinda like this; for years it had been her habit to whisper them if necessary when Racinda was around, as when a bad feeling popped up while driving, say, but otherwise she never did in her daughter's presence. But the sobs kept wracking her and Jesus was right here, wasn't he, right here by this creek? This was where he lived, this was where Amandine had *seen* him. So the syllables started coming slow and wispy and rough, staccato around the edges.

There was a certain mastery in Amandine's tongues, she rocked back and forth slowly and Racinda rocked with her, hanging on tight, here, now, not wishing for fishponds but as open as she had been that long-ago morning when the fishpond, the ground, the sky, the grasses, the branches, the air spoke to her and informed her of her birthright.

As Racinda began to understand now that wishing for that other time was useless because *this* pain was as essential as trees and air and water, she closed her eyes and listened to her mother, the water from that creek became water of that ocean again, rough in patches and glass-smooth in others, shallow enough for babies to splash in, but famished and toothed in places, too, antediluvian, able to swallow the despotic and the huge, able to devour whole worlds when their time came. Amandine's tongues spread out across this ocean and the words ceased telling a story, the words carried Racinda to this ocean beyond story, this ocean that absorbs all the stories and remains the same in its eternal variance, its eternal abundance.

And she saw me there, somewhere in that ocean. She saw me dressed up as Him, pinned to the cross, bleeding from the wrists and the forehead and the crotch. That ocean showed her villages burned into dirt, she saw rapes like her mother's, she saw knives at throats with the demand that daughters name me something else. She saw thousands of years and every continent, she saw soldiers and she saw secret, everyday assassins. She saw me up there on the wood, as Him, a reminder to her that if she listened to the stories the world wanted her to believe, she could be one or the other, whore or mommy, the ship or the safe harbor, the Magdalen or Mary, the girl with a mouth on her or the one somebody loved. But not both, not all she really was.

The little thaw on the creek was minor, and this will be the last day so warm for months to come. True winter will soon coddle the black trees and this creek will freeze across, melt, freeze across, melt. And Amandine will quiet her tongues again, out of practicality, and politeness, but when she whispers them in the car or around the house, back in California, a Friday evening in the not too distant future, Racinda won't inch away. It won't even occur to Racinda, in new knee-high vinyl boots, to roll her eyes, as she pops into the bathroom to find the purple lipstick she really needs to replace and discovers her mother speaking her strange prayers aloud, in front of the mirror, no wig on. Bald. Racinda will pat her mother on the head, and this gesture will cause Amandine to smile rather than wince. When the bell rings—too early to be Rudy, too early to be whomever Racinda is waiting for—Racinda will step lightly to the door, Racinda will pause for a moment, closing her eyes before looking out the window to see who it is. As the dusk deepens into night, as the stars blot and then saturate themselves into the blackening sky, Racinda will feel that old creek melting and freezing and melting when she sees the never-tamed vine of blond hair carried up on the breeze. Before putting her hand on that doorknob she will look up and wonder. Stars? Stars are flying and who knows where they already are by now?

ACKNOWLEDGEMENTS

So many people have helped me over the years I was writing this book and since then in getting it out into the world. Emberly Nesbitt and Tom Perrotta read versions and provided great insight. *Girly* herself, like Tinkerbell, thanks Maureen McCoy, Lynda Bogel, Wylie O'Sullivan and Judy Heiblum for believing early on. Michael Stiglitz and family: thank you. Catherine Latham and Dame Lori withstood the gale force and taught me so much. My students, my SGs, Regena. All boosters, especially Katherine Lanpher, Jen Kirwin and Sara Zuiderveen.

Kara Lichtman, Nathalie Thandiwe, Joan Arnold, Elvira Ryder, Angela Heckler and all my friends, delirious with laughter and also scooping my heart off the floor so many times. The Ithaca posse, and Amy Weber and Jenny Scott, kept *Girly's* late 90s winters toasty. Elliot Weinbaum was the Philly true believer, and in San Francisco it was Loree Anthony in that long-ago world back on Duboce Park. John Curatolo: macmagician, nail-gun expert, and last-minute printing hero. Robin Werner: we are definitely pros now. Liberation, Ben, Kira, Rachel: thank you. Cory Greenberg: kindness above and beyond. Tania Kamensky and Wendy Kenigsberg, I am so grateful to you as queens of the visual and as friends, your generosity unparalleled.

VCCA, the Saltonstall Foundation, the Cornell MFA program and all my teachers there kindly provided support and time. And the Ragdale Foundation—this book would not yet exist without your provision of time, warmth and prairie. Mrs. G, WF, TC, S, C.

Especially Carol and Jack Merrick: every page a thank you.